# EDWARD HERON-ALLEN

## &

## SELINA DOLARO

# THREE
# GHOST-WRITTEN
# NOVELS

## WITH AN INTRODUCTION BY
## DANIEL CORRICK

THIS IS A SNUGGLY BOOK

ISBN: 978-1-64525-064-7

The publisher would like to thank the Heron-Allen Society for their important work in promoting the study and appreciation of the life, interests and writings of Edward Heron-Allen.

# THREE
# GHOST-WRITTEN
# NOVELS

EDWARD HERON-ALLEN (1861-1943) was an English polymath, writer, scientist and scholar. Writing under a number of pseudonyms, as well as his own name, his works cover numerous forms of literature and fields, including those of Persian poetry, violins, chiromancy, and foraminifera, though he is probably best remembered today for his forays into fantastic fiction under the pseudonym of Christopher Blayre. His publications include *Chiromancy, or the science of palmistry* (1883), *Violin-Making, as it was and is* (1884), the volume of poetry *The Love-Letters of a Vagabond* (1889), a translation from the Persian of *The Lament of Bābā Tāhir* (1902), *Barnacles in Nature and in Myth* (1928), *The Strange Papers of Dr. Blayre* (1932), and *Asparagus as a Hobby for Amateurs* (1934).

DANIEL CORRICK is an editor, philosopher and writer. From 2010 to 2014 he ran Hieroglyphic Press and edited the journal *Sacrum Regnum*. He has published essays on various nineteenth-century figures including Hugo von Hofmannsthal, Gabriele d'Annunzio and Arthur Machen, as well as contributing articles on philosophy of religion topics to the Ontological Investigations blog. He co-edited *Drowning in Beauty: The Neo-Decadent Anthology* (Snuggly Books, 2018).

SNUGGLY BOOKS

# CONTENTS.

# INTRODUCTION.

For contemporary readers much of the pleasure to be found in the three novels making up this volume will be derived from their rich depictions of a vanished society, a sort of theatrical Victoriana peopled with the well-recognised figures of bohemian artistes, mesmerists and anarchist conspirators. But for their original audience of the late nineteenth century, who read them in cheap "softcovers" and popular magazines, they were the thrillers of the day, dealing in sensationalist "hot topic" subject matters. They also enjoyed the additional allure of a celebrity author: a glamorous *prima donna* familiar to society through her exploits on the stages of London and New York. The actual story of their authorship, though, is as complex and winding as the plots within.

The woman who would later be known to the public as Selina Dolaro was born in London to Julia and Benjamin Simmons on the 20th of August, 1840. Her father was an accomplished musician, who, over the course of his life, served as a conductor and violinist in music halls and opera houses all across the city. From a young age, Selina showed an interest in music and singing, gifts which were enthusiastically encouraged by Benjamin, who spared nothing on her education, hiring a private tutor and later paying for her to study abroad. When fifteen, she married Isaac Dolaro Belasco—a match strongly opposed by her parents on account of the Belasco family's infamy amongst the London Jewish community due to their involvement in petty crime and prizefighting. After several years of training at the Paris Conservatoire, she made her London debut in January, 1870, singing soprano at the Lyceum. This and the following performances were a great success; over the next few years Selina

"Dolly" Dolaro enjoyed a meteoric rise in fame as a burlesque singer, performing in venues throughout London and beyond (a feat made all the more impressive given that three of her children were also born during this period). Her speciality was opéra bouffe, a form of satirical light opera incorporating elements of dance and vaudeville which was the precursor to the modern musical. Later she would branch into classical opera, taking the title role in the first English rendition of Bizet's *Carmen* in 1879, a performance which, though praised, left some critics wondering whether she had the vocal range for *grande* parts.

But whilst Selina's career was flourishing, her family life was not: her husband had serious gambling problems, was absent for long periods and left the support of their four children to his stronger-minded wife and her family. Although not formally divorced until the decade's end, the two led separate lives after the birth of their last daughter, Genevieve, in 1873. One wonders what admirers the charismatic and forceful "Dolly" won (her fictional alter-ego recounts being invited to an intimate *tête à tête* with a Royal Personage—in reality the Prince of Wales did take a fancy to at least one of her co-actresses at the Lyceum). By the public, though, she was soon beloved, her picture appearing on posters, cards and cigarette boxes till the end of her life. In 1875 she added theatrical management to her repertoire, organising the first production of *Trial by Jury* by the newly formed musical duo of William Gilbert and Arthur Sullivan at the Royalty Theatre, and touring the provinces with her own "Madame Selina Dolaro's Comic Opera Company" when the London season was off.

Desirous of obtaining more prominent classical operatic roles, she turned her attention to the New World, emigrating to New York in the winter of 1879. Despite a promising response to her Carmen, American critics scorned her *grande* aspirations. Thankfully, her familiar opéra bouffe parts were more of a success; over the next couple of years she toured across the States to great acclaim. By this point her health had begun to suffer; she experienced periodic breathing difficulties which were the first signs of the tuberculosis which was ultimately to claim her life. In 1882, tired from the stress of touring and uncertain payments, she turned to literary endeavours, writing her first play, *Justine*—a domestic tragedy which she also managed, produced and starred in—which was followed the next year by *In Fashion*, a farce on the spending habits of wealthy wives.

Her last stage performances were in the spring of 1886, by which time it had become apparent to her confidantes that the beautiful actress was fast on the way to the grave. At the time of her retirement she was known on both sides of the Atlantic and received aid from colleagues and fans. Finally, on the 23rd of January, 1889, Selina "Dolly" Dolaro passed away as a result of a seizure related to her illness. Even at the end she retained her wit and force of character, reportedly turning down the offer of a complimentary ticket from a colleague on the grounds that an urgent assignation with Death prevented her from attending further performances. She may have obtained some wry amusement from the fact that several of her children were to follow theatrical paths, with her daughters Esther and Genevieve both taking roles on stage and in film.

It was in the winter of 1886, probably in New York, that Selina met the man who was most certainly responsible for those literary efforts published under her name, a polymath named Edward Heron-Allen, who had recently arrived in America at the beginning of a successful lecture tour promoting his work on chiromancy. The two became romantically involved, although how seriously the relationship was taken by both parties is unclear, as any correspondence and journal entries relating to it have been lost. A short love note from the English writer remains extant, but given the location, it is ambiguous whether it was written for the eyes of a potential lover or for those of the reading public. It appears in what was to be the first product of their relationship, both professional and amorous, the 1888 volume *Mes amours*, billed as a compilation of love poems received by the actress in which the admirer's amorous effusions are subject to mordent commentary by the object of their affection. After Selina's death, Heron-Allen conceded that the verse element was supplied with full knowledge of its destination by three of her poet friends, but, as the sole existing manuscript of the collection is in his characteristic hand with only marginal amendments by Selina, scholars are apt to conclude that it was he alone who compiled and provided the vast majority of material for the volume.

Selina Dolaro's name also appeared on several pieces for popular journals and a play, unpublished in her lifetime, titled *The Mourners*, which was also written by, or along with, Heron-Allen.

The question therefore arises as to what involvement Dolaro had with the work attributed to her.

During his later life, in the autobiographical essay "Notes Upon the Literary, Scientific, and Artistic Activities of Edward Heron-Allen, F.R.S., Extracted From His Diaries and Other Documents by Cristopher Blayre Ph.D., D. Litt," Heron-Allen said that the two novels published under Dolaro's name, *Bella-Demonia* and *The Vengeance of Maurice Denalguez*, were written by him. As for *The Princess Daphne*, though Dolaro's name has long been associated with the book, and also appears as co-author in the latest printing, by Tartarus Press, in 2001, the novel was originally published anonymously. It is easy to see why such rumours should have arisen, however, since the novel features a thinly veiled fictionalised version of the actress in Mahmouré, a pet-name already introduced in *Mes amours*. Selina must have been aware of this portrayal, even if she took no part in the writing process, as the description of the character's background includes numerous details of her early life not readily available to a stranger. The earliest attribution of co-authorship comes from the novelist Gertrude Atherton, who knew both Heron-Allen and Dolaro, and wrote a touching obituary of the actress a month after her death.

For Heron-Allen the novel represents a transitional phase in his development as a writer: it is the point at which the aestheticized social tragedies of his early fiction, with their obvious debt to the Decadent movement, give way to the fantastic themes for which he would be most remembered in literary circles. Fascination with the paranormal was with rife in late Victorian society, with the continuing vogue for Spiritualism and widespread popularisation of Eastern spiritual ideas promoted through occult periodicals and groups such as the Theosophical Society. Heron-Allen was fully appreciative of this trend, and remaining interested, albeit somewhat sceptically, in paranormal phenomena throughout his life. The central theme of *The Princess Daphne*, mesmerism and the transference of thoughts, had been treated by him a couple of years before in a not entirely serious manner in the essay "A Discourse on Mesmerism or Ye Principles and Practique of Animal Magnetism" for the delightfully named *Ye Earlie Englyshe Almanack*. Twenty-first century audiences may be apt to find the novel's fond depiction of West London Bohemia, its colony of struggling but cheerful artists with their faint glow of *l'art pour l'art*, as intriguing as its somewhat cryptic supernatural plot, though the obliqueness surrounding the episodes of the latter element lends it a favourable air of verisimilitude when compared to actual accounts of alleged psychic phenomena. Its author evidently felt this cast of characters had promise, for many of them originated from an earlier work, a play called *Told in the Twilight*, itself the basis for the novel's closing chapter, and were to return a year later as part of the framing device for many of the stories in his collection *A Fatal Fiddle*.

The second novel, *Bella-Demonia*, originally appeared in March, 1889, in *Lippincott's Monthly Magazine*, the American periodical for which Oscar Wilde wrote *The Picture of Dorian Gray*, and is the only work recognised by Selina Dolaro's biographer as her having a hand in, though she died two months before its publication. If we are to believe Heron-Allen's "The Story of Madame Selina Dolaro's Lost Manuscript," dated 7th February, 1889, which is placed just before *The Vengeance of Maurice Denalguez*, and which is referenced in "In Memorandium," placed just before *Bella-Demonia*, she originally conceived it as a drama and then later bade him adapt the plot to prose form when it became apparent that the number of acts would make it impractical to produce. The account of how the original manuscript was submitted to Belford & Clarke, Heron-Allen's usual publisher, only to be stolen by his enemies, forcing Dolaro and himself to rewrite the whole novel in a couple of days at the bequest of the concerned *Lippincott's* editor, seems rather implausible. Although no trace of the original dramatic version survives, if it actually existed, it was the subject of some controversy with Dolaro's children, her daughter Esther—fearful that the shady occultist adventurer was defrauding the estate of its rightful due—crossing the Atlantic to stage a budget rendition of the play in order to stake a claim to production rights. Despite this literary power-grab, no version of *Bella-Demonia* ever graced the stage again and, as far as we know, the Dolaro children never contested royalties for the novels published under her name.

As a literary work *Bella-Demonia* is possibly the most interesting of the three novels, not least because it is a very early example of the spy novel. Modern readers may be surprised that so many of the tropes they are familiar with from the works of Ian Fleming and other writers of popular espionage thrillers—secret decoder devices, amorous high-jinks at diplomatic parties, morally ambiguous *femme fatale* operatives and the fate of nations decided over the gaming table—were already present in the genre at its inception. The decade in which the novel was published had seen a culmination of the Great Game, the labyrinthine diplomatic power struggle between the British and Russian Empires over colonial ambitions in Asia, and although the plot deals with the Russo-Turkish War of 1877, its depiction of Russia would have accorded with popular Anglo-American perceptions of that country as a sinister police state rife with secret organisations and governmental conspiracies.

Of the last novel presented here, *The Vengeance of Maurice Denalguez*, history tells us little. It was published in 1889, and is generally documented as a ghost-written novel, yet Heron-Allen prefacing it with a long affectionate account of Dolaro's life suggests she had some connection with the work even if it only be providing mere seed-germs of the plot. It is the most polished and well-paced of three and seemingly the most conventional: a novel of adultery and intrigue in high society. The device of the indiscreet letter is a common one in Victorian literature but the main influence here is probably Maupassant. The small cast of characters and the focus on dialogue leads one to wonder whether it was also intended for theatrical adaptation or, if Selina did provide the plotting, whether she drew from an existing play.

Unsurprisingly, much has changed since the three novels were written. Whereas then they would have been consumed by a fashionable society readership, now most come to them through Heron-Allen's early contributions to the horror and science fiction genres. Well that they should: it is always illuminating to learn how a writer one associates with short, idea-centred pieces handles sustained character-driven narratives. The life of Selina Dolaro, too, is fascinating as an example of a strong personality in a milieu which is both romantic and romanticised. But if it is not surprising that the world has changed in the last hundred years, perhaps it should surprise us even less that despite all the distance in time these novels still have much to charm and excite us today. Elements that at the time of writing were topical, for the modern reader recede in significance, bringing out the essentially beguiling elements of the pieces in burnished relief.

For information on the early part of Selina Dolaro's life I am indebted to the biographical sections on her and her husband in Steven MacDougal's *Belasco: from Boxing to Theatre and Film*. Special thanks must also go to John P. Mahoney for his essays "A Genealogic Tour of Selina Simmonds Belasco Dolaro (1849-1889)" and "the Queen of Bohemia and the Passions of the Boy, Omar," and for the invaluable advice he has provided the publisher and editor in personal correspondence.

—Daniel Corrick

# A NOTE ON THE TEXTS.

The three novels contained herein were originally printed in the United States, though written by an Englishman. There is, therefore, in the breadth of the original texts, a mixture of American and British spellings. We have, in this volume, chosen, for the most part, to leave the spellings as they first appeared, though this presents many cases of inconsistency. Spellings of words are also often peculiar, and irregular, with different spellings of the same word, without any discernible reason, present even on the same page. These, generally, have been left intact. We have removed obvious errors, but have refrained from altering instances where it is unclear if it is an error, or a quirk of the author—of which there are many.

# THE PRINCESS
# DAPHNE

"Why! if the Soul can fling the dust aside,
And, naked on the air of Heaven ride,
    Wer't not a shame—wer't not a shame for him
In this clay Carcass crippled to abide?"

*Omar-i-Khayyám.*

Day after day we wandered—you and I
Amid a labyrinth of thought, nor found
The answer to the problem that we sought.
Day after day we pondered, asking why
Our twin souls sought each other, and seemed bound
Together by some strange resistless tie.
And as each answer seemed nor wrong nor right,
But all inexplicable, I forsook
The quest, and sate me down to write this book,
That peradventure may contain some light
That; thrown upon our question, may explain
The bitter pleasure and the mad, sweet pain
That we have known together. I have done
This work for you; look kindly on the flaws
That mar it, since it leads you to the cause
Why, when we met, we felt our souls were one.

SORRENTO, *March*, 1885.

19

*In lands which the stupidity of civilization regards as barbarous, there are occult powers of which contemporary science is absolutely ignorant. The materialism of Europe has not the faintest conception of the spirituality which the Hindus have reached . . . their mortal envelope is but a chrysalis which the immortal butterfly, the soul, can abandon or resume at will.*

*I have attempted to undo with magnetism the bands that join mind and matter. In experiments that were certainly prodigious, but which failed to satisfy me, I surpassed Mesmer, Deslon, Maxwell, Puységur, and Deleuze: catalepsy, somnambulism, clairvoyance, soul-projection, in fact, all the effects that are incomprehensible to the masses, though simple enough to me, I have produced at will.*

*I have fasted, I have prayed, I have meditated so long, I have domi-nated the flesh so rigorously, that I have been able to loose the terres-trial bonds. Vishnu, the god of the tenfold incarnations, has revealed to me the mysterious syllable that guides the soul in its avatars.*

*I am not an erudite in the ordinary acceptation of the word; but on the other hand, in studying certain subjects disdained by science, I have mastered some unemployed occult forces, and I produce effects which appear miraculous, though they are perfectly natural . . . By*

*watching for it I have sometimes surprised the soul . . . Armed with the force of my will, that electricity of the intellect, I vivify or I annihilate. Nothing is opaque to my eyes; my gaze pierces everything . . . We Europeans are too superficial, too matter of fact, too much in love with our clay prison, to open windows on the eternal and infinite.*

THEOPHILE GAUTIER. "Avatar."
*[Myndaert Veretst's Translation.]*

# PROLOGUE.

"Then, if I understand you rightly," said Mr. Paul du Peyral, "the case lies thus. My late friend and benefactor, Casimir Préault, makes my enjoyment of the fortune he has left behind him, contingent upon my offering myself as the husband of his second cousin, Miss Daphne Préault of New Orleans?"

"Exactly!"

"And if she refuses me, I enjoy the income only so long as I remain unmarried?"

"Exactly!"

"And should I marry anyone else, it reverts at once to that young lady, unconditionally?"

"Exactly!"

"I understand—good morning."

"Good morning;" and the senior partner of the firm of Seligman, Searcher, & Certiorari bowed Mr. Paul du Peyral out of his office on the ground-floor of No. 195 Nassau Street, New York City.

"Well," said the latter gentleman to himself, as he proceeded up-town in a brown study and a cab, "I am in a pretty peculiar position. Prospectively a wealthy man, but my wealth contingent on my offering myself to a woman I have never seen. Well, they say she is beautiful. Daphne seems inevitable! and as the inevitable I accept her. I wonder if she will accept me?"

On reaching his rooms he straightway indited a letter, laying his hand and heart at the feet of the testator's nominee. This done, he dressed himself; and, with the air of one who has manfully done his duty, he sought Delmonico's and dinner.

A week later, he received the following reply:

NEW ORLEANS, LA., *December*—, 18—.

*Sir:*

Your impertinent offer of marriage has reached my daughter, who has placed it in my hands to reply thereto. We beg, once and for all, to decline the offer with which I presume you consider that you honour us. We have already suffered sufficiently from the madness of my cousin, Mr. Casimir Préault, of Baton Rouge; we did not expect, however, that he would insult us by suggesting the possibility of an alliance between his second cousin and his body-servant. We congratulate you on the disgraceful success of your efforts to gain an ascendency over the enfeebled mind of an octogenarian, though that ascendency robs us temporarily of an inheritance which should be justly ours. Any further communications that you may wish to make to us must be made through the attorneys to the estate, Messrs. Seligman, Searcher, & Certiorari; any letter of yours to us will be returned unopened. I have but one regret, and that is, that my age and infirmities prevent my administering the chastisement that, in my opinion, you deserve.

Obediently Yours,
VICTOR PRÉAULT.

"Good!" ejaculated Mr. Paul du Peyral, as he turned to his breakfast; "I've got the money unhampered by the woman."

# CHAPTER I.
## A Bohemian Soirée.

Do you know Holland Street, Kensington? Yes? I wonder whether you do, or whether you answer me "in the air," the *prænomen* "Holland," as applied to streets, roads, parks, and gardens, in that expansive area known as "Kensington": to us, which comprises the Brompton, the Notting-Hill, the Hammersmith, the Fulham, and almost the St. John's Wood of our fathers, being so familiar as to call forth the affirmative with hardly a moment's reflection as to whether one is telling the truth or not. For Holland Street is not a very well known locality: it is hardly a thoroughfare: and unlike Holland Road, and Holland Park, and Holland Park gardens, it is not lined with the gorgeous abodes of fashionable Bohemia—but it is Bohemia all the same, Bohemia as *we* knew it, the Bohemia of Thackeray, of Jerrold, of Albert Smith, and almost of Dickens; and it is inhabited, or at any rate was, at the time of which I write, exclusively by "the boys." The men who lived there were "the boys," and wore the pepper-and-salt continuations, the velveteen or corduroy jackets, the open collars and quaint ties, the comfortable shirts and the uncompromising hats that distinguish "the boys" from their uninteresting but respectable fellow-men, all the world over. And the women, too—they too were of "the boys"; and since long before Oscar Wilde carried the costume of the *atelier* into every-day life and conventional drawing-rooms, they had worn the artistic folds and colours which have become familiar to us coupled with the adjective "æsthetic," and, in merry communion with the male artists, enjoyed a blissful immunity from the tortures of civilization, represented for them by high heels, tight waists, Mrs. Grundy, and the nineteenth-century dress-improver.

Those were happy days in Holland Street, and its Bohemian glories have not yet quite departed; its red-brick walls and ramshackle studios have not been invaded or routed by "villa residences"; its pipes have not been banished by the cigarette; it has hardly begun to be civilized, even to the extent to which Bedford Gardens and like localities have succumbed to the influence of fashionable Bohemianism, and there are many nooks yet therein, where the dress clothes cease from troubling and the opera hat's at rest. You know, of course, the church-yard of St. Mary Abbott's, and Hornton Street: those are the media of communication by which "the boys" sought the outer world when they wanted it—which was seldom. They took the little flagged footpath through the church-yard, or, when the carrying of a picture to or from an exhibition warranted or required the extravagance of a cab, they reached their classic shades *via* Hornton Street. Hornton Street is practically a one-sided affair looking due west; that is to say, throughout a greater part of its length it looks out over the gardens of Something Priory (I think it is called), and its inhabitants dread the day when this "open lot," as the Americans would say, shall be built over by greedy heirs, or by thrifty executors and trustees—for now, in the early spring, from their upper windows they can watch the birth of the year and the return of the song-birds, and later on they can open them and get the full benefit of the summer fragrance. A discreet little street is that called Hornton, where there is no danger of being over-looked by inquisitive "opposite neighbors," but not inhabited by a homeful little colony like Holland Street—or as Holland Street was in the autumn of the year 18—.

My story opens in the September of that year. Autumn seemed to have roused herself from her long sleep, and had—timorously—tentatively, as it were, laid her chilly touch upon the great city, to warn it that ere long she would be fully awake, and strong enough to take it wholly into her grasp. Already the chestnut trees in some of the parks and squares seemed to have realized that they could not store up for another year the gold they had gathered from the sun-shine during the summer, and had begun to squander it extravagantly, flinging it lavishly to earth in the brilliant bronzes and gilts of the leaves that strewed the grass beneath them; the sparrows were beginning to seek the patches of sunlight on the tree-tops, or fluffed themselves into cosy, chattering feather-balls in the warm dust of the more deserted roadways. The summer was not gone, but it was strong with life only for a day or so at a time, husbanding its strength, as it were, during the intervening hours, to display it with the more arrogance at intervals, as a temptation to the world.

But the season of the year was a matter of indifference in Holland Street. Spring meant, in its eyes, one of the male "boys," flying into the studio of one of the female "boys," and dragging her out for a walk, out toward Hammersmith and Chiswick and Barnes and Ealing; summer meant half-a-dozen of them providing their own refreshments, and going up the river—to find that each had been struck with the same original idea, viz., to bring a chicken-pie; autumn meant a cottage by a wood or by the sea, whence they should return laden with sketches and "studies" to be worked up in the winter; the winter, which represented only an increased expenditure of gas and coal, with tea and muffins at intervals during the day. How happy we were! and now that we are respectable fathers and mothers of families, a younger generation is doing the same thing behind the walls and windows of Holland Street.

Perhaps I am generalizing too much, for of course I have a particular house—a particular *ménage*—in my mind's eye. It is No. 141 on the north side of the street, one of those houses with no front to it, which gives one the idea that the builder was going to face it the other way, but changed his mind at the last moment, cut a front door looking into the back-yard, and filled up the road in front with a garden—which garden, in turn, the inhabitants had filled up with a studio. There are many such in Holland Street. Where the houses are, so to speak, right side foremost, there are little gardens in front of them, wherein old-fashioned flowers grow luxuriantly in defiance of the London smoke, and through which flagged pathways lead from the front doors to the wooden gates; and in one of these we shall seek some of the actors in this drama.

At present our attention is turned to No. 141, at whose uncompromisingly ugly door a young man is letting himself in with a latch-key. An artist obviously, by his velveteen coat, soft hat, and long hair; and a man whom one would remark wherever one might see him. His face is, perhaps, too finely moulded for a man's—there are those who declare him to be effeminate in appearance; his eyes are large and of a dancing brown, his nostrils clearly cut, his lips thin, the jaw is square, the forehead high, and the brows are straight, the whole being framed in masses of rather light brown hair. The hand and arm not occupied in opening the door are encumbered with parcels;—Gabriel Hawleigh has been shopping in High Street, Kensington. Whilst he fumbles with the key, the door is opened from the inside by a girl, dressed in a long, loose frock of chestnut brown, girt about the waist with a broad *moiré* sash, who stands on the steps and laughs at him. The front of her dress is concealed—protected rather—by a long apron, and calico sleeve-preservers are tied over her arms, from the elbow down. She is neither pretty nor plain, but her great, grave, gloomy gray eyes quarrel with the sweetness of her expression, and with the laugh which, parting her finely traced lips, displays two rows of dazzling teeth. Her hair, rather short, forms round her head an aureole of gold, which shimmers as she laughs at the "boy" on the door-step. In sooth a goodly sight are they, as she stands in the shade of the doorway, and he, with one foot on the step, looks up at her.

"Thanks, Maye," says he, as he steps into the house and she closes the door.

"Have you got the muffins?" she inquires, anxiously.

"Yes."

"And the plums?"

"Here they are; they had a narrow escape from squashing against Dick Lindsay, as I came through the churchyard."

"And the soda-water?"

"It's coming round—I won't carry soda-water bottles through High Street."

"And the coffee?"

"There!"

"And the cheese?"

"Rather!"

"Very well; go and finish clearing out the studio, and I'll come up directly;" and the girl disappears, whilst Gabriel hangs up his hat, and, passing through the little drawing-room on the right, steps through the window into the studio. Here he looks round him as one is wont to look round when one is "at home," and then produces from his apparently inexhaustible pockets a box of cigarettes, which he dumps down rather contemptuously upon the mantel-shelf, and a fat package of tobacco, which he empties carefully into a stone jar by their side.

The studio already shows signs of having been cleared somewhat, but now he continues the operation, carefully covering a half-finished picture on an easel with a cloth as he turns it to the wall, and lifting into a corner a smaller easel, the flower-painting on which, however, he does not cover up. Only, the bowl of Gloire de Dijon roses which stood on a table by its side he carefully carries out of the studio and upstairs into his own room, taking pains that their arrangement be not disturbed, so that on the morrow Maye Trevethick may have no difficulty in finishing her study from them. When he returns, an elderly lady is sitting in a low arm-chair by the window of the drawing-room.

"Ah! madre," cries he, "how are we getting on?"

"I think everything is ready now, dear. Maye is putting the finishing touches to the baked meats down-stairs, and I'm ready to receive the company, and have got all my stereotyped phrases ready to greet them with. We shall have quite an historic party!"

There was to be a party in the studio, the reader has gathered that already, and the little household at No. 141 Holland Street were quite excited at the prospect of the festival, which was to be one of those merry Bohemian orgies such as "the boys" delighted in. Let me present the host to you before the company arrives. Stay! there is a ring at the bell—some one arriving? No, only a boy with the soda-water.

The lady in the window is Mrs. Hawleigh—a sensible, clever old lady, such as young men delight in talking to, very courteous, very correct, a great reader, but a wise old lady who, having passed her later life in poverty, by comparison with the affluence of her earlier years, knows her world thoroughly, and in the parlance of "the boys," has no nonsense about her. Hermippus the Sage it was who remarked that the society of young people keeps old people young; and this was the case with Mrs. Hawleigh—the artistic colony with whom we are concerned adored her. She was a kind of mother to them all, and returned their affection with impartiality: she had only two especial favourites, and they were her son Gabriel Hawleigh and her niece Maye Trevethick. She had married, when quite young, a lieutenant in the ill-fated Light Brigade, and soon after that fateful 25th of October, when the blue and black missive from the War Office had told her that the young husband to whom she had given her whole soul without reserve had ridden "into the jaws of death, into the gates of Hell," and had left his fair young body before the batteries of Balaclava, she had given birth prematurely to her boy Gabriel. His consequent delicacy was almost a source of solace to her, as a safeguard against his joining that profession which had already torn two-thirds of all she cared for in the world from her. Mrs. Hawleigh, though possessed of but slender means, lived only for Gabriel, and had refused to marry again; had only watched with delighted solicitude the growth of her son's artistic taste, and had denied herself many a little luxury that he might cultivate it to the utmost; for Gabriel, with all his softness and delicacy, had undoubted talent in the profession he had taken up, though that talent had not as yet proved very remunerative.

Gabriel Hawleigh was an artist and a fiddler, and spent his life in the companionship of his easel and his violin. His mahlstick and his fiddle-bow were the twin sceptres of his autocratic power—in Holland Street. Often his mother feared that the one would interfere with the other, but it was impossible to make him forsake the one and cleave to the other, especially since Maye Trevethick had become a member of the household, with her enthusiasm for her paint-brush under the tuition—and the able tuition—of Gabriel, and her skilled, sympathetic touch upon the piano which stood in a corner of the studio, and on which she would often play rich phantasies by the hour, or accompany Gabriel when, for her delight and that of his mother, he would take up

> "——this small, sweet thing,
> Devised in love and fashioned cunningly
> Of wood and strings,"—

interpreting the masterpieces of the composers for his instrument, or following Maye through the chords and melodies of some daring improvisation, in which he would plead to her in harmonious whispers of things unutterable. For they were very poor in this world's riches. Ah—yi!

Maye Trevethick, the orphan and only child of Mrs. Hawleigh's only sister, had joined the household some three years before, and was now a sweet woman of nineteen. Gabriel was twenty-two. By that you can approximately fix the date of my story. When her father, Claude Trevethick, had died in India, her mother had soon followed him to "that undiscovered country from whose bourne no traveller returns," and her worldly possessions hardly sufficing for the co-maintenance of body and soul, Mrs. Hawleigh had taken the girl to her heart and home, and the *ménage* in Holland Street had become triple instead of, as heretofore, dual. Mrs. Hawleigh had never regretted her good-hearted impulse, for the pure, sweet girl had brought a rare sunshine into the little house, and was as much one of the family as if she had been in very truth Gabriel's sister. Such were the inmates of No. 141, and such, one of them at least prayed that they might ever continue, for the mother's heart read truly in the clear pages of her boy's soul, and daily she wove happy visions of a happy future.

The hour approached for which, as Maye said, "the cards had been sent out." Mrs. Hawleigh was suppressing a tendency to doze, and Maye and Gabriel were having an active row about the framing of certain works of art that at present lay around the stu-

dio in a frightfully dissolute state, when the bell rang, and Eric
Trevanion was announced by the "Empress," a good-naturedly
obese person of uncertain age, who, progressing through the
stages of Mrs. Hawleigh's maid, Gabriel's nurse, and general
factotum in Holland Street, had enjoyed the names of almost
every imperial Roman dame, and from Eudoxia, Theodora,
Faustina, Aspasia, Poppaea, and a host of others, the morals of
whose original bearers would have brought her gray hairs in sorrow to the hair-dresser's, had arrived at the simple appellative
of "Empress," from her imaginary authority in the Bohemia of
Holland Street.

Eric Trevanion, whom the Empress had just admitted, was a
Bohemian of a class much commoner today than it was at the
time of which I write. He was, as it were, an amateur Bohemian;
that is to say, he had private means of his own, an ample allowance made him by his father, a wealthy Cornish squire, enough
to prevent the necessity of his selling his pictures to live; and this
was a most fortunate thing for him, for though a royally good
fellow, Eric was not much of an artist, though he meant very well,
and covered acres of canvas, in his very superlative studio next
door, with what he called "Studies from the Impressionists."

"Mine is an untamed genius," he used to say; "I can't tram-
mel it with purity of line and rules of colour; it is enough for
me to know that my work elevates the thoughts and stimulates
the imagination. The study of my pictures is a search after the
hidden beauties of the Undefined. Look at *that*, for instance;
if you look carefully but comprehensively at it for a little while
and at a little distance, the subject will form itself for you, and
you will be astonished that you did not see it at once. Since you
are pressed for time I will tell you. This is 'A Discord in Aniline
Purples—Jimmy Whistler struck by lightning in the middle of
a sneeze.' The large canvas on the wall is a Theosophical picture. I think the idea came to me in a trance, I'm not sure; it
looks, I admit, as if it had been painted by my astral double the
morning after a drunk; but the idea is very sublime and Esoteric
Buddhism-ish—'A Nocturne in Green Apple Color—Madame
Blavatzky as a Priestess of Isis, pondering on the "Now-ness of

the When," whilst Mohini and A. P. Sinnett play three-card *monte* in the distance.' Some day I shall grow a white curl and be appreciated. At present I'm happy enough as I am."

Such was the new-comer, the first arrival, a young man dressed with scrupulous carelessness in the costume of Bohemia. Son, as I have said, of a Cornish squire of considerable means, he had adopted art as a profession for the sake of its associations and its freedom. Tall and dark, and quiet in manner, no one ever knew whether he were serious or not, or whether, like the Æsthete of historic fiction who dined with closed doors off beefsteak and onions, he laughed at himself in the solitude of his own studio; but everyone liked him, for it was whispered that his right hand did many a good action of which his left hand remained bliss-fully ignorant, among the impecunious "boys" whose pictures he would buy, ostensibly on commission for his father, and this often with such a lordly disregard of their merits as paintings, that, when Gabriel Hawleigh ate things that disagreed with him, his grisliest nightmare was always one of incarceration in the elder Trevanion's picture-gallery. His especial cronies were the Hawleighs, possibly on account of their proximity, a proximity which lent itself to his continual appeals "next door" to have buttons sewed on, or especial delicacies cooked, or the wounds produced by his amateur carpentering bandaged. Tonight he made an early appearance, with two chairs in one hand and in the other a basket.

"Do you want some more chairs?" was his greeting. "And look here; the governor sent me up a couple of brace of partridges yesterday, so I had them cooked and brought round. I get very hungry later on and require strong meats, so I said to myself, 'Come early and bring your own birds.' How are you all, anyhow?"

"Now that's what I call having a proper regard for the ethics of the situation," cried Gabriel. "Empress, here is food! Give me the chairs, and now let's greet him. How are you, Mr. Trevanion?—so good of you to come!"

"Not at all—pleasure, 'm sure," replied the Cornishman, gravely. "And whilst I think of it—before the aristocracy of

Camden Hill turn up—have you got a shoe lace? Hark! some one approaches—I shall go away and come back fashionably late. How are you, Miss Easton?—have you brought the latch-key? I've left mine on my dressing-table."

This last remark was made to the elder of two girls who made their appearance at this moment, Sylvia and Eva Easton, occupants of the floor above him next door, who were engaged taking off their hats, smoothing their hair, and giving themselves and one another little corrective pats and punches all over, in a corner with Maye, to an accompaniment of those hysterical whispers and bursts of suppressed merriment without which no properly constructed young women can greet one another after an enforced separation of—say—two hours. The elder, Sylvia Easton, was a student of "Still Life," and had been remarkably successful at getting five-pound pictures exhibited and sold in Suffolk Street, Pall Mall, and Burlington House. Her sister Eva was recently home from a two-years' sojourn in the Conservatoire at Leipsic, where she had devoted her time to the study of the violin. That accounted for the *papier maché* fiddle-case and roll of music which she dexterously concealed beneath her cloak, with one end plainly visible to guard against its being ignored.

"Let us go into the studio," said Mrs. Hawleigh, as another arrival announced himself by "tirling at the pin;" and the little nucleus of "the party" stepped through the window.

"Great Scott! Pouff!!" exclaimed Trevanion, flying to the ropes of the skylights, which he opened to their fullest extent. "Gabriel, what are you doing?"

The gaslights of "the flarer" were reinforced by half-a-dozen candles disposed around the studio, and seated on the floor before a brass Venetian lamp, Gabriel had succeeded in producing a perfume which, not having the pen of a Dante, I am powerless to describe.

"Well," said he, smiling apologetically, in defiance of the contortions of his face from his nose outward, "I thought this Venetian thing would look pretty, alight, but I can't get it to work. By Jove! if the merry Venetians always produce this effect when they try to illuminate the world, I don't wonder that they seem rather to like the Grand Canal at low water!"

"Take it out! Ouf!" vociferated Eric.

And amid the derisive laughter of the band, Gabriel removed his highly artistic but disagreeably pungent illumination; whilst Maye lit some incense in a *cinque-cento* thurible to neutralize the aromatic effects of his experiment.

Meanwhile the other guests begin to arrive. First Bernard Rawlinson, a grave, handsome creature with picturesquely dishevelled hair and an indumentary *désinvolture* peculiarly his own. Rawlinson would have been an excellent artist if he had not been a tolerable actor, and an excellent actor had it not been for his talent as a painter. As it was, he divided his time about equally between the studio and the stage, with the result that the one always interfered with the other, and precluded his reaching the summit of excellence in either.

He was followed by Dick Lindsay—a funny man. That was obvious the moment you saw him. His smooth-shaved and rather ugly face never changed its expression in the slightest degree; but from behind his light, gold-rimmed spectacles, his keen blue eyes seemed to watch everything around him, and discover the hopelessly ludicrous in whatever presented itself within range of his observation. He stood in the doorway and snuffed the gale suspiciously.

"Is anybody dead so far?" said he.

"Not at present," replied Sylvia Easton.

"Then I think I may venture," said he, stepping into the studio. "What has happened?" he queried.

"Gabriel has been making sacrifice of a sweet savour, and has just disappeared, like the ghost in the 'Antiquary,' 'with an aromatic perfume and a melodious twang'."

"Oh! I thought someone had had an accident with the chemicals;" and he subsided by Mrs. Hawleigh's side as Gerome Markham, an artist attached to the permanent staff of a comic paper, made his appearance. A small, fat man with a large income and a supremely careworn and worried expression, clothed in the most superlative evening dress, with a gardenia in his button-hole.

"Apothecary! an ounce of civet," cried Bernard Rawlinson, as Markham stepped round on tip-toe, making his choicest salaams to the company, and diffusing a faint, sweet perfume of chypre as he went.

"Yes," said he, as if in answer, "I perceived a weird aroma before I left Phillimore Gardens, and as the wind set from this direction, I thought you would appreciate my delicacy in providing a counteractive."

Others followed him, and at last about a dozen genial souls had shaken their hosts by the hand, had turned from Gabriel more in sorrow than in anger, had congratulated Markham on the picturesque splendour of his appearance, and joined in the tea, coffee, and gossip of the studio.

Suddenly Trevanion, who occupied the music-stool, swung round and said:

"Where's the Princess?"

"Echo answers where," said Gabriel.

"Then Echo is a liar or intoxicated," rejoined Lindsay, "for Echo ought to answer 'cess.'"

"But where *is* she?" persisted Trevanion.

"I saw her today," said Eva Easton, "and she said she was coming."

"I think," said Rawlinson, "that the President's dining with her;" and at this intelligence every tongue was hushed, for "the President" dining in Holland Street was an event that brought throbs to every Bohemian heart. And yet it was not uncommon, for Sir George B———, President of the Royal Something-or-other of Painters, with his fine, handsome face and silver-gray hair, was "a boy" among "the boys," and, often looked in on the colony, and smoked cigarettes whilst he made suggestions that accounted for many an admission to the holy precincts of the Academy on Varnishing day.

"Well, he's in good company," said Mrs. Hawleigh, "and Sir George is likely to stay there."

"No!" said a voice on the threshold; and most of the men rose to receive the great man himself, who stood smiling for an instant at the colony, and then bent low over the hand of Mrs. Hawleigh.

"May I come to the party?" said he, as he settled himself by Mrs. Hawleigh's side.

"Rather!" said Gabriel.

"Coffee?" said Maye.

"Thanks—both of you," said Sir George.

"I come as an ambassador or advance-guard," continued he, "to say that the Princess Daphne will be here directly; she stayed to interview someone for a moment, and sent me on—there's a ring! Perhaps it's she." Maye rose and went quickly to the door; the next moment Miss Daphne Préault—called unanimously by the colony "The Princess"—stood in the drawing-room window and looked round the studio. The men rose again with one accord, and a little murmur of satisfied "Ah's" went round.

That Miss Préault should have been dubbed "The Princess Daphne" never caused a moment's surprise to any who saw her. Who she was, and where she came from, no one knew for absolutely certain; and the combined and persistent curiosity of the entire female colony had not as yet elucidated the problem. Meanwhile they bowed before her; and though she often seemed unconscious of her empire, the sceptre she swayed was that of a rule which, all agreed, was highly beneficent to her subjects, and very genuine indeed.

A dim rumour existed in the colony to the effect that the Princess Daphne was a Creole. No one, however, dreamt of pressing the idea heavily upon her, and when suggested lightly, she would equally lightly set it aside. Since then, however, I, the writer of this narrative, have been far afield, and among the beauties who stroll of a summer's evening along Carondelet Street, or on the Levée, or in the old Rue Royale, in New Orleans, or who lounge on the piazzas of Baton Rouge and Mobile and such semi-tropical cities of the New World I have seen many a finely moulded quasi-Amazonic figure that reminded me, as nothing else has ever done, of Daphne Préault. The reader may as well be let into the secret that a Creole she was.

Daphne Préault was tall, or at any rate held herself, as many women have the trick of doing, so as to convey that impression; and this dignity of stature was still further enhanced by the grand proportions of her body, by the half-Spanish lines of the neck and shoulders, the finely rounded bust and non-atrophied waist, the curves at the hips, and the purity of the lines down to her feet, which, like her hands, were not too small. Her hands especially were a study for the artist or sculptor; not too small, as I have said, and of a respectable breadth, the flesh firm and lightly colored, the thumb not weak, as it so often is in a woman's hand, the fingers smooth and slightly tapering to a delicate squareness at the tips, the nails long and curved, the finger-tips rounded on their surfaces into that little cushion of flesh, sure sign of sensitiveness in a hand; the whole exquisitely flexible, the

> "Gentile morbida leggiadra mano
> Cui fer le proprie mani d'Aurora"

of Paolo Rossi. And, above all, her head, which for very fear I have left until last! A head not too small, covered with masses of hair that would have been black but for the reddish lights that flashed through it when she moved, hair that came low on a broad, clear forehead, bounded by straight and rather heavy, dark eyebrows, from beneath which a pair of great dark-brown eyes looked straight into one's soul. The nose straight as we see it on a Greek coin, the mouth firm, but finely, almost sensuously, curved, the jaw square and strong, the whole complexion pale rather than coloured—and there you have the portrait of the Princess Daphne. Yes! to the *cognoscenti* she could never be anything but a Creole; but nature had been kinder to her than to most of her race,—she had not, in producing perfection of form, exhausted her creative energy, but had endowed this imperial woman with a brain no whit behind her physical development; and though she was equally amiable to the entire colony among which she lived, her especial cronies realized—and fully realized—that they were lucky indeed.

"Am I too fashionably late to expect absolution?" said she, as she surveyed the group, "or has Sir George prepared a gracious forgiveness for me?"

"The Princess can do no wrong—*sta felice alla casa*" replied Gabriel, gallantly, as the girl stepped into the studio with a little laugh, and greeted the company with a series of "nods and becks and wreathed smiles."

"I have been doing combat with our natural foe, the art-dealer," said she. "The particular specimen of tonight thought to catch me in a good humour after food, and buy a miscellaneous lot by gaslight, for ready but insufficient cash. I am proud to say that I resisted, and told him to come back tomorrow, when I shall probably be suffering from this evening's dissipation, and be in too bad a temper to make him any concessions."

"There is no doubt about it," said Bernard Rawlinson; "if Art-dealers were not as a class—well, let us say—stupid, they would buy pictures on gastronomic and barometric principles. Take my own case, for instance: '*Metiri se quemque suo modulo* what's-his-name,' as the classic has it. If I have looked in on Gabriel in the morning, and feasted on half-cooked muffins, I spend the afternoon meditating an essay on the meaning of the word 'Remorse.' At such times the dealer has no chance; nor has he any luck when the weather is on my nerves; but if it is a fine day and I have had tea at the Princess's, I become kindly disposed towards him, and take his paltry shekels in exchange for works of art worth treble—in my estimation,—and merely smile a wan smile of pity when he declares that he is ruining himself to save me from starvation, on strictly philanthropic principles. To paraphrase Byron, 'Now Barabbas was an art-dealer.'"

"But why talk of funerals, physic, and art-dealers?" cried Lindsay; "let us rather make music. Miss Trevethick, won't you twankle on the harpsichord for us?"

"Certainly," replied Maye; "I'll play you a little thing of my own. I call it 'Funeral March of the Hanging Committee,' and I am going to dedicate it by special permission to Sir George B——;" and she began to run her fingers over the keys, first in playful, catchy fantasy, drifting thence into pure tunefulness, and ending with a grand, rich fugue that left the assembled crowd wondering at its meaning, so strange and suggestive was the *leit-motif* that crept into the harmonies at every moment, or anon would stand out by itself in a bit of exquisite melody. When she finished, a dead silence had fallen on the gathering, broken only by the Princess's ejaculation of, "Thanks, dear; it's very sweet of you to exhaust yourself like that for our selfish, but appreciative edification."

"What I like about Miss Trevethick's music," remarked Lindsay, "is that she gives no chances to the social fiend, the man who beats time, or whistles the air if he knows it, or insists on turning over the music."

"Poor Lindsay!" said Markham; "one would think he had been himself a sufferer, though I doubt whether he knows the difference between a piano and a penny-whistle."

"True! I have not suffered from the musical fiend; *my bêtes noires* are the Story Fiend and the Introduction Fiend. Some day I shall write an essay on Social Fiends, and clear off old scores. Yet, after all, the Social Fiend is only a product of high civilization and cultivation, and will increase, I suppose, rather than decrease."

"Explain! Define! Speech! Speech!" was the cry; and Lindsay, after looking helplessly around for a few seconds, thus held forth:

"What I mean by my introduction," said he, "is that the fiendishness of the Social Fiend generally results from the perversion of some high quality, which, kept within proper limits, would inspire our respect, e.g., musical, literary, or dramatic talent.

"The social fiend is of two classes—or declensions—the *active* and the *passive*; or perhaps it would better express my meaning if I were to say, *transitive* and *neuter*. To the former fiend one stands in some measure in the light of a foil; one's presence, and to a certain extent one's coöperation is necessary to him; one inflicts him on one's self, so to speak, and consequently he may be avoided with care, and discretion, and practice, and presence of mind. The latter, on the other hand, is a fiend all by himself; he can sit alone and exercise his fiendishness, disseminating it quasi-unconsciously all around him; he cannot be avoided; in his case, absence of body is preferable to presence of mind; you must get up and go away!

"Thus much by way of introduction. We can now, in the words of the classic, 'cut the dialogue, and come to the figures.'"

"On mature reflection I think that the most drastic and damnable kind of musico-social fiend is the man who taps with his foot when music is being played. The man (his brother *cadet*) who hums the tune in an undertone, or gently whistles an accompaniment, pales into insignificance before him. The affliction arises from a diseased musical ear, a pathological condition, I believe, unknown to the aurist. I once knew one of this class who tried to beat time to Wotan's fifty-minute recitative in the 'Siegfried' of Wagner (the sin was its own punishment—he was carried out in convulsions); but it is the slow waltz or quick march that principally draws forth his natural corruption. An air is being played;—suddenly you become aware of a little measured thud on the brain repeated at regular intervals; you tap your ear and reconcentrate your attention:—in vain! the tap, tap, tap seems to become a kind of devil's tatoo on your inmost soul: the rest of the audience also gradually wake to the fact, and a scared expression spreads itself around, whilst the entire *assistance* ignores the music, and begins searching for the fiend. At last you find him, a mild-mannered youth with a wisp of hair bristling at the crown of his head, with large hands and a pale face—absorbed, concentrated in the music; his right foot is merrily accompanying the melody; he is as unconscious as a *young* organ-grinder of the grief that he is causing; he doesn't see the cyclonic glares directed at him, not he! He is only mildly surprised that he alone applauds at the end of the performance; the rest of the audience is only waiting for the end of *his*, and merely regards the musician as a kind of accomplice. The tapper has 'queered the show,' but he doesn't realize the fact. The only person who is similarly self-satisfied is his brother fiend who has been softly whistling the air between his teeth all the time; and this improvised drum-and-fife band forms a kind of link of brotherhood—hitherto unrecognized—between them. These fiends have, as I say, fallen from a high but uncultivated musical taste, like the fiend who insists upon turning the leaves for the *pianiste*. His radius of iniquity is often more circumscribed; it may extend only to the lady playing, her chaperone who doubts his capacity, and the man who wishes *he* could perform this office for the fair *artiste*: if the leaf-turner is sure of himself it is all right for the others; but as a rule he isn't. He only does it 'to show off'; and his anxious, conscience-stricken face, as he stares blankly at the page, wondering where the deuce and all the player has got to, gradually betrays his mental state to the audience, and they sit writhing with apprehension till the *artiste* makes a convulsive bob of the head, the fiend makes a wild dive, and it is five to one he drops a leaf on the floor and replaces it upside down. If he doesn't the audience breathes freely for another five minutes, and so on at intervals, until the fiend perspires, apologizes, is frigidly thanked, and retires into his pristine insignificance to reflect upon the impression he has produced.

"There are other musical fiends that we all know:—the man who insists on being told the name of the piece played, and the man who tells him—wrong; the man who, in the dead silence that follows a performance, is heard remarking that he heard Rubinstein play—or Sims Reeves sing—that particular thing; the man who tells the lady performer, at the conclusion of a carefully learnt English song, that he is 'so fond of those weird little Arabic chaunts.' And so on—and so on—and so on!

"The musical fiend, of whatever sort, is the best specimen of the neuter declension. The most perfect exemplification of the *transitive* class are the story fiends, whether active or passive. Among the active ones, of course I will not refer to the retailer of 'chestnuts,' the man who tells you the original story for telling him which Cain killed Abel; or the man who tells a story inside out, i.e., gives you the point seriously, and wonders that you don't laugh as he concludes with the introduction thereto; or the man who tells you a story that you know of old, and leaving out the point altogether, gets mad when you bring him safely onto the track once more. All these are too common for the esoteric profundity of this sermon. The story fiend I *hate* is the man who with much pantomime tells you a pointless old yarn for the purpose of impressing with his wit and eloquence a girl across the room whom he *hopes* is looking at him and taking in his performance.

"Similarly do I hate certain story fiends of the *recipient* variety. For instance, the converse of the last fiend, who, whilst you are telling *him* your latest and best, is making eyes across the room, and gauging the effect upon *her*, and when you come to the point where you should be interrupted by a smile, and wait for it accordingly, turns an absent-minded, lack-lustre gaze upon you and ejaculates spasmodically, 'Oh! ah! yes! Haha! very good—and what became of the boy?'—or some tom-foolery of that sort. Only one degree removed from him is the man who, instead of listening to your yarn, keeps his eyes fixed on the ground about six feet in front of him, racking his brain to think of a story on his *own* account, and at the conclusion of your effort, instead of grinning appreciatively, chips in like an east wind chased by lightning with 'Ah! yes, and that reminds me of a story,' etc., etc., etc. Ugh! there's a brute for you! And yet how common!

"Then you have the fiend who tells you a long yarn, usually concerning his own prowess in the Camp of Mars and the Court of Venus, when you are dying to skip over unconcernedly and take the seat just vacated by *her* side. You are like the Pool of Bethesda; whilst the descended angel troubles you, someone else steps in and reaps the benefit.

"And again, what a fruitful field for abstract and experimental objurgation is the introduction fiend—the man who insists on being introduced to you, and the man who insists on your introducing him to So-and-So!—the man who grasps your hand with an eighty-one ton crunch and says, 'We have a mutual friend in Mrs. X.; she has often spoken to me of you.' You have never heard of Mrs. X., and don't believe in her existence, but you daren't say so, for fear that he will queer you with some pleasant acquaintance whose name you haven't caught; so you put your head on one side like a contemplative parrot, and say, 'Oh yes! And how was Mrs. X. when last you saw her?'—praying inwardly that you are not, both of you, constructively, liars.

"And then the man who says genially, 'Oh! is this Mr. X?' in much the tone of voice in which Uriah's wife is said to have remarked, on her first introduction to David, 'Is *this* the youth who slew the great Goliath?' Or the man who says treacherously, 'Oh! Mr. Z., I've heard so much of you;' you break into a cold perspiration and wonder what he's heard about you, and from whom. But, good heavens! I've been lecturing for half an hour—believe me, I apologize—somebody else do something to wipe out the memory of my harangue!"

Lindsay stopped, and the laughter which had rippled through his discourse culminated in a storm of delighted applause, in the midst of which Maye set forth the more solid baked meats, and the company proceeded to picnic.

Whilst they ate, Bernard Rawlinson recited to them, and at the conclusion of the little repast, Gabriel, with much pomp and circumstance, asked the Princess on behalf of the men to permit them on behalf of the ladies to smoke.

"Well," replied she, "of course it is understood that we all dislike smoke exceedingly, and regard the use of tobacco as wholly vile; but on this single occasion we will not only permit, but countenance, the proceeding."

So saying she produced a silver cigarette-case and selecting a cigarette for herself handed it to Sylvia Easton, who did the same and passed it on to the other girls. This was carried through with the utmost gravity, and the symposium continued amid the soft blue fumes of the weed nicotian, unsupported, however, by Sir George and Mrs. Hawleigh, who had slipped away softly, for fear of breaking up the party by their departure.

It was one of those delightful evenings in which everyone does something. The two Eastons played a duet, and after that Gabriel and Maye were persuaded to do likewise. When Gabriel played in public it was a thing to hear, for it seldom took place: his fiddle was to him his confessional, his confessor, and his confession; and if we are to accept Neil Gow's axiom, that "a mon's a player when he gar him-sel' greet wi' his fiddle," Gabriel Hawleigh was a player indeed; for his playing was the very soul, the very agony of music, and often, when he had a melancholy fit on him, he would bring tears to the eyes of his small but appreciative audience, consisting, as a rule, of Maye and Mrs. Hawleigh.

Tonight, however, he was in his more enthusiastic, fiendish mood, and tore out of his fiddle a brilliant suite of wild Czardas, drawing Maye irresistibly along with him as she played the piano accompaniment, and winding up with a wild, triumphant solo of barbaric melody, that roused his audience as if it had been a thunderstorm of harmonies.

This solo terminated in a roar of enthusiasm, during which he recovered his senses, as it were, and when it subsided he seized the opportunity to fall on one knee before the Princess Daphne, saying:

"Like the King's minstrel I crave a boon, Princess."

"It is granted,—Ser Menestrel what is it?"

"That *you* sing for us."

"Oh, you wretch!" exclaimed she. "If I had guessed—but I've promised, so I suppose I must;" and amid the delighted acclamations of the crowd, Daphne Préault moved to the piano.

"After that gorgeous performance of Gabriel and Maye's, I can't sing any of my French *repertoire* to you; here is a little Cuban suite of melodies, in the Cuban dialect; it is supposed to be a triumphal song of a woman's self-sacrifice."

She began in a low, soft minor key, a weird, half-monotonous melody of which every note seemed to thrill the very souls of the listeners; then, just as the depth of despair seemed to have been reached in the music, the major inversion of the chord was heard in the bass, the treble took it up, and the lament became a grand, almost military chaunt, that ended abruptly with an unheralded minor harmony. Daphne Préault had the pure, rich contralto of the south, and threw herself into her music in a way that used to make her listeners tremble. Like Gabriel, she seldom flung the glories of her art before the public, which made it all the more an event to remember when she did sing; and tonight undoubtedly she eclipsed herself.

On one at least of the company she had made an impression not likely to be soon effaced: he sat on a long, low, carved chest, with his head resting in his clasped hands as he leaned against the wall, his soul far away on the wings of the music, forgetful of everything save the grand orgy of sound. When the music ceased his eyes turned with an expression of dumb wonder in the direction of the singer, and, attracted perhaps by the intensity of his gaze, her eyes sought his. The Princess Daphne resumed her seat quietly. The man was Eric Trevanion.

And so, amid music and conversation, light tobacco and light refreshments, the evening wore on. To an historian much latitude and meanness and betrayal of confidence are allowed, but I do not propose to divulge the tale which was told by the clock as the last guests—Gerome Markham and Dick Lindsay—concealed about their persons a stirrup-cup proffered by Gabriel, who then, turning out the gas and contemplatively munching a biscuit, wandered up to bed. The Princess had been the last girl-guest to go, escorted by Eric Trevanion; and then Maye Trevethick had softly and silently vanished away, leaving a small male group to talk unrestrained "shop" into the small hours of the morning.

The Bohemian *soirée* was ended, and the Empress, on the following morning, expressed a hope that there might not very soon be another.

## CHAPTER II.
### Une Maîtresse Femme.

From Holland Street, London, to Forty-first Street, New York City, is a far cry,—three thousand miles or more,—but though we have transported ourselves, Aladdin-like, across the site of the submerged continent of which Ancient Egypt was a colony, and Yucatan a young dependency,—according to Ignatius Donnelly,—and have reached the commercial capital of that "great aristocratico-oligarchical democracy where all men are equal and none of the women," we are still in Bohemia, though it is Bohemia of a very different order from that which we have left behind us in the old world.

The American autumn was much like the English one in temperature; only its outward and visible signs were different. In the squares, the asphalt was strewn thick with broad golden and bronze leaves, and the water drawn off from the fountain-basins had left hideously bare the roots of the lilies and lotuses and other semi-tropical water-plants, whose flowers had been so good to look upon during the empty summer months, and whose leaves, decaying, were watched with almost vulture-like impatience by the municipal gardeners, who were waiting for their death to lift bodily the great square boxes of roots, to be put away for the winter, or to cover them with the fallen leaves. In Central Park, and in the open lots up beyond One Hundred and Fortieth Street, the crimson awns of the sumach were beginning to bow reverence to the autumn winds, and save and except that now and then summer seemed to have left a day behind; and to have come back to look for it, the new world, like the old, was preparing for winter.

In one of the lower rooms of a house on Forty-first Street, whose number lay in the first hundred, but is immaterial to our story, the morning light streams in upon a small, supple figure which lies curled up on a low divan,—a divan so colossal in its proportions that the figure looks even smaller than it is,—and illuminates a picture that tells its own story to the inquisitive sun-beams. The room, which is large, though furnished in the main with the faded elegance that announces the lodging-house, shows by a few of its more prominent objects that its occupant has come thither from haunts of luxury and taste. The observant eye can pick out at a glance the objects that are the property of the woman who lies on the divan in the reckless *abandon* of sleep, relics of former years when her footsteps fell in softer places. An inlaid piano by Steinway, a screen of rare Japanese brocade, a proof-etching or two, a masterpiece of Meissonier, and an unfinished sketch by an artist whose name gives market value to a line drawn across a sheet of mill-board, some matchless Satsuma and Kâga porcelain, and some scraps of rare stuffs thrown across chairs of bastard design, in a vain attempt to conceal their illegitimacy—all bespeak the *artiste*, the woman of refined taste. The floor is covered with a matting of scented Indian grasses, that fills the air with a quaint, pungent odour, and over it are strewn tattered but glorious Persian and Turkish rugs.

But what catches the eye and holds the senses, taking prisoner the imagination, is the divan on which the little immobile live thing rests. It is very large and very low, covered in brown satin and furs, and cumbered with huge cushions of varied but harmoniously combined coloured silks. A great sheet of rich brocade is drawn in a crumpled mass to a corner, and is falling on the ground over the edge of the divan; the cushions are doubled up and punched into numberless odd shapes, their corners sticking out in all directions; and *blottie* among them is the small, supple, sleeping form of the woman, whose individuality harmonizes to admiration with her surroundings. Her attitude, which would strike the ignorant observer as intensely uncomfortable, so curled and twisted does it seem, looks, in her case, perfectly natural and easy. She is but half undressed, and must have fallen asleep almost unconsciously, when, in the conflict of Morpheus and Eros, exhaustion had overtaken her unawares. At least it appears so; every line of the dormant figure and its minutest details reveal a delicious lassitude. One little foot, in a slipper of gold brocade, rests on the floor; the other slipper has fallen off, and the foot is drawn up under the figure. The light silk covering has slipped away, revealing a stocking of open-worked gold-green silk stretched over curves to which it clings as if fearful of marring their beauty by the slightest suspicion of a wrinkle, and heightens the dazzling tints of a glimpse of the satin-like skin, that sleep has indiscreetly revealed above the stocking.

It is only a glimpse, for a "mysteriette" of pink silk covers the rest of the figure, without hiding its delicate, sensuous curves— only making the picture more indefinite and more alluring by adding the subtle charm of the unseen to charms which the imagination grasps without difficulty.

She lies deep among the cushions, her head thrown back in a mass of shiny hair of a bronzed, burnt gold, which, uniting with the purple brown of the divan, makes an exquisite background for the pale shell-pink of her skin. The stream of light which steals into the darkened room lies in a solid ray across the divan, shedding over the sleeping figure a glow which seems not to illuminate it, but to be shed by the figure itself upon the surrounding brocades; and so, a perfectly natural effect of light seems to become a weird, spectral mystery. The dead stillness of the world, the halo environing the sleeping woman, the dim light pervading all else in the room, combine to make a picture which embodies all that there is of sensuous poesy in real life.

The delicate brows, the finely-curved lips, the curved nostrils, and subtly-rounded chin, betray the woman's Oriental origin; and if any doubt remained on the point it is dispelled when, without any start or visible effort of awakening, Mahmouré di Zulueta opens her grand, brown eyes and, with a movement of intense, unconscious longing, stretches out her arms to the empty air, and encountering naught save a tumbled cushion, grasps a fold of it with a little feverish clutch as, using her arm lever-wise, she gives her whole body a comprehensive voluptuous twist that hides the scrap of skin that dazzled the sunbeam, beneath the falling folds of silk, and sinks back into the cushions with a scarce satisfied sigh. As she does so her hand encounters something hidden among the cushions: she draws it forth and recognizes it with a smile of happy recollection. It is a portrait—it had been her last thought as she sank to sleep, and is her first on waking; and as she holds it before her, it brings a warmer tint to her cheek, a brighter glow to her dark eyes. The face before her, be it by reason of the photographer's art or of the individuality of the original, is one of great beauty, intense, delicate, and very youthful, so youthful indeed that at a first glance it might be taken for that of a mere boy, but on closer inspection one discovers in it a firmness, enhanced by the high intelligence of the brow; and the woman gazing at the picture through her half-closed eyes sees there the self hidden behind the mask. To all else he may be and is what he chooses; to her his inmost being is revealed, and through the changeless, senseless reflection, she sees the thousand flashes of the master passion which she, and she alone, has bred within him—a passion of which he had always laughingly declared himself incapable.

49

And concerning the woman herself, the supple Eastern woman with the strange Eastern name Mahmouré di Zulueta? There is, I know, something inexpressibly tedious in the "previous histories" of heroes and heroines of romance. Perhaps I ought to have made a former chapter of that of Mahmouré, for it is quite quaint enough to spur a biographer to his highest effort in this particular branch of natural history. I am not going to enter into a discussion of whether her history was stranger than her nature, or whether her nature was stranger than her history; whether her history was the result of her nature, or *vice versâ*. Without the remotest tendency to mediocrity she was neither very good nor very bad; she was always rather both, and often very much one of them; the world being divided, admittedly, into men, women and Mahmouré di Zulueta. Probably it was an effect of her home training, the tender influences of a father and mother who worshipped her, that prevented the bad in her from developing to its fullest extent. It is thus that many great characters in history are spoilt, are, as it were, still-born. Without the refining influences of her home Mahmouré would have been historic, but whether as a Vallière, a Brinvilliers, a Bradamante, or a Lola Montez, far be it from the present historian to hazard a conjecture.

Her early years were monotonous, spent between the English home where she found her level in gentle, commonplace family affection, and the continental *conservatoire* where she labored from an early age for the development of the talent that should some day make her famous; for her father, himself an artist of great enthusiasm and judgment,—two rarely concomitant attributes,—strained his every resource to fit her for the position which he felt she was bound to attain. She rewarded him for all his bitter struggles (and God alone knows what privations he had endured for her) in the usual way. Developed to womanhood at an age when most of her sex are hardly out of the nursery, she chose to fancy herself in love; and she married, when barely fifteen, a complicated concentration of the lowest qualities peculiar to half-a-dozen nationalities. The name of this mongrel was di Zulueta. A friend of the family, expert in variegated genealogies, asserted that his father was a Greek and his mother an Italian, that he was born on board a Spanish ship in French waters, and was a naturalized American citizen domiciled in England!

It is hardly worth while to attempt the impossible, or to describe the abysmal depths of blackguardism to which this gutter-bred cur had sunk by the sheer specific gravity of his own cowardly vileness; but he oozes into my narrative at this point, for he married this child—for not only in years, but in everything else save physique, she was a child; and thus her first folly, the launch of her "inconsequent" career (in the Balzacian sense), was committed. Art for art's sake, which might have been to her a gracious, generous protectress, was thrust aside, and the first step in her progress was taken.

And what a progress hers should have been with the materials at her command! A gorgeous voice, of great range and power, and, above all, of that quality so rare, a perfect sympathy—that one gift of blood and race without which the finest voice becomes "as sounding brass, or tinkling cymbals." Fantastic but dazzling personal beauty, the matchless health of a perfect constitution, were all factors in a personality that should echo her fame from world to world—and the first exercise of her will had been to fling the whole treasure of herself into the grasp of a foul-mouthed, under-bred ruffian.

The first era of her life may be said to have commenced with her marriage, which, though uneventful in itself, was a fitting probation for what was to follow. He was a hard taskmaster to his child-wife, but, brute though he was, he treated—from motives of policy—his golden goose with some show of affection: but his coarseness killed the goose. Had he been a clever rascal he might have kept the girl; as it was he never spared her, feeling sure of the obedience she dumbly gave, never looking deeper when some greater exaction than usual struck a flash from the highly-charged personality he was trifling with. He was consequently not a little astonished when, one night, in the presence of her father, she remarked coolly and with no passion or quiver in her voice:

"I am not going to live with you any longer."

Her father, who had refused his sanction to the marriage, and loathed her husband, still did what he believed to be his duty, and urged her to reconsider her decision.

"Better let me go now, when there is no man in the case. If I wait six months longer, there will be," she had said, calmly but quite characteristically.

It was not long before this that she had made her début on the stage, and that début had created a furore. Men about town had but one topic of conversation—this new girl with the great, wondering, innocent eyes; and a Great Personage (as novelists love to call libertines of the blood-royal), on his first visit to the theatre, had sent for her. She had no idea of the importance of the attention, and kept the G. P. so long waiting that the G. P. indignantly retired. This was much commented upon in the theatre, and doubtless did not escape the observation of intelligent managers. Throughout this period that husband of hers was her execrated monster; but for her father's sake she endured the burden, until month after month added feathers by the ton to her load, and at last the result came in the calm, dispassionate words that terminated her married life.

With the advent of this relief departed every moral reserve, and her vagabond, Bohemian imagination began to expand. She had no lover and wanted none—later on she had lovers and still wanted none:—liberty seemed so glorious. Experience had taught her that man would steal away from her this newly attained possession; and the word "Freedom" was emblazoned upon the oriflamme that led her into and out of every scrape that ornamented her life. She had vowed never to be enthralled again; and she all but kept her vow.

She became the fashion. Her little rooms, just close enough to Belgrave Square to swear by, and avoid the ambiguity of the euphemism, "South Belgravia," were the cherished haunt of the smartest men in town. I say "men" advisedly, for no "man" could boast one jot of possession. Her own income gave her independence, and she laughed at the Richelieus and Rochesters of the *foyer* and the *coulisses*. Of course, one or two men more enterprising than the rest sought by every means to capture what, by reason of its impossibility of capture, appeared a hundredfold more attractive than it possibly was, and by force of constant pressure came very near breaking, if not wearing away, the stone; but, on the whole, there was no getting over the fact that Mahmourd remained, through sheer disinclination, her own mistress—and nobody else's. She had plenty of "episodes" but no "histories."

Why follow her amid the thousand scenes of passion, real and pretended, that, like every beautiful theatrical Bohémienne, she passed through—amused sometimes, excited sometimes, disgusted often, but touched, never. She kept the foremost rank in her profession until, weary of the reiteration of unsought conquest, she sought the New World. With all London at her feet, she travelled three thousand miles to find the Pygmalion who should quicken this worldly Galatea of European Bohemia.

Just before she left London, a celebrated journalist, who led a light-hearted life of libel and lickings, said to her:

"Dear child, why don't you marry Lord Blank? Acting as the Countess of Blank over the water, you would make your fortune—besides, it would be such fun writing paragraphs about it; I haven't had such a lovely chance since my wife bolted with D——."

"Thanks," she had replied; "sorry I can't oblige you—but never mind. Get my obituary ready for an emergency, and I'll leave you my diary to work from."

Thus she reached New York; and there, shutting herself up, she abandoned the world which she found took such vast amusement out of her, and gave her none in return, living a life of the closest retirement, a retirement from which she only emerged from time to time with some old friend of her earlier days.

By this time Mahmouré's age was—well, never mind; I didn't intend to begin the sentence.

And thus four years sped by, during which she worked hard and successfully as ever. She was the very incarnation of health, the wonder of all who saw her, so fresh and girlish was she; for all the world judged her life—of which they knew nothing—to be what it might have been had she so willed it. For in the New World, as in the Old, she inspired deep, wild passions which to her were mere pathological curiosities. She had caprices, of course! but they were not what she wanted; and at last she became resigned and made up her mind that love, the crowning joy of woman-hood, was not to be hers.

✻

The end came terribly and suddenly. The wild, irregular years of artist life succeeded at last in undermining the gigantic constitution, and one day, in the middle of a peal of laughter, she fell to the ground, dyeing the white frou-frou of laces, the folds of silk, her white satin couch, and the masses of heavy exotic flowers with which she loved to deck herself, with the crimson life-blood that welled from some unseen injury. The picture was an apposite termination to her unconventional life, as it appeared when, lying unconscious, they found her an hour later, incarnadined as if with her very soul's self—the poor little feet now so limp in their pink satin slippers, with the crushed mass of sensuous flowers, their waxy whiteness scarce whiter than the lifeless features of what had been an hour before—Mahmouré di Zulueta.

For five long, weary months she lay between life and death, and then, her lovely figure, her overflowing vitality, her voice,—all, save her beauty, which remained, chastened and refined by her interview with the Dark Angel,—things of the past, Mahmouré realized that the end of her artist-life was come, and relinquishing the Bohemia of Thespis, she turned to that of the Muses, and drawing upon her rich store of experience, adopted a life of literature, seeking the acquaintanceship and companionship of its masters.

It was shortly after this that Paul du Peyral was presented to her in the foyer of the Metropolitan Opera House—and the introduction was a complete success.

When first Paul du Peyral had met Mahmouré di Zulueta they had immediately cemented between themselves a merry bond of good-fellowship. Each respected the talents of the other; on her side there was a certain curiosity to examine the handsome young Southerner who had led such a laughing, conquering life among the women of two continents. They had taken up their cues the first time he took advantage of her permission to call upon her, and had engaged in a brilliant little battle of epigram, in which they had talked much irresponsible philosophy and cheap cynicism, and had scoffed at love right merrily, though, in the minds of both, there arose Balzac's axiom, "*qui parle d'amour fait l' amour*," to talk of love is to make love—she, amused by the contrast between his looks and his speech, the one so young and the other so old; and he, delighted at finding that the woman he had known by sight and name so long, was gifted with a mental freedom so essentially identical with his own. And so their first interview had passed, leaving nothing but an interest inspired by each in the other's mind, with enough danger mingled with it to make them await with impatience their next.

It soon came, and was soon repeated. She used to curl herself up on the divan, whilst he walked about, and, half seriously, and half laughingly, talked about himself or exchanged epigrams with her on platonic friendship, which they professed a belief in outwardly and confessed to ridiculing inwardly. They resembled nothing so much as gymnasts delighting in their own danger, as they danced on a tight-rope of platitude stretched across the gulf of passion.

This operation was actively proceeding one evening when a footstep and a knock announced the approach of some guest or other. As she rose to open to the new-comer, almost unconscious of the significance of her words, she said hurriedly, "Sit him out, whoever he is!" and admitted an old and evidently harmless "family friend." He was one of those good, innocent creatures who attach themselves to beautiful women in this capacity, regretting every moment of their lives their harmlessness and innocence, but clinging to these attributes feverishly as their sole excuses for existence.

His entry hastens the *dénouement*. She has held herself in check when alone with the man who, in her soul, she has begun to long for with all the passion of her wild Oriental nature, and has purposely held herself at something of a tension, from pride rather than from prudery, so anxious is she not to let the wooing appear to be hers. But now she revels in the luxury of "letting go," protected as it were by the presence of Unnecessary Respectability. Her wondrously supple body, following the dictates of her scarce-formed passion, now writhes itself upon the divan into a thousand unconsciously exquisite *poses*. Slight though it is, Paul du Peyral, deeply versed in the ways of woman, sees the change, notes the deeper colour on the lips, the brighter light in the dark eyes, and he knows that the end is not far off now. She talks to the Unnecessary Friend with a freedom, an utter disregard for conventionality, and a reckless gayety that make the Unnecessary Friend's mental hair stand on end. He also cannot make out why the youthful stranger does not go away, according to the rules laid down in the "Complete Manual of Etiquette for Gentlemen," but finally, after having made several heroic attempts to dislodge him, all of which are epigrammatically parried, and leave him doubtful whether the youthful stranger is a paragon of politeness or of impertinence, he resigns himself, takes up his unwilling hat, and leaves them.

Now that they are really alone a fear arises in the minds of both lest by precipitation the analysis may be spoilt—to borrow a phrase from the laboratory. He knows thoroughly well how one false note would jar her beyond possibility of re-established harmony, so, adopting the tactics of Fabius Maximus Cunctator on an historic occasion, he waits. She has thrown herself back on the divan and signed to him to sit by her side.

"May I?" says he, and sinks among the cushions at a virtuous distance.

*Why* can she think of nothing clever to say? All she *does* say is, "Is not this a lazy lounge to lie about on?"

"Delicious!" he answers; "but then everything about you is so restful, so soothing. Do you know, for a nervous man, as I am (though it doesn't appear), it is an exquisite pleasure to be with you, to sit near you, to touch you?" He has taken up one of her hands, and is softly, nervously, playing with the fingers. "Do you mind my playing with this? it is so pretty."

"Oh, not at all!" in the same tone as she would refuse another cup of tea.

"Have you ever been magnetized? do you believe in electro-biology?" he says, gently passing his fingers up to her elbow and drawing them back with a sensuous, lingering pressure.

"I don't know—see if you can do it."

He is apparently wholly and entirely taken up with his experiment, giving her a chance to raise her guard, as it were. He does not look at her, and so, after a while, she relaxes; a languor born of his wonderful magnetic touch envelops her, and she looks at him, as she thinks, unseen. His face is so tranquil, she cannot decide if it is science which at each magnetic pass leads his hand nearer to her shoulder. Her sleeve is loose, he has raised it—for purposes of his scientific experiment. He draws his sensitive fingers down her arm very slowly as he says, "How lovely these little blue veins are! see this one, for instance."

He is evidently very much interested in "this one," for his head gets nearer and nearer till his lips touch the extended arm, and rest there warm and moist. A deadly stillness prevails, as, with an intense difficulty, she suppresses the tremor caused by the pressure of his lips; but she forgets that the very suppression has caused a contraction of the muscles that he has felt and interpreted. When he raises his head there is a humidity about his eyes which makes it very difficult for her to preserve her impressive appearance. He makes no movement, but only looks, with that sweet, damp look, till she can endure no longer. She raises herself a little from the cushions as if to speak, and then sinks back, a little nearer to the silent, imploring face.

He will not advance one step apparently. Suddenly, after a little movement, as if of pain, she takes the comb from her hair, and the glorious mass falls all over her, reminding him of the picture of the Magdalen in the Pitti Palace. Its subtle perfume seems to envelop him, and, plunging his hands among the glistening threads, he buries his face in it, almost with a sob. She remains very, *very* still. At last he whispers:

"How exquisite!—and how sweet of you to let me!" And he fills the mass of bronze gold with wild kisses, till she, with a rapid movement, clasps her hands around his neck and draws his lips to hers.

He seems all entangled in her sweet, sinuous embrace. At last he takes his lips from hers for a moment, and gazes through her half-closed eyes, and then, with a little cry, he gathers her up in his arms and clasps her, panting, and almost senseless, to his bosom.

✳

"If you would only love me a little! I know I don't deserve it; all men say that, I believe; but in my case it's true, for I was always worthless. Won't you help me to a new life?"

As he spoke he crushed the little figure again in his arms; her answer was scarcely audible, so close had she laid her head against his heart: "Do you know how near to death I am?" and, as he pressed her closer to him, the wan light died out of her face and she seemed transfigured. A moment before, when he had wound his arms about her, her features had been worn and weary, scarce showing a trace of reason for the worship that had been hers, and was hers still. True hearts had ached to see her look as she looked now, and to hear her confess the wealth of her passionate love in every quiver of her rich, low voice.

For now her face lit up with the glory of a passion hitherto unknown in her wild, brilliant life; the veil of sadness and sickness faded, and left a face, whose charm we are powerless to judge— can only feel. It is not beauty, but something so fascinating, so strange, that even the fresh young face of a beautiful girl might remain unnoticed beside it, though she is on that borderland between youth and age so dreaded by a woman who has had a far greater portion than her share of the world's admiration and man's homage at her feet.

And he who holds the little figure in so close an embrace—look at him as he stands, glorified by his perfect youth and strength. Tall, heavily but lithely built, a strong head set massively on such shoulders as woman loves to look upon, and fears, in spite of herself. A hero to the backbone, though born in some little village of Louisiana, with his long, fair hair and blue-gray eyes, handsome as a man of his size should be, though not formed on the perfect lines which constitute an artist's ideal. His mouth, soft, gentle, and sensual, is too heavily formed for beauty, though it is in keeping with himself, for it seems to promise so much in the way of individuality; the chin is firm but not too heavy or coarse, with a good-natured dimple in it which is one of the principle charms of the face. He is much older than his age; many who have lived his years are boys, but he is a man in every sense of the term. How he can have absorbed so much life as he has is a mystery, as yet; but judged, even as she judges him, by the fierce critical light of the greater world which she knows exoterically and esoterically so well, he comes unharmed through the ordeal. "*Si jeunesse savait, si viellesse pouvait!*" said the Sage. Well, his is a *jeunesse qui sait et qui peut!*

A great fire of joy is in her eyes, for she had honestly believed that no power of man could bring her back to life and love in the world, and all this shines in her face as she answers him once more: "Do you know how ill I am?" For she would not take advantage of the impulse of a moment, though fraught with such insane happiness and intoxication as this.

"I know," he answers, kissing her senses away, "I know; but you shall live again and your veins shall throb with the pulses of my love. I will give you life in which to forget your foolish fancies."

"Why have you come to disturb my life?" she says, after a pause. "I know how much older I am than you. I am not strong enough to love you as I might. *Don't* play with me." This, almost imploringly.

"What is age to us who have only just begun to live?" he answers.

And so she resists no more, but lies in his arms, just as he had lifted her up and laid her on the cushions of the divan; her lips are close to his, and then she knows of nothing save of that wild embrace, is conscious of nothing save the soft touch of his finely moulded hands. At last, as if to wake himself from some exquisite dream, he rises to his feet and looks down upon her.

At parting, whilst he holds her in his arms, he says, almost malignantly:

"Never let us injure one another by word, or deed, or thought; for two such enemies as we should be, this world is far too small."

No other words, no protestation of devotion could have given her so full a measure of joy; for a savage love is the only one possible for her, gentle though all her life has seemed to be. She stands before him, looking up into his face, on hers a wonder, a curiosity, a questioning that seems to say, "Why did you seek me? what can be the reason? How have I won you?" After a long look she murmurs, as her hands cling to his arms that are clasped round her waist:

"I think you are right—there is no middle course for us."

There is nothing very clever, or original, or significant in the few words, but a look creeps into her face which does not fit the soft features—it is the expression of some beautiful wild animal, fraught with all the jealous intensity of passion, revealing—dimly, though indeed revealing—a cruel, wild love that kills rather than relinquishes its object.

Fascinated, both of them, their lips meet and part silently, and leave them quivering and so he goes out into the night leaving her transfigured.

She looks into the glass critically, searchingly: she hurries away an instant and then, returning, looks again. The bronze-gold wrapper she had worn has fallen off, leaving her swathed in a gown of soft, clinging white silk, which is bound around her in sinuous folds—even illness has been powerless to rob her of the supple grace that she inherits from her Greek ancestors. She looks at the reflection, evidently satisfied; then a doubt grows up within her and she turns to another glass, thinking the first may have flattered:—no, the reflection is still good to look upon; her lips are crimson with excitement, and give greater beauty to her dazzling, perfect teeth: she looks fixedly, without conceit, as if appraising to its exact value each feature, seeking to justify in her dreadfully wise mind all that the last six hours have brought. With the memory, her knees give away beneath her and she stumbles into the cushions of the divan, and as she almost unconsciously continues to balance the pros and cons, the last remaining spark of reason dies amid the ashes of memory, and, with a big sigh, Mahmouré di Zulueta sinks to sleep.

With the practiced indiscretion of the romancist and historian, I have betrayed the confidence of the early sunbeams, and already the reader has assisted, in the spirit, at the waking of Mahmouré. Little by little she roused herself, and began the indolent and luxurious operation of clothing her little, fantastic body, whilst she sipped her coffee, and at intervals embarked on the arduous undertaking of crunching an atom of toast; for, like all Oriental women, it was with the greatest difficulty that Mahmouré could be induced to feed like a Christian—which she was not and had no intention of becoming. She preferred to spoil her appetite and ruin her constitution with sweets and strange groceries, which later called forth Paul's dictum that "Mahmouré lived in a state of chronic *hors d'œuvres*, physically, mentally, and morally!" It was nearly one o'clock before she was what she called dressed, and, robed or rather wrapped in crossing and recrossing folds of white china silk, with a little Greek jacket of gold embroidery on a burnt-sienna ground, she punched the cushions of the divan into a comfortable nest, and settled herself among them with a scrap of embroidery, the last novel sent her from Europe by its illustrious author, and a writing pad whereon to make a show of writing letters that never got written.

She was cuddled up thus, diffusing around her a quaint fragrance of sandal-wood, of myrrh, and of Tonquin, when a card was brought her: "*Mr. Paul du Peyral.*" "Ask him in? Certainly!" And it was thoroughly characteristic of the woman, that, instead of arranging a fold here, a ribbon there, and giving a precautionary touch to her hair, to receive the natural—enemy man, she merely stretched herself out a little more comfortably among the cushions, and held up her hand to be kissed by Paul, who had almost to kneel on the divan by her side for the purpose.

"I'm so glad you've come," said she; "it proves at any rate that it's all real. I was beginning to wonder if I hadn't been sent to sleep by the 'family friend,' and that you had both left me to a pleasing, but wearing kind of dream."

"No," replied he, "it was all exquisitely real—and, being so, what do you think of it?"

"I don't know what to think. I never felt like it before—it's all new to me. Suggest something, please."

"I wonder whether you would act on my suggestion."

"Certainly if it's feasible."

"And supposing it isn't feasible?"

"Well—I should try;" this with an air of lazy but interested curiosity.

"Let us marry one another!"

With a sudden movement she started into a sitting posture, and thus, her arms clasped around her knees, she remained, her brown eyes wide open and gazing into his with an expression of lively amazement.

"You suggest to marry me—you who know three things that would 'make the heart of the stoutest quail,' as they say in inexpensive fiction? First, my age; second, the whole of my inconsequent life; and third, that my illness has left me a mere shattered wreck of womanhood."

"Certainly and those three things I meet with three incontrovertible facts. First, a woman is as old as she looks, and you look about my age; besides, your real tale of years give you an experience that makes you more maddeningly fascinating to me than any girl between seventeen and five-and-twenty could be. Second, your 'inconsequent' life is at an end, for 1 shall be your last love, just as you are my first. Speaking properly, a woman's last love is the only kind of love that can satisfy the first love of a man. Besides, your love for me can only be terminated by the death of one of us, for I shall love you till I die, and if you were unfaithful to me I should kill you without a moment's hesitation. And third, true, your health is shattered, therefore it is necessary that you should not only be taken care of as only a husband can take care of you, but also that, should I die, you should inherit what little property I have, as only a wife can inherit. I might almost say to you, in fact, as M. Le Comte de Nocé said to Mlle. de Pontivi, '*Voulez vous être ma veuve?*'—will you be my widow?—for my life is full of dangers, and I might die any moment."

"Paul, you overwhelm me! A man of the world, such as you are, cannot be blind to the fact that marriage with Mahmouré di Zulueta would be ruin to your scheme of existence, which depends, as you yourself have told me, on your social position."

"*Chère amie*, your words are like those of a printed book with the leaves in it. What you say—as I expected you would say—is perfectly true, but why and how, you can scarcely guess. Curl yourself up among your cushions; I am going to expound my plan with a long story."

"Go on, *mon ami.*"

"I, Paul du Peyral, aged twenty-eight, descendant of a Franco-Spanish alliance, rejoicing, as few of us Creoles do, in the possession of a certificate of legitimate original birth and ancestry, live, move, and have my being by a caprice—the caprice of a cranky old Southern gentleman whom I had the good fortune to please at a moment when he had had what the Irish call "an elegant row" with his entire family. I was left an orphan at sixteen, and, more from pity than from anything else, was adopted as companion, assistant, secretary, steward, or whatever else you like to call it, by an old bachelor who lived a few miles from Baton Rouge, by name Casimir Préault, and who led a solitary, woman-hating life, engrossed in the studies of the indigenous mosquito, the cosmopolitan house-fly, and the naturalized London sparrow. He was very wealthy, and the premonitory symptoms of his demise were consequently watched with cheerful solicitude by his only living relations, the Préaults of New Orleans, of Louisville, and sundry other cities of the South. Now, this old gentleman's nearest living relative was a cousin, by name Victor Préault, whom he cordially hated, and for whose benefit he used continually to devise irritating and ingenious schemes of disappointment. The interest which I educated myself to take in the morals of the mosquito, the haunts of the house-fly, and the pathology of the common sparrow, in spite of my more absorbing interest in psychology, suggested to him a scheme for the disinheriting of Victor Préault, which, however, was tempered by a more or less genuine affection for his cousin's only daughter, Daphne Préault, whom he adored in spite of that young lady's aversion for him, an aversion which rendered futile a cherished scheme of his for the marrying of the said young person to his *protégé*, Paul du Peyral. He consequently made a will, the ingenuity of which has always inspired my profoundest respect. He made a disposition of his entire property to trustees, in trust to pay the entire income to me, on certain conditions and hampered by certain directions. First, I was directed to marry Miss Daphne Préault, whom I had never seen. If she formally refused to marry me, the said income was directed to be paid to me, so that I might be in a position to prosecute his and my hobbies in elegant independence—to wit, psychology, and the studies of the mosquito, the house-fly, and the sparrow. But the will further contained a proviso that, should I ever marry anyone other than the young lady aforesaid, the said income was to be paid thenceforward to Miss Préault; and in the event of my death the same thing was to take place, she being meanwhile invested with a power to dispose of her reversionary interest in the estate, by will, in case of her pre-deceasing me. Now, I am prejudiced against, rather than in favour of, this young woman, and this is one of the reasons I have never married, in spite of the conspiracies of designing mammas, ignorant of the provisions of my benefactor's will. The other reason is, that until I saw you I never loved any woman sufficiently to make her my wife—you alone have the mentality, apart from your exquisite personality, which tempts me to throw up everything; but I have thought of a plan that obviates this latter very painful necessity, though I have, by this time, money enough of my own to render me mildly independent. My plan is this. I am naturally very carefully watched, both by my trustees, and on behalf of Miss Préault, who is, I believe, in Europe somewhere, having gone thither on the death of her father some years ago. We must elude their vigilance, and it may be done in this way: we will go away somewhere and be married very quietly, and then we can return here and go on as we should go on anyhow, only that in the eyes of the world, should they ever guess the completeness of our connection (which is unnecessary, if we are careful), you will be my mistress, whilst between ourselves you will be my wife, and will assert your position after my death, in respect of my separate personal estate. I ask this because I love and admire you—two very different things, and seldom concomitant—from the bottom of my soul, and I verily believe that the knowledge that you *are* my wife will have an excellent effect on both of us. Only, before the world I shall be still Paul du Peyral the scientist, and what is of far greater interest to the world—the bachelor; whilst you will continue to reign in the Bohemia that is so dear to you, as Mahmouré di Zulueta. Say, then, darling, will you take this new lease of life from me?"

The woman, at the conclusion of this speech, had buried her head in the cushions. She kept her face thus hidden for a few minutes, during which neither of them spoke, then, raising her eyes to his, she encircled his neck with her arms he had sunk among the cushions beside her and drew his head down to hers, whispering:

"Paul, Paul, my darling, are you sure you will not regret this?"

"Never, sweetheart."

"But this other woman—it is not fair to her."

"Ah—bah! she is nothing to me, and you are everything. Sooner or later this property must be hers; at present she is ignorant of all; let her continue so. I wrote immediately I came into the property and offered myself to her; she refused me insultingly, and her representatives have never ceased trying to harass me; fortunately, however, though an amateur, the old gentleman was too good a lawyer. If you love me, do not let any thought of these horrible people interfere with our happiness. Tell me, is it 'yes' or 'no'?"

The "Yes" was felt rather than heard; and radiant with hopes, and looking younger than ever in her new-found happiness, Mahmouré di Zulueta lay almost unconscious in her lover's arms.

# CHAPTER III.
## "L'amour Est Enfant de Bohême."

Many are the pros and cons of London weather. It has been said of us Londoners, and I fear with truth, that we have the most horrible weather in the world, especially in autumn and winter; but we can boast with equal truth that nowhere else in the world do we find an indoor comfortableness that renders even a foggy day delightful, as we do in London—nowhere else can one be so unspeakably cosy as in a London snuggery whilst the elements practise for another Deluge, or the world outside grows white and soft with snow. Well, the day after Gabriel Hawleigh's party was "a foggy day"—and by this I mean a day as foggy as London knows how to make it when she gives her mind to the subject—a day that reminded one of the pictures of London by Leech in the early numbers of *Punch*, wherein link-boys flit like the familiar demons of the fog.

It was useless for the Princess Daphne to attempt to work, for the fog lay on the glass of the skylight in her studio roof like a curtain; so she drew an arm-chair close up to the fire, lit the gas, and took up a book—one of those cynical modern romances of immoral psychology which combine the somniferousness of the old-fashioned novel with the innocuousness of the nursery-rhyme. The warm red and brown lights flashed by the fire amid the encircling gloom, the gas-jet with its shade, and the girl's brown dress made a charming picture in the stillness of the fog; but the Princess was not sorry to have it disturbed by a ring at the bell, closely followed by the appearance of Eric Trevanion. He also had been driven by the "murk" from his soul-elevating easel, and his thoughts had brought him to the door of the Princess Daphne's cottage.

"Ah! Mr. Trevanion," said she, as she saw who it was: "to what am I indebted for the honour?"

"To the weather, Princess, which gave me an excuse I was ardently desiring."

"I'm sure you require no excuse to call on me; if you're let in, it means that I am glad to see you—or anybody. If I'm busy I 'sport my oak'! Today I am honestly dull, trying to read this miserable production. I've formulated an axiom this morning, which is as follows: 'Modern literature is the apotheosis of truism.' Formerly everything was paradox; a writer thought he had only to state the glaringly improbable or contradictory, to catch the popular taste: today he says sapiently, 'To put on one's hat wrong side foremost is very uncomfortable;' and instead of saying, 'Well, what of it? we know that!' his readers hold up their hands and cry, 'Dear me, how *true*! what an *observer* he is! why, we've often noticed that ourselves!' Yes, modern literature is the apotheosis of truism, and the criterion of its excellence is piracy in the United States. If a book is clever enough to say nothing that we don't know already, it is clever enough to be stolen in America. Such is fame!"

And the Princess laughed a little, silvery laugh, which stopped short as she saw the smile die away on the face of Eric Trevanion.

"Why, Sir Knight of the Rueful Visage," said she, "what ill news shortens the smile which I expected as homage to my tirade against the novelist of today?"

"No ill news, Princess; only I'm puzzled. I can't make you out; you're so brilliant, and clever, and—all *that*, you know— and you're so absolutely by yourself in the world, I can't account for you; you're a kind of Sphinx to us all, and yet you talk more freely about yourself than anyone I have ever known. But it's never to the point. You know what I mean, though I can't say it," concluded he, helplessly.

"Well, are you another Davus, or will you be Œdipus?"

"I don't know who Davis is, unless he's the man who bought that academy picture of yours, and I never heard of the other gentleman," replied Eric, mendaciously, so as to hear Miss Préault's definition, which was bound to be interesting if not funny.

"Well, the Sphinx, you know, was a bewildering lady with a taste for cannibalism and conundrums."

"Yes, I know that."

"Davus was the journalist of the time, the regret of whose life was that he was not Œdipus, who was the contemporary Irving Bishop, and read the lady's thoughts."

"And what good did it do him?"

"No good; he would have married the Sphinx, or what was human of her, and killed what was animal and bad, and no doubt, like many a modern husband, would have been rather sorry for himself. As it is, I believe he married his mamma."

"But you are not the Sphinx really."

"Yes, I am. I am half-human and half-animal," returned the girl, gazing abstractedly into the fire. "There is a great deal in me that is terribly human, and there's an underneath side to my character which is terribly savage. I don't know which side troubles me most; and I don't know whether they will ever be separated from one another, and if they are, which will remain incarnate in Daphne Préault, and which will fly off into space;" she raised her eyes as she finished, and found Trevanion leaning forward in his chair, his wide-stricken eyes fixed upon her with an expression that fancy had often placed there for her before, but intensified, feverish, yearning.

"Princess! Daphne—you gave me my choice a minute ago whether to be Davus or the other man—let me be the other man—let me solve the riddle of your life for you. Surely you have seen how I worship you. I never thought I should dare to tell you of it, but I can't help it—I love you." He had taken one of her hands in his and was covering it with kisses; she did not try to take it away, but merely looked down with a gaze of infinite pity at him as she replied:

"Yes, I knew it, but it isn't to be. I would love you in return if I dared; but I cannot, I dare not, trust myself to love anyone: sooner or later you would discover all my badness and weakness, and then it would be all over. The unknown is always a goal for one's ambition; I am a goal for yours, which is, I fear, more than half curiosity. So long as you see me from a distance you wonder and do not question; touch me, and you would soon criticise; and when we criticise we soon despise. Eric, my dear friend, I like you far too well ever to show you that weak underside of my nature. Be a companion, a friend to me, if you will,—you are the only man who ever had the chance to be, but a lover—never! Come, *mon ami*, we are merry Bohemians; don't let's trouble our life with the silly emotions of the outer world."

He had risen to his feet, and laying one arm upon the mantelpiece, was looking into the fire, leaning his head upon his hand. Her words troubled him; troubled him with a sensation that was neither pleasure nor pain, but confusion of thought. He brought her the armor of gold, but she refused it, almost inviting his offer of the armor of brass: she had offered him a kind of emotional Platonism, that made his heart beat high with hope, but refused his avowed love on the one plea that flatters a man whilst he will not accept it—her own unworthiness.

"But I want something more," he said; "I want your love."

"No, boy," she replied; "come to me for sympathy, for friendship, for assistance, for confession; but love—real love only comes to a man once. It has come to you, but you don't see it; some day you will, and then you'll be very grateful to Daphne Préault for not engaging your heart, your soul, but only your brain."

"What do you mean?"

"I mean that I know a girl who loves you with her whole heart. Ah! no; I am not going to tell you who it is, if you can't see for yourself: but when you are married you shall come here with your wife, and Daphne Préault will continue in the sunshine of your life the friendship that she inaugurated with you in a London fog. Now leave me alone, dear boy, and come here to tea with me tomorrow—you will have thought it over by then, and realized that it was for the best that I advised you."

So saying she gave him her hand to kiss, and with her little imperial gesture dismissed him. He stood looking at her humbly, helplessly, for a moment, and then—he was gone.

The Princess remained in the house just long enough to wrap herself in a cloak and put on a hat, and then started forth to call at the Hawleigh's. Here also she found work at the easel suspended, but Gabriel and Maye were lost in a cloud of harmony that seemed to make the very fog that had filtered into the studio vibrate with its passion. Daphne Préault did not disturb the musicians, but stood at the entry to the studio till the music should have ceased. When this moment arrived, Gabriel, violin in hand, flung himself onto the lounge, whilst Maye merely bent over the keys and seemed lost in reverie. It was Gabriel, in turning over on the couch, who first saw the magnificent figure standing in the flickering light, and springing to his feet, exclaimed,—

"*Princess!*"

At the word, Maye turned also and greeted the visitor, and then they all drew chairs to the fire and began to talk with daring originality about the weather.

"You have the advantage of me here," began Miss Préault, when this subject had been exhausted. "When you can't work you can play—sounds like a truism, doesn't it? but you know what I mean. Now *I* simply have to read or receive visits until I get tired of both, and seek congenial society here. Which do you prefer, Gabriel, the fiddle or the easel?"

"Well, really I hardly know," replied he; "sometimes I wish I'd been brought up a professional musician instead of a painter, and at others I wouldn't give up painting if the triumvirate of ghosts of Stradivarius, Tourte, and Paganini came down and implored me to become a violinist by trade."

"And who are they?"

"The Trinity of the Fiddler's worship, the Princes of Fiddle-making, Bow-making, and Fiddle-playing. I invoke their names every time I take up my violin, and beg their shades to inspire me. Ah! I should never be an artist on the instrument; I should always remain a virtuoso."

"And what is the difference?"

"Well, it's the difference between the active and the passive: the artist is master of his violin, the virtuoso is its slave. Joachim, Viardot, Vieuxtemps were and are artists; Sarasate, Wilhelmj, Paganini, were and are virtuosi. Don't you see the difference? The artist can read at sight the most difficult music, and plays by note; the virtuoso plays more, as a rule, by ear, than otherwise. The artist strives after perfection of *technique* for the interpretation of the works of the great composers for the instrument; the virtuoso, on the other hand, aims at brilliant execution for the interpretation of his own moods, his own thoughts, his own fantasies. That's what I do; and there are days when I wish I had given my whole time to it."

"Then, I suppose," remarked Daphne, "that, just as you are a virtuoso with your bow, Eric Trevanion is a virtuoso with the brush. Certainly he doesn't aim at perfection of *technique*, and certainly he tries to interpret his own moods, thoughts, and fantasies—and does so to his own satisfaction doubtless!"

"Well, yes; I think we may call Eric a virtuoso of the camel-hair; his impressions are hardly what one would call artistic—are they?"

"And what do you think about it, Maye?" queried the Princess.

"Do you know, I never thought of Eric as an artist. I look upon his profession as a colossal joke, and an excuse for keeping untidy, artistic rooms."

"What do you think of him as a man?"

"Good gracious, Daphne, what an indiscreet question! Why, I think him a very worthy person, very bright and kind and all that; but I never made a study of him. Why ask *me*?" The girl did her utmost to make her light reply as meaningless and casual in tone as possible; but the flush that came over her face as she answered told the Princess the story she wanted to know.

"I wonder he has never married," she went on, vivisectinally.

"On the contrary," broke in Gabriel, "the wonder to me would be if any girl would ever be bold enough to take him, and be painted continually as a 'Note in Black and White,' 'A Crochet in White Worsted,' 'A Quaver in B Minor,' or something eccentric of that sort."

"I think," returned Miss Préault, abstractedly, "that he'd make some girl a perfect husband. He'd be so tender, and gallant, and chivalrous, and delicate."

Maye looked at her gratefully, and would have spoken, only Gabriel cut in, remarking:

"Well, I'm glad you think that, because he's madly in love with you."

"Of course he is—so are you," replied the girl, without turning a hair.

"Of course I am, but I'm not so badly bitten as Eric; I'm only at the stage of telling you so whenever I have a chance; he's got to the point of thinking it continually."

"Don't talk nonsense, Gabriel," replied the Princess, sharply.

"I am not talking nonsense: and look here; I wish you'd marry him and take him back to Cornwall or Dartmoor or wherever it is; he's ruining me—here am *I* painting nightmare pictures now."

"Oh! *where?* Show me,"

"Under the seal of profoundest secrecy, I'll show you the great work for the next Academy."

So saying, Gabriel uncovered the canvas on which he had been at work. It represented a London street, in a dense fog. In the foreground, lighted by a yellow blotch of street lamp, a blind itinerant fiddler was playing, apparently unconscious of the state of the atmosphere. A man and a girl were passing, wrapped up snugly, and laughing at one another. Under cover of the fog they had twined their fingers together as the girl held the man's arm tightly in hers; whilst the blind fiddler played on, in apparent ignorance of all. The painting was unfinished, hardly, indeed, more than roughed in, but the composition of the oblique vista of street was perfect, the balance of the figures was masterly, and the whole thing was toned in a manner which showed high artistic skill.

"But, my dear friend," said Daphne Préault, gravely, "this is really a great work if you finish it as you've begun. What shall you call it?"

"'Sunshine in the Fog,' I think, or perhaps, 'It's an ill wind blows nobody any good.' You see, I want to convey the idea that the blind fiddler is unconscious of the fog as well as of the happiness of the young couple flirting under his blind old eyes and under cover of the darkness. It shows that it might be an advantage to be sightless sometimes—you see, to him it's apparently an ordinary day, for the sunshine is in his soul as he hears the two go laughing by."

"Gabriel," said Daphne, "this will be a great picture—mark my words."

"Well, I hope so," said the boy; "it's time my undoubted talents were recognized by the Hanging Committee and the art-dealers. If this goes well, it will make a rent in the cloud, through which I may be enabled to shove some of my lesser masterpieces—known to the vulgar as pot-boilers."

"Well—a thousand congratulations! But I must go back to work, for the sky's clearing a little."

And with this she left them. In the drawing-room she found Mrs. Hawleigh.

"What do you think of the boy's picture, Daphne?" said she.

"I think it is going to be very great. What accounts for his sudden stride?"

"Can't you guess, dear?"

"Ah! And does *she* care for *him*?"

"Yes, I think so. Gratitude would make her do so, but I don't think it is necessary. He has worked hard enough for her, poor boy! I hope nothing will happen to disappoint him; it would be his death-blow, I think."

"Mrs. Hawleigh, forgive me, but has it never occurred to you that she might care for anyone else?—Eric Trevanion, for instance?"

"My dear, I have *feared* so sometimes, but when I see Eric with you, I feel easier about it. You know he adores you, I suppose."

"Yes."

"He has told you so—no doubt?"

"Yes."

"And do you care for him?—pardon me for asking, but I'm so anxious on Gabriel's account; do you care for Eric Trevanion?"

"Yes"—this almost in a whisper.

"And have you told him so?"

"No, I have not told him so."

"Oh! why not, dear? Think a moment—if you love Eric and would tell him so when he asks you, how happy we all should be—you—he—I—and those children in there."

"That boy, you mean, Mrs. Hawleigh?"

"And the girl too, dear; she knows Eric doesn't care about her, and if she knew that you returned his affection, she would give her whole heart undivided to Gabriel, and uninfluenced by that terrible thing, gratitude."

"I hardly know myself enough, Mrs. Hawleigh. Sometimes I am afraid when I think of marriage. There are two sides to my nature, one human and the other savage"—she was unconsciously drifting back to what she had told Trevanion—"and I know that marriage would kill the one and develop the other, and unless the man were a great, strong creature, I am terribly afraid that the human, womanly side of me would disappear. It's the way with all of us Southern American women; we can rule others, but require to be ruled ourselves; and I doubt if Eric Trevanion has it in his power to rule me, to keep me in his power when he gets to know all about the real Daphne Préault, with whom the Daphne Préault *you* know is hardly on speaking terms herself!"

"Oh! you do yourself injustice. All girls do when they are in love. Go and think it over, dear; I am sure you will see that what I say is for the best."

"Very well—I'll think it over."

"That's right—and remember that by making yourself and Eric happy, you are giving a new life to Gabriel and Maye, a new encouragement to him in his work, a new bulwark of defence to Maye, against the whims of her silly little heart."

The two women kissed one another, and the Princess Daphne walked back to her cottage.

It was situated at the other end of Holland Street, and was one of the little houses with a patch of garden in front of it to which I have alluded, in describing the street. When her father, Victor Préault of Baton Rouge, died, leaving her an income which, computed in American dollars, was statable in four figures, of which the first was only one remove from an unit, Daphne, alone in the world, strongly inclined to art, and averse to governessship, had struck her camp, and migrated direct to Holland Street, where her income warranted her in furnishing the little semi-detachment in which the scene I have described between her and Eric had taken place.

Her originality of invention and daring touch had quickly assured her artistic success, and her personality had gradually made for her a throne from which she ruled the colony with a beneficent and almost motherly sway. A better friend "the boys" had never had, and rumour chaunted a variegated though monotonous Iliad—paradoxical though it may seem, written down—of the way in which everyone had been obliged to go through the tortures of unrequited affection and refusal, before settling down into the ranks of the Princess's adoring subjects. The little house was charmingly furnished, and the studio into which the goddess of the place now stepped was characteristic of its denizen as only a studio can become. It was very large, and its general appearance reminded one more of a Roman *atelier* than anything else: its solid furniture consisted of a lounge covered with an enormous bear-skin, a rosewood writing-table, a miniature grand piano by Chickering, and a renaissance cabinet filled with a collection of the silver, ivory, and porcelain toys of the eighteenth and preceding centuries. Daphne Préault painted, as regards touch and subject, with the weird independence of the modern French school; and it seemed as if into her work, which had the minutia and detail of Meissonier, combined with the sensuous fantasy of Vedder and Blake, she flung without reserve the infinite shades of her complicated personality. One of her finest works—which she refused to sell—hung over the high oaken mantel-shelf; it represented Gabriel Hawleigh in his silk working shirt of morning, and "*autres choses*" of afternoon, his collar lying open, his feet thrust into morocco slippers, reclining on the bear-skin of the lounge, with his fiddle under his arm. Evidently he had got up in the middle of his work, seized by some musical whim or other, and, at the conclusion of his performance, had flung himself exhausted onto the fur; the Princess had insisted on painting him thus, and called it after Tourguenieff's marvelous story, "*Le Chant d' Amour Triomphant*." It was an admirable specimen of her skill, and a great favorite among "the boys."

Today, however, she did not paint, but lay till evening almost motionless on the bear-skin, "not at home" to any-one, and revolving in her mind the events and conversations of the morning. A black woman—a negro servant—who had accompanied her across the ocean four years before, brought her tea at five o'clock, and at half-past seven she went forth to dine in Queen's Gate, returning to bed and to sleep soundly till the sunrise woke her next morning.

What the result of the previous day's cogitations had been not even the practised indiscretion of the novelist is entitled to impart to his readers. It is enough for them to know that, today being bright, she worked hard at her Academy picture until Clytie, the darkie woman, bringing in the tea-tray at five o'clock, announced:

"Mr. Trevanion."

Daphne Préault rose, and extending her hand, said:

"*Bon chevalier!* sit down and drink tea and eat things, and then I'll tell you a programme I've made out for our amusement this evening, if you're disengaged."

"I'm always disengaged for you, Princess."

"Very good! that's as it should be. You must go away at six, and come back at half-past seven; I've got two stalls for the Parthenon, and want you to take me to see the new play. *Vi piace cosi?* Does my plan suit you?"

"Certainly," replied Trevanion; and they chatted easily and merrily on different subjects, avoiding the one which was uppermost in their minds, until the stated hour, when the young man, with a joyful "*Au revoir*" left the girl to her important meditations, her more important dinner, and her most important toilette.

At half-past seven he was at the door with a hansom; and Eric Trevanion and Daphne Préault were bowled along in what Lord Beaconsfield, plagiarizing from Balzac, called "the gondola of the London streets," past Kensington and Knightsbridge, and down Piccadilly to the doors of the Theatre Royal Parthenon.

People may say what they like to the psychological contrary, but there is certainly something deliciously "*intime*" in the fact of driving alone with a woman, whether it be in the family coach, the discreet coupé, or the ordinary hansom. We are told that when the American young man "goes courting," he lavishes his substance on innumerable buggy rides with his young woman. I have passed much of my life in what Mr. Carnegie has called the "Triumphant Democracy," and have not observed this to be the case; but there is no denying the fact, that when, in the depth of the transatlantic winter, the snow is packed in a polished layer upon the face of the world, the transatlantic young man and the transatlantic young woman do eagerly patronize the sleigh known as a "cutter," wherein the pair sit very close together indeed, and the young man drives; or better still, the roomier form of sleigh in which, if I may be allowed the expression, they "snuggle" beneath the buffalo-robes, and the young man prevents the young woman from falling out when they turn sharp corners. The spring is consequently the season of love and marriage in America—as is, I believe, the case elsewhere, according to the poet; and the Englishman who said he preferred as being less dangerous—sitting in a draught in a rocking-chair, with his feet in a tub of ice-water, jangling a bell, to the national winter pastime, must have experienced the joys of sleighing with a well-meaning, but *male*, companion. In Canada they toboggan, and this is a still more ingenious invention (or rather collaboration) of Eros and Hymen; and these things have their efficient counterparts in England, no matter what may be the vehicle that enforces an intimate physical propinquity.

Love is to a great extent a meteorological phenomenon, that is to say, it is largely a matter of atmosphere. Who has not experienced, on entering a woman's boudoir, the sensation that the whole atmosphere is deliriously saturated with her physical as well as mental personality? To a much greater extent is this noticeable in a brougham or coupé, where the area is even more circumscribed. How keen an observer have we considered to be the French author who describes the sensations of an amorous swain on finding himself reclining in a box upon wheels, practically enveloped in the draperies of his inamorata! Such *séances* are often, like spiritualistic functions, carried on in darkness and silence; but the mingling of atmospheres produces a mental excitement that has hurried many a domestic drama to its *dénouement*. And the Londoner who understands his hansom will agree with me. *She*—the She with a capital S—not unfrequently becomes as fascinating as the "She" described by Mr. Rider Haggard (even if she was not so before), when, with a flash of ankle and whiteness, she has stepped into the expectant hansom, and we have followed her, and then, by closing the doors, have covered our knees with the outlying regions of her opera-cloak and other "things." The celibate philosopher will agree with me that to order the "cabby" to "put down the glass" is fatal; the hansom then becomes worse than a coupé; the half-doors are bad enough! It is not necessary to talk; we have most of us observed that She leans more heavily upon our extended hand in getting out than she did on getting in.

Eric and Daphne were in love with one another. They said but little during the transit, but lounged, rather than sat, crushed against one another by the narrowness of the cab, and gave themselves over to the unrestrained enjoyment of their thoughts, trusting to the rattle of the vehicle to drown the almost audible beating of one heart, if not of two. Arrived at the doors of the Parthenon their eyes flashed strangely bright in the darkness, and both felt almost relieved that the ride was over, and that the play was there to obviate the necessity of conversation.

But between riding with a woman within the confines of a cab and sitting next to her in the stalls of a theatre there is little to choose; indeed, for harmlessness, I think the palm might be given to the former. We enter and take our seats, and then, passing an arm behind her, we help her to remove her wraps and reveal—for ourselves—the ivory skin, the rounded arms, and the delicious dress which has been hitherto hidden from us by the aforesaid wraps; and, in so doing, we envelop ourselves, as it were, in a cloud of the delicate fragrance of the perfumes with which women in all parts of the civilized world love to heighten the fascination to themselves. We settle ourselves luxuriously in our seats, and the play commences; after a moment the spirit moves us to rest our elbow on the arm of the stall; we find it already occupied, and draw our sleeve away again with a thrill! Next time we are more successful; the arm is unencumbered; she has leaned forward interested in the play: in a minute or two, the strain of attention relieved, she, in turn, rests her elbow on—well, on the arm of the stall, after we have apologized *sotto voce* and once more vacated the position. Then something in the play calls for a whispered comment, and a lovely head is bent close to our own to listen, and to require the remark to be repeated; then our heads separate, and for a few seconds we haven't an idea of what the play is all about. Next, the opera-glasses fall down, and we dive amidst a maelstrom—so it seems to us—of laces and stuffs to recover the same, whilst the prettiest hand in the world holds the maelstrom aside to facilitate the search, and the glasses are gently laid back in the place whence they originally fell. Next minute, the act-drop falls, the lights are turned up, and we chatter volubly about the play, uttering commonplace platitudes against which our intelligence would revolt in broad daylight, ask stupid questions which require and expect no answers, and answer at random questions that have not been asked.

The curtain rises on the next act—the act in which the love interest of the play develops. It is getting interesting; and now—quite unconsciously—both our elbows rest upon the intermediary arm, which has by this time assumed the *rôle* of the wall which separated Pyramus and Thisbe—not touching one another; that only happens—unconsciously also—about half-way through the act; and we are almost surprised to find that it is the case, when the act-drop falls once more, and turning to one another simultaneously, each reads in the other's eyes what each—we, that is—would have done under circumstances similar to those in the play. Between the second and third acts we chat reasonably, almost confidentially, on subjects quite personal, quite unconnected with the play we are witnessing, leaning back in our stalls, our shoulders almost, if not quite, touching one another. We are interrupted almost surprised when the lights in the house go down, and the stage lights up once more. There is little or no pretence during the last act; we sit as close together as circumstances—i.e. the people behind—will allow. As the story before us draws to its climax, and everything ends happily, we fancy we can hear one another breathe; and when the concluding sentence, often the best-written in the whole play, is drowned by the rustle of people struggling into their outer garments, and groping for hats which have somehow gone off on voyages of discovery by themselves, we carefully and with procrastination—which is the soul of business, in spite of the proverb—wrap her up, in dire terror lest the night air should attack that beautiful throat, and we are rewarded by ever so slight a pressure of the hand that rests on our arm as we reach the outer world and embark once more in the insidious hansom, which we direct, with an air of luxurious proprietorship, to drive to *her* house.

On the application of the above analysis to the circumstances of my story I offer no comment. Eric Trevanion and Daphne Préault witnessed the performance at the Parthenon—and drove home to Holland Street.

"Waters, both strong and mild, with biscuits and a fire will be in the studio," said the Princess Daphne; "won't you come in for an instant before you stroll down the street?"

"Thanks! with pleasure;" and they went in.

Clytemnestra, or for short, "Clytie," the ebony tirewoman of the Princess Daphne, had removed her opera-cloak, her fan, her gloves, and other impedimenta, and had left the pair alone. Whilst Eric busied himself with the innocuous comestibles that stood on a little table by the fire, Daphne threw herself onto the lounge and sat, lazily watching him, and prosecuting a search after conversation. Between them there had sprung up a sudden restraint which was quite unusual; the pauses in the conversation were longer than necessary, the stray remarks were mostly irrelevant, the observations were spasmodic and impersonal. They who had been accustomed to compare their feelings with perfect frankness seemed conscious that a tacit understanding had been raised between them, had grown up without their knowledge, and forbade a word that might invoke—they knew not what! Who can say which hand-pressure, which tremor of the eyelid, which quiver of the lips had shown them that a chapter of their lives was ended? Who can say which lightning-flash of passion had riven the cloud of their happy *camaraderie*, showing the heaven of love beyond? Whatever might be their future, the unconscious carelessness of their past companionship was left behind forever.

And now she leaned forward and gazed into the fire, and he could look at the exquisite lines of her neck and back. Her hair grew exactly to the "beauty line," and being drawn up rather high on the head left a few lovely little soft curls at the back of the neck, their dusky warmth making her white skin still more dazzling and cool. After a moment of eloquent silence she said:

"Eric, come here."

He approached her, and impulsively he sank on his knees on the hearth-rug, at her side and a little behind her, and, feeling as though it were too good to be true—some deceitful vision that he feared to dispel—he remained in rapt wonder looking at her, scarcely breathing.

Was it a simple accident, or the unconscious magnetism of love that drew Daphne's head back toward him, back until his lips almost touched the little curls? and then, he breathed rather than imprinted a kiss, as if by accident, upon the beautiful neck. As he did so, with a strong shudder she leant back in the lounge, and with little more than curiosity in her face, though a delirious weight lay on her heart, she said in a steady, clear voice:

"My poor boy, you will only be more miserable if I kiss you— and some day you will blame me—"

Before she can say any more, he has construed her words for himself, and such a torrent of kisses rains upon her hair, her eyes, her lips, that she is unable to frame a thought or utter a word, but gives herself up to the moment. The subtle charm of the tender violence little by little overpowers her, a stifled sob breaks from her, and she turns deathly pale. If he had understood women better he would not have taken his arms from about her, as he does for an instant, and ask her if she feels faint! The sound of his voice destroys the spell; she puts him from her almost roughly, with a nervous force that surprises him, and says:

"Go—go—or I shall never forgive you;" and as he tries to speak, she interrupts him, saying, "Eric! I know I am in your power—but I am only a woman—go, for God's sake! go, and don't take advantage of that power."

It is a terrible temptation to him as he holds the gorgeous figure in his arms, and he hesitates: then his manhood conquers; he rises with a little stagger, and without daring to look at her, he hurries from the studio. The front-door slams, and he is gone. And is she grateful to him for his obedience? Ah! who knows?

With the sharp click of the outer gate-latch, distinctly audible in the stillness of the night, Daphne awoke, as from the influence of a dream. She rose, straightening and smoothing the folds of her dress as if to brush away the touch of the man, and, walking to the fire, stretched out her icy-cold fingers to the blaze. As the warmth began to circulate in her veins the softness faded from the great brown eyes, and in its place came a calm, questioning, introspective look, which would have done more to pull Eric Trevanion together, could he have seen it, than the radical brandy-and-soda that he gave himself on reaching his rooms.

Then, turning from the fire, she lit a cigarette and began pacing up and down the studio. It was characteristic of her to vivisect herself with far less mercy than she would have shown to another woman; her code had ever been, "mercy and extenuating circumstances for her feeble fellow-creatures; but for herself!— the hard, uncompromising Truth." So she figuratively placed her inmost being in a sort of glass case, put it upon the piano, turned up the lights, and proceeded to examine its intricacies critically. No flaw escaped—her no weakness was condoned—no excuse of sex was pardoned. What were her feelings as regarded Eric Trevanion?—*this* was the burden of her investigation; did she wish he had remained?

Yes, she would answer herself truthfully, she wished he had not been so obedient or so English. Why had he not forced her to say she cared for him as she had never cared for man before? Should she marry him? Was what she now felt the love she had so often read about, and had never believed in or sympathized with? Hardly. She had no more desire to marry him now than she had had before the events of the night which was now shivering with the chill of approaching dawn. No, she wanted to be free—but she wanted Eric as the companion of that freedom; but even with all her independence of spirit, could she stretch the mantle of Bohemia so wide as to cover *that*? Hardly. But the weird confusion in the glass case said plainly, "I want liberty, and what is liberty without him?—a mere simulacrum of independence." This strange Creole girl, against whom no word of reproach had ever been breathed, was sensible that before morning her vital choice would be made. She could do as she pleased on payment of the cost—Liberty and Eric. But the cost was enormous; in this one venture she was called upon to sink the entire capital of her womanhood. She brought the whole of her faculty of mental concentration—so rare in woman—to the solution of this point.

The recklessness and fatal danger of the choice attracted rather than repelled her. Her savage nature, once aroused, found an added charm in the thought of thus gambling away her most precious possession; in her perfect chastity she could look upon the commission of a sin in the eyes of the world without a shock. Why do I continue? In seeking to show the complicated nature of Daphne's personality I cannot escape being either minute to weariness or vague to incomprehensibility. It was this very confusion of characteristics that was one of her greatest fascinations.

For hours the brain battled with the heart the spirit with the flesh; and as the bell of the neighboring Carmelite Monastery roused the monks to Lauds and Prime, Daphne Préault seated herself at the writing-table and wrote to Eric:

"I have fought, and I have conquered. I am yours—come to me."

## CHAPTER IV.
### Mesmerism.

In the society of every city in the world, I suppose there must be, by some inscrutable law of nature, *some* nasty people—probably to make us appreciate the nice ones. Whatever may be the reason, however, there is no doubt that New York, at the time that I chronicle, was no exception to the rule; and even in the fascinating cosmopolitan society of the modern Gotham there were a few nasty people, of whom undoubtedly the nastiest were by common consent the Van Baulk'ems. Mrs. Odious Van Baulk'em regarded herself as handsome, and as select in her strife after social position. I have often observed that people who refuse to recognize those of their own class in life, and seek to entertain their social superiors, usually find themselves reduced to entertaining the sediment of a class superior to their own—the impecunious and shady ones, who will go anywhere for a dinner and daughters with money—and so entertaining, fondly imagine their society to be "select." Well! select it is; but it is a selection of the riff-raff of a class into the solid substance of which they would give their eyes to be admitted. The Van Baulk'ems were of this complexion, and this was the kind of society that one would meet at their house on Fifth Avenue should one be so imprudent as to pass through its portals on the strength of one of the innumerable cards that Mrs. Van Baulk'em was in the habit of flipping all over New York, *via* the "Society List," and especially among the young men who might possibly feel justified by their constitutions in "going in for" the angular and highly-coloured charms of Miss Van Baulk'em, or the clever, pretty vulgarity of Miss Parthenia Van Baulk'em, a young lady suspected of society journalism, who had been hawked round Europe and America for years, in search of an adventurous swain. But such had not turned up; and though it seemed likely that the millions of the elder might attract a penniless European of doubtful antecedents, the younger, Miss Parthenia Van Baulk'em, showed no inclination to "go off."

From this very slight sketch of a very unpleasant family, the reader will have gathered that the Van Baulk'ems' house was hardly one where Paul du Peyral would elect to spend much of his leisure time; but as, on his first arrival in the city, he had dined at the house on Fifth Avenue, and had allowed himself to be mildly lionized as a social *savant* by the family; and as, moreover, there was something essentially *piquante* and refreshing about the ready repartee of Miss Parthenia, he would periodically drop in on Mrs. Van Baulk'em's reception day, and converse with that young person for a space. One of these occasions took place about two months after his marriage with Mahmouré di Zulueta, and, in obedience to the laws of cause and effect, that visit materially influenced the course of the history I am recording in these pages. The opera season had recently commenced, and Paul had unconsciously made himself very interesting and instructive on the subject of the German school of opera, with Wagner as the text of his homily.

"Why don't we see you more at the opera, Mr. du Peyral?" had queried the fair Parthenia.

"Because I have but little time for such pleasures. My work is of a kind that appreciates, nay requires, the peacefulness of the night hours; and again, the conversation for which one goes to the opera in New York is so cruelly interrupted by the music that one has no chance of appreciating it and profiting by it."

"But don't you think it is possible to divide one's attention?"

"No, I don't, Miss Van Baulk'em. To appreciate a melody in an opera, one must have followed very carefully the harmonies which have led to it. An isolated melody is like a proverb in a foreign language, which one knows by heart, and of which one admires the meaning and sound, without knowing its literal translation."

"Well, I quite agree with you, only I wanted to get at your sentiments on the subject."

Miss Parthenia was accounted a brilliant conversationalist, and deservedly so, for she had fully realized that, in woman, conversational brilliancy consists of little else than an appreciation of the conversing man; and Paul left the Van Baulk'ems' house that day—he was but human, after all—with a pleased conviction that the girl was not so bad as she was painted perhaps, and as he stepped onto the avenue, recorded in his note-book an engagement he had made to visit the Van Baulk'ems' box at the opera on the following evening.

Two months before this, he and Mahmouré had fled New York and hidden themselves in a little Canadian village on the banks of the Niagara River, and beside that grand, placid stream, that gives so little indication, save by a dull murmur on a very quiet day, of the agony of turbulence with which it has rushed over the falls a few miles further up, had become man and wife, in the presence alone of a couple of parishioners, the parson, and God. There had followed a few weeks of pure, lovely delight, in contemplation of the turquoise water, with Ontario in the distance, reminding one by its colour and placidity of the Trasimene Lake; and then they had returned to New York to a life outwardly unchanged, but new in every thought, both to Mahmouré in her nest in West Forty-first Street, and to Paul in his bachelor apartments—not so very far off. The world remarked that they seemed to be "very good friends," and looked at them with uninterested curiosity when they appeared in public together, according to the custom of the Bohemia in which they lived; but not on that account did disinterested mammas cease to play upon Paul the shrapnel of invitations to every kind of entertainment where marriageable daughters do congregate.

The light of life seemed to be returning to Mahmouré's pale cheeks, the fire of life began to shine, as of yore, from her eyes; but Paul was unchanged, save in the eyes of one or two of his most intimate friends, who told one another that he seemed to lack in a measure his old enthusiasm, to enter less eagerly into the somewhat exhausting schemes of amusement they put before him; that his mouth was less determined, that his eye was less bright than of old, when they disturbed him at his books and at his weird calculations, at hours when domesticated New York has sought its virtuous couch.

Nevertheless, ten o'clock on the evening of the day following that of his visit above recorded found him entering the Van Baulk'ems' box, to be greeted warmly by Mrs. Van Baulk'em, who was chatting with a man on the sofa in the ante-loge, and to be "sent forward" in order to be seen talking with the dear girls in front. It was during an *entre-acte*, so that Miss Parthenia had no compunction in proceeding to draw him out, an operation in which that young lady excelled, and in deference to which Paul subsequently wrote an article dedicated to her and entitled "The Conversational Corkscrew—a study of Platitudinous Periphrasis!"

"Mrs. Lexington Park has told me," began the siren, "that you are most interesting, M. du Peyral, if one can get you to talk about transmigration of souls—metem-what's-his-name—you know."

"Metempsychosis?"

"Yes, that's it—and I have been thinking how it would be if one could suddenly change places and souls with one of those people up in the gallery. How strange it would be to find one's self suddenly full of new ideas, perhaps wondering if one can afford to come again on Friday, and whether the people down here enjoy themselves more than they do up there."

"I think, *mademoiselle*, that if you could make the change you desire, you would probably find that you were in an atmosphere of genuine appreciation of the music, whilst in your place here would appear, by the exchange, a stupid, unsociable creature who actually wanted to listen, and might even go so far as to say 'Hush!' when your neighbors talk 'small talk' and 'scandal' to the music of the 'Götterdämmerung.' Think! how terrible!"

"Do you know, I think I should rather like it."

"Are you sure?"

"Yes."

"Then look at me for a moment."

She did so, and almost immediately closed her eyes, and Paul smiled a little self-satisfied smile. Unfortunately Miss Van Baulk'em, observing that her sister had sunk from scandal to silence, and fearful lest she might rise from silence to snores, tapped her with her fan and exclaimed,

"Thenie! you're going to sleep!"

She opened her eyes, and looking at Paul, said, "How odd! I just closed my eyes, and there I was in the gallery when Nell disturbed me." And then, seeing the smile on Paul's face, she exclaimed, "You wretch! I believe you had something to do with that."

"Not at all!" returned he; and then, rising, he added, "Alas, I must be very dull today; you were nearly asleep! *Au revoir*; when next we meet tell me what you think of—the opera."

"You will come soon very soon?"

"With pleasure—good-night."

As he made his *adieux* to the mother in the ante-loge he caught sight of the man sitting by her side. A dark, handsome man with straight brows, a coarse mouth, and square jaws. Paul looked at him inquisitively, and the man returned the gaze without flinching: the next moment Paul had left the box. Outside, in the corridor, he stopped still for a moment, and then, looking on the ground, began pacing up and down, muttering the while—"Who is he? Who is he? Where have I seen him before?"

From another box, during the next *entre-acte*, he saw him again, talking in the front of the box with Miss Parthenia Van Baulk'em. Then the whole drama came back to him. Act 1. A country village, a beautiful woman, a handsome stranger. Act 2. A dishonoured wife, a wagging tongue, a hurried flight. Act 3. South Belgravia, a "scene" or two, and an outcast. That was all. And there was Charles Sturton Baker, in superlative costume, displaying his handsome face in the Metropolitan Opera House. The Van Baulk'ems had got him!

Paul remembered the example of the eminent firm of soap-boilers who made a large fortune by attending to their own business, and strolled home in the moonlight, Baker, the Van Baulk'ems, the opera, everything dismissed from his mind by a mental picture of a little, lithe figure that lay curled upon the huge divan, in Forty-first Street, looking at the clock, and wondering whether "Götterdämmerung" was one of the long operas, or whether he would be there soon.

A footstep in the hall-way, a rap at the door, and he is there, kneeling at her feet and playing with that wondrous hair, of which he used gayly to say, "the sunshine, when it kissed it, turned to darkness for very envy."

"You are tired, my poor Paul—the room is hot," she says, passing her ridiculous handkerchief across his forehead.

"No, no, sweetheart—it's not that—I don't quite know what it is; it has come on quite suddenly." He looks into her eyes until she seems to draw his very soul into hers, and then, suddenly rising with an exclamation almost of pain, he says:

"Do you know, Mahmouré, I don't think I'm as strong as I used to be? These mesmeric experiments I've been doing lately seem to take a great deal more out of me than they used to—I've been feeling tired and distracted. But never mind about me; there is something I wanted to ask you—what was it?—oh, yes. Do you know anything of a man named Charles Sturton Baker?"

"Good heavens! yes—what of him?"

"He's here, in New York. I was in a box at the opera with him tonight. What do you know about him?"

"Well, not much that is definite beyond that affair about poor little B——; you know all about that, I suppose. After she went to grief, he used to hang about the theatre, and played '*Inferno e Tommaso*' among the girls. He once had the audacity to make love to me, and I had him thrown out of the place by a scene-shifter. What's he up to now?"

"I think he's going to marry Parthenia Van Baulk'em, or rather, her money."

"Well, let him; they about suit one another."

"No! After all, she's only a fool—and he's a knave; and though, according to the dictum of the philosopher, the two would make an interesting little microcosm, she doesn't deserve such a fate as that. I'm sorry for her."

"Well, what can you do about it?"

"Nothing. But, after all, Miss Parthenia knows I've been all over the world, and perhaps she may ask me about him."

"And if she does, *cher ami*, don't know anything about the animal."

"That would hardly be fair, would it? If a fellow can protect a woman, surely he ought to do it—eh?"

"Yes, of course he ought; but if you undertake to protect a woman against an unscrupulous blackguard who happens to be her lover, you will probably find yourself in a most enterprising little mess. But *sapristoche!* Paul, since when this concern for the little Van Baulk'em?"

"Oh, I don't know. I think she's a clever little thing, for all her vulgarity; at any rate she's sharp, and I'd sooner talk to her for half an hour than to nine out of ten of these society women. Now, make me a scene of jealousy."

"Certainly! Kiss me immediately!"

※

"Paul," said Mahmouré, presently, when their conversation had turned into a more reasonable channel, "this mesmerism of yours is killing you; I'm certain of it, and you must stop it. Every time you make your experiments with me as a 'subject,' I feel stronger and better than I did before them; but simultaneously you look paler and more worn. *Mon cher*, with a physique like yours, you require all your vital force to keep it going—you mustn't waste it on me. What is the use, dear heart? I am a dying woman; your absolute influence over me shows it, if nothing else; reserve your force for some fresh young subject who won't sap your energies as I do."

"*Tiens!* listen to her! here is Mahmouré posing as a charming little vampire! Why, darling, I've a great deal more strength than I want for myself, and if I can make over the surplus to you by mesmerizing you, you ought to be as glad of it as I am. But come, we waste time. You remember that experiment we made when I sent your soul across the sea, and you told me what was going on in a house in London—well, I want to carry that experience still further. I am going to mesmerize you and to try to identify your soul with that of someone over there, and learn what that someone is *thinking* about as well as *doing*."

"But, Paul, it's not possible."

"Perhaps not, but we can try. If we succeed, after all it's only a progression in the clairvoyant experiences with which we have been so successful. It depends, I think, only on one thing, and that is, the existence of a personality over there identical with your own or mine; if such exists you will be able, if my will is strong enough to direct you, to identify yourself psychologically with some man or woman over there, for whom, if you knew them in the flesh, you would feel an affinity that would make *me* madly jealous. Come, let us try; the result, if we attain it, will be an enormous one."

"Very well, Paul—but promise not to over-exert yourself."

90

"Bah! what a timid little woman it is! Now, make yourself comfortable."

And Mahmouré du Peyral—to call her for the first time by her new, real name settled herself among the cushions of the divan.

"Look into my eyes—there!—be quiet—quiet ah!—so;" and Paul put his hand on the forehead of the woman, who sighed deeply and closed her eyes. "So you are asleep, are you not?"

"Yes."

"Where are you?"

"I don't know."

"Who are you?"

"I cannot say."

"You are in a room?"

"Yes."

"How is it furnished?"

"As a studio."

"Is there a looking-glass in it?"

"Yes."

"Look into it and describe yourself." [A pause.]

"Well?"

"A tall woman with dark hair—a man is by my side—*Eric!*"

"Who is Eric?"

"Oh! don't you know? he is my lover, my good, brave Eric."

"Is there a writing-table in the studio?"

"Yes."

"There are letters addressed to you lying on it. Read me the address of one of them."

"Miss Préault, The Cottage, Holland Street, W."

"*What* is the name?"

"Miss Préault."

"*Daphne?*"

"Yes—yes—who called me? Eric! my darling, there is some one in the room; oh, my love, help!——" and the little figure on the divan began to writhe as if in terror.

Paul du Peyral, trembling with the effort and excitement, took the beautiful head in his hands and blew softly upon the forehead once or twice. The convulsions ceased slowly, and Mahmouré opened her eyes. Seeing Paul leaning over her, she threw her arms around his neck and, in the terror and excitement of the moment, burst into tears.

"Come, come, sweetheart," said he; "I have tried you too much. Ah! but this is horrible—wicked—dangerous! Do you know where your soul has been?"

"No, dear, only I thought you were changed, over there, or here, or wherever it was, till I felt a terrible pain and woke up."

Paul was the first to recover himself. "Mahmouré," said he, "we have trifled with a great power, and its working has been more mysterious than I anticipated; more strange, more marvellous than I ever could have dreamed. Do you know that your soul found that of Daphne Préault?"

"What? of the woman you were to have married?"

"Yes."

"Oh, Paul, never let us do this again; it is not right."

"On the contrary, with your help I shall at last be able to find out something about this strange young woman—but not now; you are tired, and I must leave you. I have much to do, much to think of, tonight; tomorrow we will talk of this again. Now, good-night; in half an hour you must be fast asleep—do you hear?"

"Yes, Paul;" and after a last wild embrace, he was gone.

"At last! at last!" he cried to himself, as he reached his own rooms and began rapidly jotting down some notes in a little book with a lock-clasp. "Through Mahmouré I shall have this woman—this Miss Préault—in my power; what does it mean? Is it that the same blood runs in both our veins, as old Préault used to tell me sometimes. What it that old story of our common ancestry were *true*? How else account for the identity of our personalities? for, unless my researches have led me astray, it must be that which caused Mahmouré to single her out as the object of her search for a sympathy in Europe. Oh, Grand Principle of Life! if you are indeed capable of obedience to command, solve me your secret; whisper the solution of this mystery to me—to me, Paul du Peyral!—if only to reward me for the sacrifice to you of the best years of my life, of my health, of my very soul."

He rose and began pacing the room; suddenly he stopped, and raising his arms in the air, cried:

"Daphne Préault! if you and I are indeed one in soul, and breathe with the same life-current running through our veins, show yourself to me—to me—to me!"

Then, suddenly a wild pain gripped his heart, the room grew black around him, and there stood before the eyes of his super-excited imagination a woman such as we have described Daphne Préault, but having the features, almost the face, of Paul du Peyral. Then he fell senseless upon his face, in which condition his body-servant found him next morning.

"Not a word of this to Madame di Zulueta," said he; and the magnificently trained menial gave him an assurance, which his long experience of that individual's inflexible mendacity told him was to be implicitly trusted.

And so, for the next few days, he went about as usual, nothing altered in his manner to Mahmouré or to the world, but now and then catching his breath for an instant, and looking a trifle whiter round the eyes.

On Sunday afternoon he paid his promised visit to the Van Baulk'ems.

He had not been there more than a few minutes when the fair Parthenia, corralling him into a corner, asked suddenly:

"Do you know Mr. Baker—an Englishman?"

"Mr. Charles Sturton Baker?"

"Yes."

"Well, *no*, I can't say I do. I came across him some years ago, but though I was presented to him, I can hardly say I know him."

"He is very charming, is he not?"

"Well, that is a question entirely for you to answer; you know the English are a queer people, and have a different standard from ours; many actions which we look upon as blackguardly, they, I believe, look upon as quite the right thing to do. I am hardly a judge; Mr. Baker has done things that I think infamous, but he may be charming 'for a' that.'"

"But he moves in the best society in England—or might, only that he is a quiet, domesticated kind of man, and does not care about it."

"Well, I should say that you have formed a misconception concerning him; he is distinctly what I should call a 'fast' man. But, after all, he only takes up the opportunities afforded him by human nature in the class of society in which he moves. As for his going into 'the best society,' I should hardly say that was correct; I believe that my 'set,' in London, is pretty good, and I never met him there. I have only come across him in a rather 'rowdy' country-house, where he was having a desperate flirtation with a child of sixteen."

"Is he not very well connected?"

"No—I think not. In fact, I think that he is rather by way of being an absolute nobody; I may be wrong—if you like I'll find out for you."

"Well, I should rather like to know; but you won't mention *me*, will you?"

"Of course not!"

And so the conversation dropped, and presently Paul sought "fresh teas and houses new," and thought no more about the ten-minutes' chat that was to have such an influence upon the fortunes of himself and Mahmouré di Zulueta.

It was not till that evening that an idea on the subject occurred to him. Said he to himself: "That little girl is evidently crazily in love with Baker; I wonder if young Hawleigh knows anything about him." And the practical form his idea took was to write and ask full particulars concerning the handsome adventurer from Gabriel Hawleigh, whom he had met in a little French village some years before, and whom he recollected as a young English Bohemian, who seemed to know everybody who had ever lived, by sight, name, or reputation.

He wrote, merely asking if Gabriel knew anything definite against the man, and if he did not, to send a "kind" letter, "not as a guarantee of good faith, but for publication."

Whilst it passed across the sea, he continued his experiments with Mahmouré, learning by degrees, with an accuracy resulting from the marvellous coincidences of their three personalities, almost as much about the Princess Daphne as the Princess knew about herself.

And so the world wagged, day following day, and causes developing eternally into effects.

Now, Gabriel Hawleigh's recollections of the days he had spent in a French village on the Biscayan coast were not as distinct as those of the young American who had shared his self-imposed exile, and on receiving Paul du Peyral's letter it took him an appreciable time to remember who Paul du Peyral *was*. Gradually, however, the memory of those half-forgotten days returned to him, and he turned his attention to the object of the enquiry. Charles Sturton Baker was one of those mysterious individuals that one comes across periodically in the more careless section of London society;—one of those young men who, clustered about the door-ways of semi-public or subscription balls, compare offensive notes on the wives and sisters of their friends; who wear ribbed shirt-fronts and single studs, cylindrical collars, satin ties, and self-satisfied smirks; and who, when the hours of labor in the far-eastern "City" are at an end, take the Underground Railway, and are swallowed up by the deserts of Belsize or Bayswater, by inaccessible North-Western suburbs, miles beyond the comparatively civilized spots "where omnibusses turn round."

We have said that he was handsome; add to this that his mysterious occupation in the murky orient supplied him with the wherewithal to satisfy the lower cravings of his sensual nature, and hide the essential feebleness of his mind behind the venal adulation of impecunious clerks, and caused the said clerks to regard his triumphal progress along Piccadilly on Saturday afternoons, in a hansom, with some Lottie or Tottie of the ballet, as evidence of his claims to the titles of "devil of a fellow" and "rare good sort." The frisky matrons of his inaccessible suburb, "the squaws of the north-west frontier tribes," as Dick Lindsay used to say, hearing of his reckless lavishings in the matter of Gaiety stalls and five-shilling cab-fares, got up quite a little excitement about this provincial Lothario; and the ladies whom he honoured with dishonour were looked upon almost with reverence by the compulsorily virtuous remainder. And, by-the-by, he had crept into a calling acquaintance with the Holland Street colony, via the Miss Eastons, whom he had met at a subscripto-suburban ball, at the Kensington Town Hall.

Therefore Gabriel, though loth to commit himself, could hardly profess entire ignorance of the swain, but could not be said to know anything either for or against him. He had seen him a member of a party of men at a music-hall, and paraphrasing the saying of the French philosopher, "*La nuit tous les hommes sont gris,*" did not regard as a crime the fact that he had been disorderly, and, in vulgar parlance, "chucked out." That he was over-dressed did not matter much. After all, if one cuts one's coat according to one's cloth, one wears it according to one's income and education; and to him Mr. Baker was a tasteless young man who wore very good clothes very badly. He therefore replied to Paul du Peyral, that he knew nothing against the man as a man, and that he was a harmless, stupid kind of thing who couldn't do anyone any harm; and armed with this non-committal reply, which he thought would close the matter satisfactorily for all parties, Paul strolled up to the Van Baulk'ems', and showed it to the fair Parthenia. She received it in silence, thanked M. du Peyral for the trouble he had taken, and the incident, as far as he was concerned, was apparently terminated.

"After all," thought he, "abuse of one man by another is very much like mud splashed up by an unconscious cart; a modicum of it is sure to stick, according to the proverb; but even that modicum, black and sticky as it is when it's wet, turns white or at any rate gray when it's dry, and is easily brushed off; and I've no doubt the fair Parthenia will rather enjoy the process of brushing than otherwise. Besides, it is possible that Baker has become steadied down, and has repented the rascalities of his fevered youth."

And so he returned to his solitude and to Mahmouré, and to his absorbing interest in his psychical experiments, which he concealed beneath the ostensible search after knowledge in the studies of the Sparrow, the Mosquito, and the Housefly.

The constantly recurring "Psychical Romance" may be described as an intellectual nightmare resulting from the literary indigestion of the day, an indigestion produced by a surfeit of Wilkie Collins, Stevenson, Hugh Conway, and Mrs. Crow; and lest I lay myself open to the reproach of swelling the mass of "weird" literature of the past decennium, I beg the reader to skip the following exposition of Paul's discoveries in Mesmerism and Telepathy, but to remember that I have set them out, and to recur to them for an explanation should the spirit move him presently to fling aside the book with the exclamation, "Bah! another attempt to panoply platitude with the dim magnificence of mystery!" if he is in the habit of using this sort of language to himself.

Shortly, the result of his investigations, arrived at after months—nay years—of wasted tissue and brain-power, was as follows. The whole matter resolves itself into one of sympathy. Two persons are presented to one another: the one has a personality—a vital force—represented by the numeral *six*; the other has a vital force represented by the figure *two*. Very well! They try to converse: at first the conversation is spasmodic, choppy, uninteresting, carried on at cross purposes as it were; gradually, however, the mere physical propinquity lessens this mental discrepancy, and before long they get interested in—i.e. they understand— one another. The higher force lowers itself in proportion as the lower force rises, till at last the two are said to be "in sympathy with one another." They almost know one another's thoughts; each can almost guess what the other is going to say next: they no longer require to explain their respective meanings minutely; an unfinished sentence, a word, a look, conveys a whole thesis on the point under discussion. They are reciprocally charmed, for they feel themselves to be on an intellectual level with one another; in a phrase—to recur—they no longer represent the contrast of six and two, but each giving to and taking from the other, they represent at the end of the conversation the uniform vital force of *four each*. Mesmerism is an acceleration of this process by an effort of will; Telepathy is a higher development of it. And in Mesmerism *or* Telepathy the one mind conveys to the other, to be acted upon, the thoughts that are uppermost at the moment within itself.

In the almost clairvoyant experiences of Paul and Mahmouré, this had occurred to a high degree, and had been very powerfully assisted by the coincidences of the personalities of Paul and Daphne Préault, united as they seemed to be by some distant tie of Creole ancestry. Mahmouré being powerfully attracted to, and acted upon by Paul, there was no doubt but that Daphne would possess the same influence over her; and, following the natural laws of attraction, it was not surprising that her spirit should seek that of the Princess, living as the latter did amid associations doubtless familiar to Paul, and being, beyond all, the soul in which Paul's interest was principally centred in Europe.

People who "see ghosts" are generally looked upon either as mystics or as rather weak-minded subjects by the rest of the community; this is because we always feel a certain uneasiness in the presence of an eccentricity. If that eccentricity is one beyond our comprehension, we revere its author; if it is one that we can criticise and examine, familiarity breeds contempt, and we despise him. Reverence and despite are merely developments of fear. Ghost-seers come under either the first or the second category, according to their talkativeness. The uncommunicative ghost-seer is feared—nay, he is thought a trifle mad; the communicative ghost-seer, on the other hand, is laughed at, and considered a *raconteur* or an ass, according to his powers of eloquence. Now, following the theory of Paul du Peyral, a ghost is nothing more than a coincidence of condition occurring between two persons at the same moment, by which coincidence the illusion—or rather phenomenon—of the appearance of the one to the other is produced.

To recur to the doctrine of sympathy established between two people who are conversing with one another:—At a given point, maybe, their personalities find one another in absolute or perfect coincidence. The result of this is, as a rule, love: courtship is a continual search after a renewal of those conditions; marriage a more or less successful effort, as the case may be, to establish a new sympathy on a new plane.

However, to return: The sight of another person is merely the effort of a certain excitement on the visual segment of one's brain; when the sympathy, perfect, absolute, of which we have spoken has been established, that excitement becomes a very strong one. Two persons look into one another's eyes, and through their eyes into their souls; the impression made is necessarily very forcibly stamped on the memory, and it is not so much an impression of the outer form under contemplation, as one of the inner soul that shines out in the gaze. Now if, at any future time, by reason of the one person thinking of the other with any strong effort of cerebration, by a rare coincidence that other person finds himself in the same vital condition—at the same numeral of personality, in the same state of sympathy and degree of attraction—as he did on the occasion when the sympathy was originally established, then, the conditions of the mind being the same, the same impression will be conveyed by the optic nerves to the brain, and the effect is produced of the appearance of the one person to the other, which, for want of a better term, has become called "a ghost."

It is rare for each to appear to the other at the same time; the coincidence of thought, effort, and personal condition is *too remotely* possible: it is the person who makes the effort who either sees the object of his mental strain, or, if his thoughts are centred upon its present occupation, appears to that object.

And so, every effort of thought of which Paul du Peyral was capable being concentrated upon the woman whom, in the body, he had never seen, he was wont to call up her mental picture with a vividness that gave to her spectre all the attributes of substantial form; and adopting her as a subject for his experiments, which chance, coincidence—call it what you will—had flung in his way, he pursued his investigations with all the devotion of a *savant*, and at the expense of his life.

# CHAPTER V.
## Daphne and Eric.

The "*tempora mutantur*" principle, as far as this story is concerned, holds good in Europe as it does in America and elsewhere; and whilst Paul du Peyral and Mahmouré led their separated though identical lives in New York, time had wrought its changes in the Holland Street colony, though that time was measured by months only, and not by longer periods. Spring had arrived and was growing old; already, at intervals of a week or so, the sun shone so brightly that the shades were closed on the sunny sides of the streets, giving them the appearance of having been struck blind with astonishment at the fine weather, after the fog and rain and slush of the metropolitan merry spring-time.

In Holland Street, grimy persons had appeared, and had borne thence carefully protected canvases, to deposit them for approval or rejection at the doors of Burlington House; in a word, "Show Sunday" had come and gone, and hearts beat high with hope or apprehension; whilst "the boys" who had sent in their Academy pictures rested a little on their oars,—or rather brushes,—and awaited the official intimation—of what? Most of our personal friends—if we may call them so—had launched an argosy on the sea of public appreciation; but all of them awaited with some anxiety the fate of Gabriel Hawleigh's picture, "Sunshine in the Fog," which had fulfilled its early promise of excellence, and was regarded as the *chef-d'œuvre* of the colony.

To Gabriel himself, though he said but little on the subject, the acceptance or rejection of this picture by the hanging committee meant everything—a large word, but the only one which properly expresses the case. Into it he felt he had put the very best work of which he was capable; he knew that he could do no better, and that if this were "found wanting" he had better abandon art as a means of livelihood, once and for all; and this reflection occurring often to him in the midst of his wildest rhapsodies with his violin, he would drop his instrument from his shoulder and sink for hours into a revery on the Future—and Maye. She, on her side, said but little about the picture; but the Princess Daphne was an angel of hope to him, and never for an instant assumed anything on the possibility of the rejection of his masterpiece, but urged him to work in anticipation of his popularity as an artist, which she regarded as a very proximate certainty.

"There will be a great demand," she used to say to him; "mind the supply is ready to meet it; and, for heaven's sake, don't sell your old rejected trash on the strength of this big work of yours. You can do that later, when your hold on the public is strong enough to defy the dangers of dilution with inferior work. Remember, Gabriel, and keep Maye's happiness in your mind as the lodestar of your energies."

Maye herself was placidly content with her existence—or outwardly so, at any rate; deep in her heart, if the truth must be confessed, lay a gnawing agony that had usurped a place there ever since the "engagement" of Eric Trevanion and the Princess Daphne had been announced. Their *liaison* had been published to the colony under the title of a betrothal, though it was as impossible to get anything out of Daphne concerning her future marriage as it had been to extract information on the subject of her past history. Eric practically spent all his time with her, and seemed to have abandoned his profession of *flaneur* of the studios; and men spoke still more reverently of the Princess in his presence, standing unconsciously in something like awe of the man whom Daphne Préault had selected as her future husband—if not, as was whispered, as her present lover—from amid the army of aspirants.

He seldom touched his palette or spoilt good canvas now-a-days. They had been but an occupation for idle hours at best, and now his occupation was Daphne; and, as he had but one pleasure, and that was to sit with her whilst she worked, she had fitted up a second and more substantial writing-table in her spacious studio, and tried to make him take seriously to literature, and make some use of his undoubted cleverness, his knowledge of the world, and his very exceptional education.

Unfortunately, as a *littérateur*, Eric was an epigrammatist rather than a word-painter, and he seldom got beyond titles of striking and remarkable originality, for essays, which, when they were written, took the form of a collection of aphorisms, spicules of epigram embedded in a protoplasm of commonplace, the whole vivifying a spongy mass which absorbed the ideas of other people rather than originated new ones of its own. There are many writers—for the most part young ones—in the present day to whom this description applies, and publishers look askant upon works which are gems of literary composition rather than of imaginative construction. And Eric's masterpieces: "An Indigo Inspiration by a Blue Bard" (written in a moment of depression); his "Petrifaction of Passion, a Pathological Problem" (written when his vocabulary of eulogy of the Princess had suddenly dried up); and several similarly entitled effusions reposed peacefully in the pigeon-hole that he described as the "Walhalla of Rejected Addresses," and over which he had inscribed on a strip of gummed label, "*Lasciate ogni speranza, voi ch' entrate!*"— "Abandon hope all ye who enter here!"

Still, the ill luck of his manuscripts caused him no pity for himself, only contempt for them. The allowance made to him by his father was an ample one, and any caprices he might have had he might very well have satisfied; but as it was, he had but one thought in life—Daphne! To be by her side, to hold her in his arms and tell her all over again how he loved her—that was all he wanted; and as Daphne was of a practically identical opinion, the studio in Holland Street was certainly one of the happiest places in the world.

Eric Trevanion had perhaps but one thorn in the flesh, and that was Clytemnestra, the coloured woman, who jealously guarded her mistress' lightest actions, and strenuously objected to Eric, not so much on the ground of his being a new master for herself, as on the ground that he stood in quasi-authority over her mistress. Clytie had no moral scruples of any kind, but, with the cunning of her race, with that devotion of self and that selfishness for others that characterizes the darkie, she was convinced that her mission in life was to bring about the marriage of the Princess Daphne and Paul du Peyral, whom, though she had never seen, of course she knew all about.

Clytie had been owned by Victor Préault, his father had owned her father, his grandfather her grandfather; generation after generation of master and slave had looked after one another, and the ideas of freedom, and a vote, and the College of Surgeons were, to Clytie, iconoclastic institutions which she strenuously objected to take in place of the companionship of Daphne, her red bandanna head-gear, and her own mnemonic storehouse of Voodoo pharmaceutical knowledge.

Clytie's mind was a magazine of Creole legendary history and historic legend. As long as she could remember, Daphne had been accustomed to listen almost unconsciously, when Clytie was in the vicinity, to stories of the bayous and swamps of Louisiana, of the early settlers of New Orleans, of D'Iberville, of Bienville, of the Chevalier Le Blond de la Tour, of Indian raids, and of massacres by the Chickasaws, the Choctaws, and the Natchez. Anon her tales would be of the Spanish rule of 1760 to 1770, of the patriot merchants such as Milhet, dAbbadie, and Préault, of the landing of Don Antonio de Ulloa, and, later, of the Irish Spaniard, Don Alexander O'Reilly, "Cruel O'Reilly" as he was still called in Louisianian folk-lore, of de Unzaga, of de Galvez; in a word, Clytie could have dictated a complete Creole history, correct in its chronology, and fictitious only in its facts. But it was as the chronicler, the *trouvère* of the Préault family, to an ancestor of which an ancestor of hers had been sold in all his picturesque insufficiency of costume, that Clyde came out strong. Clytie fondly imagined that, the idol she wore around her neck had originally belonged to this ancestor—it was a shapelessly human affair, which had done duty in turn for correct and life-like representations of Voodoo, of Obi, of Gitche-Manito, of the Madonna, of Martin Luther, of the Saviour, and of Jefferson Davis—and when she lectured Daphne on her Creole ancestry, she was wont to refer to said idol, whose existence at the time said events did not take place was, to her, conclusive evidence of their historical accuracy: and it was upon one of these family legends, well known among all the branches of the Préault family, that she based her efforts to induce Daphne to reconsider her contemptuous refusal of Paul du Peyral.

103

Clyde's legend of the Préault and du Peyral families was a remarkable chronicle, based on a good deal of historic fact, and embroidered with a good deal of historic fiction. I prefer, therefore, to tell the story in my own words, shorn of much ornamental eloquence, but enriched with a certain amount of careful research among the archives of the city of New Orleans. In the year 1718, Bienville had succeeded Epinay as Governor of Louisiana, and affairs in the colony were governed principally in conformity to the requirements of John Law's "Mississippi Company"—the South-Sea Bubble that was to explode with such terrific violence two years later. Among the 800 emigrants that landed at Dauphine Island on the 25th of August, 1718, was one Hippolyte du Peyral, an engineer, who formed one of the little band of pioneers who might have been seen in 1720, headed by the Sieur Le Blond de la Tour, "garbed as a knight of St. Louis, modified as might be by the exigencies of the frontier," marking off streets and lots—planning, in a word, the city of New Orleans.

There are doubtless many of my readers to whom New Orleans would be an undiscovered country were it not for the Abbe Prévost and "Manon Lescaut." I refer to this work because, if the truth must be told, the colony was then in the condition described by Prévost—i.e., in what might be called a state of troglodytish simplicity as regards its social institutions, and the female society of New Orleans was composed, exception being made in favour of the wives of a few of the officials, and those of the French and Canadian settlers, of ladies who had loved not wisely but too well, if not too promiscuously, in France, and had, after going through a term of probation at the Salpêtrière and St. Lazare, been shipped off by a paternal government to supply the rugged colonists with the gentle influences and reproductive advantages which are the prerogatives of the *beau sexe*. Unless these ladies are traduced by their historian, they appear to have drunk, gambled, and fought on terms of perfect equality with their lords and masters, or, to put it tersely, their proprietors. But among them, a damsel of a finer mould than the generality fell to the lot of Hippolyte du Peyral, and to him was born, within a pistol-shot of the ancient and modern Place d'Armes, a beautiful daughter. This child was some six or seven years old when the gentle Ursuline Sisters established their convent and hospital on what was then called Arsenal Street; and her mother having succumbed to the ravages of the colonial climate and social laxity, du Peyral was glad enough to find there an asylum where the child would be secure from the influences of the almost primeval condition of affairs in the young city, no less than from the periodical raids of Chickasaws and Natchez.

In the winter of 1727-28—I quote from the pages of the Creole historian, G. W. Cable—a crowning benefit was reached. On the Levée, just in front of the Place d'Armes, the motley public of the wild town was gathered to see a goodly sight. A ship had come across the sea and up the river, with the most precious of all possible earthly cargoes.

She had tied up against the grassy, willow-planted bank, and there were coming ashore, and grouping together in the Place d'Armes, under escort of the Ursuline nuns, a good threescore, not of houseless girls from the streets of Paris, as heretofore, but of maidens from the hearthstones of France, to be disposed of, under the discretion of the nuns, in marriage. And then there were brought ashore, and were set down in the rank grass, many small, stout chests of clothing. There was a trunk for each maiden, and a maiden for each trunk, and both maidens and trunks were the gifts of the king. Similar companies came in subsequent years, and the girls with trunks were long known in the traditions of their colonial descendants by the honourable distinction of the *"filles à la cassette"*—the casket girls.

Hippolyte du Peyral was a substantial citizen, standing high in the good graces of the pious sisters, and he was one of the first to take to his home among the new plantations of Louisiana, a gentle, sweet-tempered helpmate, his lawful wife, a healthy Provençale of some twenty summers. This good couple lived to an equally good old age, and like the worthies of nursery romance, died regretted by all who knew them, leaving a family of stalwart young colonials who founded the du Peyral family, which had accordingly flourished in the state until war, fever, transference from one government to another, and other disturbing influences had dwindled the old stock down to concentration in the person of M. Paul du Peyral, the *protégé* and heir of old Préault of Baton Rouge. Thus, after a lapse of a century and a half, the parent stock had been thrown together again by chance; for the nameless daughter of Hippolyte du Peyral, having arrived at years of indiscretion, had run away from the convent and married a handsome, wild pioneer, by name Préault, and had scattered through the state a small but exclusively Creole race of Préaults; a family not, alas! without its place in the scandalous history of Louisiana, for the hereditary taint seemed to be fatally constant, and ever and anon the blood of the girl who had enslaved the fancy of Hippolyte du Peyral would crop out, and produce a woman of gorgeous meridional beauty and dazzling personality, half-tame and half-savage, a type that might be seen in its perfect development in Daphne Préault, the exile, the Princess of the Holland Street colony, in a word, the pure-blooded Bohemian.

Now, the historic outlines and the romantic details of this family history were cherished with true negro persistency by Clytemnestra, the ex-bondwoman; and the dream of her darkie soul was to see the old stock of Hippolyte du Peyral reunited in the persons of Paul and the Princess Daphne, and therefore, when the latter indignantly scorned the conditions of her second cousin's will, in refusing to marry Paul, Clyde held that she was flying in the face of Providence, and valourously invoked the assistance of her multi-fold deity in jade, to bring about this consummation, to her so devoutly to be wished for.

I have dealt with this family history at some length because it accounts in a great measure for the sympathy—in a way, a tie of blood—that existed between these two strong Creole personalities, separated from one another though they were, by half a hemisphere; a sympathy which led in so large a degree to the *dénouement* of this veracious narrative. It is hardly surprising, therefore, that to Clyde, from whom no secret of her mistress' life was concealed, the position of Eric in the Holland Street *ménage* of the Princess Daphne was a never-failing source of annoyance;

an annoyance that she dared not openly show to the principals in this drama, but which made itself felt continually, and especially to Eric, who, early in the game, rechristened Clytie, "Onesima, his thorn in the flesh."

Without risking the reception of a frown from Daphne, which though theoretically less baleful, was practically far more awful to Clytie, than the curse of Obi or the incantation of Voodoo, this antagonism caused itself to be very distinctly perceived on such occasions as she found it necessary in the pursuit of her professional avocations to enter his presence, as, for instance, when she would come in to lay tea at five o'clock; and then a vague feeling of easiness would come over Eric as he sat at his writing-table, from whence he could watch the Princess at her work. Underlying all Daphne's love for him, his super-sensitive nature fancied that there existed a feeling of superiority that only wanted one earthly touch to make it contempt; and this was a sensation he had never been able entirely to get over: it would impress him with a vague feeling of discontent in little scenes such as the following, which were of pretty constant recurrence.

It was five o'clock, and Eric had been enjoying himself vastly, writing an essay—high-flown, satirical, paradoxical—entitled, "The Praise of Publishers, by one of their Victims." The light was nearly gone, and Daphne sat in front of her easel painting somewhat abstractedly, playing, rather, with some of the details of her nearly finished picture. Eric had just concluded his essay with the paraphrase, "He who writes with nought to say, finds his labor thrown away," and, Clyde having set the tea-things with something like aggression of manner, he laid down his pen and looked at the Princess. She was leaning back in her chair, looking lazy and satisfied with her work, now and then making a little dab for some particular point, until the light, as far as painting was concerned, had died out. Then she laid down her palette and brushes, stretched her toes out in front of her, clasped her hands at the back of her head, and rested so, in contemplation of the canvas.

That silence fell which seems to envelop every death, even that of the daylight. No sound disturbs the stillness of the studio till the fire stumbles into a fresh fantasy of fallen cinders, the ashes burst out upon the hearth, and "new-born night begins its little life."

The day has risen and lived its life, it fades and dies, and as it dies there is a moment of stillness that proclaims its death: another life takes its place—"*Le Jour est mort; vive la Nuit!*"

Daphne yawns, stretches her long arms again, and rising, approaches the fire, where she throws herself into the big lounge as she did on the night that she surrendered herself to Eric, and by degrees settles herself into absolute comfort. Eric has been so quiet that she has almost forgotten his existence, when suddenly he startles her—if so placid a person as the Princess Daphne can ever be said to be startled—by bounding from his seat with an exclamation that partakes of the dual natures of a roar and a snort, and paces up and down the floor, until Daphne, without looking at him, remarks:

"Well! what are you playing at Polar bear in a cage for?"

"I swear!" he exclaims ("Don't!" says she). "I swear," he continues, "I'll never write another line, and I'll burn every paper that I've ever slung ink upon!" and he comes to the fire and takes up his position before her, in the attitude peculiar to and favoured by the Englishman of patriotic instinct.

Hard as steel, and with a little playful sneer, come the words from Daphne's lips:

"Why this sudden philanthropy? Why heap these blessings on the heads of undeserving publishers? Pause! reflect! gracious lord of mine, ere you inflict such privation on helpless humanity—on the world that hungers for the glorious fruit of your transcendent genius, and that has deserved no such salutary punishment at your hands. Let me plead for the world! Oh, write one more Assyrian farce, one more essay 'On the Morals and Pathology of the non-existent races of Central America,' before the fiat goes forth and the doom is sealed!" And she clasps her hands as if in prayer, as, with a fascinating *moue* of mock seriousness, she sinks on her knees from the big lounge, before him.

Eric looked down at her. He made no attempt to hide the pain her levity caused him. She saw it, and her hands fell, as she remained seated on the bear-skin rug, leaning against the sofa behind her.

"I'm blue—unhappy—disappointed," he said; "why do you sneer at instead of encouraging me?"

"Because you live in the nineteenth century and your books are those of the monks of the middle ages. Your standard works might be entitled *'Auctorum ignotorum omnia qua non supersunt'*— 'The forgotten works of unknown authors!' and your romances are simply scholarly epitomes of all that has been said by previous writers on subjects no one cares anything about. There is no boy who has just left college who could not do what you do; you write things that all scholars know as well as you, whilst as for the rest of your readers, you either bore or confuse them. Your writings, *mon cher*, are the apotheosis of the commonplace."

"It seems to me that what you want me to write *is* simply bald commonplace."

"Not at all. I don't see why you must necessarily jump from one extreme to the other. In doing that you admit that you have neither ability to originate nor industry to supply a demand."

"There you go again! You always stand up for the purely meretricious."

"My dear boy, up to a certain point everything is meretricious. Why do you suppose I sold my first pictures? Gabriel Hawleigh's early work was infinitely superior to mine, but mine sold, and his did not. Why? Because I am a beautiful woman, and painted my own portrait indirectly into everything, and with that, I painted subjects which were described as 'daring' by unsuccessful artists disguised as critics. In this way, an interest entirely apart from the work sold my prentice efforts. What you have to do is to prove yourself personally superior—as you undoubtedly are—to mere acquirements."

"In a phrase, you would have me write down to the morbid craving for sensation that characterizes the literary taste of today."

"Nonsense! Genius is universal, and requires no dictionary of its own. I tell you to forsake the display of erudition, and cultivate imagination. If I hadn't wit enough to give the public what it wants, and to give it art as well, I should be admitting that I am like every unsuccessful struggler who gives them pure talent—which is a drug in the market. If I could write I *would* make a success, for the reason that I should conceal art so well that those who cannot appreciate it would not find it. A fine lady can wear gingham and homespun, and be called 'chic'; but Clyde couldn't wear my terra-cotta wrapper. Apply this to your erudition. Gild your pill, *tres cher*, gild your pill!"

"Daphne, are you quite sure that you know—that you understand—what you are talking about?"

"Oh! I am absolutely sensible of my own ignorance, but I live in this nineteenth century of ours, and I desire to live comfortably—luxuriously—and to be 'somebody' into the bargain. My plane is immeasurably below yours, but whilst you cannot look down on me—though you are over my head—I can look up to you and appreciate you. I live on earth, you live in the clouds, and your work is no use there. You haven't yet reached Heaven, so you can't be sure that your works would sell there; and with the present moral obliquity that exists with regard to international copyright, though you might be celebrated, you would probably reap no advantage from your celebrity beyond a pair of first-quality wings and a more than ordinarily curly trumpet."

He turned away almost petulantly.

"What have I done," said he, "that you should talk to me like this? I'm a fool—a sensitive fool—I know; but, by Jupiter, you know exactly where to hit, and you hit hard."

"What have you done? What have you done? You have made me love you, darling, that's all." And she went to him, putting her arms about his neck, and pressing him closer, closer to her heart, until her head sank upon his shoulder, and her voice died away to a whisper in his ear, that she caressed softly with her lips.

Eric was deeply—obstinately—wounded, and he held her in a loose, distracted embrace. He was thinking so much of himself and of his own woes, and it hurt him beyond bearing that she did not worship him blindly—uncritically.

"Suppose," she went on, "you were not rich enough to be independent of your work. Would it be right to throw away the talent you have, on work that is gratifying only to yourself? Be sure, your want of success lies in yourself, not in other people. The cant phrase, 'writing above the heads of the herd,' is all rubbish. Fame is the justification of Talent; strive after it, buy it at any cost. Oh, I know the difference between Fame and Notoriety, and how much easier it is to gain the latter than the former. But to be heard, to be listened to, is the first consideration; make your crowd listen to you, and when you have got them in your grasp, give them what *you* like; but spare no means, however false they may seem to you, to get them there."

"But, sweetheart, you are arguing that Art should acquiesce in its own suppression."

"No—I argue that art should give you the superior force to conquer your tendency to sacrifice everything to it. Don't think I am cruel when I hurt you like this—I am so proud of you, and of your talents. Oh, love, I *must* see you rise above your disappointments. *You* are satisfied to know your own worth; *I* shall never be satisfied until the world acknowledges it. Forgive me, sweetheart, if I seem sordid and mercenary for your sake."

Though Eric adored Daphne, there was always this grain of worldly wisdom in her that jarred upon him; it was indefinable, but intense. But while it was repugnant to him, he was too reasonable not to acknowledge that in much of it she was right. It was almost humiliating to realize that this woman, who was only educated up to the ordinary feminine standpoint, could sound blindly, unthinkingly—with a rush,—as it were the depths of human nature, whilst he, with all his scientific and classic lore, took ten times as long to arrive anywhere near the same point. It came out strongly in her pictures. With all her profound artistic talent, she knew how to leaven the excellence of her work with a something that arrested the eye, with details of human nature which, though admirably executed, he still felt to be essentially meretricious. The word was his nightmare; it was her bank-account.

It was irritating to him to argue with this woman, who, like all self-supporting workers, had a confidence in her own efforts which, being based on practical experience, was unanswerable. He was forced to admit that her instinct was unerring, and that, in spite of her sordid expressions, she was inherently artistic; she could produce with a touch effects that, in others, demanded hours of labor. And above all, she worshipped him, and he knew it; he was her god, and though she strove often to hide the fact, she was mentally on her knees before him, adoring him wildly, and more appreciatively than any milk-and-water maiden who might have flattered him more by listening to and memorizing his incomprehensible poems, effusions which he loved to garb in the jargon of the unintelligible. She was of that type of woman who makes a man what he is. For what? That he may straightway go from her to fling himself at the feet of some pretty specimen of puerile femininity, and in the enjoyment of its inane worship, wonder how he could so long have endured the rather trying criticisms of a woman whose fibre, though passionate and maddening, "was somewhat coarse of a woman not fit to enter the same room with his Colinette—his Colinette, so pure, so holy, so—" bah! etcetera! etcetera! etcetera!

'Tis a weird world, my masters!

But Eric had not yet found his Colinette. He was enthralled by a personality stronger by far than his own, in all save that she adored him; he was content to live with only one thought in his mind—Daphne! Daphne!—and had anyone told him that the time might come when he would tire of the electric light, and seek the comparative gloom of the unexhausting ozokerit, he would have regarded the prophet with a contemptuous wonder, and would have returned to the dazzling fascinations of the gorgeous Creole with something like pity in his heart for the inexperienced philosopher "who had evidently never *loved.*"

Certainly nothing of this could have been foreshadowed by anyone who saw Eric Trevanion take Daphne in his arms, at the end of the conversation I have recorded above, and lose consciousness of the whole world in the thought that this matchless woman was his, and his alone; and as usual, they parted happier than ever in their fool's paradise of varied sensations. It is probable that a man of Trevanion's character would never have been chained as he was, if the course of his love had run perfectly smooth; and it was perhaps Daphne's art of criticising and correcting him that made her tenderness so infinitely more precious to him than it would otherwise have been. An American writer—Edgar Saltus—has said very justly, "The secret of never displeasing is the art of mediocrity;" and certainly one might wander for a lifetime amid the labyrinth of attributes before selecting for Daphne Préault the adjective "mediocre." She was grand, intoxicating, sublime, and infinitely soft; but never "affectionate." The word "affectionate" is too frequently a synonym—an euphemism—for "indifferent"; and Eric was Daphne's very soul, her only thought, her unique religion. And he left her today to go to some dinner-party or other, more bound to him, soul to soul, forever; for the instinct of maternity that unconsciously mingles itself with love in every woman's heart told her that this man was destined to be—nay, already was—a thing of her own creation. After dinner she went to his writing-table and spent a couple of hours with his impractical, high-flown manuscripts. He was a Quixote of literature; his essays were gems; not the diamonds, the rubies, the sapphires eagerly bought by the public who understand such things, but the cameos, the avanturines, the labradorites, and chrysoberyls of language, infinitely dearer than diamonds to the collector and connoisseur, but in no wise understood or appreciated by the people.

Whilst she was thus occupied, a thought struck her: she was reading an essay of his on the social customs of the Mayas of Yucatan, as contrasted with those of the people of Atlantis; an ingenious dissertation in which two people perhaps in the whole world—Dr. Le Plongeon and Ignatius Donnelly—would have revelled. She took up Eric's pen and rewrote the entire thing, discarding nothing of his, but adding a quantity of her own, until she had practically produced an essay on the Aztecs of the Parisian Boulevards and the Regent Street and the Piccadilly of the capital of Atlantis; and in its new and almost sacrilegious form, she posted it to the editor of the leading monthly magazine of the English-speaking world. This done, the Princess Daphne, though as yet it was early, went to bed.

Daphne Préault was a physically perfect woman. She had read of heroines of novels who took chloral, and she knew weak-minded women whose prayers for rest, on going to bed, took the practical form of bromide of potassium. To the Princess these things were the romance of the Pharmacopoeia. Having wrapped her exquisite body in the clinging silks of her night attire, she was in the habit of falling asleep almost the instant that her head touched the pillow; and with the regularity of clock-work, pre-cisely eight hours afterward, she made one bound from her hardly tumbled bed-clothes into her bath. Thus, at something before six o'clock on the following morning, the Princess surprised Clytie by stepping into the studio, where the spring-morning rays had just acquired sufficient strength to be properly called the light of day.

Swathed in her loose morning-wrapper, she was carefully cleaning and polishing her palette, when suddenly a strange, faint sensation seemed to travel all over her, and a strong shudder shook her from head to foot. She grasped her easel to prevent herself from falling; everything seemed black around her, and when the momentary mist had cleared away, everything seemed changed.

Was it herself or the studio? She touched her hair, and it seemed as if she were touching the hair of another woman: in an agony of terror, as if to identify herself, she staggered to the looking-glass; yes—there she was—the same hot black hair and Southern eyes; but something seemed altered; another *soul* seemed reflected from the eyes in the mirror, and, looking round, the very furniture seemed unfamiliar, though she recognized it all. Good God! was she going mad? Was she still herself? She even went to her writing-table and took up some of the letters that lay thereon. She read, half-aloud, her name and address on one of them, and—oh horrible!—it seemed, in some weird way, strange to her. Then her eyes fell on Eric's table, just as she had left it the night before, and in her agony she cried aloud, "Eric!—Eric!"

"Eric!"

Clytie, hearing the cry, rushed in, to find her mistress lying in a dead faint on the floor of the studio.

It was one o'clock in the morning in New York, and at that instant of time, Paul du Peyral roused Mahmouré di Zulueta from her mesmeric trance.

"Sho, honey! Sho, there! What is it, chile? Tell yo' Clytie what de mattah. You moughty po'ly, fo' shuah; yu's up too early, my pretty"—such were the words of her darkie nurse that rang in her ears as she recovered consciousness, to find the faithful old woman rocking herself to and fro over her prostrate body, and muttering incoherent prayers to her jade idol for her mistress' recovery.

"Be quiet, Clytie," said she; "I'm quite well, only I've been frightened. I ought to have eaten something before I got to work. Get it me quickly; and mind! don't speak of this to Mr. Trevanion."

"Sho' 'nuff," replied she.

There was little fear of her volunteering her conversation to Eric, whom she in some way connected—she knew not how—with this unprecedented state of her mistress' nerves. And Daphne sat down before the fire, unable for some mysterious reason to rid her mind of thoughts of her early life, of Baton Rouge, and of the would-be husband she had never seen—Paul du Peyral.

By ten o'clock, when Eric arrived, she was herself again, calmly at work, the obsession of her mind having departed as quickly and mysteriously as it had supervened. She had, as a precautionary measure, sent for her doctor as soon as it was fair to rouse him to his day's work, and he had completely restored her equanimity. There was no doubt about it—he was reassuringly positive, as doctors always are on points they know absolutely nothing about—she was quite obviously suffering, said he, from a touch of indigestion. She had eaten something—he could not say what—that had not agreed with her!

That was all.

"By-the-by, Eric," said she, after he had been there some time, "I was reading over some of your stuff last night, so as to secure a good night's rest, and I found that article of yours on Yucatan and Atlantis. I liked it better than ever, and have sent it to the editor of *Smith's Monthly*. Do you mind?"

"Not at all; it is a mere matter of form—he's had it once, and we shall have it back again. I might have saved you the trouble of sending it; but it really doesn't matter, sweet-heart. What a good child you are! You're always thinking of me."

"Oh, it's not that—but I *will* make, these editors appreciate you."

He came over and kissed her, and went back to his work feeling that the whole world was nothing to him so long as he kept the love of this wonderful woman. Still, was it not strange that she should have suddenly warmed to an appreciation of that article of his?—for he remembered her laughing it to scorn when first he read it to her; but perhaps she was at last acquiring a taste for his work, and he regarded it as a good omen.

Of the curious obsession of her mind that morning neither the Princess nor Clytie whispered a word, and it is probable that, had it never been repeated, he would never have heard anything about it at all; but to Daphne's bewilderment and Clytie's alarm, the symptoms recurred at intervals, generally late at night, and sometimes with such strength that it was hours before Daphne became quite herself again. After such attacks Eric would find her altered in some strange, indefinable way; her manner was hardened, her ideas were more independent and brusque, her whole personality was coarser, as it were, but at the same time touched over with a more languorous sense of luxury, a carelessness that was at the same time more subtle but more pronounced. They had almost ceased to alarm her, for the doctor before mentioned, having been once more consulted, had confirmed his previous opinion on the case: It was impossible to say exactly what the disturbing influence was—probably the home-sick fruit of the Kensington green-grocer; the effect, beyond all doubt, was a certain congestion of the blood-vessels of the cerebellum produced by a disordered state of the stomach. There was nothing to fear in any way. Seven-and-six for the visit—during which he acquired artistic dinner-party conversation for a week—and two of these pills after every attack—too late to prevent the attack true!—but quite sure to prevent its recurrence—for a time, at least. Er—thank you!

116

It was one afternoon, about three weeks after her first seizure, that Eric suggested suddenly:

"Daphne, do you remember that night we went to the Parthenon together?"

"Do I remember it? *Cher ami*, do you think I shall ever forget it?"

"Let's go there tonight and see the new piece for—'auld lang syne,' as it were."

"Certainly, boy; will you dine here, or shall I dine with you?"

"Oh, come down to the Bristol with me, and then we shall not have to hurry so."

And so it was arranged, and six o'clock saw them flying down Piccadilly again, as on the night when they gave up the world for one another.

They were supremely happy, and they showed it. A brighter spark appeared to gleam in Daphne's eyes as she sat by Eric's side; whilst, for his part, a sensation of utter and absolute contentment seemed to pervade his whole being. He hardly noticed the play, and was only conscious of a lover-like regret that the fall of the curtain chased them once more into the open air. Arrived once more in Holland Street, he was following Daphne into the studio, when suddenly she sprang back, exclaiming,

"Eric! there's somebody there."

"What!" he cried, and strode past her into the studio.

The fire-light threw shadow-shapes, gaunt and monstrous, upon the walls; the imprisoned air seemed heavy with the sensuous perfume of the Princess Daphne's personality; but that was all.

"Bah!" said he, as he struck a match on the sole of his shoe, and lit the gas, "there's no one here. Tell you what it is, Daph; you're getting nervous, and I don't like it. Let me give you something strong; what shall it be?"

She did not answer, and he looked round. Something in her look arrested him as he stepped towards her. She had curled herself up as it were on the hearth-rug among the pillows that had fallen from the lounge, a position, picturesque, passionate, beautiful, but not *hers*. A strange, yearning look was in her eyes, her half-parted lips wore a feverish crimson, and, revealed by the cut of her corsage, he saw her bosom heave as if she suffocated under some strange excitement. It was Daphne, and yet not Daphne; the figure that lay before him was too soft, too sinuous; the position was too undignified, too wild—if such an expression may be applied to a posture—for the calm, cool Princess. He flung himself on his knees by her side, exclaiming,

"Daphne, my darling, what is it?"

For answer she gathered his head in her long white arms, and drew it down to hers, crushing him in an embrace that was almost suffocating, till he could feel the tumultuous beating of her heart as she whispered:

"Oh, Paul, Paul, my darling!"

"Paul!" he exclaimed, as he started from her. "Who's that?"

"What?"

"You said 'Paul.' What do you mean? Come, child, get up, and be sensible."

"Sensible! What do *you* mean? Aren't you Paul? Oh, no; you're Eric. And yet I seem to know a man named Paul. Isn't it you? No. Ah! but what does it matter? Oh, don't look at me like that, dear; put your arms round me, to tell me you are here. Oh! Eric, if you knew how I love you!"

"Yes, yes. But what is the matter with you? You look—you act so strangely."

"Well, never mind—kiss me!"

"No, you are not yourself; let me get you something."

"Oh, don't trouble yourself," said she, rising suddenly and flinging herself into a chair. "No I'm not myself—I don't care—it pleases me to be someone else for the time. What does it matter? You are not Eric, as far as I can make out—everything seems topsy-turvy—so much the better; it makes a change. Come!"

He stood still, a few paces from her, as if terror-stricken—spell-bound. Was this his grand, graceful Daphne, whose calmness had so often chilled the flame of his love when it blazed highest? Was this the woman who, in the pure devotion of herself to him, had become his, to the nethermost thought of her soul? Good God! the woman who looked at him from the arm-chair through Daphne's eyes was almost coarse—almost animal—in her expression. He turned away and looked into the fire, as if to find there the explanation of the transformation that had taken place before his very eyes. She nudged him with her slippered foot.

"Don't you want to kiss me, darling?"

"Oh, hush, hush!" he murmured, taking a few steps away from her. She sprang to her feet.

"My God! what a fool I am to love you so! I ought to be a sickly, sentimental school-girl, ready to weep with you, laugh with you, dance with you, and sigh all day at your lightest frown. But I'm not. What I am, I am; if you don't like it you needn't take it; there are a hundred men as good as you within as many yards. I must have been mad when I made up my mind that you were the only man in the world. Ah! but the difference between you and Paul!"

That name again! He turned sharply upon her, just in time to see her sway to and fro for an instant, and then to catch her as she fell into his arms.

He laid her on the lounge. Hardly had he done so, when, with a choking sigh, she opened her eyes, and seeing him bending over her, she said, with a half-frightened look, as she saw the hard, cold pain in his eyes,

"Eric, my darling, what is it?"

"You ask *me* what is it. Good heavens! that's what I ask you!"

"What do you mean? Oh, Eric, I feel so strange; just as if I'd had one of those stupid fainting fits of mine. What has happened?"

"Upon my life, I don't know. You seem to have been possessed for the last twenty minutes. Who is 'Paul'?"

"Paul?"

"Yes, Paul. You have been talking—raving—about him, and saying the most awful things to me."

"To you? oh, my love!" Then, after a pause, she covered her face with her hands, and said, in a broken whisper, "My God! am I going mad?"

Eric made no answer.

"I feel," continued she, "as if I had been somebody else, somewhere else, and I thought that you were that horrible man who is in America—Paul du Peyral. Oh, Eric, what does it mean? I can't bear it;" and for the first time since he had known her, she burst into tears.

He knelt by her side and put his arms round her, torn hither and thither by a weird feeling of violent attraction and equally violent repulsion. What was the mystery attaching to this incomprehensible woman?

Little by little she became quieter, calmer—herself again; and when he left her, there was no trace remaining of the manner that had horrified him so, no recollection of the incident which, on his mind at least, had left an impression of uneasiness, if not of positive alarm. He slept but little that night, but determined to learn, without delay, all that he could of this Paul du Peyral, who seemed to cross his path continually, and who seemed to be in some mysterious way entangled in the skein of his existence, and of that of the Princess Daphne.

His opportunity came sooner than he expected it. A couple of days later the Eastons gave a tea-party to the colony, and as their studio was smaller and less picturesque than his, he placed the latter at their disposal, and found himself to a certain extent in the position of host with regard to their guests. If it had not been for this, he would probably have hardly noticed the good-looking vulgarian who was presented to him by Sylvia Easton as "Mr. Charles Sturton-Baker"—the name in full. Mr. Baker had promoted himself from the obscurity of Belsize, N. W., to the dignity of a hyphenated name, and of a manner which he fancied was more suited to the punctuation. Miss Easton, not quite sure of her suburban Adonis when transplanted into Holland Street, exploded a mine in her good-natured endeavour to supply him with a cloak for his personality, by saying sweetly as she presented him,

"Mr. Baker—er—Mr. Sturton-Baker has just returned triumphant from the conquest of social New York."

"This may be my man," thought Eric, as he shook Mr. Baker's hand, and invited him to look at his sherry and bric-a-brac with him.

"So you have been in America, Mr. Baker," said he, by way of opening the conversation; "how did it impress you?"

"Don't you know that thousands of Americans lose their lives yearly by asking that question of foreigners?"

"Indeed! why—how?"

"Because it is the question that one is asked from the moment one lands till the moment one re-embarks, and after a few days, killing the man who asks it of you becomes merely justifiable homicide."

"Indeed! I wasn't aware that I was either transgressing the laws or courting danger when I asked the question. But seriously, it must be a very interesting country. I have always heard that its social institutions are quite unique."

"Well, in what way?"

"Why, that all classes of society are mixed up together inextricably, and you never know whether you have a millionaire driving your horse-car, or a car-driver receiving you in a millionaire's mansion."

"That is to a certain extent true. I have met in my American travels car-drivers and bar-tenders whom I should be proud to call my friends, and millionaires and social magnates whom I should be sorry to have black my boots. Excellent sherry this, Mr. Trevanion!"

"Er—yes. Have some more. I suppose no one ever inquires into his friend's antecedents in the land of the brave and the home of the free."

"Oh, no. A sort of *Fifth-Avenue oblige* keeps them quiet on questions of paternity and grand-paternity. It is only the members of the *haut* Knickerbocker *régime* who discuss their pedigrees; and the descendant of a Dutch adventurer thinks he confers a great honour when he marries the millions of some commercial magnate. The funny part of it all is, that when said descendant of said Dutch rapscallion wants to be particularly insulting to the working-bee in the hive, he describes the latter contemptuously as 'a Dutchman.'"

"And did you come across the Creole element of society at all?"

"Hardly at all. Few Creoles inhabit the North and East, and when they do, one seldom knows them to be such. Now and then one meets a handsome, stormy-looking man or woman, and hears that it is a Creole—that is all."

"I wonder if you ever came across a Mr. Paul du Peyral?"

The vulgar face became convulsed by an expression that was half astonishment and half leer, as he replied:

"Why, yes—I have come across him; what of him?"

"I know nothing of him, but I should like to."

"Mr. Trevanion, if I read your expression right your feelings toward du Peyral are hardly friendly."

"Well, no; he keeps a dear friend of mine out of a very large fortune, and seems, in more ways than one, to lie across my path—though I have never seen him. You know, it happens so sometimes."

"Then I have the advantage of you, for I have stayed in a country-house with him, and can only say that he was personally very offensive to me."

"Ah! a gentleman, I suppose?"

"Well, yes—I suppose so," replied Baker, on whom the gentle sarcasm was completely lost. "He's one of those affected, half-mystic people who think the world of themselves here, and will want frills on their halos hereafter."

"You evidently don't like him, Mr. Baker—have some more sherry."

"Thanks! No, I don't; in fact, between you and me, old man, he did his best—and failed—to spoil a very pretty little game of mine over there. There is a little girl in New York who thinks herself a second Madame Récamier, but isn't, and who is madly in love with me—all New York rings with it. Now, as she has millions of her own, I have gone in for them, and in a few months you'll see me making her American dollars fly right merrily. Now this du Peyral wanted her for himself, so he abused me to her like mad, and then had to take it all back, as they say over there. Naturally, I should like to get even with him."

"He wants to marry this girl, you say?"

"Well, he wants to marry her money; I don't fancy he is rich himself. Unfortunately, there is an obstacle, I understand—some *liaison* he has formed over there."

"A *liaison*?"

"Yes—see here—I only heard about it by this morning's mail—here's my little girl's letter."

"But, my dear sir, I don't want to read your love letters!"

"Oh, that's all right; go on. Women shouldn't make fools of themselves if they don't want it known. However, if you don't care to know what you ask about, you needn't read it, that's all."

Eric, seeing that the man was in earnest, took the letter, and read as follows:

"My own sweet darling, etc., etc., Charlie! You know that your little girl is unhappy, for when you are away, etc., etc. When you come back—and you *will* come back, won't you, Charlie? etc., etc., etc.—I shall have such lots to tell you that you won't want to hear, etc., etc., etc., naughty boy! etc., etc., etc., darling! etc., etc., etc., married, etc., etc., etc. And I am your own etc., etc., etc., Parthenia, P. S.—I had almost forgotten what I wanted to tell you, darling. The other day that loathsome man, du Peyral, called—like his impertinence!—and, oh! my darling, etc., etc., etc., he said the most dreadful things about you. Of course I didn't believe him, because I know in my etc., etc., etc., that you are etc., etc., etc., and I thought no more about it; but he wrote to a gentleman in England named Gabriel Hawleigh, whom I should like to etc., etc., etc., who wrote back the truth about you, which was lovely. And du Peyral was so dreadfully frightened of what you would do to him that he gave me the letter to read, with a perfectly grovelling apology for having slandered you. I hope that, when you come over again, you will etc., etc., etc. The idea of his daring to call at a decent house, when everyone knows that he is somehow connected with that dreadful woman, Mahmouré di Zulueta, who you know was etc., etc., etc., and is etc., etc., etc." And then, with renewed expressions of admiration, of the domestic servant order, the postscript closed.

"What do you think of that for a letter from a girl with five millions, my boy, eh?" remarked Mr. Baker, as Eric returned him the communication, with an expression of supreme disgust on his face.

"Well, it is hardly a letter that I should think your million-heiress wants hawked round to flatter your vanity; but you certainly seem to have cause to dislike Mr. Paul du Peyral. What are you going to do about it?"

"Ah! that's it. First of all I am going to find out all I can about him and the Zulueta through Murray Hill, an American friend of mine, and then I shall marry my little gold-fish."

"*Je vous souhaite de la chance!*"

"Eh?"

"Good luck to you!"

"Oh! certainly, thanks—great heavens! who is that woman who has just come into the room? What a clipping gal!"

"That is Miss Daphne Préault," said Eric, very stiffly.

"Well, she's A 1, ain't she? Do you know her?"

"Yes."

"I say introduce her to me, will you?"

"I will present you to her, if she cares about it. I'll ask her, if you like."

"All right, old man; go on. And, I say, do you know—it's a queer coincidence—she's the living image of that man we've been talking about—Paul du Peyral!"

※

"My goodness, Eric," said the Princess, as they entered her studio together an hour later, "why on earth did you introduce that horrid-little cad Baker to me?—I believe he was half tipsy."

"He was all you say he is, *chère amie*, but I owed him some favour, and that was the one he claimed. He had been giving me very useful information about the man who I believe is what the Germans call your *doppelgänger*—Paul du Peyral. He hates him, and if there is anything wrong with Monsieur Paul, he'll find it out through an idiotic but love-lorn American heiress, who is negotiating the purchase of Mr. Baker for her very own, and will, in this manner, save us a good deal of trouble and expense. I've asked him to come and report progress to me. *Il faut souffrir*, you know, *pour être au courant!* One must suffer, to be well-informed."

"Well, it is a devotion on your part which I highly appreciate;" and the conversation drifted on to other subjects.

It was about half-past nine that evening that Eric and Daphne were sitting before the fire, playing *écarté*, when Gabriel sprang into the studio suddenly, pale and out of breath.

"I am going to be hung," he cried, sinking into a chair.

"Good God! Whom have you killed?" exclaimed Eric.

"My picture, I mean—see!" and he produced the notice from the authorities at Burlington House, which told him that its hospitable portals would be thrown open to him on Varnishing day, at the Private View and at the Academy Soirée.

A season of genuine congratulation ensued, which became general a few moments later, when the postman arrived bearing similar intelligence for the Princess Daphne; and as Gabriel rose to leave, having been warmly felicitated by Eric, the Princess took both his hands in hers, and leaning over, kissed his forehead, saying,

"Gabriel, dear friend of ours, I am proud to be the first to salute you on your accession to greatness. A new era has opened for you and—for Maye. May it be eternal, and may we all live long to congratulate ourselves on being the intimate friends of one of the greatest artists of his day."

It was with a tear in each eye that Gabriel rushed from the studio to go on spreading his good news. As he did so, the door slammed violently behind him, and a little mirror that hung by its side fell with a crash, and was shattered into fragments.

"*Absit omen!*" ejaculated Eric. And he rang for Clytemnestra.

# CHAPTER VI.
## An Anglomaniac.

In a delicately-furnished male apartment in the hotel which he had come fondly to imagine had been named after himself, sat Mr. Murray Hill, an American gentleman of Spanish appearance and French manners, the aim and object of whose existence was to be taken for an Englishman. With this purpose in view, he clothed his symmetrical form entirely in British clothes, was virulent in his abuse of all things American, turned up his trousers in New York when the weather reports announced rain in London, spoke with an amazing drawl, stuck an eye-glass of a perfectly innocuous and supererogatory description in his dexter optic, affected with enthusiasm the society of wandering Englishmen, and was consequently a centre of adulation and imitation in the sacred precincts of the Pantaloon Club, within whose exclusive portals the gilded youth of Manhattan origin strove to hide their honourable Dutch ancestry beneath a varnish of acute anglomania.

From the above description the casual reader might be inclined to write Mr. Murray Hill down as an ass, but the casual reader would be vastly mistaken. A better fellow never showed himself at Delmonico's than Mr. Murray Hill; a gentleman in every modern sense of the word, the shady members of the English snobocracy who yearly came to New York for the winter, and who ought to have been proud of his friendship, were seldom fit to be spoken of in the same breath with him; and by those who understood him at his proper value, his little transatlantic idiosyncrasies were readily forgiven, on the principle of "*Nullum magnum ingenium sine mixturâ dementiæ!*"—a great genius is always a trifle mad!

It was unfortunate, however, that his knowledge of Great Britain was not of a kind complete enough to show him what should have been apparent to the merest observer, viz., that Charles Sturton Baker was a cad in the most practical and onomatopoetic sense of the term, for, meeting that person one day at the Sunday menagerie of the Van Baulk'ems, he was led away by his somewhat aggressive personality, and nearly succeeded in launching him in the best society of the modern Gotham. After Baker's return to the land of his obscure birth, he kept up a correspondence with Mr. Murray Hill for his own selfish purposes, a correspondence which he garnished freely with extracts from *Truth*, *The World*, and *Vanity Fair*, on the culinary principle of "flavour to taste, and serve quickly on clean paper."

It was with a lazy tremor of joyful anticipation therefore, that, on the morning of which I speak, Mr. Murray Hill took up the envelope that lay beside his chocolate, and whose postmark, "London," was in no sense—for him—qualified by the letters "N. W." that bespoke its evangelhurst origin; and, breaking the seal, he commenced, with much appreciation, the string of second-hand and original (though imaginary) gossip of the back-stairs and of cheap society journalism. That H. R. H. should have worn in his button-hole at "The Private View" the entire spike of a double hyacinth bloom was, to say the least of it, thrilling; but it paled into insignificance before the intelligence that a Royal Duke had expressed to Mr. Baker, on the steps of the Marlborough Club, the opinion that, if that sanctuary were conducted more on the lines of the Pantaloon Club in New York, his Brother (with a capital B) would have nothing left to wish for in the world. It was therefore with a new thrill of pleasure that he received Mr. Baker's commission, which was couched in the following terms:

"A few days ago I was talking about you to my bosom friend, Lord Trevanion, and he said to me, 'I wonder whether Mr. Murray Hill could find out for me anything about a man named Paul du Peyral, who lives in New York. He is, I believe, an adventurer of the deepest dye, and should he by any chance be married quietly, it would be a scrap of intelligence that would entitle its author to sincere gratitude in *High Quarters*?'" [Capital H. Q., and underlined.]

Now, Mr. Murray Hill had traversed the world from China to Peru—proceeding in a westerly direction, of course—and consequently Paul du Peyral was not only well known to him, but was also, in the lucid intervals when he was free from anglomania, an object of intelligent admiration to him. But the mania was strong upon him this morning, and he determined, in a social but drastic manner, to enquire into that gentleman's "record," and report accordingly. Mere personal admiration must not be allowed to interfere with patriotic *esprit de corps*, and, posted as he was in matters transatlantic, Mr. Murray Hill had almost come to look upon himself as an Englishman!

His toilet carefully completed, therefore, he sallied forth—that, though hackneyed, is the only expression that ever conveys adequately to my mind the progress of the American dandy down Fifth Avenue—to the Pantaloon Club, in the classic gloom of whose reading-room he found a selection of the gray-headed youth—the *jeunesse argentée* of New York, and of him who seemed to him the best, or rather, the most promiscuously, informed, he inquired for data concerning that traveller-mystic, Paul du Peyral. The answer was prompt and precise.

"Du Peyral? Oh, yes. A queer chap, but interesting in his way. He was at Mrs. Lexington Park's last night, and he and Eugene Stiggins had rather an interesting discussion on mesmerism. You know, Eugene is awfully good at it, but he confessed himself nowhere in the presence of du Peyral. Why, there was a woman there who humbugged him about it, and said she did not believe in it, and our mystic just looked at her for a minute and then said, 'You can't stir an inch, hand or foot;' and, by gad, sir, she couldn't! I never saw a girl so scared in my life. She began to beg off, and he simply said, 'Hush! you can't speak;' and, by gad, sir, she couldn't! It was wonderful. Then he clapped his hands and said, 'Now you're all right;' and she was. She didn't chaff him any more, but followed him about the room with her eyes all the evening, as if he had bewitched her."

"But who is he, anyhow?"

"I'm not quite sure, but they say he's a Creole by birth. He came here a few years ago, and his ostensible occupation is a study of 'Skeeters and Bluebottles, or something of that kind; but they say that's only a blind—that he performs weird rites in his own rooms with that queer foreign woman, Mahmouré di Zulueta. He'll get his head broken by someone some day, if he performs promiscuously on other people's best girls."

"What's the tie between him and la Zulueta?"

"Well, that is a mystery too, and a rather delicate one. He hasn't known her very long, but they're awful thick—nearly always together, and people say—well—you know! Tom Morrison was catching bass on Lake Ontario some time ago, and saw them together at Niagara, and put them down as a pair of honeymooning turtles."

"Honeymoon?"

"Well—sort of. However, there's no fear of Paul marrying the dazzling Mahmouré, for if he does, all his money goes to the Préaults of New Orleans. Claude Préault was telling me about it the other day. Naturally they wish he'd marry, but du Peyral's too foxy, and doesn't bother about buying the tree when he can always pick an apple."

"Oh!"

Mr. Murray Hill lunched pensively, and then wandered down the mountain side till he reached Paul du Peyral's rooms. He was greeted with effusion, and presented to Mahmouré, who lay in a sort of happy lethargy on a lounge. It was not long before he spoke of the phenomena of the preceding night in terms of admiring interest, and followed an established principle by giving a biased opinion on a subject he knew nothing about, to the grave amusement of Paul, who itched to give him a practical illustration, but withstood the temptation manfully.

When he was gone, Mahmouré looked after him and said:

"Paul—who's your friend?"

"Male variety of the genus American—sub-order, Dude—class, Anglomaniac. A harmless, gentlemanly fellow, with a lot of good stuff in him, masked by a morbid fear of letting it get out."

"Don't trust him."

"Good gracious, why?"

"Because he is your enemy. Probably he doesn't know why himself, but the way he looked at me and watched you told me that he had some *arrière pensée* in coming to see you. Depend upon it he didn't come here for nothing."

"What an anxious little woman it is! Well—don't be afraid, dear; he can't hurt me, and he's one of the few men I should care to have around. He has seen the world, and it makes him interesting, because he understands it."

"That's the very reason you shouldn't be too thick with him, *cher ami*;" and could Paul have seen Mr. Murray Hill, as he proceeded up-town on a broad grin and a horse-car, he would have been inclined to agree with her. As it was, all he said was:

"Well, the only thing I know against him is, that he was a friend of Charles Sturton Baker's when he was over here."

"That's another name that always frightens me for no earthly reason, when I hear it; depend upon it, Paul, the combination of those two men is bad."

"Well, it doesn't affect *me* if he chooses to keep bad company; you can put it down to a phase of anglomania. But, by Jove! one must have it strong if it blunts one's perception of the moral and social qualities of Baker. But come, let us make an experiment. I wonder whether I could make you 'appear,' as it is called, to Daphne Préault, who seems such a friend of yours over there."

"Oh, not today, Paul; you look so tired. It takes too much out of you."

"Nonsense, little one," replied Paul; but his wife was quite right. The rings round his eyes were increasing in circumference and deepening in shade, and sometimes even Paul himself felt uneasy at the lassitude that crept over him. Mahmouré, on the other hand, seemed to be gaining strength every day—her new-found happiness seemed to restore to her the life she had almost relinquished through sheer indifference to it; and sometimes a horrible feeling came over her that, Hermippus-like, she was slowly but surely sapping his vitality, was living with a life drawn in some mysterious manner from his.

"Nonsense, child," repeated Paul; "I am a little tired this morning; that's the result of the mesmerism at Mrs. Lexington Park's last night; but this afternoon or this evening I shall try to make the fair Daphne see a ghost."

"Doesn't it seem a shame," said Mahmouré, pensively, "to worry her in the way we must, when we are living on money that ought to be hers?"

"Good heavens! what do you mean?"

"I don't know. Somehow I seem to have identified myself with her lately, and feel sometimes as if I were ashamed of myself for having been a party to such a dishonesty—for that's what it *is*, Paul, you can say what you like. I can't help looking at it from her point of view; it's the result of our experiments, I suppose—but sometimes it makes me miserable!"

"Don't be ridiculous, girl," replied Paul, almost brutally. "I have a mission to fulfil in the world, and that mission is the perfection of mesmeric science. I could not get money enough by fair means to live in the luxury which is necessary to us for the purpose of our experiments, so having got it by foul, I keep it. I don't care how I get it, so long as I have it."

"Oh, don't talk like that. I'm quite serious—and it makes me feel as if I were a thief."

"Oh, indeed! Why this high moral tone all of a sudden?" said Paul, with a sneer. "I suppose you want me to play the restitution game, and all that!"

"Yes, Paul."

"Great heavens! and it's for *this* that I married you. It's for *this* that I've tried to satisfy for you the scruples that every woman naturally cherishes. Mahmouré, you will oblige me by not mentioning this subject to me again *never*. You hear?"

"Yes, Paul. There's only one last question I want to ask. If you hadn't this money, should you have enough of your own for us to live on?"

"Yes, I should; but I don't choose to live less comfortably than I do. I don't mind telling you that most of the income of old Préault's money is put aside to provide for you in case I die. But I won't hear any more infernal nonsense about proclaiming myself to the world as a swindler. Now we will change the subject, if you please."

In this little scene all the unscrupulousness of du Peyral's race came out, and it was a kind of poetic justice that Mahmouré should have got such an idea into her head. There is no doubt that it was due to the identification of Mahmouré with Daphne through his own agency. The continual communion of the two souls had made the one woman sympathize with the other, thinking almost with the same mind as she. But neither Paul nor Mahmouré realized this. *He* thought it a sickly sentimentality that must be crushed out; *she* fancied that it was a natural sympathy for the wronged heiress. It was the commencement of a very pretty complication in this history—a complication, in fact, on which the entire history was destined to turn.

If Mr. Murray Hill could have fully realized what was going on in Mahmouré's mind, his task would have been much lightened. As it was he re-arrayed himself in new and more patriotically English garb, and went and called on Miss Parthenia Van Baulk'em.

It happened by good or ill luck that, when he was announced at the Van Baulk'ems' mansion, Miss Parthenia was seated in her boudoir, engaged in transferring the gold stamped band bearing the magic name of Pingat-Laferrière from a ball-dress purchased some years ago in Paris, to the waist of a home-made production of the family dressmaker. Miss Van Baulk'em was about to visit friends at Tuxedo, and felt that this band, carelessly exhibited as the gown hung from its appointed peg, was more calculated to impress her friends than the "unsigned" work of art of her more economical *modiste*. Engaged in this work of indumentary diplomacy, the fair Parthenia was equally busy making confidences on the subject of Mr. Charles Sturton Baker to her "greatest girl-friend"—for the time being—and giving full scope to her venomous little tongue on the subject of M. du Peyral. It was therefore annoying that Mr. Murray Hill should come at that particular moment, but as he was a combination of three things strange among the male adherents of the Van Baulk'em menagerie, to wit, a gentleman, a scholar, and a friend of Mr. Baker's, she deemed it expedient to deviate from the strict path of mendacity, and confess that she was "at home."

Virtue, she felt, was on this occasion its own reward, for Mr. Murray Hill opened the conversation, in terms which were balm to her wounded soul, on the subject of Paul du Peyral, and together they speculated on the possibility of du Peyral having married the beautiful Mahmouré on the quiet. However, the question occurred—what could be his object in doing it?

"Well," said Mr. Murray Hill, in answer to her question, "there could be only one explanation of the thing. In the first place, if report is not, as usual, a liar, la Zulueta is singularly fickle in the bestowing of her favours, and requires chaining; in the second, du Peyral has evidently been infatuated by her; and in the third, he is mad on this mesmeric business, and she is his champion 'subject.' Now, everything seems to point to the fact of his being an utterly unscrupulous adventurer, so, to keep his victim bound to him, and to steal the Préault inheritance into the bargain, it is quite possible that he has married her somewhere without saying anything about it. What we want to get at is evidence of this, circumstantial and documentary. And that is what I propose to do, if I can."

"My heartfelt wishes for your success go with you," responded Parthenia. "If that man isn't what he pretends to be, the sooner he is hounded out of New York with his ballet-dancer—well, actress, if you like—the better. Here he has been, for the last three or four years, swelling about the place as an independent gentleman, making love to all sorts of girls, and marrying none of them, besides creating no end of scandals with married women; so you will be doing a good action to society at large, and a very great favour to me." And the beautiful Parthenia put her hand on Mr. Murray Hill's arm with the coyest little pressure imaginable, and looked with her great brown eyes deep into his.

Mr. Murray Hill was only a man after all, and "Phenie" Van Baulk'em, though vulgar, was very pretty, and when she let him carry her hand unresisting to his lips—for the benefit of "Charlie" of course—he felt that he was indeed a Galahad; and should "Charlie" prove to be a King Arthur, he was perfectly prepared to become a Sir Launcelot to her Guinevere. Mr. Murray Hill was only a man, after all!

That evening Paul du Peyral made his grand experiment of acting through Mahmouré upon Daphne as she slept in Holland

Street, Kensington, W., with a measure of success duly to be recorded in the next chapter.

In her mesmeric trance on this occasion Mahmouré retained her own personality, and gave Paul a description of Daphne that astonished him vastly. Was it possible that the Creole heiress resembled him so marvellously in appearance? or was Mahmouré confusing the two personalities, and describing *him* to himself as Daphne Préault? It was a problem that he reserved to time and himself for solution.

On the following day, as Mahmouré lay curled up among the cushions of the divan, to her amazement Mr. Murray Hill was announced! At first she was going to reply with an indignant "Not at home!" when it occurred to her that if this was an enemy, she might as well cast around him her wiles, to make him declare himself. So he was shown into the snuggery on Forty-first Street which is already familiar to our readers.

"An unexpected pleasure, Mr. Hill," said Mahmouré, as that gentleman seated himself at a respectable distance from the lounge on which she lay curled up as usual.

"A pleasure, Madame di Zulueta," replied he, "that I should have denied myself on the grounds of etiquette, for I know I ought to have asked permission before venturing to call, had it not been that, though I only had the pleasure of making your acquaintance yesterday, my thoughts turned somehow instinctively to you for sympathy as I passed your door."

"For sympathy?"

"Yes, for sympathy with an indignant man; though I have no right to be indignant, for my indignation is on account of other people's business, not of my own."

"But how interesting to find someone so altruistic as to be indignant on someone else's account!"

"Yes, it is, rather, especially as indignation is a very wearing emotion, and produces gray hairs and wrinkles and things."

"Are you not going to tell me its cause? I always thought that you Englishmen never had emotions."

"We *what?*"

"You Englishmen."

"What do you mean?"

"Why, you are English, are you not?" (Oh! the wily Mahmouré!)

Mr. Murray grew pink with pleasure, and as nearly as possible hauled down his colours as he stammered:

"Well, no!—I'm not *quite* an Englishman. Of course my family were English, and that makes me very un-American, thank God!—and I've lived over there a good deal and—"

Mr. Murray Hill would have gone on with his Macaulayesque history of himself, only that Mahmouré, having made her *coup*, didn't care a jot about the fiction she had encouraged, and so merely cut in with:

"But your cause of indignation?"

"Ah, yes," said Mr. Murray Hill, coming back to fact or rather, abandoning one fiction for another—as he remembered his business: "I have been very much disturbed this afternoon by a very strange case. A young Englishman is over here, slaving at almost menial literary work for a living, compelled to this course by the unscrupulousness of an American blackguard, who, living in England, has contrived to rob him of an inheritance that is justly his."

"Oh, how abominable! can't you suppress the American blackguard over there?"

"Well, blackguard is rather too strong a term. I was led away by my feelings—foolish things to have, are they not? I should have said adventuress, for the swindler over there is a woman."

"A woman? how shameful!" cried Mahmouré, getting interested, and feeling all a woman's vindictiveness against the misdeeds of one of her own sex rising within her as she spoke.

"Yes," said Mr. Murray Hill, reflectively, "it is shameful, for the boy over here ought to be living in elegant independence, as they say, instead of starving to satisfy the low caprice of an utterly unworthy woman over there."

"Caprice? What do you mean?"

"Why, no doubt we should be able to work upon her sense of right and wrong, but she has married over in Europe some hound of a man whom she supports, and therefore there is no chance of inducing her to surrender her ill-gotten wealth."

"Really, Mr. Hill, this is the most abominable story I ever heard. How can a woman be so wicked? and how can a man be so mean?"

"Should you think it any better or any worse if the case were reversed?" said he, rising and walking towards the window. "I mean, suppose a man kept a hard-working woman out of her inheritance to support himself and another woman in luxury?"

This was a stunner! It was her own case exactly, and in the light in which it constantly occurred to her. She looked quickly and keenly at the gentle, courteous creature who was playing with his gloves, at the window, standing so that his back was turned to the light. Was this really a true story he was telling her? or was he, like some modern Machiavelli, touching off a torpedo of truth by firing a fuse of fiction? If he were, not the slightest indication thereof appeared on Mr. Murray Hill's interesting but impassive face, and Mahmouré, lulled into a sense of security, felt a certain relief at having someone to whom she could express her views on her own case, and who would turn a sympathetic ear to the cry of her artificially aroused conscience. Artificially, I say, because had she not become so mysteriously identified with Daphne Préault she would never, in thought, have swerved from her allegiance to Paul and his schemes for his own welfare. So after the first shock of astonishment was over, she replied quite calmly:

"I don't think that theoretically it would make any difference to the morals of the situation, but practically speaking, I think it would make all the difference in the world. For a man can always support himself, and a woman cannot respect a man who lives upon her. If the position were reversed, as you suggest, I am certain that the woman who was supported with someone else's money could be acted upon by sympathy for her fellow-woman, and would herself try and induce the man to make restitution. If he would not do it, and the case were properly presented to her, she would even make restitution herself—supposing, that is, that the man could support himself without the other unfortunate woman's money. And even if he couldn't, I believe the woman would try, even if it came to working for herself. Ah! Mr. Hill, I know we women are awfully hard on one another when we are in independent circumstances, but pity for a really ill-used sister is a very strong factor in many of our actions."

Mr. Murray Hill was very clever, and knew exactly where to stop—he was not like the amateur gardener who stirs up the seed he has sown, with a stick, every day, to see how it is getting on—so he stopped here and proceeded to change the subject. We have remarked above that he was only human after all, and Mahmouré, attractive as she was, even when she was nearest to death, was doubly so now that life was beginning to blaze once more from her beautiful eyes. So Mr. Murray Hill was stricken with the brilliant inspiration of killing two birds with one stone, and replied, coming close to the divan:

"Ah, madam, I thank you from my heart; it is such women as you that make one think better of humanity in general, and of your sex in particular. I bless the day that broke for me when I had the honour of making your acquaintance. A friend of mine used to say that he never knew but one woman who could understand reason, and *she* wouldn't listen to it. You are unique, for you both listen and understand." And he took her hand and carried it to his lips.

Mahmouré drew it away somewhat hastily, and arranged herself more stiffly on the divan.

"Why do you take away your hand?" said Mr. Murray Hill, trying to get hold of it again. "You cannot be so cruel as to refuse my homage and with such eyes as those that were made to look in love, with such lips as those that were made to smile and kiss."

"Mr. Hill!" exclaimed she, standing up, with a look of terror in the eyes he had insulted.

Mr. Murray Hill believed most of the stories of the "inconsequence" (Balzac again!) of Mahmouré, and fancied that the assumption of dignity was conjured up to spur him to fresh ardour. At that moment Mahmouré heard the click of Paul's latch-key in the outer door of her "apartment," and the look of terror gave place to one of malicious courage. Mr. Murray Hill noted the change, and, misinterpreting it by reason of the inferiority of his ear, flung himself on his knees and tried to clasp her in his arms.

"Mr. Hill! how dare you? Paul! help me!"

Paul had burst into the room, and with one bound had caught the enterprising anglomaniac by the collar. Paul was wiry if not muscular, whilst Mr. Murray Hill was a small man. Calmly, and apparently without effort, he dragged the gay Lothario to the front door, and applying a well-aimed kick to that portion of Mr. Murray Hill's person especially constructed for the purpose by Providence, launched him airily into Forty-first Street, to the delight of a small crowd that was listening to the elevating strains of an itinerant band, and then, returning, took Mr. Murray Hill's hat, gloves, and cane, which he cast after him onto the sidewalk.

"I'm a fool," soliloquized Mr. Murray Hill; "but I have suffered in a good cause. Firstly, it is clear that those two are something more to one another than merely casual lover and mistress; secondly, that being the case, la Zulueta is conscience-stricken over living on the Préault money; and thirdly, I'll break that blackguard du Peyral with all the greater joy for this thrilling episode. My God! let him look out for himself if his record isn't all right!"

Meanwhile Paul, the excitement over and the strain relieved, had sunk exhausted onto Mahmouré's divan. Strange, surely, that a man of such physique should pant so after a trifling exertion like the ejection of Mr. Murray Hill!

"I don't understand it," said he, in answer to Mahmouré's anxious inquiry. "If, like Gautier, I could believe in 'avatar,' I should think my soul were getting, in some mysterious way, separated from my body. I think, if my bodily strength would weaken off with it, the balance would be maintained and my vitality would not be so worn-out, as it were; but it seems to me as if my soul were too weak for my body. I'm not ill; I'm not even tired; but all the same, everything seems an effort to me now."

"Oh, Paul, Paul, are you sure it isn't this mesmerism?"

"No, dear, of course not! or if it is, it is only so in a very slight degree. Something is sapping my vitality, but what it is, and how the change takes place, I cannot hazard a conjecture to explain."

In this respect Paul resembled many a student in psychology. Absorbed in the contemplation of the result, his eyes were blinded to the cause, proximate or ultimate. A less profound student than he would have suggested immediately that the repeated concentration of his whole vital force upon Mahmouré and its transference, through her, to Daphne Préault, was gradually robbing him of his very soul. The effect was visible in his decreased vitality, and in the gradual resuscitation, as it were, of Mahmouré, who, day by day, regained the physique which had been hers before she became, as every one supposed, a chronic invalid. In Daphne Préault, a thousand leagues away, the change was visible in an infinity of almost inappreciable ways. Her Creole nature kept coming out more and more strongly; little coarsenesses, little brutalities, piquant, almost bewitching as they were, would crop out here and there in her language and in her manner of life; and had not the eyes of Eric Trevanion been blinded by his love, he would have noticed a fact that did not escape those of Mrs. Hawleigh, namely that the Princess Daphne was losing dignity.

And Paul? In him the change was the more curious, the more complicated. The loss of his vitality, of his soul-power, as it were, not being the result of any bodily ailment, of any pathological condition, his physique remained identically the same. His figure retained that blended grace and strength which had bewitched Mahmouré, as it had bewitched many a woman—though in vain—before her. His muscular development was unimpaired, but the motor being no longer of a sufficient strength for the machinery, a certain listlessness began to steal over him, which was attributed by his friends to a kind of nervous prostration, by his enemies to discouragement and an evil conscience, and by Mahmouré—and she was perhaps nearest the truth—to exhaustion caused by his unremitting labors of the mind.

It is to this listlessness that may be attributed his indifference to the proceedings of Mr. Murray Hill and Miss Parthenia Van Baulk'em, for though during the next few weeks after the episode above recorded at Mahmouré's, he heard vague rumors of the animosity of that siren and of her henchman, and of enquiries they had set on foot concerning himself and Mahmouré', and their respective antecedents, he did not bother himself to surmise whither those enquiries might lead, but devoted his time, in the privacy of his own apartments, to the tabulation of the notes for his great work on "Psychic Forces, and the influence of Mind upon Matter," which was rapidly approaching completion since he had taken to himself, by chance as it were, so singularly gifted a *collaborateuse* as Mahmouré di Zulueta.

The spring of the year was growing old, and the machinations of Mr. Murray Hill were slowly but surely progressing. Little by little, with the assistance of Mr. Charles Sturton Baker, who, acting in concert with Eric Trevanion, kept him posted on the condition and position of Miss Daphne Préault, he had pieced together the history of Mr. Paul du Peyral, and, this task accomplished, all that remained was to prove the marriage of that individual and Mahmouré di Zulueta. This task he set about with enthusiasm, receiving, by way of advance reward, the approbation of Miss Van Baulk'em, from an interview with whom he one day set forth to find the before-referred-to Tom Morrison, his pulses dancing wildly, his fingers still warm with the pressure of the fair Parthenia's unresisting if not encouraging hand, dazed with the minion of divers blandishments which not even the indescretion of the novelist can reveal, and which had been lavished upon him by the siren, "for the benefit of Charlie," of course, but in no wise the less fascinating to Mr. Murray Hill on that account. *Entre nous*, dear reader, it had dimly occurred to Mr. Murray Hill that, in the first place, his own income was only sufficient for his own maintenance in elegant leisure; in the second it was a pity that Miss Parthenia's millions should be bestowed upon an alien; and—Miss Parthenia having been more or less successfully chaperoned through a London season by a lady who had hidden most of Parthenia's vulgarity beneath the ægis of her own pure-blooded aristocracy of birth and nature, the said young woman having in turn suppressed her failures and exaggerated her successes with artistic mendacity—in the third, that it would be an excellent scheme to marry that young woman himself, preparatory to carrying her over to London, where, according to her own account, she had a certain apocryphal social position, and where he could gradually cut himself and her free from the associations of her horrible family.

He knew that it would be difficult if not impossible for him to hold, personally, any further communication with Mahmouré; but he bore very minutely in mind the recollection of the way she had received his carefully prepared story of the ill-used Englishman, and felt that, if properly approached, she might become an ally most important in the subversion of Mr. Paul du Peyral; and having occupied a few more weeks in collecting evidence in a manner which is too obvious to need recapitulation here—such as searching the registers at Niagara and so on—Mahmouré was one morning aroused to the contemplation of her matutinal coffee, flanked by an envelope bearing upon its upper left-hand corner the name and address of an eminent legal firm, addressed to her in the alarming legibility of the Remington type-writer.

There is only one thing that alarms a woman more than a mouse or a telegram, and that is an obviously "business" communication. Little wonder therefore that Mahmouré, rousing herself into vivid wakefulness and a sitting position among the pink-silk sheets of her pretty *dortoir*, neglected the ridiculous in favour of the sublime, and forgot her coffee in contemplation of the "lawyer's letter."

If the outside had disturbed her, how much more the inside, which read as follows:

Offices of SELIGMAN, SEARCHER,
& CERTIORARI.
No. 195 Nassau St., NEW YORK CITY.

[*Two enclosures.*]                    *23rd* May, 18—

DEAR MADAME:
    Information which has recently come to hand prompts us to write to you for corroboration or explanation on a subject which is of the last importance, both to clients of ours and to yourself, and

we trust you will answer our communication in the spirit in which it is made, with a view to saving all parties concerned the annoyance and expense of complicated legal proceedings. Without wishing to trouble you with details upon a matter with which you may or may not be already familiar, it is necessary to state that the marriage of Mr. Paul du Peyral entails certain consequences and duties upon the executors and beneficiaries of the estate of the late Casimir Préault of Baton Rouge in Louisiana. From information which has been put into our hands it appears that in the fall of last year you were privately married to this gentleman in the village of Niagara, Ontario, Canada. We shall be glad if you will sign and return to us one of the enclosed documents, to wit, the acknowledgment of that marriage, or its specific denial.

We are, dear Madame,
Yours faithfully,
SELIGMAN, SEARCHER,
& CERTIORARI.

To MADAME DI ZULUETA,

No.— West Forty-First Street, City.

To say that Mahmouré was frightened by this ominous missive is to employ a miserably inadequate term, and one in no sense fitted to the state of the case. Hardly conscious of what she was doing, she dressed herself with lightning rapidity, and flew as fast as an American hansom could take her, over the boulderous moraines known in New York by the euphemism, "streets," and arrived breathless with excitement, at the door of Paul's flat, where she admitted herself with her latch-key. Into the dining-room, lest he should be at breakfast—Paul was not there; into the study, lest he should be already at work—Paul was not there;

142

through the *portières* of the study, into his bedroom, lest Paul should not yet have risen and there she found him.

Asleep?—surely not; for he lay motionless and senseless as she flung herself on her knees by his side. In vain she strove to arouse him from his lethargy; in vain she implored him to open his eyes, which she covered with kisses. In an agony she tore down the bed-clothes and laid her hand upon his heart; a feeble, intermittent beat was the only sign which her husband gave her to tell her he was still alive.

Paul du Peyral lay dying.

# CHAPTER VII.
## Clouds.

"What I say is this," remarked Gerome Markham, as he dallied with a muffin and a cigarette in the Eastons' studio, one warm spring afternoon: "morality is a question of geography, and whilst not, perhaps, advocating the same latitude of action as that implied by the motto of the monks of Medenham, '*Fay çe que vouldras*,' still, in the Bohemia of Holland Street, the red, white, and black flag covers a multitude of trifles that would be sins in West Kensington, crimes in the provinces, and eminently good form in St. James's. And on the principle that we have adopted as a precept, 'live and let live,' I don't see what we have to do with Eric Trevanion and the Princess Daphne."

"Well, to a great extent I agree with you, but it does seem strange that Daphne Préault, who has rather gone in for taking a high moral ground, should get herself so very unpleasantly talked about," responded Sylvia Easton. "Give me of your light, for like that of the foolish virgin, my cigarette has gone out!"

"After all, you know," observed Dick Lindsay, who, from a distant corner, beamed through his spectacles on the other three, to wit, Sylvia and Eva Easton and Gerome Markham, "a little scandal—*un tout petit scandalorama*, as Vautrin would say, has the inestimable advantages of an advertisement, and would give an additional value to the Princess' autograph."

"Well, you'd better collect it at once," said Eva Easton, "for Mr. Baker says she's got a grand lawsuit coming on in America, which will probably make her retire into wealthy insignificance. Do you collect autographs, Mr. Lindsay?"

"Not personally; I used to collect them once for a great-aunt from whom I had 'expectations,' but when one day I sent her a slab of plaster, with 'Mene, Mene, Tekel, Upharsin' scratched on it, and signed '*Belshazzar*', she left off collecting, as she said it was too great a strain on my inventive faculties. She then proceeded to make a new will and die—I got nothing but her autograph album."

"Well, you ought to be thankful for small mercies."

"Yes, like the man who had gout in both feet and thanked God he wasn't a centipede! But unfortunately I'm not. I'm sure I was meant to live a life of dignified ease, not to drive myself melancholy-mad by writing cast-iron humour from morn till dewy eve, from dewy eve till deuced late. But still, it might be worse. Just fancy being 'something in the city,' like your friend whom you mentioned just now, Mr. Charles Sturton-Baker."

"I'm sure," said Sylvia Easton, "there isn't much the matter with Mr. Baker, except the hyphen in his name—and that's harmless. He makes a great deal of money, which is more than we do!"

"Ah, you'd better get his recipe for us," observed Markham.

"Go to the ant, thou sluggard," said Eva; "consider her ways and be awakened to the error of your own."

"That's just it," returned Lindsay; "I haven't got any aunt and when I had, I used to wake her up a good deal more than she did me."

"Oh, how dare you? To pun is human; to forgive, divine. However, I'll forgive you," said Sylvia, "and if you're good, I'll get Mr. Baker's recipe for you—or Eric's."

"Well, I don't know that I want either of them, for they seem very similar. Baker is always swaggering about some drivellingly idiotic American heiress or other, that he declares is madly in love with him, poor little thing! And it strikes me that if Trevanion *père* knew much about his hopeful son, he'd cut off the supplies; perhaps that's why Eric is so anxious to secure the Princess' fortune for her."

"For shame, Dick!" said Eva. "If you could catch an heiress, you'd do it on the spot, I know."

"Not at all," replied he, shamelessly. "Why, here I am, positively dying of love for *you*, Eva, and we've nothing to live on but bread and cheese, with kisses, whereof the first is not nice in excess, and the second isn't nourishing in *any* quantity."

"Sorry I spoke," remarked Eva, blushing nevertheless a lively crimson, as Dick Lindsay continued to beam on her through the gold-rimmed spectacles.

"Those two will quarrel in a minute," said Sylvia; "they always do. Tell me, Mr. Markham, how are the Hawleighs getting on?"

"Ah! there's a happy family for you, if you like. There's no getting over the fact that 'Sunshine in the Fog' is *the* picture of the year; and now Gabriel floats in golden seas. Dealers and amateurs vie with one another to buy his work, and unless his health gives out, we shall see our dear boy both rich and celebrated in a very short time."

"Ah! and then I suppose he'll marry Maye Trevethick?"

"Oh, *tiens! tiens! tiens!* how indiscreet you are! The idea of a young woman announcing as a fact what we all know but keep to ourselves. Of course he'll marry Miss Trevethick, and he'll be a jolly lucky fellow; but we shall all be delightedly surprised when it's announced."

"Do you know," said Eva Easton, pensively, as she bent over her work, "I always had an idea that she was in love with Eric."

"I hope not, for all their sakes," returned Gerome Markham. "In the first place, Eric has only one idea in the world, and that's Daphne Préault; in the second, it would break poor Gabriel's heart; and in the third, it would be very ungrateful of her, for without the Hawleighs she'd have been obliged to go out as a governess or companion, or something."

"Pooh!" exclaimed Eva, with a quick glance at Dick Lindsay; "what has gratitude to do with it?"

"Unfortunately nothing," replied Markham, gravely; and he rose to go.

Lindsay followed his example, and the two men left together.

Outside the door Lindsay remarked: "I say, Markham, I don't like the look of things in this street. The Princess is compromising herself badly, and Eric's letting himself drift; one of these days he'll be pulled up short. And I'm afraid there's something in what Eva said about Maye Trevethick caring about him."

"Well," replied Markham, as they parted to go in opposite directions, "all I can say is, I hope not. I should be sorry to see Gabriel and Maye wreck their lives; but I fear Eric is doing that same, even now. 'Who lives will see!' *Au revoir!*"

From the above conversation, which was only one out of many like unto it which the eaves-dropping walls of Holland Street overheard about this time, the reader will have gathered to a certain extent how matters stood with the quartette in whom we are mainly interested. The doors of Burlington House had opened on the first Monday in May to a crowd that were unanimous in their verdict upon Gabriel's picture as "the picture of the year," and Gabriel had the remunerative work of a lustrum on his hands, in the commissions showered upon him by European and American patrons of art. The days of struggle and genteel poverty seemed to have ended for him, and it was with the new light of a great tenderness in his eyes that, nowadays, he would watch Maye at work in her corner of the studio, whilst Mrs. Hawleigh regarded the consummation of her hopes as practically within her reach, and felt that she was amply rewarded for the sacrifices she had made at the altar of her son's genius.

As for Maye, the only change in her was one which was sedulously hidden from the outer world, for she concealed the excitement that an intuitive sense of the approach of a crisis in her life caused her in her heart—her heart, which concealed also the dull, deathly pain that she suffered when she thought, or anyone spoke to her, of Eric. But her home-life seemed even purer and sweeter than heretofore, and filled her often with a dim, soft melancholy, when, at the death of the daylight, she would sit down to the piano in the studio, and Gabriel would follow her into an ecstasy of music with his violin, which was now his one fondly cherished recreation.

Often they would wander among the harmonies of Chopin, of Beethoven, of Kalliwoda, of De Beriot, of Brahms, and of the other masters; but more often Maye would lead off with an improvised theme, and Gabriel, taking it up, would follow her through its variations and modulations, until, trembling all over, he would fall on the lounge in the altitude of the painting in Daphne's studio, and lie silent and happy, whilst Maye resolved the harmonies of the theme as it died away under her fingers.

"Maye," said he, one day, as the music ceased, "how strange it is that you and I should think as it were with one brain when we play! Do you know, dear, it seems to me sometimes almost *eerie* that such a perfect sympathy should exist between us. How is it, do you think?"

"I hardly know, Gabriel," she replied, a strange feeling seizing her heart, and driving the blood, it seemed to her, into her throat. "I suppose it is that we live here in such perfect accord—we three—that the same thoughts occur to us when we play, and express themselves in our music."

"Ah! pray God that you speak the truth, Maye. Sometimes, do you know, the thought comes to me that it may all cease suddenly, and that we might be separated; and the thought is almost more than I can bear. Maye," he continued, earnestly, and coming closer to her, "you have been more than a sister to me since you have been here with us; you know, don't you, dear, that I feel more than a brother to you. For I love you very dearly, sweetheart; you have guessed that, haven't you? I've never told you so, for we've been so poor, though it's been on my lips a thousand times, and in my heart always. But now, thank God, it seems as if a change had come, and even if we are not rich, we shall be quite independent. Can you love me a little in this newer, sweeter way, darling? Heaven knows that the only joy I can find in my life lies in the thought that I can lay it at your feet—will you take it, dear?"

"Oh! Gabriel!"

"Perhaps I ought not to have spoken so soon, but to me it seems as if I had waited, oh! so long, for today; but I have an excuse for speaking, dear—I love you so." He sank on his knee by her side, and slipping his arm around her waist, covered the hand that lay in her lap with kisses.

She looked straight before her, with a dry, far away look in her eyes, answering never a word, but clasping the hand that encircled her waist, as if in doubt whether to draw it closer round her, or to fling it away.

"Answer me, darling, won't you?—or shall I wait?" said he at last, trembling for her great silence.

"No, you must not wait any longer, dear; what can I say to you? You and the madre have been so good to me that if I can make you happy in return, I have no right to deny what you ask of me, even though it be my life—myself."

"Oh, no, no, not like that," he cried, springing to his feet; "don't think of gratitude, dear. You know that I shall love you just the same, even if you cannot think me worthy of you as your husband. If you will come to me and be the light of my life, let it be in love, and not in dull, cold gratitude. Oh! tell me that you love me, darling."

There was a moment's pause as she also rose to her feet, and turning, faced him as he stood, a great half-fearful joy in his eyes. And then she put both her hands on his shoulders, and looking up at him, answered, gravely:

"Yes, Gabriel, I love you very dearly, and I will be your wife if you want me to."

His answer was to clasp her wildly in his arms, and then, as she broke from him and ran out of the studio, he sank once more upon the lounge, almost unconscious with the exquisite joy of the moment that made her his.

And she?

She ran up to her own room, and flinging herself upon her bed, burst into an agony of tears.

She had never realized perhaps till that moment how she loved Eric Trevanion.

※

Meanwhile the days that came and went brought little change to Eric and Daphne, so far as their love for one another was concerned; but already there had crept into it those tiny carelessnesses which seem to be the fate of love after the first flush of its dawn has paled into the broad day-light of custom. This, however, did not affect Eric so much as the terror that sometimes took possession of him—a terror that some horrible change was taking place in the soul of the Princess whom he had elevated to be his Queen.

There is no doubt about it, humiliating as is the confession, that there is something singularly unpleasant to man about maladies of all kinds. If anyone shows symptoms of faintness or other distress, in a party, the men get perfectly miserable with nervousness. Not so the women; they, as it were, gird themselves together and watch, vulture-like, for the moment at which their services will be required. This difference comes out equally in conversation. What is so interesting to the female mind as a discussion of the maladies to which the conversants and their friends are subject, the epidemics of infantile diseases which have attacked such and such families of their acquaintance? Not so the man. Man A. says to man B., "How's C?" "Oh, C! poor devil! something wrong with him, I believe. Had measles and went out riding, got thrown and broke three ribs, got a chill lying on the grass, and the worry of it all gave him brain fever! Come and have a glass of sherry—going to the D.'s this evening?" Now this would have formed the subject of an hour's conversation to *Mrs.* A. and *Mrs.* B., with illustrations of what happened to C., what Dr. E. had said about him, and the remedies exhibited.

From all of which the reader will gather that the nervous and sometimes almost hysterical state into which the Princess Daphne was getting, by consequence of her repeated "mad attacks," as Eric used to playfully say and seriously think, was not so much a cause of pity to him as one of nervous irritation; and when he saw them coming on he would dissemble and fly; and when she described them to him, he used to pay little or no attention, or laugh at her. Therefore the account of her visions fell flat when she told him of them, and he merely put them down to a higher development of her nervous condition, which the doctor who has before been mentioned still ascribed to "a trifling indigestion, a slight derangement of the stomach which this draught will effectually,"—etc., etc. "—seven-and-six-pence thank you!"

But Clyde listened with weird-struck ears to the account of how, three times at least, Daphne had been awakened by an indefinable sensation that something was looking at her—of how, on clearing from her eyes the mists of sleep, she had seen before her the figure of a lithe, supple, but withal beautiful woman who looked at her out of great soft brown eyes, which, so far from frightening the Princess, rather attracted and soothed her than otherwise; and Eric felt almost alarmed at the importance she ascribed to these visitations, and almost annoyed at the quasi-affectionate interest she took in what she playfully called "her ghost."

However, a more serious consideration had crept into the politics of the Eric-Daphne *ménage*. We have said that Eric lived in somewhat princely style in the colony, on the liberal allowance made him by his father. Now the elder Trevanion was an individual most easy to get on with so long as he wasn't contradicted; but differ from him on a course to be adopted, and the firmness on which he prided himself, castled in his old Cornish manor, became divided from pig-headedness by a line of demarcation that was fearfully slight.

In the earliest days of the love of Eric and Daphne, Trevanion *père* gave an entertainment "to the county," and as was his wont, sent for Eric, as his son and heir, to assist in entertaining the innocuous magnates who (their names beginning, almost to a man, with the ancestral Cornish syllables, Tre, Pol, and Pen) considered that to be a Cornishman was to live, whilst to be anything else was merely to exist—on sufferance. Eric, like an historic prototype, answered that "he could not come," and having nailed his colours—or rather Daphne's colour's, the red, white, and black of Bohemia—to the mast, just didn't. Trevanion *père* was much annoyed, and began to make enquiries into what could possibly keep Eric in London when he wanted him at Trthwwsthpllgg

150

Manor. The result of his enquiries was that his letters to Eric began to hint at a proximate return to Trthwwsthpllgg, and an ultimate marriage and culminating respectability of behaviour, with solemn dinner-parties and grandchildren at recurring intervals. To these suggestions Eric replied at first not at all, then playfully, then sarcastically, then seriously, with a point-blank prayer to the governor not to talk bosh.

As an immediate result, Eric was apprised that if he did not at once return home and marry a Cornish maiden, and give other trifling evidences of submission to parental authority, the supplies would be cut off, and the commissariat would dry up. "There can only be one excuse for you to remain in London," papa Trevanion had said in this letter, "and that is, that you have found idiots sufficiently weak to buy your pictures, or editors sufficiently courageous in their ignorance to buy your articles on the 'Potentiality of the But,' and so on. You therefore can get on without an allowance from me, and from this quarter it ceases."

And so Eric found himself in the exciting condition of having to make his own living—or dying—by his own unaided exertions.

Here was naturally food for thought, and for a couple of days Eric was very thoughtful. At the end of that time, as he sat idle at his desk in Daphne's studio, she came up behind him, and, putting her arms about his neck, laid her cheek against his and said:

"Eric, you are not kind; there's something on your mind that you haven't told me anything about. What is it, old man?"

"Oh, nothing of importance, dear," he had replied, a little wearily.

So she had insisted, using the thousand arguments and persuasions that a woman who knows her power can use with impunity, until at last, taking the letter above referred to from his pocket, he handed it to her without a word. In similar silence she read it through and returned it to him.

"Well?" he said, finding that she made no remark.

"Have you any money of your very own—independently of the governor?"

"Not a penny."

"Good! you will have to make some."

"How?"

"Why, by writing stuff that will sell, of course."

"Well, I've been trying to do that for months," he replied, "and I don't seem to have got the knack of it yet."

"Of course not," returned Daphne, "because you haven't absolutely required to sell your work. *Now* you do, and you must adopt a different style."

"It strikes me I shall have to adopt a different style of existence altogether. I don't see how I am to go on spending a thousand a year on nothing per annum, paid quarterly."

"So much the better for you, Eric. Your days of amateur literature are over; you must descend from the altitude of transcendental essay to the dead level of the pot-boiler. You must write stories for the magazines and articles for the reviews; paragraphs for society papers, and political squibs. You are no longer Samuel Rogers, you are Lucien de Rubempré."

"What's the use, Daph? the editors will 'regret that want of space prevents,' etc., etc., as heretofore. I was never Samuel Rogers, and I won't stoop to copy Balzac's gentle hero. Why, only yesterday I got a letter with the stamp of *Smith's Monthly* on it. I didn't even open it, I knew so well what's in it."

"Where is it?" asked Daphne, a queer look coming into her eyes, as she held out her hand.

"Oh, it's here somewhere—here it is," said he, giving it to her.

"Ah!" said she, opening it; "this was unimportant yesterday or the day before. It isn't so insignificant now. Your article on 'Atlantis and Yucatan' is accepted, and you will get the proofs in a day or two."

"What!" he exclaimed; "why, those people refused it once."

"Well, they've seen the error of their ways, that's all," replied the Princess, with a little laugh. "Now, look here, Eric; you've got to take this matter into your own hands 'right now,' as we say in America. This letter proves that if you will only take my advice, you'll get on all right. In the first place, you have the finest studio in Holland Street. You don't paint, and you don't want it, except to spend money in; you haven't got the money to spend now, so you don't want the studio, and you must give it up. Oh! don't make faces; I know what I'm talking about. Just opposite, there are a couple of rooms both vacant and cheap. You can make them very pretty and comfortable with some of the stuff you've got in your studio, and you must move in at once and set to work in earnest."

"But, Daph, I can't suddenly proclaim myself a pauper."

"That doesn't alter the fact that you *are* one, dear."

"Please, don't."

"But you *are*, Eric."

"Well, if I can't afford to live in the old place, how can I in the new?"

"Why, very easily. In the first place you are going to make money by writing, and until you have made it, I have plenty. Besides, my solicitor, or rather the solicitor to my second cousin's estate, tells me that he thinks that that money will come to me after all, in a short time. I suppose Paul du Peyral has grown tired of bachelorhood at last. We have plenty to live on, in any case."

"Thank you! I don't want it to be said that the moment I got poor I married you for your money."

"Married! Good heavens! who talks of marrying? we're very happy as we are. The only difference will be that when you were rich you spent your money on me, and now you are poor, I spend mine on you. Nobody need know anything about it!"

"Daphne! by Jupiter, you *do* want me to become Lucien de Rubempré in a hurry. Do you imagine that I—*I*, Eric Trevanion, am going to live upon *you?* Hush!—not a word more if you please on the subject; you insult me—unintentionally, I know; but your proposition is an insult all the same. Don't you *want* to marry me?" He had risen and was pacing feverishly up and down the room. At her answer he came to a dead full stop in front of her.

"Not in the least!" she said, calmly; "I prefer to remain as I am!"

"Good God! what am I coming to?" he cried. "Never dare to make such a suggestion to me again—you hear!—never *dare*."

"Eric—I dare anything. I love you, and I intend to make a great man of you. You have all the possibilities, and if you will take my advice, you are bound to succeed. For the moment, however, you want my help. It is yours to take and mark me, my mind is made up."

"Well—so is mine. It is useless to prolong this discussion—we shall not agree. I am going home now to think matters over a little. When I come back, don't let me hear any more of this preposterous thing. Perhaps I *am* going to be successful—well, success means independence, and I will be independent. *Au revoir.*"

"*Au revoir,*" she said, lazily stretching herself in the divan as he left the studio. And ten minutes after, the Princess, with a little ironical smile on her lips, had fallen fast asleep!

Later in the afternoon he burst in upon her, pale with anger, and with a roll of proof-slips in his hand.

"What have you been doing with this article of mine?" he exclaimed, by way of greeting.

"Making it salable, *cher ami,*" she replied, with a grin.

"Making it vulgar, you mean. How dare you interfere with my work? You can talk as much as you like; fortunately I have sufficient self-respect not to take your advice; but oblige me by leaving my work as I finish it. I shall alter these proofs so as to make them resemble, at any rate, my original manuscript—let this be the first and last performance of this little comedy."

"Do as you like, Eric. If you like to make a fool of yourself, do. Your stuff will only be re-rejected at the last moment."

"Time will show. Now, let us drop the second unpleasant subject that has arisen between us today. I wonder you can worry me so, when you know I have so much on my mind!" he concluded, querulously.

"Well, well, darling, I did it for the best, and I hope that in time you will come to look at things as I do; meanwhile we won't talk about it. Oh! don't be angry, dear; I love you so."

But he *was* angry. He returned her caress in a very half-hearted way, and his manner hurt her finer nature, which happened for the moment to be in the ascendant. Presently he broke the silence again by saying:

"I've been thinking over what you said about moving out of the studio, and have been seeing exactly how I stand. By the time all my bills have come in, I shall be pretty hard up, until some of these editors pay me for my work; so it will be better for me to move. I don't see why I should be ashamed of being poor. I'll see about the necessary arrangements at once."

"Good!" she replied, drawing him down by her side on the lounge. "I am almost glad the governor has cut up rough, do you know, dear; I shall have you more to myself now, and I shall be more a part of your life in future."

It was almost with a sense of discomfort that he listened to her words, and presently he disengaged himself to go over to his own writing-table. And in the long silence which followed, the thoughts of the two were taking an identical direction: both realized that a new era had dawned in their lives, but they looked forward into that future with very different feelings—feelings, however, that they did not express to one another.

In an hour Eric had removed from his article almost every trace of the Princess' handiwork, and had posted his corrected proofs to the editor of *Smith's Monthly*, feeling almost satisfied with himself. She had meant well, he said to himself; she was a good girl, and he was very fond of her. Ah! the world? Ah—yi! Let us remark, *à propos de bottes*, that between "*une femme qu'il aime*" and "*une femme qui l'aime*" there is only the difference of an apostrophe—and what is punctuation in a love story?

And so Eric settled down to a new life. Of course his abandonment of the gorgeous studio next door to the Hawleighs was a theme for great wonderment in the colony, but it became generally understood that Eric had had reverses of some kind, and, being no longer the merry plutocrat of hitherto, had cut down his expenses and had taken to literature in search of a livelihood. This did not in any way impair his position in the colony; on the contrary, they liked him the better for it. There were few, if any, of "the boys" who did not know what it was to be periodically "broke," and that Eric should come to the same complexion seemed to draw him still nearer to them, and went far toward abolishing a certain feeling that had existed in holes and corners, to the effect that the wealthy amateur had no absolute right to share the pleasures and sorrows of the colony, but was admitted rather on sufferance than otherwise.

Eric had, in these first days, but little doubt of his ultimate success as a man of letters, though it struck him as decidedly odd when he got a polite communication from the editor of *Smith's Monthly* to the effect that in its altered form his article was not suited to the requirements of the magazine, and asking should it be inserted as it stood in the duplicate proof sent therewith, or should the article, in its new form, be cancelled? Now, Eric wanted the money somewhat, and the magazine paid well and promptly; should he pocket his pride and accept what he called the Princess' "garblement"? After much consideration he decided so to do, and, to the sorrow of all persons concerned, be it related that this was apparently, for a long while at least, Eric's first and last literary success. From this time forward, so surely as he sent an article or story to any periodical, so surely was it returned to him. Once or twice he posted a many-times-returned manuscript to some third-or fourth-rate magazine of no antecedents and doubtful future, and got it in, but never got paid for it, considering it something gained to have got rid of it at all.

And thus did Eric's literary apprenticeship begin, with all its trials and disappointments. Who is there of us who woo the Muse of Literary Fame, who has not been through it? The stories of young writers who, reduced in circumstances, have made a wild sensation, and sprung to the first rank with a first work, have ever been, to me, purely apocryphal, as they must ever be to anyone who has adopted literature as a profession and not as a recreation, and who has pitched his literary tent, so to speak, day after day in that "Elysium of the Literary Unwashed," the Reading-Room of the British Museum. The dogmatist who laid down the paradoxical axiom that "No man can make a living by letters until he is dead," exaggerated of course—exaggeration is the prerogative of the inculcator of axioms; but it is equally true that, except in a few very rare instances, men who have written standard works for all time, have been men in absolutely independent circumstances, whose works cost them far more to write than they ever brought home to their authors in the form of publisher's cheques. Now and then one hears of a great success made by a writer of fiction who has never before seen the light of day as it shines upon a book-stall. If we only knew his esoteric history, we should find that his book is made up of the few good things that have brightened three or four previous still-born productions; and our opinion in the matter is usually confirmed by the subsequent publication, "on his reputation," of the sweepings of the waste-paper basket to which he had consigned his "Rejected Addresses."

For the man who has the pluck to destroy his rejected manuscripts and start fresh, regarding his futile efforts merely in the light of "practice," I have always reserved my choicest salaam; I have known but few such. And if it is an agony to the wealthy amateur to see his works, like the curses of the proverbialist, come home to roost, can ye imagine, "ye gentlemen of England who live at home in ease," what are the feelings of the young writer who has put off importunate landwomen and tradesmen with a promise of payment "on receipt of a cheque from his publishers," when he arrives home late at night from some Bohemian entertainment or other, and sees on the table in the hall, by the dim light of the frugally lowered gas-jet, an oblong package, with a letter tucked under the string which secures it, and he thinks to himself, as, without looking at it, he carries it upstairs in the dark, "Which of them is this?" and presently unwraps some pet essay or other, on which he counted with all the fondness of a confiding mother? Ah, sirs! *then* is the moment of tears, not of tears which flow from the lachrymal glands, but from the tear-well in the heart, as one asks one's self the question, "Am I a failure?—shall I ever be able to write for a living?" We of Bohemia know what it is—we have suffered, *nous autres*! and I am not writing these lines for the eyes of the specialists who periodically write an article to order, on their hobbies, or for the public characters whose signature covers a multitude of literary sins that are unpardonable in the scholar, but for the earnest student who has apparently wasted the best years of his youth acquiring an education that seems utterly useless when he tries to earn five pounds with a prostituted pen.

And this was the case of Eric Trevanion, who now for the first time realized that heretofore, to him, apocryphal condition, of being "hard up"; who learnt to climb upon the knife-board of a Kensington omnibus in lieu of waving his umbrella at the passing hansom; to spend hours in the dingy book-shops of Holywell Street, instead of sending a peremptory order to Quaritch or Bumpas; to cast an interested glance at the prices marked on the goods in a grocer's window, instead of sauntering into the antique silver shops in Hanway Passage to see if there was anything he could buy. And Eric felt it all keenly, all the more so when he found himself returning a compulsatory negative to postulants who had always found him hitherto "good for a fiver," under the euphemism of a loan. And with it all he became more and more of a recluse, more irritable with the Princess, when she would suggest subjects to him which he considered beneath his dignity as a scholar to discuss in print, and more sensitive than ever when she would make any remark that seemed tinged with an inquiry on the question of finance.

And Daphne felt it more keenly still. She used to scheme to lighten his worries in a score of ways, whose principal difficulty lay in that of their concealment. Thus, one day she said to him suddenly, "By the way, Eric—what rent do you pay opposite?"

And when he told her, she replied, "That's just like you! you're the most casually extravagant creature I ever knew. Why, So-and-so, who has the corresponding rooms in the next house, only pays a third of that sum. I shall have a talk to your landlady about it."

And Eric, who stood in some awe of the said enchantress, whom he constantly feared he would some day be compelled to ask to wait for her rent, replied grimly:

"Well, don't let me rob that person of the pleasure of a conversation with you."

"And you know," continued the Princess, "the bachelor-man is the natural prey of the London washerwoman. I shall send

Clyde over to you for your clothes every week, and you must pay *me*. I will *not* have you robbed all round as you are now."

And to Eric's astonishment, a few days later, his whilome terrible landwoman informed him that, as she heard that he contemplated moving next door, she would be glad to have him stay, and pay the next door rent, which was, in fact, one-third of what he had hitherto been paying. About this time also Daphne grew captious about dining with him in town, preferring vastly to have him come and picnic with her in the studio; or anon she would burst in upon him in his own rooms, carrying the complete outfit of dinner in a basket, and exclaiming:

"Eric! I'm bored, and tired of my old studio; I've come to picnic with you—here's my share; what have you got?" and then she would ransack his cupboard in search of potted comestibles and other trifles which she knew Eric kept "on the farm." And she did it all so charmingly, that Eric never dreamt that she had any motive ulterior to her own amusement, or that "the rent next door" was precisely the same as what he had always paid.

It was on one of these occasions, when she had descended upon him, the bearer of more than ordinarily good cheer, that she said at the conclusion of the meal, when they had drawn their chairs to the fire, which was now almost rendered unnecessary by the advancing spring:

"Do you know, boy, I've got a scheme for you. I was sitting the other day at a dinner-party next to a provincial journalist, and he told me all about an undertaking that made me think at once of you. He is the editor of a big concern in a big midland city, and is starting a magazine to be written by London journalists. They are going to pay very well—two pounds a page—because all the articles are to be strictly anonymous, so anonymous, in fact, that not even the contributors are to know the name of the magazine, or where it's to be published. The articles are to go to him, and he sends a cheque on receipt of the corrected proofs. Well, I offered at once to write for him, and he jumped at the offer. Now, I *can't* write, but you can, and as we're very poor we must pocket our pride. You shall write the articles, and I'll put in a touch here and there. I promise not to alter what you write, and when he sends me the cheques I shall claim twenty-five per cent, for my share of the work, and as negotiation fee. You mustn't ask any questions about it, because I swore I wouldn't betray him—will you go into it with me?"

"My dear girl," answered Eric, "I'll do anything that'll make money. I've come down to that. What do you want for a start?"

"Oh, dish up any of your old impossible stuff a little, and hand it over. I'll see that it gets in all right."

And so Eric set to work again. The Princess was as good as her word, and hardly "garbled" his manuscript at all, and he returned his first set of proofs, feeling that at last the tide had turned a little. For a space the cheques came in with cheerful regularity and liberality, and Eric and the Princess used to laugh together over what he used to call "The Mysterious Magazine," which they used sapiently to agree could never pay its proprietors, so absolutely in advance of the merits of the "copy" was the price they paid for it. And for a couple of months Eric seemed to be in a position to laugh at his former troubles, especially as not only did he make a good thing by writing Daphne's articles for her, but also the editor of a leading weekly had betrayed a disposition to accept, publish, and pay for a few articles of which Eric declared himself heartily ashamed, but which necessity made him sink his personal feelings and write.

At the end of that time he sat one day in the Princess' studio finishing an article for her, and scribbling some letters, when he found that he had not an envelope left in his pigeon-holes. He rose and went over to Daphne's table to find one, and not seeing any in the place where she usually kept them, tried to find, without troubling her, the reserve stock. In pursuance of his quest, he opened a drawer in whose lock the key stood invitingly, and the first thing that met his eye was the whole set of his articles for "The Mysterious Magazine," the corrected proof of each neatly folded up with the manuscript. A horrible, sickening sensation took possession of him as he took them out and verified them, and, white to the lips as the ghastly truth flashed across him, he rose and, presenting them to Daphne as she sat at her easel, which had hidden him from her as he stood at her table, said, in a deadly, quiet voice:

"Daphne, what is the meaning of this?"

Her face was scarcely less white, her eyes scarcely less troubled and dry than his, as she made answer to him:

"Oh, Eric! where did you get those from?"

"I was looking for an envelope; there was none in your case; I opened the top drawer, and the first thing that caught my eye was this packet. Well—answer me—what have you to say?"

She kept silence, looking dumbly at the bundle, and he continued:

"Does the magazine of which you have spoken exist? Did you ever meet such a man as you described the editor to be? In God's name, Daphne, answer me, or I shall go mad!"

She covered her face with her hands, and sobbed forth her answer:

"Oh, Eric, my love, forgive me—forgive me! I can say nothing, only that I loved you, and it made my heart ache to see you so poor—to see you suffer so. I knew that some day, when you had made a name, they would be valuable, and anyone would be only too glad to take them from me for you. I was only buying them in advance—it was an investment, Eric."

For answer he flung the packet at her feet, and strode from her presence. When he returned twenty minutes later, his eyes flaming with passion, she was sitting in the same position, her brushes lying with the manuscripts at her feet.

"So," he began, "you have lied to me from the beginning, and you have cheated me into living on your charity. I did not ask your alms—I refused them, as I refuse them now. My God! how can I have been so blind? You thought that that wretched woman over the way would keep your secret well, so she might have done had I not by good luck chanced upon these papers. I trust you are satisfied with the success of your scheme. Egad! it was well contrived very well contrived. How dared you insult me so?—do you hear me?—how dared you?"

She had sunk upon her knees before him—she, the proud Princess Daphne of a few short months ago—her face hidden in her hands.

"Don't speak to me like that, Eric I can't bear it—you are killing me. It was for the best—it was for the best—I loved—I love you so! Ah! won't you forgive me, dear?"

"Never!"

She rose slowly to her feet and staggered to the hearth. There her forces left her, and she flung herself on the lounge in an agony of tears. And Eric Trevanion, his face deathly pale, his brows contracted as if with physical pain, stood looking at her.

And as he stood, no sound breaking the silence but her sobs, amid the hideous humiliation of it all there came over him the realization of how great a love was this of hers for him. Few men can withstand tears, if they are genuine, and well from a breaking heart; so at last he drew nearer to her, and kneeling by her side, put his arms about her prostrate body. As she felt them, she turned and flung hers round his neck, burying her head upon his shoulder.

"Come, Daph," he said, at last; "don't be so unhappy about it. I know it was only your true, loving heart that made you do as you did. It is I who should beg for forgiveness, and I beg for it here on my knees. I spoke harshly, cruelly, just now—I had no right to do so. You can understand my feelings a little, can't you? I know yours, and I forgive you the moment's worry you caused me—forgive you from my soul."

And so, little by little, her sobs became more intermittent, and at last ceased entirely, as, lying in his arms, she raised her beautiful eyes to his and he kissed away from them the last tears that trembled on her lashes.

When they were both comparatively themselves again, they fell to talking naturally; and when at last he saw that she had quite recovered from her paroxysm, he rang the bell, and Clytie brought in tea and lit the gas. Her sharp eyes saw that the Princess had been weeping, and she levelled at Eric a look of undisguised hatred, which, however, he scarcely noticed, though, unreasonably, he felt this afternoon more than usually inclined to reciprocate her aversion.

When she was gone, and they had settled themselves comfortably, he said:

"Now, Daph, let's talk business."

"Yes, Eric," she exclaimed, eagerly, "that's what I want you to do. I knew that you'd never consent to accept this money from me—and see—I have kept an exact account of everything I have spent for you. It has been nothing to me, for you know I am quite well off. Very soon you too will be rich and prosperous, and then, never fear"—this with a little laugh—"I'll exact it from you to the uttermost farthing—I promise you I will."

And so they calmly discussed the question and their mutual arrangements for the future. The past was irremediable, the money was spent that she had given him, and with her sweet casuistry he came almost to look upon her future loans as not so shameful after all, for he felt within himself that his present poverty *must* soon come to an end.

They were thus employed when, suddenly, a distant report shook the studio, and some fragments, apparently of glass, fell upon the skylight in the roof.

"Great heavens! what's that?" exclaimed Eric.

"Goodness knows," returned the Princess, anxiously; "what do you think it is?"

"There has been an explosion somewhere—let's hope it's only the boiler of some conservatory or other, I tell you what—I'll run out and see if it was in Holland Street." And he disappeared.

In ten minutes he returned, looking very grave.

"Oh! what is it, Eric?" cried the Princess.

"It was an explosion of gas, dear—and I'm sorry to say it was in Gabriel Hawleigh's studio. It had got turned on somehow, and when he went to light it, it exploded, blowing the whole of the skylight out."

"And Gabriel?"

"I'm afraid he is terribly hurt. Fortunately there was no one else in the studio at the time."

# CHAPTER VIII.
## Transmigration.

Yes! Paul du Peyral lay dying.

So said the doctor for whom, in an agony of terror and grief, the distraught Mahmouré had sent Paul's body-servant. He might live, said the doctor, for hours, or for days, but most probably it would be a question of the former: it was the beginning of the end; and after having made the most thorough examination possible, the medico was forced to admit that he was absolutely and completely baffled by the nature of the disease which showed such alarming symptoms.

Mahmouré, being questioned, gave the fullest possible particulars of Paul's habits of life—which were regularity itself. She told all she knew of his studies, of his scientific and psychological pursuits; and concerning these latter the doctor made especially minute and interested inquiries. At last his examination—during which Paul had lain in a state of semi-consciousness—ended, and the doctor rose and took his leave, saying to Mahmouré as he went:

"The case to which you have summoned me, madam, is one which appears to be unique in my professional experience, and which cannot be dealt with by any form of pathological treatment that is familiar to me. I am not, however, of that class of physicians who will gladly see a patient die rather than yield a point of etiquette, and meet in consultation a doctor of the Eclectic school. If I may be allowed to suggest I would ask you to send for Doctor Schuyler Van Boomkamp, a young practitioner whose *specialité* is psychological complaints, and who has made a profound study of them in Paris, Berlin, and Leyden, from which latter school he is a graduate. If you will beg his attendance here at three o'clock, by that time Mr. du Peyral will most probably have regained consciousness, and I will be here soon after that hour to consult with Dr. Van Boomkamp."

During the day, as the doctor had predicted, Paul recovered consciousness, though his weakness was so great as to be almost paralysis, and noiselessly Mahmouré came and went in his room, ministering to his wants, and rewarded now and then with a few half-articulated words of thanks. The thought of what she had originally come about never once entered her head, nor did it until she was reminded thereof in her conversation, that same afternoon, with Dr. Van Boomkamp. As he is a not altogether unimportant actor in the development and conclusion of this drama, a word about him may not be out of place.

Schuyler Van Boomkamp was a man of thirty-two, tall, but with a pensive stoop in his shoulders, and a grave inclination of the head forward and sideways, that was habitual, a smooth-shaven face, and hair of an uncertain colour that had become slightly touched with white, eyes rather deeply set and of an intense steel-gray, a clearly cut nose and thin lips, his whole personality completed by a pair of icy-cold, long, white hands, with beautifully formed nails, and a pair of equally icy-cold pince-nez, from behind whose gold rims the steely eyes literally froze the prevarication ere it gushed from the fountain of the brain. He always dressed exquisitely, but invariably in the fashion of a few years ago; and today, when Mahmouré was summoned from Paul's bedroom to speak with him in the study before he saw the patient, she realized, the moment she saw him, as he courteously handed her a chair, and in smiling showed her a set of teeth as fine and white as a woman's, that she was in the presence of a man who, like Paul, was *the* unique specimen of his kind.

After giving him the same general particulars as she had given to Paul's own doctor, Schuyler Van Boomkamp asked her question after question concerning the mesmeric phenomena in which she had been the percipient, investigating them with a minuteness that almost appalled Mahmouré, and examining into causes, agencies, and effects in a manner that might almost have made her fancy he had been present at their *séances*. As he concluded his examination—of which he had taken copious notes—a ring at the bell and a step in the parlour announced the arrival of the senior medico. Mahmouré was about to summon him, when Dr. Van Boomkamp, arresting her with a gesture, said quietly:

"There is one final question that I must ask you, Madame di Zulueta—on what day were you married to Mr. du Peyral?"

"Dr. Van Boomkamp!" She had turned and faced him, her eyes stricken wide with apprehension.

"Do not be distressed, *madame*, I beg of you; and I assure you, though the assurance is hardly necessary, that the information will rest as profoundly confidential as the rest of our conversation. Of course I know that you are legally married to our patient; you have told me so unconsciously fifty times this afternoon; but it is important that I should know the exact date."

"On the 25th of September, last year, in the village of Niagara, Ontario, Canada."

She made the answer almost mechanically, under the spell of those terrible eyes. Schuyler Van Boomkamp made a last note on his *carnet*, and joining his *confrère*, the three entered Paul's bed-room together.

Paul lay propped up by pillows, very weak, hardly able to articulate a word, but yet conscious, and the moment Dr. Schuyler Van Boomkamp entered the room he fixed his eyes upon that gentleman, never letting his gaze wander for a moment. After verifying the diagnosis of his older colleague, Van Boomkamp said to the dying man, in a low but deadly distinct voice:

"I am about to ask you some questions; can you concentrate your mind upon the answers?"

An inarticulate whisper broke from the patient, in which the words "understand"—"too weak" were alone recognizable.

"Madame di Zulueta," said the doctor, "I must ask you to restore temporarily a portion of the vitality you have unconsciously drawn from our friend here. Kindly take your seat close to the head of the bed here. So—thank you. Now place the tips of your fingers under the patient's head, so that they lie along the spinal column at the point where it leaves the brain. So—good! Kindly make an effort of will to transfer some of your very abundant vitality to him. Mr. du Peyral, you are feeling stronger—can you answer my questions now?"

A flicker of light returned to his dull eyes, an infinitesimal tinge to his hollow cheeks, as he replied in a weak but perfectly distinct voice:

"Certainly, doctor."

The older and more orthodox physician sat petrified with amazement, but watching the proceedings of his young colleague with fascinated interest. Then the examination began.

"Are you in pain?"

"No."

"Do you feel in any way light-headed?"

"No."

"Are you in full possession of all your mental functions?"

"Yes—in a way."

"You mean that your brain works with its usual clearness, but without its wonted rapidity?"

"Exactly."

"Have you ever had an attack of this kind before?"

"Once only."

"And that, I presume, was immediately after some more than ordinarily violent effort to compass some psychological end?"

"Yes."

"What was its nature?"

"I had summoned to my mind a picture of the subject upon whom I have been making my experiments in Europe."

"Ah! and you saw her?"

"That was my impression."

"To return to your present condition: there is apparently no alteration in your physical condition?"

"No."

"No loss of weight?"

"Not an ounce."

"No emaciation—no loss of muscle?"

"None whatever."

"Raise your leg in bed."

"I cannot."

"Raise your arm above your head."

"I cannot."

"Ah! Kindly remove your fingers from his neck, *Madame*." Mahmouré did so.

"Now tell me, what are your sensations?"

A contraction passed over his features, but though his lips moved, no sound came from them.

"Be so good as to replace your hands, *madame*. So—thank you. Now take a deep breath, put your lips to his, and breathe softly, so as to fill his lungs if possible with your own atmosphere."

Mahmouré did so, and a strong shudder shook the dying man.

"Doctor," he said, "do not let her do that again—she cannot bear it. I know that it must be my life or hers; let it be mine—my work is ended. But I know yours, doctor, and I beg you, if you will, to take up mine where I have left it." As he said these words his voice had almost regained its natural strength, and at the conclusion of his sentence the muscles of his face relaxed once more, and he sank still deeper among the pillows that supported him.

"That will do, *madame*," said Van Boomkamp, rising. "We cannot arrest the end; it must come in a short time now, probably in a few hours. You wish to remain with him, I presume? Pray do so, but do not touch him more than you can help; the excitement will be too great for him. Now, doctor," continued he, turning to the older man, "I shall be glad of a few minutes conversation with you." And he led the way into the study, closing the doors behind them carefully.

"What is your opinion on this case, sir?" he began, when they had seated themselves.

"Dr. Van Boomkamp," returned the other, "when I diagnosed the condition of our patient this morning, I am proud to say that I found that my experience and medical skill were wide enough to tell me that I was completely baffled. As you see yourself, there is no tendency to a diseased condition of the heart, liver, lungs, spine, or brain; it is not nervous fever; it is not hypochondria or lymphomania. If disease is here, it is a disease of the life, of the soul; and at the amphitheatres of anatomy, a life, a soul, has yet to be dissected—we know nothing of it. Though, therefore, the name of Schuyler Van Boomkamp is one that causes the orthodox faculty to look somewhat askant (as you know), your fame as a psychologist has reached me from sources that I respect in Paris and Berlin, and especially from the more esoteric schools

168

of Leyden University. I therefore counselled Madame di Zulueta, who takes an interest in this young man that we can perhaps understand, to consult you, and having assisted at your examination I can only say that I am proud to meet you in consultation on a case which, I frankly confess, is beyond the range of my orthodox and perhaps old-fashioned experience and studies."

At the conclusion of this exordium Schuyler Van Boomkamp bowed respectfully, though without rising, to his senior colleague, and then, removing his glasses, he wiped them thoughtfully and readjusted them. Then he made answer in the slow, measured terms of one who is stating a collection of carefully ascertained and determined facts.

"Sir, I have not been in the habit, as you know, of encountering this frankness in my consultations with the faculty, or rather that branch thereof which you represent. I will answer you with equal frankness, and I hope lucidity, strange as must appear to you my unalterable convictions on the nature of this case.

"We have here a man of very rare and very highly developed psychological powers, whose name is about to be appended to the already almost interminable roll-call of the martyrs to science.

"He is bound by ties, earthly as well as spiritual, to the very highly magnetic woman who is with him at this moment, and through her he has become connected in a manner, mysterious to the ordinary mind, with another woman, who, though a thousand leagues distant from him, is probably also connected with him by some half-forgotten tie of blood, and is certainly connected with him by the bond of a coincidence of personality which strikes even myself as being almost miraculous. Madame di Zulueta is an extra-ordinarily receptive woman, and when first their *liaison*—let us call it that for the sake of definition commenced, she was at the lowest ebb of vitality, physically and psychologically. The absolute regularity of his life has left his physical constitution unimpaired, but by dint of continually hypnotizing his companion, he has gradually transferred his vitality to her, and it is practically with his *soul*, with his vital force, that she is living now, has regained her health, her strength, almost her youth. But of this vitality which he has poured into her, only the grosser atoms have remained as fuel for the machine of her life; the more ethereal, the more subtle portion he has transferred, through her, to this woman on the other side of the ocean, by name, it appears, Daphne Préault.

"Your diagnosis of his condition is of course"—and he bowed again—"pathologically, scientifically correct, but the vital condition in which he finds himself at this moment is this. Pray follow me very carefully. His magnificent and unimpaired physique requires a commensurate strength of vitality, of soul, to support it in the condition known to us as 'Life.' That soul he has gradually transferred, until what is left of it is insufficient to maintain the 'life' in so powerful a physical machine. If his body had weakened with his soul, he would undoubtedly have continued to live, though upon a lower plane of vitality; but it has not done so, and now the remaining vestiges of soul are about to leave him, and produce, in a perfectly healthy body, the phenomenon known to us as 'Death.' The problem which is about to be solved before our eyes is this: into which of these living personalities will the final transference take place? It may be into that of Madame di Zulueta, but I hope not, for she is not physically strong enough to bear the burden, and it would probably result in some form of mental aberration with her. I am inclined to expect that it will be the body of Miss Daphne Préault that the residue of his soul will seek. You doubtless think that I am expecting a kind of metempsychosis, a kind of reincarnation such as formed the basis of the Pythagorean philosophy—well, in a measure, I am. I have once seen such a phenomenon take place in a little village in Poland; we are about to witness its repetition, and, in the interests of psychology, we may congratulate ourselves on our almost unique experience."

He ceased speaking, and for a few moments the elder man kept silence. At the expiration of those moments he rose and said:

"Dr. Van Boomkamp, the theory you have expounded to me is so unexpected, so marvellous, that I am absolutely unable to give an opinion in exchange for yours. Excepting as an observer— and as a deeply interested one, believe me—I have nothing more to do with this case; I see that I cannot arrest the finger of death, and I leave our patient in your hands, for—though against my will and judgment—I am bound to confess that you have laid before me an aspect of the case which, extraordinary though it be, I am not in a position to controvert. When do you expect that death will supervene?"

"In about four hours."

"You will be here?"

"Certainly—and you?"

"With your permission—yes."

"Good! we will meet here then at about half-past seven."

And, leaving a message to that effect for Mahmouré, the two physicians left the house.

When they returned, at the time agreed upon between them, she was sitting where they had left her, at the foot of the bed where Paul du Peyral lay, also as they had left him, half-conscious, and apparently paralyzed. His pulse was thin, hard, tense, and rapid, and as Schuyler Van Boomkamp replaced his hand upon the bed, he looked significantly at his companion and said:

"It is a matter of minutes."

Mahmouré buried her head in her hands, and for the first time burst into a flood of tears.

The two men took their seats by the bed in silence, the younger making rapid notes in his memorandum-book.

The profound silence of the room was only broken at intervals by a convulsive sob from the woman, and Van Boomkamp shaded the lamp more carefully to make the twilight complete. Suddenly the dying man moved, and all three riveted their attention even more closely upon him.

His lips moved, and a sound escaped them, the purport of which the listeners could not catch. Then, suddenly, half rising into a sitting posture, his eyes opened wide, a flush of colour mounted to his cheeks and as instantaneously died away again, as he stretched his arms before him, and crying, in a grand, ringing voice, "Daphne! Daphne!" he fell back upon the bed. They turned in the direction his eyes had taken, and Mahmouré cried out in terror:

"There! there! do you not see her?"

"Who? Where?"

"Daphne—Daphne Préault," she murmured, and then added, as she covered her face once more, "Ah! she is gone."

Van Boomkamp took Paul's wrist for a moment, put his ear to his mouth, and then placed his hand upon his heart. He glanced at the older physician, and then, laying his hand on Mahmouré's shoulder, he said softly:

"It is over—he is gone."

"Dead! Oh, God!" she cried, "and his last thoughts were of her. Oh! Paul, Paul!" and she buried her head upon the dead man's breast.

During the four days that elapsed between the death of Paul du Peyral and his funeral, Mahmouré never left her husband's body, refusing to see anyone, to be comforted, almost to sustain life, and would not arouse herself from her apathy to gratify the curiosity which the circumstances of Paul's death had excited.

New York rang with it for at least three days. The sudden death of the man who had been such a problem in society, the sudden appearance on the scene of a wife, the stories of the colossal fortune Paul had tortiously enjoyed by concealing the marriage which had taken place, said the gossips, immediately on the death of his *first* wife ten years ago, all were weirdly interesting, and formed the staple subject of conversations at dinner-parties, germans, the opera, in church, and in other places where the School for Scandal of New York meet to paint their neighbours the deepest possible black, in the hope that its own members will look a shade grayer by comparison. Miss Parthenia Van Baulk'em looked upon it as a visitation of Providence, a direct interposition of Divine power in her favour, and almost took to herself the credit of having killed the man who had dared to form a true opinion of her tinsel troubadour. And when Mahmouré du Peyral, as she was now called, refused to place herself on exhibition, and give particulars on the subject of Paul for a small fee, popular indignation reached its zenith; and, from the altitude of Fifth Avenue, descended with full force on her unconscious but beautiful head.

She denied herself peremptorily to all save Schuyler Van Boomkamp and Paul's man of business, and in the settlement of his estate the latter gentleman had his hands full. It was a complicated affair. Paul had saved money, and had bequeathed everything to his wife; but the difficulty lay in separating from the property that was undeniably his, that portion of the proceeds of the Préault estate that had fallen to his lot since his marriage with Mahmouré. Representing, by way of amateur "*amicus curiæ*" or "guardian *ad litem*" in the interests of social justice, Mr. Charles Sturton-Baker, and so, indirectly through Eric, the Princess Daphne, Mr. Murray Hill, with the assistance of Messrs. Seligman, Searcher, & Certiorari, was making himself very officiously offensive; and as his reception by Mahmouré du Peyral was a matter not to be thought of for a moment, he was thrown back on the congenial companionship of Parthenia Van Baulk'em, who was making her arrangements to spend the season in Europe, where she fondly imagined she would find "her young man" in society, and whither Mr. Murray Hill felt anxious that she should go in the capacity of *his fiancée*, though he still kept up the fiction that it was entirely "for her and Mr. Baker" that he had started rolling the nucleus of the snow-ball of worry that was weighing upon the mind of the erstwhile desired Mahmouré.

The last instructions that the solicitors of the Préault estate had received, had been to extract to the last cent from the estate of Paul du Peyral the proportion of income that had been received by him since his marriage with Madame du Peyral; and Mr. Murray Hill, smarting under the memory of Mahmouré's contemptuous rejection of him and of Paul's *argumentum ad caudam*, not to mention the encouragement that twinkled from Miss Parthenia's reddish eyes, had started a wild rumour that Paul had been secretly married before this marriage with Madame du Peyral—indeed, there were people who thought that he went through the marriage ceremony clandestinely with someone about once a week—and filing affidavits, managed to tie up the whole estate for months prospectively, and to put Mahmouré into what was practically, for her, a position of considerable embarrassment.

Through all her troubles she had one staunch and true friend, a friend who had come accidentally to her side, and who had made a complete study of her case, legally, personally, mentally, and physically. That friend was Dr. Schuyler Van Boomkamp.

After the funeral of Paul du Peyral he had come to her and said:

"Madame du Peyral, I have taken the liberty of enquiring somewhat into the circumstances of the case which has been preying on your mind since the sharper anguish of your husband's death has been softened. You will naturally want a friend to represent you in many matters that a woman cannot well manage alone. I offer myself as that friend, at the same time as I offer myself as a physician."

"As a friend, Dr. Van Boomkamp," she had replied, "I accept your offer gladly, and as frankly as it is made, and I know what I have to thank you for when I see the columns and paragraphs about me in the papers; but regarding you as a physician, I hope I can decline your offer, for, now that I am rallying a little, I find myself returning to the health I enjoyed before my husband's death."

"Exactly," replied Van Boomkamp; "but you must be careful. Your health is a very curious problem, even to me; you live practically by means of a transmitted vitality, a vitality that excessive excitement would seriously impair, and that must therefore be very carefully nurtured. You do not allow the newspapers to worry you, I trust; I fear the case of the 'Préault du Peyral' estate is going to become a *cause célèbre*."

"Oh! I don't mind them, Dr. Van Boomkamp. You see, I have no friends in New York to speak of. The imaginative efforts of American journalists seldom, I think, worry their objects. They can never be more than weapons in the hands of one's enemies wherewith to annoy one's friends. I have enemies, for some mysterious reason, it seems; but I have no friends to whom they can send clippings from the morning papers day after day, as is, I believe, the custom over here."

"Well—that's good! I shall look in periodically to see how you are getting along, and whenever I hear anything that in my judgment you should know, you shall know it. At present it seems as if all that has to be done is a subtraction from Mr. du Peyral's residuary estate of the income paid to him since last September, so that in a few weeks you will have nothing more to worry you in any way whatever. What are your plans?"

"I am going home," she said, a far-off look stealing into her great brown eyes.

And then, seeing that the doctor maintained silence, as if waiting for an explanation, she added,

"To Greece, you know; that is where my people originally came from; we have always called it 'home.' My village lies between Pyrgos and Corinth, on the Gulf of Lepanto. I shall buy a villa near the old place, and die forgotten under the same skies that looked down upon the hardy men of Argolis, my forefathers, when they gave up their lives for the freedom of the Peloponnesus."

"Your resolution, madam, is an excellent one," returned Van Boomkamp, gravely; "the climate of the Morea is the one that will give you the completest rest"—he had been about to say "the longest life," but he changed the expression for fear of alarming her.

To the young eclectic physician, Mahmouré was a study of intense interest; living, as she did, at second-hand, as it were, everything depended upon her remaining in a quiet frame of mind. Under those circumstances she might live to be an old woman; but should any unforeseen occurrence make too heavy a draft upon her precarious vitality, he had grave fears for her reason, if not for her life. When, therefore, the new complication arose—the throwing of the whole estate into Chancery, or its American equivalent, for the purpose of making enquiries—and he saw that not only might Mahmouré be put to inconvenience and expense for many months, but she might be even seriously embarrassed by a course of action of whose effects he felt certain that Daphne Préault, the person principally concerned, was in ignorance, he came to Mahmouré one day, and finding her nervous, irritable, worried, he made to her a proposition which was sound on the face of it.

"You can do no good," he said, "by remaining here. The atmosphere of antagonism that surrounds you is bad; besides, the hot weather is at hand, and you must leave the city anyhow. Why not go to Europe? to London,—*en route* for Greece? Your affairs do not in any way require your presence here; you can safely leave them in the hands of your attorney, whom I have ascertained to be a man of absolutely unimpeachable rectitude. By such a course many objects would be served: in the first place, you will obtain the change of air and scene in great need of which you stand at present; in the second, you will see, if you like, Miss Daphne Préault, and doubtless come to some understanding with her which will be to your mutual advantage; in the third, you will be nearer your ultimate destination, and the rest in London will serve the double purpose of shortening a journey that might overtax your strength, and of enabling you to complete many arrangements before you proceed to the Peloponnese. I may add, that I have myself accepted an invitation to proceed at once to Paris to assist Dr. Charcot in certain observations important to mental science which he is making at the Salpêtrière. I shall stay in London for some weeks before crossing the channel, and shall therefore be able to keep an eye on you, on your health, and on your business, with a beneficial result to all three. Think it over."

Mahmouré du Peyral thought it over, with the result that, the next time Schuyler Van Boomkamp called upon her, her mind was made up, and her arrangements were completed; and a fortnight later the passenger-list of the Royal Mail Steamer *Anatolia* contained the names of Schuyler Van Boomkamp and Madame du Peyral; and a grave, ascetic-looking man with steel-gray eyes and gold *pince-nez* might have been seen pacing her decks as she ploughed across the Atlantic in proper "Cunarder" style, in the company of a woman, small but exquisitely made, with an oval, oriental face, great, soft brown eyes, and a mass of tawny hair, with which the north-west wind seemed to love to play for very wantonness, to display its glossy beauties to the gulls and petrels.

# CHAPTER IX.
## The Reincarnation of Daphne.

"Well, and what does Critchett say?"

"Hardly anything; he says that by a miracle there might be enough of the optic nerve left on which to form the basis of a hope that, when the inflammation has gone down, sight may be partially restored."

"And are both eyes equally injured?"

"Yes, or apparently so."

"Poor old Gabriel!"

"Yes, it's hard, isn't it? just at the moment he had made a name. However, let's hope for the best."

The speakers were Bernard Rawlinson and Eric Trevanion. They had met just as Eric left the Hawleigh's house at the conclusion of a visit of enquiry, about a fortnight after the explosion in Gabriel's studio. A novelist is not allowed by the Canons of the Cult to sympathize, himself, with his heroes, but it must be conceded that a sadder tale was never told than that of Gabriel Hawleigh's blindness. For an artist to be blinded is certainly a tragedy of the saddest sort; but how much more sad if that artist be at the outset only, of a successful career! Here was Gabriel, however, poor and in love. The moment had arrived when his anxieties seemed to be at an end. Fortune, won at length by his persistent wooing, had smiled upon him and extended her hand, and at the moment that he stepped forth to grasp it, the blow fell that shattered in an instant every hope that he had built up for himself; and, boy as he was, sitting for the most part alone in his darkened room, the first threads of gray began to peep among the strands of light-brown hair that fell in picturesque confusion over his brows.

Mrs. Hawleigh seemed—as well she might—crushed by the blow which had fallen upon them, the culminating point of all these years of struggle against poverty. For the moment, fortunately, money was not lacking, for the great Academy picture having been purchased by a celebrated amateur for what, to Mrs.

Hawleigh and Gabriel, seemed a vast sum, the news of his accident spread like wildfire, and it being currently reported that Dr. Critchett had declared his blindness to be incurable, dealers and collectors alike had contended for Gabriel's previous works, which, by the advice of Sir George B——, were sold by auction at Christie's, and brought prices such as Gabriel had never dreamed of in connection with his own work; and such is the irony of fate—many a canvas that had been rejected by the Institute, the Academy, and the Grosvenor, went for prices even higher than that realized by "Sunshine in the Fog." The fact that Sir George B—— bought the first picture in the sale, and "Miss Préault, the eminent lady-artist," the second, may have contributed to this result; at any rate, on the Monday following the sale, Mrs. Hawleigh received a cheque that relieved her mind of any anxiety as regards either the proximate or immediately ultimate future.

The eminent oculist who had taken charge of the case offered but one shadow of hope: as soon as he could be safely removed, and could without danger be exposed to the light of day, Gabriel was to be taken to a little cottage on the borders of Dartmoor, almost on the boundary line which divides Devonshire and Cornwall; and after a few months of this quiet, pure, and invigorating atmosphere, the best or the worst would be known, and Gabriel Hawleigh would know irrevocably whether he might one day look again on the faces and scenes he loved so well, or whether he were doomed to be led through life blind!

And Maye? Maye Trevethick—what of her? Ah, sirs! who shall pry into the secrets of a woman's heart? How shall I dare to say what were her thoughts as she sat in the dark with her poor blind Gabriel, holding his hand in hers in silence, or talking gently to him of their plans, of the events in the colony, such as she knew them, of the rumours from the world outside Holland Street which came to her and which she memorized in case they might interest the boy whose light had become so great a darkness. In all the unwritten history of faithful women, no story is sadder than hers, no devotion more heroic, no love and duty more sacred: to tend Gabriel, to anticipate his needs and humour his sick-man's fancies, had become her life; and she lived it, showing no trace of aught but a gentle, feminine devotion to the lot that had become hers, whilst well—! who shall pry into the secrets of a woman's heart?

And so the days passed on and grew into weeks.

Of Eric Trevanion in these times some of those who had eyes saw very little, whilst again some who had eyes saw a good deal! He did not mix very much with the colony now; he was poor, and, like every man who from affluence has come to poverty, he felt it almost as a disgrace, and no longer held his head high in the air with a merry word or a proud little laugh for everyone.

The Princess Daphne watched him with a light of deep anxiety in her great grave eyes, as he would sit at his desk, often for hours together, crushed, as it were, beneath the load of disappointment that began to take a tangible form in his increasing penury. Little by little his bric-a-brac, his pictures, his curios, his Eastern carpets had been sold to pay the landwoman, the baker, the grocer, and other people necessary in the scheme of even an artist's existence. And every time the Princess made him accept some small loan, the operation became more and more distasteful to him. He had even begged the elder Trevanion to give him another six months' law, but in vain. "Return here, settle down, and marry a county girl," had responded the Autocrat of Trthwwsthpllgg Manor, "and I'll pay your debts, and you shall be a man of independent means; but I refuse to keep you, as you are living now, in opulence, luxury, and debauchery"—and Eric would look round his little retreat with a bitter smile, and wonder what the governor's ideas of opulence, luxury, and debauchery were.

"Well?" the Princess would query sometimes, after a more than ordinarily protracted pause.

"Nothing—capital and labor don't seem to be hitting it off together in my case, Daph. An author seems to me to be very like a man who has found a well of natural gas on his farm, but hasn't the capital to lay down the pipes which shall conduct it into the houses of the community. The pipe-man is the publisher, and I haven't found one to undertake my gas yet."

"But the gas exists all the same—stop the flow until the capitalist comes along."

"I can't; it's too strong. At present my books are in the limited edition of one manuscript copy, as Alexander the Great used to insist upon Aristotle's works being produced. It won't do *me* much good if three thousand years hence my writings become as popular as his. Even the Chaldean author who cut his work on the wall of a palace at Nineveh had a better 'show,' in the American sense, than I; and the gentle Babylonian who wrote romances on a cylindrical seal, had at least the satisfaction of knowing that a copy of his book reached the world every time the owner sealed a letter. It isn't good to make a living by literature, dear."

"It's better than making it by the means that so many men employ, Eric. The easiest way to make a living, to my mind, is by inheritance, the next is by marriage, and the next is by being a bachelor—all of them nice, easy occupations. Wait a bit, old man, and you'll coin money."

"It seems to me that if I wait a bit I shall have to—and take the chances of being caught at it! I quite agree with the philosopher who said, 'Poverty is no sin, but all the same it's damned uncomfortable.' They talk about the merry Bohemianism of a literary life. Egad, Daph! I feel about as merry as a stuffed bear with corns, put out in the rain as a furrier's advertisement."

"Well, try something else—promote companies like the Eastons' friend, Baker, and take the chance of imprisonment for fraud as he does."

"Ah! I think I might get up a good sporting company or two. I had an uncle once—a bishop—who got up a joint-stock concern for bringing about the fulfilment of scripture prophecies. He was great on the law and the prophets, but when the other directors found that he wanted to lay down all the law and take up all the profits, they didn't sink the capital, and consequently (paradoxical as it may seem) the company didn't float. And as for the bishop! Solomon in all his fury was not enraged like one of these."

"Eric, I believe you're descending to the kind of joke which is called a pun. When I said 'do as Mr. Sturton-Baker does,' I meant in finance, not in vulgarity."

"I don't see why you should be so hard on Baker; it's through him and some friend of his in New York, to satisfy some private grudge or other, it would seem, that we got on the track of Mr. Paul du Peyral's marriage, and recovered for you the fortune which is to be yours in the course of a week or two."

"Well, I'm very sorry he had anything to do with it. Couldn't you have got anyone else?"

"Nobody so cheap."

"All right! as you are the person principally concerned in that money that I don't want—I——"

"Daphne! how dare you?" cried Eric, flaming up at once; "how dare you insult me so? True, I have the misfortune to owe you a certain sum of money that you cheated me into taking. That is no reason why you should insult me by suggesting that I have any thoughts for myself in watching your interests in America."

"Then why bother yourself? *I* didn't ask you to."

The old dangerous light was coming into her eyes as she spoke, and finally, starting to her feet, she cried, in a hard, altered voice:

"Good heavens, man! can't you tell the difference between love and egotism? If I'd wanted this money of my cousin's I'd have married Paul du Peyral—sometimes I wish I had. Anyhow, he's man enough to be a good scamp, instead of a desponding, faint-hearted creature who won't raise a finger to help himself except in his own useless way. Bah! I'm tired of your high moral tone!"

Eric rose, and took his hat preparatory to leaving in silence—hurt to the bottom of his soul. As he turned, the Princess Daphne, pressing her hands to her head, fell forward upon the floor.

In a moment he was at her side, had raised her gently and laid her on the lounge. Not a sign of life! not a throb of the heart! Her face was deathly white, her hands were tightly clinched. He had never seen her like this before, and with a strange feeling of terror he sent off post-haste, not for the doctor without an idea beyond indigestion, but for an eminent physician, whose waiting-rooms are the rendezvous of half the queens of London society. As good luck would have it, the great man was at home and alone, and within an hour of the Princess' seizure he arrived in Holland Street.

Daphne had been put to bed by the distraught Clytie, and after making a rapid and silent examination, Doctor P—— joined Eric in the studio.

"Your wife?" queried he, briefly.

"No."

"Ah!" and he took a scrap of paper to write a prescription.

"Has she ever been like this before?"

"Never. She has had curious fainting fits; there have been times when she has apparently suffered from a kind of obsession but it has never been protracted and profound like this."

"Ah! Who is her regular attendant?"

"Dr.——; he lives opposite."

"Send for him."

In a few minutes the doctor we already know arrived, and metaphorically grovelled before his superior, to whom nevertheless he remarked immediately and consequentially:

"It is, I presume, one of Miss Préault's recurrent fainting fits—resulting from a slight stomachic disorder. I have been in the habit of exhibiting——"

"The spectacle of a schoolboy playing at being a doctor," rapped out Dr. P——. "It has nothing to do with faintness of any kind; and as for indigestion—pooh!"

"You think it grave?" said Eric, anxiously.

"Very grave," replied the physician. "The cause is beyond me —the effect is only too apparent."

"And that is?"

"What are you to Miss Préault?" said Dr. P——, taking Eric aside.

"She is dearer to me than anything else in the world."

"Sir, I am sincerely sorry for you—I can give you no hope."

"None whatever?"

"None."

"When will the end come?"

"At about midnight."

Eric turned, burying his head in his hands.

"If, when she recovers consciousness, as she may do, there is any delirium, let her have this prescription," said the physician, on leaving. "I can do no more—I regret to have been able to do so little. Good afternoon." And he left the house, obsequiously attended by the local G. P., whom he indignantly ignored.

At midnight a single lamp burned dimly in the Princess Daphne's room, and Eric, who had been sitting motionless beside her since the moment her death-sentence had been pronounced, rose and bent over her as, with a sigh, she opened her eyes and looked into his—speechless—motionless—but conscious of his presence. Once or twice, in answer to the appeals he made to her in a passionate whisper, her lips moved as if she would fain have answered him, but no sound broke the silence in answer to his prayer, save the gurgling sobs of the black woman, who crouched upon her knees in a corner, alternately choking and muttering incomprehensible invocations to her poly-personal deity in jade.

This continued until a quarter to one; then, on the night air, there was borne to his ears the last swell of some chaunt that died in the Carmelite church near by. Roused by this, a dog howled behind the house, a fretful, unhappy howl, broken by little yaps before it settled into its lugubrious breve and descending semi-breve. The Princess moved and seemed to say something, but if so, her whisper was drowned by a burst of drunken laughter that rose from some band of revellers who had taken Holland Street on their way home.

When all was still, a faint flush came into Daphne's cheek, and Eric, his heart bursting with grief, laid his head close to hers, lifting her beautiful arms and circling them around his neck as he enfolded her body in a last distracted embrace. Clytie had risen and was standing at the foot of the bed.

"Eric—my love——" whispered the Princess Daphne, royal still, though in the arms of death, "I am going—remember—I loved you, and none but you—you were my life—my religion—I had no thought that was not yours. Good-bye—keep the old place where we've been so happy. I can't see you, darling—but I know you are there. Good-night!"

The head fell back as he held her in his arms he could feel her dying as he held her. The already cold body grew colder, the *live* feeling seemed to die out of it, the eyes opened and then half closed, the lips parted a little, and a sigh escaped them which Eric caught in a wild, agonized kiss. The body was heavy. The arms had fallen from about his neck. The Princess Daphne was dead!

※

As he held her in his arms, her head lying back upon his hand, the silence of the death-scene was broken by a shrill cry from Clytie:

"Oh, Gord! Mars' Eric—look dar!"

Her white eyes shone in the darkness, as she pointed with a withered black finger to the side of the bed opposite to Eric.

Nothing!

"What do you mean, woman?" said Eric, angry through his grief at the interruption.

"Yaas, dar—yaas, dar!—oh, Mars' Eric—don' yo see 'um? —dar, now he touch my honey chile oh,—Missy Daph!"

Eric had turned his head to where the black woman's finger had indicated a figure invisible to him. Now he turned again to Daphne. Good God! was he mad? A spark lit the great eyes, which had opened a little farther; the lips gave utterance to a little gasp, as the woman swallowed and sighed; a single strong beat announced the reawakened heart, as Daphne Préault gave a wild look in the direction of Clytie's unseen Thing, and exclaiming, in almost her strongest voice:

"*Paul!*" fell back upon the bed insensible, but alive.

Alive! Eric rose to his feet, an icy cold sensation of terror seizing in its grip every fibre of his body. What had happened? He hardly dared to think. Clytie was once more crouched in her original corner, no longer sobbing, but praying volubly to the idol returning thanks doubtless for his recent performance.

Eric seated himself and wrote on a leaf of his note-book: "*Crisis over—she is alive—must see you—can you come at once?*"

"Clytie," said he, "you love your mistress; if you want to save her life, take this to Hanover Square at once. Don't lose a second—find a cab at the church;" and with a nimbleness that Clytie would never have confessed to being capable of, the darkie idolater was gone.

In half an hour she was back with another slip of paper. "*Am in bed—very sleepy—will come in the morning—a miracle has happened—she will live—give my prescription if necessary.*" That was all—and somehow Eric felt that it was enough.

The Princess was breathing peacefully her unconsciousness seemed to have given place to sleep. And she slept till morning. She was restored to him from the dead. Restored, did I say? Well, hardly! "The Princess" had reached that undiscovered country from whose bourne no traveller returns. Daphne Préault came to life! She was never "The Princess Daphne" again.

The traces of fire faded slowly from Gabriel Hawleigh's face. The agony of inflammation had left his cicatrized eye-balls, and, with carefully shaded eyes, the happy young artist of a month before felt his way timidly about the house and studio he knew so well. With trembling hands he would lightly touch the furniture and hangings, and a sharp contraction of pain would come over his features when his hands met his paint-box or palette, or other artistic paraphernalia. The absence of the pictures which had lain about seemed to hurt him, and they kept him as much as possible out of the studio, whilst "the boys" would come in and sit and talk with him, avoiding with all the tact of which they were capable, the subject of his affliction. Sometimes unconsciously someone would bring his mind back to it by accident, and then a sharp spasm of grief used to shake him, whilst Maye or Mrs. Hawleigh dexterously turned the subject.

The doctor whose fiat had gone forth that Gabriel was to be removed as soon as possible to the moors, was not one of those immortalized medicos who

"come in haste,
To suit their physic to the patient's taste;"

for the thought of leaving Holland Street, which he knew so well, for a place that he might possibly never see, was a perfect nightmare to the blind man. But Dr. Richardson was inexorable on the point: setting aside the benefit that he hoped might be derived from the pure, heath-scented atmosphere of Dartmoor, the continual brooding over familiar surroundings that he could only feel, even in the weeks which preceded his departure, began to have a perceptible influence on Gabriel's mind—he was becoming irritable, fretful, impatient, as blind men are apt to do when ill-health added to their infirmity; and therefore, as soon as it was possible to move him, they started for the cottage that they had found with the assistance of Eric Trevanion's knowledge of the neighbourhood, for it was comparatively—for Dartmoor—close to Trthwwsthpllgg Manor.

No better description of their retreat could be given than that contained in Mrs. Hawleigh's first letter to Daphne Préault. "Here we are," she wrote, "on the borders of Dartmoor, three hours' drive from the nearest town, and a Sabbath day's journey from London. I do think Dr. Richardson might have sent us to some more civilized corner of the world. I feel as if I were banished forever from everyone I have ever known in my life; but I don't complain, as it is for my poor boy's sake. Miles of moor all round us! and I fancy the nearest civilized habitation is the convict prison—if one can call that civilized. For my part I live in constant dread of a sudden invasion of escaped convicts, in horrid, unbecoming striped stockings, and with things like bluebottles, supposed to represent broad arrows, all over them. But the air is lovely, and already Gabriel seems less fretful than he was in Holland Street."

And so, for a time at least, the Hawleighs seemed to have gone out of the life of the Holland-Street colony, and Eric, for one, had perhaps realized what a loss they had sustained in the departure of the genial matron and the grave-eyed maid who raised the little house from a studio to the sweet dignity of a home. Yes—he missed them, for since the recovery of Daphne, an indefinable and almost weird change had taken place in her personality.

Even to Eric the change was inexplicable. Daphne Préault was, if possible, even more beautiful than she had been before her illness, but it was a different kind of beauty.

Her carriage had lost dignity and had acquired grace; her great, dark eyes were matchless as of yore, but their look was no longer calm and imperious, as it had been when she raised them to his, at the conclusion of her song on the night of Gabriel Hawleigh's Bohemian *soirée*; the lovely curves of her mouth had lost much of their firmness and had acquired a certain soft, flickering smile that was inviting in its subtle mockery, but no longer benign and pitying as it had been when first she smiled upon Eric Trevanion; and in her attitudes, as she lounged about the studio, there was a languor which she had not possessed before. In her music there was a quaint, sensuous harmony that had not characterized it when she was "The Princess Daphne"; in her speech, a word here, a glance or a smile there, betrayed a lower standard of intelligence; and in her painting the detail of Meissonier had given place to the morbid minutia of Van Beers and of the latest French school. She would devote hours to painting some demi-mondaine, sleeping carelessly the sleep of exhaustion in an absolutely "esoteric" attitude; and at the conclusion of her work she would draw a brush full of bright vermillion across the canvas, and tell Eric that it was a painting in his school "An Impression of Humanity in Primary Colours." Into her caresses there crept a *je ne sais quoi* of inexplicable earthliness, that almost repelled whilst it intoxicated him. The change she had announced as possible in her had taken place. The savage side of her nature seemed to have got the upper hand.

She was less womanly, and more female.

These were dark days for Eric. His poverty told upon his spirits; he no longer cared to go into society, as heretofore, and it was only at rare intervals that he could be tempted forth into the world of men. Another factor which conduced to his distaste for society was that Daphne betrayed a tendency to cross-question and catechise his going-out and coming-in; she would chaff him about the women he met at dinner-parties, and almost make him "scenes" about them—in a word, he was beginning to feel a little friction of the chain that bound him to Daphne Préault. It is a horrible thought for a man that he is bound to a woman by ties of financial dependence, even when the accord between them is perfect; but when a certain uneasiness has sprung up between them, it becomes frightful; and Eric began to experience a horrible feeling of revulsion when Daphne began to claim as a right the little services he had felt himself so honoured by her accepting as favours. Of one acquaintance of his she was especially jealous: this was the eminent Doctor P——, who had apparently taken a fancy to this grave young man, and had asked him to call upon him in Hanover Square, an invitation of which he had eagerly taken advantage. One day Dr. P—— had called, semi-professionally, he said, upon Miss Préault, and after he had gone, she had said:

"I never want to see that man again—I don't trust him; he seems to be watching us all the time he talks; he'd like to separate us if he could—and I'll take good care he doesn't. Mind that, Eric!"

The speech had jarred upon him, more in its tone than in the words she used, and the next time he called upon Dr. P——, he said nothing about it to her. It was the first action of his life, since he had known her, that he had not told her all about.

One day she was lying on the lounge, reading a newspaper, one shapely foot trailing on the floor, the other lying on a cushion at the foot of the lounge, when suddenly she looked up and said, "Eric, we must see this new play at the Prince's Theatre; let's go on Wednesday."

"Very sorry, *chérie*," he had replied, "but I can't."

"Oh, that's all right," returned she; "*I'll* get the tickets; it won't cost you anything."

He turned very pale, and then very red, as he answered:

"It's not that, dear; I have an engagement."

"Oh—indeed! you didn't tell me—what is it?"

"A dinner-party at Dr. P——'s in Hanover Square."

"Ah!" returned Daphne, "I don't wonder you said nothing about it: you're always with that odious man, it seems to me—he interferes with everything."

"You can hardly say that, Daphne; it's only the second time I've dined there. Surely you don't mind my going; one meets interesting people at his house, and this dinner is in honour of a celebrated American doctor who has just arrived."

"Come and sit down here."

He sank on the lounge by her side, a little nervously, and she put her arms round his neck and drew his head close down to hers.

"Don't go, darling," she whispered; "stay here with me—I'll give up the play, if you'll give up the dinner—I don't want you to go—that doctor doesn't like me, and I know he'll separate us if he can."

"But, my dear girl—I *must* go. I've accepted, and I can't put off a man like Dr. P—— at the last moment."

"You are determined?"

"Well yes, dear."

"Oh, very well, then! go to your horrid dinner-party. Anything to get away from me, and go about flirting with other women. I wonder you don't give in to your dear father and go and marry 'a county girl,' in Cornwall—it would about suit you. You'd probably suit *her*, now I've made a man of you, and you've got tired of me."

She pushed his head roughly away from her, and turned her face into the cushions of the lounge, pretending to go to sleep. Eric sighed deeply as he returned to his writing-table. But his mind was made up—he would dine at Dr. P——'s on the following Wednesday.

Until the evening in question nothing more was said, on either side, on the subject. When seven o'clock on Wednesday evening arrived, however, and Eric was just leaving the house to go home and dress for his party, as he passed the dining-room he saw, through the open door, the table rather coquettishly laid for two—just as in the first days of their love. His first impulse was to return to the studio and ask for an explanation; his second was to do nothing of the kind, and with a little proud toss of his head he passed on and across the street. Whilst he dressed, however, the one thought that surged through his brain was, "Whom does she expect?—whom does she expect?"

He had almost lulled his mind to rest by the artificially produced conviction that Daphne, having been stricken with a horror of being alone, had sent for Sylvia or Eva Easton to dine with her. But why had she not told him? This was a question which solved itself as he stood at the looking-glass in his window tying his cravat. It was just half past seven, when a cab drove up to Miss Préault's door, and Mr. Charles Sturton-Baker, springing out, disappeared into the house. It was with a queer, strained sensation, like a nasty taste in his mouth which he could not get rid of, that Eric Trevanion took an omnibus at St. Mary Abbot's and proceeded, by way of Bond Street, to Hanover Square; and though the dinner was interesting, and the American doctor was in every respect a remarkable man, his soul was in Holland Street all the time, and as soon as the first lady gave the signal for departure at eleven o'clock, he also made his escape to regain Holland Street on foot, in the fresh air of the cool summer night.

Miss Daphne Préault's house was quite dark, and he stood on the pavement in front, deliberating whether to go in as usual, or not, for some minutes, his latch-key in his hand, his heart beating with that strong, measured thud that the coolest of us have experienced in moments of agitation, however impassive and unconscious we may outwardly appear to be.

At last he persuaded himself that to refrain from going in would be, in the first place, cowardly in him, and in the second, an insult to Daphne, so he turned the key and stepped through the house into the studio, which he could see from the hall-door was illuminated. As he walked down the little passage, how he prayed that he might find her alone! and, such is the contradictory nature of man's feelings, the moment he stepped into the studio he felt he would have given worlds to have found Mr. Baker still there.

The ex-Princess Daphne was lying asleep on the lounge in an attitude of the most delicious lassitude. She was wrapped in one of her softest and most easy *négligés*, her head thrown back on her hands, which were clasped behind it. She did not wake as he stood on the hearth-rug, his back to the empty fireplace, looking at her, just as he had stood on that other night that seemed already so long, long ago; and as he looked at her, a feeling of horrible, undefinable dread stealing over him, he went back in his mind over all the short past he had trodden with her, and which had seemed so exquisite to him. Was it all over—was it irrevocably ended, tonight? A voice deep within his heart—so deep that he could not reach it to stifle it—told him that it was so indeed; and then a great, profound pity surged up in his mind, and his eyes filled with tears. He knelt softly by the sleeping woman, and, bending over her, touched her lips with his. Without opening her eyes, and with a little sigh, she returned his kiss—ah! so sweetly, that he was about to fling his arms round her, when she raised the lids from the grand brown eyes he had so often closed with his lips, and, seeing him, uttered a little exclamation of surprise, in which he detected a ring of mingled disappointment and alarm, as, turning her head away so as to avoid him, she said:

"Oh! it's *you!*"

He sprang to his feet with a strangled gasp of pain and rage, and stood staring down at her as she slowly turned her head and looked him defiantly in the eyes.

Not a word was said for a few moments.

It was Daphne who first broke the silence:

"Well," she said, "did you enjoy your dinner-party?"

"No."

"No?—Why?"

"Because, strange though it may appear to you, I would sooner have killed myself, or have been struck blind like poor

Gabriel Hawleigh, than have seen that man enter your house this evening."

"Ah! you spy upon me?—Well—I presume I am at liberty to ask whomever I like to my own house when you are away amusing yourself elsewhere."

"Oh! of course—My God!—has it come to this?"

"Why, certainly, *mon cher*, why not? Why can't you live and let live."

"I don't live—this is worse than death to me. Since when has that man been coming here in my absence?"

"Since you have made it a recurring practice to be absent—how selfish you are! He has my interests at heart, and comes to consult with me on my American affairs. You know he is in some way interested in them himself, and you surely have not forgotten that it is through him that I have obtained, or shall obtain, the fortune Paul du Peyral cheated me out of."

"I congratulate you," said Eric, bitterly, "on the means whereby you have obtained his skilled coöperation. Good God, Daphne, how changed you are! I have felt it ever since your illness—it needed but this to convince me. I could almost believe that *you* are the subject of a marvellous story that was told us tonight by the American doctor who arrived in this country only yesterday."

"Ah! a story? What was it?"

"I am not in a mood to tell stories."

"But I am in a mood to hear them. Tell me this one."

"He told us of a man whose death-bed he attended in New York—a man who was the incarnation of all that was unprincipled; who had by some supernatural means projected his soul—his vitality—into some woman over here, by means of his mistress, over whom he had obtained a marvellous mesmeric power. I could almost believe, looking at you as I see you now, that you are the woman."

"I am."

"What do you mean? Daphne! do you want to drive me mad?"

"Not at all, my dear boy. Your American doctor's name was Schuyler Van Boomkamp, was it not?"

"Yes—how did you know?"

"Inductively, through Mr. Baker. The man over there was Paul du Peyral; his mistress was in fact his wife, Mahmouré du Peyral, *née* di Zulueta; and I am Miss Daphne Préault of New Orleans, his blood relation and, by a coincidence, apparently his double, at your service."

Eric stood looking at her in horrified amazement for a few moments longer, and then, without a word, turned and left the house. Daphne Préault rose from the lounge and spent an hour with her thoughts before going to bed.

The whole thing, from Eric's entrance, seemed to be a twisted version of that other night in the preceding autumn.

On the following morning Eric did not make his appearance as was his wont. The hours crept by, filled for Daphne with idleness; lunch-time came, and still no Eric.

"Well," thought Daphne, "he's in a huff about something or other. Really, that man becomes wearisome—assommant. Heaven defend me in the future from a rich man who's grown poor!—they're the worst kind of paupers, because they're so impracticable. Heigho! I hope kind fate will send me some visitors—I'm bored with myself."

As if in answer to her prayer Clytie entered the studio at this moment, bearing a card. With a feeling of genuine relief Daphne stretched out her hand to take it, hoping that it was a man, or at the least an interesting woman, with whom to while away the hours of afternoon; she did not feel inclined to go out; she would far rather sit and chat lazily at home.

As she looked at the card, a sudden grip of pain seemed to seize her, and a flush rose to her brow which as quickly gave place to a white, hard, stern look that augured ill for the reception of the visitor.

The name on the card, printed in tiny block letters, was "Madame du Peyral."

We have none of us heard or thought much of anyone without making to ourselves a strongly defined mental picture of their personalities, a picture, as a rule, so widely differing from the truth that the difference, when we see how great it is, strikes us as a keen disappointment, if not as an insult to our intelligence. Since the news of Paul's marriage to an actress had reached her, Daphne had conjured up an unvarying picture of Mahmouré. She expected to see a rather loud-looking woman—tall, voluptuously formed, with a handsome, bold, foreign face—a face to suit the name, Mahmouré di Zulueta. She had seen the type in all its glory at Nice, at Monte Carlo, at Ems, at Aix: they are usually called "Mine, la Princesse de Quelquechose," and are generally to be seen dashing up and down the most frequented *allées*, in wildly luxurious landaus or victorias, whose panels bear highly emblazoned coats of arms, and the cockades of whose coachmen's hats are decorated with little scraps of divers-colored ribbon. They are also usually attended by quiet, dignified men, all of them built alike—that is to say: complexion ivory white, hair and moustache white and trimmed *en brosse*, perfectly dressed, patent-leather boots, light gloves, tightly buttoned in drab-coloured frock coats, white hats, canes with gold heads, the air of "Diplomacy" stamped indescribably but unmistakably upon them, the whole arrangement identified with and known by some noble Russian name. The type pays little attention to the woman by its side, whom one catches one's self wondering vaguely—about whether it be his wife, sister, or *chère amie.*

This was the kind of woman whom Daphne Préault prepared herself to snub, as a gentle frou-frou of skirts heralded the entrance of Mahmouré. The door closed and the two women, animated by such different feelings, faced each other; but instead of advancing, by a singular and simultaneous impulse each stopped as if transfixed.

Perhaps no one ever belied a name as did Mahmouré, dressed to go into the world. She had essentially that undefinable pose which only the true gentlewoman can possess, whilst so many gently-bred women lack it altogether. Always dressed in an absolutely original arrangement of the very last fashion, she would have been remarked anywhere, but not, as is usually the case, in consequence of her gown per se, for she had the art of subduing and rendering harmonious the most bizarre "creation," and for "form" would have been singled out from any crowd. Where this little foreigner got her manner from was a marvel to the envious; it seemed in no sense acquired, but instinctive.

Daphne's hand which held the card dropped mechanically to her side, and the pasteboard fluttered to the floor. Her eyes were fixed on Mahmouré's face in questioning wonder—where had she seen this stranger before? The face seemed perfectly familiar, yet unknown; and it was attractive to her with an attraction beyond the power of words to describe. She remembered nothing of her indignation; the thoughts of resentment she had felt due to Mahmouré faded away. She felt as if a new era had sprung up in her feelings since the moment her eyes first rested on the small sable-clad figure that stood motionless before her, the pale face, framed in its burnished bronze hair, standing out weirdly from the dark surroundings.

This strange sympathy that took possession of Daphne was the more absorbing from the fact that it was quite new to her—for she was not given to what is called "gushing" over women. Though she liked them very well, she never made nor needed "greatest girl-friends." The affection which seems to be such a necessity, such an all-absorbing *lien*, between some women had always been a matter for wonder to her. In her school days, when some girl or other had sought her in friendship, and had drifted into adoration, as girls will drift, Daphne had never been able to understand why she should be expected to waste her time in promiscuous osculation. She would submit in a gracious manner to being kissed; it seemed to please the other girl, and didn't hurt her—but why?—*but why?*—she would question. After she had grown up, and after she had begun her Bohemian life among "the boys," women betrayed a tendency to like, to admire, and to adore her—her magnetism seemed to reach them to an extraordinary degree. Their liking may have been due to the fact that, fascinatingly beautiful as she was, sensuously and a trifle masculinely formed, she had admitted no man before Eric to her close friendship. However it was, certain it is, that in society she was run after by all the women whose names were most quoted as associating at ultra-fashionable functions; and the tributes to her talent which reached her in the form of letters and bouquets, each year, after the opening of the Academy, were almost invariably addressed in the fashionable female hand, and scented *an point de dèlire*. She sometimes wondered at it, for she never strove for their patronage or friendship. At last she accepted it unquestioningly, thanking her feminine admirers for the many charming afternoons they gave her, and passively permitting herself to be loved, as is always the *rôle* of one principal in a great friendship.

Therefore was she the more amazed to find herself drawn irresistibly to this little woman, whose big eyes were fixed on her with a strange, far-off look. Her prejudice faded, her fancied anger fled—all were merged in an uncontrollable desire to comfort and welcome the sad, sweet-faced woman before her. She roused herself and advanced a little, stretching out both hands so as to take Mahmouré almost in her arms as she said:

"You must let me welcome you to England," and for the first time in her life offered her lips to be kissed by a woman, impelled by a fascination which was stronger than herself, and which was wholly due to the strange magnetism of her visitor's personality.

And Mahmouré, who had remained meanwhile as one in a dream? As she gazed, an almost supernatural look flamed from her eyes—at first it was one of questioning, then by degrees the questioning turned to recognition. It was the woman she had seen at Paul's bedside at the moment of his death! Her eyes became moist, and lit up vividly; the pupils dilated till the colour of the iris seemed blotted out; a weird, sullen darkness filled them, heavy and soft; and then, as Daphne's lips touched hers, a flash illumined them before they closed, as she leaned upon the other woman, murmuring in a sigh as she threw back her head, almost unconscious, "Paul!"

Instantly both women recovered themselves. Of what inscrutable influence had they been the sport? Both were confused, but Mahmouré, whose momentary aberration was the more easily understood and explained, was the first to regain her ordinary equilibrium.

"This is a strange meeting, Miss Préault," she said, "and I fear I frighten you; pray forgive me. I don't know quite why I should lose my head on meeting you. I came to talk severely business. If I tried to explain why you affect me so strangely, you would laugh at me."

"Oh, no! Believe me, I am as astonished as you—but somehow I seem to know you, madam."

"And I, you," replied Mahmouré. "The instant I saw you all recollection of time, place, and circumstance seemed to leave me. I seemed to be in a dream, for I saw in you the man whose name is so familiar to you, and who was so dear to me, Paul du Peyral! I should feel bitterly ashamed of my folly were I not sure that you will forgive and forget the weakness of an invalid."

"But I am not angry at all," returned Daphne. "Come, let us sit on the lounge here, and you shall tell me all about yourself. As you can imagine, I have been anxious—not to say curious—to see you in the flesh, for—I too have a confession to make that will seem foolish and hysterical to you. I seem to have seen you before—in a dream, or somehow—so we are not strangers—what does it mean?"

"I don't know how I can explain it, Miss Préault—"

"Call me Daphne—won't you—Mahmouré? Yours is such a beautiful name that I should love to call you by it in exchange."

"Please, do. Well, to continue: I think the sympathy between us rests on our having both been influenced by the same man—who resembled *you* as if he were your twin and who was *my* husband. It is of that I came to speak to you—I have wronged you deeply—can you forgive me?"

"There is nothing to forgive; we shall be great friends, I know."

"Ah! how good you are!" exclaimed Mahmouré; and she kissed the hand that Daphne extended to her.

They were seated close together on the lounge, and though an ordinary observer would not have seen anything strange in the appearance of the two women, one of them at least had by no means recovered her self-possession. It was Daphne who could not reconcile her own conflicting sensations—she could find no reason for the intense, soft satisfaction that she felt under the influence of Mahmouré's presence, of her touch, of her gaze, of her kiss.

It seemed like a new obsession, and it troubled her; but at last she explained it to her own dissatisfaction as being natural magnetism—or madness. But she thought that if Mahmouré was mad, she was a singularly interesting maniac; and as the low, tender voice spoke on, the desire to befriend her and to love her grew stronger and stronger, till at last she gave herself up to the moment, and she and Mahmouré plunged, confidentially, into stories of their past lives, of the events that had established such a sympathy between them, and had finally brought them together.

The afternoon was drawing to a close with tea and chatter. Daphne had denied herself to every visitor, and the two women, completely at their ease, sat, or rather lounged on the divan, exchanging confidences as the hours sped by.

"Very well, then," said Daphne, as if concluding an arrangement; "that is settled; so long as you are in England you must spend much of your time here with me. The questions of business that exist between us can be disposed of in a morning, and we must see all that we can of one another whilst we can. You cannot think how strangely happy I am that chance should have thrown us together like this. Our friendship, though sudden, must be lasting; promise me, Mahmouré, that it shall be."

And Mahmouré, lying among the cushions, looked up into Daphne's beautiful eyes and said:

"I promise you!"

For answer Daphne bent and kissed the beautiful lips that had framed the words, as if to thank them. A sudden noise made her raise her head suddenly, and Mahmouré also started up into a less "easy" position.

Eric Trevanion stood before them.

Daphne blushed scarlet, for no earthly reason that she could give herself, as she rose, and, going to the tea-table, said:

"Madame du Peyral, this is my great friend and ally, Mr. Eric Trevanion. Eric, this is Mme. Paul du Peyral."

Eric bowed profoundly and raised his eyes to Mahmouré's. What was the intense feeling of antipathy that surged over him as he met her steady gaze? He could not tell. But he grew pale as he took his tea-cup from Daphne, and he felt that, whatever might be the character of this beautiful little Oriental woman, she was an enemy to him, a barrier to be, between himself and Daphne.

He could not reason it out, but as he put Mahmouré into her hansom when she took her departure, and she leant upon his hand in getting in, the same electric thrill of intense antagonism shot through him, and he turned back into the house.

# CHAPTER X.
## The Autocrat of Trthwwsthpllgg.

On the few occasions when I have time to think at all, I have often thought it strange that so few Englishmen know anything of one of the most glorious districts of their native land, save from the pages of "Lorna Doone" and the writings of Baring-Gould. The Amateur Pedestrian is a strongly English institution, but the proportion of pedestrians who explore the beauties of Dartmoor is ridiculously small by comparison with the army of knapsack-fiends who yearly invade the lake district of Cumberland, the Peak scenery of Derbyshire, and Scotland generally. I am not going to challenge comparison with Blackmore in a description of Dartmoor. Had Gabriel Hawleigh been able to see the beauties that were bathed in the exquisite heather-scented atmosphere that day by day brought back the colour to his wan cheeks, he would have made many a study of landscape from the neighborhood of the little cottage in which the Hawleigh household found itself installed just beyond the borders of Cornwall. But Gabriel was blind, and it was in vain that Mrs. Hawleigh endeavoured to discover any sign that the veil that hid the life around him from his eyes showed any tendency to lift, and give back to her son the glorious gift of sight.

The cottage that they had found was little short of an artist's paradise. A little house of one story, shut out from the lonely moor-road by a privet hedge, and sheltered from the winds by high elms and poplars, which bowed their heads in sage appreciation of the secrets whispered to one another by their intermingling branches, when the moor winds woke them to murmur.

Their lives were as quiet and uneventful as lives can be. Maye and Gabriel made music together a good deal. Fortunately, Gabriel, virtuoso as he had laughingly declared himself to be, had the faculty of playing by ear, and from memory, highly developed. Now that the faculty had become a necessity, it had increased wonderfully, and they spent long, happy mornings together, lost in the clouds of harmony with which they filled the little cottage, playing over all Gabriel's old repertoire, learning new masterpieces, which Maye would play on the piano for Gabriel to pick up on the violin, and yet more often breaking into the wild, passionate improvisations that had been the delight of the favoured few in the Holland Street colony who had been permitted to hear them.

In the afternoon, the two would go out for walks on the moor, arm-in-arm, chattering gayly over the points of landscape which Maye described, as minutely as she could, to her poor blind boy. And when, as sometimes happened, Gabriel had a return of his old listlessness and disappointment, and wanted to be left alone with his mother or with his thoughts, Maye would wander forth alone, and explore the country for new spots to which she might lead Gabriel when next they took the air together. It was on one of these solitary excursions that she made an accidental discovery that was the beginning of the end of my story.

She had been practising with Gabriel all the morning, and in the afternoon he had felt tired, and had gone to his room instead of taking his customary stroll on the moor, and Maye, feeling hipped and cramped in the little house, had shod herself with the uncompromising boots which she reserved for such excursions, had armed herself with the ground-ash sapling that was her constant escort in her country walks, and had started out alone, along a new road, which led she knew not whither.

As she walked, the girl's mind was busy revolving the changes that had come into her life, analyzing her feelings with a calm introspection that would have done credit to the Princess Daphne herself. She loved Gabriel Hawleigh with all her soul—but did she yield her heart to him? Though she was as steadfast as ever in her purpose to marry him and strive to make his life lighter for him in his blindness, yet a vague questioning mood would sometimes come over her, which frightened her, though she took it in hand, and never let it interfere with her course along the path of what she considered to be her duty. Were I writing a romance—telling of things that never happened—I should have caused my ideal maiden, Maye Trevethick, to love her betrothed husband all the more wildly, all the more devotedly, for his blindness, but I am speaking of a real, living woman—a good, pure, English maid, with all the real feelings of her age and sex strong in her healthy young soul. Maye was not a girl to idealize, or to hide her feelings from herself. She was nineteen, and full of life and of wonder at the world; she had all the curiosity, the enthusiasm, of her age; and she had bestowed her fair young self, a tribute of gratitude, upon the boy whose life she was, whose light she was to be in every sense of the word, whose mother had been a mother to her, and to whom she was bound by every tie of recognition. Yes! My ideal maiden should have loved the boy the more dearly, the more devotedly, for his affliction; but Maye, though strong in her single-hearted purpose to marry Gabriel whenever he should wish it, realized that her life was doomed to be blotted out, to be devoted to the care of an invalid whose only knowledge of her fresh young beauty must be the memory of the face he had so often fixed upon his canvas—the face that went laughing by in the darkness, in his picture "Sunshine in the Fog," whilst the blind man made music for her laughter that it joyed him to hear, but whose smile he would never see.

"Oh! Gabriel—Gabriel!" she cried out sometimes in her great loneliness; "if only I could give you my eyes, and my life with them, my poor blind love! You will never see me again—and after we are married it will be the same—darkness—darkness always—always. Oh, God! I am a wretch to feel it like this, to think of it even for an instant; but the thought is sometimes terrible—terrible. If only I could think of nothing but his faithful love, his strong, true-hearted devotion to me before he became a great man—and blind; but I can't—I can't. What use is it that I am young, and that people tell me that I am fair? he can never see me now. What use will it be to make our home beautiful around him? Oh! why has my love changed so? I do not love him less ah, no! not less; but the love is not the same. Would that I could be his servant instead of his wife?—but that cannot be. Even when we were in town Eric Trevanion was more useful to him than I; and now he constantly wishes that Eric was here with us. Pray God he may not come—but no, he cannot—he has only one thought, and that thought Daphne! Ah! why do I not hate her?—but I can't—she loves Eric so dearly—and I?—well, well, I felt like a fiend before I left London, when I wished that *I* were blind that he might lead *me* about and read for me, as he did for Gabriel. Oh, Gabriel, Gabriel, why is my love for you changing?—for I can feel it changing, here at my heart; and the thought is killing me."

And, wondering thus, she walked along the Cornish roads, buried in thought, and not noticing whither her wandering feet were leading her. She was roused suddenly from her reverie to see the sun slanting to the west, and knew that it was time she returned home. Returned home! Yes, certainly; but where was she? She appeared to have reached the borders of the moor, and not a human habitation was in sight, not a human being of whom she could ask her way.

After considering the matter profoundly for a while, at a place where three roads met, she decided at last to follow one of them, in the hope of meeting someone who could put her right, and started off, feeling a little bit frightened, and, to tell the truth, a little bit tired. But she dared not acknowledge this to herself, for she knew that she had a long way to walk home, even after she got the direction, and that she must not increase her worry by the confession, even to herself, that she was weary.

She had walked along the road she had chosen for upwards of a mile without seeing any sign of human occupation of the county, and was beginning to feel a singular tendency to cry—for Maye was only a woman, after all—when, the road taking a sudden turn, she found herself confronted by a high gate leading apparently into a park. There was no lodge, but the private road inside the gate showed such signs of cultivation that she concluded that it must lead to a house, and so, mustering all her courage, she opened the gate, which was fortunately not locked, and went in.

Where *was* that house? The drive, for drive it appeared to be, seemed interminable. Tired as she was, it seemed as if she had walked for hours between the high and carefully trimmed hedges of rhododendron and laurestinus, and she was just preparing to give up in despair and retrace her footsteps, when suddenly the hedges stopped, opened, and the road dipped. I say dipped, because she found herself standing on the summit of a steep declivity, where the road suddenly plunged into a great hollow, at the bottom of which lay what seemed to Maye to be the most beautiful old house she had ever seen in her life. The precipitation of the incline was modified for wayfarers by the road curving round it to reach the bottom by an easier slope; and it stopped at a moat, a veritable moat, the mediaeval appearance of which was only modernized by its being crossed by a comparatively new stone bridge, which seemed to be carefully gravelled.

On the moat itself a few swans and innumerable ducks sailed hither and thither, leaving broad fan-like wakes behind them on the mirror-smooth surface of the water; and, apparently surrounded by the moat and standing in a sweet, soft lawn that resembled green plush as she looked down upon it, there rose a lovely old house, built half of gray stone and half of grand old ruddy brick, with here and there an excrescence in the form of a wing of a more modern style of architecture. The whole seemed softened and tender, as if its angles had been rounded off by the gentle, continuous kiss of Time, which had spread over the crevices of the masonry an embroidery of soft lichens, with here and there a tuft of saxifrage or a golden ball of stone-crop. Into the deathly stillness of the summer afternoon a perpendicular column of blue smoke rose here and there from the clustered chimney-stacks, and gave a touch of life to this old-time manor-house; and as she stood stricken motionless by the beauty of the place, she espied a gardener driving a mowing-machine over a far angle of the inner lawn. A gentle whirr rose into the air from the machine, and then she saw, dotted here and there on the slopes that surrounded the house, lying lazily under the oaks and elms that protected this elysium from the winds of the moor, a few great black oxen, which gave no sign of life save an occasional sway of the head as they reached for some hitherto unnoticed tuft of clover.

A feeling of intense repose stole over her weary senses as she prepared to descend into the hollow and ask the man who was mowing, where she was, when suddenly her purpose was checked by the sound of wheels behind her. Whatever it was that approached, humanity, in some form or other, must accompany it, so she waited until the vehicle should reach the spot where she stood as if enchanted. The sound of the wheels drew nearer, and at last a dog-cart turned the corner, driven by a man. Maye's first feminine spasm of apprehension was banished as, on a second inspection, the man appeared to possess the requisite number of years to allay her sexual alarm. It was an *old* man, and the dog-cart perceptibly slackened its speed as its occupant caught sight of the girl standing there, looking at him.

As he saw that she was about to speak, the driver stopped his horse, and the trim servant who clung to the back seat jumped down and posted himself, tigerwise, at the animal's head, as the old gentleman, with an awkward movement, jerked off his hat and threw it on again.

"I have lost my way," began Miss Trevethick, quailing a little under his questioning look, "and I came up this drive hoping to find someone who could direct me. Can you tell me how to get back to the village of Arthisham-by-Dartmoor

"Arthisham-by-Dartmoor! Do you wish to walk back there this evening, young lady?" said the old gentleman, with a look of astonishment.

"Yes—if you please—is it far?"

"It's nine miles."

"Nine miles!—oh dear! what shall I do?—they will be so anxious about me."

"They?"

"My aunt and my cousin. I live with them about a mile beyond Arthisham. I came out for a walk, and missed the road home—oh! how can I get back?—will you please direct me?"

"But, my dear young lady, it will be nearly dark before you get back; you will miss the road again. Dear, dear, dear—what an unfortunate occurrence!"

"I think, sir," said poor Maye, striving hard not to burst into tears, "that if you could send a servant a little way with me, to see me on the right road, I can find my way back. I am accustomed to going about alone."

"But you should have brought your cousin with you; pardon me, has it not been a little imprudent of you?"

"My cousin is blind."

"Oh!—Forgive me, pray;" and the old gentleman's face was crossed by a look of perplexity as he glanced from the young girl, looking so pretty and so piteous before him, to his steaming horse.

"I tell you what, young lady; I hardly know what to say to you; but if you will jump up here, we will go down to the house, and whilst my man harnesses another horse to a phaeton, my housekeeper will give you some tea—you must want it—and then my man here will drive you home. No, I will take no excuse; I haven't any daughter of my own, but I should be very sorry, if I had one, to let her walk twenty miles."

And so Maye got up, her weariness almost dazing her, a feeling of infinite comfort and safety stealing over her as she took her place at the old gentleman's side, and reached the front door of the old house across the moat.

"What a lovely old place——" she began, but her admiration was cut short by the appearance of an eminently respectable housekeeper, who, after giving her a searching glance of strong disapproval, took her in charge and carried her off, after a few words of explanation from her master, to perform the mysterious rites of the brush and comb.

When she came down again to the great hall, whose polished floor was strewn with fine old English rugs, her unexpected host was ready to do, bachelorwise, the honours of the tea-table, and whilst she chatted with him about her adventures of the afternoon and the old-time pleasance in which she found herself by such a lucky chance, she was almost sorry when a most modern and comfortable phaeton drove up to the door, and a pair of strawberry roans pawed the gravel as if impatient to carry her away from this Eve-less paradise.

Maye rose, and thanking her host, prepared to go.

"If you will not be bored by an old man's company, my dear, will you let me drive you home? I shall be able to reassure your aunt—er?"

"Mrs. Hawleigh."

"Exactly—your aunt, Mrs. Hawleigh, on the subject of your long absence. She must indeed be uneasy about you."

"I shall be delighted, I am sure," said Maye, a feeling coming over her that she liked this gruffly courteous old Cornishman very much indeed.

And so they got into the phaeton, and her elderly Galahad took the reins.

"I am quite gratified at the accident that has procured for me the pleasure of your acquaintance, Miss Hawleigh," said he, as they reached the top of the hollow and began rolling swiftly down the drive she had walked up with such very different feelings half an hour before.

"My name is not Hawleigh," corrected she; "Mrs. Hawleigh is my aunt. My name is Trevethick, Maye Trevethick."

"Trevethick! why, that's a Cornish name," replied her escort.

"Yes—my father was a Cornishman."

"*Was* a Cornishman?"

"Yes—my father died in India five years ago."

"God bless my soul!—you are not going to tell me that you are the daughter of Claude Trevethick, of the Indian Civil Service."

"Yes—did you know him?"

"Know him! Why, yes, very well—and his wife too—she——?"

"I am an orphan."

"Dear, dear, dear! poor child! But I'm right glad to have met you, my dear, and am more than ever thankful that you lost your way this afternoon. Dear, dear, dear! I wonder if you ever heard your father speak of Eric Trevanion of Trthwwsthpllgg Manor?"

※

Eric Trevanion! Eric Trevanion! She was driving home with Eric's father—"the Autocrat of Trthwwsthpllgg Manor," as she had so often heard Eric laughingly call him.

Her feelings at the strangeness of the situation the varied emotions that it roused in her soul, combined with the weariness that was beginning to take effect on her poor, tired little body—caused her almost a feeling of faintness, and she sank into a reverie which Mr. Trevanion, taking it for natural exhaustion, forebore to disturb with any attempt at protracted conversation. So they drove along almost in silence—the old gentleman periodically ejaculating:

"Dear, dear, dear! what a little world it is!—just think of it! —how strange!—who would have dreamt of it? Egad! it's like a novel. So you are Claude's child?—dear, dear, dear!"

And so they reached the cottage, where they found Mrs. Hawleigh and Gabriel in an agony of apprehension, which changed into a chorus of gratitude and satisfaction as Maye disappeared, thanking "her preserver" once more for his charity to her.

Mr. Trevanion remained but a few minutes, but before he left he had heard the latest news of his son, whom he was astounded to find was a friend of the family; and he took his departure, promising to return next day to inquire after the maiden whom he had rescued so fortunately, and in whom he expressed an interest that was more than paternal.

On the following day, true to his promise, and on many days following, Mr. Trevanion came over to see the Hawleighs and

Maye, till at last Gabriel laughingly declared that he was getting quite jealous of Eric Trevanion, senior, and should send for Eric Trevanion, junior, to keep his father in order. It was a hard trial sometimes for Maye when old Trevanion would pour forth his solitary woes to Mrs. Hawleigh, in the little cottage parlour, on the text of his son's absence.

"He has a comfortable home waiting for him here, my dear madam; why doesn't he return to it? Starving! I've no doubt he is; he was never made to get his own living, and never will. I don't ask much of him—only that he should come down here and live with me, part of the year, at any rate; and then, it's high time he married—we Trevanions have always married young, and never out of the county. I don't know who that Miss Préault is, that he seems to be so fond of, but I won't have my boy marrying an American adventuress."

"Miss Préault is hardly an adventuress," mildly expostulated Mrs. Hawleigh. "She comes of a very fine old American family of the South—she is certainly very beautiful, and very fond of Eric," concluded she, guardedly.

"That is all very well—that is as it may be, of course—but a Trevanion must marry a Cornish girl. Trthwwsthpllgg Manor has never been shared by a foreigner, and, please God, it never will. Tell me—did my son know your niece before she became betrothed to your son?"

"Oh! yes, Mr. Trevanion. We have known Eric ever since he came to London."

"Is it possible?—is it possible?"

Maye rose and joined Gabriel on the veranda, where he loved to sit for hours at a time, listening, he said, to the world-sounds, differentiating, with all the super-sensitive keenness of a blind man's ear, between the innumerable murmurs that filled the quiet summer air.

Left alone with Mrs. Hawleigh, Mr. Trevanion returned to the charge.

"Tell me, my dear Mrs. Hawleigh," said he; "what truth is there in the stories they tell of my boy and this Miss Daphne Préault? What is the meaning of this infatuation of his?"

208

"Really, Mr. Trevanion," was the still guarded answer, "I cannot tell you more than you already know. They are great friends and constant companions, and Eric seems very anxious to marry her."

"Good heavens! when he might have married your niece! I tell you, my dear madam——"

"Hush!" exclaimed Mrs. Hawleigh, in an undertone; "Gabriel will hear you; his ears catch almost every sound now; it is his keenest sense."

"Well, well!" returned Eric's father, in a lower tone, "it's no use crying over spilt milk in that direction, and I should be very sorry to see my boy rob another man of his sweetheart; but I confess to you that I'm very uneasy and anxious about Eric. We are not children, my dear madam; my boy says nothing about marriage with this woman, and there is only one interpretation to be put upon it. I know he must be very poor, and sometimes I have a horrible dread that he is indebted to her for material assistance. Will you not help me? I'm hasty and bad-tempered—a little too authoritative with him, perhaps; can you not soften my methods by supplementing them with yours?—can you not help me to get him down here?"

"I will try, Mr. Trevanion."

"And then I want you all to come over and live at Trthwwsthpllgg until your son's sight is restored, or sufficiently so to enable him to return home. You are cramped and lonely here; at Trthwwsthpllgg there are distractions of all kinds, even for a blind man. Ah! do not say no, my dear madam; it is an old fellow's whim, and it is for my son's sake that I ask it of you."

So Trevanion *père* wrote another and more urgent prayer to his son, to leave his modern Circe, or Helen, or whatever she was to him; and Mrs. Hawleigh wrote him a long letter full of entreaties from Gabriel, who longed to have him come and read to him, and talk to him as he had done in the last days in Holland Street. But Eric was enthralled by his own morbid sensitiveness, and had not the moral courage to break the chain that was beginning to gall him so fearfully.

His honour, rooted in dishonour stood,
And faith unfaithful kept him falsely true!"

Well, well, he was not so very much to blame—he was only a man, after all, and I never knew a man who was morally as strong as the weakest woman I ever met. This is a fact which has been remarked by far profounder observers than I, and the explanation has yet to be found for it. I suppose that it is the compensation that is given to woman for her physical inferiorities and infirmities; perhaps it is in consequence of this physical inferiority that she is always more or less on the defensive, and has realized the advantages of delay and patience. At any rate, the man has yet to be born who can scheme towards an end, can wait behind his defences, can act with the pitiless directness, and if necessary bear the mental and physical agony that every woman can bear—*not* in consequence of her education or determination, but simply because she is a woman! Woman always acts on her convictions, unless she is in love; and she is nearly always right to do so. This is doubtless why women always ask for a reason, and never listen to one. This is, however, by the way; let us return to our story.

One of Mr. Trevanion's greatest delights was to come or send over for Mrs. Hawleigh, Gabriel, and Maye, and keep them at Trthwwsthpllgg Manor all day, sending them back the last thing at night; and Gabriel seemed to revel in the quiet that filled the hollow round the old manor-house. His host had fitted up, for the special purpose of receiving the family, a boudoir that had belonged to Mrs. Trevanion,—who had died when Eric was quite a child,—a little room situated in an angle of the house, with a conservatory leading out of it; and in this conservatory he had arranged a lounge shrouded by ferns and high plants, where Gabriel could lie when he felt weary, revelling in the moist, soft perfume which filled the place. There he would remain for hours, as he did on the verandah at the cottage, whilst Mrs. Hawleigh and Maye explored the hidden treasures of the grand old building, from haunted garret to subterranean passage leading nowhere, below the moat. The whole place was a perfect paradise to Maye, who was always discovering new nooks and beauties in it, and in her frankly expressed appreciation, came nearer and nearer to the old man's heart as the days collected into weeks. Even the old housekeeper got over her suspicion of this new face about the house and Mr. Trevanion used laughingly to call her "the fair Chatelaine of Trthwwsthpllgg." It may also be mentioned that Maye had given further evidence of her Cornish origin by being the only person about the place, with the exception of Mr. Trevanion, who could say "Trthwwsthpllgg" quickly, without premeditation, and without immediately suffering from paralysis of the tongue.

"I envy you your children," said their host to Mrs. Hawleigh; "upon my soul, I envy you. I wish my boy were more like yours, and I wish Maye Trevethick were going to be my daughter-in-law instead of yours."

And Mrs. Hawleigh would laugh it off, though sometimes she threw an anxious glance in the direction of the pair as they walked round the moat arm-in-arm, Maye chattering gayly and describing it all to Gabriel; he with his blind brown eyes fixed on the darkness before him, whilst he smiled at his conductress and played with the fingers of the hand that held his own.

They had been living happy in this new phase of their exile for about three weeks when an anxious day dawned for Mrs. Hawleigh. Dr. Richardson, Gabriel's London physician, had determined to come down to Dartmoor to report on the progress of his patient towards recovery. It had been almost impossible to say, before the Hawleighs left town, what Gabriel's chances really were. His health was so impaired by the shock that a perfect diagnosis was almost impossible, and Dr. Richardson had promised to come down, when the grand air of the moor should have had its effect upon Gabriel's bodily health, to make a new examination of his eyes. The long-looked-for visit was now expected, and it had been arranged that Maye should spend the day at Trthwwsthpllgg Manor, returning only after the departure of Dr. Richardson in the evening for London. He could not stay over until the following morning.

Accordingly, "the Autocrat of Trthwwsthpllgg" had driven over early and carried her off, taking her for a long drive round the neighborhood before they arrived at the manor-house for lunch.

In the early afternoon the old gentleman and the young girl were sitting together on the lawn within the moat, when suddenly he startled her by saying:

"Have you any definite notion when you are going to be married, my dear?"

"No," she had replied, suddenly awakened from a delicious reverie about nothing at all.

"Supposing this blindness of Gabriel Hawleigh's should prove to be really incurable after all?"

"Well?"

"In that case would you still become his wife?"

"Oh, yes! Mr. Trevanion. How could you doubt it for a moment?"

"And what would you live upon, my dear?"

"I—I—don't know," faltered Maye, helplessly. "I never think about it."

"But surely you *must* think about it, my child. Do not think me inquisitive or impertinent, but I think I understood Mrs. Hawleigh to say that the only means you have consist of her annuity and what Gabriel made by his painting."

"Yes—that is true."

"And if Gabriel can never paint again? Supposing (which heaven forbid!) Mrs. Hawleigh should die? What would you young people do?"

"I—I don't know," answered the girl. "I can paint a little, and I can play the piano. I could teach—and—and—I suppose we should get along somehow," she concluded, vaguely.

A long pause ensued, which was broken at last by Mr. Trevanion saying, as if to himself:

"What an affliction! what an affliction!—for an artist of all men, too! Just as he had planted his foot on the first rung of the ladder of fame—to be blinded, with only his art as a means of support! Well—well! how capricious Fortune is! There is my son

212

Eric; he might be rich and prosperous, and can see as well as you and I can; whilst poor Gabriel, who depends on his eyes for a living, is blinded at what is practically the very commencement of his career."

"Oh! do not speak of it, I beg of you, Mr. Trevanion it is all so sad—so sad—and so hopeless."

"Well—there! I won't say any more about it. But—Maye, my dear child forgive me if I say that if you could have loved my boy, and he had been worthy of you, I should have been the happiest man in Cornwall—nay, in the world! If only you could have loved him!"

If only she could have loved him! Ah—yi!

And deep in her heart Maye knew that the love of her whole life had been given, long ago, to the son of the man who sat by her side pleading for his boy—who had never known—and asking nothing better than to end his days in his beautiful old manor-house, whilst the woman by his side laid her touch upon everything there to brighten it, and the old oak-panelled corridors echoed with the laughter of his grandchildren.

✳

The drive back was accomplished almost in silence. Mr. Trevanion left her at the garden gate, promising to drive over in the morning to hear the news about Gabriel.

The news about Gabriel! Dr. Richardson had come and gone; had gone away looking very grave, and leaving with Mrs. Hawleigh only a very slender remnant of the hope she had brought with her from Holland Street. He was to hold another consultation with the eminent oculist in London, and in a week or ten days, at most, was to write Mrs. Hawleigh his final opinion and Verdict on the case of Gabriel, her son.

This was the news which the laird of Trthwwsthpllgg heard next morning when he came over to the cottage—news which he received with genuine expressions of grief. Only Gabriel seemed unaffected by his lot—he wandered about the house quietly as heretofore, now and then playing a few bars on his violin, which lay ever ready to his hand in the little parlour, or strolling out into the garden among the flowers, which he had come to know by their perfume and touch.

Before he left, Mr. Trevanion said:

"By-the-by, in my concern at receiving your news I almost forgot to give you mine. Eric, my boy, has at last yielded to our prayers—he is coming down to Trthwwsthpllgg. I am going to meet him at the station on my way home."


# CHAPTER XI.
## Attraction and Repulsion.

"It is a long lane that has no turning," said a philosopher whose name is, I believe, lost to the posterity by which he is quoted. The critically-disposed may say that the turning is of little use to the traveller if he does not reach it before he falls from very weariness. Another proverbial philosopher has said that, "When things are at their worst, they are sure to mend." This dogmatist had more reason than the other, and if he thought of it at all before he said it, he had probably observed that things mend when they are at their worst, because it is then and not until then, that, throwing everything aside, and sacrificing our feelings to the instinct of self-preservation, we are forced to make the supreme effort which, made earlier in the game, would have obviated the progression of "things" to their possible worst. It must not be supposed that I recommend the utilization of the supreme effort one moment before it becomes absolutely necessary; on the contrary, *nec deus intersit, dignus ni vindice nodus*, as the Classic says. Never—despite the axiom—do today what can possibly be put off till tomorrow. Procrastination, as I have before remarked in these pages, is the soul of business, notwithstanding the oratorical assertion of the copy-book to the contrary.

Things were not yet at their very worst for Eric Trevanion. It was fortunate for him and for my story that he did not know this. Had he imagined that it was possible for him to be more supremely wretched than he was when we left him last, he would assuredly have killed himself. His feeling for Daphne Préault was only one of the profoundest pity—a pity that was reflected upon himself.

Eric Trevanion was pitiably poor: he had rebelled against receiving assistance from Daphne, and was living, miserably, on what he could make by his pen. His pride being crushed, he no longer wrote in the high-flown, debonair style of the scholar and man of the world: he had turned his talent to baser uses, and had made it pay him, inadequately to his bare needs, but still it paid him. His poems, which were sicklied o'er with the stupidity and incomprehensibility of the decennium in which he lived, came home to him like curses, send them where he would: at length he had made a holocaust of them, and in sheer cynicism had scribbled off a set of rhymes of social small-talk, with a slang refrain. These he sent to a society paper, which accepted them, paid for them at once, and asked him to write more. An idyllic story which his soul had loved more and more every time a magazine editor returned it to him, he had ruthlessly cut to pieces, interpolating a series of incidents that turned it into a glaring advertisement of a patent medicine. He sent the MS. to the proprietors of said specific, and received by return of post a cheque which cleared his landwoman's scorbutic physiognomy of the scowl it had worn for a month past. With the exception of his lodging-bill he kept out of debt, and for the most pertinent of all reasons—he could not get into it. Things got bad by degrees and beautifully worse, and Eric became a literary hack. The position had one advantage: the occupation of his days, spent among his kind in the Reading-room of the British Museum, took him far from Daphne, who idled away her life in Holland Street in practically no companionship save that of Mahmouré du Peyral, with whom she had struck up an intimacy that caused Eric a mingled feeling of fear, jealousy, and disgust. It seemed to him that the society of the penniless horde of scribblers who practically lived in the Museum, he breathed a purer atmosphere than that which filled the perfumed studio in Holland Street.

It was at this period of his history that I first got to know him well, for I also was one of the gang that day after day breathed that invigorating atmosphere of book-dust, penury, and ink. We adopted Eric as one of us, for he was as poor as the poorest of the crew, and today, when we are most of us respectable members of society, we often talk together of what Theophile Gautier called, with perfect truth, "those happy days when we were so miserable!"

And our misery *was* happy. What a merry crowd we were! There are men whom I meet today, rich, respected, and celebrated, who were then poor, disreputable, and obscure. I remember one day in particular, when a man who now commands whatever price he likes to ask, for anything he writes, came down to the Museum, his haggard face irradiated with a smile of triumph—he had not tasted food for forty-eight hours, and I don't believe that the lot of us possessed a pound between us. We crowded round him to hear the news. He had a commission to write a special article for a leading review. He had received five pounds on account, and was to receive fifteen on delivery of the manuscript—and the manuscript was to be delivered next day. He was an incorrigible idler, and we banded together to make him knock off the article, inviting ourselves to dine with him on the following night. Then we left him alone, and in the afternoon I went to his seat to find out how he had got on. He was entrenched behind a fortification of reference-books and authorities; and the article well!—not a line was written; he had spent the day in writing a Latin ode in exquisite elegiacs, which I still possess (it hangs, framed, on the wall of my study), on the contrast between the colour of the Superintendent's hair and Fitzgerald Molloy's neck-tie. He went home that evening without having approached the subject of his article, and we were in despair. He owed me five shillings, and hope had been telling me a flattering tale all day, to the effect that I was going to get it back. Next evening, at six o'clock, he took down to the office of the —— *Review* a positive masterpiece, which practically laid the foundation of his present fame; and "the gang" dined with him at Rampazzi's in Soho, and adjourned for an all-night sitting at his rooms in Great Ormond Street, Bloomsbury. That is how we lived, and Eric Trevanion with us.

We soon "licked him into shape," and gradually he sank with us from literature to journalism, as a preliminary towards rising from journalism to literature by the ladder of advertisement. He was not quite a stranger among us, for I had met him in Holland Street, and Bernard Rawlinson was intermittently one of the crew. It was through him that Eric joined us, and it was to that versatile genius that he owed his first lesson in practical journalism. Eric had been sitting idle at his seat all the morning, when Rawlinson came and asked him why he didn't write, instead of gazing on vacancy in search of inspiration.

"I have nothing to write about that anybody wants to read," replied he, dolefully.

"Well, what of it?" replied the Bohemian; "write about nothing."

"What bosh!" exclaimed Trevanion. "I defy anybody to write about nothing."

"Defy anybody, if you like," was the answer, "but don't defy me;" and, so saying, he sat down and wrote the following, which, short and fabricless, was completely to the point, and sold for one pound ten!

## NOTHING!
### A Study of Modern Journalistic Art.

A boy whom I left in a little country town, beloved of parents who were quite unparentally charming, wrote to me a few months ago, and asked my advice as to whether he should give up his obscure and uninteresting, but comparatively lucrative position on a stool in a provincial bank, to embrace the profession of letters, to matriculate in journalism and graduate as a literary man. I sent him at once Balzac's "Bible of the Journalist," to wit, the two volumes of the 'Illusions Perdues' and "Splendeurs et Misères des Courtisanes," accompanying this gift with two grains of pure aconitine in a gelatine capsule. I instructed him to read the first, and then, if he still felt himself endowed with a constitution, mental and physical, that warranted him in living or dying on what he could get out of letters, to find a spot where it was not untidy to die, to lie down, and swallow the alkaloid.

He wrote back shortly afterwards, returning me the poison and announcing that he had decided to follow the fortunes of Lucien de Rubempré, rather than be warned by the fate of Balzac's hero. In vain I pointed out to him the fact that nowadays Coralies and Mlle. de Grandlieus are scarce, if not an extinct race; he abandoned his regular hours and salary, and began to starve on the potential proceeds of precariously launched articles that interested no one, and that editors betrayed a tendency to refuse consistently to buy. Nay more; so badly was he bitten, so profoundly did he develop the hydrophobia of literature, that, realizing his small possessions, he came up to London, like a modern Lucien, and proceeded to starve in the great metropolis.

Proud as Lucifer, he confided his penury to no one; it had no outward and visible sign save in the poverty of his lodgings, to which he admitted never a soul; and he died in my arms a fortnight ago, of combined starvation and nervous prostration.

Why? Ah! that is the point. He died because he had nothing to write about, and yet could not write about it. He—died of starvation, here in Bloomsbury—because he could not write unless he had a subject to write upon.

The man who cannot write about nothing at a moment's notice cannot make a living as a journalist.

Priggish societies with ridiculous names have met and discussed learnedly—if chaotically—'The Nothingness of Everything': a literary *coterie* that will establish the "Everythingness of Nothing" has yet to rise, Phoenix-like, from the ashes of unsuccessful journalists. It is a solemn and an undeniable *fact*, that unless one can write a column on Nothing at all, and do it more or less attractively, one has no right to attach one's self to the permanent staff of a journal—in point of fact, one can't get there.

It is the age of journalistic commonplace; one must idealize commonplace trifles, or one cannot expect to be understood. This state of things arises from the *blasé* condition of the modern reader's faculties. The literary exaltation of Nothing is the only pabulum which the debilitated intellects of a large class of readers today are capable of assimilating. Therefore let us establish schools for the development and study of mental anaemia, that a new generation of writers may arise in our midst, whose works shall be 'easily understanded of the people.' because their end is the glorification of Nothing at All.

[Signed] BERNARD RAWLINSON.

"There," said the picturesque Bernard, as he handed over the manuscript with a smile, "that is how to write about Nothing. Go, thou, and do likewise."

But Eric found it very hard to "go and do likewise." He went through the whole gamut of literary insuccess. Often editors—cultivated men—would be charmed by the epigrammatic way in which he would present the most uninteresting matter, and, on the spur of the moment, would accept his manuscripts; but he scanned their journals in vain in the hope of seeing himself in print, and finally, when he called upon them or wrote on the subject, they would return him his work with something like shame, "regretting that want of space prevented them from utilizing his articles, for the offer of which, however, they thanked him, and remained faithfully his," etc., etc., etc.; and at the conclusion of his day's contemplative quietude in the Museum, he would return to Holland Street, almost dreading to enter the studio which had become associated in his mind with so many sweet and bitter thoughts.

One evening, when he arrived at Daphne Préault's, a surprise awaited him. He had divested himself of his impedimenta in the hall, and penetrated to the studio. As he did so, a man who was sitting chatting with Daphne and Mahmouré rose and held out his hand.

"What!" he exclaimed; "Dr. Van Boomkamp! this is indeed an unexpected pleasure."

"I was waiting for you," returned the psychologist, scrutinizing him keenly through his gold *pince-nez*. "Miss Préault and Madame du Peyral are deep in business matters. I have hoped to meet you again, and tonight my hope is realized. Will you do me the pleasure of taking dinner with me at my hotel, and we can continue the conversation that we began at Dr. P——'s?"

Eric looked at Daphne, and she answered his look by saying: "Yes, Eric. Madame du Peyral and I have some important business to discuss, and some correspondence to go through. We shall be glad to have you out of the way, *tres cher*."

"In that case," said Eric, "I am quite at your service, Dr. Van Boomkamp;" and so it was arranged.

Towards seven o'clock the two men took their departure, and left the two women together.

It was not until they found themselves seated comfortably after dinner in Dr. Van Boomkamp's room at the Hotel Metropole, that they approached the subject which was of the deepest interest to both of them. It was the American who opened the conversation by saying:

"Miss Préault and Madame du Peyral seem to have taken a great fancy to one another, do they not?"

"Yes—it is a very strange sympathy, and one that I cannot understand," replied Trevanion. "As you know, doubtless, without my telling you, Miss Préault and I have been, and I trust are still, very great friends. I know her life very well for the last four years. Until now no woman has ever been her intimate friend;

220

this Madame du Peyral seems to possess a strange fascination over her."

"Strange—yes—to the casual observer, but to the psychologist not so strange. You are, I know, the intimate friend of Miss Préault. Owing to circumstances into which it is not necessary to enter, I know a great deal concerning Madame du Peyral, and their friendship interests whilst it fails to astonish me. It is of this that I wish to speak to you."

"You knew Paul du Peyral?"

"I saw him die."

"Ah!"

"You doubtless remember my recounting a curious psychological case at Dr. P——'s on the occasion of our first meeting?"

"Yes."

"The man and woman in New York, to whom I alluded, were Paul and Madame du Peyral."

"And the woman in Europe?"

"Was Miss Daphne Préault."

"Good God! She said something to this effect herself, when I repeated your story."

"In all my experience with the workings of mental science I have never encountered a stranger case. Accident has gathered all the threads into my hands, and I have postponed my visit to Paris for the purpose of watching the *dénouement* of the drama, for drama it is, in every acceptation of the term."

"What do you want of me?"

"Well, it is needless to say that whatever you will be good enough to say to me, will remain under the seal of a professional confidence. I want you to tell me all you know of Miss Préault— of her life from the moment you became—er—connected; of her mental state, of her physical illness—everything."

"So be it."

And Eric gave to the American doctor, who listened intently, every now and then making an entry in his note-book or asking for a date, a complete account of the circumstances which had puzzled, had frightened him, with regard to the woman who, before her most serious attack, had been "The Princess Daphne."

At the conclusion of his recital, he said:

"Now, Dr. Van Boomkamp, I have been eminently explicit with you; may I ask for an exchange of confidence? What is your explanation of these phenomena?"

Schuyler Van Boomkamp rose and paced the room in silence for a few moments. Finally, re-seating himself, he spoke as follows:

"The case turns upon a strange coincidence of personality existing between Miss Préault and Paul du Peyral. She was almost what the Germans call his *doppelgänger*, and on his death his personality became merged in hers."

"Then——?"

"Miss Daphne Préault is Paul du Peyral."

"For heaven's sake, explain yourself!"

"Psychological science, founded as it is upon neurology, despite the labors of Georget, of Charcot, of Bell, of Bain, of Kollmann, and a host of others, is practically in its infancy. Mesmerism is a phenomenon which the conditions of its existence render very difficult to examine scientifically. Here we have two people, who, though separated by half a hemisphere, were practically identical with one another, speaking psychologically. Through the medium of this strange foreign woman their souls found one another, and little by little Paul du Peyral transferred his psychic force to Miss Daphne Préault. The completeness with which this was done was due to the fact that, springing from a common ancestry, they have, by a freak of heredity, "thrown back," as it were. The exact physical process it is impossible to describe—the result has been apparent in what we will call, for the sake of definition, Miss Préault's fits of obsession. These occurred coincidentally with Paul du Peyral's experiments. The culminating phenomenon occurred with the death of du Peyral: his illness was answered, as it were, by Miss Préault's, and at the moment that he died he fancied that he *saw* her; at the moment of her apparent death his soul seems to have sought hers, and was seen, or apparently seen, by the black woman Clytemnestra, who has always been closely allied with her. His wife, by reason of his repeated experiments with her, has become strongly identified with him, but his *soul* sought that of his *alter ego*—Miss Préault. He was a man of little or no principle; in Miss Préault the good and the bad seem to have been about equally divided; the good was dying out in her when its place was taken by the salient features of his personality. She lived again with his soul, but the strain has been too great, she is overburdened by a vitality from which she cannot escape, and which she cannot bear; his wife sapped his physical attributes, Miss Préault his mental ones. They are both disordered, ill-regulated, mentally diseased in consequence; Miss Préault is, and has been, in a state of physical and mental hysteria ever since this transference took place; Madame du Peyral, robbed, to use a nautical simile, of her steering apparatus, her guiding principle, has been vainly seeking for it ever since. She has found it; she—though she hardly realizes it herself—fancies that Miss Préault is well, she recognizes in her new friend the vitality, the attributes, the *personality* of her dead husband."

"Explain yourself! What do you mean?"

"I mean that the position requires the most careful supervision, for though they neither of them know it, and though orthodox doctors would be at a loss to admit it, both these women, when in the presence of one another, are *mad!*"

"My God—how awful!"

"Not awful, but deeply interesting."

"They must be separated, of course."

"No—for that would probably either kill them, or drive them dangerously insane in the ordinary sense of the term."

"What then?"

"They must quarrel, and part naturally."

"But how can that be brought about?"

"It will bring itself about in the ordinary course of events. They will probably quarrel over *you*. When that takes place, Madame du Peyral will pursue her journey to Greece, which has been interrupted by this meeting, and I hope that Miss Préault will regain her health and ordinary mental equilibrium."

It was close upon midnight when the two men parted, and Eric trudged home—save the mark!—to Holland Street.

Seeing a light burning in Miss Préault's vestibule, he went in, and passed through to the studio, where he supposed he should find her alone.

The Creole was not alone. As Eric stood motionless in the doorway of the studio he saw Daphne lying in a lazy, languorous attitude upon the lounge, whilst Mahmouré du Peyral sat by her side, her arms twined round her, looking into her eyes. Daphne was playing lazily with the masses of Mahmouré's hair, which she had unbound, and which were floating in tawny billows all over her as she lay among the cushions. Neither woman spoke, but the silence was far more eloquent than words—and Eric, as he stood looking at them, felt his heart swell with a dull, impotent rage against this Greek who had come and thrust herself between him and the woman he had loved. The slight sound he made in entering was unnoticed by Mahmouré, who had her back turned to the door, but Daphne opened a little wider her half-closed eyes and said:

"Ah! Eric. Is that you? I didn't suppose you would come in again tonight."

At the sound of her voice and her words Mahmouré started away, but Daphne, restraining her by winding her arms about the supple little figure, said:

"Don't go away, dear. He isn't going to stay. Eric, *mon cher*, come in the morning, will you? Madame du Peyral is staying here with me tonight. We did not get through our work till it was too late for her to think of going home alone."

Eric turned and left the studio. He had not spoken a word since he entered. Mahmouré du Peyral had not turned her head in his direction. He was glad of it.

Arrived at his own rooms he spent an hour feverishly pacing up and down, reviewing the position and criticising himself, nothing extenuating, nothing hiding. Week by week, month by month, he lived over again the period of his liaison with the fascinating Creole. It had begun with her song at Gabriel Hawleigh's Bohemian *soirée*; it had ended—ended?—with Dr. Schuyler Van Boomkamp's *précis* of the case of the Princess Daphne, and its corroboration before his very eyes half an hour ago. Hardly more than half a year, but in that time what multifold experiences had

224

been his! Every month seemed an age as he looked back upon the time: he had passed through every phase of worldly condition and every *nuance* of the thing called "love." And what had he now? From affluence he had fallen to poverty—sordid, grinding poverty—and from passionate adoration to a feeling very near akin to profound disgust. Daphne Préault had declined from her altitude as queen of his soul, to a weird, monstrous, unnatural problem; and as he thought of the interview next day great beads of perspiration started to his forehead. What would the morrow bring forth? He felt that, before another sun would set, his future course would be definitively shaped and in what direction? He could not tell—he dared not surmise.

He passed a restless night, and next morning waited, watching the door of the cottage opposite for Madame du Peyral's departure. At length it came, and ten minutes later he confronted Daphne Préault in her studio.

"I am glad you are alone," he began; "I have been watching for that woman to leave you. I have something serious to discuss with you."

"Have you?" replied she, her womanly scent giving her premonition of a "scene," and drawing herself into a position of aggressive attention. "If you have a great deal to say you had better begin at once, for she will be back here very soon."

"Back here?"

"Yes I have persuaded her to come and stay with me for a few days—perhaps till she leaves England."

"Oh! indeed! then that makes my way clear before me."

Daphne Préault had selected a cigarette from her case, and, lighting it, had settled herself in the lounge, like some beautiful wild animal, crouching on the defensive, whilst Eric stood looking down at her.

"Daphne," he began, his voice growing stronger and his manner more determined as he went on, "you and I must distinctly understand one another. Our love for one another is not, alas! what it was, and sooner or later we must speak plainly—better today than tomorrow!"

"Certainly, my dear Eric go on."

"You have made life very beautiful for me all these months, and from the bottom of my soul I am grateful, dear; but there should be no question of gratitude between us. A love such as ours has been must live upon itself alone—by itself, and of itself; it cannot decrease, it can only change; and once changed—God help us!—it is extinguished. I have asked you to be my wife. I love you still, in spite of the troubles that have come between us; if you love me in return, I ask you again to share my life with me, and proclaim ourselves one before all men."

"My dear boy why should I?"

"For every reason in the world for your purity, for my honour, for our happiness."

"But, my dear Eric, I am quite content to remain as I am—free—unrestrained Bohemian. Love is for me an ecstasy—I will never make it a bondage."

"Then the love you offer me is not the love I ask of you! It is not love at all—it is mere passion."

"Call it what you will," replied the woman; "it suits me as it is."

"And you would insult the name of love by giving it to an emotion that is capable of no sacrifice?"

"Sacrifice!—have I made no sacrifice already? What would you have of me now?"

"First and foremost that you should give up the friendship of this du Peyral woman. It is infamous, disgraceful, unworthy of you. Then that you should come with me as my wife somewhere, anywhere, to your own America, if you will but to a spot where no one shall be able to whisper about us as they do here."

"Really, Eric—I think it is as well to be as frank with you as you are with me. Your programme does not suit me. I like you—I am rich enough to indulge my likes or dislikes—you shall share my home, my fortune, if you will—but I will not be bound down by any laws. And mark me I will not be dictated to. As for Madame du Peyral or 'the du Peyral woman,' as you contemptuously call her—she attracts and she pleases me. I shall keep up my acquaintance with her in any form I please."

"Very well, then," rejoined Eric, turning a trifle paler and looking yet more determined; "you will have to choose between her and me."

"Exactly!"

"And your choice is?"

"*Mon cher ami*—she has all the charm of novelty!"

"Novelty!—Good God!"

"Yes novelty. If you must know the truth, you weary me with your sermons on honour, your tirades upon virtue and all that. You took me as I am."

"No—as you were!"

"Well, then," exclaimed Daphne, her eyes flaming at last, "I am changed—you are changed—we are changed we are tired of one another—let us part! I prefer this woman to you—there! —you wanted the truth—you have it!"

"Great heavens! is it possible?"

"Not only possible, but existent. Let this be an end of it—let us square our accounts and part."

"Our accounts?" Eric turned a vivid crimson, and then became deathly pale. He thought that she referred to the material issues between them, and as he turned away, he added, in a broken voice, "True, I owe you money as well as gratitude—you are right to remind me of it; though I never forget it, night or day."

It was an insult; an accidental one, it is true, for she had not dreamt that he would so construe her expression. Under its sting, she turned upon him and exclaimed:

"Very well, then—since you reduce it to that level, so be it. Give in to your father; he will welcome his prodigal son, and sell his fatted calf to pay your debts. This is the end of everything between us—I despise you, Eric Trevanion!"

"You do well to despise me, Miss Préault," he returned, bitterly "I am a despicable object, and you have a right to tell me of it."

What she would have replied to this taunt he never knew, for at that moment Clytie appeared at the door of the studio announcing "Madame du Peyral."

It was the culminating point of the scene. Eric recovered his composure as he bowed to Mahmouré, and, taking his hat, turned to Daphne, who was greeting the new-comer as if they had been parted for years. He said:

"I will say good-bye now, Miss Préault; I will send you over a note during the afternoon;" and so saying he bowed and left the studio.

Mahmouré turned after him an enquiring look.

"*Tiens!*" said she; "there has been an unpleasantness?"

"Yes."

"You have quarrelled?"

"Yes."

"About?"

"You."

"*Chérie!*"

A couple of hours later Daphne received a note from Eric Trevanion: it was short, and read as follows:

> I write merely to say good-bye—the scene of this morning leaves no other course open to me to us. I leave for Cornwall tomorrow. We have a few little matters to settle; I think that I have them clearly stated; you shall hear from me from home in a day or two. I thank you from the bottom of my heart for all your kindness to me, and should you ever want a friend you can count upon me. In any other capacity—good-bye.
>
> ERIC TREVANION.

With a little laugh Daphne handed the note to Mahmouré.

"Ah!" said the latter, "now I am really happy. Do you know, *chère amie*, I loathed that man from the first moment I set eyes upon him."

## CHAPTER XII.
### "Splendide Mendax!"

The return of Eric to Trthwwsthpllgg was an occasion of profound rejoicing to two people, and of anxiety which bordered on misery to two others. The former were his father and Gabriel; the latter were Mrs. Hawleigh and Maye. Poor Eric, broken in spirit, and bereft of all his old careless merriment, saw only the pleasure that his presence gave to Trevanion *père* and the blind boy. He was too recently arrived from the scenes of the deepest agony he had ever suffered, to take note of the care with which Maye avoided being alone with him, a care that was almost frustrated by Mrs. Hawleigh in her endeavours to the same end. The time for which the cottage had been taken had elapsed, and it had been impossible to resist Mr. Trevanion's prayer that its inmates should move over *en masse* to Trthwwsthpllgg. Mrs. Hawleigh and Maye were strongly opposed to the change, but poor Gabriel—poor, blind Gabriel—received the invitation with the first transport of joy he had known since the accident in the studio. To Mrs. Hawleigh's mild arguments against the advisability of such a step, he had querulously replied:

"Why, mother, why not? I'm tired of this pokey little cottage; every time I walk two yards, I run up against something—it's narrow, cramped, *étriqué*; and besides, we see so much of the Trevanions that we might just as well be with them altogether. I don't want to go back to London—not until I can see again. I *shall* be able to see again some day—I know it—and I want to look at Dartmoor before I leave it. We must leave the cottage anyhow—why not go to Trevanion's place with the unpronounceable name?—they really want us to. It must be an awful tax upon them, bringing them over all this way every time. Besides, I *want* to go there—I adore that old place—it's lovely to wander about in, even for me, and *I* cannot see it. Do accept, mother—do accept."

There was no refusing him, and so it was settled, though Mrs. Hawleigh's heart sank within her, and Maye's soul was filled with a vague terror of she knew not what. Only, during the last days before they moved she devoted herself more assiduously than ever to her poor, blind lover. Did he appreciate her devotion?— who knows?—he had become accustomed to being attended to, waited on, to have his lightest wish anticipated. Accustomed— ah!—there it is. Accustomed!

And so they went to Trthwwsthpllgg, and found themselves at home at once. In the little boudoir Mrs. Hawleigh would sit with Mr. Trevanion, whilst Gabriel lay on the lounge in the conservatory, and Maye sat talking to him; or more often she would sit with Maye, whilst Eric and Gabriel went for strolls round the place, or for long drives into the country, from which he would return radiant, and full of Eric's descriptions of the scenery through which they had passed.

"Really, do you know," he used to say, enthusiastically, "Eric ought to have been a real artist instead of a toy one. If his picture-painting equalled his word-painting he'd be famous in no time. He has been describing the landscape to me. There has been such a lovely sunset; a gorgeous blaze of crimson and gold, melting out of the blue heaven into the purple and browns of the moor—the most beautiful thing I ever saw," he would continue, forgetting himself, his affliction, everything, in his artist's enthusiasm; "and the very next picture I paint—Ah! what am I saying?—what am I saying?" And a tear would gather in his sightless eyes as he turned sadly away, to fling himself upon the lounge, or to play a mournful bar or two upon his violin.

Constantly this would happen: happy in the companionship of Eric he would lose all memory of his blindness, to be suddenly reminded of it and stabbed to the heart by the recollection; then he would become fretful, and Maye would soothe him into peace again. Sometimes on these occasions Eric would look at her with something like startled wonder in his eyes at the spectacle of this fair young girl devoting her life to a blind man's care; and if Maye caught his look she would turn a shade paler, and her heart would give a strong, convulsive throb as she turned to hide her face from him.

What is love but contrast? The adored one is different from all the women one has ever met. What a difference there was between Daphne Préault and this sweet, pure maiden who stood before him in all the majesty solemnity of her matchless self-sacrifice! He looked at her, and his look was that of the Catholic to the crucified Christ; and she returned him a look that seemed, in deprecating his adoration, to beg for mercy at his hands. It was the Prince-god Siddartha and the maiden Yasodhara once more:

"So their eyes mixed, and from the look sprang love!"

And the days passed by, and with them weeks, but more slowly. Eric would absent himself for longer at a time, and Mrs. Hawleigh's heart was filled with a vague terror. Mr. Trevanion was as blissfully ignorant of the struggle that was proceeding beneath his roof as the blind boy himself, and quite innocently strove to throw his son and Maye together, that he might appreciate the difference between this pure English girl and the delirious Creole he had fled from in London. Of Daphne, Eric had heard nothing. With something like a fear that he was insulting her he had repaid to her the loans which he doubted whether she regarded as such, and she had answered never a word. Only he received a line or two from Schuyler Van Boomkamp, who still lingered in London, and who told him he had done eminently right in leaving Holland Street; that the intimacy of Daphne and Mahmouré du Peyral showed little or no signs of abatement; and that he began to entertain grave fears of how it might end.

And Maye? Ah, sirs! who shall pry into the secrets of a woman's heart? If ever she allowed herself to think, it was only to add a new incentive to her imagination in devising new duties for herself that should draw her nearer, should make her more necessary, to Gabriel; and the love that was growing in Eric's heart would probably never have found an answer in that which lay deep and stifled in her own, had it not been that one day Mrs. Hawleigh brought it before her in all its truth.

Maye was sitting alone in the little boudoir, reading a little volume of verse which Eric had brought from London. She had just read a poem which had shaken her to the soul, had terrified her, so close did its possible application seem to her own case, when Mrs. Hawleigh entered the room, and, seeing her sitting—the open book in her lap—looking straight before her, apparently plunged in a reverie so profound that her entrance did not disturb it, broke the silence by saying:

"Where are Gabriel and—and—Eric?"

"Oh—out in the woods and gardens, as usual," replied Maye; "I heard them go laughing over the bridge more than an hour ago."

"I don't know what we should do without Eric; it is really wonderful the way he manages and takes care of Gabriel, reading to him and telling him stories by the hour, and never minding when he grows irritable, poor boy! Curious, is it not, that he should forsake his shooting, and his house-parties all over the county, to stay here and take care of a blind man and amuse his companions? Very creditable, of course, but strange in such a fashionable and rich young man."

"Very," replied Maye, faintly, as she felt her aunt's eyes riveted on her face.

"I hope—for his sake"—continued Mrs. Hawleigh, coming close to her, and laying her hand gently on her shoulder "and ours, my dear child, that there is no *other* attraction that keeps him here."

"Oh, auntie, of course not," returned Maye, very hurriedly, and growing deathly pale as she continued, with a visible effort; "how could you suggest such a thing? I respect Eric Trevanion for his devotion to Gabriel, and like all men, it pleases—it flatters him, to be respected by a woman. It flatters his vanity. And being such a friend of Gabriel's, he likes me almost as a brother would. But beyond that—nothing—oh, nothing!"

And the girl rose and left the room to run out into the grounds, where she might be alone with the soft, black cattle, and her heart-agony.

Left by herself, Mrs. Hawleigh stood for a moment at the window, and saw Maye run out across the bridge. As she settled to her work, she said to herself:

"Well, I hope Eric is not falling in love at last with Maye. What a calamity it would be!—and yet—poor child!—perhaps—well, well, Eric told me that, when Dr. Richardson's final report came, he would accept some of his country-house invitations, and go away from here, so that Gabriel might get accustomed to perpetual darkness, or that he might grow gradually well under Maye's gentle care. But it struck me that he didn't talk of leaving them together with much enthusiasm. Oh! why doesn't Dr. Richardson write?—his letter is *days* overdue, and the suspense is terrible."

The end was nearer than she supposed. It came on the following afternoon.

Day after day Mrs. Hawleigh waited and watched for the arrival of the post. Daily, from the post-office in the little village, a decrepid courier, known as "the post boy," started on his weary round, bringing in the letters for Trthwwsthpllgg soon after lunch; and often, the minute the meal was finished, Maye or Eric would start for the village, and get the letters before the post-boy had consigned them to his sack, for delivery in their proper turn.

Today Maye had undertaken this duty at Mrs. Hawleigh's earnest request, and her aunt anxiously awaited her return. And as she waited she soliloquised:

"Dr. Richardson must write today, and then we shall know. Poor Gabriel! I hope I shall get as reconciled to his affliction some day as he is now; but at present there is hardly a moment of the day that I can banish the thought of it from my mind, and when I think of it a pang shoots through my heart which is almost more than I can bear. Poor little Maye, too!—poor child!—poor child! How long Gabriel was in love before he asked her to be his wife!—and then that dreadful gas-explosion in the studio which blinded him! Dear, faithful little nurse! she has shown us since then what a good, true girl she is; what should we have done without her? Still, it seems hard that she should be condemned for the rest of her fair young life to taking care of a poor, blind man, and looking after his helplessness. Besides, what will they live upon if this blindness proves really incurable? Thank God! I can just support him and myself; but she has nothing, and he is no richer than she. I see nothing but starvation in front of them."

At this point her soliloquy was interrupted by the entrance of Maye.

"Well," exclaimed she, as the girl took off her hat, "have you got the letters? the post has not been here."

"No," replied Maye, "I just missed them. That poor old man they call the post-boy had just started on his round in the opposite direction, but I thought he would have been here by now, for I walked slowly, and have been doing a little gardening since I came in. Ah, there! he has just appeared at the top of the slope. I'll run and save him the walk down and up again."

Five minutes later she returned, exclaiming, "Here you are, auntie! Two letters for you, and one big one for Eric. Heigho! there has never been anybody to write to me but Gabriel, and now I write his letters for him. I can't very well write love-letters to myself. Poor Gabriel!——"

"Ah," interrupted Mrs. Hawleigh, "here is Dr. Richardson's letter. This will put us out of our suspense about him. Dear child, I can hardly hold it in my hands, I am so nervous. Do you read it to me. Oh, heaven! if I could only know, without opening it—the best—or the worst!"

She had given the envelope to Maye, and Maye, opening it, had run her eyes over the first lines of the letter. Her face, as she did so, became deathly white, and she said softly:

"You must sit down, auntie darling; I'm afraid the news is not going to be good. Shall I begin now? yes? Very well."

And she read as follows:

"My Dear Mrs. Hawleigh:—I have had a long and final consultation with Dr. Critchett since I saw your son at Dartmoor, and I regret to say that I fear I must destroy even the small hope which I was able to give you then. There is no longer any doubt that the nerves of both eyes are destroyed, and, this being the case, it would be dealing unkindly with you were I to hint at the possibility of an ultimate recovery. You were good enough to make me the recipient of your confidence, and to tell me of your son's approaching marriage when this accident befell him."—The reader's voice died out for a moment, and then she resumed: "I feel that this must be a terrible blow to his intended bride, for he will never be able to see her again, and I can fully realize what it will be to you to break this news to her. Please accept my sincere sympathy with this sad affliction which has fallen upon you, and believe me to be, with kind regards,

Always very faithfully yours,
E. Clifford Richardson."

234

As she finished reading, she rose, and, moving to the window leading into the conservatory, she leant against it, struggling to suppress her emotion. Mrs. Hawleigh, who had burst into tears, came to her, and, winding her arms about her, kissed her silently. Then, taking the letter from her, she left the room.

Maye returned to the seat she had occupied before, and sat, dry-eyed—tearless—gazing into the future.

Blind!—hope was extinguished—Gabriel was incurably blind!

And whilst she sat, the twilight deepening over her soul, she heard a burst of laughter in the conservatory, and Eric and Gabriel stood on the threshold. The former, seeing the girl sitting there, a wild, white look in her eyes, started forward a step, forgetful of the blind man's hand upon his arm.

"Why, what's the matter, old man?" exclaimed Gabriel; "I'll trouble you not to stumble when your two eyes have to direct four legs. Is anybody here?"

Maye tried to speak, but her parched tongue refused to articulate immediately. Seeing the struggle, Eric answered:

"Yes—yes—Miss Trevethick is here."

"Then why don't you answer, Maye?" said Gabriel, irritably. "I wish you wouldn't play with me as if I were Caleb Deecie in 'The Two Roses.' Ah! I *saw* 'The Two Roses.' Well," he continued, recovering himself, "you've missed such a treat; you should have come out with us. Eric has been reading me some lovely poems out of a new little book called 'Tares.' They are beautiful—he must read some to you. And we have had another exquisite sunset. You ought to have seen it." And he took up his violin, which lay as usual on the piano, and began playing to himself, "Told in the Twilight," the refrain of the song, "Close to the Threshold."

"Poor fellow!" said Eric, in an undertone to Maye; "it's hard to believe sometimes that he doesn't really see the things he describes to one. Do you know, Miss Trevethick, sometimes he describes you to me so perfectly that I actually see you before me—he delights in doing it. Really, if you heard him you would be both interested and flattered, believe me."

"And believe *me*, Mr. Trevanion," returned Maye, with a wild effort at merriment, as she made him a courtesy, "I am. But seriously, how can we ever thank you for your kindness to him and to us? It is only with you that he forgets that he is blind. What would I not give to be able to be to him what you are!"

What Eric would have answered I know not; what he thought was: "And what would I not give to be to her what he is! I wish that I were blind when I see them together." It was her own thought repeated.

They were interrupted by Gabriel suddenly laying down his violin and saying:

"Now, then, what are you two conspiring about? Don't you know that it's very rude to whisper before third parties? I suppose you imagine that I don't count—ah, no, I don't mean that," added he, as Maye went quickly to his side and touched him; "I was only chaffing. Come! what have you been doing since lunch?—and where's the mother?"

"Oh," replied Maye, turning cold and confused at the thought of the imminent explanation, "I walked down to the village because auntie wanted to get the letters quickly, but the post had started, so I came home and tied up those creepers which hang down and annoy you when you come in at the conservatory door—and then the post came in—here's a letter for you, Mr. Trevanion—and then the mother left me alone and went to her room—I think. How far did you walk?" concluded she, desperately changing the subject.

"Tell me," said Gabriel, not heeding her question, "was mother's letter from Richardson?"

"I—I think it was."

"Did mother tell you what was in the letter?" pursued the blind man, with a strong effort to appear calm. "Richardson was to write and say how soon I shall be able to see again."

"No," replied Maye, with forced prevarication, "*she* did not tell *me* what was in the letter."

"I must go to her at once—take me to her, Maye;" and the two disappeared.

236

Left alone, Eric drew his letter from his pocket. It was directed in Schuyler Van Boomkamp's characteristic fist, and was a bulky letter enclosed in a foolscap envelope. It was with a vague, sickening feeling of apprehension that he tore it open and brought to light a closely written manuscript, headed "*The Narrative of the Coloured Woman Clytemnestra*" and a letter from Schuyler Van Boomkamp. The letter was short, and to the point. It read as follows:

> My Dear Trevanion:—Miss Daphne Préault is dead. The circumstances attending her death constitute, I fear, a horrible tragedy, of which the details are contained in the narrative I have compiled for you, from the account given by the coloured woman who attended upon Miss Préault and witnessed her death. To that narrative I have nothing to add, save that I was able to certify that death ensued from naturally-produced asphyxia, in which certificate a singularly ignorant practitioner, who announced himself to me as Miss Préault's regular medical attendant, concurred, knowing nothing of the case. I am making arrangements for the return of Clytemnestra to New Orleans; she is amply provided for under the will of Miss Préault, the bulk of whose property is bequeathed to you. Finally, as regards Madame du Peyral, if it became necessary at any future time, I could certify that she was mentally deranged, and not responsible for her actions; in any case, under the circumstances, the death of Miss Préault—certainly unpremeditated— might have been accidental. Madame du Peyral left England the same night as the tragedy occurred. I forbore to enquire whither she was bound— possibly to her original destination in Greece. I do not think it will be necessary for us to ascertain; she will certainly not return. I leave, myself, for Paris this evening. Should you wish to communicate

with me, a letter addressed, care of His Excellency, the American Minister, will reach me safely.

A word in conclusion, in case we should never meet again. You and I have been the witnesses of, and to a certain extent actors in, one of the most startling, nay terrific, psychological dramas that it has ever been my fate to encounter in all my experience in mental science. I shall prepare a report thereon, which I shall send you for signature; any details that you can add will be valuable. I think we had better keep our own counsel in the matter, closely and completely, until the story of Daphne Préault and Paul du Peyral shall have become a chapter of forgotten history. I wish you health and prosperity, and shall remain always, my dear Trevanion,

Very faithfully yours,

SCHUYLER VAN BOOMKAMP.

White to the lips, Eric Trevanion looked from the letter he held in his hand to the manuscript, which had fallen to the floor. He picked it up and hastily glanced through the sheets until he reached the last page. Then his eyes dilated with horror, his pallor increased, and he felt as though he would have fainted, had he not fled forth into the air. There his senses seemed to return to him. Composing himself with a violent effort, he returned into the house, and, going to his own room, he locked away carefully Schuyler Van Boomkamp's letter and manuscript in his dispatch-box.

And then a great sense of misery and loneliness came over him, and flinging himself onto a sofa, he cried aloud in the agony of his soul: "Oh, God! and is this the end? Is my life utterly wasted? —utterly spoilt?—Blind—blind fool that I have been!—Had I but known where my happiness lay—had I not been stupefied by my ghastly folly—you might have loved me— Maye, my darling, my pure, beautiful love! And now—what is left for me? Ashes—ashes! I am not fit to enter your presence—and yet—I have fancied—but no, she is pledged to Gabriel—God forbid that I should break his heart—should wreck his life more completely than it is wrecked already! I will go to her—perhaps the sight of her sweet, true face will chase this nightmare from my brain—may save me, after all, in spite of myself." And then the lines recurred to him this—time with a new hope in every word:

> *"I hold it truth, with him who sings*
> *To one clear harp in divers tones,*
> *That men may rise on stepping-stones*
> *Of their dead selves to higher things!"*

And so Eric Trevanion sought once more the little boudoir, where he found Maye alone in the twilight, standing at the window looking out into the deepening shadows across the moat.

As he entered the room she turned quickly. The evening light slanted across his drawn, white face, and she exclaimed:

"Mr. Trevanion—Eric—you have had bad news!"

"Bad news!—bad news?—I wonder whether it be bad. Terrible news—yes! but bad!—I wonder——?"

"Oh, what is it?"

"Daphne Préault is dead."

"Dead!"

"Yes."

"How dreadful!—how did she die?—tell me about it."

"She died in one of her curious fainting-fits. She had had many of them in the past year, and since her serious illness a short while ago she has never been her old self."

"I am so sorry—Eric."

"Nay, do not be sorry for her, or for me, Miss Trevethick. Perhaps it is better thus."

"But—you loved her so."

"Loved her—did I love her?—no; I think—God help me!—that I was bewitched, possessed—mad!"

"But surely——"

"Do not let us speak of it—I beg of you. It is all too sudden, too ghastly. Let us speak of something else."

There was a moment of deathly stillness, and then Maye, womanlike, recovering herself the first, said:

"What are these poems that Gabriel speaks about, that you have been reading to him?"

"A little volume by a young author," answered he, drawing it from his pocket as he spoke. "They are light, of course; but some of them are very pretty. It has been lying about; have you not read them?"

"No—I took it up yesterday, but I was interrupted. Will you not read me one, as Gabriel suggested?"

"Certainly, if you wish it. No, do not ring: there is light enough here at the window. What sort of poem shall I read you?"

"Had you not better go on where you left off?"

"Very well. I was just going to read this one, when it struck me it was getting chilly for Gabriel, and we got up to come home. It is called "*Nachtstuck*" and runs thus:

*"I will lie still, here in the shadow, and turn my face to the wall;*
*Mine eyes shall behold no other since they may not mirror you,*
*Since I may not hear your voice mine ears shall be sealed too,*
*And my lips are mute to all!*

*"But you—oh, my fair, sweet love, you must walk far afield, in the*
*light,*
*Not quite forgetting my soul that aches in the darkness here,*
*Though Time's soft, dead hand puts me from you, each day less dear*
*Grow the tender mem'ries of night.*

*"And that shall be well!—I—am only a wraith from the past,*
*No more may my glad arms cradle your drooped gold head,*
*To you—and because to you,—to all am I henceforth dead.*
*[And you knew not that kiss was our last!]*

*"And that is well too!—to the last was our summer sweet,*
*To the very end no pale cloud obscured our exquisite days,*

*Our sun, for the last time, set in a warm, wild blaze,*
  *Making earth and heaven meet!*

*"False? Ah, no! hardly that—dear heart, you are not to blame;*
  *[Who carps at the sun, or the transient rain, or the fleeting*
    *ev'ning dew?]*
  *And I cavil not at your fair young soul that would fain, but*
    *could not be true,*
    *And I love you, aye, the same.*

*"That you do not ask it, I know, and I would not, alas! but must*
  *Lie here chained and tortured by mem'ry forever; but you, dear,*
    *are free:*
  *And the welcomest gift that this wide, blank universe holds for me*
    *Is a little handful of dust!"*

As he read, his voice grew lower and more tender. Every word
ate into her soul. It seemed as if Gabriel himself was speaking,
and it was more than she could bear. The spell of the words lay
over Eric too, and he realized every word and its meaning. Had
it not been for this they would have heard the slight noise that
Gabriel had made as he raised himself on one elbow, to listen as
he lay upon the couch in the conservatory. He had come in from
the garden just as Eric entered the room—they had not heard
him—and now, with a blind man's acuteness of ear, not a word
that they had said had escaped him.

Even now he might have made his presence known to them,
but that, as Eric's voice ceased, Maye buried her head in her
hands, and moaning, "Oh! Gabriel!" burst into an agony of
tears. Gabriel waited and listened—hardly daring to breathe in
the gloom of the conservatory.

It was Eric who spoke first within the room:

"Ah, Miss Trevethick," he exclaimed, "I have pained you,
Maye! This poem has touched you—then it speaks to you as it
speaks to me. Poor Gabriel!—of us three I do not know whom
I should pity most. You do not answer. Alas! that I should speak
so, when every prompting of honour urges me to keep silent.

I have no right to speak, as my heart bids me, to the affianced wife of my best friend—least of all when he is afflicted, helpless, as poor Gabriel is, but—I am going away now, and I cannot go without a word."

"Oh, Mr. Trevanion—I beg of you——"

"Ah! don't stop me now—I am leaving you, perhaps forever. Every day that I have been here I have been drawing nearer and nearer to the truth, that I love you—aye! love you more than words can say—than eyes can speak; and that when I leave you—as leave you I *must*—poor Gabriel's blindness will have fallen on my soul. God help me, for I am utterly helpless myself."

"My duty—my duty——" began the girl, but he interrupted her:

"Yes, your duty and mine; but when I think of your fair young life tied to his in one ceaseless continuance of care for his infirmity, even as you have tended him hitherto; when I think that his eyes can never see you, that you must be chained for all your life to the side of a man whose only knowledge of you is—memory—the remembrance of your beauty, which cannot give brilliancy, for one moment, to the darkness before his eyes, my heart is ready to burst. Ah!" he continued, desperately, losing himself in the torrent of his words, "let me go to him and implore his forgiveness for myself, for *us*. Why should we wreck three lives—as wrecked they must be—without doing any good by the sacrifice? I cannot believe that I have been mistaken—that you care nothing for me—oh! come to me, and be the light of my life."

He had fallen on his knees by her side, burying his head in his hands in the agony of his despair—and she laid her hand gently on his shoulder, as she answered him in a cold, miserable voice:

"Hush, Eric! hush! I can never be the light of your life, if, indeed, that might be, for I have promised to be the light of his. You have spoken truly—he will never see me—you—any of us, again; the letter from Dr. Richardson has destroyed our last hope—Gabriel is incurably blind, and this, if nothing else, makes my path clear before me."

He raised his eyes to hers, and stayed there, on his knees, gazing into her soul, as she pronounced the death-sentence of their love.

"We must not misunderstand one another, dear friend," continued she, "but I would gladly have spared both myself and you this full knowledge of the truth. I am, as you know, without relations, without friends, save for Mrs. Hawleigh and Gabriel; without means of subsistence save what I can gain by my own work. Auntie rescued me five years ago from absolute penury, and whilst I lived with her, Gabriel loved me in silence—during all that weary time. It was only when he became famous and was becoming rich that he asked me to link my life with his; and I consented. What else could I do?—besides—I loved him very dearly—though not as I *could* love. Hush! do not speak! His accident, as you know, has destroyed all his prospects; would you have me desert him now? No, no! We must go away from here—for I own to you, Eric, that you have stirred a deeper feeling within my heart than I knew existed there. Ah! why should I pretend ignorance of my own weakness?—it *is* love! But you are his friend *and mine*—are you not? Help me, then, by your example, to do my duty to our poor, blind Gabriel."

She ceased speaking, and Eric, rising to his feet, took her hand and kissed it as he would have done homage to a saint. Then he said, controlling his voice with a violent effort:

"Then—it is all over. Thank you for this grand lesson you have taught me, and may you be as happy in your new life as you deserve. Forgive me for what is past, dear, and forget, if you can, that I ever asked you to be untrue to your promise to Gabriel. I leave here tomorrow. Think of me kindly, if you can, sometimes. For myself I cannot regret this trial, for it will make my life better, purer, to have loved you as I have come to do. See—I will tear this poem from this little book; and he—must never know! Perhaps we shall never meet again. In that case—good-bye— God in heaven bless you, Maye Trevethick."

He kissed her hand once more, and the next moment he was gone. The silence that he left behind him was broken by a tiny noise in the conservatory. Maye's heart gave a violent bound, and for an instant she seemed to stifle; then she went into the conservatory—it was empty—and flinging herself upon Gabriel's lounge, she sobbed as if her heart would break.

The dinner at Trthwwsthpllgg that night was a silent meal save that Gabriel made a superhuman effort to appear gay as usual. He and Eric kept up a cross-fire of conversation, in which Maye alone detected the false note. When it was ended, and the Trevanions, father and son, and Gabriel had joined Mrs. Hawleigh and Maye in the little boudoir, Gabriel said:

"Are we all here?—yes? That is good I have something very serious to say to you all. Yes, mother," he said to Mrs. Hawleigh, who came and laid her hand on his arm, "it must be said sooner or later, as I told you. Sit down and keep silence, all of you, please, till I have done. Maye!—mother has been reading to me Dr. Richardson's letter, and it has decided me to say what I have been on the verge of saying to you—for many weeks—for many weeks. You now know that I can never recover my sight, that I can never again see the landscapes in which I have revelled, the flowers and animals which I have loved; can never again see *you*, save as the beautiful model whose features I fixed upon my canvas and my brain last, before my light became a great darkness. I am poor—very poor—and blind. That, I know, makes no difference to you—but, alas! this physical infirmity has altered my whole being—in a moment, as it were—in a moment—and I should be doing you a grievous wrong were I to conceal my altered feelings from you and marry you notwithstanding. Hush! do not speak—I beg of you. Only forgive me. I *cannot* marry you to make your fair young life one of slavery, even if I *would* do so; and you must not think me fickle or untrue; it is my infirmity— my infirmity, that has altered my whole life."

Maye flung herself on her knees by his side, and put her arms about him:

"I cannot leave you like this, Gabriel—I cannot leave you!" she said.

"I know—I know, dear," he replied; "but it must be so. Eric—your voice, when you have spoken to me of Maye, has told me far more than your words have said—we blind men have keen intuitions and infallible instincts, you know; will you guide for me this child-friend of mine through her pure, sweet life?—and the knowledge of your happiness will be a light to my life which has become so dark."

Eric Trevanion rose in his turn:

"Gabriel—dear old man," he said, "you must not make this sacrifice—we cannot bear it."

"Yes, old friend," he replied, "it must be—it is better so. Mother, dear we shall not be separated, after all, you and I. We will go back to the old studio, to our old life and my music, and Eric and Maye will come sometimes to tell me of the world they—*see*—around them."

*Splendide mendax!*


# EPILOGUE.

Many years have passed since the day that the story told in the foregoing pages was closed with Gabriel Hawleigh's magnificent lie. The Hawleighs, mother and son, are both dead. Gabriel Hawleigh died in Naples—or more accurately speaking, at Sorrento, whither he had fled in search of quiet, and recovery from a malarial fever caught in Rome—but not before his fame as a musician had rung from one end of Europe to the other, as would have rung his fame as a painter, had not his career been cut short by his accident. There lingers probably in the memory of many of my readers the fame of a violinist who stirred the heart-strings of his audiences as no one has stirred them since Paganini and Sainton stayed their magic fingers under the grasp of death. He was a miracle for he was blind. And under the *nom d'artiste* which he adopted and inscribed indelibly upon the roll-call of glory, only a few people in England recognized Gabriel Hawleigh the painter.

His mother was with him to the last, but she did not long survive her son. She died in the old studio-house in Holland Street—shall I say of a broken heart? Now-a-days I fear to say it, for, now-a-days, hearts do not break.

Dick Lindsay married Eva Easton, but Sylvia never married anybody: she lives on the Schiavoni in Venice, and paints pictures that are eagerly sought for in the index of the Academy catalogue. Bernard Rawlinson is a great actor now, and never paints at all; Gerome Markham still individualizes the pages of a leading comic paper, and dresses five times a day—he does not look an hour older than he did the day on which I first saw him; and Mr. Charles Sturton-Baker has disappeared. There was a little difficulty about the prospectus of a joint-stock company, which brought about his enforced seclusion for a few years at the expense of Her Majesty's government. When he had served his term he sought fresh fields for his peculiar industry in the United States, exchanging them subsequently, owing to circumstances over which unfortunately he had control, for the pleasant security of Canada.

He did not marry Parthenia Van Baulk'em.

That young lady came over to England to inspect Mr. Charles Sturton-Baker's position "on the ground"—so to speak, and finding that the swain had given to an airy nothing, a local habitation and a name, returned to Fifth Avenue the betrothed of Mr. Murray Hill. They were married in the spring following and people say that he beats her.

It was only last summer that I went down to Cornwall, to rest at Trthwwsthpllgg Manor, at the conclusion of a more than ordinarily hard spell of work, and gave that terrible polymonosyllable to my publishers as my address for a couple of months. The Autocrat of Trthwwsthpllgg is a grand old gentleman, autocrat now only in name, for the reins of government have fallen to Eric, who is the typical young country squire, very proud of his place and his horses, and on his knees to his wife, who has not aged an hour—I swear!—since I first met her in Holland Street. And in the early morning I used to be awakened by a chorus of shrill shouts from the lawn beneath my windows, proceeding from the throats of Eric's children, to wit, his daughter Dorothy, a young woman of decided and advanced opinions, and her twin brothers, Eric and Gabriel, whom she rules with a rod of iron. They are her juniors by a couple of years, and it is an understood thing that Dorothy is to make haste and catch me up, and then we are to be married!

One evening I was sitting alone with Eric in his armoury, dignified by the name of "study," when our conversation turned upon the old colony in Holland Street, on the Hawleighs, and on "the Princess Daphne." The old wound had long healed over, so I knew that I could approach the subject with impunity.

"By-the-bye," I said, "what a dreadfully sudden thing Daphne Préault's death was! did you ever hear any of the details?"

"Yes—all of them."

"How did she die?"

"My dear fellow," said Eric, very gravely, "the death of Daphne Préault was one of the most horrible tragedies that the world has ever witnessed: Fortunately for everybody concerned she had been attended by Schuyler Van Boomkamp, the American psychologist, and he arranged matters."

"Why, what do you mean?" I exclaimed; "I never thought there was any mystery. I always understood that Miss Préault was subject to fits of some kind, and that in one of them she had died."

"If you like," said Eric Trevanion, not answering my remark, "I will place in your hands a complete account of her death. It reached me and I read it the day that I proposed to Maye, my wife. From that day to this it has lain undisturbed."

So saying, he turned to a dispatch-box that lay on the table, and, unlocking it, he took thence a few sheets of paper, folded up, and getting yellow with age. These he placed into my hands. I unfolded them and read as follows:

THE NARRATIVE OF THE COLOURED WOMAN CLYTEMNESTRA: GATHERED FROM HER LIPS BY SCHUYLER VAN BOOMKAMP, M.D., LEYDEN, PARIS, AND N. Y.

I was born in the service of the late Victor Préault of New Orleans, on the Belles Fontaines plantation, Louisiana, U. S. A. After his death I came to

England with Miss Daphne Préault, and have been with her all the time she has been in this country. Madame du Peyral began coming to the house early in this summer, and she and Miss Préault seemed very much attached to one another. Whenever Mr. Trevanion was not here, Madame du Peyral used to come and remain with Miss Préault. One day Madame du Peyral brought her things and came to stay in the house. The next day Mr. Trevanion left London. I have not seen him since.

Madame du Peyral was here about three weeks; she occupied the room adjoining Miss Préault's on the first floor, and connected with it by a door. They used generally to sit up talking late into the night in one room or the other, and in the morning, at nine o'clock, I used to carry up the breakfast. Often Madame du Peyral would be in Miss Préault's room, and then I used to carry the chocolate in there for both. A few days after Mr. Trevanion had left, a letter came from him, and I took it up to Miss Daphne on her tray. Madame du Peyral was there, sitting on the edge of the bed talking, and the moment she saw the letter she tried to snatch it. Miss Daphne was too quick for her, and she did not get it. I often heard them speak of it afterwards, Madame du Peyral always wanting to see it, and Miss Daphne never showing it to her.

The last morning before Madame du Peyral left the house I took up the chocolate as usual, and as I went into the room I thought I heard their voices raised as if in anger, and when I got in, Miss Daphne was lying in bed looking very pale, and I was afraid she was going to have one of the fainting-fits she used to have. Madame du Peyral was sitting on the bed by her side, looking at her—her face was red, and she had a dangerous look in her eyes that frightened me. The bed-clothes were disarranged, and the two looked as if they had been struggling. Neither spoke whilst I was in the room, and instead of going out again by the door onto the landing, I went into Madame du Peyral's room, intending to arrange it a little, and to be within call. In a moment, however, I heard footsteps, and Madame du Peyral, coming in by the connecting door, said:

"You need not arrange my room yet—wait till I am dressed."

I went out, but came back as soon as I heard them talking together again, and listened at the door, which had been left ajar between the two rooms. Madame du Peyral was saying:

"Why won't you let me see it? I am sure there can be nothing to conceal. I know Mr. Trevanion dislikes me, and that if he mentioned me at all, it was unpleasantly."

"But he didn't mention you at all, Mahmouré—what a child you are!" said Miss Daphne.

"Not such a child," she said, "as to be deceived in that ridiculous way. I know what was in the letter—he wants to make peace with you, and he wants you to give me up. Well, it is very simple for you to choose. You are tired of me."

"Don't be so silly," was the answer; "there isn't a word of truth in what you say!"

Then I peeped through the door-crack, and saw Miss Préault take Madame in her arms. The latter struggled away, exclaiming:

"No—you are tired of me."

"I am not."

"Then give me the letter."

"I can't."

And then Madame du Peyral began to cry.

"Come, Mahmouré," said Miss Daphne, "you excite yourself too much. You are overtaxing your strength. We carry our gossip too late into the night.

Even *I* am not so strong as I was. Every night I determine to send you to bed, and not let you sit here and chatter; but then we forget all about the time. I have been feeling unlike myself for days, and this morning I have a dreadful headache. Come, stroke my temples for me, dear."

Madame du Peyral's face was turned in my direction, and as she leaned over Miss Daphne, the same horrible, frightening look came into it. I could see that Miss Préault's eyes were shut. Then the other got up and, creeping across the room, pulled down the blind, and came back to the bed, where she lay down and began passing her fingers across Miss Préault's forehead and through her hair.

Miss Daphne did not move, and gradually Madame du Peyral drew herself into a crouching, sitting position, watching, watching, watching, as she played with the other woman's hair. Suddenly Miss Daphne gave a gasp and struggled a little. Madame, seeing her move, flung herself suddenly upon her, and gripped her round the throat—I did not dare to stir—I was frozen with terror.

Then she began to mutter rapidly and incoherently in a harsh, forced voice.

"No, no!" she said, "you shall not die—I will keep your life in you; it shall not escape;" and she still held Miss Daphne's throat.

The latter moved a little, then a little more. Then her movements grew weaker again, and at last she lay quite still. Then Madame du Peyral stooped lower and began kissing her. I went into the room. As I entered, she looked up like a wild animal just going to spring, and cried, "Go away!—how dare you come in here?"

I was terrified, and put on my things and ran for the American doctor who has been here sometimes. When he came he told me Miss Daphne was dead.

I say that Madame du Peyral killed her.

Her

CLYTEM X NESTRA.

Mark

At this point the manuscript was signed with the mark of Clytemnestra, witnessed by Schuyler Van Boomkamp. A few words were added by the doctor to the effect that Miss Daphne Préault had died of a sudden cerebral congestion produced by over-excitement, and the narrative closed with his signature and the date.

THE END.

# BELLA-DEMONIA

## A DRAMATIC STORY

We are but pieces in the game He plays
upon this checker-hoard of nights and days,
Hither and thither moves, and checks and slays,
And one by one back in the closet lays.

*Omar-i-Khayyám*

# DEDICATION

## TO A. A. PALMER, Esq.,

### Palmer's And Madison Square Theatres, New York:

To you, to whom I owe so many a kindly word and deed, at times when Fate pressed hardest,—given with gentle, simple courtesy, as if the service rendering were a boon receiving,—to you, whose unspoken sympathy has brought me comfort in my darkest hours, I have naught to give in return, nor ever shall have, save remembrance. Will you accept it?

SELINA DOLARO.

# IN MEMORANDIUM.

## *SELINA DOLARO*

Yon rising Moon that looks upon us in twain,
How oft hereafter will she wax and wane,
How oft, hereafter rising, look for us
Through this same Garden, and for *One* in vain!

And when, like her, O Sákí, you shall pass
Among the Guests, star-scattered on the grass,
And in your joyous errand reach the spot
Where I made *one,*—turn down an empty glass!
*Omar-i-Khayyám*

She said to me one day, not long ago, "I wonder whether I shall live to see my book come out, and hear what critics say? I fear I shall not." And her doubt proved just. Madame Dolaro, of whose *self* the world knew but one aspect, that which strove to please its fickle fancy on the mimic stage, has left a world of friends to mourn a loss that few, who knew her not, as some of us, can realize.

Born but a few months more than thirty-five years since, she lived her life with all its disappointments and its joys—neither of which were few—calmly serene in every purpose of her earthly span. When, on the morning of the 25th, we buried what was left to us of her, quietly, as she wished, among the graves of those who died in her ancestral faith, in a green nook among the Cypress Hills, the honored few who, with her to the end, heard her last words and caught her dying breath when on the world she closed her weary eyes, felt that her time had come, and thanked the

God in whom through all her pilgrimage on earth she placed her trust with gentle, simple faith, that He had suffered her to end the work she had begun, and, merciful at last, had let her fall asleep in "perfect peace that passeth understanding." For in death, as she had been in life, she lay a sweet ensample to her children and her friends.

She married early—in her fifteenth year—one who, like her, was of the Jewish faith; he traced his ancestry, without a flaw, back to a family who from their home in Spain were thrust in 1492 and sought a safe retreat in Italy. Finding a refuge at Belasco, thence they took their name, discarding that which Spain had known them by,—Miara.

Her artist life began in '70, after some three years spent developing her matchless voice at the Conservatoire of Paris, and she made her first *début* upon the stage that year in "Chilperic" at the Lyceum Theatre. Success crowned every task she 'tempted from the start; the artist world flocked eager to acclaim this prima donna who was but a child, and all the press of England sang the hymn of her rare triumphs in light opera. Later, in "Zampa" and in "Fleur de Lys," in "Madame Angot" and "La Perichole," she showed the public that in opéra bouffe there may be something more than vulgar jest, suggestive quip, and veiled indecency, throwing around burlesque a zaimph of art. Under the circumstances, 'twas not strange that, presently discarding such light *rôles*, she trod at last the operatic stage under Carl Rosa's management, and then it was that, conscious of her power, she re-created "Carmen," and at once took, as it were of right, the place reserved for her.

Her "Carmen" first was played in '79,—in February,—and from that time forth it seemed as if her future were secured; but circumstances which proverbially are out of our control ordained that she should cede her place in opera to some one else less fit for it than she had been, and soon we find her once again, with all the cares of management upon her hands, leading her company in opéra bouffe,—only, however, for a while; for next we find her singing "Carmen" in New York,—this time in Italian, and now surrounded by an envious foreign *clique* who strove to hinder her in all she did, till, weary of their petty jealousies, she sought once more her English home for rest. In 1883 she came again, and shone among us here in comedy. She played in "Caste," and those who saw how she won every heart with Polly Eccles' tears have since sought vainly for her life again. Since then until her soul declared itself, she played a vast variety of *rôles*, comedy, burlesque, drama, opéra bouffe, and charmed us with her tears as with her smiles,—for even in her most Cimmerian hours, Madame Dolaro smiled upon the world that was the better that she lived therein, but used her with such merciless despite, until at last when luck had seemed to turn and some of her desires began to bask in realization, then the strained cord snapped. Her health, which had left much to be desired, gave way without the warning of an hour, and she who yesterday had been the queen of opera and comedy was laid upon a bed of sickness from which those who saw her there ne'er dared to hope that she could rise again, and plucky though she was, she too made up her mind she was to die.

'Twas only in her later years that I was privileged to know her, when the blow had fallen that deprived her of the power to revel in the glorious gift of life; but even then her bravery was such that high above misfortunes such as most men would succumb to, she triumphantly rose, and began her work in life anew: her voice, her strength, much of her sweet self, gone, she turned her hands and brain to other work. Early in '87, when at first her fragile body rallied from the shock of her first seizure, she took up the pen and put the final touches to a play called "Fashion" which she wrote some years ago, but which had never been produced. Hearing the play was ready for the stage, her friends came round her and entreated her to let them act it for her benefit, and A. M. Palmer, foremost of them all, lent her his stage and its accessories wherewith to mount her brilliant comedy. In May—the 19th of the month—this work received its first production, and was played as perfectly as any drama could, by a well-chosen cast of faithful friends who strove their utmost to make "Dolly's play" a great success. How they succeeded has been written in the annals of the stage. Now she could rest awhile, and by the sea Madame Dolaro and her daughter lived a few short months in perfect peace, and so when she returned to town it almost seemed as if she might be with us soon again as once she had been, but the daily cares, the constant wonder where to turn for work that she could do, began to break again the skein of life that rest had almost weft.

When in the winter-time of '87 her drama "Fashion" was produced and all its beauties marred by rank incompetence of some of those who played it, and "the press" who in the spring had chanted in its praise turned round and said that " Dolly's play" had failed to please the public, then she realized that she must seek more uncongenial work to make her daily bread, and so she wrote articles, stories for the magazines, and made that book entitled "Mes Amours" out of the poems and the doggerel rhymes that she had written and that faithful friends wrote for her, giving her their leave to print their verses. Not content to wait and trust to Fortune for some unexpected gift, she turned at once to the most arduous task of all her life,—"Bella-Demonia." With loving care she labored at her book, reading authorities and histories, and, having gathered her materials, she took them to the sea-shore. There we wrote (hers was the brain and mine the hand alone) "Bella-Demonia: a Dramatic Tale." The world has read how when this book was done and publishers had read it and agreed to publish it the manuscript was lost,—was stolen from the office of *The World* by some malignant fiend whose wickedness the patient lightnings yet have failed to blast. Up to that hour her health had seemed to us improving daily, but this frightful loss seemed such a shock to the poor fragile soul that from that day the end began, and as she bravely sate her down and wrote again her book from memory (for she kept no notes), the hand of Death seemed to be drawing her away from us. The book at length was done over again, and then the Lippincotts made her an offer that she could accept, so that the latter months were lived at least in comfort, if not luxury.

Meanwhile, she made another drama of her book, which still awaits production; it is called "Bella-Demonia," like her novel, and in it she voices the dramatic scenes through which the people of her novel pass. This done, she did not "fold her hands for sleep," but set to work once more and wrote a new novel, which just two days before the end began was finished. She had been down town to see about its publication, when, chancing to call upon her with a friend, we found her lying crimsoned with her life that ebbed from the old deep-hidden wound. That was upon the 19th, Saturday, and from that time with all the care we knew how to bestow we tended her, though we, her children and her friends, knew well that this was the beginning of the coming end.

All Sunday and on Monday just a gleam of hope lit up the twilight of our grief, but Tuesday afternoon the tired soul began the final struggle to be free. On Wednesday her sharper sufferings ceased, and in the afternoon the look of pain died from her face and one of exquisite contentment took its place. She was so fair! Then, at a quarter after six o'clock, she tried to speak to us just once again, and, gentle, trusting, loving to the last, she ceased to strive to hold her little life, and, weary of her day's work in the world which for her tender frame had been so hard, she laid her down to rest and trustingly gave back her soul to God—and fell asleep.

Edward Heron-Allen.
26th January, 1889.

# PROLOGUE.

## CHAPTER I.
### The Honorable John Vyvian Fane.

"But indeed, Excellency, the fare is three roubles."

"Away! and quickly."

"But indeed——"

"What! still whining? Here! take that!"

The sharp shriek of a man in pain rang out in the wintry air, and was lost on the snow-clad Prospect. An *isvoshtshik*—a sleighdriver—had been struck across the face by the passenger who had just descended from his droschky, at the top of the Newski Prospect.

The *isvoshtshik* was a miserable specimen of the Russian *moujik* or peasant class, clad in the ragged fur coat and pleated boots of his profession, and, as he cowered against the side of his droschky, formed a wonderful contrast to the man who had struck him. The latter stood illumined by the oil lamp that lit the curb hard by (I am talking of the Petersburg of twenty years ago), a figure of military erectness, clad in a long and tightly-fitting coat of dark cloth, heavily trimmed with Astrachan fur; the cap on his head and the gloves on his hands were of the same material, and his feet were encased in high polished leather boots whose simplicity bespoke their English manufacture. The face illuminated as the man turned, by the oil lamp, was finely cut and of an ivory pallor. What was visible of the closely-cut hair beneath the fur cap was of a jet-black, as was also the stiff military moustache which, drawn to fine points on either side, disclosed a thin, pale, cruel mouth. The man looked down at the trembling *moujik*, one hand upon his hip, the other holding a light rattan which still quivered with the force of the blow which had just been laid across the *moujik's* face.

There was nothing very noteworthy—especially at the time of which I write—in a droschky-driver being struck by his client, but the stillness of the air in the keen frost of the Russian winter seemed to accentuate the bitterness of the cry that rang out. At any rate, it attracted the notice of a man who, stepping from the shadow of a neighboring gate-way, approached the group.

"Come, come," said the new arrival, in the tone of one accustomed to command, "men are not flogged in the streets of Petersburg for nothing. What is the meaning of this?"

The man who had struck the sleigh-driver turned on his heel and confronted his interrogator. The manner of the latter immediately changed, and, straightening his figure as he raised his hand in military salute, he exclaimed, in a tone of surprise,—

"The Gospodar Vyvian Fane! We are punctual!"

As he spoke, the *moujik*, who had fastened his eyes on the newcomer's face, sprang upon the driving-seat of his droschky, exclaiming under his breath as he did so,—"Dmitri Keratieff, of the Secret Police! Holy St. Katerine, what an escape!" And, before either of the pair could turn, he had started his horse and disappeared down one of the by-streets leading out of the Newski Prospect.

"Yes," said the man whom Keratieff had addressed as Vyvian Fane, in answer to the Police Agent's ejaculation, "my business is of a kind that demands punctuality on my part, promptitude on yours. No need to trouble about this scoundrel—ah! he is gone; it is well. He tried to claim a double fare: he mistook his man."

And the Honorable John Vyvian Fane laughed, a little hard laugh that parted his thin lips over two rows of small cruel teeth.

"You have brought the papers?" queried Keratieff.

"Here they are," replied Fane, drawing a letter-case from his pocket and taking thence a folded sheet. "This one will be more than sufficient. It is a letter from Alexis Dorski, the Terrorist leader, to the Prince Ladislas Galitzin. You will see that it proves the intimacy of the two."

"That will indeed be sufficient," returned the Police Agent; and, hastily unbuttoning the cloak which was wrapped about his somewhat stunted form, the light of a small flat lantern shone out, instantly lit by some chemical process, and illuminating the sheet which Keratieff perused attentively.

"It is more than enough," observed he, as he extinguished the light and refolded the paper, which he, in turn, placed in his pocketbook. "How does the Prince Ladislas come to have let this fall into our hands?"

"He had intrusted it to his sister, the Princess Carita Galitzin, for safe custody. It is from her that it was—obtained."

The Chief of Police glanced quickly and keenly at the impassive face of the Englishman.

"Ah!" he ejaculated. Then, after an instant's pause, he asked, "When do you desire that this arrest should take place?"

"At once. Within an hour he must be safely lodged in the Fortress of St. Peter and St. Paul."

"So soon?"

"Yes. The young fool was so ill-advised as to attempt to make a scene at the Club tonight. The matter must not be taken up again tomorrow. He must have disappeared. You understand?"

"Perfectly."

"And mark me, also," continued Fane, lowering his voice, though in the moonlight it was plain that no one was near. "Once in the fortress, he must not come out. There must be no trial."

The Police Agent smiled: "Have no fear, Gospodar Fane. Prisoners who take the groundfloor apartments of St. Peter and St. Paul seldom come to trial. The place is damp. Life is uncertain. The Prince Ladislas is delicate. By the bye, you might like to assist when—when the time comes. A prison funeral is an interesting thing—to a foreigner."

"Are you sure you can lay your hand upon him at once?" queried Fane, not appearing to notice the other's words.

"In an hour he will be safely lodged," answered Keratieff, echoing the Englishman's words.

"Where is he now? He left the Club at once."

"He is with his wife."

"*What!*"

"With his wife. The prince has been more than a year married. A *mésalliance*, Excellency."

"I did not know of this."

"Nor anyone else, with the exception of Dmitri Keratieff and the Princess Carita his sister."

"The deuce!"

"There is yet time in half an hour, should you change your mind."

"Change my mind! Never! the revenge will be all the finer. What a chance!"

Vyvian Fane was about to leave his companion, when the latter stopped him, laying a hand upon his arm.

"This is a terrible revenge, Gospodar Fane," he said. "It strikes his sister and his wife with him."

"Well?"

"It will probably kill both these women."

Vyvian Fane had bitten the end from a cigar and had struck a match. As he held the flame close to his face, his dark sinister eyes flashed into those of the Police Agent.

The cruel smile disfigured his face again, as he threw down the match and without a word turned on his heel and strode off into the night.

"What a devil!" said Keratieff to himself, as he looked after the retreating figure. "But all the same an invaluable member of our Third Section." And then, hailing a droschky which had been hovering about as if anticipating a fare, he sprang into it, and disappeared in the direction of the police head-quarters.

As the sound of the sleigh-bells died away in the distance, the moon shone down upon the Newski Prospect and the square of St. Nicholas, which were once more deserted in the frost-bitten air.

# CHAPTER II.
## Husband and Wife.

Of St. Petersburg, as of every other city of the world, the most magnificent and the most squalid dwelling-places abut upon the river. Just as the late Tuileries and the Louvre, in common with the obscurest tenements of the Quartier Latin, look upon the Seine,—just as the Houses of Parliament and Somerset House, in common with the 'long-shore hovels of the city, look upon the Thames,—so in Petersburg the Winter Palace, in common with the warrens of the *moujik* population, looks upon the Neva.

In these warrens live for the most part the students of the city; here it is that the majority of Nihilist intrigues foster and spread, and here it is that the domestic spy, the *dvornik*, or *concierge*, is most looked after and best paid by the Secret Police. It is here also that tenements can be found whose *dvorniks* are better paid by the tenants than by the police, and where individuals who desire to efface themselves conceal their identities behind passports either fictitious in themselves or issued to worthy citizens who have died or disappeared long ago.

In a blind alley leading from the inner court of one of the most intricate blocks of buildings we find with difficulty a low door, announcing a squalid interior, to all appearance a stable or warehouse. We might knock here for an hour without evoking any sign of human habitation, but draw a stick or stone lightly across the door and we are answered by a single word whispered inside. A couple of these passwords are exchanged, and the door opens noiselessly.

Immediately the foot-fall is muffled by the furs with which the hall-way is strewn. We pass through heavy curtains and reach the innermost room of this abode, which, lit entirely by sky-lights and softly-burning lamps, is a very jewel-box. The apartment into which we have penetrated is carpeted with Ukraine and Siberian skins, the walls are hung with silks from Ispahan and embroideries from Damascus. The furniture is of the carved ebony from the banks of the Indus, ancient weapons of Turkish origin are festooned upon the silken walls, and on the tables are scattered the gold and silver trinkets of Indian and Persian master-workmen. An inlaid lute of Venetian craft lies upon a chair, an Angora cat is stretched asleep upon another, at opposite ends of the room hang masterpieces of Flemish and French art, in a corner stands a marble statuette from some Florentine *atelier*: in a word, all that luxury and taste can conceive is grouped here as a proper setting for the woman who lies upon a huge divan, nestling among the piled-up cushions in her garments of soft clinging silks,—waiting.

The woman who waits is the Princess Nadine Galitzin, once the handmaiden of the Princess Carita, and now the wife of the young Prince Ladislas.

Yes, the Prince Ladislas Galitzin had made what the world would have stigmatized as a *mésalliance*, but no one would doubt for a moment, looking at the woman as she lies on her divan, that some strain of noble blood, a bar sinister if you will, made her worthy to share the title even of the last Prince Galitzin.

As she lies waiting the advent of her husband, her mind wanders back over all the ecstasy of the past two years. She lives over again the happy days in the chateau by Ladoga, where she lived more the companion and sister of the Princess Carita than her handmaid,—the arrival from college of Prince Ladislas,—the gradual awaking in her soul of the conviction that this was the Kamar-al-Zaman of her dreams, the King of the Time for her. She remembers the steps in their courtship, the first time that their eyes met and rested in each other, and the death thenceforth of the indifference of the maiden to her mistress's brother; their sudden meeting in one of the corridors, when the prince had clasped her in his arms and kissed her for the first time and then fled without a word; then the progress of their secret betrothal, so sedulously concealed from the old Prince Galitzin; the misery with which she learned of his approaching departure to take up his commission in the Tzar's body-guard, the Regiment of the Transfiguration, and how the prince persuaded his old tutor the family chaplain to marry them secretly in the chapel of the chateau; their flight to Petersburg; the joys of the year that had elapsed since then,—the greatest of all, perhaps, the day when the Princess Carita had come to her hiding-place to welcome her by the sweet name of sister.

The concealment of their marriage had been a matter of vital necessity. The young Prince Galitzin, last of his branch of a family exalted throughout the history of the Empire, had in his wild student days been suspected of liberal views, and the Tzar had designed for him a brilliant marriage with the daughter of one of the oldest conservative families of his realm. Hence his position in the body-guard; hence the necessity for the concealment of his marriage. Only one besides his sister knew of it, and that was Dmitri Keratieff, Chief of that Third Section,—the secret police that, even today, make life in Russia a perpetual terror. But Dmitri Keratieff owed much to the Galitzin family, and with him the secret was safe until such time as its keeping should conflict with his devotion to his master.

The Princess Nadine lay anxiously awaiting her husband: her state was delicately precarious, and the mystery that surrounded her sometimes told hard upon her. Suppose anything should happen? The secret police, she knew too well, acted blindly like the Council of Ten upon denunciations made by unknown enemies. If such a fate should befall her idol, what would be his doom,—and hers? At the thought, recurring as it did tonight with tenfold persistence, she buried her head in the cushions and groaned rather than cried,—

"Husband! husband!"

A rattle of the rings of the hangings, a strong step upon the piled-up furs, and he is with her.

"Nadia—*matiouchka* [little mother], beloved! I am here!"

She is in his arms in an instant; all her misery, all her apprehension, is lost in the ecstasy of his kiss. Yes, he is safe,—safe from all harm; for no one can disturb them here. Their secret is too well guarded. She has no fear.

"I have been so frightened, Ladislas: every hour that you are not with me I torture myself with fears for you. Suppose they should discover me? Perhaps they would look upon your disobedience to the Tzar as cause for your arrest,—for—for anything. Oh, be careful, beloved; should anything befall you it would kill me,—would kill us both. Think of that other life that shall be so dear to us, Ladislas."

"Courage,—courage, Nadia!" he replies. "There is no danger. We cannot be discovered, sweetheart. I know how lonely, how dull you must be. Well, tonight I have a surprise for you: we expect a visitor."

"A visitor?" A look of alarm creeps into the beautiful eyes as she echoes his words.

"Yes. You have heard me speak of Alexis Alexandrovitch?"

"Alexis Dorski, the Nihilist!"

"The same. My old college companion, unknown even to the faction of which he is the leader, comes to Petersburg tonight. I want him to see my wife, my pride. He is coming here."

"Oh, Ladislas, how imprudent you are!"

"Not at all. I have the fullest knowledge that his presence here is unsuspected. Nothing can ever assail Alexis Dorski if he so wills it. Have no fear, darling."

As he speaks, the old servant who alone waits upon the Princess Ladislas Galitzin enters the room.

"What is it?"

"A peddler, an old man armed with the passwords and countersign, desires to speak with your Excellency."

"Admit him."

The servitor retires, and a moment later, lifting the hangings, gives entrance to a bent figure carrying a pack. As soon as the servant has left them the peddler rises to his full height. With a gesture he flings off his disguise of hair and beard and stands before them a young giant.

"Alexis Alexandrovitch!"

"Ladislas Ladislaievitch!"

And the two men are locked in each other's arms.

# CHAPTER III.
## The Arrest.

"At last, after so many years, old friend!" It is the Prince Ladislas who speaks, holding the other by the hand. Then, turning to the woman whose frightened eyes are fixed upon the new-comer, he says, "Nadia, this is my old friend Alexis Alexandrovitch Dorski."

"I have heard much of you from my husband, Alexis Alexandrovitch," said she, raising her eyes once more to Dorski's, and addressing him in the familiar Russian fashion. "Welcome to our hiding-place and our home."

"No doubt you fear me, princess," returned Dorski; "but your fears are groundless, believe me. No word or act of mine can implicate your husband. I sought this interview to tell you so."

"I pray that it be so," said the Princess Nadine.

"Well, and how goes the cause?" put in Ladislas Galitzin, cheerily.

"Bravely," replied the other, "both here and in the provinces. We have friends at court, high up,—very high,—in the Regiment of the Transfiguration, as in all three sections of the police. A few years, maybe, a few months, perhaps, and Russia shall be free. What Alexander the Second has done for us already he will do again. He will add to his reforms, and Russia will be free. If not,——"And his sentence closed with significant silence.

The princess turned a look of fear towards her husband.

"Have no fear, *matiouchka*," replied the latter, interpreting her look. "I am no conspirator. Alexis and I are friends, but no more. I am not one of his lieutenants. By St. Katerine!" continued he, with a laugh, "I care too little for it all to risk my neck. I am too much at peace with the world, too happy with you, sweetheart, to bear ill-will towards any man, be he Tzar or *moujik*. No, I was never made for a Terrorist. I left that all behind me when I left college; and when our secret society that was to do such wonders was broken up without my being implicated, why, I thought myself well out of it, and settled down as a respectable married man." And he laughed again carelessly as he threw himself on the divan beside his wife.

"Right!" exclaimed Dorski. "That is as it should be. Do not let us say anything more about it. See, I have brought you something." So saying, he drew from his pocket a little leather case. Opening it, he disclosed a portrait of himself set round with opals, which he handed to the princess.

"It is a little wedding-present, though it comes late for the wedding," said he. "But it may serve to impress upon your mind the features of a man who would willingly give up his liberty, and, if needs be, his life, for your husband."

"I thank you, Alexis Alexandrovitch," replied the woman. "I shall cherish your present. But why did you let them set opals round it? I think they will bring us misfortune. Am I not foolish?"

"Yes, indeed," cried Ladislas, "by all the saints, a most excellent portrait, old friend. It shall be one of our greatest treasures."

The three stood together looking at the miniature, when suddenly the stillness was broken by three heavy blows upon the outer door, and by a voice crying, in the silence of the night,—

"Open, in the name of His Majesty the Tzar!"

Every face became white as they exchanged glances; Ladislas hurriedly thrust the portrait into his pocket, and Dorski exclaimed,—

"Great heaven! I am discovered! And yet,—it is impossible. My presence is undreamt of. No matter; hide me,—somewhere,—anywhere."

"Here,—here,—quick," whispered Prince Ladislas, pressing a spring in the frame of one of the large pictures. The picture swung out from the wall, disclosing an open space behind it, contrived in the building. "In here; and do not utter a sound."

"Do not betray my presence by word or look," whispered Dorski, gathering up his pack and his disguise, and stepping into the recess. "I will not be taken alive."

Ladislas Galitzin hurriedly closed the picture, and took his place on the divan beside his wife, who was more dead than alive with terror. Meanwhile, the blows on the outer door and the summons were repeated.

"Open, in the name of His Majesty the Tzar!"

"Open the door!" cried Prince Galitzin, loud enough to be heard outside. "There is no reason why the inmates of this house should fear the mandates of our father the Tzar."

Footsteps sounded in the corridor, a clank as of arms was heard, and Dmitri Keratieff stepped into the room.

"What is the meaning of this?" demanded the prince, haughtily. "See, you have terrified my—my—mistress almost to death. We harbor no suspected persons here."

"My business is with you, Excellency."

"Indeed! Name it."

"I hold a warrant for your arrest on a charge of treason against the sacred person of His Majesty."

"Of treason!—I? Monstrous! Of what am I accused?"

"Of complicity with the traitor Alexis Dorski."

"He is not here! he is not here!" cried the princess, recovering consciousness in time to hear the police-officer's last words.

"I know it," replied the latter. "The police is well informed of his movements; he is now in the Ukraine. The prince is arrested, however, on the evidence of a letter he has received from Dorski, and which is in the hands of the police."

"His letter!" exclaimed the prince. "How——"

"Enough said," broke in the officer. "We cannot enter into explanations. Your Excellency will follow me?"

"Yes." Ladislas was about to follow him, when suddenly the portrait of Dorski flashed across his mind. Quick as thought his hand sought his pocket where it lay; but the keen eye of the Chief of Police caught the action, and, supposing the prince to be in search of some weapon, he sprang upon him, crying out as he did so a word of command in Russian. Two soldiers entered the room. At a sign from Keratieff they seized the prince's arms. Then Keratieff, putting his hand into the prince's pocket, drew forth the miniature!

"Ah!" he exclaimed, "there needed but this. A portrait of the traitor himself carried on the prince's person. Come. Let us go."

"Send out your soldiers for a moment, Keratieff," said the prince. "I have something to say."

Keratieff gave the word, and the soldiers retired.

"Where am I to be taken?" asked Prince Galitzin.

"To the Schlusselburg."

At the word the prince turned paler yet. Then, commanding himself, he said,—

"Keratieff, you and I know too well what this means. This lady is my wife: let me be alone with her for five minutes. You will not refuse me. I give you my word that I will await you here."

"So be it," returned the Chief of Police, softened in spite of himself as he took in the condition of affairs at a glance. "In five minutes I will return." And he left the husband and wife alone.

As soon as he was gone, Ladislas Galitzin flung himself by the side of his wife, and whispered eagerly in her ear:

"Nadia,—*matiouchka*,—look up, beloved. All may yet be well. They have no suspicion that *he* is here. When I am gone, aid him to escape. Tell him that this is Vyvian Fane's work: I insulted him in the Club tonight. If anything should befall me, bid him avenge me, and you. My poor darling, how can I leave you thus, now? Send at once for Carita. She will care for you till I am free,—and longer, if need shall be. Come, come, be brave. See! I am not afraid!"

And so in agony he tried to soothe, to comfort the paralyzed woman. It seemed like an instant only when Keratieff appeared, pale and silent, at the door.

They went out together.

In the outer street a droschky awaited them, into which Keratieff stepped with his prisoner. The two soldiers followed on horseback as the party moved off in the night.

An hour later the same droschky drove away from the ferry landing of the Fortress of the Schlusselburg. As he made for his hovel by the Neva, the *isvoshtshik* said to himself,—

"So that was your business with the Gospodar Keratieff, son of a dog! Ah! scoundrel, ah! filth, you would strike me with your cane, would you? We shall see; we shall see. The Terror is sometimes as powerful as the Secret Police!"

# CHAPTER IV.
## A Nihilist Leader.

Meanwhile, as he heard the sound of the sleigh-bells vanish in the distance, Alexis Dorski, opening the picture-frame from the inside, stepped into the room in which the arrest had been made.

The Princess Galitzin was lying motionless upon the divan. Kneeling by her side, the Terrorist endeavored to rouse her.

"Princess," he whispered, "rouse yourself, I implore you. The night grows old, and I must away. Rouse yourself, and listen to me."

Raising herself as if with great difficulty, the eyes of the princess met those of the Nihilist. As they met, she shrank back with a start, exclaiming,—

"Leave me! leave me! I cannot bear to look at you! It was for you they took him."

"Nay, Nadine Fedorovna, it was not for me. Some private revenge has been at work tonight, and—hear me—I swear by the Holy Saints and my devotion to the cause of Liberty that I will avenge your husband. Tell me, has he never mentioned any enemy by name?"

"Yes, yes: he bade me tell you! It has been the work of the Englishman, Vyvian Fane. Swear—swear to me that if they kill Ladislas you will avenge him!"

"I swear it. If this charge is proven against this Vyvian Fane, should it be the work of my whole lifetime, I will punish him. I have sworn it!"

"Thank you,—thank you, Alexis Alexandrovitch! Ah! but what agony!" And with a convulsive movement the woman buried her head in the cushions once more.

Alexis Dorski stood looking down at her. In an instant his keen instinct had taken in the gravity of her condition: he realized that if a triple murder were not to be the work of the night's arrest, aid must be summoned immediately. Bending over her prostrate form, he whispered, in a tone whose softness would have made his desperate followers marvel,—

"Tell me, Nadine Fedorovna, have you no friend that I can call,—no woman———?"

"Carita! Carita!" she moaned, between her clinched teeth.

Rising and hastily resuming his disguise, Dorski went out into the night.

✳

Half an hour later the *dvornik* of the Galitzin Palace was roused by a knocking on his door.

"Dog of a reveller, what wantest thou at such a time?"

And there came back through the door the almost whispered words,—

"In the name of His Majesty and of the Third Section, a message for her Excellency the Princess Carita Alexandrovna."

Hastily tumbling out of his improvised bed, the *dvornik* opened the door. There stood on the threshold an old peddler.

"Deliver this to one of the princess's women at once. It must reach her hand immediately. You understand?"

"Yes, Excellency," replied the *dvornik*, accustomed to seeing the emissaries of the secret police in every form of disguise.

And half an hour later the *troïka* of the Princess Galitzin swept out from under the gate-way and disappeared in the direction of the Neva.

It still wanted three hours of daylight, and the peddler, having delivered his summons at the Galitzin Palace, thought for an instant, and then stepped off at a brisk pace down the broad Prospect, towards the square of St. Katerine, where three or four droschkies stood, awaiting the chance of a night-customer.

As he passed the group of *isvoshtshiks* that stood smoking in a door-way he laid one hand upon his hip, the fingers pointing earthward, raising the other to his ear. As he did so he ejaculated the familiar greeting,—

"*Zdrastvouitai*" ("Good-night").

And one of the group answered with a guttural "*Choroskho*!" ("All right!")

The peddler pursued his way.

The moujik who had answered his salutation, after a moment's delay, bade his companions good-night, and, mounting the driving-seat of his droschky, started off in pursuit of the peddler. He passed him under a lamp, and as the peddler repeated the motion he had previously made, the moujik drew his horse towards the curb, and held out a hand palm upward, as if ascertaining whether it rained or not.

"The night is fine," said the peddler.

"The air is free," said the *isvoshtshik*.

"The air is Russian," said the peddler.

"Men must have air,' said the isvoshtshik.

"*Choroskho!*"

The droschky drew up, and without a word the peddler got in and was driven a few yards down a by-street. Here he said, "Halt!" and the droschky stopped. The peddler alighted, and, drawing a small object from beneath his arm, held it up to the *moujik*. It was a small gold disk on which was enamelled a red cross.

"Holy St. Nicholas!" ejaculated the *moujik*: "it is the Chief. What are my lord's commands?"

"One of the *isvoshtshiks* of Petersburg drove a prisoner from the Neva to one of the fortresses tonight. You will bring him to this address at ten o'clock in the morning." And the peddler wrote a few words on a slip of paper, which the isvoshtshik read carefully and then destroyed.

"If he be alive, he will be there, Excellency."

"Good! Salutation and freedom!"

"Amen. Salutation and freedom!"

And the pair parted once more in opposite directions.

At the time appointed next morning, Alexis Dorski sat before the stove in a room of one of the houses of a quiet suburb of St. Petersburg. He was immersed in thought, but looked up expectantly as the clock struck. He had not long to wait. Almost immediately the *moujik* whom he had accosted on the Newski Prospect entered, accompanied by the one whom we met at the opening of this history.

After casting over him a keen glance of inspection, Dorski and the new-comer exchanged three or four almost imperceptible signs and countersigns. He was apparently satisfied with his examination, and said,—

"Last night you were employed by the police."

"Yes, Excellency."

"To what ferry did you take the prisoner??"

"To the ferry of the Schlusselburg, Excellency."

"Good God! Know you anything of the arrest?"

"Yes, indeed, Excellency," answered the *moujik*, eagerly, "that do I. Earlier in the evening a foreigner hired me to take him to the head of the Newski Prospect. There, when I demanded my fare, he struck me with his cane: see, here is the scar: it will be weeks healing. There he was met by the Gospodar Keratieff of the police, and, burning with fury, I hung about. When they parted, Dmitri Keratieff took me to police head-quarters, thence to the Neva, and thence with his prisoner to the Schlusselburg Ferry. Ah! dog of a foreigner! wait for me!"

"Did Keratieff address the foreigner by name?"

"Yes, Excellency: it was—it was—Ivan—something."

"Vyvian Fane?"

"Yes! yes! that was it, God be praised! I could not remember."

"Good! That will do. Your name?"

"Rodia Pouschkoff."

"It is well. Good-day. Salutation and freedom!"

"Amen. Salutation and freedom!"

The two *moujiks* left the room.

"Now, Vyvian Fane,—since that seems to be your name,—the issue remains between you and me. If the fate of the Schlusselburg befalls Ladislas Ladislaievitch, beware! The world is not wide enough to hide you from the talons of the Terror!"

278

# CHAPTER V.
## The Princess Carita.

Two days have elapsed since the events occurred which are recorded in the preceding chapter.

In one of the lower rooms of the Galitzin Palace, fitted up as a boudoir, the Princess Carita Galitzin sat at her writing-table, her head resting on her hands. She was dressed in black, and her sable garments served to heighten the pallor of her face no less than the red eyelids that announced the fact that she had been weeping.

Every few minutes she would eagerly look through the papers on the desk before her, as if in search of something which she sought in vain.

At last she is roused by a footstep in the corridor. The hangings of the door part and fall together again, and the Honorable John Vyvian Fane enters the room unannounced.

"Well," he says, by way of greeting, as he flings himself into a chair, "at last Madame la Princesse is good enough to send for her devoted slave, after an absence from home of forty-eight hours. Pray, what new intrigue, what new *amourette*, is engrossing the Princess Carita 's attention?" The cruel sneer is on his lips, a tone of raillery is in his voice.

"I have been at the death-bed of two of your victims," she replies, never taking her eyes from his.

"You speak in riddles, princess."

"No, I speak plainly. You have killed a woman and her child by way of revenging yourself upon a man who never harmed you, whose only crime was to know your true vile self."

"What do you mean?"

"I mean that you have caused the arrest of my brother by means of a letter that he confided to me for safe-keeping, and which you, cowardly thief that you are, have stolen from this bureau."

"I am sorry, of course, to hear of your brother's misfortune, but a man who is in communication with traitors to the Tzar has no business to get married,—especially clandestinely."

The princess rose and came close to him.

"How did you know?" said she, "that I was speaking of my brother's wife?"

The man saw his false step immediately, and endeavored to retrieve it.

"I did not know," he stammered: "I only assumed. You seemed so excited that I concluded——"

"Cease lying to me, John Vyvian Fane! I do not expect you to show mercy, but I look at least for shame, even from you. What have you done with the document you have stolen?"

"Really, princess, this scene is beginning to pass the possibilities. If your brother has been arrested for treason, I am of course sorry, for it must naturally entail unpleasant consequences upon you. If he has been so foolish as to make a secret marriage, I am of course sorry for his wife. If, as you say, she is dead, I think she is better off than she would be as the wife of a convict with a 'wolf's passport' to Siberia. This is all I have to say."

"You hound!"

"Take care, princess. I am not accustomed to insult of this kind, and I will not allow it even from you. Do you hear me? I will not allow it! Do you think that I am a man to be played with? I think I have given you proof ere now to the contrary. Be good enough to remember what I say!"

For all reply the princess pointed to the door.

"Go!" said she, "and never let me see your coward face again. Go, I say, or I will summon my servants and have you thrown out,—ay! thrown out,—and I will take the consequences of my action. Do you think I, Carita Galitzin, fear you, police spy though you have proved yourself to be? You hear me. I am ready to take the consequences, I tell you."

"In any case," returned Fane, with a violent effort at self-control, "I see that it is useless to prolong *this* interview. I leave you now; but I will return when you are prepared to listen to reason. I deny all your charges against me, and at some future time I will prove to you that any trouble your—relations may be in they have brought upon themselves. Good-morning. Mind! when I return you will be civil: at present I can make excuses for you."

And, with a feeble attempt at nonchalance, the Honorable John Vyvian Fane left the room.

Left by herself, the Princess Galitzin buried her head once more in her hands and resumed her interrupted chain of thought. At last she rose, and, hastily effecting some changes in her toilet, she prepared to leave the house. Whatever was to be her brother's fate, she must seek an interview with him at once; and well she knew the difficulties that lay before her in encompassing her end.

All that day she flew from official to official, from minister to minister; she even sought and obtained an interview with the Tzarewitch himself, and nightfall saw her, provided with the necessary passes, at the ferry of the Schlusselburg, accompanied by a captain of the military police.

## CHAPTER VI.
### In the Fobtbess of the Schlusselbubg.

On one of the islands that cluster in the mouth of the river Neva rises a gaunt pile of buildings, within hailing-distance of which no boat save one ever approaches. It is the dreaded Fortress of the Schlusselburg, one of the great prisons where political suspects are incarcerated. The other is the Fortress of St. Peter and St. Paul. The Schlusselburg has been dramatically described by an American writer as follows: "The guards are so thick on the banks of the island that they can speak to one another, and their orders are, as they pace their beats, to shoot any person who attempts to land. No warning is given, no password is asked. As soon as the foot of a stranger touches the turf on the banks of the island a bullet is fired at his heart. His body falls into the stream and floats down to the sea. No questions are asked. Only one boat is allowed to land on the island; that is painted black and belongs to the police. No one has ever returned from that prison. People may have been released from it, but if so they have never confessed the fact; and the popular belief is that whoever lands there once never leaves alive except to go to Siberia."

It was hither that the young Prince Ladislas had been brought, and at nightfall on the day of which we speak the Princess Galitzin took her seat in the boat to gain the fortress on a visit—an unheard-of concession—in company with the two officers.

She was met at the entrance to the fortress by the chaplain of the prison, an old parish priest, a *batiushka* who had found his way thither twenty years before for having sympathized with and ministered to some dying Nihilist.

The old man's face was inexpressibly sad as he greeted the princess with the benediction of the Church.

"We must be brave, my daughter," he said. "The prince your brother is grievously ill. On the night of his arrival he was confined in one of the lower cells, and the cold and damp attacked him. You must be prepared for a great change."

"My God! is he dead?"

"No, my child."

"He is dying?"

"We are in the hands of God!"

She laid her hand upon his sleeve:

"Tell me, *batiushka*. They have poisoned him?"

The priest made the sign of the cross as he replied once more,—

"We are in the hands of God, my daughter. Come with me.

They have moved him into one of the upper rooms."

In a room looking out over the city, whose lights twinkled across the water, the Prince Ladislas lay dying. That was obvious to the princess the moment she laid her eyes upon the wasted form and drawn features. The film of death was growing over his eyes. For a moment he hardly seemed to notice her; then, raising himself with an effort for an instant, only to fall back upon his pallet exhausted, he whispered,—

"Carita—you! Nadia,—where is she?"

"Ladislas,—brother,—my God! how can I tell you!" And she sank on her knees by the dying man's side.

He raised himself again on one elbow.

"Where is she? Why do you not answer? Holy Mother! has he killed her, too? Yes! yes! She is dead,—my wife, Nadia; is it not so?"

He was answered only by the broken sobs of the prostrate woman.

"Carita," he whispered, with fast-failing breath, "you will avenge us, you and Alexis. Listen: it was the Englishman Vyvian Fane that betrayed me. He stole the letter from you: how he did it I cannot tell; it matters not. Keratieff has it. You swear this?"

"I swear it, brother!"

"Thank God! Come closer. I cannot see you, but you are there, are you not, *matiouchka* beloved——"

A deep sigh ended his sentence, which his sister caught in a last wild kiss.

The Prince Ladislas was dead.

She had arrived but just in time.

The clocks were striking midnight as the princess landed once more at the ferry pier.

Her troïka awaited her, and she was swallowed up by the night.

# CHAPTER VII.
## A Woman's Vengeance.

Early in the day that succeeded the death of the Prince Ladislas Galitzin in the Fortress of the Schusselburg, the Chief of the Secret Police, Dmitri Keratieff, sat in his office, pondering over the events of the last few days. The Chief was not satisfied with the turn that affairs had taken. In the exercise of his duties as commander of the dreaded Third Section many a cruel task had fallen to his lot to perform; often he had known himself to be the instrument of private vengeances which he had had to work out or be himself suspected of sympathy with the omnipresent agents of the Nihilists. But this time he felt that he had been the compulsory party to a crime that surpassed any in his official experience in cold ferocity. It was therefore with a new feeling of distaste and apprehension that he read on the card that had been brought him by one of his subordinates the name of the Princess Galitzin.

Still, there was no reason that he could allege for not receiving her, whilst there existed, as he knew, many why he should do so, and finally he gave orders that she should be admitted.

She entered the room a moment later, and seated herself opposite to him. Thus placed, they regarded each other in silence for the space of a full minute. At last the Police Agent spoke:

"What can I do for you, madame?" said he.

"You can do me the first and last favor that any member of our family will ever ask of you in return for all or any that we have done for you, Dmitri Semenovitch."

The Chief of Police fidgeted uneasily in his chair. He did not like the proem; but all he said was,—

"Pray proceed. Anything that I can reasonably do for the Princess Galitzin shall be done."

"Good!" replied she. "This is what I require. My brother, as you know, is dead. His arrest was the death-blow of his wife, of whose existence you alone besides myself were aware. She died in my arms, and her child with her, the night after Ladislas was taken from her. I demand from you the documents on which he was arrested."

"Princess," replied Keratieff, "in the first place I do not admit the existence of any document that led to the late Prince Galitzin's arrest; but, even if such were the case, what you ask would be impossible. Supposing that such documents existed, I should be responsible for their safe custody, and were they to leave my hands I should get in exchange for them 'a wolf's passport' as they say. And the Siberian mines at my time of life are not a thing to be played with."

"One moment," returned the Princess, "and I will prove to you that I am already well informed. The Prince Ladislas Galitzin was arrested in consequence of a letter written to him by the Nihilist leader Dorski. This letter was stolen from *me* and delivered to you by one of your foreign agents, the *Honorable* John Vyvian Fane. By all the rights of common gratitude I demand this letter of you, as a man."

"Princess," replied Keratieff, imperturbably, "I am not in a position to admit the correctness of your—surmises. I do not know, as a man,—the capacity in which you make this request of me,—that Mr. Vyvian Fane has any connection with this department. If you have nothing more to urge, I must beg you to conclude this interview, which, believe me, is as painful to me as it is to you."

For a few moments the princess remained in silent thought. Then, as if with an effort, she made up her mind, and, turning once more to Keratieff, who had risen as if to terminate the conversation, she said,—

"Dmitri Semenovitch, I will say no more of the relations which have existed between our respective families. I appeal to you as a man no longer. But as head of the Russian police you have been made perforce the repository of many family secrets, many details of domestic dramas reach your ears. I am going to recount to you the incidents of a tragedy more bitter than any you yet have heard within these walls. Listen!"

An hour later, at the close of her story the Chief of Police rose from his seat, and, going to an iron chest that stood in the corner of the room, he took thence a paper, which he handed to the princess.

"What you have told me," said he, gravely, "convinces me of your right to this document. Here is the letter stolen from you by John Vyvian Fane: he confessed the theft to me when he delivered it to me as the *pièce d'accusation* on which the arrest took place. Make your mind easy, madame. This Englishman will leave the country at once, never to return. In three days from now he will cross the frontier."

"At last! at last!" thought the princess, as she was rapidly borne through the streets of Petersburg, ten minutes afterwards. "I have my proofs, and you shall be avenged, Ladislas, and you, Nadia, sweet sister mine. My God, I thank thee!—I thank thee!"

Five days later St. Petersburg rang with the news that the travelling-carriage of the Honorable John Vyvian Fane, whose figure had been a prominent one in the festivities of the past season, had been attacked by brigands just over the Polish frontier, and that the Englishman had been massacred.

That night the Princess Galitzin fell on her knees in the oratory of the Galitzin Palace and cried aloud to God,—

"Vengeance is mine! vengeance is mine!"

And the chaplain, entering the oratory a moment after, found her in floods of tears, the first that she had shed since the murder of her brother.

# BOOK I.
## *VIENNA.*

## CHAPTER I.
### A Masquerade Ball.

The grand masquerade at the Vienna Opera-House, of the 15th August, 1876, was at its height.

Round about the corridors, in and out of the boxes, over the floor, the stage, and the balconies, surged the bedlamite crowd of foolishly-dressed men and dominoed women, who were enjoying, or trying to enjoy, or pretending to enjoy, the "grand masquerade." The scene was gay enough, as novelists say, in all conscience, but it must be confessed that unless one is a member of a large and merry party, or unless one has some particular intrigue to carry to its more or less lurid termination, a masked ball is the deadliest, dullest, dreariest affair that was ever invented for the torture of the long-suffering and ironically so-called "gay world."

On no mind did this circumstance impress itself with drearier persistence than on that of Captain the Honorable Aubyn Goddard, some-time of the Twentieth Hussars, and now occupying the uncomfortable but none the less on that account eagerly-sought-after position of Queen's Messenger.

Captain Goddard was the ideal guardsman of the young lady's dream. Well over the regulation six feet in height, and broad in proportion, his well-balanced head was covered with close-cropped fair hair; his irreproachable moustache was carefully trimmed, and the look of intense boredom on his handsome face gave him a certain Byronic expression that evidently found favor in the majority of bright eyes that flashed from beneath dominos of all colors; or at least so it would seem from the persistency with which the fair—or dark—artillerists attacked him, with nod, beck, wreathed smile, nudge, punch, and apology.

But Captain Aubyn Goddard seemed invulnerable, for no irritation or challenge seemed able to rouse him from his apathy as he leaned against one of the pilasters at the foot of the grand staircase and slightly yawned as he watched the procession before him and wondered vaguely on the chance that found him there when he would infinitely rather be in bed.

I use the word "chance" advisedly.

In his capacity of Queen's Messenger he had arrived in Vienna bearing despatches the previous evening, and early that morning had delivered his despatches at the Austrian Foreign Office. He was to leave on the following afternoon.

For the previous five years the political world had been in a ferment over that time-honored bogie, the Eastern Question. In 1871 Mr. Gladstone had sat calmly in Whitehall, and uttered no protest, whilst Russia, repudiating the Treaty of Paris of 1856, converted the Black Sea into a Russian lake, and the effete demagogue whom Lord Beaconsfield has handed down to posterity in his famous epigram, as "a sophisticated rhetorician inebriated with the exuberance of his own verbosity," had rendered the taking of Sevastopol vain, and surrendered all that Europe had won with her blood in the Crimean War. From that time (1871) a cloud had begun to gather in the East, which now threatened to burst and engulf the Balkan Peninsula, and called forth the historic "Andrassy Note" in December, 1875, following on the rising in Herzegovina.

At the sound of Count Andrassy's clarion, Europe awakened from the sleep into which she had been lulled by successive Liberal governments and Gladstonian croonings, and throughout 1876 there had been almost daily interchange of despatches between London, Berlin, Vienna, and Constantinople. As a natural consequence, trusty messengers were in increased demand, and Captain Aubyn Goddard, having, unlike the majority of men of his years, spent his days as a subaltern in the study of European politics and languages, had been one of the first to receive a commission as one of Her Majesty's postmen, and to commence the nomad career of Queen's Messenger specially detailed for Oriental service.

Things were quieting down, and Europe might have had peace, when the deposition and suicide of Abd-ul-Aziz, and the ten days' sultanate of the imbecile Murad the Fifth, once more gave the malcontents in the Balkan Peninsula the opportunity they had looked for, and brought the present Sultan Abd-ul-Hamid the Second to the throne, determined to put down the disturbances that threatened to rend asunder the empire founded by the first Othman and consolidated by Suleiman the Magnificent.

Some cruelties practised by the Turkish soldiery at Batak in Bulgaria afforded Mr. Gladstone the Irrepressible an opportunity to fulminate which no consideration for the welfare of Europe could allow him to let slip, and accordingly he published his incandescent pamphlet on "Bulgarian Atrocities" that in course of time plunged Europe in war and gave Russia the opportunity she had so long desired to encroach in the southeast and southwest of her dominions.

European Cabinets were preparing for the Conference at Constantinople of January, 1877, and thus we find Captain Aubyn Goddard in Vienna in the August of the preceding year.

As the bearer of important despatches, the Queen's Messenger had not thought it expedient to look up any of his convivial acquaintances in the Austrian capital, and after delivering his despatches in the morning he had taken a long and solitary drive, idly wondering how he should kill the hours of that evening and of the following day until he should return to the Foreign Office.

On his return from his drive his question was answered for him. As he entered his hotel an envelope was put into his hand.

He turned it over and over, profoundly perplexed. What could it mean? Whom could it be from? He had apprised no one of his arrival, and the handwriting was entirely unfamiliar. But that he was known was evident; for the superscription was in full:

*To—Captain the Honorable Aubyn Goddard.*

There was nothing to indicate whether the note was addressed in a male or a female handwriting: at last he came to the conclusion that there was only one solution for the mystery, and that that was inside the envelope.

Accordingly he opened it.

Nothing! not a word of any kind. Only a ticket for the masked ball at the opera-house that evening.

Well! there was his evening accounted for. But whence could the ticket have come? Who had brought it? A servant in a black livery that gave no indication of his master's rank or nationality.

"Anyhow," thought the Queen's Messenger, "I'll go. There can be no harm in that. I know how to take care of myself. No doubt my mysterious host will reveal his—or her?—incognito, at the ball."

And so he had dined, had strolled out on to the Prater and watched the motley passing panorama of people as he listened to the strains of "unser Strauss," and when the last chords of the march from "Tannhäuser" had exploded into the blue vault of the sounding-board he stepped into a cab and was deposited at the doors of the Grand Opera-House.

But that had been two hours previous to the moment when we first set eyes on him, and as yet no solution of the mystery of his presence there had offered itself. The ball was at its height, and would presently wane. People who had come on business had transacted it and gone away, people who had come after intrigues had found them and were developing them, and people who had wandered in, unattached and for no particular reason, were beginning to have had enough of it and were turning their thoughts homeward.

Among these latter, as we have said, was the Honorable Aubyn Goddard, and he had just stretched himself and was casting a last look round, after the manner of the man who is about to depart, when a woman passed him.

Her figure, which was gorgeously proportioned, was entirely clad in a tightly-fitting domino of black satin, heavily brocaded with a raised black embroidery. A hood covered her hair, and a black half-mask rendered more brilliant a pair of grand black eyes that caught his for an instant as she passed, and the rich crimson of a rather stern mouth. The jaw was massive, and the complexion colorless. Thus much Goddard had had time to notice, when his attention was diverted to a shambling awkward figure that seemed to be following her. It was that of a man in the costume of a mediaeval jester, that accorded well with his sinister, ugly face. As the woman disappeared in the crowd, Goddard saw the hunchback address her, and saw her shrink from him with a gesture of repulsion, leaving him biting his nails as he leered after her for a moment before starting in pursuit.

Captain Goddard for the first time since his arrival felt an awakening interest in the scene, and resumed his place against the pilaster, waiting for the brocaded domino to pass again.

Suddenly he heard an exclamation behind him, and, looking round, saw the same woman hastily descending the grand staircase. At the same moment the hunchback appeared, shuffling down after her, evidently in hot pursuit. He caught her at the foot of the stairs, and as he passed slipped a piece of paper into her hand which she instantly dropped. Next moment both hunchback and domino once more disappeared.

By this time thoroughly aroused, Goddard stooped and picked up the twisted scrap of paper, though not without a certain sensation that he had no right to do so. He opened it.

The paper was blank!

"Egad," said he to himself, "this is getting interesting. But, despatches or no despatches, that little beast mustn't be allowed to insult that glorious creature." And Captain Goddard—who was only a man, after all—started off in the direction the pair had taken.

His towering frame forced for him a passage through the throng, and he had hardly got half-way around before he found himself immediately behind the brocaded domino.

Where was the hunchback? Ah! there he was. He had passed the domino, and was just advancing as if to address her, when the woman turned sharply and was almost thrown into Goddard's arms.

"I beg your pardon," said she in English without a trace of foreign accent, as she stood irresolute before him.

"I beg yours," replied Goddard. "Can I be of any assistance? I see that you are being annoyed."

"If an utter stranger may so far trespass upon the goodness of a gentleman, may I beg you to conduct me to my carriage? I am alarmed and foolishly upset by this man's persecution."

"Certainly," answered Goddard, extending his arm, as he looked round in search of the hunchback, who had disappeared.

Together they made their way to the entrance. Suddenly the woman spoke:

"I beg that you will forgive me, and I hope you will not misunderstand my object in begging your momentary protection, but I felt that as an English gentleman I could trust you not to look upon me as—as—one of these."

"Of course; of course," replied Goddard, feeling nevertheless vaguely disappointed.

They had reached the grand entrance, and Goddard made as if to turn.

"Not that way," said the domino. "My carriage is at the side-entrance."

"Oh!" returned the Queen's Messenger, his spirits imperceptibly reviving.

She led him down a narrow passage to a door that opened upon a side-street. At the curb stood a perfectly-appointed black coupé, with a single horse of the same color. Goddard opened the door, and she stepped in.

"Will you not accept my protection as far as you have to go?" said Goddard, seeing his "adventure" vanishing into thin air. "You may not yet be safe."

"No," said she, raising her hand as if to stop him. "I am quite safe now."

"Can I direct your coachman?"

"He needs no directions."

"At least you will allow me to call and ascertain that you are quite recovered from your alarm," pleaded Goddard, despairingly.

The woman appeared to reflect for a moment, and then she said,—

"If I give you that permission, will you promise not to make any inquiries about me, and to forget afterwards that we ever met?"

"Yes,"—this desperately.

"On your honor?"

"On my honor."

"Very well." And she took a card from the rack before her, and scribbled a word or two on it in pencil, saying, as she handed it to him, "Do me the pleasure to breakfast with me at this address at twelve tomorrow, or rather today."

"I will be punctual."

"That is well. And now good-night. *Au revoir*, and a thousand thanks, *Captain Aubyn Goddard!*"

His name! she knew it! He started back to get a better view of the carriage. Instantly the door was slammed from the inside, and the coupé dashed off and was lost in the dimly-lighted street.

Goddard took the card which he held in his hand to the nearest lamp. On it was engraved, in tiny capitals,—

THE BARONESS ALTDORFF,

and an address was added in pencil.

"Well, I'm damned!" remarked Captain Aubyn Goddard to himself, as he lit a cigar and walked round to the main entrance of the opera-house as a point of departure for his stroll home in the moonlight.

# CHAPTER II.
## The Baroness Altdorff.

Notwithstanding the late hour of his return from the ball, and the fact that after his return he had spent an hour in fruitless wonder on the events—or rather the event—of the evening, it was a good two hours before mid-day when Captain Aubyn Goddard left his hotel and proceeded to stroll almost unconsciously in the direction of the place of his rendezvous.

To say that he was interested and perplexed is to use a miserably inadequate form of words; but the main outcome of his reflections was that he put the whole thing down as a *bal-masqué* intrigue of a rather more than usual interest, as regarded its commencement at any rate.

There was something indescribably baffling about the woman he had escorted to the street, and whom he hoped to see again within a couple of hours. There was nothing in her voice or manner that betrayed aught but perfect gentleness of birth and breeding. The idea of risking a word of reproof from those wonderful lips, or a look of disdain from those amazing eyes, was quite out of the question; and yet she had made his acquaintance in almost orthodox *bal-masqué* style, and had given him a rendezvous for the morrow in *quite* orthodox *bal-masqué* style. To the Queen's Messenger on service, adventures of all kinds are necessarily a forbidden luxury, and yet Goddard would not for one moment admit to himself that he was running into any personal danger. He could not retrospectively satisfy himself of the woman's nationality. She spoke very perfect English; and yet there was a pretty uncertainty about her *r*'s that betrayed either foreign birth or long residence abroad.

Of the manner of his coming reception, however, he had no doubt. He would be ushered into a boudoir from which daylight would be carefully excluded, a scent of musk or something equally sensuous would hang in the air, the room would be hung with soft silks and decorated with heavily-perfumed exotic flowers, and the woman herself would either be reclining on a divan,

294

or would enter the room with the upward sweep of a shapely arm through velvet *portières*, clad in some bewitching and lace-covered *négligé*. The woman herself, he felt certain, would be dark, and of a heavy, sensuous type of beauty. The face would be not quite innocent of the *veloutine* of Fay, and would be either of a brilliant coloring or of a properly improper ivory pallor.

Together they would partake of a delicate and *recherché* repast, and after breakfast she would sing to him, accompanying herself on the piano, or more probably on the guitar. And then——Well, why anticipate?

He was sufficiently "experienced" to know exactly what to expect.

His reflections were suddenly cut short by his arrival at the very house, "The Villa Altdorff," which the *incognita* of the night before had inscribed upon the card she had given him. It was situated quite on the outskirts of the city, where the suburbs begin to assume a distinctly rural appearance. A high quickset hedge divided and hid the grounds of the villa from the road, but a barred gate opened upon a curving drive that led up to the house. A glance at the house did not serve to enlighten the Queen's Messenger. It had the appearance of being deserted. All the windows were closed with heavy shutters. No smoke rose from the clustered chimneys, no sign of life appeared within the gate, which was securely fastened.

With difficulty restraining an exclamation of surprise, and forgetting, in his astonishment, his promise not to make inquiries, Goddard turned to a municipal gardener who was sweeping under the tulip-trees that lined the quiet suburban road.

"What is this house?" he asked.

"That," returned the man, eying him suspiciously, "is the Villa Altdorff."

"And who lives here?"

"No one."

"How? No one?"

"No. It has been closed ever since the death of the Baroness Altdorff, three years ago."

"But it does not look neglected."

"No; the family keep the gardens neat, but it is never occupied."

"You are sure?"

The man vouchsafed no answer. He had turned once more to his work, and studiously ignored his questioner, whom he probably took for a gentlemanly burglar compiling notes for a campaign.

So this was the end of his adventure! Better so, after all, thought the Queen's Messenger, since he had to be at the Foreign Office at four to receive Andrassy's despatches. The end? Stay! it wanted yet an hour of mid-day; he would continue his walk and return at the time appointed: at least should chance ever throw him against his dazzling domino again she should not be able to reproach him with not having fulfilled the terms of her invitation.

The Honorable Aubyn Goddard walked on, beyond the outer fortifications.

Punctually at twelve o'clock he found himself once more at the gate of the Villa Altdorff; and now a new surprise awaited him. The gate stood open! He entered. As he walked up the drive he noted with ever-increasing wonderment that the shutters were all thrown open, as were the lower windows. From one chimney a column of smoke rose into the air. On the veranda in front stood two chairs, and some Oriental rugs lay before them. On one of them lay a shawl and a book, giving evidence of recent occupation. From one corner of the rug a very British fox-terrier rose, stretched himself, and trotted down the drive to meet him and assure himself that the perfume of the visitor was a friendly perfume.

As he readied the door it was opened by a grave butler in the correctest black,—not by the pert Parisian maid he had anticipated,—who ushered him at once into a drawing-room matted with Indian grass and furnished throughout in the white-gold style ascribed to Louis XV. Dazed beyond the power of expression, Goddard was walking to a window to inspect the exterior, when the full soft voice that had been echoing in his brain for the past ten hours said behind him,—

"Captain Goddard."

He turned, to see his hostess advancing towards him with out-stretched hand.

True to his anticipation, she was dark; but there the correctness of his anticipation began and ended. The gorgeous figure was held with stately erectness, and was clad from throat to foot in the most correctly fitting of tailor-made suits ("Turned out by Morgan, for a fiver!" ejaculated Goddard to himself), at the throat and wrists a collar and cuffs of the snowiest linen, secured by plain gold buttons. Her only ornament was a crimson rose thrust into the bosom of the dress. The raven-black hair was carried smoothly off the high white forehead and drawn to a simple coil at the back of the head.

The vision before him was one of ideal health, perfect womanly beauty, and eminent "good form." Aubyn Goddard stood speechless. The Baroness Altdorff was, of course, perfectly self-possessed.

"You are punctual, Captain Goddard. That is well. We shall have the more time in which to make each other's acquaintance,— or rather to improve it."

"Pardon me," said Goddard, in reply, "if for a few moments I am too bewildered to talk rationally. You have me at a great disadvantage. Will you tell me where we have met before today?"

"Not now. But before we part,—yes. Let me see: at four o'clock you must be at the Foreign Office, at five you leave Vienna. I am right, am I not? Yes? Then I propose that we breakfast at once and talk afterwards."

"I am completely at Madame's service."

"Don't make any rash announcements! you ought to mistrust me profoundly. Admit at least that my conduct has been highly irregular."

"Well, I——"

"The fact is," broke in the woman, in a serious tone, "I have long wished to make your acquaintance. The opportunity arrived for me to do you a service, unknown to yourself, and in doing it I killed two birds with one stone: I took the part of Captain Aubyn Goddard in a diplomatic war, and made his acquaintance into the bargain. All is fair, you know, in war!"

"And in love!" concluded Goddard, with a nervous laugh.

"Exactly," replied the Baroness Altdorff, with a slight blush, "but at present the former alone engrosses our attention. But come; breakfast is ready. Will you follow me? Unlike most women who make gentlemen's acquaintances under romantic circumstances, I am ravenonsly hungry."

She led the way into the dining-room, where a breakfast was served in perfect taste but supreme simplicity.

"At least you will begin," said Goddard, as he seated himself, "by giving me a few words of explanation. First, how did you know my name? and, second, did you send me the ticket for yesterday's ball?"

"I know your name, for in the society of Vienna not to know Captain Aubyn Goddard, of Her Majesty's Diplomatic Service, is to argue one's self unknown. It *was* I who sent you the ticket for last night's ball, for reasons that I will explain to you presently. I am very much interested in the questions that have brought you to Vienna four times in as many months, and chance favored me last night in bringing about a meeting to which I have long looked forward."

She spoke with charming frankness, looking him straight in the eyes, and it was with a, to him, altogether new sensation that he replied, with a little inclination,—

"Whatever may have been your motive, baroness, believe me, I congratulate myself, more profoundly than I can say on so short an acquaintance, on the chance that has thrown us together—at last."

A ring of intense earnestness had come into his voice as he answered, returning her gaze. The woman flushed perceptibly as she turned the conversation:

"Your profession must be a strangely interesting one. You are so much behind the scenes. The Powers will unite in conference about December or January, will they not?"

He glanced at her keenly. "I cannot tell," replied he, cautiously, "but it looks like it at present."

"It seems so strange to me that England should submit so calmly to the dictation of Russia. I should have thought that your government would have despatched a fleet to the Levant."

"That would not take place unless the Conference should prove abortive."

"Ah! then the step is already considered?"

"I do not know," replied Goddard, shortly, as he suddenly perceived that he had been led into an important disclosure. Then he added,

"You seem vastly interested in European politics. Ladies do not usually trouble about such matters."

"Oh, I adore them," replied the baroness, with a laugh; "but it annoys me when I see your English interests calmly flung into the lap of Gortschakoff by your Mr. Gladstone."

"Mr. Gladstone will have nothing to do with it," replied Goddard, dryly. "The entertainment of 1871 will not be repeated, I can assure you. So long as Lord Beaconsfield lives, you may be sure that the Pruth will bound Russia on the southwest, and Batoum and Constantinople will *not* become Russian military seaports." He spoke with quick indignation, for Goddard was of the true Tory faith, and the light tone of this foreign woman stung him in a sensitive place. The Baroness Altdorff plunged her eyes deep into his, and leaned forward as she replied,—

"That is how I like to hear a man talk. *That* is the substance of your despatches, on this mission?"

Goddard was about to lie promptly in expressing his ignorance, but something in the woman's look made his heart leap into his throat, and he answered nothing, as the color rose to the roots of his hair.

"That is right," she said, softly. "I could not imagine you lying to me."

"No," answered the man, shortly: "I cannot lie to you."

The Baroness Altdorff rose.

"Let us go into the drawing-room," she said, with a sudden change of manner. "We have yet an hour before you need start. At half-past three my coupé will take you to the Foreign Office, and thence to the station. Will you oblige me by sending my man from the Office to settle your bill and bring your luggage from your hotel? I do not want you to return."

"Really, I feel ashamed to take advantage "began Goddard.

"Promise me! promise me" she interrupted, eagerly.

"Certainly, it shall be as you wish. But, in heaven's name, give me some explanation of all this mystery."

"Very well," replied she; "I will. I need not tell Captain Goddard that diplomacy in Russia sticks at nothing. I happened to have learnt that an effort would be made to detain you in Vienna by the Russian agents there. You were to be summoned from your hotel last night. They laid their plans well. I sent you the ticket to insure your absence, and came myself to the ball to see that you were safely there. The hunchback whom you saw persecuting me adopted that course to mix you up in a most unpleasant *esclandre*. He knew that an English gentleman would not suffer an unprotected woman to be insulted in his presence. It is needless to say that he was a political spy. Had we left the opera-house by the main entrance you would have found yourself this morning in a duel or a police court. It was necessary to hide you today. I thought of this place as we sought my carriage. They have watched for you at your hotel all day. Remember, you have promised not to return there with your despatches."

"Do you think I am going to run away from the creature?" said Goddard, indignantly.

"It is your duty to guard your despatches," answered the woman, calmly.

"You are right," answered he, simply, after a pause.

The conversation took another turn. Her interest drew from Goddard—almost, I was going to say, the story of his life, and when the clock struck half-past three it was almost with a start that he recalled himself to the present.

It was the Baroness Altdorff who cut the conversation short. "It is time for you to go," she said. "I am sorry."

"And I too, baroness," replied Goddard. "I have not half expressed to you my gratitude for all you have done for me, still less for these charming hours with you."

"Then you forgive my plot against your liberty?"

"Yes," replied he, boldly. "All is fair, as we said, in love and war, and—and both are here."

The Baroness Altdorff crimsoned despite herself.

"Good-bye," said she, holding out her hand again.

"Not good-bye, I trust," pleaded he, as he held the delicate white hand in his. They had reached the front door, where the presence of the grave butler holding open the door of the coupé which stood in readiness placed a restraint upon the wild declaration he was tempted to pour out to her. "Not good-bye, baroness, but *au revoir*. Is it not so?" And he leaned forward as he pressed the taper fingers.

"I hope so,—believe me," replied she, and her pallor intensified.

"Then I go not altogether in despair," said Goddard, gayly, as he descended the steps.

As he took his seat in the carriage he turned to where she stood on the veranda.

"I forgot!" he exclaimed. "You said you would tell me where we met before today. Where was it?"

"At the ball last night."

The servant slammed the door, and the carriage whirled off down the drive. As it turned out of the gate, Goddard looked hastily out of the window. The windows of the Villa Altdorff were once more shuttered as they had been in the morning. No smoke rose from the chimneys. All signs of human habitation had disappeared.

The Villa Altdorff seemed deserted!

Captain the Honorable Aubyn Goddard flung himself back on the cushions of the coupé.

"By Jove!" he exclaimed, "this carriage is real enough, or I should believe the whole thing was a dream."

Whilst he transacted his business at the Foreign Office, the coupé went to his hotel for his luggage.

The servant brought back word that two gentlemen refusing to give their names had been waiting for him since mid-day.

They were waiting still.

# CHAPTER III.
## The Power Behind the Throne.

The police system of Russia is divided into three sections, the First Section, consisting of the ordinary patrol of *gendarmerie*, the Second Section, consisting of what are called the Political Police, originally instituted by the Tzar Nicholas to control corruption among officials, but now, and at the time of which I write, a vast organization having its representatives in almost every city of the world, and the hated and dreaded Third Section, of Secret Police, having its spies in every house, in every restaurant, in every public place, almost in every family. The three are united under one head, and during the crisis of 1876-77 that head had, as may be supposed, more than enough to occupy it.

One of the largest suites in the Public Offices of Petersburg is devoted to the Ministry of Foreign Affairs. Adjoining it is the Ministry of the Interior. Connecting the two are two small rooms, one an inner room opening upon the vestibule, the other looking out upon the Newski Prospect, These two rooms are devoted to the use of the Chief of Police—"The White Terror," as he is called—and his personal staff, consisting of a private and two ministerial secretaries.

In the outer room sat Prince Schouloff, the Chief of Police, and the position he occupied between the two principal Ministries indicated his importance in the affairs of the Empire.

No one who saw him seated in his great leather-covered chair before his table could fail to be impressed with the personality of the man. Though he sits huddled up, as it were, there can be no mistaking the massive proportions of the man: his hand alone, as it lies on the table before him, gives overwhelming evidence of his tremendous physical strength. He is a comparatively young man,—not more than forty years old,—despite the fact that his closely-cut hair is almost snow-white, and that the clearly-traced lines round his eyes and mouth give evidence of years of anxiety, if not of physical suffering. In startling contrast to his white hair are his thick eyebrows and elaborately-pointed moustache, which are of the intensest black. At this moment his keen gray eyes look straight before him from beneath the heavy brows, and his face wears the expression habitual to it in repose,—one of concentrated watchfulness.

Before him—it is morning—lies a heap of letters, which for the past half-hour has been slowly diminishing as he opens one after another, and, after making a note upon each in pencil, for the direction of the secretaries, lays them in two heaps, one to the right of the pile for the political secretaries, the other to the left for future private reference. At this moment the morning task of looking; through the mail has been arrested,—arrested by the paper that he holds in the hand that lies on the desk before him. He is not looking at it. It would be useless, for it is not of an ordinary kind. It is written on a large square sheet of thin blue paper; in the upper left-hand corner, arranged within a diamond, appears the following design, in Greek capitals:

Incomprehensible to the uninitiated, Prince Schouloff reads within the lozenge the word "Bella-Demonia. A.H.2.R.", and, having progressed thus far, he has laid down the paper and is plunged in thought. The letter is in cipher, and is sealed to him until the arrival of his private secretary, who has the custody of the key to the enigma.

He has not long to wait. A slight noise behind him causes him to turn his head. A young man has entered the room, and has silently taken his seat at a smaller desk in the corner.

"Ah, Dmitri Dmitrievitch, is that you? I am waiting for you."

"A despatch from Bella-Demonia?"

"Yes. Have you your dial?"

"Here it is, Excellency."

"Set it: A.H.2.R."

"It is done."

"Read me this." And the Chief of Police hands the document to his private secretary, and turns once more to the unopened letters before him. For half an hour no sound breaks the silence, save the slight squeak of the cipher-dial, as, letter by letter, the young man interprets the despatch.[1]

---

## 1 BELLA-DEMONIA'S CIPHER-DIAL.

The cipher-dial referred to in the text, the original of which is in my possession, is an instrument of great interest and ingenuity, and an explanatory note may not he out of place at this point. It is a mode of cipher-construction that practically defies solution, like a combination-lock, and was used by the staff in command of the forces in Asia Minor during the Turko-Russian War, on whose main outlines the story of Bella-Demonia has been constructed.

All that is necessary, for two people who wish to communicate in cryptograph by its means, to bear in mind, is a key or combination, such as is used by Bella-Demonia in the text,—to wit, A.H.2.R.

The instrument consists of an outer dial, AA', out of which a circular chamber has been cut which receives a smaller dial, BB', which falls into its place so as to be level with the raised rim of the dial AA'. It is further kept in place by a little pin, D, which falls into a hole in the centre of the dial AA', as at E. The dial BB' may be rotated in the dial AA' by means of the milled knob C. The alphabet and a few numerals are engraved round the edges ot the dials, as seen in the illustration.

Now, supposing Bella-Demonia to be writing the despatch referred to above, on the combination A.H.2.R. She sets the dial as in the illustration. The H of the inner circle falls under the A of the outer. The "2R" means that the dial BB' must be rotated two spaces to the right, to find each letter in the cryptograph message. "III" would mean, one space to the right; "3L," three to the left, and so on.

We will assume that Bella-Demonia wishes to write her own name on the formula A.H.2.R. The dial is set as in the illustration.

304

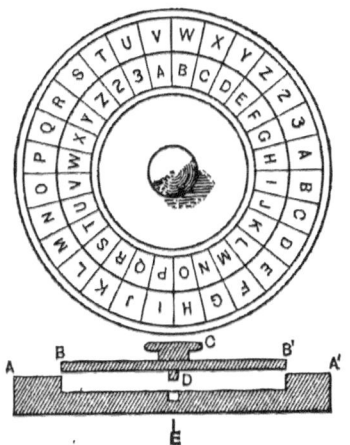

She turns the dial BB' to the right, so as to find the second space from the B in the upper or outer circle (of the dial AA'). It will be found that the letter that falls under B is G. G, therefore, is the first letter. Now to find the equivalent of the second, E; without moving the dials she finds E in the outer circle, turns the dial BB' two spaces to the right, and finds the letter H has come under the E. H is therefore the second letter of the word Bella-Demonia. Next the L. L is found on the outer dial, the inner is revolved two spaces, and M is the letter found. Now for the second L. The dial BB' is once more shifted two to the right, and the letter K represents the second L. Following the rule, and always turning the dial two spaces to the right, A is found on the outer and in turn Z on the inner circle, so that the letters 6HMKZ represent the word BELLA; and, proceeding in the same way, DEMONIA is represented in cryptograph by the letters 2.Z.D.D.A.V.L.

BELLADEMONIA=GHMKZ2ZDDAVL.

Now, Prince Schouloff *receives* the letters Ghmkz2zddavl, and to find out what they mean sets *his* dial A.H.2.R.,—i.e., with the A of the dial AA' over the H of the dial BB'.

In *reading*, the above process is reversed only in the fact that the *letter to be interpreted* is sought on the inner circle (of the dial BB'). He finds G on the dial BB', rotates it two spaces to the right, and finds over it, on the dial AA', the letter B. Next he rotates the H on BB', and finds over it E on AA'. The M on BB' rotated two spaces gives him L on AA'; and K on BB' rotated two spaces gives him a second L. Z treated the same way gives A on AA', and thus out of "Ghmkz" the first half "Bella" is produced, and in the same way the whole word, and the whole despatch.

At the end of that time the secretary rises and lays before his chief a paper on which appears the following, in French:

VIENNA, 25TH AUGUST, 1876.

> Captain the Honorable Aubyn Goddard, Twentieth Hussars, especially detailed Queen's Messenger for Oriental affairs. Age about 34. Single. English gentleman in every sense of the word. Unapproachable by ordinary means. Passed through Vienna August 15 and 16, bearing despatches for Foreign Office.
>
> In the event of Conference, England will maintain armed neutrality. In the event of Russia taking meditated action, will occupy the Bosphorus. Integrity of Ottoman Empire will be supported: particular attention to Batoum and Trebizonde. No further details.
>
> Leave for Petersburg tonight.
>
> BELLA-DEMONIA.

"H'm!" ejaculated the Chief of Police, as he carefully folded the cipher message and its translation and placed them

---

The great point to be noted is that by this means the same letter never means the same thing twice, so that the principal means of deciphering cryptograms—i.e., the observation of the most recurrent letters and substituting for them the commonest vowels and consonants—is destroyed. Without ever going more than two spaces to the right or left, 4010 different combinations can be formed; whilst if the persons in possession of the dials choose to read upward for writing and downward for reading, instead of as above downward for writing and upward for reading, 16,080,100 combinations can be formed, and it is that number of chances to one against anybody but the right person hitting on the formula.

Of course any arrangement of the letters of the alphabet, and any number of numerals, omitting the 1 and the 0, can be engraved on the two dials, so long as they coincide exactly with each other.

SELINA DOLARO.

in his pocket-book. "This is important. 'English gentleman. Unapproachable by ordinary means. No further details.' I don't like that. Bella-Demonia does not usually stop half-way in her inquiries. She is coming here. That is well, and I shall meet this marvellous woman at last!"

And, the current of his thoughts evidently changed by the receipt of the despatch, he altered some of the notes on the letters before him, and as one of the secretaries took away the bundle for distribution he said to him,—

"Inform the secretary of His Excellency the Minister for War that Prince Schouloff will wait upon his Chief in an hour's time."

When this latter had left the room, the prince turned to Dmitri Dmitrievitch Keratieff, his private secretary, and remarked,—

"You are sure that you never heard your father, Dmitri Keratieff, refer by name to this Baroness Altdorff,—'Bella-Demonia,' as they call her?"

"Never, Excellency. After the attempt upon the life of His Majesty in which my father received his death-wound, he spoke to me of a woman who possessed his cipher-dial, but never mentioned her name. I was very young then."

At the private secretary's words Prince Schouloff's face clouded. The attempted assassination of the Tzar in which the late Chief of Police lost his life was a subject which the present Chief—for state reasons, he said—never allowed to be mentioned in his presence. However, his private secretary, as son of his predecessor, and Prince Schouloff's especial *protégé*, considered himself a privileged person. At the time of his father's death Dmitri Dmitrievitch Keratieff had been one of the junior clerks in the Department of Police, and when his father met his death in the abortive attempt of the followers of Alexis Dorski, Prince Schouloff, who came to Petersburg to take the direction of the police, sought out his predecessor's son and appointed him his confidential secretary. Dorski had disappeared,—he was reported killed at Odessa soon after,—and his society had been broken up. From that moment his conspiracy had been a forbidden subject, like many others, in the Department of Police.

Now, however, the Chief did not silence his secretary, but remarked, with the air of a man who dimly recalls a half-forgotten incident,—

"How did he refer to her?"

"Though it was eight years ago, I remember his words as if they had been spoken yesterday. 'Dmitri,' he said, 'you are too young now to understand the workings of the section in which you are a subordinate; but some day you may be called to a position of trust therein. There exists a duplicate of the cipher-dial with which I construct my political correspondence. Should ever a woman communicate with you by its means, lay the matter at once before your Chief, and tell him that I, Dmitri Keratieff, left for him the injunction that she was to be considered. Trust her utterly: the welfare of the Holy Russian Empire is in her heart, and may be in her hands.' I believe this Bella-Demonia to be the woman, Excellency, for my father would never have intrusted his cipher-dial to anyone who would either duplicate or misuse it."

"I think you are right," returned Schouloff, as he reconcentrated his attention upon the papers before him.

That day he devoted to important interviews with the Ministers of War and of Foreign Affairs, and at the closing of the office at four o'clock another step, and an important one, had been taken in the policy that was to eventuate in the war of 1877.

The office was closed. The secretaries had gone, a servant had placed a reading-lamp upon his table, and Prince Schouloff was alone.

He stretched his arms above his head in the manner of a man concluding his work or turning to some lighter employment. No one looking at him as he sat, idly for the moment looking out over the Prospect that teemed with life below him, would have dreamed that the hard, ascetic-looking man, with "diplomacy" written on every line of his face, the man whose word could at any moment send families to Siberia with a 'wolf's passport,' or plunge the Cabinet in international complications, had been, eight years before we see him in the office of the Police—Alexis Dorski, the Nihilist!

It was he. But of this circumstance only two living souls were aware, and those were Prince Schouloff himself—and in after-years, people who know have said, *One other*.

# CHAPTER IV.
## Bella-Demonia.

Prince Schouloff rose, and, walking to the window, looked out over the Prospect of Alexander Newski, seeking a momentary relief from the cramped position to which he had been constrained by his work during the hours of toil. For a few minutes he stood idly watching the droschkies and troïkas that crossed and recrossed one another, listening to the jangle of their bells and to the vague murmur of the *isvoshtshiks'* voices as they apostrophized and harangued their ponies, after the manner of their class. Then he drew down the blinds to shut out the remainder of the already dying daylight, and seated himself once more at his bureau.

From a carefully-locked drawer he took a small bundle of folded blue sheets, and placed at the bottom thereof "Bella-Demonia's" despatch of the morning, and was about to replace the bundle, when a second thought struck him, and he unfolded them all in turn, running his eyes rapidly over their contents as he did so. All the originals were in cipher, but the translation was attached to each in his secretary's handwriting.

"This is a most marvellous woman," soliloquized he, as he concluded his cursory examination of the bundle. "I wonder how she is to be accounted for. Among all the political agents of the Russian administration, of her alone nothing is known: as a rule, the Holy Empire is well informed as to the antecedents of its—spies; but in the case of this woman it is different. Who is she?—or, rather, who was she? Who is—or was—the Baron Altdorff? I have sent Dmitri Keratieff in turn to London, Berlin, Paris, Vienna, in search of information regarding her. I have inquired into all her aliases in vain: everywhere we are met and assisted by her work, but by the woman herself—never. Well, well, notwithstanding the mystery, I would trust her where I would not trust Dmitri Keratieff himself. The treasury of the Department has been at her service for five years. A mere adventuress—my English agent Emily Dashton, for instance—in her position would long ago have realized a million or so of roubles and disappeared. But Bella-Demonia is true to her trust under all circumstances: her motive, whatever it be, must be a strong one, and in due time no doubt she will elect to present herself. She says in this last despatch that she is coming here: when will she arrive? By St. Nicholas! I—I, Schouloff, confess that I am curious—nay, anxious—to see her.—What is it?"

The concluding words of his soliloquy were addressed to the *dvornik* of the office, who had entered the room after a premonitory-knock.

"A lady," replied the *dvornik*, "desires to speak with your Excellency." And he handed to the prince a card on which was engraved "The Countess Laroche, Avenue de Jena, Paris," and in pencil had been added, in Russian, "Hôtel d'Europe,—*Evropeiskaya Gosstinnitza*."

"You told her that the office was closed?"

"Yes, Excellency, but she insisted that I should inquire if you were still here."

"Did she state her business?"

"No, Excellency, she said only that she had just arrived from Vienna."

"From Vienna? Ah! Admit her, and order two of the guard to station in the secretaries' office, before she comes through it."

Prince Schouloff had twice narrowly escaped assassination in this very room, and was prepared for emergencies.

Two minutes later a woman entered the room. She stood for a moment at the door, and said, interrogatively,—

"Prince Schouloff?"

"I am he," returned Schouloff, scrutinizing her narrowly. "Be seated, *sodaini*." He spoke in Russian, and his visitor answered in the same language:

"I see you have placed your Cossacks in the anteroom. I should have saved you the trouble by announcing myself as the Baroness Altdorff. It suits me, however, to be the Countess Laroche, travelling for her health: so I gave to the *dvornik* the name by which

I am to be known so long as I remain in Petersburg." There was a simple, commanding dignity in her words as she spoke, seating herself the while in the chair indicated, opposite to the Chief of Police. Prince Schouloff had remained standing.

"Bella-Demonia!" he said, simply.

"I am she."

Without another word, he went to the door, and called out, "*Choroskho! Ogon!*" ("All right! Go away!") and the footsteps of the two soldiers were heard retiring down the corridor. Schouloff returned, and, seating himself in the great leather-covered chair, remarked,—

"I will not waste time in trivial compliments. I can only say that it affords me a profound satisfaction to meet Bella-Demonia face to face. You will explain the object of this visit in your own words and at your own time."

"It was time for us to meet. The negotiations at Vienna are practically closed. You will find that Bismarck and Andrassy are acting together, have done so from the first, and will do so to the end. The policy of Great Britain is cut and dried. Their plans are formed. It is time to form ours."

"Ours?"

"Yes,—yours and mine."

Schouloff thought for a moment. Then he said,—

"Madame von Altdorff, let us understand each other from the commencement——"

"Countess Laroche, if you please," corrected she.

"Very good,—Countess Laroche. You are staying at the Hôtel d'Europe. Have you a passport?—but of course you have."

"I have five," returned she, simply.

"I beg your pardon!"

"Here they are," said she, taking a thin packet from the bosom of her dress. "Two of them are, as you see, countersigned by yourself. Here is that of the Countess Laroche, dated, issued, and visa-ed in Paris; these are respectively those of Mrs. Damian, issued and visa-ed in London; of the Baroness Altdorff, signed by yourself, in Berlin; of the Baroness Altdorff, similarly signed, in Vienna; and of Madame Raezewitz, issued, and so forth, in Constantinople."

The Chief of Police seemed thunderstruck.

"Madame," said he, "in two minutes you have impressed me as I have never been impressed before. May I ask your nationality? Your Russian is perfect, but foreign; your French is the same."

"I am cosmopolitan. I am in turn English, French, German, Russian, and, what is most to our present purpose, Roumeliote, but always and everywhere Bella-Demonia. Do I make myself clear?"

"To me—perfectly. Your identity established, pray consider the Department of Police at your service. And now, what have you to say?"

"More than can be said now. One question, however, before we terminate this interview. When do we declare war?"

Schouloff started, despite his training, despite himself.

"War?" he echoed.

"Yes,—with Turkey."

For reply the Chief leaned forward and raised the shade from the lamp, flooding the room with light. He fixed his eyes on Bella-Demonia's face. She returned his gaze unflinchingly. She was dressed from head to foot in some black-beaded material, with here and there a flash of crimson, in a lining, a ribbon, or a feather. The Chief was apparently satisfied with his scrutiny.

"When the Porte shall have rejected the conditions presented by the Conference."

"They will not be of a nature that the Porte *can* accept?"

A moment's pause, and then Schouloff answered, shortly,

"No!"

"Good! That is enough for today. Tomorrow I will lay *my* plans before you. Is it agreed?"

"Perfectly."

Ten minutes later Prince Schouloff sat alone in his sanctum, buried in his complicated reflections.

# CHAPTER V.
## A Plan of Campaign.

On the following afternoon, when the secretaries had gone and the offices had been closed to the world, as the bells of the neighboring Cathedral of St. Isaac's tolled the hour of five, Prince Schouloff sat once more in his sanctum, in conference with the Baroness Altdorff.

"As I understand the position," Bella-Demonia was saying, "our plans stand thus. The conditions laid before the Ottoman Cabinet will be of a nature that will render their acceptance impossible. When this is an accomplished fact, and the Powers have protested by protocol, Russia will cross the Pruth, and enter Asia Minor by Batoum or Kars without further notice."

"Exactly."

"What opposition shall we meet?"

"In Europe, little or none. Roumania will join our cause, and probably Bulgaria. In Asia we shall probably have difficulty with Moukhtar Pasha."

"And where shall we station our political observatory?"

"Probably at Odessa."

"That is wrong. It is too far from Stamboul."

"Has Bella-Demonia anything better to suggest?"

"Certainly, or she would not be here. Give me a map of the country."

Schouloff laid a chart of the Balkan Peninsula on the table, and together they bent over the sheet, the woman demonstrating with her finger as she spoke quickly and decisively, in the tones of one stating a case with which he is entirely familiar:

"Immediately on the declaration of war, long before we reach the Danube, the Buda-Pesth, Giurgevo, and Varna route to Constantinople will be closed. The ports of the Black Sea will be blockaded, the sea-route from any other port will be impracticable. The only line of communication between the Powers and the Porte, therefore, will be across the Balkans by way of the Shipka Pass. To reach this point, messengers must pass through Belgrade, Widin, and possibly Plevna. From Shipka they must reach Stamboul by Eski Saghra and Adrianople. On the road between the two lies the village of Deve-kini. At that village Madame Helen Raezewitz, a Roumeliote lady, must take a hunting-villa at once. By the time our armies cross the Pruth she will be firmly established there, and his Excellency Prince Schouloff will always be a welcome visitor."

As she ceased she looked up into Schouloff's face to mark the effect of her words.

"Then you propose——" said he.

"To found a political observatory, away from large cities or military centres, though within a certain radius of Eski Saghra,—an observatory, however, on the inevitable line of route between Stamboul and Europe."

"But between this and next year I have important duties that call me to Paris and London. I could not occupy the chateau of which you speak."

"But I could. I propose to be there within a month."

"You know the state of a civilized country on the first outbreak of a war and before military control is established. Do you fully realize what would be the condition of affairs in Bulgaria? The good Gladstone was nearer the truth than is his wont in his *brochure* on Batak."

Bella-Demonia's lip curled scornfully.

"Do you think," said she, "that a woman who has lived the life of Bella-Demonia is likely to flinch at the thought of a sojourn in a country notoriously Russophile? Besides, inquire at Philippopolis and Sofia concerning Madame Raezewitz: you will be satisfied, I think, that I am safe among the Balkans."

Prince Schouloff had resumed his seat, and now remained silent for a few moments, watching the woman opposite him.

"Madame von Altdorff," said he, at length, "I do not ask a confidence which apparently you are desirous of withholding, but it is obvious that it must have been some terrible cataclysm in your life that plunged you into the whirlpool of political intrigue."

"A cataclysm indeed!—one that shattered every womanly feeling within me; one that turned my life into one protracted longing for excitement and distraction. When, on the death of Dmitri Keratieff at the hands of Alexis Dorski's band, *you* took his place in the councils of the nation, a month of keen observation of your methods satisfied me that under your chieftainship the office of political agent would be no sinecure. I wrote to you: you gave me my first commission, and in an hour my womanhood, my past, was laid aside,—in a word, I became—Bella-Demonia!"

"I would that we had met sooner, baroness. With such a partner as yourself, there is no height to which an ambitious man might not aspire."

She looked at him for an instant as if in alarm. Then, resuming the cold, hard tone that was natural to her, she said,—

"It is just as well that we did not meet then, for I am incapable of aught but hate. You understand me?"

"Perfectly," replied Schouloff. And the conversation changed.

A fortnight later the "plan of campaign" was settled. Day after day the Chief of Police had been closeted with the Baroness Altdorff, and nothing remained to be discussed, of the policy of the Chief and his *lieutenante*. "The Countess Laroche" was making ready for her departure; and in two days' time Prince Schouloff would have left Petersburg for Paris *en route* for London.

They sat, as usual, in the bureau of the Department of Police, and Bella-Demonia had just folded up her last sheet of notes, written in the cipher under which we first made her acquaintance.

"So!" she said, "all is finished."

"Almost," replied Schouloff.

"How? almost? Have you anything else to say?"

"Yes. Give me your attention, if you please, for a few moments longer, baroness: what remains to be said is not unimportant." He paused for a moment, as if searching for words: then he resumed. "You have never enlightened me, baroness, on the subject of your past, and for my part I have no desire to be enlightened. I only know that you are incomparable as you are incomprehensible; I only know that, whatever your birth may have been, you would add lustre to any name that you would deign to adopt. The family of Schouloff is second to none in the Russian Empire, and since before our history began the Schouloffs have ranked side by side with the Romanoffs, the Dolgouroukis, and the Khristovs. This name, in all humility, I offer to you. Will you be my wife?"

Bella-Demonia had risen and walked to the window.

There, she turned and faced Schouloff, who sat, nervously—for him—twisting an end of his moustache.

"Prince Schouloff," said she, "I regret from the bottom of my soul that you should have honored me with this proposition. I can never be more to you than I am now. I know that I am in your power, I have expressed my willingness to place myself still further in your hands, and I have no fear for the result. But more than your adjutant I can never be. Let us forget this scene, and resume our old positions with regard to each other. I can never be your wife."

A sharp contraction passed across the man's features, but he regained his old icy composure as he replied,—

"I know you too well to urge my suit. Some day I hope, however, that you may reconsider your decision. Should that day ever arrive, I leave it in your hands to tell me of it. Meanwhile, I am always your obedient servant."

She inclined her head in silence.

"I think there is no more to be said," he resumed. "So, *au revoir*. Early in the year I will join you in our Bulgarian observatory."

"Good!" she replied, simply. "I shall look forward to your coming. *Au revoir!*"

# BOOK II.

## CHAPTER I.
### A Committee of Ways And Means.

"But, my dear girl, for heaven's sake be reasonable. How the deuce do you suppose I can get ten thousand pounds?"

"How should I know?"

"Very well, then: don't be absurd."

And Major Homer Carteret and Mrs. Bradley Dashton sat looking at each other as if hoping to derive inspiration from each other's ingenuous countenances.

They were excellently well matched, this brother and sister: he was a gentlemanly adventurer, and she was a garrison hack. This is perhaps a trifle crude. Let us explain.

Major Homer Carteret was "society runner" for a syndicate of Oriental gentlemen who promoted companies in the far-Eastern city. His was the task of snaring ornamental directors with high-sounding titles, and moneyed youngsters with plethoric bank-accounts: no one in the business had so keen a scent or so sure a hand, no one was so innocent a (professional) victim or so enthusiastic a (professional) supporter as Major Homer Carteret, and, though Dick Saville and other ribald spirits who had suffered by and with him averred that his military commission was one in the Salvation Army, there was no denying that, diplomatic and deprecating to the last degree, Major Carteret was a most useful member of the society which for a consideration he adorned.

To explain yet further, the major owed his rank to some obscure Indian regiment, and according to his own account had seen much service in the Empire; but a majority in a Sikh regiment is not a lucrative post, nor is it one in which the undoubted talents of the major found full scope, and he took the first opportunity to seek the mother-country as the pioneer of a queer gold-mining company, and, having found the work profitable and congenial, realized that *this* was his proper sphere, and settled in London, where his fame spread among wealthy but unpresentable financiers, as purveyor of directors and social "drummer" for the stocks of his employers. His business found an able co-operator in the person of his sister, when she too forsook her all—to wit, all the officers in Bengal—and established herself in the cosey little house in Mayfair where we find her sitting on this bright November morning, in conference with Major Homer Carteret.

Their tactics were such as to compel the admiration of all who suffered by them. The major and his sister were "devilish good fellows," both of them: did any gilded youth desire to meet any particular damsel *en petit comité*, Mrs. Dashton could always be depended upon to give a little dinner, at which she and her brother counted for little save as hosts. During dinner Mrs. Dashton, with some excuse or apology for talking shop, would deftly draw from the major a few enthusiastic words regarding his last "investment;" over the wine and the first cigar the major generally managed to re-introduce the subject, and the gilded youth, as a rule, bit at the bait and "went a hundred" in company with the major, "just for fun." The company generally turned out to be one of unlimited liability, and in due season burst with more or less explosive force, and the major when reproached would express the most awful consternation, but "as a friend of the directors" would manage to limit the gilded youth's liability to a "few" thousands, whilst he, poor old chap, was absolutely ruined, and in his despair would borrow five hundred for a month to set himself on his feet again. As the five hundred was always punctually repaid, he always got it, and with it the commiseration and absolution of his unconscious victims. For the supply of ornamental directors he had a fixed ascending scale: a baronet, so much; a baron, so much; a viscount, an earl, a marquis, a duke, so much apiece, according to the standing of the title in the financial Debrett which financiers keep locked up in their strong boxes.

For her share in the proceedings Mrs. Dashton charged a regular commission, with now and then a bonus. At this moment she wanted a bonus, but the bonus she wanted was ten thousand pounds, and at this moment it was decidedly inconvenient. The major was "filling the cast," to put it dramatically, of a company for the exploitation of some absolutely inaccessible copper-mines in Asia Minor, and, though the syndicate was wealthy, the major had run through about as much "petty cash" as the concern could stand.

He was consequently constrained to remark,—

"For heaven's sake, be reasonable!"

"Well, it's your own affair, Homer. If Arlingford doesn't have this ten thou. by Monday, 'up he goes' at Tattersall's and the Club; and that means the extinction of Arlingford; and the extinction of Arlingford means the extinction of the Ararat Mining Company."

"But, hang it all, he's had between fifteen and twenty thousand already, and the company is beginning to look into the accounts."

"Well, what if he has? you've had the value of your money. Without his house for head-quarters you'd never have filled your board of directors, and you certainly wouldn't have got young Saville, or young Midas, to 'go a hundred for fun,' as you call it. Besides, you *must* get this American Briggs. He's a millionaire, and so long as Arlingford's on his feet you can always strike him there. He's to be at this dinner there tonight to say good-bye to Goddard."

"Goddard?"

"You argue yourself unknown. Twentieth Hussars, Queen's Messenger, most popular man in London."

"Never met him."

"No, you wouldn't: he hasn't got any hundreds 'to go for fun'."

"Keep to business, if you please."

"I *am* keeping to business. I want ten thousand pounds."

"Well, I haven't got them, and can't get them. There."

"Well, what are we going to do?"

"I don't know. Can't you borrow it from Schouloff? These Russian princes are always fabulously rich."

"Schouloff could certainly get it me if he wanted anything in return for it. He told me at the Ackerlys' last night that there was a favor I could do him; but I can't do him ten thousand pounds' worth of work in three days."

"Still, you could try him. See what he wants."

"I shall certainly do that this afternoon; but it's a forlorn hope."

There was a minute's silence, and then the brother broke out:

"Don't sit saying nothing! Suggest something, for goodness' sake."

"I was just about to do so," returned Mrs. Dashton, her eyes fixed on the fire. "You go straight into the city and move heaven and earth to get the money. I'll write to Schouloff to get him here this afternoon. Write from the city to Lady Arlingford to say you are detained, but will come in after dinner: I'll write later on and say I'm ill, but will also come in afterwards. Meet me at Arlingford's at nine o'clock, and before they're out from dinner we'll compare notes. I haven't much hope."

"Nor have I."

"Well, do your best, anyhow."

"You bet I will."

And Major Homer Carteret took up his hat and left the house.

As soon as he had gone, Mrs. Bradley Dashton sat down and wrote a few lines.

"Take this," said she to the servant who appeared in answer to her summons, "to the Russian Legation, and wait for an answer."

This done, she walked to the fire and held out her fingers to the blaze.

Mrs. Bradley Dashton was an extremely handsome woman in the luxurious blonde style of beauty. Her eight-and-twenty years sat lightly on her fuzzy brow, and the ravages of the Indian climate, and the excitement of her life as the successive flame of every subaltern in the Bengal Staff Corps, had left no trace upon her regular features.

This had not escaped the notice of the Earl of Arlingford when he visited India on a hunting-tour, a couple of years before, and, unmindful of the existence of his wife in England, or perhaps relying on that lady for protection against the ultimate wiles of the siren, he had easily persuaded her to abandon Bengal for London; and in her secret soul Emily Dashton cherished a hope, founded on a light promise of Lord Arlingford's, that so soon as her ladyship should seek redress of her wrongs through the medium of the divorce court, she, Emily Dashton, should graduate as the Countess of Arlingford in the peerage of England.

Hence her anxiety to aid his lordship in the present strait, hence her late conference with her brother the major, and hence her summons to Prince Schouloff, whose ally she had been, off and on, ever since her return to England.

The answer to the latter arrived promptly, and with a little sigh of satisfaction Mrs. Bradley Dashton proceeded to lunch.

## CHAPTER II.
### A Political Commission.

At three o'clock that afternoon, clad in the most bewitching of wrappers, Mrs. Bradley Dashton lay curled up in an arm-chair before her fire, expectant. It cannot be said that her features were free from care, for there's many a slip 'twixt the fingers and ten thousand pounds; still, she was more hopeful than she had been in the morning, for Schouloff's prompt reply to her note and his obedience to her summons pointed to the fact that there was something she could do for him, and Prince Schouloff 's service, though one of danger and intricacy, was excellently well paid.

The miniature cathedral chimes of the carriage-clock on the mantel-piece had hardly struck thrice when Mrs. Dashton heard a hansom checking its mad career at her door, and, a moment after, Schouloff entered the room. She did not rise, but extended to him her hand, which the Russian bent himself reverentially to kiss.

"And how goes it with my charming ally?" he began.

"Pretty well, thanks. At this moment I'm bored. I want something to do,—something exciting. That's why I asked you to call."

"Ah! I thought as much. Well, how much is it this time?" he asked, in a matter-of-fact tone of voice.

"Ten thousand pounds."

"Dear me! is that all?"

"That's all for the present," said she, ignoring the sarcasm.

"Only ten thousand pounds!" repeated Prince Schouloff.

"Can I have it?"

"Well, I hope so. It will depend on yourself."

"You don't mean to say," she said, eagerly, "that there's anything I can do for you that's worth ten thousand pounds? I want it by Monday."

"If you will do what I want, your work will be done by midnight. At one A.M., unless you fear I might compromise you by so untimely a call, I will come here and pay you ten thousand pounds, in notes or gold. How do you want them?"

"Don't play with me, Schouloff," said the woman, nervously: "I can't bear it. I want this money awfully badly."

"I am not playing. I was never more serious in my life. I heard that his lordship needed ten thousand pounds, and obtained the money yesterday in the hope that you could earn it."

"Earn it! It's a large sum!"

"An *enormous* sum,—the greatest I have ever paid for an individual service."

"I suppose you want something impossible."

"To a woman so beautiful and talented as Mrs. Bradley Dashton, nothing should be impossible."

The woman sat watching him. She knew her man, and the thought that the money was within her reach was so sweet that she postponed as far as possible the stating of the condition which she felt sure must shatter her hopes.

"Well," she said, at last, "what do you want me to do?"

Schouloff became suddenly very grave.

"Emily Dashton," he said, "I know no Englishwoman who can work with your promptitude and finesse. You have often served me in what may be called police-cases: I have never employed you in political intrigue. I am going to give you a commission higher than any you have executed hitherto."

"Why don't you give it to Bella-Demonia?" asked she, suspiciously.

"Because the Baroness Altdorff is at this moment in Turkey,—for her health."

"Well, what is it? I'll do your commission,—whatever it is," concluded she, desperately.

"Good! If you *can*, I know you will; but it is something higher than the stealing of a letter or the extortion of a confession. Listen! You are bidden to a dinner at Lord Arlingford's tonight."

"Yes."

"To meet Captain Aubyn Goddard."

"Yes."

"He starts by the night-express from Charing Cross by Dover, for Vienna, en route for Constantinople, with governmental despatches of the highest importance."

"Yes, yes. Go on."

"He must not go."

"WHAT?"

"He must be detained."

"And who is to detain him?" asked the woman, with an expressive shrug of the shoulders.

"You."

"*I!*"

"Exactly."

"Prince Schouloff, do you realize what you have asked?"

"Do you realize that you have asked for *ten thousand pounds*?"

"Do you know Aubyn Goddard?"

"By reputation,—well."

"And how do you suppose he is to be prevented from doing his duty?"

"I have not the vaguest idea. If I had, I should save ten thousand pounds."

For a full minute the two sat looking at each other, the man deadly calm, the woman evidently profoundly agitated. At last she spoke.

"If this is the price of the money, I had better abandon all hope of it. The thing is grotesquely impossible. You know, as well as I do, that from the moment he leaves Arlingford's till he enters the train at Calais he will be watched by armed men. How can he be stopped?"

"He cannot be stopped. Besides, I do not want him stopped,—only detained: till tomorrow morning will be sufficient. The delay of his despatches for a few hours is all that is necessary. Force is out of the question: he must not start."

"And you expect me to prevent him,—to keep him in London?"

"You knew him in India, did you not?"

"Yes," answered the woman, with a flush, "but that was all over years ago. I have no more power over him than—than you have."

"Well," said Schouloff, looking at his watch, "I must go. It is four o'clock. Between this and midnight a woman like you might wreck an empire. Think it over: do not throw down your cards before you have played a single one. I dine at the Duke's tonight: at ten I shall drop in at the Arlingfords'. At eleven you will put your scheme, whatever it may be, into operation. At twelve the mail will go without the Queen's Messenger,—I hope. And at one I shall have the honor of waiting upon you with ten thousand pounds,—I hope. Now, *au plaisir* and *à bientôt*."

And before Mrs. Dashton could say another word he had left the room. As the rattle of his cab-wheels died away in the distance, Mrs. Dashton dropped into her chair, and lay there motionless, her eyes fastened on the wall before her.

# CHAPTER III.
## Captain Aubyn Goddard.

It was nine o'clock.

In the drawing-room of Arlingford House, Piccadilly, Mrs. Bradley Dashton sat in a low arm-chair before the fire in much the same attitude as we left her at her own house in Mayfair. The lights were turned low, but the butler was making a tour of the room, turning them up one by one.

"Dinner is not over yet, Cookson?" remarked she.

"Not yet, ma'am. Dinner was late."

"When Major Carteret arrives, show him in here."

"Yes, ma'am."

To judge by the expression on Mrs. Bradley Dashton's face, her plans had not undergone any simplification since the afternoon, and she had evidently arrived at that point at which there is nothing to be done save to await developments from external sources. It was therefore with a sigh of relief and anticipation that she rose and moved towards the door as Cookson a few moments later drew aside the *portières*, announcing,—

"Major Carteret."

"How late you are!" she exclaimed, hurriedly. "I began to be afraid that you wouldn't get here before dinner was over"

"What! doubt *me*? And after so much devotion to the cause,— after foregoing a charming dinner here and rushing through my solitary one at the Club on purpose to serve you? Really, my dear child"

"You're too civil to have any good news," interrupted she. "Keep your society manner for Lady Arlingford. You're only truthful when you're disagreeable. Be disagreeable now; for I want the truth. Have you been able to raise the money?"

"I regret to say that it was impossible."

"Well, what's to be done?"

"I don't know. There's only Schouloff left. I saw him this afternoon, and he hinted that you could be of service to him. I suppose you've seen him?"

"Yes, I've seen him."

"And can he help us?"

"Yes, if——"

"If! Good God! listen to her! As though there could be any 'if'! Of course you'll do what he wants. What is it?"

"Captain Goddard leaves tonight for Vienna with despatches——"

"Well, what has it to do with *him?*"

"Schouloff wants him detained. That's all."

"*Oh!*"

The tone of Major Carteret's exclamation spoke volumes.

"I'm getting bored with this Goddard," said he, after a pause.

"Of course I regret that," said she, "but he's an old sweetheart of Alice Arlingford's, I think. That should make him interesting to you."

"Indeed! Why?"

"Because you have been laboring under the delusion that you might, by the employment of much strategy, induce Lady Arlingford to care for you or compromise herself. You have not succeeded, nor are you likely to succeed. You are not her 'form' even did she intend to be so charming as to give her husband cause for alarm,—which does not, I grieve to say, seem likely. You forced your *entrée* here by lending Jack Arlingford money. Well, you are here. What advantage have you gained?"

"You are delightfully frank,—I might almost say rude. Why?"

"Because you're no use to me: so why should I be civil?"

"An admirable reason; but you might reflect——"

At this juncture Cookson the butler entered, and put an end to the colloquy by saying to Carteret,—

"His lordship desires to know if you will join them in the dining-room."

"Oh! very well," replied Carteret. "Yes." And he went.

"Who's here, Cookson?" said Mrs. Dashton when he had gone.

"Mr. Cincinnatus Q. Briggs, an American gentleman, ma'am,

Master—erghem!—Mr. Charles Middleton, and Miss Middleton."

"Is that all? What made dinner late?" asked Mrs. Dashton, in quick alarm.

"They were waiting for a gentleman who sent a note at the last moment, ma'am."

"Do you know who it was?"

"I think it was——"

"Captain Goddard."

A footman made the announcement, cutting his superior short as Captain Goddard entered the room. Mrs. Dashton had resumed her seat before the fire, and the new-comer did not notice her.

"Not quite finished dinner yet, sir," said the butler. "Would you like to go into the dining-room?"

"Thanks, no. I'll wait here."

"And I'll keep you company!"

The words were spoken by Mrs. Dashton, who turned as she spoke and held out her hand. Seeing her, Goddard uttered an exclamation of surprise.

"Hullo, Dashey!" he cried. "How are you, old lady? How stunning you look! Egad! and deadly respectable, too,—for you."

"Hold your tongue. We're not in India now; and please remember it's something like seven or eight years since we met there."

"But"

"Don't! Don't look at me and say it's impossible to remember seven or eight years. I'll take all your compliments for granted,— and I'll take a little discretion and prudence at the same time, if you please. Do you understand me, *Captain* Goddard?"

"Perfectly, *Mrs.* Dashton," replied he, gravely. There was a moment's pause, and then he added, with a quick intonation of suddenly-aroused suspicion in his voice,—

"What are you doing here?"

"In England?" queried she, meeting his tone with one of subdued defiance.

"No: in this house."

"Oh! on a visit."

"Whose invitation?"

"Whose business?"

"That depends."

"On what?"

"On you."

"Not on you?"

"That also depends."

The little colloquy was made with laconic rapidity. As silence reigned again, Mrs. Dashton eyed her opponent keenly, as if measuring their respective strengths. Finally, seeming to satisfy herself of her own inferiority, she resumed, in an altered tone,—

"Well, what do you want to know?"

"How you got into this house."

"By Lord Arlingford's invitation."

"So I thought!"

The woman bit her lip.

"Well, next?" she asked, containing herself with an effort.

"How long have you known Lady Arlingford?" was Goddard's next question.

"Since I arrived in England from Nice."

"So I supposed! How long is that?"

"About two months."

"How do you like her?"

"I don't know. I haven't thought."

"How does she like you?"

"I don't know. I haven't cared. How does she like *you*?"

"Well, I hope."

"Good! I'm glad to find some one she *does* care for."

"You don't like Lady Arlingford as well as her husband, do you?"

Mrs. Dashton rose with an impatient gesture.

"I'm getting a little tired of your questions," she said, petulantly. "Tell me plainly, is it 'Pax' between us?"

"Yes, if you behave yourself. Now look here, Dashey," he continued, frankly, "it's a rough thing to hurt a woman's feelings, and I hate to be hard on you, but Lady Arlingford is my cousin, and a dear friend into the bargain, and—and—well, hang it! you've no right here in the same house with her, and if you give me cause I shall be compelled to drop her a hint, and then most likely she'll——"

"Do as her husband bids her,—as all dutiful and obedient wives should!"

"Oh!" The intonation which Goddard threw into the ejaculation was unmistakable.

"*Exactly,*" said Mrs. Dashton, as if in reply. "It *is* 'Pax' isn't it? Let us forget, forgive, and shake hands over it. I'm not going to stay long: I go abroad in less than a month: so you needn't be alarmed on Lady Arlingford's account. I must have a pleasant life, if I die for it, and if Lady Arlingford won't ask me to her house,—why, Lord Arlingford must,—that's all. I'm very little in England, but to keep my Continental friends going I must have a good house in London at my back."

"Do your Continental friends care much?"

"Of course they do,—Prince Schouloff, for instance, who entertains so charmingly, whose yacht, opera-boxes, villas everywhere, are always at my disposal. He sees me here; he likes to come to Lord Arlingford's informal little gatherings after his stately dinners and ceremonials. For Arlingford's little parties are not particularly ceremonious, are they?"

"Well,—erghem!—you're here, aren't you, old lady? so you ought to know."

He spoke lightly, but in his heart he was thinking, "Poor Alice! I wonder how I can help her." What Mrs. Dashton would have answered remains uninvented; for at that moment a rattle of the rings of the *portières* announced the arrival from the dining-room of Lady Arlingford and Miss Kitty Middleton.

The Countess of Arlingford, rapidly taking in the pair that rose as she entered, bowed icily as she greeted Mrs. Bradley Dashton, who returned her bow with something of defiance in the gesture of her head. The enmity of the two women was obvious to the merest observer.

Turning to Goddard, however, her manner entirely changed.

"Ah, Aubyn!" she exclaimed, "I am so glad to see you! What a long while it seems since you went away! You remember Kitty, of course, and—Mrs. Bradley Dashton—Captain——"

"Captain Goddard and I have met before," said Mrs. Dashton, with a smile, "and we have just been re-cementing our friendship."

Goddard looked for a moment at the gold-headed Kitty, who stood staring at him, and then said,—

"Kitty, kiss your old pal at once!"

"Let me see," mused Kitty: "what is it the Yankee says? Oh, yes! Why, cert'nly." And with much deliberation Miss Middleton proceeded to kiss the handsome Queen's Messenger.

"Kitty," said Lady Arlingford, "do be more careful—before strangers."

"Oh," replied the girl, turning saucily with her arms still round Goddard's neck, "Mrs. Dashton won't be scared at a kiss—more or less," she added in Goddard's ear.

"So you're as wild as ever?" said the latter, who was suffering from mingled amusement and embarrassment.

"Worse a great deal," put in Lady Arlingford. "If you could have heard her at dinner——"

"Well," explained Kitty, "you wanted someone to wake you up. *You* looked like a block of marble, and you ought to be very much obliged to me for being so disreputable a person. What do you suppose I asked the Yankee, Aubyn?"

"Something more awful than usual, or you would not be so much amused. Go on: I'm ready to be shocked."

"I put on my most serious face and asked what he did when he found a more than usually high mantel-piece. He looked puzzled, and waited for an explanation: so I explained by asking if, under the circumstances, he stood on his head, so as to get his feet up, in the national attitude."

"What did he do?"

"Sold me dead. Instead of being a bit amazed or amused, he said, "Is that out of *Punch*?"

"Poor Kitty! how crushing!"

"Never mind. I shall survive the blow, and come up smiling for the second round. I'll get Mrs. Dashton to tell me about Prince Schouloff's adventures and crimes. I'm always so interested in anyone with a Russian name,—sort of blood-curdling, isn't it? You'll tell me of the beautiful murders he's committed, won't you, Mrs. Dashton? It'll cheer me up."

"If the prince heard you," said Lady Arlingford, with a smile, "you would probably be sent to Siberia for life."

"Who is your Russian curiosity you're so keen about?" asked Goddard.

"Prince Schouloff, the Russian plenipotentiary. You know him, surely?"

"I know *of* him. An unprincipled scoundrel, from all accounts,—utterly unscrupulous,—a relentless, indomitable autocrat; in short, a thoroughly typical diplomat, who bears the reputation of uninterrupted success in his career by never having fallen a victim to the tender passion. There's a hearsay description for you."

"In that case," said Mrs. Dashton, "his days of success are numbered *now*."

"And who is the conqueror?"

"Why, Bella-Demonia."

"And who's Bella-Demonia?" pursued Goddard.

"Oh, come on, Mrs. Dashton," broke in Kitty. "You can tell him about Bella-Demonia presently."

"You should not bore Mrs. Dashton, Kitty," said Lady Arlingford.

"Don't mind her, Mrs. Dashton," said the young woman, drawing her victim towards the billiard-room, that was separated from the drawing-room by heavy curtains. "You got to where the two spies crept out from the window-curtains, their daggers gleaming!—EEEH!"

Kitty Middleton's sentence closed with a scream. She had run into Cookson, who at that moment entered through the curtains with coffee. Recovering herself, however, she took her cup and disappeared with Mrs. Dashton.

Left alone with Goddard, Lady Arlingford seated herself by his side, saying, as she did so,—

"How long it seems since you went to India! And by what a strange collection of accidents it is that we have never met since!"

"Do you remember the day I left?" said he, in reply. "We were dreadful spoons, weren't we? Ah, I little thought then that I should come back to find you had forgotten your first sweetheart!"

"How do you know——"

"That I was your first? Why, you were only three years old when we met."

"Well, how do you know I have forgotten? But, seriously, you were in hopes of getting into active service. I heard General Saville say something of your getting a command. Is that true?"

"Partly. I expect to get an appointment that may lead to a command. General Saville's awfully fond of me,—dear old chap! He'd do anything for me, and he has great influence at head-quarters."

"Of course your knowledge of Eastern languages will help your promotion."

"Well, yes, to a certain extent. I must say that I look forward to active service as my greatest luck. I can say it to you, Alice: I feel that if the chance comes I can make a career, and my chance has come, I think. The mission on which I start tonight is of the greatest importance. Vital issues depend on the prompt delivery of my despatches: the loss of an hour might prove fatal to their effect. I am the more anxious to carry through tonight's job sat-isfactorily, as it will be my last service before retiring."

"But, in spite of all that, I shall hate to see you leave for Afghanistan."

"Ah, but you don't know how tired I am of being a toy soldier. I'm only a sort of postman, after all!"

"Nice thing for a Queen's Messenger to say!"

"Well, denuded of the swagger, it's much the same. I carry despatches; so does the postman. He works harder and gets worse paid,—that's all. There has been one thing about it lately, however,—an adventure that interested me immensely, and I had made up my mind to see the end of it, but I shall probably be prevented by this very stroke of good luck. And I'm just disappointed. Human nature, you know——"

"An adventure? Tell me about it."

"I will. This last August, waiting in Vienna for despatches, I went to a masquerade, and, after having been thoroughly bored by the usual round of stupidity, was just leaving, when a woman who I had noticed was being followed and annoyed by a man put herself under my escort to regain her carriage unmolested. The voice was unmistakably gentle: no one, even in that questionable place, could have presumed to be impertinent to her. You felt at once that she feared no insult: even in asking a service she had the air of conferring a favor. The charm of this confidence in herself and in me was so profound that I forgot everything else and could only speculate on the mystery. She hurried me forward till we reached a side-door and found ourselves in a lonely street, apparently far from the general entrance. Here a brougham was waiting. She jumped in. Aghast at the thought that the adventure was to end there and then, I begged to be allowed to see her again. In reply she made me promise to ask no questions of or about her, and then, giving me an invitation to breakfast the following day, said, 'Good-night, and many thanks, Captain Aubyn Goddard!'"

"She knew you! Who was she?"

"To this moment I have not the vaguest idea, beyond that she is called the Baroness Altdorff. By the time I had read her name and address on the card she had given me, her brougham was out of sight."

"You take away my breath. It is fascinating; but I suppose I need ask no more?"

"You are mistaken. Equivocal as the adventure appears in the beginning, to the end I can tell you every detail."

"Did you go to breakfast? But of course you did. What a question!"

"The address was in the suburbs. I found a little house hidden in a garden that at first appeared deserted, but at the appointed time I was admitted at once. A simplicity and elegance that bespoke the owner pervaded this charming nest. The whole place was a dumb repudiation of the feverish adventure of the night before,—all was such rattling 'good form;' there was that crisp, get-up-early appearance which boded more the advent of a healthy English girl in her spotless cuffs and collar than of my heroine, whose entrance put an end to my reflections. She was quite unknown to me. I will spare you all description. The confidence that had been her chief attraction the night before saved a world of awkwardness. She had a strange charm, and, intelligent and often profound as her conversation on current events was, I give you my word I entirely forgot that I had never seen her before. It seemed as though we were old friends."

"What was she like? Very beautiful?"

"I really don't know."

"What an absurd answer!"

"But I mean it. I don't know if she is what is called beautiful; I don't know if she is what I thought beautiful. I only know that that is a point one ignores in her presence. I doubt if anyone could describe her after seeing her."

Lady Arlingford smiled.

"You *have* described her, by not being able to describe her," she said.

Aubyn Goddard colored.

"My dear Alice," said he, "you show me I've been making an awful fool of myself."

"Aubyn," returned the woman, earnestly, "the love of a man is not foolish, in my eyes."

He started.

"Love?" said he.

"Yes, love!" she replied.

A dead silence fell between them.

# CHAPTER IV.
## A Game of Écarté.

It was broken by the sound of a boyish voice exclaiming behind them,—

"Hullo, Goddard! you back again? I heard my governor say you were going to Afghanistan. Is it true? I wish I could go with you." Charlie Middleton had just entered the room.

"I hope it's true," replied Goddard, pleasantly. "I think so. Are you going into the service?"

"No. The mater always begins to cry when anyone says 'soldier,' and a fellow can't make his mother cry, can he?—beastly bad form. Where's my beastly sister? She's always in the way when one doesn't want her. The other day I was talking to Mrs. Dashton, and—well, catch Kitty giving a fellow a chance!—not she. Deuced fine woman, Mrs. Dashton, ain't she? I say, has she got any *Mr.* Dashton?"

"The memory of man runneth not to the contrary," quoted Goddard, a quaint look coming into his eyes. "You take my advice, Charlie, and give Mrs. Dashton a wide berth."

"Well, I think a good many people are a good deal too hard on her. She's a woman not easily understood. Now, I *do* understand her," said Charlie, with the superiority of his seventeen years.

"Come and talk to your May Queen, Charlie," called Kitty from the door of the billiard-room at this point.

"Oh, you! vulgar beggar," ejaculated Charlie, coloring helplessly. "There's a sister for a man to have!"

"Come to its May Queen, mother's darling," reiterated Kitty, laughing herself into the room. "You didn't know Charlie was his mother's darling, did you? His mother ought to have heard him calling Mrs. Dashton the May Queen."

At this point Charlie Middleton's overtaxed forbearance became too much for him: he made a wild rush for his escaping sister which took them both out of the room.

"What a good girl that is," said Lady Arlingford," in spite of her wild tongue! I don't know what I should do without her."

"Is it true that she's to marry Dick Saville?"

"Yes: they were made for each other; but I shall miss her sadly. She is always ready with a cheery word to dispel the very worst attack of blues. My life would be much worse without her."

"Worse?"

"I—I mean—I meant to say I don't make friends quickly: you know I am not what the French call 'expansive,' and as one gets older——"

Goddard had been watching her color come and go as she strove to retrieve her slip of the tongue, and now he interrupted her gravely.

"Alice," said he, "what does all this mean? You are not like your old self. We were boy and girl together for as long as we can remember; friendship and affection like ours do not fade with the years that pass us by,—no, dear,—and my affection for you tells me more than I dreaded to hear. I have kept silent long enough,—too long, it may be. Vague rumors have reached me, which I have not heeded, thinking that you would speak if there was aught to say. Tell me, what is your trouble?"

"Trouble? Why, what an alarmist you are!"

"That is no answer. Look here, Alice: I am going away tonight, possibly for months, and I must come straight to the point. We will speak plainly. It is no use pretending not to know what the world says of Arlingford. The world is not always—or often— right; but—what is Mrs. Bradley Dashton doing here? why do you admit her?"

"I—my dear Aubyn, you know very little of Jack Arlingford, to ask me such a question. He invites his own friends, and Mrs. Dashton is one of them. Let us talk of something else."

"No, we will talk of nothing else. I want to hear something of your life since your marriage. In all your letters you have been strangely reticent on this subject. Lots of gossip, but not a word of yourself. I believe I am the only man whose relationship to you gives him a right to question your husband."

"A right! My dear boy, you are so impetuous. If I do not complain, why should you? Why insist on pursuing an unpleasant subject? Do you not see I am content? I made a mistake, that's all."

"That's all! When I heard of your marriage—I was in Calcutta at the time—I wondered how your puritanical mother's consent had been won. Everybody knew Jack Arlingford's past. It would not have been telling tales out of school, in his case, and I wished that at that time I could have been in London. When I came home soon after, you seemed happy, and—and—I think I must have been a fool not to look deeper into my old play-fellow's heart."

"And if there was no heart to search?"

"Ah! but how you are changed! You will not complain, you are too brave, and I was wrong to ask what you desire should remain unasked. Forgive me; I'm a blundering soldier; but remember, dear, I'm always your friend, and if you can ever break the ice that binds your confidence, count on me. Count on me, dear, to the last."

For an instant Lady Arlingford's lips trembled; then, breaking down, she hid her face in her hands.

"Oh, why has God so punished me?" she murmured. "I thought I was stronger."

"Now I have made you cry! Don't give way," said Goddard, helplessly. "What have I said?"

"Not you,—not you," answered the woman. "I thought I was hardened; but—if you only knew what my life has been."

"Won't you tell me? Perhaps you think things are worse than they really are."

"*Think*! There *is* nothing worse than my life. God never condemned a creature to misery more deep than mine. But come! forget what I have said. Don't be frightened; you see I am unstrung. I am not ill, but I think it is good to unburden my heart: it is not so hard to confide in you. But I had made up my mind never to speak of my trouble: I have no patience with women who have but one idea of relief,—the divorce court. I would sooner die than show the world my sorrow."

"You may carry that reticence too far. I would stake my life you are not to blame."

"You might hold me blameless. You know me, have known me all my life. But can you say to the world, Here is a girl, brought up by a good simple mother in the simple faith of marry, love, and obey your husband,—an honest, uninteresting creed that thousands of women live up to. This girl is married to 'a man of the world.' She is full of belief in the holy bond; her illusions are unbroken, and her faiths supreme. One by one they snap, as all in her finds no response in him. She fades and withers. The world asks, 'What is his crime?' It seeks a crime punishable by law, as if the atmosphere of his presence were not crime enough!' Oh, the curse of our false, worldly society, which demands position at *any* cost, which admits a man with *any* past, nor inquires further than his *title!* 'Her ladyship' makes up for all shortcomings. Of *this* is the world created by Fashion, but it is not the world created by God."

"Poor girl! poor girl! what can I say? How can I advise you?"

"There is no advice I could take,—for the child's sake. My poor little girl would be the worst sufferer. How can I brand the father without branding the child? For her sake I will endure; but it is almost beyond endurance. I have told you so much that I may as well tell you the last infamy. I missed my pearl necklace some days ago. The same evening, that woman, who was going to the theatre with us, was standing in front of that glass as I came into the room. As she saw me she hastily unclasped something from her neck. My heart stood still; I cannot tell why, but I am convinced she had my necklace!"

"You do not think she stole it!"

"Not for a moment. *He* gave it her."

"I cannot believe that any man, no matter how bad, could be so lost to shame as to offer any woman such an insult!"

In the excitement under which they both labored, neither had heard a slight movement beyond the curtains of the billiard-room. Unperceived by them, Mrs. Dashton had been about to enter the room, when the instinct of her class bade her listen. She was eagerly drinking in the whole conversation.

"I am *not* mistaken," resumed the countess. "My shame comes to me a thousand times over as I speak of it. How I have endured that woman's presence so long I do not know. Do you think because I look passionless that I do not feel, that I cannot see, the scarce-concealed sneers of the women, the open, half-proffered pity of the men around me? I have borne it all till now; but the end has come, and if my suspicion about the necklace should prove correct——"

"Yes, yes," interrupted Goddard, eagerly, "sometimes a momentary impulse may determine what has been a long and weary struggle; and should such an impulse come to you, do not hesitate to command me. There is nothing I would not sacrifice for you!"

"Boooh!"

"Goodness! how you startled me!"

The speakers were Kitty Middleton and Mrs. Dashton. The former had come running in through the billiard-room, and had seized the latter round the waist as she came.

"I'll lay an even tenner," said the girl, cheerily, as they entered together, "that Mrs. Dashton's been listening. You know the proverb? How do you come out, Mrs. Dashton?"

"Kitty, you're too bad!" expostulated Lady Arlingford. "I hope Mrs. Dashton will excuse you."

"Of course she will," returned Kitty. "I've got a capital story to tell her while we put our hair straight and powder our noses. It's mildly improper. Come along. The men are coming in."

And before Mrs. Dashton could say a word, she had been whisked out of the room again.

At this moment there entered from the dining-room, laughing and talking together, Lord Arlingford, Major Carteret, and Mr. Cincinnatus Q. Briggs.

"Ah, Goddard! glad to see you again," said his lordship, shaking Goddard by the hand. "Sorry you were detained. Major Carteret, Captain Goddard—Mr. Briggs. Mr. Briggs will be glad to ask you some questions about Berlin that I couldn't answer. I know you can. He is doing Europe; and I tell him no one is better able than you to give him the information he seeks."

"Only too happy," replied Goddard, bowing. "I fancy I knew a brother of yours, Mr. Briggs. He was painting at Leipsic— Horace I think his name was. Am I right?"

"Perfectly," replied Briggs. "He often spoke of you, and he gave me a letter of introduction which your absence from London has prevented my using."

"I need not say, command me. I am, unfortunately, obliged to leave town tonight, on urgent business; but I hope to be back in about a fortnight. Come and have a chat then and tell me what I can do."

"Thank you. I shall come with pleasure."

Mr. Cincinnatus Q. Briggs was a most disappointing American,—that is, from the English point of view of Kitty Middleton. His clear-cut face was innocent of goatee, his clothes, though of Gothamite origin, fitted him with a precision worthy of Saville Row or Conduit Street, his full deep voice was guiltless of the least suspicion of twang, he neither hazarded "guesses" on subjects under discussion nor spent his time in vain "calculations" concerning the affairs of life. He never "reckoned," nor did he "enthuse." He ate with a fork in the regulation manner, and, whilst justly proud of the Yellowstone Park and the Yosemite Valley, did not dismiss Vesuvius with the reflection that his country boasted a waterfall that could extinguish it in two minutes. In fact, instead of being an American gentleman, he was a gentlemanly American; and Kitty Middleton, who watched to see him put his feet on the table and wave a handkerchief embroidered with the stars and stripes, was disappointed and annoyed.

As he turned to Lady Arlingford, the master of the house remarked to Goddard,—

"You go tonight, I understand? Things seem pretty lively at the Foreign Office. 'What's to be the end of it all?' is the only question one hears nowadays, and no one seems able to answer it. By the way," continued he, lowering his voice, "Mrs. Dashton tells me you knew her in India."

"Yes: most of our fellows can claim that—honor. I scarcely expected to meet her here,—or in the same house as any man's *wife.*"

The words were spoken with bitter emphasis, and the speaker turned on his heel, to be immediately tackled by Charlie

Middleton, who had entered with the men. Arlingford looked after him and muttered between his teeth,—

"You shall pay for that, you puppy!"

Mrs. Dashton, entering the room at that moment, caught his expression, and came up to him with a mischievous smile on her face.

"Tt-tt-tt!" said she. "Has he been scolded by his wife's friend,—naughty boy? Goddard's affection for Alice is really quite touching, isn't it?"

"Don't play the fool!" was the courteous rejoinder. "What did Schouloff say? Can he let us have the money?"

"Ye-es."

"What does he want for it?"

"More than I can do."

"Nonsense! you must do anything he says. I *must* have it."

"He wants Goddard detained tonight. He must be delayed at any cost. This is the price of the loan."

"Oh!"

"Exactly. What do you think about it?"

"How *can* he be detained?"

"I think I know a way, if you will consent."

"If! when you know I must have the ten thousand by Monday or be posted!"

"Very well. Let me wear the pearl necklace tonight. I brought it with me."

"The necklace! Why—how——?"

"Ask no questions. Yes or no?"

"No,—not that,"

"All right: manage for yourself."

"Hang it, Emily! don't be angry with me."

"Then don't be a fool!"

"I'll—I'll decide in ten minutes." And Arlingford turned and walked into the billiard-room.

Left alone, Mrs. Dashton's face was crossed by a look of triumph.

"So, my lady," said she to herself, "pure and passionless as you pretend to be, you can feel! So can I, when I am unwelcome.

You have sneered at me long enough. What did you say? If your suspicions about the necklace were true, your patience would not last. We shall see! and you, Captain Goddard, will have an opportunity of making your sacrifice for friendship."

Then she joined the group at the fireplace.

"That's right; go on,—pitch into me," Kitty was saying from her position on the floor by Lady Arlingford's side, "but all my escapades are knocked into fits by Bella-Demonia's. Mrs. Dashton has been telling me about her. Who knows her?"

"By reputation, everybody," said Major Carteret.

"Everybody but the Wild Westerner," put in Briggs; and then, as they looked at him for an explanation,—it being prior to Buffalo Bill's visit to London,—he went on: "Miss Middleton told me I should have appeared in my native costume,—that is to say, beads, feathers, wampum, and a tomahawk,—and wanted to know if we hunted buffaloes on Broadway and Wall Street. I revenged myself by treating her to the dear old stand-by about Bears being the indigenous animals of those jungles. She didn't know what I meant."

"Didn't I!" said Kitty, indignantly. "But I knew you were making an old stock joke, or I'd have said I was Irish, just to get in the Bull."

"Mr. Briggs," said Lady Arlingford, as the American was about to reply, "as an old friend of Kitty's let me tell you it is hopeless trying to 'sit on' her. She will not be sat upon."

"I am patient," replied Briggs. "But may I not know more of Miss Middleton's latest shock, Bella-Demonia?"

"I did not suppose," said Carteret, "that there was a man who had not heard of her. To tell all her adventures would fill another 'Arabian Nights.' Strange that her name should be unknown to you! No woman is more talked about, and personally less known: she is more abused and praised than any living creature; I never heard her name spoken in any society that her defenders were not as earnest as her abusers. One thing is sure enough, she must be a very remarkably intelligent woman, for she certainly puzzles both friends and enemies alike."

"Did you never meet her?" asked Briggs.

"No. I believe she has never been known to receive anyone on simply social grounds. Politics are her sphere, and it is remarkable that she never makes a mistake. A man may be admitted to her circle who has apparently no more value as a politician than I have as a milliner, but it always turns out that he was the one man who was vitally necessary to this or that plot. Volumes could be filled with stories about her."

"But the stories told about her are generally untrue," put in Mrs. Dashton. "*I* know her well. She is one of the most generous creatures imaginable. If anyone in distress wants *anything*, off they go to Bella-Demonia."

As she said this, Arlingford entered the room unperceived, accompanied by Prince Schouloff, and remained in conversation with him in the background. The prince's tall figure was clad in evening dress, the black-and-red ribbon of St. Vladimir across his waistcoat, and the jewel of the order hanging below his cravat.

"She must be rich, to live as she does," resumed Briggs.

"Fabulously," replied Mrs. Dashton. "I must confess, I envy her. A woman with unlimited money and brains is rare enough to excite that feeling in anyone. But we are boring Lady Arlingford horribly; You do not care to hear of interesting people, do you, Lady Arlingford?"

"When they are not reputable,—no," replied her ladyship, quietly; "I am sorry to say I cannot so far live up to the times as to admit those people to be interesting."

"What do *you* say, Captain Goddard?" said Mrs. Dashton. "Don't you think Bella-Demonia interesting?"

"Yes, and no," replied he. "My principal feeling is one of pity,—of sorrow. I cannot forget that she is a woman, and a woman who fights against the world must at best be the loser."

"The sentiment I should expect to find expressed by so brave soldier as Captain Goddard," said Prince Schouloff, "whom," he continued, as Lady Arlingford presented them, "I have long hoped meet, and am charmed to know."

The two men shook hands.

"May I add to your information?" pursued the prince. "Much has been said, and much has been written, of Bella-Demonia.

She is relentless in her hate as she is gentle in her love. Revenge is her life,—revenge for her wrongs. Once hear her speak of them, and the name she is known by suits her to perfection."

"But what is her real name?" asked Briggs.

"No one knows," replied Carteret.

"Or no one who knows tells," put in Mrs. Dashton.

"Bella-Demonia never lets anyone know what she wishes to remain unknown," concluded Prince Schouloff; then, turning to Goddard, he added, "I have just come from the Duke's, where I heard of your probable promotion,—from General Saville. Let me congratulate you."

"Thanks."

"Will you call on me tomorrow?"

"Very sorry, I can't. I leave London tonight."

"Well, it is a pleasure deferred. A soldier is always the slave of his duty. If I were a woman I would never have a soldier lover. I am sorry we cannot improve our acquaintance now: however, call on me when you return,—or in Berlin. I shall be there in a week, and I will present you to Bella-Demonia."

Goddard bowed and rejoined the others. The prince looked after him.

"Perhaps you will not go," said he to himself; and, taking a telegram from his pocket, he read, "'The despatches carried by Captain Goddard contain ultimatum; their detention imperative. Explanation and further instructions by messenger.' Well, well, life is uncertain: the young man thinks he will start tonight on his mission,—*I* think he will not. Which of us is right, I wonder?" And he seated himself by a bookcase and began idly turning over the leaves of an album.

"I say, Mrs. Dashton," cried Charlie Middleton to that lady, who was conversing with Lord Arlingford, "you promised to play me a game of billiards. Come now, while they're not looking, and we'll study the game."

"Will you be very good if I do?"

"Awfully!" replied the boy, and started for the billiard-room.

"Will you spare me to this bad child?" said she to Arlingford, as she rose.

"I wish I were the bad child!" returned he, and as he spoke he took the hand that hung by her side and pressed it. The action was not lost upon Lady Arlingford, who happened to be looking in their direction, and Goddard, noticing her change of color, followed the direction of her eyes and grasped the situation.

Lord Arlingford walked over to Prince Schouloff.

"I am afraid, prince," said he, "that you find it dull."

"Oh, no," replied Schouloff, looking him straight in the eyes.

"We shall all be much amused, I hope, presently. When one has an object to serve, all things are amusing. Er—Captain Goddard must soon go. So will I." And he returned to the study of the album.

"What did Emily mean, I wonder?" reflected Arlingford, recalled to actualities by the prince's words and manner. "Can it be that if she wears the necklace Goddard will resent the affront and delay his departure? Ah!"—and a new light broke in upon him,—"she's right, as usual. We shall see; we shall see."

"It seems as though when you go," Lady Arlingford was saying to Goddard, "I shall be at the mercy of that creature."

"Cheer up, little woman," he answered. "Don't give way. Pretend you don't care: it's the worst punishment you could inflict."

"Come and see a catastrophe," broke in Kitty. "I'm going to spoil sport. I want to show you how Mrs. Dashton teaches Charlie billiards. Nice game, billiards. Listen! not a sound. Follow me."

She started towards the billiard-room, accompanied by Carteret and Briggs, and Lady Arlingford pursued her to prevent the accomplishment of her vile purpose. Goddard was following, when Arlingford, who had been watching for the opportunity, stopped him.

"Look here, Goddard," said he, "you are an old friend of Alice's. I wish you'd advise her to be more civil to Mrs. Dashton."

"You must do your own dirty work," replied Goddard, hotly; "and, by God, sir, *that's* not the advice I would give your wife, even if I had less regard for her than I have! You ought to send that woman away."

"Really, Goddard," answered Arlingford, haughtily, "upon my word I don't understand you."

"Yes, you do! and you make my position doubly difficult by evading the question."

"By what right do you *dare* question my actions?"

"By the rights of blood and friendship!"

"For my wife! I fail to recognize the right. Now look here: I've been patient long enough. I'm sorry you're in love with my wife——"

"In love! Stop——"

"But she *is* my wife," continued Arlingford, imperturbably, "and I forbid you to see her any more. Do you hear?"

"You hound!" cried Goddard, "if I didn't respect her feelings, I'd thrash you in your own house." Then, as the others, attracted by his tone, re-entered from the billiard-room, he added, "For her sake, no scene now; but later on you and I will settle."

"What is the matter?" said Lady Arlingford, anxiously, as she came between them. "You are quarrelling!"

"No, no," said Goddard; "only arguing."

"A trifle warmly, perhaps," added Arlingford. "We were disputing a point at écarté. We will settle it now, if you like, Goddard. I'll bet you a hundred pounds I'm right."

"So be it: we shall see."

Kitty Middleton, who saw that something was amiss, busied herself with Charlie getting the card-table ready, whilst Arlingford rapidly sorted out the unnecessary cards from the pack and threw them on a side-table. Throughout the above scene Prince Schouloff had sat apparently absorbed in the album he had taken up. Arlingford and Goddard seated themselves at the table and began to play. Carteret and Briggs were standing in a bow-window, discussing American finance, Lady Arlingford was alone by the fire, and Kitty sat at the piano close beside her, running her fingers lightly over the keys.

As the game began, Mrs. Dashton strolled in from the billiard-room. As she did so, the prince looked at his watch. It was eleven. In a quarter of an hour Goddard must be gone. Mrs. Dashton came to Arlingford's side, and whispered,—

"Well? The prince grows impatient. Am I to aid you?"

"Wear the necklace!" said he, desperately.

"The despatches will be detained: you will get the money," she whispered, adding to herself as she left the room, "Goddard will be ruined, and 'Dashey' will have scored one!"

As she went out, Prince Schouloff strolled over to Lady Arlingford's side.

"Lady Arlingford," said he, "I do not see you much in society now, and you look pale. I hope you are not suffering? You should go abroad for a time. Lord Arlingford must bring you to Nice, and you, Miss Middleton, must come also."

"Kitty will not be Miss Middleton for long, prince," answered Lady Arlingford for her.

"Then I shall look forward to welcoming Mr. and Mrs. Saville wherever I may be," answered Schouloff, with a bow to Kitty.

At this moment Mrs. Dashton entered the room, wearing a row of magnificent pearls round her neck. Lady Arlingford, catching sight of them, started violently, and Prince Schouloff said, in the quiet careful tone that alone betrayed the fact that he was a foreigner,—

"What beautiful pearls you have, Mrs. Dashton! Excuse me, but I had not noticed them before."

"Yes," answered she, carelessly, "they *are* pretty. A present."

Goddard turned his head, and his eyes fell on the necklace. Lady Arlingford was steadying herself with difficulty against her chair.

"You cowardly blackguard!" he hissed across the table at Arlingford.

"You are my wife's champion, it would seem," sneered he. "Defend her!"

"Come and see the game, prince," said Mrs. Dashton, moving over to the card-table, where she was joined by Mr. Briggs and Major Carteret. Meanwhile, Lady Arlingford had crossed to the table where the useless cards had been thrown down, and, taking up one of them,—a two of clubs,—wrote on it hurriedly in pencil, "*I will not stay another hour in this house. I go with you.*"

Mrs. Dashton had watched her closely.

"Much on the game?" asked she, carelessly.

"For so much excitement," said the prince, "there should be at least ten thousand pounds!"

Lady Arlingford came over to Goddard's side. There she dropped her handkerchief, and as she stooped to pick it up slipped the card on which she had written into Goddard's lap. He took it stealthily, unconscious that Mrs. Dashton had followed every movement.

Suddenly the latter stooped and whispered in Arlingford's ear.

"What is that you have hidden?" cried he to Goddard.

"I—I do not understand," stammered Goddard.

"You have a card there, and I demand that it be shown!"

"I cannot show it."

"I did not suppose you could," sneered Arlingford, slipping a card from his hand unobserved into that of Mrs. Dashton, and flinging the rest on the table. "You see I do not hold the *king*."

"What do you mean?" cried Goddard, growing deathly pale.

"I mean that I do not play cards with a man who cheats!" howled Arlingford.

Goddard started to his feet.

"My God!" he exclaimed, pressing his hands to his head. As he rose, an elderly military-looking man had entered the room. It was General Saville.

"Well, how are you all?" he exclaimed, comprehensively. "Aubyn, I bring you good news, my boy. Tonight's mission will be your last. I have gained my point with the Duke, and he has confirmed your staff-appointment." Then, observing for the first time the dead silence and the dismayed faces round him, he continued,—

"What is the matter? Why don't you speak, some of you?"

"I repeat," said Arlingford, with deadly distinctness, 'your methods' are not such as to permit gentlemen to play cards with you, and I must desire that you leave this house at once."

"Arlingford," cried General Saville, "how dare you! You must be mad. I demand an explanation."

"Captain Goddard holds a card that was not dealt to him, which he refuses to show, and which I assert is the king of clubs."

348

"Good heavens! Deny it, Aubyn: tell him he lies!"

"Mrs. Dashton and Prince Schouloff also saw him take the card from his lap," continued Arlingford, calmly.

"Answer!" thundered the general, growing purple.

"It is a lie," said Goddard, quietly.

"Then show the card," said Arlingford.

"Yes, show the card," cried the general.

"I cannot."

A dead silence fell in the room. It was broken by the sound of a fall. Unobserved, during the above scene Lady Arlingford had been struggling to speak. An iron grip seemed to be upon her throat, and she struggled in vain. As Goddard spoke, she fell senseless to the floor.

"Captain Goddard," said General Saville, stiffly, "it will be obvious to you that there is only one course for you to pursue. I will save you the trouble of resigning your commission, and your diplomatic post is vacant. You will take your name from your Club lists tomorrow, and—God! boy," concluded the old gentleman, all but breaking down, "I'd sooner you'd been a murderer than a black-leg."

General Saville turned, and, seeing Schouloff, went towards him. Goddard looked round him for a moment, and, seeing even Kitty's face averted as she bent over Lady Arlingford, exclaimed,—

"Ruined! God help me!"

And he rushed from the room.

An hour later, in the little May fair drawing-room Prince Schouloff paid over to Mrs. Bradley Dashton ten thousand pounds in Bank-of-England notes.

Not a word was said on either side.

# BOOK III.

## CHAPTER I.
### In A Political Observatory.

The political crisis which opened the year 1876 with the "Andrassy Note" closed it with the Conference at Constantinople of January, 1877. By the middle of that month the Cabinets of Europe had realized the fact that the Conference had been met by a rejection of its proposals on the part of the Sublime Porte, and at the end of March the Six Powers forwarded to the Sultan their ultimatum in the form of a Protocol. Turkey, however, pursued her time-honored policy of masterly inactivity, and on the 24th of April Europe was startled by the news that Russia had declared war against the Sultan in defence of the Christian populations of the Balkan Peninsula, had crossed the Pruth into Roumania, which had promptly declared itself on the side of the Muscovite, and had entered Asia Minor at Batoum, Kars, and Bayazid.

The only explanation vouchsafed to Europe was contained in the circular note of Prince Gortschakoff, and the Powers, after entering their formal protest, assumed a position of armed neutrality.

The campaign opened, as is familiar to the student of modern history, with a series of Russian successes both in Europe and Asia. General Gourko crossed the Danube without opposition in June, and invested Tirnova on the 7th of July, preparatory to crossing the Balkans at Yeni Saghra five days later with a flying column. It was not till then that Russia saw the mistake she had made in overlooking Plevna, and turned in that direction to find it occupied and fortified by the greatest general of the Ottoman forces, Osman Pasha. On the 20th and on the 31st of July two desperate assaults of this position resulted in the total defeat of the Russian arms, and Gourko was driven back beyond the Balkans, whilst in Asia Moukhtar Pasha gained his first decisive victory at Kars.

Thus, in August, 1877, when our story reopens, the Muscovite advance had received a temporary but serious check, Todleben had been called to the investment of Plevna, and the nations looked at one another with apprehensive glances as they asked themselves and one another, "What next?"

Meanwhile, the principal post of observation established by Russia in the Balkans was at the village of Deve-kiui, on the road from Eski Saghra to Adrianople, where, snugly established in the Villa Kristov Hisar, Prince Schouloff and the Baroness Altdorff anxiously watched the successive turns which events were taking.

A few weeks before this they had been joined by Mrs. Bradley Dashton, who since we parted from her in London had suffered a series of reverses in the prosecution of her plans. Indeed, important events and changes had taken place in the lives of most of the actors in the drama with which we are concerned, all resulting directly and indirectly from the tragedy enacted at Arlingford House on the night that saw the successful issue of the plot concocted against Captain Aubyn Goddard.

For weeks Lady Arlingford had lain unconscious between life and death. In her delirium she had raved much about that fatal evening, but her utterances had been ascribed to the state of her brain; and when she recovered from the blow and emerged into the light of reason, Goddard was to all intents and purposes lost to the world. As soon as she could be moved, Alice Arlingford had been taken to her mother's house in Berkeley Square, and here Kitty Middleton had been her only *confidante*. To her she had told the whole dismal story as soon as she was sufficiently herself to do so, and both agreed that to publish the facts now, in the absence of Goddard, would be to lay themselves open to the charge of having invented the story to clear the man whom Arlingford had—though vainly—tried to brand as his wife's lover. So they had waited on in the hope that Goddard might be heard of again, and that he might be summoned home to assist in his own exculpation from the charges brought against him by the Earl of Arlingford, Mrs. Dashton, and Major Homer Carteret.

One step, however, had been taken which the events of the evening and the episode of the necklace had rendered inevitable: this was the divorce of the Earl and Countess of Arlingford, which went by default in the absence of his lordship and upon the admissions of Mrs. Dashton. Soon after the disappearance of Goddard, Arlingford had found that the glances bestowed upon him in club-rooms, never of the warmest, had become arctic in their frigidity. He found that men refused to hear the name of Aubyn Goddard spoken by his lips, and that his efforts to deepen the cloud which rested over the ex-Queen's Messenger were practically abortive. Under these circumstances, his lordship had betaken himself to the more congenial atmosphere of Nice and Monte Carlo, whither Mrs. Dashton had shortly after followed him, and, after passing six months of varied fortune at the tables, found himself in the, to him, familiar predicament of being "cleaned out." It was then that the summons of Prince Schouloff had seemed to Mrs. Dashton laden with the pleasant perfume of hope, and, obeying it, armed with passes through the Russian lines, she had joined the Prince and Bella-Demonia in their political observatory, anxious to serve the Chief of Police for the furtherance of her own plans, which seemed to have encountered a serious and abiding check.

The divorce of the Countess of Arlingford and the marriage of Kitty Middleton to Dick Saville had taken place almost simultaneously, and thus a powerful ally had joined the campaign for the rehabilitation of Aubyn Goddard.

Of Goddard himself the news had been at first scanty, then depressing, and finally overwhelming. What might have been the effect on European history had he started on that fatal night with his despatches, it is not for us to conjecture. He had reached Charing Cross five minutes too late, and had laid his despatches with his resignation on his chief's table at eight o'clock on the following morning, and they had left London with another messenger by the ten-o'clock mail. Later in the day he had had a long interview with General Saville, from which the sturdy old warrior had emerged with something very like a tear in the one eye that active service had left him, and had emphatically remarked to a Club crony,—

"Damn the boy! I love and admire him more than ever. He won't tell me anything about it, but I'll swear"—which he did with unction—"that a more honorable fellow never lived. Some day we shall get to the bottom of this miserable affair; meanwhile, we can only wait and hope for the best."

General Saville took upon himself to lay Goddard's resignations, with a statement of the circumstances, before the committees of his various Clubs, and those illustrious bodies had decided to hold his membership in abeyance, pending an inquiry and explanation.

On the following day Goddard had started for America, bound for a ranch owned by General Saville in Dakota Territory. A few months later, one of the periodical revolutions having eventuated in Central America, Goddard's soldier instinct overcame him, and he had placed himself at the head of a regiment of *filibusteros*, on the side of the existing government. In one of the decisive engagements he had performed deeds of unheard-of valor, and had been reported dead,—killed by a stray shot at the moment of victory,—and so he had gone out of this history, and his record was to all intents and purposes closed.

Things were in this condition when our story reopens at the Villa Kristov Hisar in Bulgaria, in the month of August, 1877.

Prince Schouloff sat in his study, which looked out upon the veranda of the villa, going over a bundle of despatches, and ever and anon consulting a map that lay before him. At his elbow stood his private secretary Dmitri Keratieff, awaiting the attention of his chief.

"Well, said the prince, looking up from his map, "what have you to report?"

"Mrs Dashton tried to open the mail-bag early this morning: she said she had enclosed a letter by mistake. I opened it for her: there was no letter of hers in the bag. Madame von Altdorff sent a despatch by her courier-secretary before daylight."

"Ah! Know you its contents?"

"No, Excellency. I am more useful alive than dead, and I never question the incoming or outgoing of Rodia Pouschkoff."

The secretary laughed as he spoke, and Schouloff nodded his head gravely but approvingly.

"Did you see him start?"

"Yes, Excellency. He took the direction of Eski Saghra."

"He has not returned?"

"Not yet."

"Anything else?"

"Mrs. Dashton bade me present her compliments and say that she desired to speak with your Excellency as soon as you should be at leisure."

"Where is she now?"

"On the terrace."

"Ask her to honor me with a visit, here and now."

The secretary retired.

"Ah, Emily Dashton," soliloquized the prince, "you are unable to control your curiosity: you are madly eager to know why I sent for you. Take care! You are an excellent servant, but you can never direct. Examine my mail-bag! how *rococo*! The method has neither novelty nor ingenuity to recommend it, and still, undaunted, you play your little, your *very* little, tricks."

And Prince Schouloff, leaning back in his chair, laughed aloud, as Mrs. Dashton appeared at the French window leading out upon the terrace.

"Alone, and amused?" said she, looking at him from the window. "Happy man!"

"Sensible people," replied Schouloff, "never depend upon anyone for anything, not even for their amusement."

"As usual, your sentiment is flawless. But are you sure you are as independent as you think?"

"It has been the study of my life to be so."

"And, like most students, you have absorbed yourself so much in the study of others that you have left no time to study yourself. You leave that for fools like me."

"Do you find me interesting?"

"Er—urn—ye-es. But not so original as I expected."

"Well," said Schouloff, in the altered tone of a man desirous of changing the subject, "I will try to do better. So much for your amusement. Now for your business. I understand you wished to speak to me?"

"Yes," answered Mrs. Dashton, her manner also altering. "I am not satisfied with the way things have turned out. You offered to help me, and I carried out my part of the bargain. I knew that when Lady Arlingford saw her pearls on my neck she would do something foolish that would detain Goddard. She did more; but I am no nearer the realization of my hopes. I am getting tired of scheming, and want rest."

"Why reproach me with—pardon me!—your own folly? I wished Captain Goddard detained, and was willing to pay for it. You undertook to effect the delay, and received the payment for so doing,—an enormous sum: is it not so? It is with Lord Arlingford you are not satisfied, not with me. Come, be frank; what did he promise you? You do not answer. Well, he promised that if you would help him, he would drive Lady Arlingford to claim a divorce, and would then marry you. The first he has done; the second he has not."

"How do you know this?"

"I did *not* know; but you betray your own secrets. But your ambition is a wrong one. As a woman you are charming, as a wife you would be stupid."

"Do you suppose," broke out the woman, impetuously, "that because I have led a rough life I have no feeling? You have guessed half the situation, so hear it all. I am *fond* of Jack Arlingford. I know he's a bad lot; perhaps that's why I like him: I'm not such a very good lot myself!—and good people make me angry. He cares for me, I believe, and if everything had not gone so contrary, I think he would have kept his promise; but after the divorce everything went so wrong that I was obliged to leave London. I joined him in Nice, and now he is broke there, and cannot move a step till he gets money."

Prince Schouloff smiled.

"Shall I prove to you," he said, "that he will *not* keep his word—even so far as he can—to you?"

"How? Do you mean that he does not really care for me? If I thought that——!"

"Lord Arlingford is at this moment trying to marry a rich American, a cousin of the Mr. Briggs whom we met at his house. He cares for *nothing* save gambling, and his affection for you will be regulated by the amount you subscribe to the fund. Now, let me know the amount necessary to—your happiness, and try to find out for me accurate details as to the death of Captain Goddard. I am much interested in him."

"In Goddard? Where did you lose sight of him? Let me see: where did you lose sight of him? I think I remember. After the scandal he started for Dakota, for a ranch belonging to General Saville. There the soldier got the better of him, and he joined that Central American revolution, and was reported dead. Is that right?"

"Perfectly: you are accuracy and clearness to perfection, as far as our information goes; but I should like the details. Now, I have a charming villa at Mentone, of which I should like to make a wedding-present to the bride who can give me accurate details of Captain Goddard's death. The certificate of the marriage is not necessary to secure the gift."

"Which means, translated——?"

"What you please! Mrs. Dashton, you are a clever woman, especially so where the finesse of a woman's nature is concerned: witness, for instance, your instinct in Lady Arlingford's case, where you judged exactly the moment to strike. I should value your opinion just now. Erghem! I see a great change in Bella-Demonia. She takes no interest in anything. I have sought in vain the reason: can you help me?"

"You once said, 'Bella-Demonia never allows anyone to know what she wishes to remain unknown.' That is my answer *now*. I am a woman of fairly strong nerve; but ask Bella-Demonia a question about herself?—excuse me! See," continued she, rising, and moving to the window, "there she is on the terrace. She looks gentle enough; but when she chooses to freeze you, her cold stare of wonder at your audacity would daunt a braver woman than I. But be sure that if I can help you I will. She is coming this way. Shall I go?"

"Not yet. See if her manner helps you."

And the prince walked to the window to meet the object of his recent conversation.

"Who, to see her sweet soft face," thought he, "would believe that she could be so hard to conquer? Yet for close upon a year I have fluttered like a moth in vain around the flame of her fascination,—I, Alexis Schouloff!"

Two quickly successive reports, the boom of a distant gun, reverberated dully on the air, as the Baroness Altdorff stepped into the room, giving her hand to Prince Schouloff as she did so.

"Those were the cannon of Eski Saghra, prince. It is true, then, that the Flying Legion has arrived in the neighborhood?"

"Such are my last instructions, baroness," returned the prince, gravely, looking at his watch.

"What a picture you made there, baroness!" put in Mrs. Dashton at this point,—"a living embodiment of tranquil power in repose. Dreaming pleasant things, I judge by your expression. You are a true subject for an artist."

"You evidently have not remarked, Mrs. Dashton," interrupted Bella-Demonia, icily, "that I do not like flattery. From a woman it means either nothing or a great deal too much. Prince, I shall have, I think, great news for you before the afternoon is over. Mrs. Dashton, you have not yet visited me in my own apartments: you must come and see me there. The prince is good enough to let me have an entire wing to myself, where no one ever comes save at my request."

"I shall look forward to coming and seeing you *chez vous*. I have so much yet to say to you and ask you."

"You will find me a bad gossip——"

"But I will do all that, and I am positively dying for a good long talk. This place, with all respect to Prince Schouloff, is so far from civilization! Upon my word, it's as hard to get here as—as—as it was for poor Goddard to get himself killed."

She said the last words after a hesitation, as if she had been searching vainly for a simile. As she concluded, Bella-Demonia turned deathly white, but controlled herself with a violent effort which did not escape the narrow observation of Schouloff.

"What a singular comparison to make!" said she, at last.

"Perhaps it was," said Mrs. Dashton, reflectively. "I don't know what brought him to my mind at that moment. Strange break, his,—a man who was apparently just reaching the zenith of his career, or, if not quite that, with every promise for the future, to ruin himself so completely!—it is inconceivable. But why should I wander on so, about a stranger to you?—but then, you see, I knew him so well."

"You knew him?" put in Bella-Demonia, eagerly; then, recovering herself once more, she added, "*What* was the name?"

"Aubyn Goddard. I'll tell you all about it some day, when I come to see you in your own rooms."

"That will be very soon," said Prince Schouloff to himself. Then he added aloud to Bella-Demonia, "You are interested, baroness?"

"Naturally! A man who ruins himself at the very moment that his prospects seemed most bright must have had the usual cause,—a woman. Hence the story must be at least amusing."

"Then you believe," said the prince, "that when a man is ruined, a woman is always the cause. Oh, fie!"

"Not at all, in the way you put it. A man may be ruined by many causes but when he brings about his *own* ruin it is pretty safe to assume that there is a woman."

"Well," said Schouloff, "I will argue that point later."

"It must be nearly time our bold travellers arrived. I must watch from the terrace for them, in case there be any young man in the party whom I can make my own. Who are these visitors, prince?"

"They shall announce themselves to you, Mrs. Dashton."

"Well, no doubt it's some pleasant surprise you have in store for me. I won't be inquisitive. I hope I don't shock you, baroness?"

"I shocked!" returned Bella-Demonia, in an accent of ironical surprise, "I,—the byword of Europe! My right to censure or extol was stolen from me years ago."

"And *I* don't believe I ever *had* that right. Well, *au revoir*. I must go and get ready."

And Mrs. Dashton disappeared from the room with a laugh.

"Who are these visitors, prince?" said Bella-Demonia, when she had gone. "You have told me nothing."

"Because there was nothing to tell, till this morning. A Mr. Saville and his wife,—charming people: they will interest you. They want to see me,—and you,—and, arriving at the frontier two days since, applied to me for passes through the lines. They arrived at Eski Saghra last night, and are coming on this morning. The proximity of the Flying Legion has made me nervous about them."

Bella-Demonia dismissed the subject with a little shrug.

"Tell me," said she, "why did you ask that woman, Mrs. Dashton, here?"

"Because I thought she would amuse you."

"Because you wanted her to find out something for you, from me,—from *me!*"

"If you know, why ask?"

"To give you a chance of being honest with me. You know I hate lies and the cowardice that begets them. Ask *me* what you want to know. Have I ever been wanting in courage to speak?"

"You are irritable, baroness; yet I have been patient, and not—not ungenerous?"

"Forgive me, if, in the weariness I feel, I forget how much I owe you. When I first sought you I was seeking distraction: you offered me politics, absorbing as heart or brain could desire. I had nothing to live for till you brought me within range of your vast world of schemes. By degrees the fascination of your power gained on me. To see great nations tremble or rejoice, to see life or death meted out, was the breath of life to me. For years of feverish oblivion I have to thank you, and I do. But I am still a woman, and my very being is weary. See the traces!" As she spoke, she turned to the mirror over the mantel-shelf, and leaned upon it. "If only my revenge had not been torn from me, I would have served an eternity. If heaven had but been just to me!"

"My hope," said the Russian, gently, "has been to bring yon more than oblivion. Must that hope always be vain? Will you never forget the cares, the sombre side of life, and remember but the glowing sunshine which is yours by right of love?"

He had risen and approached her as he spoke. She drew away, as she said,—

"I thought our compact was clear. Must I remind you? When I accepted your service, I knew that I risked my life in a service of danger; that life I sold you,—if need should come, my death; but I did not sell you myself."

"No, that you only give. Oh, it is only 'Bella-Demonia' who is dead to love: to find mercy, the mother of love, one must appeal to charity. 'Carita'—it is a sweet name, and I would call you by it."

"The name was my mother's: it is sacred to me. But come! do not let us speak in riddles. You know some part of my secret, you would know more. I tell you frankly you will learn nothing through that woman. *You* have the better chance. Question me! I may reserve what I like, but I will not lie."

For an instant the two stood silently looking at each other, and then the prince spoke.

"Did you care for this man Goddard?" said he.

"With my whole soul!"

"Why did you never speak of him?"

"That which lies near the heart is far from the lips."

"Do you know what has become of him?"

"He is dead, if that woman spoke true. Well, so much the better for you and for your work. You will find me the better destroyer now that the one touch of womanhood is laid at rest forever. Direct, and I will execute. Let me think only of wrongs and the blight they bring. I told you I would give you news. I have news for you,—brave news."

"Tell me, what is it?"

"The Russian arms have received a serious check. For the last month your best-laid plans of campaign have been frustrated by the unerring precision of the movements of this Flying Legion of which we hear so much and see so little: is it not so?"

"Perfectly. The latest despatches of Skobeleff are to that effect."

"Well, the chief of the Flying Legion, Beyaz Murad Bey, will be in my power tonight. What is his capture worth?"

"Murad here! It cannot be possible!"

The prince rose to his feet and commenced pacing up and down the room. The Baroness Altdorff smiled as she leaned back in her chair.

"Is that a reflection?" said she. "You are not complimentary to my powers of fascination, to say nothing of my skill as a diplomatist,—some say 'decoy.'"

"You are in earnest!" exclaimed Schouloff, coming to a full stop before her.

"Perfectly. I came to the conclusion that he must be taken out of your way. But for him, we should be in possession of the Shipka Pass. He is advancing upon Plevna. Once let him join Osman, and we shall see what the Grand Duke, Todleben, and Skobeleff can do,—such a three against such a two! I shall remove him, this terror, Beyaz Murad,—Murad Bey."

"Not easy——"

"No, not easy, but—— Well, never mind my plan of action: the result is all that you need know. Admit that I chose our location here with forethought, three months before hostilities commenced. After much delicate work, I have caused the report to reach the Chief that in consequence of your weakness—of *your* weakness!"—and she laughed a little—"I was in possession of important strategic secrets, that I had expressed great admiration of his bravery and was impressionable,—*impressionable!*—in short, that *he* might learn all I knew with a little trouble. The Flying Legion encamped last night near Eski Saghra. They are short of provisions, and knowledge of our movements is imperative. Well, by my arrangement he has laid a trap for me into which he will fall himself."

Prince Schouloff's eyes glowed with admiration.

"By St. Nicholas! ingenious as only Bella-Demonia could be! Perhaps this is the only one line that could have snared him. What marvellous tact! what instinct! Ah! if you are not for me, what a pity you were not born a man! You are sure he will come?"

"I await only a letter by my courier-secretary Rodia, to confirm what I say."

"Tell me, how were you inspired to such a glorious plan?"

"I wanted to earn your supreme gratitude, and, so, my freedom. I had hoped—till *she* dispelled my dream——. But never mind: since he is lost to me, no danger can appall me. I thought for a brief hour that I might know the joys denied me and given to others; but no! like the fabled Jew, so must *my* pilgrimage last forever. No peace! no love! naught that woman counts her right. Well, so be it!"

She covered her face with her hands as she became silent, and the interview was interrupted by the entrance of a servant bearing two cards.

"Ah, baroness," said Schouloff, as he read the names of Mr. and Mrs. Richard Saville, "our expected guests are here. They will amuse you. Mr. Saville belongs to a very good family, and finished his eccentric career by marrying an eccentric young lady,—a Miss Middleton. They call them 'The Shocks;' and we are indeed fortunate that they arrive so opportunely to enliven us."

Then, turning to the servant, he said,—

"Inform Mr. and Mrs. Saville that Prince Schouloff and the Baroness Altdorff will wait upon them immediately in the hall."

## CHAPTER II.
### Dick Saville.

Dick Saville was an excellent specimen of the young Englishman whose personal qualities cause him to be universally dubbed "a devilish good fellow." Only son of General Saville, he had elected not to follow the profession of arms, but became Aubyn Goddard's chum at Oxford, where, with widely divergent tastes, they were as inseparable as circumstances would permit.

Goddard had been a reading man and an athlete, Saville had been an athlete, but there their similarity of pursuits had ended. Notwithstanding his multifarious escapades, indulged in with the object of emblazoning the gray old university town a lively heraldic *gules*, Dick Saville was an inveterate favorite with the dons, and even in that paradise for women Dick suffered a positive embarrassment of attentions from the petticoated inhabitants of his *alma mater*. Still, the process of compelling an objectionable proctor and his bull-dog to take a midnight bath in the college fountain and proceed home in each other's clothes turned inside out is not calculated to act as an example of discipline to undergraduates, and Dick Saville returned to the bosom of his father,—who, I regret to say, roared with delight,—to spare the authorities the heart-rending task of "sending him down" covered with ignominy and unpaid bills.

At the premature close of his academic career Dick started for the Cape *en route* for Seringapatam, and, having returned home via India and Egypt, met Kitty Middleton at a dance at Lady Arlingford's.

In five minutes Dick realized that he had met "that other self," and historians tell us that Kitty became kissed. This duty performed, he started for Madagascar *en route* for Persia and Russia, with two flannel shirts, a tooth-brush, and a photograph of Kitty. He escaped from a horde of Koords with nothing but a pair of tattered trousers and the photograph—also tattered— of Kitty, and when he told her of his escapes observed that she grew dreadfully white and didn't laugh at or abuse him for a whole quarter of an hour. Announcing his intention of starting for New York *en route* for Japan and China, Kitty put her foot down firmly, and asked what was the maximum of luggage that *she* would be allowed to take. Dick argued that she would have to camp in very rough places, to which Kitty replied that so long as he took a thick rug and plenty of quinine she didn't care. And so at the end of the season of 1877 the *Morning Post* announced that at St. Peter's, Eaton Square, Richard Arthur Chenevix Saville, son of General Sir Richard Saville, V.C., K.C.B., had married Catherine Maude, daughter of the late Sir Cyrus Middleton,

K.C.M.G. It was a "marriage," not a "wedding," and Mr. and Mrs. Saville started for Paris and Monte Carlo with one object alone in view,—to wit, the exoneration of Goddard.

So long as there was any hope of Goddard's return, Dick had agreed with Kitty and Lady Arlingford that they must wait for his assistance to this end; but now that he was dead, Dick announced his intention of taking the matter into his own hands and extorting a confession from Arlingford and Mrs. Dashton. Dick was no fool. The presence of Prince Schouloff on that fatal night, the delay of Goddard's all-important despatches, and the immediately subsequent clearance of Arlingford's most pressing liabilities had given him a clue, and when he found that nothing was to be done with Arlingford or the Dashton, he wrote for passes to Prince Schouloff, whom he personally knew, on the plea that he was anxious to pay a country-house visit in the middle of the seat of war.

Thus on this eventful afternoon Mr. and Mrs. Dick Saville found themselves in the hall of the Villa Kristov Hisar at Devekiui, near Eski Saghra, awaiting the appearance of their host and hostess.

They had not long to wait before Schouloff appeared with Bella-Demonia.

Schouloff greeted Saville and his wife warmly.

"Let me present you," said he, "to the Baroness Altdorff, Mrs. Saville,—Mr. Saville."

"I am charmed to see you," said the baroness. "We owe a great debt to Providence for having brought you safely to us. I have ordered some tea immediately. I learnt the custom in England and Russia, and never enjoy it so much as when I am far from civilization."

"It's contrast that gives the charm to everything," replied Kitty. "Dick and I pass our lives in search of it. It was to find a contrast to the deadly respectable that made us become so disreputable. You know, we are called 'The Shocks' because we keep people in a continual state of excitement. I tell them it's good for their health. They probably consider it heroic treatment; but it's quite necessary for some complaints."

"For instance?" queried Bella-Demonia, who was equally astonished and amused.

"Dullness and stupidity! There is no doubt we are good for our own people, but better still for the world. Nothing amuses Dick and me so much as to devise some awful escapade,—that is, what the world is pleased to consider awful. Time after time we say, '*This* is sure to settle us: we shall be ostracized,—kicked out.' Not a bit of good. Dick's too rich: people look upon it as a new and charming eccentricity, and that's all. But I must be boring you dreadfully. Somebody must stop me talking, or I shall go on forever."

"Don't stop!" exclaimed Bella-Demonia: "you are more than delicious. I will only interrupt you for a moment, to ask how and by what accident you are here."

"By no accident," said Dick Saville. "We came to find you, baroness, and Prince Schouloff."

"Indeed? You surprise me. What can we do for you?"

"Mrs. Saville has been telling you of some of our follies," answered Dick. "How long we should have continued to afford amusement to our friends is uncertain, because an event occurred which changed the current of my idiocy."

"Well, we won't contradict you," said Bella-Demonia, "it is so refreshing to hear you display your superior intelligence in your own way."

"Intelligence! I am trying to convince you, baroness, that I am a fool."

"I am afraid you are not succeeding very well. Still, I would not interfere with the amusement of any living creature: so I promise to assume anything you please, if you promise to continue your story."

"Oh, Dick doesn't need any inducement to talk," put in Kitty: "he runs *me* very close, and I've killed several people."

"The last time we met, Mrs. Saville," said Prince Schouloff, "I tried to make you promise to visit me at Nice. I did not expect that you would ever wander so far from the world as to make that visit here. But I am none the less indebted to you, believe me."

"You are too good, prince. It is to remind you of the time of which you speak that we have come to take you by storm."

"Since you have come so far to find us, I presume, like the Baroness Altdorff, that there is some service we may render you. For myself, pray command me; and I am sure that the baroness feels with me."

"Most assuredly," said Bella-Demonia.

"Well, then," said Dick Saville, "since I cannot convince you that I deserve to be called a fool for my pains, let me at least convince you that I can be a hard-working friend; and it is on behalf of that friendship that I have come in search of certain information and assistance. The prince has spoken of his last meeting with Mrs. Saville. On that occasion a tragedy was enacted which ruined the career of the best fellow that ever lived. I speak of Aubyn Goddard."

"Goddard!" The speaker was Bella-Demonia, who leaned forward, her eyes eagerly fixed on Dick's ugly but sympathetic face.

"Doubtless you, madame," said Kitty, "heard of the affair. I was present. It was terrible."

The Baroness Altdorff bowed her head in silence.

"It is to clear my dead friend's memory from a foul stigma," continued Saville, "that I have determined to prove his accusers guilty of the vilest conspiracy ever formed. Captain Goddard was accused of cheating at cards at the house of Lord Arlingford."

"But surely," put in Bella-Demonia, "it must have been easy for Captain Goddard to disprove the accusation?"

"There is the mystery. On investigation, there is no doubt that he had a card in his possession which he refused to show. This, in face of the fact that the king of trumps—they were playing écarté—was not to be found, gave color to the charge; though every one knew that Arlingford was quite capable of managing the cards well enough, even if he had been unaided by confederates: he had two on that occasion, a Major Carteret and his sister, Mrs. Bradley Dashton."

"Mrs. Dashton!" said Bella-Demonia. "She is in the house at this moment."

"Here! now?" answered Saville. "May I ask you to say nothing of my mission, and allow me to make my request of you before I meet her?"

"I will see that no one enters," said the prince, rising, and moving towards the door. As he passed Bella-Demonia he said, in an undertone, "I have given orders to Kapiodovitch to have an escort ready to receive our visitor of this evening."

"You make a grave charge against this Lord Arlingford," said she to Dick Saville.

"I am sure of my facts, however—morally sure. But proof to establish those facts is absolutely necessary. I believe that you, madame, and Prince Schouloff, can help me."

"I? but I never heard of Lord Arlingford."

"It is of Jack Vyvian Fane's career in St. Petersburg that I wish information."

"Vyvian Fane!"

It was more a gasp than an exclamation that broke from the Baroness Altdorff as she spoke the words. Prince Schouloff sat narrowly watching her, a shade of perplexity enveloping his brow.

"You remember him?" asked Saville.

"Remember him!" answered the baroness. "Perfectly. He was the cause of a terrible tragedy, and paid with his life for his treachery."

"You are mistaken, baroness. Vyvian Fane is alive, and is now Lord Arlingford. The title came to him, it is true, very unexpectedly."

"And *this* is the man who ruined Captain Goddard? In St. Petersburg he betrayed an innocent man to death,— a man be loved by all, a man who knew no wrong,—and struck down his wife and child with the self-same blow. Oh, you did well to come to me! I can give you all the information that you want. Listen!"

At this moment a servant entered.

"Your Excellency's secretary has returned," said he to Bella-Demonia.

"Admit him."

The giant form of Rodia Pouschkoff entered the room. Delivering a note to his mistress, he waited whilst she read it, and then, receiving a hurried command in a low tone, left the room once more. The Baroness Altdorff turned to Dick Saville.

"I must ask you to wait until tomorrow," she said, "for the details. A sudden call interrupts us." And she rang for a servant.

"Conduct Mr. and Mrs. Saville to their apartments.—*Au revoir*, Mrs. Saville, and I hope *à bientôt*."

Dick Saville and his wife left the room, accompanied by the servant. When they were gone, Bella-Demonia turned to the prince:

"Beyaz Murad is here, at the gates. Follow me." And she led the way to her own wing of the chateau.

# CHAPTER III.
## The Snare.

The boudoir-study of the Baroness Altdorff was a large room opening upon the terrace. When she entered it, accompanied by Prince Schouloff, it was illuminated by a couple of lamps, that served to intensify the gloom beyond the radius of their light.

"This omnipotent general is here," she said, turning to the prince as she closed the door. "I will admit him by this window. Once here, you will have the house surrounded by Kapiodovitch's men, and when I have learnt all I can of his plans I will give a signal. I have my revolver here: I will fire once."

As she spoke she threw open the shutters that guarded the windows, and the light of the rising moon poured into the room; then she came close to the prince, and said, looking him deeply in the eyes,—

"What will you give me for this man's capture?"

"Whatever you choose to ask. What shall it be?"

"*The life of one man, taken or given when and how I shall decide!*"

"Baroness!"

"Don't wonder; don't be surprised: only promise,—promise me by all that you hold holy."

"It shall be as you wish."

"Good! Now go!"

Prince Schouloff left the room, and she listened to his footsteps growing fainter down the corridor.

"At last," said she, as she loosened the fastenings of the window,—"at last I shall be avenged! He lives! How has he escaped all these years? But what does it matter? Ah! how I could have vindicated you, Aubyn Goddard, had *you* too lived! but I can show the world that your honor was stolen from you by a felon; *and I will!*"

She sank into a low chair before the fire, which blazed despite the season, her back turned to the window, her face hidden in her hands.

A slight noise as the window is pushed open from the outside, and a man steps into the room. He is dressed in the simple but striking costume of a Turkish staff-officer. His black military frock is buttoned to the chin, relieved only by the star of the Medjidieh which blazes on the left breast, and thrown into shadow by the folds of his voluminous military cloak. One arm, which is evidently wounded, rests in the breast of his coat, and his feet are cased in high boots which bear the traces of hard and rough riding.

The woman lowers her hands and turns slowly with a little smile upon her face. As their eyes meet, she starts violently and springs to her feet. A cry breaks from her:

"Aubyn Goddard! You! Living! Here, and called Beyaz Murad! What does it mean?"

On his part he is no whit less astounded. He advances towards her:

"The Baroness Altdorff! Is it real? My God! at last I see you again! Is this a dream?"

Quick as thought she has flown to the door and double-locked it, then to the window, which she hastily bars once more. At last she turns and comes to him.

"Would to God we never might waken!" she whispers, in a frightened moan.

As for him, the object of his coming, all, is forgotten in the ecstasy of seeing her again.

"If you only knew," he says, "how often I have prayed that I might live to see you once more! Through all the wild excitement of fighting, *that* hope has been my talisman. I have thought how foolish I was to obey you and not try to find you again in Vienna, till it was too late! When I made up my mind to tell you that I could no longer keep my promise, that I must try to win you back,—that, wild and impetuous as was the dream, its strength swept my reason from me,—ah! I felt that I must return and read once more in your sweet face a promise that——"

"For pity's sake——"

"I sought you too late: you had gone, and left no trace behind. It was a moment of bitter despair, for I thought you would have smiled pardon upon me, and I felt I should not have had to beg in vain. Was I wrong?"

"Oh, forgive me, Aubyn! Why did I not know? Let me speak now."

"Not yet! Let me tell you first, before I touch your lips, that I am ruined, disgraced,—that I have been robbed of name, fame, honor—no! hardly that. But *you* will believe that no fault of mine has exiled me."

"You will break my heart!"

"You have heard how, and why, I left England?"

"Yes,—but just now."

"Do you believe me guilty of the crime of which I was accused?"

"I *know* that you were not, and all the world would have known the same, if you had demanded an explanation."

"And that I could neither demand nor give."

"Oh, you were wrong! You must have been mad not to see how base a suspicion you allowed to take root. Why did you keep silent?"

She had come close to him and laid her hand upon his arm,—the wounded one. He became deathly white, and staggered at her touch.

"What is it?" she exclaimed. "You are ill."

"No, no; it is nothing. Give me some water. Ah! Nothing serious,—only a bit painful. I was wounded a few days ago, and as I was riding here my horse stumbled; I had only one hand, and he threw me. I—I think the wound has opened again. Don't be alarmed: it's all right. It does not pain me now."

He paused and caught his breath.

"It's stupid of me to get knocked over so easily," he continued, "but I've been ill some time, and I suppose that's why I got faint. You were asking me something?"

"Are you better?" she asked, anxiously.

"Yes,—yes. Listen! You asked me why I did not explain how I got that card. I could not. It meant the loss of honor for a woman or for me. The whole thing was a plot, but I could not have proved any conspiracy. This woman was cruelly wronged; I had known her from a child; she was helpless and alone:—can you wonder that I chose even disgrace to save her?"

"But she was wrong to let you do so. How could she keep silent and let you ruin yourself? It was cruel!"

"Don't blame her; she was not to blame, and it can do no good now. I only tell you this because I could not bear that a thought of suspicion should be between us. I had a card on which she had written a message,—innocent enough in itself, but which those who sought to entrap us both could have made to appear guilty. This is the secret of my crime. Do you believe me?"

"As I believe in God!"

"My darling!"

They were in each other's arms, the world forgetting in the glory of the moment that they knew each other's love.

"And you will tell me that there is nothing to prevent you resting here upon my heart forever. The war can't last much longer, and I shall be free. Then will you help me to forget the weary time before I knew you? Ah!"

The cry was wrung from him by his agony.

"Ah! you are badly hurt! you are hiding it from me!" she said.

"It is true," he gasped: "the wound is deep, and I am more hurt than I thought. It's only the loss of blood, however. Don't come near. It will frighten you."

At that moment a slight noise upon the terrace outside struck her ear, and recalled her to the present. It was the light clank of a rifle as it touched the gravel.

"My God!" she exclaimed, "there is danger here. You must try to keep strong,—to get away. Heaven forgive me! you are betrayed! Can't you walk? Try. Come here into my room: it is your only chance of safety."

Her words and tone recalled him too to his senses.

"Why are you here?" he said; "and where is the woman I came to see?—Bella-Demonia? I don't understand."

"Don't try to understand. I will tell you when you are safe. Come with me."

"What do you mean? I can't——"

A footstep in the corridor. Quick as thought the woman seized his wounded arm, and with the pain he fell senseless to the ground. Then she fired her revolver,—twice. A knock on the door! She drew his pistol from its holster and laid it on the floor, drawing his cloak over his face as she did so. With a crash the door fell open, and Prince Schouloff entered the room.

"For God's sake get help!" she exclaimed. "When he found he was betrayed he would have killed me. I shot him. He was going to escape. I tried to keep him: he was desperate—then I fired. *He is dead!*"

"I was wrong to let you risk such an interview," said the prince, looking at the prostrate form. "I will see myself that no one enters till he is taken away."

He was moving to the door. Then he turned and came back. "Perhaps he is only wounded," he said, laying his hand upon the senseless man's heart. He was just going once more, when he saw the revolver on the floor. He picked it up and pointed it at the still form.

"Better make quite sure!" he said.

He was about to fire, when Bella-Demonia flung herself upon the body.

"No! no!" she cried, "I have lied to you! I have betrayed you both!"

The cloak fell from Goddard's features. The prince looked at him.

"Captain Goddard!" he exclaimed.

"Yes, yes! It is Captain Goddard. Listen! For this man's capture you promised me the life of one man given or taken how and when I should decide. *I claim his!*"

# CHAPTER IV.
## Face to Face.

For the next few days the inhabitants of the Villa Kristov Hisar lived in a state of suppressed excitement. Prince Schouloff's first care was to send Mrs. Dashton off to Nice, armed with all that was needful to bring Lord Arlingford back to London, but ignorant of what had taken place at the villa. Of the amazement of Dick Saville and his wife it is unnecessary to speak. Kitty and the Baroness Altdorff relieved each other in the care of Goddard, who woke from his swoon in a high delirium.

The prince said but little, biding his time and waiting for Bella-Demonia to speak.

At last, one day when Goddard was fairly convalescent, she sent for him to her boudoir. She was sitting listlessly before the fire when he entered, and, looking up, gave him her hand, which he respectfully kissed.

"Be seated, prince," she said. "The time has come when some explanation is due to you. I wish to give it to you now."

"You are not overtaxing your strength, baroness?"

"No. I am as eager to question as I am willing to answer."

"I am all attention."

"Had you any suspicion that Beyaz Murad Bey and Aubyn Goddard were one and the same man?"

"Not the faintest."

"You believed him to be dead?"

"Implicitly."

"What has been the result of his detention here?"

374

"The result has been the beginning of the end. The Flying Legion, suddenly deprived of its leader, has lost its position as an independent army corps. Radetzky and Gourko have at last defeated Suleiman, and the Russian standard floats in the Shipka Pass. Suleiman is trying to regain his position, but in vain. Meanwhile, Skobeleff refuses to take warning from July, or advice from Todleben, and is preparing to attack Plevna once more, now that Osman's reinforcements have been stopped."

"It has been a great work," said the baroness, drearily.

"For which a great price has been paid, baroness."

"A great price?"

"The life of Captain Goddard given and taken when and how you decided," said Schouloff.

"Ah! it was fortunate for Lord Arlingford, his betrayer, that it was so! Had it not been Goddard's it would have been his."

"You have plunged me in a whirl of wonder, baroness. The afternoon that Mr. and Mrs. Saville arrived you expressed your ignorance of Viscount Arlingford. Five minutes later the sound of his name caused you the first strong emotion that I have ever known you to betray. It is with John Vyvian Fane that you are concerned,— John Vyvian Fane, now Viscount Arlingford. You have cause to hate him. Tell me about it: I can help you, and I will."

"You?"

"Even so. Lord Arlingford was at one time in the employ of the secret police in Petersburg——"

"I know!"

"He was expelled for making it the instrument of a private vengeance——"

"I know!"

"He implicated an innocent man in the socialist schemes of one Dorski——"

"I know!"

"You know! you know!" exclaimed Schouloff. "How do you know?"

"You ask me how I know. You ask me why I have sworn an oath of vengeance against this Lord Arlingford, once John

Vyvian Fane. Ask me rather the question you have spent time and money in vain to have answered: ask me rather who I am."

"My God! what do you mean?"

"*I am the Princess Carita Galitzin!*"

"Holy St. Katerine!"

Prince Schouloff rose and went successively to the doors leading into the corridor, and into Bella-Demonia's apartments, to make sure against eavesdroppers.

Then he returned to her side, and, bending till his eyes were plunged in hers, he took her wrist in his soft irresistible grasp and said, in a low, distinct voice,—

"*And I am Alexis Dorski!*"

❊

For some minutes a dead silence reigned in the room.

The Princess Galitzin, to call her by her real name, had sprung to her feet, pressing her hands to her throbbing temples, as she looked down at the man who, after intrusting her with the master-secret of his life, had resumed his seat calmly.

"The mystery of the cipher-dial is at last explained," said Schouloff at length.

"And his son,—Dmitri Dmitrievitch Keratieff,—does he know?"

"No one knows, save the Princess Galitzin, and Schouloff, the Chief of Police."

"Why have you told me?"

"You have a letter of mine."

"True: here it is." And, rapidly unfastening the bosom of her dress, she took therefrom a tightly-folded paper, which, opening, she laid before him.

"That is your handwriting?" she said.

"No; it *was* the handwriting of Alexis Dorski the Terrorist. It was missing from among the secret papers of Keratieff. It was to obtain it that, primarily, I obtained his position. I have sought it ever since. It was to obtain it that I made his son my confidential secretary. Had I known in whose hands it lay, I should have rested easy."

"It is at your service. Now!"

"Now?"

"Tell me: Vyvian Fane was reported assassinated on the Polish frontier."

"True; but it was his valet who was murdered and mutilated beyond recognition. His connection with the Third Section gave him means of learning the conspiracy against him. He boarded an English cruiser which lay off the Fortress of the Schlusselburg. Arrived in England, the unexpected reversion of the title and estates of Arlingford served more completely to conceal him: the name of Vyvian Fane was dropped. I alone of the Department have kept track of his lordship, and I have surrounded him with such a network that when the time comes to strike, he cannot escape me!"

"Cannot escape *you*?"

"Yes, me. Over the senseless form of your brother's wife I swore to avenge my friend Ladislas Galitzin. It was I who apprised you of her condition that fatal night. Since then I have made Arlingford my tool in many a plot, only the more surely to shatter him when I turn down my thumbs and cry, like the Romans in the arena, '*Habet!*"

"When shall you strike?"

"As soon as the war is over and Captain Goddard can return with us to London. I have sent Mrs. Dashton to take him thither supplied with the necessary funds to bring him within our grasp. I summoned her here to obtain information of Captain Goddard's death. I confess to you that I would have given ten years of my life to get it; for then I dreamed that perhaps you—well, well, that is over now. I will show you that I am grateful to 'Bella-Demonia.' I will show you that though I cannot be your lover I can still be your friend and ally, and my power is as much yours as it would be were you mine. No, not a word! I do not wear my heart upon my sleeve, but, princess, I love you more than I shall ever tell you. Now! it is over. There! we will change the subject."

The princess had risen as he spoke. When he became silent she moved to his side, and, sinking on her knees beside him, she took his hand in hers. A strong shudder passed across his frame, as the woman bent and pressed her lips to his hand and a hot tear fell upon it.

Then, as she raised her head and looked at him, he bent his reverently, and for the first and last time kissed the marble-cold brow that was upturned to him.

# BOOK IV.

## CHAPTER I.
### Sowing the Wind.

When our story reopens in the month of April, 1878, great changes—almost cataclysms—have occurred in Europe. The Treaty of San Stefano has been signed, and the Powers, walking to the enormity of its conditions, are preparing for the Congress of Berlin. What might have been the end of the Turko-Russian war of 1877-78 had the Flying Legion succeeded in reaching Osman Pasha, it is impossible to surmise. The dispersal of that mysterious organization seemed to mark the turning-point of the war. Osman's last supplies reached him from Sofia in November, and on the 9th of December, driven to despair, he made his heroic and historic sortie, which would have undoubtedly been successful had not treachery from within the bastions of Plevna apprised Todleben of his intention, and enabled the Russian general, at the cost of the Siberian regiment, to force the surrender, with all the honors of war, of the greatest soldier that Turkey had known since the days of Mahmoud the Reformer. New Year's day, 1878, saw Gourko across the Etropol Balkans, and on Twelfth-Night he supped in Sofia. At the end of the month Adrianople was reached, and a British fleet entered the Bosphorus under a protest which England's Greatest Statesman utterly disregarded.

In this way was Constantinople saved the ignominy of becoming a Russian watering-place.

Meanwhile, the actors in our drama had reassembled in London, where the last act was to be played out. Goddard had recovered from the effects of his wound only after months of patient nursing on the part of his soul's idol. Lord Arlingford had returned to town, and Prince Schouloff, present ostensibly on diplomatic service, was shifting the strings of the web he had drawn around his victim, from finger to finger, as the development of events required.

Our story reopens in the little drawing-room of Mrs. Bradley Dashton's cosey *maisonnette* in Mayfair. Two men are present, one pacing irritably up and down, the other comfortably ensconced in an arm-chair.

The first is Viscount Arlingford, the second is that promising soldier of the array of financial martyrs, Major Homer Carteret. Lord Arlingford comes suddenly to a full stop.

"Why the deuce," says he, "did you let Emily come back to England, least of all at this most critical juncture? You know how impetuous she is, and among the ways out of our present difficulties you know very well that there is no choice."

"And you know very well, my dear Arlingford, that I can't control her any more than you can. She appeared to come to the decision in an instant, and declined to allow me to argue the point. I've always warned you that she would be dangerous if the spirit so moved her, and yet you allowed the Briggs affair to get into print. Indeed, it was sheer folly of you to make the running in that direction at all."

"You put the case charmingly, my dear Carteret, only you seem to forget that at the time I went for the little Briggs there was no other course open,—indeed, that it is only within the last twenty-four hours that circumstances have permitted me to drop her out at all. Another trifle that you overlook is that neither you nor I could have foreseen the extraordinary turn affairs have taken. I shall be able now to pay all my debts and start for Algiers as soon as possible."

"That is, supposing Emily to be tractable."

"You leave me to manage her: she's not likely to give me much trouble. What a time she is! I shall be late. I promised to go and look at a horse: they tell me he's a clipper, and up to my weight,—can jump anything. Look here! I wish you'd go down to Rice's and tell him I can't come till tomorrow, but that if his horse is all he says he is, I'll take him."

"But I thought you said you were going to Algiers?" remarked Major Carteret, with an interrogative inflection.

"Yes, so I am. But I fancy I can win a bit steeple-chasing before I go. Featherstone, who's ordered out to India, has offered me a couple of horses that have been running wonderfully well at some of the small meetings. He only wants three hundred and fifty pounds for 'em,—dirt-cheap. The three will do me very well; and when I go I'll give you the lot, if you like, and you can hunt this year."

"Thanks, old man," replied Carteret, rising. "I'll go and inspect my future property; but, egad! I'm afraid my creditors will do most of the hunting."

"Oh! all right. Say they're still mine. Good-bye. Be in time tonight."

"Yes. Good-bye."

And his lordship was left alone. Not for long, however, for a moment later Mrs. Dashton entered the room.

"Aren't you glad to see me, Jack?" she said, advancing with both hands outstretched. "I've so much to forgive you that—I daren't begin. Suppose I absolve you blind, without going into the details. Tell me, weren't you surprised to know that I was here?"

"Yes,—deucedly surprised. And I wish you hadn't come."

"How horrid of you to say that! and it's such a long time since I've seen you, too, you bad boy!"

She had come up behind him and put her hands on his shoulders as he sat. He disengaged himself a trifle impatiently.

"My dear girl," he said, "I wish you wouldn't do this. You know it bores me. You shouldn't have come over: you'll upset all my plans. Why didn't you stop in Paris?"

"Because I am fool enough to care for you, and weak enough to believe you cared a little for me. But don't place too much reliance on my folly. I tell you, Jack, that the day I make up my mind that you mean to throw me over, it will be a bad day for you!" She had come close to him, and her tone changed from one of intense earnestness to one of ugly cynicism. "I'm afraid you'll make me lose my temper. Don't! I'm not nice when I'm angry."

"Now, look here, Emily: this tragic tone is out of place. You know it's no use acting with me."

"When I do *act* with you, it will be forcibly enough to claim your attention; but before that happens, I want you to explain one or two things. I came here expecting that you would be glad to see me. I didn't believe the stories I heard about an American girl; and now I want to know from you how much truth there was in them. That you would be unscrupulous enough to deceive me I don't doubt, but that you would be fool enough to arouse my enmity I doubt very much. But, bah! I didn't come to England to threaten. Are you going to marry the girl?"

"No!"

Mrs. Dashton heaved a sigh of relief.

"Ah! I was sure of you," she said. "Why do you try to make me jealous? You shouldn't do it, Jack,—you shouldn't do it. Well, the trouble of the journey is well repaid, now that the suspense is over. Of course I *knew* it wasn't true; yet I couldn't rest until I was sure."

"Now, look here, Emily," exclaimed Arlingford, rising to his feet: "let us put an end to this. I'm going back to my wife."

"What! You're not in earnest?"

"I am,—perfectly."

"Very well! so am I. *You shan't do it!*"

"Don't talk nonsense, but listen to me. An aunt of my wife's has left her her fortune and advised her to make friends with me. You don't suppose I am going to chuck away such an opportunity,—especially as everything is as bad as it can be at home? My agent can't get me a penny. Now make up your mind to accept the situation. I'll go to Paris as soon as I can; meanwhile, I'll see you get all the money you want——"

"Do you suppose," broke in the woman indignantly, "that I am the kind of woman to be ordered about?—to be a pensioner on *your* wife's bounty? Undeceive yourself! It's your turn to listen to *me*. I would have endured any privation for you and with you—for love. That is over: you make it a business transaction. Very well: you must accept *my* terms. I have disgraced myself long enough for you. You will marry *me*."

"Don't be a fool," was the brutal response. "One must draw the line somewhere, and I couldn't fly in the face of the world as far as that. I have a few friends I must consider, and——"

"So! I am not good enough for you,—you, who cannot enter a decent house in England,—you, the sharper,—the thief! Do you forget I know how you ruined Goddard?"

"I don't care a damn what you know. I was willing to take care of you; you refuse help. *Soit!* A woman who lets a married man make love to her always gets the worst of it in the long run. I am going to become respectable, and in five years no one will remember that I was ever anything else. You might have known, as I didn't ask you to come, that I didn't want you——"

He was cut short by the entrance of a servant with a note. Mrs. Dashton tore it open and glanced through it, visibly excited. Hastily writing a few words at her *escritoire*, she handed the answer to the servant, who left the room. Mrs. Dashton appeared to have recovered all her composure.

"I thought we knew each other pretty well," she said, "but it appears that we are both destined to make discoveries. Your new fad for respectability is a little startling. My determination may be equally astonishing. I simply decline to take the place you assign to me."

"My dear Emily, the great charm about you *was*, that you were so thoroughly sensible. You are not like yourself today. I've told you what I mean to do."

"In other words, you defy me. Now I'll tell you what I mean to do. I can't make you marry me, but you certainly shan't marry anybody else. I have helped you in your dirty work, I have done things for your sake that no money in the world would have induced me to do, and if you suppose that you can calmly say, 'Good-bye, I've no further use for you,' and expect that that is the end, you are vastly mistaken. So your idea of a sensible woman—such as you are good enough to call me—is one who is always ready to subscribe to your pleasure or income as necessity demands? So long as her sense is used for your benefit, she is charming, but you are always surprised when she exerts it in her own behalf. I *will* be sensible, and mind you don't regret it. So I am to wander away an outcast,—*déclassée*,—whilst you become a respectable member of society? Charming!"

As she spoke, Lord Arlingford had risen, and, taking his hat and cane, had moved to the door. Seeing him on the point of departure, she ran to him and flung her arms about him.

"Oh, Jack, Jack," she cried, "don't go like that! I was only desperate. Say you did not mean what you said. You don't really mean to throw me over, after all your promises?"

"I've said all I have to say," answered the man, roughly. "Let me go. You know 'scenes' bore me. Let me go, I say!"

He flung her from him, and went out. Her foot catching on some piece of furniture, she fell heavily to the ground. For a moment she lay as if dazed; then a great sob escaped her, and with difficulty she rose and staggered to her writing-table. Her eyes fell upon the note that lay where she had left it.

"Ah, Jack," she said, aloud, "if you had known who was waiting an answer to this letter, you would have been more—more discreet."

She touched a bell, and the next moment Captain Aubyn Goddard entered the room.

"I am glad you are here," she said, recovering herself as she went to meet him. "You have been very kind to me,—much kinder than I deserve, for until this moment I had no intention of repaying you."

"Poor old lady!" answered Goddard, soothingly. "Why, how upset you are! What has happened? Can I do anything to help you?"

"Always the same kindly sympathy, Aubyn. How good you are! I see by this note you came over to get a confession from Jack Arlingford. You want my help. You value this vindication very much, do you not?"

"Of course I do. Until his confession is obtained, there may be those who doubt me; and, more than the opinion of all, there is one whose faith in me must be justified. There is to be a meeting tonight at Briggs's to endeavor to bring it about, and you can help it, I know. You've known me for years, old girl, and you know I was innocent, don't you?"

"More! I will prove it. But you must go now, for I expect a visitor. Give me the address of your friend where the explanation is to take place, and you shall have proof,—all the proof you want. And don't judge me too harshly for my share in the matter: I have had but one excuse,—I did it for him. And just now he struck me down!—Oh!"

"He struck you!"

"Yes."

"My God! What a brute!"

"Never mind now: you must go. I—I am engaged. But we shall meet tonight."

Goddard left her. When she was alone, she moved once more to her desk, and, opening a locked drawer, took from it an envelope, at which she gazed for a few moments motionless.

Then hurriedly she tore it open and took from it a playing-card.

It was the king of clubs.

## CHAPTER II.
### The Vengeance of Three Women.

As she stood looking at it, the servant entered, bearing a card on a salver. She took it up with an air of lazy indifference which quickly changed to one of strong emotion.

"Lady Arlingford!" she exclaimed; then, turning to the servant, she added, "You did not say that I was in?"

"No, ma'am," answered the domestic. "I said that I would see."

"Say, not at home." Then, as the servant was leaving the room, she added, "Stay!"

She stood, twirling the piece of pasteboard in her fingers.

"What can she want of me,—that woman,—here in my house?" Then, apparently making up her mind, she hastily concealed the playing-card in the bosom of her dress, and said, "Show her in."

Lady Arlingford entered the room, and the two women bowed without speaking.

"You are surprised to see me," said Lady Arlingford, recovering herself the first. "I owe you, perhaps, an apology for intruding upon you, but I felt that I must come. I—I have a favor to ask."

The concluding words were spoken with an obvious effort, and Mrs. Dashton, with an inclination of her head, signified that she was listening.

"You have heard that there is to be a meeting tonight for the exoneration of Captain Goddard?" said her ladyship.

"Yes."

"You will be there?"

"Yes."

"I—I—you have heard that I desire to re-marry Lord Arlingford?"

"I have heard it."

"Mrs. Dashton, it is better to speak plainly. I know that Lord Arlingford's position in the matter will depend greatly on what you will say. I know what your feelings under the circumstances must be. I hope—I believe—that he will make every possible reparation. I have come to beg that you will hold your hand so far as you can."

"What do you wish me to do?"

"Am I right in supposing that your evidence can ruin his lordship?—I mean, in the matter of the card?"

For all answer Mrs. Bradley Dashton slowly drew the king of clubs from its resting-place and laid it on the table.

As Lady Arlingford's eyes fell upon it, she exclaimed,—

"It is as I feared. I have come to beg that you will not confront him with that card. It will be my care that Captain Goddard shall produce the card which he actually held,—the one on which I wrote. Will you not be merciful?—will you not shield my husband so far as not to add this horrible evidence to mine?"

"Lady Arlingford," returned Mrs. Dashton, "you have been frank with me; I will be equally so with you. An hour ago I would have guarded this card with my life; but within this hour things have altered."

"But surely——"

"No! let me think."

Her reflections were interrupted by the re-entrance of the servant.

"The Baroness Altdorff is below," said he to his mistress, in a low tone.

"Ask her to come here," said Mrs. Dashton; then, turning to the suppliant woman before her, she said,—

"A lady is below, who calls by appointment. On what she will say my decision must in a great measure depend. If you will step into this next room, I will tell you what that decision is when she has left me."

"You say that she can influence you: will you not let me try to influence her? A woman should be merciful to one of her sex."

"Perhaps. At present I cannot tell. Step in here, however, and in ten minutes you shall know."

There was no time for parley, and the Countess of Arlingford stepped into the adjoining boudoir. Mrs. Bradley Dashton stood looking at the card that lay upon the table.

"Ah," said she, as if apostrophizing the pasteboard, "I wonder into whose hands you will eventually fall? Those two men and that woman who have just left this room would give a good deal for you, and Bella-Demonia wants you more than either of them. Ah, baroness, you want my assistance in unmasking Lord Arlingford! You little know how much I can serve you, and how willingly I will do so."

The next moment Bella-Demonia was announced.

"You are punctual, baroness," said Mrs. Dashton, coming forward. "That is good, for it seems we have much to do. You will believe, I am sure, that I appreciate the confidence you have reposed in me, and I will justify it."

"You have already justified it by guarding the secret of Captain Goddard's identity with the Turkish general who reached the Villa Kristov Hisar just before you left us."

"But I never knew it until after Lord Arlingford had left me in Paris and returned to London."

"It was as well, we thought, that you should get some suspicion of what kind of man this Arlingford really is, before you knew so important a secret. You know, we women, when we love——"

"Yes, yes; I know all that you would say. Your letter of yesterday tells me I can help you further."

"Yes; and I trust we may count upon you?"

"I know what you want, and—yes, you may count upon me. I will meet you tonight at Mr. Briggs's in Hereford Street at nine o'clock, and, believe me, Goddard will have no more valuable ally there than Emily Dashton."

"I supposed," said Bella-Demonia, "that I should have had a hard fight to gain your aid. I will not ask why you are so unexpectedly won over, but I want you to know that my gratitude shall be no empty form of words. I will endeavor to prove to you how I value your sacrifice. May I speak frankly?"

Mrs. Dashton had seated herself in the low arm-chair, and bowed her head silently. The other woman continued:

"Captain Goddard's vindication must be in a great measure due to you and what you will say. I know that the words which will give joy to us will bring pain and grief to you. Mrs. Dashton, I can't be a humbug, and it is not for me to preach to you. The part you have played in the drama which is to end tonight will cost you many a pang. You are a woman, alone in your struggle with life. I should like you to feel that you can always count on one woman who will sympathize with, will assist, and, if necessary, protect you, and that that woman is she whom you have known as Bella-Demonia."

Mrs. Dashton had not raised her eyes.

"Don't give me too much credit for speaking the truth tonight."

"I can see that you are much upset. Let me beg you to take a little rest now. I will send my carriage for you at nine o'clock."

"Thank you. I will be ready."

388

"I suppose I am right in thinking that you still possess the card that Lord Arlingford gave you to conceal,—to destroy?"

Mrs. Dashton pointed to the table.

"There it is!" she said.

"Ah! you will give it me?" said Bella-Demonia, eagerly.

Mrs. Dashton smiled.

"In that room a woman awaits your departure to renew a request she has made to me. She also desires this card, that she may destroy it."

"A woman?—who?"

"The Countess of Arlingford."

"No? I am most anxious to meet Lady Arlingford in this way, informally," said she, eagerly. "You would oblige me very much by asking her to come in here, and by presenting us to each other."

"I should like to do as you wish, but I am afraid to trust myself in such a meeting."

"If you will do as I ask and make some excuse to leave us together for a short time, I promise you that you shall be spared the embarrassment of ever meeting her again."

"You are mysterious as usual, baroness, but I know if you promise, that you can perform, and I will do as you wish. Is there anything in particular that you wish me to say?"

"No; only, as soon as you can, make some excuse and leave us."

"Certainly. And by what name do you wish me to present you?"

"By my own."

"The Baroness Altdorff?"

"No; the Princess Galitzin."

"What!"

"That is my real name, which you and Prince Schouloff alone have heard."

There was no time to express her surprise, as Mrs. Dashton opened the door of the boudoir and the Countess of Arlingford entered the room.

"Lady Arlingford," said Mrs, Dashton, "let me present you to a friend. The Princess Galitzin—Lady Arlingford."

The two women bowed to each other.

"I must be going immediately," said Bella-Demonia. "I think my carriage must be back."

"If you will excuse me, I will go and see," said Mrs. Dashton. "I have some orders to give."

And she left them together.

"I think, Lady Arlingford," began the Princess Galitzin, "that we have a mutual friend in Captain Goddard. I may tell you that I shall be present at the meeting which is to take place tonight. It will be painful to you, but at least it will have the advantage of proving the innocence of our friend."

"You know him? Oh, I am so glad!" replied Lady Arlingford. "I think he is the embodiment of all that is honest and true in man. I had, alas! the misfortune of doing him the greatest wrong that was ever done——"

"I am sure you exaggerate your share," put in the princess, gently.

"Of course I was innocent of the intention, but the result is the same. It seems so hard that after bearing my burden for so long I should have broken down at that moment, as you know. Just as I was about to tell how I had given him the card, I became insensible. I never shall forget the horror of that moment. I could have exonerated Aubyn with a word, and that word I could not speak. I tried—I fought, it seemed to me, for hours, till the blank of insensibility came over me. Oh, it was cruel!"

"Are you not afraid of overtaxing your strength, Lady Arlingford? Would it not be wiser to avoid such an explanation as must take place tonight? Your friends might represent you, and save you much pain."

"No, I must be present, for a reason so strong that nothing can overcome it. It is not alone to vindicate my old friend that I go. I go to intercede for one who will find no defenders,—one who I feel is so alone that his need has won my sympathy,—my husband!"

"You can plead for him? But he is no longer your husband: you are divorced."

"He is my child's father: what divorce of law can alter that? You will think that I am very weak, but I have my own opinions. There is nothing of the Bohemian in my disposition."

"Bohemian! May I ask what you call 'Bohemian'? You do not answer. Let me define it for you. It is something distinct from 'a lady.' A lady means one who is well born, tenderly nurtured, carefully educated; always placed—that is, presumably placed—beyond the knowledge of evil, she is sheltered from contact with the sufferings and sorrows of her less fortunate sisters. The woman who enjoys these advantages is called a lady,—a title which signifies, not the individual, but the manner of her training. A Bohemian, as you intend it, means one who is outside the pale of respectability, an object of suspicion, one whom you only consent to meet when she can be of service to you. Yet I have known many 'ladies' the names of whose lovers are better known than the inner life of the reigning Bohemian. You would be surprised to know that Bohemians look down on certain sections of 'society' in amazement and pity."

"You have evidently made your experiences in unfortunate examples," replied Lady Arlingford. "Do you not believe that there are ladies who are good women?"

"God forbid that I should not! There is a sweet old-world title that brings to my mind all that is noble and good in womanhood,—a title that lives in my heart, shrouded in reverence,—a title that fits the beings who have rendered the name of mother sacred. That title is 'gentlewoman.' *That* title I believe in, and it is found in Bohemia as well as in society."

"These are strange expressions for the Princess Galitzin, who can know but little of these people except by force of imagination."

"You are mistaken. *My* flag bears the red and white of Bohemia, and has seen good service, believe me. Perhaps you will understand me better if I tell you that *I am called Bella-Demonia.*"

"Bella-Demonia!" Lady Arlingford had risen to her feet.

"You appear shocked," said the Princess Galitzin.

"I am a little startled, I confess. I was not prepared to meet so—so—public—a character."

"And you would not have cared to meet me, if you had known who I was. Would you?"

"I will admit—as I do not share your opinions—that I should have refused to meet the bearer of the name 'Bella-Demonia:' a meeting would not be pleasant for either of us. Still, I feel bound to say that you are quite different from what I should have expected."

"Thank you for your generous admission: you are good enough to imply that there is nothing in my appearance or manner to deprive me of the inestimable boon of at least *looking* presentable. You are a good woman and capable of noble impulses, but charity for your fellow-women seems to be no part of your creed. Is it ignorance or intolerance that makes you condemn without even one expression of regret a woman of whom you know nothing?"

"Nothing? I have heard——"

"Heard? I said *know*."

"Pardon me for reminding you that you have only yourself to blame for the impression formed of you. If a woman has no husband, and yet——"

"If respectability is based upon the possession of a husband, then I am worthy of your highest esteem. Lady Arlingford, I am about to tell you a story which may—I hope will—interest you."

Her ladyship bent her head, and the princess continued.

"My mother died when I was very young. I lived with my father at our chateau in the province of Ladoga, alone save for the companionship of a young girl, the daughter of a serf mother. She was my companion and friend rather than my attendant, and we were romantic and impressionable, both of us. One day we had wandered far from the chateau, among the woods. We were about to return home, when a crashing in the bushes announced the presence of some large animal. An instant later one

392

of our mountain bears bounded into the clearing. We clung to each other almost senseless with terror, when suddenly we heard the report of a rifle close to us, and the beast fell dead. A moment after, a man sprang through the bushes, congratulating us on our escape, and apologizing for his sudden apparition and the alarm he had caused us. He escorted us home, and was welcomed by my father, the more warmly when it transpired that he was of good family. He was an Englishman, on a hunting-tour, he said. He was staying close by, and became a constant visitor at the house. The sequel is—*banale*. I fancied myself in love. My brother, to whom the stranger was personally antipathetic, had contracted a secret marriage with my late companion, and they had gone to Petersburg, where my brother was commissioned in our Regiment of the Transfiguration. Left alone, we were not long in following my brother's example: we were married secretly, on account of my father, whose pride of race was worthy of a Galitzin, and in the winter the family moved to Petersburg. There my brother's suspicions were aroused, and, determined to drive this Englishman from Petersburg, he sought an opportunity of quarrelling with him. One night there was a terrible scandal at the Club. My brother accused my husband of cheating, and a meeting was arranged. Late that night he caused my brother's arrest. Oh, in my unhappy country it is not difficult to rob a man of liberty and even life on the merest suspicion! I will spare you my tears, my distraction, and give you the facts briefly. I learnt that my brother had been denounced by my husband. He was doomed. I never saw him again: *he died*. When it is inconvenient to substantiate a charge against a political prisoner in Russia, he has a convenient way of dying. From that moment I had but one thought, but one passion,—revenge! My husband was expelled from the country, and on the frontier his carriage was wrecked by bandits, and himself—as I thought—assassinated. I sought oblivion of my wrongs and plunged into the sea of politics. I became Prince Schouloff's most able lieutenant. In a word, I became 'Bella-Demonia.' My desperation made me famous; but, though employed by the government, my sympathies were always with the oppressed, and many a life have I saved when it has been to all intents and purposes doomed. But why continue? Even such feverish excitement as mine becomes wearisome, and just when I was most weary I met Captain Goddard. For the first time I felt glad that I had been spared the commission of a crime, that my hands were innocent of my husband's blood."

As she finished speaking, Lady Arlingford rose.

"You have forced me to listen to a discourse," said she, coldly, "that cannot possibly concern me and can only be painful to yourself."

"You will change your opinion," answered the Princess Galitzin. "I told you this story to illustrate the point of our discussion. I tell you it is well for you that all people do not gauge a woman's virtue by the possession of a husband; for *you* have never had one, and are unfortunate enough to be the mother of a child not born in wedlock."

"I! How dare you——"

"How dare I? Why, the man who murdered my brother and with him his wife and unborn child, the man whom I hounded hungry for his life, is alive! Because the man you think to be your husband *is mine!*"

"My God! it is not true!—it cannot be true!"

"I tell you that the man who robbed me of name and dignity, of my very birthright of gentlewoman, who made of me a character for such women as you to sneer at, is alive. He *was* John Vyvian Fane; he *is* Viscount Arlingford."

"Ah, you are only saying this because I offended you. I did not mean to be so cruel. See, I kneel to you to ask you for the truth. Will you swear to me that what you have said is true or untrue?"

"It is true, so help me God! And I will prove it."

When Mrs. Dashton entered the room, Lady Arlingford lay senseless at the feet of the princess.

# CHAPTER III.
## Weaving the Web.

When, half an hour later, the Princess Galitzin entered her rooms at her hotel, she found Prince Schouloff seated, patiently awaiting her arrival.

"I came to tell you," said he, rising to meet her as she entered, "that there are new complications, of which you are ignorant, and which it would be well for you to know."

"Well?"

"Lord Arlingford's position with regard to his wife is considerably altered since yesterday."

"I think not."

Schouloff looked at her critically for a moment, and then resumed: "I learn that her ladyship is willing to forget and forgive everything, and proposes to be re-married to him."

"You are wrong in your facts, prince," answered she, with a hardly perceptible smile. "Lady Arlingford is *not* willing to forget or to forgive, and she has no intention of re-marrying him, for she has never been divorced."

For a brief moment it flashed across the prince that the woman's mind was wandering; but, if so, her placid smile belied the fact. He contented himself with answering simply,—

"I do not understand you: you speak in riddles."

"Of which you would like to have the solution."

"Where is that solution to be obtained?" queried the prince, patiently.

"Why, of Lady Arlingford, of course."

"I should like to see her," said Schouloff, reflectively. "Do you think she can receive me at this time?"

"I am sure she will be charmed, prince."

"And where is she now?—can you tell me?"

"Here."

"Here! Where?"

"In this room,—before you."

"In heaven's name, what do you mean?"

"I am she."

The words were said simply as the princess dropped into a chair.

For a minute not a word was said. Then the prince sprang to his feet and exclaimed,—

"I see it all! You married this man in Russia, did you not?"

"Yes."

"It was thus that he had access to your apartments and stole— my letter?"

"Exactly."

"Does anyone else know of this? Of course not."

"Yes. I have seen the woman he pretended to marry this afternoon, and I told her. It was time."

"How did she take it?"

"As you might suppose."

"Well, what are you going to do about it?"

"It is the last weapon I hold in reserve to compel Arlingford to confess his share in the plot that ruined Goddard. Until that confession is obtained, I hold my rights over his head. Once Goddard is free, the annulment of our marriage is an easy task; the time that has elapsed, the circumstances,—everything will assist; and *you* would require no assistance."

The prince had been standing staring into the fireplace. Now he turned, and, looking her full in the eyes, he said, calmly,—

"And then?"

She blushed violently, and answered not a word.

"Never mind," continued the prince. "I have shown you that I have your happiness, rather than mine, at heart: I will prove it yet further to you. We shall meet at Mr. Briggs's at half-past nine. In spite of the snares we have tangled around the feet of Arlingford, he may yet brazen his way out, at least temporarily. I will come prepared with the last and most coercive resource, which we have in the Russian police."

"You will dare?—here in England?"

"You forget that John Vyvian Fane was a duly-enrolled member of the Third Section?"

"Forget it!"

"Well, though no formal extradition treaty exists, the arm of His Majesty the Tzar is long enough to reach his servants, wherever they may be. Leave it to me."

"Willingly. Till tonight, then?"

"*Au revoir.*"

# CHAPTER IV.
### An American Citizen.

It was shortly after eight o'clock, and Mr. Cincinnatus Q. Briggs sat at his table in the library of his house in Hereford Street, busily engaged in writing.

From the point of view of the ordinary English novelist, whose knowledge of the American gentleman is bounded on the East by his steamer acquaintance with the travelling salesman and on the West by the charming stories of Bret Harte, added to the occasional "gun" stories of more or less inventive bar-room loafers, whose daily bread—or, more accurately speaking, whose daily whiskey—is obtained by their ability to amuse the crowd, Mr. Cincinnatus Q. Briggs was a most disappointing American. His rooms were furnished with the tasteful simplicity of a scholarly traveller's den. The carpets were unsullied by promiscuous expectoration, the walls were decorated with a few proof etchings and here and there a masterpiece in aquarelle; there were no caricatures of colored deacons, nor were there portraits of fast trotters and the whiskers of Mr. Vanderbilt to be seen. With the exception of a small revolver which lay in one of the pigeon-holes of the desk, there was not a "gun" of any kind to be found, the arms and legs of the furniture had not been whittled into fanciful designs under the bowie of their owner, and the paraphernalia of cocktail-manufacture were conspicuous by their absence.

Mr. Briggs laid down his pen, and, leaning back in his chair,—which, by the bye, he did not tilt upon its hinder legs,—took up the letter which he had just completed.

"I think that this will do," said he to himself, as he read over his composition:

My Dear Mr. Saville,—

I regret to say that Lord Arlingford refuses to avail himself of the opportunity of flight. He has evidently some strong weapon in reserve. He means to fight; and, unless yours are stronger, I fear my stupid cousin will succeed in ruining her life. He is a clever scoundrel, and has adopted the surest means of making her his defender, by affecting to confide in her all that is detrimental to him, and so cutting the ground from under every one else's feet. I send you this as arranged, that you may bring all your batteries to bear at once. I expect Lord Arlingford at any moment.

Faithfully yours,
Cincinnatus Q. Briggs.

He put this letter into an envelope, and, addressing it to Dick Saville at Claridge's, touched a bell.

"See that this goes at once," said he to the servant who appeared at the sound of the bell and took the letter. This done, the American turned once more to his papers.

"Let me see," soliloquized he: "where is that girl's letter? Ah! here it is. My dear cousin,—*You are very kind, but I am quite old enough to take care of myself.*—Yes, quite old enough, but, unfortunately, neither ugly nor poor enough.—*If I had wanted you to take care of me, I should have married you years ago.*—How devilish cruel a woman can be when she thinks fit!—*I don't like to say hard things of a woman, but I am sorry to say I cannot sympathize with the lady who was Lord Arlingford' s wife,*—you surprise me, my dear cousin!—*and I must take his word before hers,*—naturally, poor little girl! Um—m. That young woman means business: we Briggs's generally do. It's lucky for her I came to Europe when I did; otherwise she'd have flung herself away on this fellow to a certainty. But I think, my lord Arlingford, that you have reached the end of your rope, and I'll lay odds that

398

it isn't from any scruple of your own that it doesn't hang you. Well, I came to Europe for excitement, and, egad! I'm likely to get a genteel sufficiency of it tonight. Thanks to you, my lord, I witnessed the beginning, and am about to witness the end, of one of the liveliest sensations that London has known for a good many years."

At this point Mr. Briggs's soliloquy was interrupted by the entrance of a servant announcing Dick Saville.

"Mr. Saville!" exclaimed Briggs, "delighted to see you. You're early; but you can't have got my letter yet?"

"Letter?" replied Dick: "what letter? No. I only dropped in on my way to fetch my wife, to ask how things were going on. I dined at the Club to try and find out if anything fresh had happened. I've brought the papers for Arlingford to sign: here they are in duplicate."

Mr. Briggs took them and glanced over one.

"I think Captain Goddard must be a remarkably forgiving man, to consider such a reparation sufficient," observed he. "On my side of the water a man in his position would, I fear, fill a man in Arlingford's with leaden bullets, and the jury would differ singularly on the verdict to be returned."

"I said something of the sort to him," returned Saville. "But he pointed out to me that there was nothing to be gained, but rather the reverse, from greater publicity. All he insists upon is that Arlingford should sign this Statutory Declaration and leave the country at once."

"Do you think that he will do it?"

"I think he will; but one can never be sure of such a blackguard. I shouldn't be very much surprised if at the last moment he didn't turn up."

"He told me he would be here at nine o'clock, but I confess I shouldn't be astonished if he weakened at the last moment. I must say, he has reduced the art of bluff to an applied science. When I advised him to give up my cousin, telling him we had the means to compel him to do so, his defiance was superb. I hope for all our sakes that the Baroness Altdorff possesses the power she promises to use with such effect. I tell you, dealing with him is no child's play! No, *sir!*"

"Well, I congratulate you on being quit of him as far as your cousin is concerned."

"How? quit of him?"

"Yes," replied Saville: "owing to very singular circumstances, he will make no further attempt to marry her."

"Is that really so? And these circumstances are——?"

"Eight thousand a year! Did you ever remark, Mr. Briggs, that the greatest scoundrels always get the best kind of love, and that a certain kind of good woman will cling to the man she has chosen—in the face of every reason why she should *not*—with a strength that she would display in no other cause? Well, such a woman is Lady Arlingford. She insists on going back to him."

"No!"

"It is so nevertheless. She has come into eight thousand a year, and proposes to invest it in Arlingford and connubial respect-ability. This relieves you of all personal anxiety. Lady Arlingford is ready to leave England with him. It only remains for us to see that he signs this document."

"And when will the Baroness—Bella-Demonia—arrive?"

"In good time. She is a capricious mystery, that woman, but her power is enormous. She demands that we unquestioningly submit to her instructions tonight. She refuses to tell us what power she holds over Arlingford, and exacts a meeting with Lady Arlingford before her identity is made known. Altogether, the evening promises to be eventful. By Jove! it's time I ran round for my wife. *Au revoir!* I'll be back inside a quarter of an hour."

And Dick Saville left the room. As he did so, the servant entered with a card, which Briggs read, an expression of perplex-ity crossing his face.

"Carteret?" he said,—"Major Homer Carteret? The name seems somehow familiar, but I can't place the man."

"The gentleman said he would be much obliged if you could see him for one moment," said the servant.

"Well, for one moment—show him up."

Major Carteret swung into the room on his best stride.

"I must apologize for calling at this unseemly hour," said he. "You don't remember me, Mr. Briggs. We met at Lord Arlingford's—er—some time ago."

"No apology is necessary," replied Mr. Briggs, gravely. "I remember perfectly. Pray be seated. Er—you wished to see me?"

"It is by Lord Arlingford's request that I am here. I came to say that he cannot be here so soon as he anticipated. Most important business——"

"So I expected," interrupted Briggs. "I think it very judicious——"

"Pardon me, Mr. Briggs," interrupted the major, in turn, "you are mistaken. The business that detains Lord Arlingford is as unexpected as it is urgent,—so urgent that he was unable to keep his appointment with me at the Club: he sent me a line asking me particularly to come here at once, fearing that you might misconstrue his absence. Erghem! I am very glad to have this opportunity of talking over this unhappy affair. I saw Lady Arlingford yesterday afternoon, and after we had discussed the matter she decided to make Arlingford an offer which I shall advise him to accept."

"May I ask if the offer concerns me in any way?" observed Mr. Briggs.

"Most certainly. Her ladyship's offer will cause Lord Arlingford to resign Miss Briggs's hand. Erghem! I have always had a great regard for Lady Arlingford, and it is her wish to re-marry her ex-husband."

"I have heard something of this a few moments ago."

"She looks upon it as the right thing to do for the child's sake, and, though I don't profess to be better than my neighbor, I must say that I agree with her."

And the major inflated his chest till he looked like a police-sergeant.

"I believe," said Mr. Briggs, drily, "that the amount of Lady Arlingford's income through the recent death of her aunt is now eight thousand a year. Am I not accurate, Major Carteret?"

"Quite; but——"

"As Lord Arlingford's *friend*," pursued the American, in the same tone, "you understand, of course, that on the interview of tonight depend his personal liberty, and, consequently, his *ability* to accept his late wife's offer."

"His liberty?"

"He will have to make full confession of his share in the conspiracy by which Captain Goddard was ruined. Er—*please* be seated. We shall spare Lady Arlingford as much as possible, but Captain Goddard's vindication is the first consideration. Frankly, if he refuses we shall convict him—and his accomplices—of conspiracy and criminal libel. Er—please be seated. I have been drawn into this matter by my cousin's unfortunate infatuation for Lord Arlingford."

"Mr. Briggs," replied the major, "I—I feel it is only due to myself to say that though I am, as you observe, Lord Arlingford's friend, I am deeply grieved at the part he took in that unfortunate business."

"I expected as much, and I am sure you are. Your good feeling in the matter simplifies a request I am about to make. Er—we are perfectly prepared to do without your testimony against him, but it might hasten matters to have it. How much do you want for it?"

Mr. Briggs leaned back complacently as Major Carteret sprang to his feet.

"Sir!" shouted he, "how dare you? I—er—er——Five hundred pounds."

"*Please* be seated."

The major sat down.

"You shall have that amount tonight after the meeting. For the present, good-evening. You will be back in half an hour, if you please."

"Certainly," replied the warrior, and, taking his hat, he took with it his departure.

Mr. Briggs looked after him for a moment, his head slightly on one side.

Then he carefully selected a cigarette, which he thoughtfully lit. Then, walking to the fireplace to deposit the match, he slowly winked at himself in the pier-glass.

# CHAPTER V.
## Reaping the Whirlwind.

Mr. Cincinnatus Q. Briggs's complacent appreciation of his own diplomacy was interrupted by the sudden irruption of Kitty Savilie, followed by Dick.

"How d'ye do, Mr. Briggs?" was her greeting. "Dick wanted me not to come. The idea!—as if I would miss seeing my old friend Aubyn Goddard set right. What a long time it is since we met, and how queer that we should both be mixed up in this dreadful business! I little thought, when I sat next to you at dinner and was so impertinent to you, that night at Lord Arlingford's, that the evening would end so tragically. I suppose you heard about Lady Arlingford's long illness?"

"Yes, but not the whole of the trouble," replied Briggs, surprised at finding himself getting in a word edgeways.

"Well, you know, when she recovered she did nothing but blame herself for the whole affair. I believe that if Lord Arlingford had not been so careless of all decency, she would have begged his pardon. Her people insisted on a divorce, though, and she was too weak to oppose it, and when she got well she confided to me that if ever she found an opportunity she meant to ask him to marry her over again."

"But why?"

"For the sake of her child. Oh, what silly women these good women are! I'm so glad I'm a bad one! I was so impatient with her that we nearly quarrelled; and now that Dick has determined that Goddard shall be set right, she has begged to be allowed to come and give Arlingford one more chance. Oh, that woman is too much of an angel——"

"My *dear* Kitty," mildly expostulated Dick, "will you confine your attention to the matter in hand, and not expand on your personal feelings?"

"My *dear* Dick," was the reply, "will you let me say one word without interruption? Mr. Briggs is an old friend of mine: we met but once, it is true, but it's all the same; we should have been old friends if we had met more frequently: shouldn't we, Mr. Briggs?"

"My *dear* madam," answered the American, "you overwhelm me. To have met you but once, is both a privilege and a privation. It is to have lived and to have ceased living at the same moment. It is———"

"Mr. Briggs! if you finish that sentence I shall have a fit! I'm not accustomed to it. Dick when he intends to be most polite generally says, 'I say, old gal, you're not looking half bad tonight,' or when he means to be most affectionate, 'Here, Tramp! come and be smacked.'"

"Really, my dear," broke in Dick at this point, "these domestic details,—really———" And, at a loss for words to balance his wife's eloquence, he raised her hand deferentially to his lips.

"Why, Dick," exclaimed she, looking at him in alarm, "you're not well. All this excitement has been too much for you. Sit down, and don't talk. Oh, Mr. Briggs, I had a most mysterious little note from Lady Arlingford, just as I was starting to come here. Let me see: what did I do with it? Ah, here it is."

She took a letter from her pocket and read as follows:

"*I have heard terrible news this afternoon, and am nearly mad with hope and fear. I will explain all to you. I must speak to the lady whom you call Bella-Demonia alone: so when we meet tonight make some excuse to leave us together for a few minutes. Read this to Mr. Briggs, and ask him to manage with you to do as I wish.*—What does it mean?"

She laid the letter down on the writing-table. As she did so, she uttered a little exclamation, and, turning to Briggs, quoth very gravely,—

"Oh! I am so much obliged."

"I am charmed, of course; but *why?*" returned Briggs, in amazement.

"Because at last you've satisfied me that you *are* an American. Now, I wonder if you got this purposely for me, or if it's a toy?"

Her glance had fallen on the little revolver, and, taking it up, she brandished it with glee.

"Be careful, for gracious' sake!" exclaimed Briggs, in alarm. "It's loaded; and, though it's very small, it would kill at this range."

"Oh, goodness!" cried Kitty, as she dropped the weapon among the papers in comic consternation. "But come, what do you make of Lady Arlingford's note?"

"I can make nothing of it. At all events, her request is simple enough. They will both be here in a few moments, and if you will come into the library I should like to show you some etchings I have bought,—a Seymour-Haden, a couple of Wilfrid Ball's, and a Haig or two. I am told they're very fine."

"I should like to see them very much," returned Kitty, "though I don't understand them a bit."

Mr. Cincinnatus Q. Briggs was a most disappointing American. Instead of buying diamonds or pictures to sell, he spent his spare cash on rare bric-à-brac, etchings, and engravings to keep. You might be with him for twenty-four hours and never hear what anything he possessed had cost him. He had not the vaguest conception as to the price of his wines, and, though as ardent a collector of early-printed books and first editions as the most uneducated Westerner settled in New York, he positively knew what books he had, and had "read at" all of them. It is probable that had he been a married man the house he lived in would not have been made over to his wife to cheat his creditors in the event of financial shipwreck.

Kitty was still pondering when Lady Arlingford was announced. Briggs advanced to conduct her to a chair.

"I hope you are not fatigued, Lady Arlingford," said he. "Have you seen Captain Goddard yet?"

"Not yet," replied she. "I expected to find him here. Ah, Kitty, how happy you look! I'm so glad, dear! You got my letter?"

"Yes, dear, but I don't understand it. Have you seen the Baroness Altdorff?"

"Yes,—this afternoon, by accident; and I learnt from her the truth."

"The truth?"

"Yes. She told me who she was and is."

"Who is she? what is she?" exclaimed Dick and Kitty both together.

"You do not know?"

"No. Who is she?"

"*The Princess Galitzin.*"

The words were uttered by a servant who at this moment threw open the folding doors and admitted Bella-Demonia to the presence of three people whose faces took on an expression of unspeakable amazement.

"Oh, Dick," whispered Kitty, "who is she going to turn out to be next? Are you sure—are you *sure* that she is not Mrs. Richard Saville, among other things?"

"I swear she isn't," replied the no less astonished Dick, in the same tone.

"She'll be somebody else in a minute. I know she will."

"Probably."

Meanwhile, Mr. Briggs, leading the new-comer forward, said to Lady Arlingford,—

"Lady Arlingford, allow me to present to you——"

"The princess and I have already met," said her ladyship.

"Yes," returned Bella-Demonia, "and Mrs. and Mr. Saville I already know. How are you?"

"I was just going—as we have a few minutes yet—to show Mrs. Saville some pet etchings of mine," said Mr. Briggs. "Would you care to see them, princess?"

The Princess Galitzin exchanged a glance with Lady Arlingford, and then answered,—

"Thank you; I would rather see them later, if you will allow me, but do not let me deprive Mr. and Mrs. Saville of the pleasure. I do not feel quite up to enjoying etchings just now."

"Nor I," said Lady Arlingford.

"Well, then," pursued Mr. Briggs, "if you will pardon us for a while?"

"By all means."

As Kitty left the room, she whispered to Lady Arlingford,—

"Are you sure you are strong enough? Shall I stay?"

"No, no: leave us," was the reply, and the next moment the two women were once more alone.

Lady Arlingford rose. "Will you give me your hand?" she said. "After hearing your story, I don't feel fit to touch you. I must have provoked you beyond endurance by my ignorance. Can you find it in your heart to forgive me?"

"If I could wipe out your injuries as easily as I can forgive you,—if indeed there is anything to forgive,—I do so a thousand times over. Can you believe that in knowing your trouble I have forgotten my own? How I wish I could help you! how I should like to prove the depth and reality of my sympathy!"

"You can prove it, and, if you will, you can give me all the peace I can hope to gain out of this sad life. If I should ask something of you that will tax your goodness to its depths, would you grant me my prayer? God knows I feel I have no right to expect so much from you; but——"

"There is no effort I would spare to help you. What can I do?"

"I implore you to give Jack—Lord Arlingford—one chance to clear himself of some of the charges of which you think him guilty. That horrible story you told me—there must be some explanation. Let him speak in his own behalf. I *know* he will do his utmost to repair the injury he did Aubyn, and I am sure Aubyn will bury the past, if only for my sake. Will you not do the same? Influential, protected as you are in your own country, surely you have only to ask for the annulment of your marriage with my—my—husband, to obtain it. Is it not so?"

"Yes; but why do you ask?"

"Because I would help him to atone for his past; because if you will give him his freedom I will still take him back. Oh, don't shrink from me! Hear what I have to say before you condemn me. Remember, I have a child. It is my duty to do all in my power to bring her father back to her."

"And you would live with that man, despising him as you must, because you feel it to be your duty?"

"Even so! It is the least I can do to atone to my little girl for the wrong that has been done her. I should be unable to meet her eyes, as she asks for her father, if I had not done all in my power to redeem him. Will you do what I ask?"

The Princess Galitzin rose, and, walking to the window, appeared to reflect deeply. Then she came back, and said,—

"For your sake, I promise that so far as my own injuries are concerned I will forgive him. But his ruin of Aubyn Goddard I cannot—will not forgive. Not upon me, but on his confession tonight, will depend his liberty. His fate is in his own hands."

"Ah! how can I thank you? I am confident now."

At this moment Mr. Briggs entered the room.

"Captain Goddard has just arrived," said he. "Shall I bring him in here?"

"One moment," said Lady Arlingford. "I—I can bear no more tonight. May I ask you, Mr. Briggs, to let me rest awhile in another room, and then I will go home."

"Certainly: it shall be as you wish," replied Mr. Briggs. "Come in here. I will see that your carriage is ready at any moment."

Her ladyship turned to the princess and extended her hand as she said,—

"May I see you once more before I leave England? I don't know if I am doing what is right, but I hope so."

Bella-Demonia bent her head, and Lady Arlingford left the room with Mr. Briggs.

Left alone, the woman looked after the departing form, and said, half aloud,—

"Who shall say that you are wrong? Not I, indeed,—I who have forgotten my revenge in my new-born dream." She pressed her hands to her head, and turned, just as Aubyn Goddard entered the room.

They faced each other for a few moments without speaking, and then Goddard, advancing, took both her hands in his.

"So I am to thank you for honor as well as for life," said he, gravely.

"That sounds almost like a reproach," replied she. "Have I not done everything I could to atone for my share in the disaster I so unwittingly brought on you? Besides, it was your delirium,

408

and not the prince, that detained you at Deve-kiui. As far as he was concerned, you were free to go as you had come."

"He is a wonderful man. Having caught me, I wonder he did not kill me: I had given him trouble enough. Besides, he would have been killing two birds with one stone,—or rather two men with one bullet. That evening when I lay unconscious at your feet—yours and his—the scene must have been terrible: it is never out of my mind."

"It is one of the few moments of my life that I am ashamed of. When the prince recognized you and I knew my trick to save you had been useless, I gave up all hope, and in the desperation of the moment I offered to buy your life from him. 'Only let him escape,' said I, 'and I promise never to see him again, and I—my life—shall be given to you!'"

"My God! And what did he say?"

"He said, simply, 'I have loved you as long as I have known you, and you evidently do not understand that emotion as I do. I hope to show you that I can be at the same time a disappointed lover and—a gentleman.' That was all that was said till you were on the high-road to recovery and we laid our plans for the trapping of Arlingford. I am not ashamed to say that I fell on my knees and asked his pardon. It was he who planned and devised so that your capture and whereabouts should be kept a secret from Skobeleff."

"How generous!"

"It was well for you that your wound proved so dangerous, and that before you could be moved peace was proclaimed at San Stefano."

Aubyn Goddard raised her hand to his lips, and said, in a voice that betrayed the depth of his emotion,—

"And you have borne all this for me! I wonder why?"

"Why?" answered Bella-Demonia, with a quick smile and shake of her head. "Because you are personally very distasteful to me; because, in short, I do not like you; because we are antipathetic to each other; because you have been so nobly treated that you deserve no sympathy. Are these reasons enough, Aubyn?"

And the man, who was just a man and no longer Aubyn Goddard the Hero, clasped to his breast the woman, who was just a woman and no longer Bella-Demonia the Mystery, as she lay in his arms and gave up her soul to the ecstasy of his kiss.

They were very nearly caught by Mr. Briggs, who entered the room at the moment, or rather just after it.

"Princess," said he, "Lord Arlingford is here. Shall he come in?"

"Wait one moment," returned she. "My plan is much upset by Lady Arlingford's strange determination, but I have promised her my aid. If he signs the papers I am willing to avoid seeing him, and it will be best that he should not know that I have found him. Let me retire for a while, where I can hear what he has to say. This conservatory will do."

"It shall be as you wish," answered Mr. Briggs, showing her to a little conservatory built out over the porch of the house, communicating by a French window with the apartment. As she turned towards it she gave her hand to Goddard, who bent and kissed it.

"Oh!" observed Mr. Briggs to himself. "Ah!"

Then he went to the door and admitted Dick Saville, accompanied by Arlingford and Major Carteret. The gallant major was evidently very nervous: he stood a little apart from his principal and twisted his moustache spasmodically, a fit subject for an artist who might desire to make a "Study of a Man, ratting."

Mr. Briggs motioned the four men to be seated, and took his place at the writing-table. Then, slightly clearing his throat, he observed,—

"As we all know for what purpose we are here, it will, I think, only be necessary for me to read this statutory declaration, which has been drawn up in duplicate for the signature of his lordship."

Arlingford signified his attention, and Mr. Briggs continued:

"The declaration reads as follows: 'I, John Vyvian Fane, Viscount Arlingford, do hereby solemnly declare that the charges made by me against Captain the Honorable Aubyn Goddard were false; that I made the said charges knowing them to be false, and with a specific purpose which was accomplished in the failure of his mission.' Now, Lord Arlingford, if you will affix your signature in the presence of witnesses, we can terminate this very painful meeting."

Arlingford sprang to his feet.

"Sign that!" he cried. "I refuse to sign it! I am willing to say that to the best of my belief I made a mistake; but sign such a monstrous production as that? Certainly not!"

"You know the alternative, Lord Arlingford," said Dick Saville.

"I have told you what I will do," retorted Arlingford, turning upon him, "and there is no power on earth that can force me to do more."

"Perhaps *I* can persuade Lord Arlingford to sign," said a quiet, rich voice behind them, as Bella-Demonia stepped into the room. Hearing the words, Arlingford started violently and turned to meet the woman's stare.

"Carita Galitzin!" he exclaimed. "My God!"

"Hardly that," replied the princess, in mock deprecation, "but, unfortunately, your wife."

"His wife!" The exclamation broke forth simultaneously from the other four. Goddard started as if he had been shot, and went quickly to the woman's side.

"What do you mean?" he said, in a husky undertone.

"Wait," she replied.

Meanwhile, Arlingford, with a violent effort, had recovered his self-control.

"You will have," said he, sneeringly, "some difficulty in proving that the very hurried form that we went through was a legal marriage, even in Russia, and you will doubtless be too sensible to risk proving yourself to have been my mistress."

Goddard, with a half-cough of rage, sprang at him, but was restrained by Saville and by the princess, who stepped between them.

"Unfortunately," said she, in a tone of withering scorn, "to have been your wife is, if possible, the greater disgrace. You overestimate the honor of a marriage with yourself, and you underestimate the fact that you are in no position to oppose my slightest whim."

"Indeed? Because——?"

"Because on me depends not only your ability to obtain the means of subsistence, but your liberty, your very life itself, belong to me. I have but to hold up my finger and your doom is sealed. You will sign that document *at once*."

"Charming!" returned Arlingford; "but we are in England now, and I am prepared to defend any action you may choose to bring. I refuse to sign. Do your worst! I defy you!" he concluded, violently.

"Mr. Briggs," said the princess, "I saw Prince Schouloff's carriage below. Will you be so good as to call him? Thanks."

And Mr. Cincinnatus Q. Briggs left the room.

"In all the years," resumed the princess, coming close to Arlingford, "during which I sought for the murderer of my brother, I thought that nothing but his death could appease me. Now, however, fortunately for you, I have found a man whose honor is as pure as God's blessed mercy, a man by comparison with whom you are too unclean a thing even to kill."

She turned on her heel and returned to Goddard's side as Mr. Briggs re-entered the room, accompanied by Prince Schouloff.

"Prince," said Carita Galitzin to the Chief of Police, "will you kindly tell Lord Arlingford that if necessary we shall not be wanting in proofs to substantiate our charges of bigamy, nor shall we shrink from the publicity consequent on taking steps to frustrate his present plans?"

"The prince will doubtless remember," said Arlingford, with a cool assurance that was sublime, "that the onus of disproof lies with the accused, and that I am in my own country and therefore have the best chance of assuming the character of accuser. You, as foreigners, will have to go through certain formalities before being able to institute legal proceedings. I shall therefore proceed at once to prove that yours is simply an attempt at blackmail."

"I am compelled to admit that Lord Arlingford's view of the legal position is entirely correct," replied Prince Schouloff, quietly.

Had a thunder-bolt fallen among them, the consternation of his auditors could not have been more lively.

"You agree with him!" exclaimed the princess.

"I am so sure of his accuracy," returned the prince, calmly, "that I have taken the very position he so clearly points out to be the best. The negotiations pending between our respective governments have enabled me to procure a warrant for the immediate arrest of John Vyvian Fane, Viscount Arlingford, and it will be in Petersburg—not in London—that his lordship will have to answer the charge."

"What charge?"

"Murder."

"Murder!" echoed Arlingford, his air of cynic assurance suddenly changing to one of alarmed concern. "You can scarcely charge a man with that of which he is ignorant. You can *charge* him with whatever you please, but I learn for the first time that I have killed anyone. Preposterous! May I know whom I murdered?"

"You will find all duly stated in this warrant," answered the prince, handing him a paper. "Your long residence in Russia, and, above all, your connection with the police, render you sufficiently conversant with our code to convince you that we are acting within our right, and," added he, significantly, "that we seldom act in vain."

"Your methods are at least expensive," ejaculated Arlingford.

"You are well able to judge of that point. My officers are below: you will, I presume, accompany them without further trouble.—Mr. Briggs, will you allow me to write some instructions? Thank you."

And the prince seated himself at the writing-table, whilst Arlingford stared dazedly at the warrant that he held in his hands. A servant appeared and handed a slip of paper to Mr. Briggs, who whispered to the princess. The latter left the room, as Dick Saville approached Prince Schouloff and remarked,—

"Prince, this is a desperate accusation,—and so unexpected."

"Desperate diseases," returned the prince, "require desperate remedies. I feared that he might be unmanageable: so I took this precaution."

"But shall you be able to prove him guilty?"

"That is quite unimportant," was the answer. "Lord Arlingford will doubtless be glad to sign any document before his trial, rather than return to Russia. You understand?"

"May I ask," said Mr. Briggs, who had joined them, "when and where this murder was committed?"

"God knows: I don't," returned the prince, laconically, as he turned once more to his writing.

Mr. Briggs's free and enlightened American mind was confused.

"But surely——" he began.

"My dear fellow," said Dick Saville, taking him aside, "what the deuce is the use of being a Russian prince if you can't prove a man guilty of anything you like on an emergency?"

Meanwhile, Aubyn Goddard had approached the diplomat.

"I am much indebted to you——" he began.

"Not at all," interrupted Schouloff. "I was unfortunate enough to be a party—for reasons of state—to your trouble; it is but right that I should be a party to your vindication. I repeat, for reasons of state I was compelled to act as I did, knowing that I could vindicate you at the right moment. That act was as repugnant to me in the manner of its performance, as to give you my assistance today is a pleasure."

Lord Arlingford had finished the perusal of the warrant, and had scribbled a few words in his note-book which he gave to Major Carteret for delivery to his wife. Now he moved towards the door. There he turned and faced the five men. The Princess Galitzin and Mrs. Bradley Dashton entered the room behind and unobserved by him.

"You calculated with perfect certainty," said his lordship, with a brave show of defiance, "and I am not fool enough to resist you and give you the chance of killing me 'in self-defence.' Fortunately, my wife is in a position to institute proceedings, which will be done at once. Egad! you're all very clever, but I observe that Captain Goddard's little card-trick remains still unexplained. The disappearance of that king of trumps *was* queer, wasn't it? Let me see: I think the suit was clubs."

"You need not tax your memory," said a voice—Bella-Demonia's—behind him. "The card is here!" She laid it on the table, and all bent forward to look at it. "You see," pursued the princess, "that this card is one bearing on its back the monogram of a gambling-club to which Lord Arlingford belonged, which was immediately afterwards broken up. The other,—the one held by Captain Goddard,—a two of clubs, will be forthcoming if required. *This* card was given to Mrs. Dashton to destroy, that night, by Lord Arlingford. Fortunately, she did not do so. The reason of Captain Goddard's refusal to show that two of clubs has been explained: so that the signing of this declaration is no longer necessary."

"You will state fully," said Dick Saville to Mrs. Dashton, who was leaning against the writing-table, "how and when this card came into your possession?"

"In any terms you choose to dictate," she said.

Arlingford had been staggered for the moment, but came up to time, game to the last.

"I congratulate you all," said he, with an evil sneer, "on the value of *Mrs. Dashton's* word!"

"You will find that it is to be depended on," said Mrs. Dashton, quietly. "I told you this afternoon that——"

"That I was to do a great many things," broke in Arlingford, in his former tone. "Among others, that I was to marry *you.*"

"No; I told *you* that you should marry no other."

"And *I* told you that a man does not marry his——"

"Stop!" cried the woman, her eyes blazing with fury. Her glance fell on the revolver lying under her hand: quick as thought she raised it and fired. Lord Arlingford fell heavily to the ground, mortally wounded.

Amid the general consternation, the Princess Galitzin went to Mrs. Dashton's side. She was fainting.

"Whew! what shall we do now?" said Dick Saville to Prince Schouloff.

"Mrs. Dashton is one of my witnesses," returned he. "I will see that she leaves the country at once. She will never return."

A door was thrown open, and Lady Arlingford rushed into the room. Seeing her husband lying on the floor, she flung herself by his side.

"My God!" she cried, "how did this happen?"

Arlingford, with a supreme effort, raised himself, and, making a sign imposing silence on the others, addressed his wife:

"I—I—the game was up," he said. "I—I—shot myself. Poor little woman! you are well rid of me."

He sank into her arms.

John Vyvian Fane, Viscount Arlingford, was dead.

THE END.

# THE VENGEANCE
## OF
## MAURICE
## DENALGUEZ

# SELINA DOLARO
## *A BIOGRAPHY.*

"I see there is nothing left for me to do but to write my own obituary. Modesty will prevent my ornamenting it with much eulogy; but if I may be forgiven what in any other sketch would be conceit, I will endeavor to make up in truth for other deficiencies."

"I will paint two pictures,—let those who love me choose which they will. Both are from life, both are true.—A woman still young, with a love of life as strong as death, but whose understanding grasps the awful fact that the down grade is steep, and that she is being hurried forward; but that tender hands await the final step that shall bring her to the bottom.—The same woman, young, but with youth stamped out for all but those who love her well enough to read her soul 'between the lines.' Through all steals the peace love brings. If she has lost her place in the world's strife she has gained in compensation, affection, consideration, generosity, that few have known. She has been the light, lightening the great good for good's sake that the good have done."

"I thank God that I was never so one-sided as to be reduced to mourn for a past that *was* past. I have loved my work, but it has never excluded all and every other thought. I am grateful that I can, and always could, forget the wonderful and all-absorbing *I*—remembering how small a thing was that *I*."

The above prolegomena were written by Selina Dolaro at different times during the past lustrum; and I feel that I cannot do better than copy them from her slips as the only comment necessary upon the biographical sketch which follows, all that is to be said of her as a woman having been indicated, though inadequately in the preceding "*In Memoriam.*"[1]

Selina Dolaro was born on the 20th August, 1849. She was the daughter of an accomplished musician, by name Benjamin Simmons, who, living in London today, follows the profession that he adopted as a youth. At a very early age his only child betrayed a violent passion for music, and she used herself to tell a story of her having been found one night, when she had escaped unobserved from home, drinking in the strains of *La Favorita* in the gallery at Her Majesty's Theatre in London. Her passion for music was so strong, that at the age of fourteen she was placed under the tuition of an Italian maestro named Salvini. At the age of sixteen (in 1865) she interrupted her studies by marrying one of her own faith, by name Isaac Dolaro Belasco. His ancestral name was Miara D'Olivares, and he came of an old family of Spanish Jews whose home was in Aragon. On the expulsion of the race from Spain in 1492, the family took refuge in the Italian town of Belasco, where they dropped the name Miara, and took that of the town of their adoption—D'Olivares meanwhile becoming Italianized into Dolaro. This was the name Madame Belasco adopted when she made her *début* in 1870, and this is the name which she made famous in two continents.

In 1866 she determined to turn her marvellous gifts to account, and going to Paris, was admitted to the Paris Conservatoire, where for three years she studied under Auber.

---

1 Since the same "*In Memoriam*" was also used in *Bella-Demonia*, it has been omitted from *The Vengeance of Maurice Denalguez*, where it was placed directly before this biography. The document can be found on page 257 of the current volume.

Her studies completed, she was not long in finding an opening, and she made her *début* on the 22d January, 1870, as Galsuinda in Hervé's "Chilperic" at the Lyceum Theatre, the first opéra bouffe, properly so-called, ever produced in London. I have before me an old and tattered collection of press notices that attest the *furore* created by the first appearance of this finished *artiste*, who was hardly more than a child—in years. She rose with rapidity to the leading part of Fredegonde in the same opera, and then created (in English) the title *rôle* in "Genevieve de Brabant." It was at this time that her second daughter was born, and the child was christened in the name of her mother's latest triumph. From this moment her future as a *prima donna* was secured, and in the mouths of all the *cognoscenti* there was but one name—hers. Meanwhile four children had been born to her; and then, realizing that she had drawn a blank in the lottery of love, she sought for and obtained a divorce from her husband, and thenceforward devoted her life to the cultivation of her art and the care of her children.

In the year 1872 she appeared (October 2nd) as Camilla at the Court Theatre in T. F. Plowman's opéra bouffe "Zampa, or the Buckaneer and the little Dear." The opera was justly condemned as mediocre, but the success that Madame Dolaro wove out of the unsatisfactory materials at her command was admittedly phenomenal. It was in this opera that she first gave her celebrated rendering of Chaumont's song "*La Première Feuille.*" On the 17th May, 1873, she appeared in the title *rôle* of "Fleur de Lys" at the Gaiety Theatre with W. J. Hill, Edward Righton, and Emily Soldene in the cast; and in the December of that year (the 23d) she made her first appearance as Clairette in "La Fille de Madame Angot," for her own benefit, at the Philharmonic Theatre, On the same occasion she played a scene from "The First Night" with H. F. Montague. Encouraged by her success, she made a tour of the provinces with her own company in the summer of 1874, playing Clairette to the Ange Pitou of John Chatterson, who has since achieved fame and fortune as Signer Perugini, The tour comprised Nottingham, Manchester, Sheffield, Bradford, Liverpool, and other great Midland and Northern cities; and at its conclusion we find her playing the part of "Sibyl Cobb" in "The Black Prince" at the St. James' Theatre. "The Black Prince" was adapted from MM. Labiche and Delacour's "*Voyage en Chine*" by H. B. Farnie. Prior to this appearance she played a short season of "*La Fille de Madame Angot*" at the Lyceum Theatre in London prior to Emily Soldene's departure for the United States. I find among her papers the following sonnet, dating from this period of her triumphs:

SONNET TO MISS SELINA DOLARO
(On Her Impersonation of Clairette.)
*Le Comique, le vria Comique, n'est jamais mechant.*
—Montesquieu.

"The truly comic never is profane:"
So spoke the sage, in accents which have reached
Far down Time's steep and echoed o'er the main.
And, lady, thou dost practise what he preached;
For thou hast churlish bigotry impeached
With thy bright smile, and mirth-provoking art,
And laughter-stirring glances and arch grace.
Pale Care's sworn foe art thou—he has no part
In the soft beams that radiate from thy face
And pierce the secret chambers of the heart,
Lulling to rest sharp pain with all her smart.
True art and genius this—which all embrace—
To cheer poor nature where it darkling lies,
And raise it joy ward—nearer to the skies.
NOTTINGHAM, APRIL 27, 1874. C. C. HARRISON.

On the 30th January, 1875, Madame Dolaro commenced her career as the manageress of a London Theatre, and opened the Royalty Theatre (in Dean Street, Soho), of which Miss Henrietta Hodson was the then lessee, with Offenbach's "*La Perichole*" supported by Walter Fisher and poor Fred Sullivan, who died soon after the termination of this engagement. It is needless to tell of Madame Dolaro's triumph as "*La Perichole*," which, with the exception of "Mademoiselle Lange," was perhaps her greatest part, and is familiar to playgoers on both sides of the Atlantic.

Perhaps the most interesting circumstance connected with this production is a modest announcement that appears on the programme in the following terms:

NOTICE.
In preparation, a New Comic Opera, composed expressly for this theatre, by W. S. Gilbert and Mr. Arthur Sullivan.

This new comic opera was "Trial by Jury," the inaugural effort of the Gilbert-Sullivan partnership, which was produced by Madame Dolaro on the 25th March, 1875, with Miss Nelly Bromley as the defendant. London awakened at once to the new possibilities of legitimate Comic Opera, and to the critic nothing can be more interesting than the mass of notices there-anent which lie before me as I write.

At the termination of a most successful season she took her company on tour, playing "*La Perichole*," "*La Fille de Madame Angot*" and "*Trial by Jury*," in Manchester, Salford, Leeds, Nottingham, Sheffield, Liverpool, Newcastle, Birmingham, and Dublin; and on October the 12th she re-opened the Royalty Theatre with the same bill. It was during this tour that she first played "Mademoiselle Lange" instead of "Clairette" in "*La Fille de Madame Angot*" and from that moment the "Lange" of Emily Soldene and Cornélie d'Anka become forgotten history.

The next record that I find of Madame Dolaro's career is an announcement of her "first appearance in Comedy," on the afternoon of January 17, 1877, as Lady Teazle in "The School for Scandal." Of her success or failure in the part I can find no particulars, the next set of papers and cuttings referring to what was perhaps her greatest and most legitimate triumph, to wit, her performance of the title *rôle* in "Carmen," under Carl Rosa's management, at Her Majesty's Theatre, on the 5th of February, 1879. This was the first presentation of the opera in English, and such was the *furore* created by Madame Dolaro's impersonation, coming as it did after Trebelli's and Minnie Hauk's, that "Carmen" ran on almost into April. Durward Lely was the José, and Julia Gaylord and Snazelle were also in the cast. At the close of the season Col. Mapleson determined to send her over the following autumn to play "Carmen" in New York, this time in Italian, with the Campanini company; but in the mean time Madame Dolaro, who, partly from virtue and partly from necessity, was never happy unless she was in harness, opened the Folly Theatre with an opéra bouffe called "The Dragoons," a version by Hersee of Maillart's "*Les Dragons de Villars*" on April the 14th. On the opening night of the season she was seriously ill, but all the notices before me unite in praise of her performance; and by April the 20th, being fully recovered, a fresh crop of criticisms announced the triumph of her efforts. This production was followed by a revival of "*La Perichole*" in which she was supported by Fred Leslie, Harry Nicholls, and Frank Wyatt, and this was in turn followed by a run of Savile Clarke's and Lewis Clifton's burlesque of "Drink," entitled "Another Drink," in which she played Gervaise, supported by Miss De Grey and G. W. Anson. It was in this burlesque that she originated her celebrated imitation of Sarah Bernhardt, for which she was singularly adapted by her features and Parisian training; and until the day of her death it remained a never-failing source of wonder and amusement to her friends. At this point in her mass of documents I find a laconic entry, in her own handwriting:

"*Here she departed for America.*"

She arrived, in this country in October, engaged by Mapleson, to play "Carmen" to Campauini's "José," at the Academy of Music. She arrived to find herself an object of dislike, suspicion, and envy on the part of a company of Italian professionals, who, from Campanini down, did all in their power to thwart her every endeavor. A noted New York manager has often told me that he attended the dress rehearsal, and that the way the Italians heaped ridicule that verged upon insult on the poor little woman made the blood of the English and Americans present boil. It is little wonder, therefore, that on October 27th, at her first appearance, singing under such circumstances, in a language that was strange to her, in a theatre twice the size of the largest English opera-house, she was pitifully nervous; and though many of the papers recognized her exquisite *technique* and dramatic intensity, her impersonation of "Carmen" was not a triumph. On Saturday, November 1st, she sang the *rôle* again at a matinée; and though the papers now united in paying tribute to her acting and vocalization, Madame Dolaro, accustomed to nothing that fell short of perfection, threw up the engagement and returned to England to resume the *rôle* in English under Carl Rosa.

Early in the following year (1880) she signed a contract with one M. B. Leavitt for a tour of the United States, to commence that autumn. In the July of that year she gave a performance of "Twelfth Night," at the Gaiety Theatre, supported by Conway, in which she played Viola to his Sebastian. This was always one of her favorite reminiscences, and I find among her archives the following couplets, written by a well-known songster, on the occasion:

### TO VIOLA: A WELCOME.

> Sweet Songstress, who first showed the charm
> > That Bizet's genius left below,
> And Carmen's nature, wild and warm,
> > Portrayed,—a child of love and woe,—
> Thrice welcome is thy brightsome face
> > To light the gloom of Drama's day.
> Let dull Convention now give place,
> > And musty Precedent make way;
> For Nature takes our hearts by storm,
> > And will not brook denial. Ah!
> She breaks through futile rule and form
> > Incarnated in Viola!
>
> > > > > E. R. S.

On September 13, 1880, her first American tour began; and all over the States she played "Olivette," "Little Carmen," "La Grande Duchesse," "La Filledu Tambour Major," "La Fille de Madame Angot," and "Orpheus." Mr. Leavitt seems to have had a talent for disagreeing with his entire company, and his combination broke up in Chicago in March, 1881,—not, however, before Selina Dolaro had established herself the Queen of opéra bouffe from the State of Maine to the Pacific coast. She at once determined to make this country her home, but before returning to England to settle her affairs, desiring to play in some real success, she played in April and May a run of "Olivette," with the Strakosch-Hess Acme Opera Company.

In May she returned to England, closed her affairs there, and went over to Paris, where the composer Audran, deeply impressed with her power, wrote especially for her the comic opera "The Grand Mogul," which, on October 29th, was produced at the Bijou Theatre by Col. McCaull, under the title of "The Snake Charmer." At the close of this run, i.e., in May, 1882, she took the Bijou Theatre, and produced there "The First Night" and "A Lesson in Love," supported by Harry St. Maur. The venture was unsuccessful, owing to the season, and in November we find her playing her own play "Justine," at the New Park Theatre (now Harrigan's), under the management of J. A. Stevens. This was her first effort at dramatic authorship, and it was at about this time that she wrote "Fashion" in its original form, founded on a play of Eugene Scribe.

She disposed of it first to Shook & Collier, for production at the Union Square Theatre, but they not having produced it within the stipulated time the property reverted to her; and on April 17th (1883) she appeared as Polly Eccles in H. M. Pitt's "Caste" company, Eben Plympton, Fanny Addison, and William Davidge forming part of the cast. This was her greatest comedy success, and had it not been for the unfortunate season of the year, this revival of the Robertsonian Comedies would probably have become historic. As it was, the company disbanded in June. I have before me a letter written to Madame Dolaro by Sara

Jewett *apropos* of this performance, which is a remarkable tribute paid by one great actress to the talent of another.

The years 1884 and 1885 were passed in varying fortunes, in gleams of hope and cruel disappointments, and Madame Dolaro kept but few and fragmentary records of them. She made many appearances, as she was ever ready to do, on behalf of her unfortunate fellow-actors; and in September, 1885, she made her last important appearance before the public with Minnie Maddern in Steele Mackaye's version of Sardou's *"Andrea"* entitled "In Spite of All." It was at the close of this engagement that, reduced to a condition of financial embarrassment, she conceived the idea of giving for her own benefit an entirely original form of entertainment, which she entitled an "Impromptu." This took place on the 3d March, 1886, in the University Club Theatre, and consisted of a series of impromptu "acts," performed by people who left their seats in the audience for the purpose, among whom were Sophie Eyre, Caroline Hill, Lillian Russell, Kyrle Bellew, George Riddle, Louis James, Frank Wilson, and, of course, Mr. Marshall P. Wilder. She followed this with an original duologue, entitled "Reading a Tragedy;" and the proceedings wound up in the small hours with a dance. The whole entertainment is described as having been singularly fascinating in its decorous *désinvolture*.

But, alas! here was the foreshadowing of the end. During the evening Madame Dolaro tried to sing her famous *"La Première Feuille"* and was compelled to abandon the attempt; and ten days later a friend entering her rooms on Twenty-third Street found her bathed in her life-blood, and apparently dying. The doctors who consulted over her case gave it out as their verdict that she could not live three months. Dark days had fallen upon "Dolly," and she resigned herself patiently to await the end.

Her friends rallied themselves together, and on the evening of the 26th of April a great benefit was given her at Wallack's Theatre (now Palmer's), which relieved her for a time of material cares, and of the anxiety consequent on the expenses of her illness. For a year she rested physically, but worked mentally at her play "Fashion," which was finally produced by her friends for her benefit on the 19th May, 1887, at the Madison Square, A. M. Palmer giving her his theatre and all its accessories for the purpose. She has said a hundred times to me: "I have believed in God, and prayed to him all my life; and as a reward, when I wanted them most, he sent me Palmer and Donahue. Remember that!"

The latter gentleman was her faithful friend and physician, who remained with her to the last—George H. Donahue, M.D., of Gramercy Park, who, in spite of his own verdict on her case, kept her alive and in comparative freedom from pain for nearly three years. Selina Dolaro paid her tribute to Mr. Palmer in the dedication of "Bella-Demonia;" it is here that I pay her no lesser tribute to Dr. Donahue.

Of recent events it is not necessary to speak at length. Of the enthusiasm created by "Fashion," on the 19th May, 1887; of its failure when produced at Wallack's under H. E. Abbey's management, on the 28th December, 1887; of the causes that contributed to that failure,—it is not for me to speak now. Suffice it to say, that Madame Dolaro, in speaking of the manner in which her play was saved from utter damnation by two of the cast, used to say: "Were it not for that man and that woman, I think I should have died of grief with the New Year, 1888."

It was at this time that she produced her remarkable "Bachelor's Guide," entitled "Mes Amours: Poems Passionate and Playful, with my answers to some of them," which called down a storm of adverse criticism, and accusations of *mala fides*. Now that she is dead, it may be said that these poems were written entirely by two literary friends in years gone by, who gave her full liberty to use them in the book, and the balance were written by herself and by a friend for the volume itself. It was not a publication of her love-letters, but was none the less humorous on that account.

Her next work was the making of "Bella-Demonia," about which book so much has recently been written and said. I think I cannot do better' than to reproduce in this place a letter which I wrote to *The Journalist* on the subject, and which I entitled

# THE STORY OF MADAME SELINA DOLARO'S LOST MANUSCRIPT.

The announcement made by Messrs. Lippincott of Madame Dolaro's novel "Bella-Demonia," coming, as it did, simultaneously with her death, has naturally been made the subject of considerable comment in literary and dramatic circles, and among the notes written *apropos* of this book one that has attracted the most attention has been the story of its loss at the moment that arrangements had been practically completed for its publication. As certain irresponsible persons have taken advantage of this tragic occurrence to give their own distorted versions of the story, it seems to me that I cannot do better than to tell, as her literary executor and co-worker, the facts of the case as they exist in my own absolute knowledge, supported by documentary evidence.

Immediately after the production of "Fashion" at Wallack's Theatre, Madame Dolaro turned her attention to the completion of a drama that she had long contemplated, entitled "Bella-Demonia." The plot of the play dealt with the period of the Turko-Russian War of 1877-8, and particularly turned upon certain dramatic incidents in the lives of Col. Valentine Baker, and of Fanny Lear (Hattie Blackford), of which Madame Dolaro had peculiar and esoteric information. As the drama unfolded, she continually deplored to me the fact that she was bound down to four acts at most, whilst the story she was engaged upon would fill ten at least had they been practicable. It was on this subject that she had her little humorous tussle with Mr. Dion Boucicault in the *New York Herald* of the 25th and 26th July, 1888. It was then that she conceived the idea of elaborating her play, which was about a quarter finished, into a romance with a prologue impossible in a drama, and the writing of her novel was begun on the 14th of July. It was finished on the 20th of August, having occupied about eight hard-worked hours every day, and the conclusion was sent to New York—the previous three quarters having been already sent to Messrs. Belford, Clarke & Company, and accepted for publication in book form. On the 31st, Madame Dolaro received a letter from Col. Cockerill, telling her that his reader "passed a very favorable judgment, thought it a very interesting story, and recommended its publication." She was in the seventh heaven of delight and hope. On the fourth of September she went to New York to see about it, and greeted me at the Sayville station on her return with the words, "Bella-Demonia is lost!" She told me of Col. Cockerill's dismay, and of his efforts to find the thief, for that it had been stolen there seemed no doubt—a MS. of 200 leaves does not get mislaid; and Col. Cockerill had laid it, for safer keeping, among his most valuable papers. On the ninth a letter confirmed the loss, and on the tenth the MS. was begun again from the first page—for we had kept no copy, so anxious (and with good cause!) was Madame Dolaro to deliver the MS. and obtain the emolument offered her in more than one direction.

The law in the matter is clear. A newspaper is not liable for any MS. not actually contracted or paid for, but in a subsequent interview with Col Cockerill, that gentleman offered *himself,* most liberally, the sum of one hundred dollars to pay for a stenographer to retake the novel, and gave himself much trouble to find one for her. I have his letters on the subject before me. On the tenth the MS. was begun again, and on the twenty-sixth of October was finished. By that time, of course, arrangements had been made with other authors, and after another chat with Col. Cockerill, whose literary advice was ever at her disposal even when he was most occupied, she sold the magazine rights in the story to the Lippincotts on the 8th of November.

To the day of her death she was never weary of singing the hymn of Col. Cockerill's kindness to her. There is no doubt that this terrible disappointment would have proved more speedily fatal had it not been for his brave words of encouragement and unremitting efforts to repair her loss. It was my privilege to defend her when she was alive from more than one Grub-street attack, and I do not propose to allow anyone to grind their axes over her grave with any perversion of the story of her relations with *The World*. The editor does not exist who was her enemy; but Col. Cockerill was one of the editors whom she felt proud to number among her personal friends.

EVERETT HOUSE, N. Y. C., 7TH FEB., 1889.

The story of Selina Dolaro's life is told.

> "Spring will return and woods grow green
> From shore to shore,
> But she, unseeing and unseen,
> Returns no more!"

Thus wrote William Winter on the death of Ada Clare, and his poem might have served as Selina Dolaro's Epitaph. The story of her last sickness and death is told in the preceding "*Memoriam*." At the request of some of her friends I append a set of couplets published in Alfred Trumble's paper, *Today*:

# TO HIS DOG.

Well, well, old doggie? You wag your tail, and if you could
    only talk,
You'd say with your tongue what you say with your eyes—that
    you want to go out for a walk.
You know not (how could you?) the hand that you loved, that
    you warmed with your soft, moist breath,
Will never caress you as once it did, for it's quiet and cold in
    death.

You can't make out why I don't talk back, as you climb up on
    to my bed,
And don't stretch out my hand to stroke you, and pat your
    woolly head.
There's a world of sympathy, dog-like and mute, that shines
    from your purple eyes,
But you don't understand (how can you, doggie?) that anyone
    ever dies.

You'll want for a time to go to her house (you could find your
    way alone),
And wag your tail and whinny to her, and ask her to give you
    a bone.
But that's all over, those days will never come back for you or
    for me,
Those days that we spent all together, boy, in the summer-time
    by the sea.

*You* surely remember those days, old dog, how she scolded you
    when you leapt
To greet her each morn with your muddy feet, from her door-
    mat where you slept?
How she lay in her hammock with you underneath, never
    lonely, and knew no fear
When I was away, for you guarded her well, and let not a soul
    come near.

But you and I have the memory, boy, of the love that to us she
    gave,
And we shall prize it more dearly now that they've laid her in
    her grave.
You didn't see her, but *I* did, doggie, she lay so marvellous fair,
With lilies strewn on her hands and feet and framing her
    bronze-gold hair.
You didn't see when she went away, oh! so far away, and alack!
She's gone where perhaps we may follow her, doggie, but she
    —will never come back.

EDWARD HERON-ALLEN,

NEW YORK CITY, MARCH, 1889.

# CHAPTER I.

"I wonder why we do this," observed Sir Reginald to his companion, as they turned for the twentieth time that morning at Hyde Park corner, and set their faces for the Westward traverse of Rotten Row. "It has always struck me that it would be an interesting thing to find out who was the first man who ever 'did the Row' in the morning."

"I neither know nor care," returned his friend, a man considerably older than Sir Reginald Faithorne; a man who might, in fact, have been his father. "I neither know nor care; and as it amuses me afresh every day, I do not choose to analyze the subject further."

"Egad! Mr. Wurmsley, I congratulate you. What you can see amusing in pacing half a hundred times up and down a broiling walk, like geese training for *pâté de foie gras*, I cannot see. One sees the same men and women, and one cuts the same men and women and is cut by the same men and women, day after day. It is enough to make one commit suicide—social suicide, at any rate. Why, I have sympathized often enough with the Frenchman who shot himself because he was dead tired of constantly buttoning and unbuttoning. I wonder some Englishman does not take Prussic acid as a protest against this everlasting walking up and down."

"Well," replied the older man who had been addressed as Wurmsley, "I don't agree with you. Every woman that we know becomes interesting anew to me, every time she puts on a fresh frock; and every man becomes the same every time he walks with a new woman. Look there, for instance," continued he, stopping at the railings as he and his companion raised their hats to the occupants of a barouche which passed at the moment; "look at Ethel Marsden, for instance. What a bewitching bonnet!"

Sir Reginald Faithorne made no reply.

"Why, Faithorne," said his friend, "this apathy is strange, coming from one whom they credit with being so stanch a friend of the fair Ethel," and an imbecile smile spread itself over the middle-aged features.

"I was not looking at Ethel," returned Faithorne, at last, "but at the companion, to whom, I presume, the barouche belongs. I never saw anything so lovely in my life. Just at this moment I feel as if I would give an empire of liabilities, for an introduction; though as she is under the wing of the charming Thello, I do not suppose it would be a very hard end to accomplish."

Whilst he spoke, Mr. Wurmsley had been showing visible signs of impatience, and at last he broke forth, in a tone laden with all the dignity he could command at a moment's notice, "I think it as well to inform you, Sir Reginald, that that is my daughter."

"Your daughter?"

"Yes, my daughter, Mrs. Warburton;" and a moment later the old gentleman sought a hiatus in the stream of passing carriages, and made his escape by the Albert Gate entrance.

"By Jove!" said Sir Reginald, to himself, as he looked after the retreating figure. "I wonder whether old Worms was in earnest." A few moments later he was accosted by a club acquaintance to whom he remarked,

"Did you see Thello Marsden, driving past just now?"

"Well, rather," replied his friend. "I should like to see Thello in the Park, *not* aggressively visible to the naked eye."

"Well, who was the woman with her?"

"I do not know her myself," was the reply, "but Gray, who knows her, said that it was old Wurmsley's daughter, a Mrs. Warburton."

"Dear me," replied Sir Reginald, "you don't say so. Where has she been all this time that we have not seen her before?"

"With Warburton, I presume."

"Oh!" ejaculated Sir Reginald. "And who the deuce is Warburton, when he's at home?"

"My dear fellow," said his friend, suavely, laying his hand on the baronet's arm, "all that I know of Warburton and all that I care to know, is this: Mr. Warburton is a man who allows his wife to drive in the Park in a barouche with Thello Marsden."

Sir Reginald Faithorne was silent for a few moments. Then, turning abruptly to his friend, he said, "Well, good-bye, I must leave you now."

"Where are you off to?" said the gentleman addressed.

"I am going down to the club for an hour or so, and then I am going to call on Thello Marsden."

"All right—good by! and good luck."

## CHAPTER II.

Ethel, or as she was more familiarly called, "Thello" Marsden, was a type of woman not uncommon, but always surprising— like some peculiar forms of marine vegetation, not however that the fair Thello was ever marine in her capacity of giving credence to the histories of her friends, or that she was ever at sea in her calculations.

Thello Marsden lived in Hans Place; in a tiny house, it is true, but a charmingly comfortable one withal. She seldom entertained, but when she did so, it was with a perfection and a science which made her dinners the talk of the town. Thello's dinner parties consisted invariably of herself and seven guests, two of whom were women and five men.

"You see," she used to say, "when you get five men together, two of them are bound to want to talk to each other about something, whilst the other three attend to the women; and then a woman can keep up a conversation and listen to that of another at the same time, with the greatest ease. But a woman *cannot* converse herself and take in the remarks of two other women at the same time; so that my dinner parties are politically and geographically, perfect."

Thello Marsden never received in state, but was at home on Saturdays, and on Saturdays the little house in Hans Place became an Eveless Eden of the best known and most sought after Adams in town; whilst to be asked to call upon Thello on Sunday, meant that you were anything from a leading socialist to a cabinet minister. Thello Marsden spoke five languages with perfect correctness; she played the piano in a manner that left one speechless, and before she became Thello Marsden a maiden aunt is reported to have said that when Thello sang, it was neither more nor less than an indecent orgie of sound. However, Thello seldom either played or sang to her visitors, and used her music rather as a lethal than as a soothing accomplishment. For if she invited a man to her house for the purpose of entertaining him with music, she would perform, clad in the severest black, her mass of red hair parted severely but becomingly down the middle, her face white, and her eyes black. It is reported that no man between the ages of five and twenty and fifty had ever withstood this combination of science and art.

Thello Marsden wore the most weird and bewitching toilettes. What jewellery she wore—which was little—was of a quality that would make a stockbroker's hair stand on end. It may be remarked in conclusion that Max Marsden, her whilome spouse, had died five years before, leaving her a net income of three hundred and fifty pounds a year.

On the afternoon when my story opens, Thello lay in a happy, indolent attitude, in a huge lounge, that occupied about three-fourths of her microscopic drawing-room. The lounge was covered with a maroon plush; Thello was covered with old-gold plush and coffee colored lace. In the pauses of her conversation, she was idly smoking a cigarette, and her bronze-stockinged feet, in their gold brocaded shoes, were fidgeting with a cushion upon which she had thrown them. Altogether the artistic effect was such that even Sir Reginald Faithorne, who sat in a low armchair in front of her, was impressed with a sense of the harmonious whole, and remarked with an airy irresponsibility, due, doubtless, to his Irish descent, "By Jove! Thello, if I had not seen Mrs. Warburton in the park with you this morning, I should not know that she existed, looking at you here."

"So Mrs. Warburton is your latest and best, *mon beau sabreur,* known only by sight, but to anticipation dear," and Thello gave the cushion at her feet a little mischievous kick, as she grinned and showed a double rank of tiny white teeth to her listener.

"Now, don't chaff, Thello," said Sir Reginald. "I want to know something about this beautiful young creature whom you have taken under your protecting wing. Who is she?"

Thello Marsden paused before she spoke. Then she said, "Edith Warburton is the wife—I might say, aggressively the wife—of Philip Warburton, of St. Nicholas Lane, in the City. He is a stockbroker, and an enormously clever one to boot. I am cultivating his wife because I want to know him; that is to say, to know him sufficiently to get him to help me in some of my investments. You know I have to be very careful about such matters, so as to eke out my three hundred and fifty a year."

"Oh, ah, yes, of course," said Sir Reginald; "that goes without saying. You know it is quite amazing the way you do it." He did not allow a single muscle of his face to twitch, as he made the remark, but went on in the same tone. "When you desire to attach a man to your body-guard, you do not generally do it through his wife, Thello. What is the meaning of this new departure?"

"The meaning of this," replied the woman, "is very simple, and it lies in my opening remark, namely, that Edith is aggressively the wife of Philip Warburton, and Philip Warburton has only one idea in the world, beyond stocks, and that is his wife."

"Oh!"

"So you see," pursued Ethel, "you have rather a hard task in front of you."

"A hard task? What do you mean?" enquired Sir Reginald.

"Nothing at all," replied the woman. "By the way," she continued, as if changing the subject, "Mrs. Warburton asked me this morning to run down and see a new place that her husband has bought at Wimbledon. What do you think of taking me down there tomorrow afternoon? We will take Clare Beaufoy to play propriety, and we will go early, so as to catch the dragon away in the city."

"Tomorrow," replied Sir Reginald, as if searching his memory for previous engagements. "I think I have tomorrow free, in which case, if I can be of any service to you, pray command me."

Thello burst into a silvery laugh. "You dear old man," she said. "What a fraud you are!"

At that moment a servant entered the room, bearing an envelope on a tray. "The messenger waits," said the grave domestic, and with a whispered, "Excuse me," Thello opened the missive.

"Dear me," she said. "This is the most inconsiderate thing I ever knew Veloutine to do. She seems to think that she has only to write out bills for me to pay them. However, I suppose, like all unpleasant duties, it must be gone through. Charles," turning to the domestic, "give me my check-book, it is on the writing-table; and my stylograph," and lying back among the cushions, Thello Marsden drew a check and handed it with the bill to the servant who left the room. A moment later he reappeared.

"The messenger says, ma'am, that Madame Veloutine would be much obliged if you would let her have the amount in notes, as it is after banking hours, and she has a heavy bill to meet this afternoon."

"How absurd," began Thello, but she was interrupted by Sir Reginald, who observed,

"Perhaps I can change your check, how much is it?"

"Three hundred," said Thello.

"Well, it happens I have got that," said Sir Reginald, "in view of a little game we are to have tonight at the club. However, I had as soon spend my money on one little game as on another. Give me your check, and here are the notes."

"Thanks, Rex," said Thello, as the servant left the room. "You are sure it won't inconvenience you until tomorrow?"

"Not in the least," was the reply. "I am charmed to be of any assistance, even temporarily." A few moments later, after completing their arrangements for the morrow, he left her alone.

As he stepped out upon the pavement, Sir Reginald Faithorne threw back his head and laughed long and loud. "She is incomparable," said he to himself, as he took the check from his pocket and tore it into little pieces. "London and Westminster Bank," ejaculated he, as the last pieces fluttered over the railings among the shrubbery. "I wonder if she ever had an account there. If I were the villain in a book I should keep this to brandish it over her head at the right moment, and should then probably discover that she had dated it by accident ten years ago when she really *had* a sovereign there." And taking up the laugh again, where he had dropped it, Sir Reginald Faithorne jumped into a passing cab and was driven back to the Raleigh Club.

## CHAPTER III.

Wimbledon Lodge was, perhaps, the most beautiful of the many beautiful houses that would look out over Wimbledon Common, were it not for the bank of high elms that screens them from the road.

Wimbledon Lodge stood in some eight or ten acres of ground. About two acres were laid out as flower gardens; another two as labyrinthine shrubberies and the rest was as nearly wild as possible. Some artistic masterpieces of American sculpture, such as Bates, Elwell or St. Gaudens might have cut later, were disposed here and there among the shrubs, and a terrace of little cascades led from the drawing-room windows into this suburban paradise. Everything that art could do to assist nature, had been done under the watchful eye of Philip Warburton, to make his wife's house a casket worthy of the jewel it was to contain.

The jewel had only deposited herself in the casket three weeks previously, and on the afternoon of which I write, her father, Mr. Botolph Wurmsley, and his second daughter, Marion, were paying their first visit to the apparently enviable Mrs. Warburton. The chatelaine of this retreat was still putting the finishing touches to her afternoon toilette, when the two descended the steps into the garden.

"A very pretty place," the old gentleman was saying. "A very pretty place, indeed. Ah, my dear Marion, your sister, Edith, has made a most excellent marriage. Philip Warburton is a man of a thousand—a splendid fellow, and quite a gentleman. A little old, perhaps, but then she needs the care of a *man*."

"Old!" interrupted Marion. "My dear papa, what are you talking about? Phil is quite young."

"I mean," returned her father, "old in manner, not in years. The fact is, he has given so much time to business, and is so steady and respectable, that he seems almost to belong to a past age. His very language is old-fashioned, and if he has a fault, it is that he is too serious."

"I am sure," broke in the girl, impetuously, "Philip has *no* faults!"

"Well, well," returned the old gentleman, "faults would be too strong an expression, and I have every reason to be satisfied with Edith's marriage. Now, if you were to become Lady Something-or-other——"

"Lady Something-or-other, indeed!" said Marion. "What an old match-maker you are; and who is Lord Something-or-other to be?"

"Oh," returned her father, "my lord has not arrived yet, but with the chances which Philip's wealth give you, my greatest wish may yet be gratified."

"Ah," said Marion, "you do love a title, don't you, father?"

"Marion," replied Wurmsley *père*, sententiously, "a father's ambition is not a fit subject of ridicule."

They had reached the bottom of the steps, as Marion replied, "You dear old thing! I was not laughing at you, but you made me think of Aunt Jane. She said, the other day, 'Ah, Dora made a good marriage as far as money is concerned, but what is money? Can money buy ruins?' and I said, 'I don't know, aunt, but it might be useful to repair them,' and she was so horrified that she nearly sat on her last new bonnet, and positively gasped as she said, 'There spoke your father, the commoner. Both you and Dora inherit much of my beauty, and should have made great successes in the society of which I am a member. But Dora married *wealth*,'—she said 'wealth' as if it were slightly improper,— 'and it now remains for you to bring a title into the family.'" The girl interrupted herself with a light laugh, as she continued, "As if Philip were not better than all the titles in the world. There," added she, as she drew her father's head down by his whiskers and kissed him, "I am going to run away from you now, to look for Edith. Why, goodness me! there is Philip. Where is Edith, Philip?—All right I am going to find her," and the girl ran away as Philip Warburton descended the terrace steps.

Philip Warburton was a man of five and thirty, and everything about him bespoke the keen man of business. A clear-cut face, smooth shaved and lit by keen, black eyes; the hair, worn rather short, was slightly tinged with gray, and, unlike the average man in his own country house, he was buttoned up in the most irreproachable of frock coats.

"I am glad to see you at our new house," said he as he shook his father-in-law's hand. "How do you like as much as you have seen of it?"

"It is perfectly delightful," returned Wurmsley. "I had no idea it was such a big place. But don't you find it a little fatiguing going to and from London every day, eh?"

"No," replied Warburton, "not enough to matter. Edith wanted to come into the country, and truth to tell, I was not sorry to get her away from some of her friends who are in too good society to be good either for her or for me. She does not seem to be in such good spirits lately."

The two men seated themselves on a rustic bench, as the younger continued, "She was most enthusiastic when she came here, but her enthusiasm seems to have dropped off. I wish you would find out for me if there is any wish, whim or caprice that she may hesitate to let me know. She said something about owning some property, the other day, which made me think it might amuse her to play chatelaine, so I have made over to her this place, and I mean to give her the title deeds as her birthday present today. Do you think she will be pleased?"

"My dear Warburton," was the reply, "you indulge her caprices too much. You spoil her."

"I hope not," returned Warburton, gravely. "If she can, one day, look back and recall no act or thought of mine, in which she was not all beloved, she may learn to value my worship as I pray she may. Sometimes I think I was wrong to marry her, so young, but I can take care of her—I think I can take care of her."

"Dear me," said Mr. Wurmsley, rising, "do you know I had entirely forgotten that it was her birthday. It was most inconsiderate of Edith not to have reminded me of it. I am going straight back to London to get her something."

"But you will see her first," said Warburton.

"Not for worlds," answered his father-in-law. "I will be back in time for dinner. I do not want her to know I had forgotten it. But I must see Marion before I go."

"Won't you go and see the new stables I have just built?" said Warburton.

"Yes," replied the old gentleman. "Send Marion to me there. I want to see her alone. Where are they?"

"Go straight down that path," directed his son-in-law, "and you will arrive there in time, and you can order the carriage for yourself."

The old gentleman started off as Warburton turned to the house. As he did so, he caught sight of Marion Wurmsley at the drawing room window. "Your father wants to speak to you, at the stables," called he. "Go to him there. I am going to look after Edith's birthday present. The lawyer must be here by this time; don't say anything to her about our surprise. I would not give up the pleasure of today for anything."

He entered the house as Marion tripped down the steps and disappeared in the direction which her father had taken.

"What a great, splendid nature he has," said she to herself as she went. "How happy Edith must be."

As she said these words, the object of her reflections appeared at the window leading out upon the terrace, and Mrs. Warburton emerged to join her sister. Arrived at the bottom of the steps she threw herself into the bench which Mr. Wurmsley and her husband had just vacated, and stretching herself into an attitude of languid discontent, she exclaimed, as if in answer to her sister's thought,

"Oh, how wretched I am!"

The two sisters as we see them together on this sunny afternoon, present a striking contrast; Marion Wurmsley *petite*, and essentially "cosey-looking," save for the mass of golden curls which spiritualized her appearance; Edith Warburton, on the other hand, stately and tall; of a figure such as French painters love to idealize in their work, with finely modelled hands and feet, her raven black hair carried straight off her high, white forehead, and a pair of deep, grave eyes, enhancing the severity with which the nose and chin were cut, a severity, tempered, however, by the delicate chiselling of her lips.

"How wretched I am!" exclaimed this royal-looking creature, as she threw herself upon the bench, and her sister Marion stood listening to her, as if petrified with amazement.

"Wretched!" she echoed. "Wretched! you of all women in the world? Only two years married, to a perfectly charming man, a man enormously rich, who has but one wish in life, and that to anticipate yours! What is there that you can possibly want?"

"I don't know," replied Mrs. Warburton, "I am bored to death, that is all. I am filled with indistinct, vague wishes; but when they shape themselves I find nothing that I do not possess or that my own husband would not give me, so I have come to the conclusion that I have a deeply-rooted disease, which for want of a better name we will call 'boredom.'"

"It appears to me," said Marion, gravely, "that all this discontent is very sudden. You were not like this a few months ago, and I cannot see what can have given you such ideas." The girl had dropped into a chair as she spoke, and sat with her great, blue eyes fixed upon her sister's gloomy face.

"All the women I see," said Edith, looking at the ground before her, "know how to arrange their lives so that they shall be their own mistresses. Clare Beaufoy, and Ethel Marsden, for instance, who are my best friends, and perfectly devoted to me."

"Well," said Marion, "I think we women have rather the best of the bargain. We not only are the better half, but we have a better half, and all we have to do is to open our mouths and shut our eyes, and allow ourselves to be made happy."

"Nonsense," said Edith. "These are but the dreams of a child, that you can never realize."

"Why?" queried Marion. "It seems quite possible to me—and I am just about to try its possibilities."

"How?"

"Do you remember," said the little girl, edging her chair closer to her sister, "a great friend of Philip's, a Captain——"

"Denalguez? A Spaniard, or looked like one—a dreary looking creature, if I remember rightly."

"But," said Marion, "he was so wretched then, and though he appeared to hate every one, he seemed to like me——"

"And that flattered you, of course," put in Edith.

"It made me very happy."

"He made love to you?"

"Not one word of love was spoken between us," replied Marion thoughtfully. "Yet I think we understood each other, for when he went to Russia he said, 'Will you wait three years, and answer me a question then, that I cannot ask you now?' and I am sure I know what he meant."

"Have you heard from him since?" said Edith, aroused to some show of interest by her sister's recital.

"Of course," said Marion, a trifle nervously, "without asking any questions I have heard scraps of news about him. Some mines or something he had in Russia have turned out well. You know he is in the embassy at St. Petersburg. A big letter, bearing the St. Petersburg post-mark came yesterday for father. He has not spoken to me about it yet, but I am certain it asks after me."

"What makes you so sure?" said Edith.

"Don't you see," returned her sister, "it only wants six months to complete the three years he asked me to wait?"

"And you would marry Captain Denalguez?" said Edith.

"With all my heart," replied her sister, as she rose and turned towards the house.

"Then Heaven defend you!" said the elder, rising too. "If you only knew what marriage meant! Hush!—here's my husband. You see one never has a moment to one's self." Philip Warburton had appeared at the window as she spoke.

"It is good of you, Marion, to come and stay a few days with us," he said to his sister-in-law. "Edith, are you still angry with me? She was *so* cross this morning," explained he to Marion.

"So I supposed," answered Marion, "but I hope it is all over now."

"Never," said Mrs. Warburton, emphatically.

"Never is a long day," said Philip Warburton. "My only crime, as far as I can make it out, is to have brought you into the country, which is exactly what you asked me to do till I have done it."

"I did want to come into the country," said Edith, peevishly, "but not alone."

"And I," said Philip, with a smile on his lips, but pained look in his eyes, "am I nobody to you?"

"Oh, what nonsense!" said Edith. "A husband and wife are one, and I hate being alone."

Philip Warburton's face took on a harder expression as he answered, "An argument well taught, and well learned, but which I do not think it necessary for me to notice."

"A husband's tyranny, to which I shall certainly not submit," said Edith in imitation of the same tone.

"Tyranny!" remonstrated the man. "Give me one instance, and I will never offend again."

"A thousand, if necessary."

"Well?"

At this point Edith Warburton broke down.

"Oh, how miserable I am!" she sobbed. And Marion, drawing close to her, slipped her arm around her waist.

"Ah, ah," said her husband, rising with something like impatience in his tone and gesture, "at last we get to something definite. Edith, for some time you have been receiving a number of people of whom I disapprove entirely. A woman is never lost through herself, but through the influence of the so-called society friends who surround her. Their bad example is the current which hurls her into the maelstrom of ruin and degradation. You follow these friends who belong to this modern pest of society, 'the advertised Beauties', this imitation of womankind bereft of its womanhood. But I am responsible for your honor, which belongs to me. I must keep you from falling into the abyss which threatens you—with gentleness if you will, with force if you compel me. Is not this my crime? This," continued he, turning to Marion, "is the reason she is angry with me?" And then laying his hand on his wife's shoulder, he said, "Darling, you know it pains me to have to speak to you so. I hate to give you any annoyance, but," and his face hardened again, "I have made up my mind."

"Oh," said Edith, looking up, "you have? You have made up your mind?"

"Yes," said Mr. Philip Warburton, "as I am obliged to be away a great deal, I do not wish your friends—you know the ladies I allude to without my having to mention their names—to visit you, except by my invitation."

"And you would never invite them."

"Quite true. Some of them are only weak, silly women, they are the least dangerous, but the others are altogether impossible—Mrs. Marsden for instance."

"But her husband was in a very good position," expostulated Edith, "and did business with you."

"Yes," said Warburton, "and a very good sort of a business man he was. One whom I should like to see every day in my office or his. But that does not necessitate your seeing his wife, of whom I disapprove. Be reasonable, Edith. As for Mrs. Beaufoy, your other friend, I *forbid* you to receive her."

"Forbid me?"

"Yes, and one day you will thank me for it. Be sure, dear, I will repay your sacrifice."

"I don't want anything," said Edith, snappishly.

"But you will do as I ask, won't you, Edith?" said Philip Warburton, with something like pleading in his voice. "You know that I will indulge your caprice to any extent, but do not go any further. Marion, I want to speak to you a moment."

"Why, of course," said Marion, going to him. And Edith, who had risen, and was idly tearing up a flower and throwing it into the cascade, piece by piece, said in a scornful tone of voice,

"More conspiring against me, I suppose."

"Probably," replied her husband, "but my accomplice should reassure you." He took her hand, and was raising it to his lips when she drew it away pettishly. Philip Warburton sighed, as he took his eyes from those of his wife, and then beckoning Marion, he disappeared into the house.

Edith turned and sauntered slowly down the middle of the lawn. "And am I to submit to such tyranny?" she said to herself. "Am I to obey him, when all the women I know *command* their husbands? Well, hardly. It is not likely, and it is not possible. I never can go on like this, and one way or another, there must be an end to it. Good gracious!" She stopped at the end of the lawn as an unexpected vision rose before her, apparently from the depths of the shrubbery.

## CHAPTER IV.

"How are you? I supposed I should find you meditating on your sins. How are you, hermit?" said a voice, and Ethel Marsden, for it was she, slipped her arm around Edith Warburton's waist and kissed her with an effusion which would have struck an onlooker as almost genuine.

"Just fancy your coming such a long way to see me!" said Edith. "It is very good of you."

"Oh, it is only about five miles," replied the adorable Thello, who, clad in the whitest and filmiest of summer frocks, was looking her very best. "And as you would not come to me, I had to come to you. It is a case of Mahomet with you, and as no true believer travels without his carpet, I have brought mine—my carpet-baronet. Where are you, carpet?" she concluded, raising her voice.

"What do you mean?" said Edith.

"Why, Rex—or I should say, Sir Reginald Faithorne," answered Thello. "He is my carpet-knight—or carpet-baronet. I suppose he is seeing after the horses. That is why we came in by the stable entrance. One of them fell at an awkward turn just before we reached your gates."

"No injury, I hope," commented Edith.

"No, nothing serious," replied Thello, "just enough to tell one that one has a heart, by setting it jumping a little."

"And who is Sir Reginald Faithorne?" said Edith, as they reached one of the benches in the shrubbery and sat down.

"A delightful youth," replied Thello, "of the Crœsus persuasion. Why, what is the matter with you, have you been crying?"

"Oh, Thello," said Edith, her eyes beginning to sparkle again, "I am in such trouble."

"What is the cause?" said the new arrival.

"You ask me that?"

"Oh, I see—your husband, of course."

"I want you to set me right," said Edith, leaning forward, and laying one hand on her friend's knee as she spoke, looking her earnestly in the eyes. "I want you to set me right. You know so much more than I do about the world; you seem to have such fun, and you always do as you please. If I try to assert myself I get sat upon and snubbed. You always tell me that I am dowdy and out of fashion. Your husband always allowed you to do as you liked—mine bullies me. How did you manage to get yours into such wonderful order? You say all women to be in the fashion should have from one to half a dozen admirers. I don't see how you get men to waste their time over you; but then I am so heavy, I never did know how to flirt, and if a man were to say he loved me, I should be dreadfully sorry for him. You, I suppose, would not care a bit. You don't pity the wretched creature you have encouraged."

"Baby," interrupted Thello, with a bewitching little laugh, which showed her pretty teeth, and the tip of her tongue, "do you suppose a man of the Rex Faithorne type deserves pity? Amusing as the game of flirtation is, it is one of 'kill who can.' Choose your fate, my dear. For my part, I prefer to kill. Take things easier. Faithorne is a delightful person, has loads of money, which he spends and lends with equal freedom. I don't know how I should have managed Veloutine's last bill if he had not come to the rescue."

Edith Warburton clapped her hands to her ears. "Oh, Thello," she said, "you do say the most dreadful things. If a stranger were to hear you, what would he think? You must not talk so wildly. The idea of your taking money——"

"Well, I pay, of course—when I can."

"You are so clever," pursued Edith, dismissing the problem of Thello's financial arrangements. "You might help me so much. Won't you?"

"My dear child," replied Mrs. Marsden, "I never prevent any-one's seeing what I do, or how I do it, but as to advice, I never give it."

"Well, I think you might in this instance," said Edith.

"No," replied the other, "my principle is fixed. Besides, what is the good of talking sense to a child."

"What do you mean by 'a child'?" asked Edith indignantly.

"Exactly what I say," retorted Ethel. "You are just what you were when you left school."

"Nonsense," exclaimed Edith.

"Not a bit of it," returned Ethel. "You are just a child from top to toe, only that all your fun is lost, your name is changed, and you have a new master, who substitutes slavery and solitude for grammar and geography."

"Well," said Edith, getting a trifle exasperated, "how can I re-lieve myself from my servitude, which will be harder to be borne than ever, now that he wants me to give up my friends."

"Give up your friends!" echoed the confidante. "You are not serious, surely?"

"But I am, perfectly," returned the chatelaine of Wimbledon Lodge. "He has begged me not to see you again, and has forbid-den me to receive Clare."

"Oh," said Ethel, grinning again. "He has only begged you not to see me. What a charming distinction. It is one for which I am most grateful. I hope you laugh at him."

"I don't dare."

"She don't dare! Delicious. If that is the case, I had better go," and Thello made a pretence of rising.

"You are angry at my weakness?"

"Oh, no," said the woman, "I think it charming. Such a good story is a positive boon. How lucky it is that Clare came with me."

"Oh, what *shall* I do?" said Edith.

"Choose for yourself, my dear," returned her mentor. "Obey your old-fashioned husband and 'chronicle small beer,' as they say, or take your proper position, and be your own mistress. Rex Faithorne can make you the envy of Mayfair. He is the most amusing man you ever knew. A type—his reputation is so well known that his name alone is enough. A pretty woman does not exist until she is a friend of Faithorne's. She is the chrysalis and Faithorne is the sun that warms it into the butterfly. Interesting, isn't he? He is a tremendous adorer of yours."

"Of mine," echoed Edith, her eyes dilating in astonishment.

"Yes," pursued Ethel Marsden, in a matter-of-fact tone, "he is always running after you, trying to get presented, and as he has hitherto failed, in sheer desperation he pursues me and Clare and adores us both, because we are your friends. Is not that devotion with a vengeance?"

"I will not receive him," said Edith, rising. "It is not right, and now after what you tell me of him, I am determined that I will not."

"*You* determined?" said Thello, with a little mischievous laugh, "not a bit. It is only an indirect way of obeying your husband's orders."

"You know better," said Edith indignantly.

"What rubbish!" said her friend. "I know you better than you know yourself. However, now is your chance to show your wifely submission, for here come Clare and Sir Reginald."

As she spoke, the two persons she had named, turned the corner, into the alley, at the end of which Thello and Edith found themselves.

"Delightful, charming," Clare Beaufoy was saying to her companion. "Is it not a lovely place?"

"Lovely," replied he with conviction, his eyes fixed upon Edith as she stood a few paces from him with Ethel Marsden.

"Let me present Sir Reginald Faithorne," said the latter. "He has given me no peace until I brought him."

"It is very good of you," said Edith, a trifle ceremoniously "to come so far simply to say 'How do you do?'"

"Far," exclaimed Faithorne, "it is only a charming drive."

"I cannot tell you all the pretty things that Ethel has been saying of you, Sir Reginald," said Edith, as the quartette turned towards the house. And then turning to Ethel she whispered, "I will tell him that you called him a hearth-rug—or a mat—which was it?"

"What do you say to our unexpected visit?" said Clare.

"Why, it is perfectly delightful," answered Edith, a troubled shade crossing her face as she thought of the coming explanation with Philip Warburton.

"It is delightful, indeed," said Sir Reginald. "It has brought back all Mrs. Marsden's good temper."

"Why, has she been annoyed?" said Edith.

"Very much," replied the man. "When I called on her this morning she had just seen by the papers that a very important appointment had been given to a man she detests, a Captain Denalguez."

"Of the embassy of St. Petersburg?" said Edith turning to him.

"You know him?" said Ethel, opening her purple eyes wide, as she turned to her hostess.

"Oh, yes," said Edith, "he is in love with my sister. I speak, of course, in confidence."

"You have the advantage of me," said Thello significantly. "I do not know the gentleman personally."

"No," said Faithorne thoughtfully, "I believe it was a brother of his who had the honor of being your friend."

"That is enough!" said Ethel rapidly to the baronet.

"Why," remonstrated he, "I never disguise my hate or my love, and I should like to believe that you were as frank. You may just as well admit that Captain Denalguez and you are mortal enemies."

"You have really never seen him?" said Clare Beaufoy to her friend.

"Never," replied Thello laconically.

"Gracious," said the lively Clare. "A man you have never seen is your enemy? This is most interesting. Fancy being able to hate in this hot weather! How charmingly young!"

"And upon my honor" put in Faithorne, "I pity him, for Madame is merciless. She is really a most refreshing hater. She brings back a perfume of the Borgias, or of any other bygone criminal epoch."

"Are you trying to irritate me, Faithorne?" said Ethel, a dangerous light coming into her eyes.

"On the contrary," replied he, "I am complimenting you."

"Well," said Clare, "I am glad you told us."

"You know," said Faithorne, coolly, "one must have some coloring to distinguish one from the idiots of the world."

During the above conversation they had reached the terrace in front of the house, and as they turned at the corner of the walk, they were met by Marion, who was running out, but who stopped short as she saw the group before her.

"Hush! be careful," said Edith, hastily. "My sister Marion, allow me to present to you Sir Reginald Faithorne."

Marion bowed stiffly to the man, and shook hands with the two women. Then turning to Edith, she said, "Come quickly. I have just seen in your room a large, legal-looking envelope addressed to you in Philip's hand. It has a sort of birthday appearance."

"Your birthday?" said Thello gayly. "We did not know it."

"Shall I bring it here?" queried Marion.

"No," said Edith. "I will go myself, but I cannot leave——"

"Oh, I will look after Mrs. Marsden," put in Marion.

"All right," answered Mrs. Warburton; "I will be back in a minute."

"I want to write a note," said Clara Beaufoy to Edith. "May I go with you?"

"And I want to smoke a cigarette," said Sir Reginald. "May I sit at the top of the steps?"

"Why, of course," said Edith, as she went into the house with Mrs. Beaufoy, and Ethel Marsden seated herself with Marion.

Faithorne gained the top of the steps and threw himself into a rocking chair. He had placed himself so that he could hear every word that Mrs. Marsden said, and watch the effect upon her auditor, whom he examined carefully from head to foot.

"A very nice family, this," said he to himself as he lighted his cigarette.

"I am so glad, Miss Wurmsley," began Thello Marsden, "to have an opportunity of thanking you for your contribution to my last charity."

"Don't mention it, I beg," returned the child. "It is a real pleasure to assist anyone so devoted to good works as you are."

"Well," replied Ethel thoughtfully, "this charity is at least deserving, I can vouch for it. A poor, young girl, an orphan—betrayed."

"Hullo!" said Faithorne to himself at the top of the steps. "What is *her* little game?"

"In fact, worse," continued Ethel, raising her liquid, purple eyes to Marion's. "Abandoned. I will not say by whom, though I know his name. It would not matter much, for he is in Russia, now."

"In Russia, did you say?" said Marion, leaning forward.

"Yes," replied Ethel, with apparent unconcern, as she narrowly watched the effect of her words. "He is in a very good position, and Denalguez could certainly have afforded——"

"Denalguez——" echoed Marion, rising.

"What, did I mention his name?" said Ethel with a tone of surprise. "I did not intend to, but it is quite in confidence; for the young girl is really of excellent family. You shall judge for yourself——"

"No, Mrs. Marsden," said Marion, growing deadly pale, "it is useless."

"Besides," continued Ethel, mercilessly, "it may be his intention to come back and marry her. We must not despair. Why, what is the matter? You are ill."

"No, nothing," said Marion, "only it is rather cold, with the water falling here—a sudden chill. Excuse me, I will be back directly," and she staggered rather than walked off in the direction of the shrubbery.

Sir Reginald Faithorne arose from his rocking-chair and throwing his cigarette into the fountain-basin to the unconcealed disgust of half a dozen gold-fish that rose eagerly to inspect it, he walked down the steps and planted himself before Mrs. Marsden.

"I will make a bet with you," said he.

"Oh! what about?"

"That there is not one word of truth in all that you have been saying."

"Indeed! what makes you think so?"

"Firstly, because you have said it. Anyhow, it is a fairly good invention to ruin Denalguez in the estimation of his *fiancée*, but take care, if you ever give me cause, I will justify him."

"You threaten me?"

"No, I only warn you. One must always be fully armed where you are concerned."

"Oh!" Thello looked into her companion's eyes, as it to measure the full scope of his intentions; then she said, "Take me across the lawn. I want to see some more of this place."

Meanwhile Marion had reached the stables where she found her father waiting for her. "How dreadful," she had been repeating dully to herself. "How dreadful! I wonder why I should be so punished."

"Well, there you are at last," said Mr. Wurmsley. "You would not have kept me waiting so long if you had known what I wanted to say to you. Come here." He had seated himself upon a broad stone just inside the carriage gates, and now he drew her to him.

"You are not looking very cheerful," said he, glancing at her, "but we will see what difference my news makes to you. You know I received a letter from Captain Denalguez?—Well, well, don't you want to know what he says? He asks me to give you to him." The girl turned her head and furtively wiped away a tear.

"What?—silent?" said the old gentleman. "Yes, I suppose I shall have to lose you, for 'silence gives consent.'"

"You are mistaken," said Marion, in a broken voice. "Please reply that I refuse."

"What," said Mr. Wurmsely, "you refuse? But from his letter he seemed to feel confident of you. Am I to give him no reason?"

"None," said the girl, "only that I refuse. No one knows of this offer and you must promise me not to speak of it."

"Do you know he has come here for his answer? He was in the stables with me, and he is waiting in the wild-garden."

"I will not see him," said Marion hurriedly. "Promise not to let him find me. I do not wish it. You will tell him I do not wish to see him," and before her father could add another word she ran away, down the path by which she had come.

"What extraordinary creatures girls are," said the ex-merchant to himself as he disappeared in turn, in the direction which he had desired his daughter in vain to take. "I would have sworn she cared for him, but I suppose I must go and do the unpleasant thing, and make myself unpopular. Oh, how inconsiderate people are!—especially girls."

## CHAPTER V.

Meanwhile, Edith Warburton had walked into the house, at her sister's suggestion, saying as she went, "Ethel is right. I will take her advice. I *will* receive my friends, I will be my own mistress in my own house, and they *shall* stay to dinner. Once the plunge is taken, my husband will obey like the rest. I do not see why he should be unlike others. I see no reason why because he thinks himself better, he should be really worse." As she passed through her husband's study to gain the hall, she saw him sitting there, apparently waiting.

"What," she exclaimed, "you are back?"

"Yes, darling," answered Philip Warburton, gently. "I could not make up my mind to leave you, so I sent a message to that effect to the office. Business must do without me until tomorrow, for birthdays do not come so often. Will you put this deed away? There! Do you feel much taller, now that you are a freeholder, a real-estate owner, you little goose?" and he drew his wife's head to him and kissed her.

"It is very good of you," said Edith nervously, "and does this place really belong to me? Is it my very own?"

"That deed," returned Warburton, "is the legal evidence of that astonishing fact." A knock at the door announced the presence of a servant.

"For how many shall dinner be laid?" said the latter as he obeyed the summons to "come in."

"For seven," answered Edith, nervously.

"For seven," echoed Warburton, with astonishment, as the servant left the room. "Why, I thought we were to have a family party, but I see—you are going to surprise me, and you have invited some friends."

"Yes," returned Edith, "some friends."

"And who are they?" said Philip. "Unless, of course, it is a secret. If it is, I promise you to be tremendously surprised when the time comes."

"Perhaps you will," said Edith nervously, as before.

"Why?"

"Why——"

"Well——"

"I don't know quite how to tell you, Philip, but honestly, I could not help it. They asked me to ask them."

"They—who?"

"Mrs. Marsden and Mrs. Beaufoy, and a friend of theirs."

"You are not serious," said Warburton, looking her squarely in the face, "you do not mean it?"

"Yes, I do," said Edith, "I have invited them, and there's an end of it." She walked to the window. "Thank heaven that's over," she said to herself.

"Edith," said Philip Warburton, gravely, "you did not mean to defy me surely? Say that you forgot what I asked you, say so, only say so——"

458

"No," said Edith, "I cannot say so. Your command was as unjust as it was unjustifiable, and it would only be humiliating to myself to send away my best friends in such a manner."

"Your best friends," echoed Philip Warburton scornfully. "Nothing hurts me so much as to hear you give them such a title. I pray that you may some day learn who really *is* your *best* friend."

"I don't want to learn," interrupted Edith, excitedly. "I know that my best friends are those who seek to lighten my bondage, and I have a right to defend them against their calumniators."

"Good God!"

"And to prefer them," continued Edith, "to people who are always annoying and tyrannizing over me. Do you wonder?"

"No," replied her husband bitterly. "I have ceased to be surprised at anything. I do not see why I should be surprised at such ingratitude. I was wrong to let you see how you wound me."

"Reproaches! Have I not done my duty?"

"Great heaven," said Warburton to the empty air, "I speak to her of love, and she answers me of duty."

"What more do you expect?" asked his wife, turning to him. "It is not my fault, if I have no more to give."

"Nothing then," said Warburton, rising. "From now, duty is all that I will ask from you. Let us see how well you fulfil it. Your first step on the new path you have chosen is to obey me. Mind you do not stumble at the start."

"Oh," said Edith. "Then this is to be the beginning of the reign of terror?"

"If you will have it so," said Warburton, with a bitter laugh.

Edith reached the door. "Woe be to him," said she, as she left the room, "that attempts such a government over me."

"Poor child," said her husband, looking after her. "May you not bring woe to yourself by your rebellion?"

As he spoke a servant reëntered, announcing a visitor.

"What!" exclaimed Warburton, as he rose to meet the newcomer, "Denalguez? I did not expect to see you for some time. What brought you here so soon?"

"Oh, the usual cause," said Denalguez, shaking the proffered hand, "a woman," and he dropped wearily into a chair.

Maurice Denalguez was a Spaniard and a soldier. He looked the latter, but not the former. Tall and heavily, though lithely built, he might have served as the beau ideal of a woman's dream. His hair, which was of a rich brown, curled lightly all over his head, and was parted on the wrong side. His eyes varied in color as he spoke of varied subjects, and were alternately of a deep gray, and of a steel blue. The moustache, whose ends were loosely combed out, overshadowed the mouth, which, in speaking, seemed almost too finely curved for a man's, but which in repose became thin and hard-set. A strong jaw gave indication of his strength of will, and a nervous habit that he had of playing with one end of his moustache drew the attention irresistibly to the tremendous physical power shown by his muscular white hand.

"A woman!" echoed Philip Warburton, as he seated himself opposite his unexpected guest. "Well, whatever the cause, I hope you will stay with us now. Is it true that you leave the diplomatic service? Why, I read only today of your promotion to St. Petersburg."

"Quite true," answered Denalguez, "but I sent my resignation not half an hour since. I resigned for a very different reason than that which brought me here. I sought neither the honor nor the emolument for myself, and now I have no further use for either."

"Well," said Warburton, cheerfully, "you have fortune enough, if not wealth, to be independent. I wrote you some time since, that the money you left with me for investment has considerably accumulated."

"Ah," said Denalguez, bitterly, "the proverb is right once more. 'Unlucky in love'—you know the rest. You can do what you like with the money. I take no further interest in it now."

"But suppose you should marry," said Warburton, growing more and more astonished at this, to him, new phase of his friend's character.

"God forbid," interrupted the latter. "I know the sex too well. Do not be surprised at my bitterness, I have been singularly

460

unfortunate, as you will allow. It was a woman who denounced my father in the political crisis that caused our banishment from Spain. My first love was fatal. The woman at whose feet I poured out my wealth of youth and hope was the cause of my challenging my earliest friend, and as his life flowed out with the blood I had shed, I learned that she had betrayed—deceived me—and that I was a murderer, where I had thought to be a chivalrous defender. To most men, woman is a fate, but to my race, woman has always been a fatality. My brother, Prosper, poor boy, might have been alive today but for that fatality. Can I ever forget that his bright, young life was ruined, his honor involved, and only redeemed by his early death? I came back from my long exile in South America, full of plans and projects for the boy's future. I left him a child, but I found him——" and he paused before he continued, "the slave of a woman's caprice, bewitched by a fiend into the dishonor he was too blind to see. I tried to save him—I but hastened the end. I pointed out to him the treason. The woman was married—not an uncommon case, you will say—I would have saved him the inevitable remorse, but he believed she cared for him. I had not been in Paris twenty-four hours before I knew that she did not. It is so easy to deceive a boy of twenty."

"And you proved the deceit to him?" said Philip Warburton, who had forgotten all his own trouble in his sympathy with his friend's despair.

"Conclusively," replied the other. "God knows if I did right; at least I thought so. I shall never forget that look of pain that his face wore, when, with a few bitter truths I shattered his faith. But the world's like that, Warburton. How often do we lavish the best blossoms of our heart's garden on creatures who crush the very essence of our manhood, and do it by means of that innate cruelty which the world has called by courtesy; 'coquetry.'"

"Was she really fond of him in her way?" queried Warburton, "for I take it he was not rich enough to be of much use to her."

"You are mistaken," returned Denalguez. "He inherited a small fortune from his mother, the greater part of which she designed to possess in the shape of a set of diamonds just ordered at a fabulous price. The discovery following my arrival robbed her of the gift. She did not care for the boy, but his reckless generosity made life easier to her. She will never forget my share in despoiling her. We have never met face to face, but I feel that we shall meet some day, and mark me, Warburton, the debt between us will be heavy of settlement."

"I should like to know," said his friend gently, "if you can tell me without distressing yourself, how he took his life?"

Denalguez was sitting, his hands clasped between his knees, staring out into the garden which separated the house from the road. He continued without a change of tone,

"I went to his room, armed with proofs which he could not doubt. He listened in silence to what I had to say, his eyes fixed all the time upon a picture of the woman. I asked his promise to leave Paris and break the chain which was dragging him down. For some moments we were both silent; I waiting and hoping for the promise that should begin a new life, he still looking at that woman's face as though he would ask mercy of it—his head resting on his hands. It was a solemn silence, old friend. And I felt he was choosing his course. The young face was so sad that even my eyes became dimmed for a moment. A rapid movement, a sharp report, and he fell at my feet—dead! *He had chosen.*"

For a few moments a profound stillness ensued between the men; Denalguez strung up to a pitch of nervous tension by the effort of recital; Warburton horror-struck at the recital itself. It was he who finally broke the silence.

"And the woman lives, I suppose," he said, "and has, I suppose, forgotten. Who was she?"

"He left a letter," replied Denalguez, "begging me to hide her name. I have respected his wish, and no one but she and I know that the cause of the tragedy was—Ethel Marsden."

Warburton had sprung to his feet, and stood looking at his companion as if a thunderbolt had fallen between them.

"You can form no idea of this woman's evil nature," continued Denalguez. "What do you suppose is her fixed resolve?"

"I cannot imagine."

"Why, to subjugate *me*, as she did my poor brother. Well," continued he, rising and pacing up and down the room, "she will have her opportunity. I have determined to humiliate her as never before was woman humiliated in this world."

"She is too clever to give you a chance," said Warburton. "Your name alone would be enough to warn her."

Denalguez laughed. "Do you suppose," said he, "that I am not prepared for that? My plan is quite clear. I make my first attack at once. Today, probably, if not, immediately on my return. I have a letter which gives me an excellent excuse for calling on her and it is as Count Guerravillia I shall present myself."

"True," said Warburton, as a new light seemed to break upon him. "I had almost forgotten that that was your name."

"No wonder," returned the other, "for I never used the title. After the insurrection in which my father was implicated, our property was confiscated, and from his arrival in England we bore our name only. That is foreign enough in all conscience. In this case, however, my ancestral honors stand me in good stead, and I believe I shall succeed. It is a case of 'diamond cut diamond.' She sought to entrap me, she will entrap herself. Oh, these women—these women," concluded the man, as he laughed a mirthless, cynical laugh, and turned to the window.

"My dear fellow," said Warburton, following him and laying his hand upon his shoulder, "your only trouble is that you have chosen badly. All you have now is to——"

"Wait a moment and hear the end. Having hardened myself against the whole world, I found a young girl, pure as an angel, honest as—*you*, promising me nothing, yet promising me all. At last I had found an exception. She belonged to a new sex, called 'Truth.' I believed in her, as I believe in you."

"And you were deceived?"

"I might have expected it. I loved her too well. I accepted my Russian appointment in order that I might gain for her both fortune and position. I had succeeded. I wrote, proposing to her father for her hand; the reply was merely that she refused me, that she could not love me. I do not blame her, mark you, for refusing me, but for having made me believe—and believe most honestly—that she cared for me."

"Well, my dear old man," said Warburton, in a tone of one about to change the subject. "After all it is possible that matters might have been worse. She might have accepted you first and deceived you afterwards."

"There, there," said Denalguez, "don't let us speak of it any more. To pleasanter things. Your happiness, for instance, for I presume you are happy as the day is long."

"Remember," said Warburton with a gravity such that his friend could not quite decide it to be real or assumed, "I have been married for three years."

"That sounds like a pretty definite 'no,'" said Denalguez, his bitter smile showing his strong teeth again underneath the now twisted up moustache.

"You are mistaken," returned Warburton. "I am happy enough. That is to say, I am as happy as I can be."

"I do not believe you."

"Well, that's pretty strong, when I say——"

"Philip, something is wrong," returned his friend. "You are not as frank as I."

"What can you expect," said Warburton, speaking rapidly. "The probe will hurt the wound, even when a friend's hand guides it. You have guessed well—I *am* unhappy. I have chosen for my wife—well there! don't let us refer to it."

"That you should have chosen such a woman," said Denalguez, as if to himself.

"Oh," said Warburton, speaking in a tone as cynical as that of his friend had been, "she is of the majority. I forget you have been away so long. Since your departure there is a new tribe existent; one of the lost ten, perhaps, though its origin is English. My wife, with numberless others, belongs to it. They have institutions of their own, as have other communities, clubs, sports, and the rest of it. But the chief sport, the great event, is 'The Married Woman's Hunt Cup.' All members of the tribe can enter for this race. All jockeys, gentlemen or professionals, are eligible, except the husband. The Cup is quite pretty and unique,—it is beaten out of the husband's golden hopes and bright anticipations, with Misery in strong relief, and it is filled with the cries of despair his heart's rending gives forth, though his lips be mute. The tribe is called 'Professional Beauties.' There was a time—which is how ancient history—when motherhood and womanhood existed, when the beauty of the wife was the glory and warmth of her husband's life, but, God help us! we are in an age of progression and obsolete customs must give way to improvements."

As he finished speaking, he fell into the chair that he had lately vacated, and Denalguez rose.

"Things are worse than I expected," said he as he took up his position in front of his friend.

"You know her," returned Warburton. "We often visited her father's house together before you left. Mr. Wurmsley, you know."

"Wurmsley," said Denalguez, controlling himself with an effort. "Yes, I remember."

"You frequently spoke of her beauty," continued Warburton, "and of her sister's. Do you remember her too—Marion?"

"Marion," echoed Denalguez, with a stronger effort. "Oh, yes. I think I remember."

"Edith was so lovely," continued Philip Warburton, not noticing his friend's agitation. "I could not bear to think what might be her fate. Her father is a strange old gentleman, always absorbed in some hobby or other; good sort of fellow in his way, but utterly unfit for the care of such a girl. It has been a long fight, and I have suffered a little, but now I have forbidden one or two women the house, women who were her most dangerous companions, and I hope peace will be restored."

"And happiness?" said Denalguez.

"That is out of the question. Of course it is my fault, at least I suppose it is, but the spell is broken. I see Edith as she is, and it seems to me my love is dead. Don't let us say anything more about it. Egad, how mournful we are! I positively insist upon changing the subject. You have come to stay with us, of course."

"Not now, thanks," answered Denalguez. "I am only in London for a few hours on my way to Madrid; but I shall be back in three or four weeks, when I shall be a comparatively idle man, and then my first visit will be to Mrs. Marsden."

"You have really decided to leave the service?" said Warburton.

"Positively. I shall return only to settle my affairs. I must go now. Make my excuses to Mrs. Warburton, and say I shall hope to meet her on my return."

The two men walked together to the front gate, where the hansom which had brought Denalguez was waiting to take him back. With a final hand-clasp to his friend, he sprang into it, and was driven away.

## CHAPTER VI.

When Edith Warburton left her husband, she sought once more the garden. "I wish they had not come," she said to herself. "But what can I do? I cannot be made the subject of Clare Beaufoy's stories to every man in town for the next month; and though I do not think that Sir Reginald Faithorne is the kind of man to talk about me in the clubs if the friendship he professes for me is genuine, it will be very unpleasant for him to be brought into the affair. Well, I suppose I must let things shape themselves as they will. Sir Reginald seems to be a man of the world. If I can find him alone, I will get him to help me out. He shall have an opportunity of proving the nature of his friendship."

She stepped out on to the verandah, outside the drawing-room windows, and the first person that she found was the fascinating baronet, himself.

"Ah, at last," said this latter gentleman, as he arose. "I had lost everybody, but, thank heaven, I have found everybody again."

"Oh, Sir Reginald," began Edith, not heeding his words. "I want you to help me."

"Willingly," broke in the baronet, "what can I do?"

"Please go at once."

"What?"

"Yes, yes. Make an excuse, and take the others away."

"But why?"

"My husband has returned, and has been making a fearful scene. It must seem strange, but I beg you will excuse my apparent rudeness; I will explain it all another time."

"Ah!" said the baronet to himself. "There will be another time. I wonder when?"

"If you were to meet him now," continued Edith, "I am sure it would be most unpleasant for all of us; so please go, for my sake."

"Believe me," said Sir Reginald, "I would do anything in the world for you, but my obedience will cost me the delight of your presence. Besides, to tell me that you are alone, comparatively defenceless, is hardly the thing to make me run away. I want to tell you so much—it is very cruel of you, and very unhospitable, too. Must I go?"

"Yes, you must," said Edith, nervously, "and I can never see you again."

"At your own house," said Sir Reginald, "I can quite understand that that might be the case, but at your friend's, at Mrs. Marsden's?"

"Oh, I am half dead with fear!"

"One word of hope, and I will go. If not, I stay."

"Go, go, I entreat you."

"Well, if it will please you, say *au revoir*, and I am off."

"*Au revoir,*" said she nervously. Sir Reginald bowed over the hand which she extended to him, and passed through the house. Edith's heart gave a throb of relief as she heard the door close behind him, and she sank wearily into the chair which he had just vacated. At this moment, Clare Beaufoy and Ethel Marsden appeared by the opposite path to that by which they had effected their retreat.

"Why," said the former, as Edith descended the steps to meet them, "why, we are just where we started. Your grounds are charming, Mrs. Warburton, your shrubbery is the most discreet piece of landscape gardening I ever saw, and your wild-garden is positively paradise. One can lose one's self as if in a labyrinth. Indeed, I congratulate you on your birthday present, after having thoroughly examined it. It is almost worth while to keep a husband when he makes one such royal gifts."

This was by no means what Thello wanted, so she nudged her friend with her heel as she continued carelessly the sentence which Clare Beaufoy had begun.

"So he gave you this place for a birthday present, did he? Well, why shouldn't he, he is rich enough in all conscience. It is a fairy bower in every sense of the term, dragon included. I am glad we did not encounter the dragon, however. The dragon is in the city, I suppose?"

Philip Warburton, after seeing Denalguez off, had come through the house and stood at the top of the steps, as Mrs. Marsden finished her sentence, and his clear, incisive tones cut in upon her eloquence, as he said gently,

"No, Madame, he is not in the city."

"Good heavens," said Thello, turning her adorable grin on the lord of Wimbledon Lodge as he descended the steps. "You were there, were you? Nothing is so disagreeable as to be over-heard, excepting, perhaps what one overhears. However, you will forgive my little pleasantry."

Philip Warburton stood at the bottom of the steps looking at her, an expression of unconcealed dislike upon his sharply cut face.

"I have given myself the pleasure," answered he, "of ordering your carriage, Mrs. Marsden, as, I regret to say, my wife's arrangements are such that she cannot give herself the pleasure of entertaining you at dinner today."

Edith had stepped to his side as he spoke.

"Take care," said she in an undertone. "If I am not mistress in my own house I will be nothing else. My friends will dine *here*."

"They *will* not," said Philip in the same tone.

"They *shall*."

"They shall *not*. Am I to speak plainer?"

"As you please," answered Edith. Then raising her voice she continued: "You can keep your house, and everything else. My friends, this house is my husband's gift to me, and this parchment is the transfer of title which he had put into my hands immediately before I joined you here. The transfer of title to a house where I may not ask my friends to dine! Do you suppose," continued she, turning to her husband, "that I am to be deceived by such a shadow? So much for your gift," and she flung the parchment into the basin of the cascade.

This time the gold-fish did not rise to investigate the disturbance, naturally mistrustful of so voluminous an offering. Of the four people present, Thello Marsden alone retained her presence of mind.

"I am so sorry," said she to Philip, "that you are unwell, and on your wife's birthday, too, of all days; but I trust that when we meet again you will be entirely recovered. Good-bye," and she held out her hand until Philip had to take it mechanically, and calling Clare Beaufoy to follow her, she disappeared. Philip Warburton escorted them to the door, and his wife was left alone.

## CHAPTER VII.

It was some time later that afternoon when Sir Reginald Faithorne called again at the house in Hans Place. To the servant who opened the door, he had given his card, and was saying:

"Tell Mrs. Marsden that I propose to call upon her tomorrow, and say I shall be much obliged if she will write me a note to say whether it will be convenient, when she comes in this afternoon."

"Mrs. Marsden is at home, sir," said the servant as the baronet was turning away.

"At home?"

"Yes, sir. Mrs. Marsden returned about half an hour ago."

"Then show me upstairs," said Sir Reginald.

"Great Scott! Thello," was his ejaculation as he entered the room. "Of all the extraordinary people I ever came across, you are, of course, the most extraordinary, but what in the world is the meaning of this?"

"The meaning of what?" returned Thello.

"Why, the meaning of your being in town, when I left you at Wimbledon?"

"*Mon cher*, I might as well ask you the same question, seeing that I left you at the same place."

"Pardon me," returned Faithorne, "my fall came before yours. I had the start of you in being turned out of paradise, I should think, by a good half hour. You *were* turned out, weren't you?"

"Yes," replied Thello, "Clare and I were turned out in the calmest manner imaginable by that brutal idiot, Philip Warburton. He don't think that we are good enough to associate with his dunce of a wife. However, I will make him sorry for himself, if ever man was sorry in this world. When do you want to see her again?"

"My dear Thello, you go so fast——" began Sir Reginald.

"I have never been given to understand," interrupted Thello, "that Sir Rex Faithorne went particularly slow. I presume you are not going to stand there, with an ingenuous smile upon your countenance, and tell me that you made no progress with that little schoolgirl, with all the opportunities you had of being alone with her?"

"On the contrary," replied Faithorne, "I made such good progress that we became friends and allies at once, and the first service that she claimed of my friendship, was that I should go away—a rather rough 'first service' for an ardent adorer."

"Never mind, poor old man," returned Thello. "You shall be avenged. She will be very sorry for herself, and shall tell you so. When do you care to meet her for the purpose? Will tomorrow suit you?"

"Certainly," replied Faithorne.

"She will be in town, and she will lunch with me."

Faithorne took his hat, and with it his leave. Left by herself, Thello paced once or twice up and down her boudoir, and then coming to a full stop before the empty fireplace, she remarked to her reflection in the glass,

"So, my beautiful Edith, you allow your idiotic husband to humiliate me before Clare Beaufoy. All right, my beautiful, proud, prim, proper, punctilious and prudish young person! Since you are so fond of this husband of yours, you may as well be, yourself, the instrument of my revenge."

She forthwith sat down, and indited the following note:

*My Poor Darling Edith:*
    My heart bled for you yesterday when I saw you so grossly maltreated by that husband of yours; but though I am prepared to admit him the soul of chivalry that you declare him to be, he did, perhaps, forget himself a little this time. Please rest assured that I quite understand the condition of affairs, and am not in the least angry at the cavalier way in which we were turned out. I have also represented the whole affair to Clare Beaufoy in such a way that she will not talk about it.
    Come up to do some shopping tomorrow afternoon. I want your assistance, so lunch with me here at two o'clock. Remember above all things that I am always your loving and sympathetic friend,
THELLO.

"Confound her!" she added to herself, as she sealed up the letter with a vicious thump that made the knick-knacks on her writing table rattle.

True to her promise to Sir Reginald Faithorne, Thello Marsden had, next day, the pleasure of entertaining Mrs. Philip Warburton at lunch. To the events of the preceding day, she referred but little, electing to treat the whole matter as a colossal joke, and when Edith tried to turn the subject in that direction, she would waive it aside with a little merry laugh, a few words of condolence with her friend on the possession of such a husband as Philip Warburton, and a phrase or two of simple eulogy on the way in which Sir Reginald had got them all out of an unpleasant predicament by making good his retreat at the critical moment.

When they came up from luncheon, a little shriek of surprise burst from Thello's lips.

"Why, I do declare," exclaimed she with a merry laugh, "here is our *preux chevalier*, himself. You could not have arrived more opportunely, Sir Reginald," said she, "though where you come from, heaven only knows. I thought you were out of town. Here is Mrs. Warburton, positively *dying* to express the relief she felt when you made good your retreat yesterday."

"Indeed, Sir Reginald," began Edith, "I hardly know how to apologize——"

"I beg that you will not say a word about it," interrupted Sir Reginald; "so far as I was concerned, the matter is of the supremest unimportance. I only went down to Wimbledon to have the honor of making your acquaintance, and since I succeeded in that object, it mattered not how soon or how abruptly our first interview terminated. I can only congratulate myself that fate has so befriended me as to bring about our second so soon."

"There, there, don't talk any more about it. But you, Sir Rex, be good enough to make yourself useful."

"Why, of course," answered the gentleman addressed. "I shall be charmed, but how?"

"Entertain Mrs. Warburton for half an hour whilst I dress. We are going out shopping, she and I."

"Can I not come and help you?" said Edith nervously.

"Not for the world," returned Thello. "I always dress myself and it makes me positively miserable to have anybody else in the room whilst I perform the mysteries of the comb and powder-puff. *Au revoir,*" and Thello disappeared.

An hour later, she came down, dressed for the drive, and found Sir Reginald and Edith discussing Swiss scenery—at least Sir Reginald was.

It did not escape Thello's observation that during their drive that afternoon, Edith Warburton was singularly silent.


# CHAPTER VIII.

An hiatus of six months occurs at this point in the tale I am unfolding, during which the names of Sir Reginald Faithorne and "the new beauty," Mrs. Philip Warburton, were invariably coupled together in the *chronique scandaleuse* of the modern Babylon. It seemed to Edith that she could go nowhere without meeting Sir Reginald Faithorne, and it struck her as odd, as she did not realize that Faithorne having made her the fashion, contrived that it should not be otherwise.

The curtain rises on the drama at the end of this period, and discloses the same scene upon which it fell, namely, the boudoir-drawing-room of Thello Marsden. Thello is sitting in an armchair before the open window, and Sir Reginald has just entered the room unannounced. There was always a great deal to engross the observation of a philosopher in the greeting of Thello and her companion. There was such a complete lack of ceremony or cordiality in the process that the most casual observer would have realized that the partnership between these two promising specimens of humanity was essentially of an offensive and defensive nature.

"Well," was the first word spoken by Faithorne.

"I expect Edith every minute," answered Thello. "I told her you would be here, and I made her promise to come. I think that I play propriety in a most exemplary manner, don't I? Though, upon my word, you ought to have been able to dispense with me by this time. It is perfectly outrageous! Here are you, the most worldly man of the world of your day, dangling after a vain, silly woman for six months, and still needing a chaperone; doesn't it occur to you that you are paying for a dog and doing the barking yourself?"

"I am, you are, it does," replied Sir Reginald, answering all her observations in a lump. "But I am free to confess that I am getting bored to death with the beautiful Edith. She is, without exception, the heaviest woman I ever met, and I get simply worn out, being kept at high pressure from week's end to week's end. You see, she has started with thoroughly bad training, and I do not feel like wasting any more time on her instruction. In other words, she has been playing the fool with me as long as I feel inclined to stand it, and I propose to say 'good-morning' before she says 'good-morning' to me. By the way, Thello, I fancy— unless I am mistaken, I think you said I could be of some service to you. How much this time?"

Thello replied with her light, grinning laugh, the laugh which showed all her teeth and the tip of her tongue. "What a nuisance I am," said she, "but I have overrun my account again. I wish you would just attend to this for me until next month," and she handed him a folded blue paper.

"Hum," ejaculated Sir Reginald, as he looked over the bill. "Thornhill ought to pay *you*, instead of asking you to pay *him*. Dear me!—cigar-case, cigar-case, scarf-ring, scarf-pin, cigarette-case, match-box, match-box, match-box, cigarette-case; dear, generous, little woman. Which regiment is it?"

"You abominable tease," said Thello, laughing as she snatched the bill out of his hand. "I do wish you would look after it, and not chaff about it, for I shall have the man dunning me again."

"I am sure I shall be most charmed," said Faithorne; "I shall be passing this afternoon, and I will look in." Then as an after-thought seemed to strike him, he said, "Oh, I find on reflection that I have to go in the other direction. Would it be bothering you awfully if I asked you, as you are going down Bond Street, to look into Thornhill's and pay a bill for me? It won't take you a moment," and drawing his letter case from his pocket, he took thereout the bill he had just received, together with a bundle of notes, several of which returned with the bill to its original owner.

"Thank heaven," said Thello to herself, "he has got tired of Edith. There certainly never was a man who did these things so prettily before." Then she added aloud, "I hear the door-bell, and I expect that that is Edith. If you are going to have a row I will wait until it is over," and Thello left the room.

"If," said Faithorne to himself, as he strolled out of the little drawing-room into the smaller apartment beyond, "the fair Edith thinks she can go on playing me like this, she is vastly mistaken." He walked to the mantel-piece and adjusted his cravat in the glass.

Meanwhile, Edith had entered the drawing room, and looking around gave a little stamp of impatience at finding the room empty. "This must end," she said to herself. "I am perfectly wretched, and if something doesn't happen, I shall go mad. Oh, there you are," continued she aloud, as Faithorne entered through *portières*, "it is very nice of you to keep me waiting, after all the risk I run to get here at all."

"Risk?" answered Faithorne, "rubbish! How can you run any risk here at Thello's? Besides, I have not seen you for more than a week."

"So much less excuse for being late," said Edith snappishly.

"I have been driving this morning," said Faithorne calmly. "The horses went very well, but I do not think Cora is quite fit."

"Who is Cora?"

"My new mare. I gave an awful price for her—a wonderful animal—"

"Bother the mare," exclaimed Edith, rising. "Do you know you nearly kept me waiting?"

"Nearly," echoed Faithorne. "You delightful autocrat! You seem like a small Catherine of Russia. You have some of her characteristics."

"What do you mean?"

"Last night at the opera, Lord What's-his name, and the Austrian chap, were in your box all the evening. Their attention was perfectly obvious, but the most amusing thing was your trying to make each believe that he was the most favored."

"Oh you do me the honor to watch me?" said Edith with an ironical expression.

"Accident—pure accident," returned Faithorne coolly.

"Who were you with?"

"Alone, of course. Now look here, Edith, let us understand one another. I am not at all satisfied with your manner."

"What do you mean? By what right——"

"The right you give me," said Faithorne rising.

"You have none," broke in the woman.

"Really," continued he, imperturbably, "I think it is best we should come to an understanding. I have remarked your coolness and reproaches for some time, and I can see that you are tired of me. I don't blame you—oh, no. It is your nature. I am constant and faithful, great faults with you, because the sameness wearies you. It is a great misfortune, but I am resigned. One must bear despair and abandonment, but what I never *will* bear is ridicule."

"Sir Reginald, you are insolent."

"You see I am not your husband. In such cases the husband cannot help himself; it is a fatality that he has to submit to. It is his mission in life, but for—the other—it is a gratuitous affront which he is not obliged to submit to—by law. And I tell you frankly, that if you were to take your noble lord or your Austrian diplomat into high favor at your court, I would blow out the brains of either of them without the slightest compunction,"

Edith clapped her hands to her ears. "This is horrible!" she said. "And to think that it is for this that I have jeopardized everything."

"To avoid being thought ridiculous, that is all."

"Oh, I see clearly enough," said Edith, desperately, "that you have desired this break——"

"No, upon my honor, you never appeared more lovely than you do now. Every one is talking about you, and I never worshipped you more."

"Because it flatters you," broke in Edith. "Thank you. I don't want that sort of love. Oh! what miserable spirit of coquetry induced me to accept attentions from you which may have compromised my whole life? I thought that I was harshly treated by my husband, and you all fostered that belief. Where I sought consolation, I find only insolent vanity. Why did you varnish your reality so thickly that all was invisible beneath the surface? Look at me, look at me, Rex—a great victory, truly, but one that will scarcely repay you. You have been good enough to show me the means of retreat, and I thank you."

"What do you mean?"

"You asked me to be frank, you ought to understand,"

"You love me no longer?"

"I render to you no account. You wished to be warned, take the warning now."

"My dear Edith," began he—at this moment Ethel Marsden came in from the inner room.

"Heavens! what a disturbance," said she.

"He is making a dreadful scene," said Edith hysterically.

"A quarrel?" queried Ethel. "Well, it will be all the sweeter to make peace."

"It is useless," said Edith, "it is all over."

"Very well," said Sir Reginald, "but give me your reason."

"Reason, indeed! There is no lack of reasons. Your vanity, your rudeness, your faults——"

"Faults," interrupted Faithorne, sarcastically. "That is nothing new. I always had them, and I never hid them."

"Besides—your heartlessness," continued Edith; "there is your utter want of feeling. The day before yesterday, for instance, when I was walking with you, you dared to bow to a—a—person."

"Very slightly!" interrupted Faithorne with humorous rapidity, "very slightly, I am sure!"

Thello Marsden stuffed her handkerchief into her mouth to prevent herself shrieking with laughter.

"I saw the same—person—come out of the Albany once——"

"She was teaching me a polonaise," said Faithorne, gravely; "she is a dancer, and a capital teacher. Let me recommend her to you. For goodness' sake don't pretend to be jealous. You know that my fidelity has always been unimpeachable."

"Well, I release you from any further fidelity," said Edith. "I only beg that you will send me back my letters and my portrait."

"You see," said Faithorne to Ethel, "you hear——"

"Well, I see," began Ethel.

"This is premeditated," continued Faithorne. "It is a cold-blooded way of getting rid of me. My servant shall bring you your letters at once, here; as for the portrait, which never leaves me, I did not think you would ask me for that, and I cannot bear to part with it. But here it is—take it," and he took a case from his pocket and handed it to Edith.

"At last," she exclaimed, opening the case. "Oh!" and she let it drop as she covered her face with her hands.

"What?" said Faithorne, as he stooped and picked it up. "Is it possible? Dear me! I took the wrong one this morning. It is a dreadful thing, but one does get mixed sometimes."

"And your fidelity!" said Edith through her fingers.

"Anticipated yours, that is all," said Faithorne. "You see we are so—sympathetic. You don't want this?" continued he, pointing to the portrait. "She is very popular just now. Well, if you won't have it, I will keep it, and I promise to send you yours here at once, and your letters. I will take care that there is no mistake this time. Adieu. I will come in this evening, if I may, Thello?"

"Certainly, delighted," returned his hostess, and Faithorne bowed and left the room.

"That is a charming fellow," said Thello, as the door closed behind him, "and you are very stupid to be so hard on him."

"I have my reasons," began Edith.

"Well, I don't know," interrupted Thello, "but I fancy I can guess."

"For some time," continued Edith, not noticing the interruption, "he has assumed an air of proprietorship which irritates me beyond measure, and which would end by ruining me. And now, more than ever I must be careful. My husband's friend, Captain Denalguez, arrived yesterday from Madrid."

"Denalguez," echoed Ethel, with an appearance of intense interest. "What is he like? I have heard so much about him that I am curious to see what sort of a man he is."

"Hideous," said Edith.

"I supposed he was handsome."

"He may be so; I believe, in fact, he is well favored enough, but to me he is horrible. He brings a shadow—a presentiment of evil. There is something about him that I abhor. It is indescribable, but it is too strong to overcome."

A servant entered the room at the moment. "Mrs. Warburton's maid is below," said she, "and would like to speak to her."

"Shall she come in?" said Thello.

"No, I will go and see her," answered Edith as she left the room.

"When Mrs. Beaufoy comes," said Ethel Marsden to the servant, "show her straight in here." She seated herself at the writing table and scribbled a note which she sealed up. "Send this letter at once to its address," said she to the servant, who left the room as Edith reëntered it.

"Anything important?"

"I am afraid so," said Edith, who was pale as death. "Marion came to the house just after I left. She seemed greatly excited. Philip went out with her, and they drove to father's."

"Well," said Ethel, "what of it?"

"Why," said Edith, "I said I was going to father's when I came here. What am I to do?"

"Can't you think of anyone," said Ethel, "who would 'father' your little misrepresentation? Some old friend, surely."

"My old friend, Mrs. Satterthwaite might, if I——"

"Sit down there and write," interrupted Thello, promptly.

"What am I to say?"

"Sit down. Write this: If you should see my father or my husband before seeing me, do not forget that I came to your house today and was taken dreadfully ill. I send you my muff to send to me tomorrow by your maid, who is to go for news of my health. Don't fail. Sign and date it. Now do you understand? When you get home, be awfully ill; I will answer for the rest."

At this moment the servant reappeared. "A gentleman wishes to see you, ma'am," said he.

"I am out," said Ethel. She signed to the servant to go, and he laid a card on the table. "By the by, who is it?" added she in an uninterested tone.

"A strange gentleman," replied the man, who says he is in London for a day only, and that he brings Madame letters from Prince Zourokoff."

Ethel thought for a moment. "Let the gentleman wait, I will receive him." The servant went out.

"The only thing that worries me now," said Edith, "is the letters and the picture that Reginald has, which he is to send here."

"It is your own fault," said Ethel, "I have told you fifty times never to write a line."

"I wish," said Edith bitterly, "that you had never told me a great many things."

"What do you mean?"

"Why," returned Edith, who was on the point of bursting into tears, "I mean that I should never have been in this trouble but for you." She did not observe the fact, but the adorable Thello was on the point of losing her temper.

"In what way am I responsible?" said she dryly.

"I do not say that you are altogether responsible," said Edith, not noticing her tone, "but you sneered at what you called my 'pastoral life,' till you made me feel that I was a martyr. What a fool I have been!"

"Yes, my dear," said Ethel, complacently, "what a fool you have been! And a fool you seem likely to be. But do not comfort yourself with the thought that I led you from the domestic hearth. If you had not wanted to go, you would not have gone."

"But you are older than I am, and might have prevented me."

"Older, well—I am. Prevented you, indeed! I am not your nurse, and though I am *older* than you, I wager that you will be old enough to make your youth an excuse for your inclination."

Edith saw that she had gone too far. "Perhaps I spoke hastily just now," said she. "Forgive me."

"You had better not lose any time getting home," said Mrs. Marsden, dryly.

"I *must* wait for those letters," answered Edith. "I shall not feel safe until they are burned. He said he would send them at once."

"As you please," returned Ethel. "But I think you had better go now, and, if you can, come back for the letters later. I will leave them in this pigeon hole of my writing-table, so that if I am out, you can take them."

"You are right," said Edith, "I will go at once. I say, don't forget to send my muff and my letter to Mrs. Satterthwaite."

"Oh, all right," said Mrs. Marsden, and Edith started for the door, meeting Clare Beaufoy as she came in.

"What, are you going away?" said the new-comer to Edith.

"Yes." Then turning to Ethel she said, "Don't forget," and left the room.

"Great goodness!" said the lively Clare, dropping into a seat. "What is the matter with Edith?"

"Oh," replied Ethel, "she is overpowered with her own innocence!"

"What are you talking about?"

"I mean it literally. She says I have led her from the bosom of her family. What do you think of her?"

"Why, what I have often told you. Give me a rogue before a fool, any day. I knew Edith was just the kind of woman to go her own way and then blame her friends for helping her along. I made up my mind long ago to give her no chance of annoying me, and you see if you do not get the worst of it in the end."

"We shall see. Do you suppose I shall let *her* get the best of *me*? Oh, no! You do not know your little Ethel."

"It is no question of getting the best of it," returned Clare, hunting for a cigarette among the bric-a-brac on the little table. "She will always play the 'innocent lamb' led away by wicked companions, and let you in for the unpleasant thing at last. I had enough of it at that birthday party, when she let her husband turn us out—perhaps you forget?"

"Forget?" echoed Ethel. "Not exactly. I have worked steadily from that day with one object. Warburton shall suffer for my humiliation. It has taken what seems to me a long time, but my turn is near at hand." She turned as she spoke and looked at Clare Beaufoy, an incarnation of malignant fury as she stood thus.

A servant entered with a packet of letters. "A messenger from Sir Reginald Faithorne," said he, "he has left this packet for you, ma'am," and he left the room. Ethel looked at it, her purple eyes sparkling. "Ah, ah! Philip Warburton," said she, "here is my dagger. It is composed of these innocent looking little bits of paper, but it will wound you as deeply as I wish."

"What are they?" said Clare, blowing a blue cloud into the air.

"Listen," said Ethel, as she opened the packet, and after a moment's hesitation broke the seal of a letter that lay on the top addressed to Mrs. Philip Warburton. "'I return your letters, but I keep your peace of mind. Reginald Faithorne.' Now for Edith's," added she as she opened the inner packet.

"Oh, Thello!" said Clare. "You ought not to have opened it. Edith will be furious."

Thello gave a nasty, little laugh, and ran the tip of her tongue lightly over her lips. "Edith will have other things to think of," she said, "for Philip Warburton will have these letters before twenty-four hours have passed."

"Well," said Clare, rising, "you know your own business best. I must go. I have a heap of things to do. Are you going to the concert with me?"

"No," replied Thello, "I also 'have a heap of things to do.' You don't mind?"

"Not in the least," returned Clare, moving to the door. "I shall see you soon. Goodbye."

"What luck I have," said Thello, looking at the bundle that she still held in her hand. "I can strike both my enemies at once, Philip Warburton and Maurice Denalguez; for a blow that strikes Warburton will reach his friend. I feel quite excited at the nearness of my triumph." She was passing from the room, when her eye fell upon the card which had been brought in some time previously. "Good heavens!" said she, taking it up, "I forget all about the stranger." She picked up the card, "Count Guerravillia. Guerravillia? I don't know the name." She rung the bell and a servant appeared. "Where is this gentleman?" said she.

"In the next room, ma'am." She walked to the *portière* and peeped through a crack.

"Gracious me!" said she, "he is very good looking, but he is fast asleep. Henry," she continued, turning to the servant, "Wake up the gentleman who is waiting in there, and ask him in here. I shall be back here in a minute." And carrying the letters with her, she left the room.

Immediately afterwards, the servant ushered into the room, where the above scene had taken place—Maurice Denalguez.

# CHAPTER IX.

"Thanks," said Denalguez, as he stepped into the room, suppressing a yawn as he came, and then as the servant retired, he looked around him. "A most satisfactory arrangement of rooms in this house! How could a woman of such cunning have given away such a chance of overhearing her plans! Could any more wonderful accident have happened than this? I knew these people were in danger, but I did not suppose that my fears would so soon be realized. How can I keep these letters from Philip, and how can I find out if Edith Warburton is worth saving? Faithorne is evidently the man; I must find him. It is all very dark as yet, but the light will come—the light will come," and he threw himself into an arm-chair. He was almost immediately disturbed, however, by the entrance of Ethel. She still held in her hand the bundle of letters, and laid them upon the table by the divan as she bowed to the stranger.

"A thousand excuses for having kept you waiting," said she.

"Not at all, Madame," returned Denalguez. "To tell the truth, I have just completed the journey from Madrid to London, and I fell fast asleep in your charming boudoir. I have brought a letter from Prince Zourokoff——"

"I am charmed to think that Prince Zourokoff holds me in such grateful remembrance as to afford me the pleasure of making your acquaintance, Count Guerravillia. What a number of letters you have," said she, as Denalguez took several from his pocket and selected one, which he laid on the table.

"Yes," said Denalguez, "I am a social person, and always like to be prepared to make myself at home in whatever city I may find myself. Some of them, however, are a little difficult to deliver, as I have only the names. Here is one, for instance, Mr. Fernheim, Banker—nothing else——"

"But," said Ethel, "he is so well known anyone can direct you."

"Then here is another," said Denalguez, "Sir Reginald Faithorne——"

"F, 3, Albany," said Thello. "Can you remember the address?"

"Oh, yes," said Denalguez with a smile of meaning which was lost upon his hostess. "I shall remember it. I am sure I am very much obliged to you for giving me this assistance; I do not know how I can sufficiently thank you."

"By giving me news of Prince Zourokoff. How did you leave him?"

"In very bad spirits."

"I met him six years ago," continued Thello. "He was perfectly charming."

"I know," said Denalguez. "He told me you found him perfectly charming."

"He told you?"

"He told me that Mrs. Marsden was the most fascinating woman in London, and as amiable as she is beautiful. I confess, I envy the Prince."

Thello threw him a rapid glance out of her purple eyes as her lips parted over her little teeth. "I think you are very impudent," said she.

"But I bring you Zourokoff's letter," said he, taking it up and holding it out.

"Ah!" ejaculated Ethel as she came forward to take it.

Denalguez drew it back. "But I repent having undertaken this commission," said he, "for after having seen you, it is cruel to have to bring you from another the homage that I would fain lay at your feet—to see you read before my very eyes, words that doubtless I dare not whisper to you."

Ethel Marsden turned on him again. "Do you suppose," said she, "that I am going to let you say such things to me on two minutes' acquaintance?"

"Well, here is the letter," said Denalguez, "but do not open it until I am gone. Won't you grant me so small a favor as that?"

Thello looked at him, a gleam of intense amusement crossing her face, and then she threw the letter down upon the table unopened. "I expect I must keep up my reputation for amiability," she said, "though I think the Prince is most indiscreet. I do not deny that I was very much fascinated by the brilliant charm of the Prince's manner, but I ought not to have given him the merest chance of compromising me."

"Compromising you," echoed Denalguez. "At present I regret that our acquaintance is slight, but I am sure you are far too clever a woman to allow anyone to compromise you. I am rather proud of myself as a judge of character, and I would give a great deal to study yours, even by the new science which doubtless you laugh at,—palmistry." He took her hand as he spoke, and looked at it. "So far," said he, "I can see indomitable resolution and patience to attain an end. Let me study you more deeply, and I wager I will tell you exactly what you are."

Thello drew away her hand, and walking over to the divan, threw herself upon it.

"You understand women pretty well," said she, "or at any rate, it seems so. I should like to hear your verdict."

"You think it is strange," said Denalguez, "that I should dare to speak so—but to confess the truth, I saw a picture of you that the Prince had, and from that moment I have been wild to know you. I have been in London several times since, and have seen you only to admire you more each time; but never have I been lucky enough to meet you. It seems as if I had known and worshipped you for all time."

"Good heavens!" said Ethel, raising herself on her elbow, and bringing to bear the full fire of the purple eyes upon her visitor. "And you expect, I suppose, to be rewarded for such devotion? Pray how long are you going to be in London?"

"As long as you will let me stay," answered Denalguez boldly.

"You do not suppose, my dear Count," said Ethel, "that I believe you would stay if I asked you?"

"Ask me—you would not dare——"

"And your country?——"

"A woman is a man's country," answered the visitor impetuously, as he arose and crossed the room to throw himself into a little chair at her side. "What is life worth if we reduce it to the commonplace pattern dictated by hard, dry rules which people call conventionality? Is life worth living without impulse—impulse? The whole glorious, fiery sunlight of the world—what can compare with it? And you are not the woman to crush impulse. No," he had seized her hand, and continued rapidly: "See, your hand trembles, your eyes glisten, and they answer me, though your tongue refuses——"

"I entreat—I beg—Count Guerravillia, you will make me extremely angry." She rose, and he rose with her.

"Ah," said he in a regretful tone, "may I not even kiss your hand? Do not be cruel. Of course if you say you are angry, I must go," and he took up his hat. "But think how much I need study." He put his hat down again. "And of how much knowledge you are depriving an enthusiastic scholar."

"Nonsense, let us talk of other things."

"There is nothing else. You know it is not possible for a man to be with you and think of anything but you."

"Upon my word," said Thello, "if you are not better behaved, you shall never come to see me again. And now I am going to send you away."

"May I call again soon? You had better say yes, or I won't go."

"You are certainly a most dangerous man. I am not quite sure whether you amuse me very much, or make me very cross."

"Don't be cross. Do you know what we do with a woman in Russia who is too cruel? I will tell you. We carry her off without further ceremony, so take care you do not come to Russia."

"I am not quite sure that I am safe *here*. You frighten me. I am always obeyed, and you must go at once. Good-bye."

"And you won't even let me kiss your hand?"

"No."

At that moment the voice of the servant was heard in the hall, saying: "I do not think Madame is at home." Ethel arose hastily, and moved towards the door, dropping her handkerchief as she did so. Denalguez, following her, stooped and picked it up, at the same moment he snatched the bundle of letters from the table and put them in his pocket. He reached the door at the same time as she did, and as she gave him her hand, he raised it to his lips. "You must let me come and see you again now," said he, showing her the handkerchief which he had kept, "if only to return this. And when you see me again, you will treat me differently," and he moved away.

As he left, Ethel fell into a divan. "Well, upon my word," said she, "if that is the way they make love in Russia, I am very thankful that I am in England. It is perfectly awful."

Denalguez, as he left the house, lit a cigar.

"Not so bad, I think," said he to himself, "for a first engagement.

# CHAPTER X.

It was with decidedly mixed feelings that Maurice Denalguez reached his rooms on the afternoon that he had left Thello Marsden in a condition of mind scarcely more lucid than his own. He was on the horns of a dilemma, as to the precise action that it was advisable to take, first, as regards the letters written to Faithorne, which he had rescued from Ethel Marsden, and secondly as to what course he should pursue with regard to the Warburtons, themselves. Like many a wise man before him, he decided he would sleep on the matter so that in the morning cool reflection might come, and accordingly on the following day his mind was made up. Made up, at any rate, in so far as he could himself compel events, and conscious of the perfection of his preliminaries, he decided to let things develop upon the basis that he had formed.

Accordingly, it was not long after breakfast, which with Denalguez, was an early meal, when he sat him down and wrote the following note:

"Captain Maurice Denalguez, having found some letters belonging to Sir Reginald Faithorne, will call to return them to him at 12 o'clock, unless otherwise notified."

This laconic epistle he sealed up and sent to the Albany, and then his eye fell upon the slip which had accompanied the ill-fated missives.

"I return your letters, but I keep your peace of mind. Reginald Faithorne."

"A threat!" ejaculated he. "The coward! Poor old Philip, how can I save you? Much of course, will depend upon this man, Faithorne, but in any case it will be better to trust him, than to leave this weapon in the fair Marsden's hands. But why does he threaten? Ah, Marion, if you had but been true and had given me the right to defend your sister! What is to be done? I cannot challenge him; besides, even if I could, that would not serve Philip Warburton as I wish. I must know this man better before I can decide any future step. It strikes me I have undertaken more than I bargained for. So far I have played spy, eavesdropper rather, and though the act was unintentional, the fact remains. Does the end justify the means? Yes, I think so, if the end be successful. How can I make best use of my feloniously recovered letters? Well, Mrs. Warburton, if your penitence be true, you shall destroy all trace of your folly as far as you are concerned. As for Faithorne, I must ensure his silence in spite of his threat."

Denalguez turned once more to his writing. He was astonished when he next looked up to find that it was growing late. "Ten minutes to twelve," exclaimed he, starting up. "Goodness, how time flies! I must go. Good luck attend me."

As he made for the door, it was opened from the outside, and a servant announced "Sir Reginald Faithorne." The two men bowed, Faithorne with rigid politeness, Denalguez with unconcealed amazement.

"To what do I owe this unexpected honor?" said he.

"To your own peculiar proceedings, Captain Denalguez," returned Faithorne. "I have my own reasons for reading between the lines of your note to me, and choose to believe that your motive must be strong for having obtained possession of my property, or I need hardly say that I should have taken advantage of the good fortune that you are a foreigner, and should have sent a friend to demand satisfaction where I now ask for an explanation."

Denalguez bowed, and motioned his visitor to take a seat, resuming his own as he did so. "I beg you will believe," said he, "that I should not shirk the penalty of any act of mine by which you may consider yourself aggrieved."

"That assurance from you, Captain Denalguez," returned Faithorne ceremoniously, "is unnecessary. Er—how did you—er—*find* my letters?"

"I stole them."

Faithorne did not move from his place. He looked at his boots one after the other, and then removed a fleck of dust from one knee; then he arranged his stick between his legs, and shifted his hat from one hand to the other. Finally he looked up at Denalguez, and said coldly,

"You must, of course, expect that I shall require a very good reason for so extraordinary a proceeding, as you must, of course, realize the unpleasant position which you have made for yourself."

"I appreciate my position fully," returned Denalguez, "and I am prepared to abide its results. Sir Reginald Faithorne, you remove much cause for embarrassment by the way in which you have taken this altogether unusual episode. You rightly judge that such a course as mine could have been adopted only for extreme reasons. Had I waited to inspire sufficient confidence in Mrs. Warburton to allow me to extricate her from her difficulty, who knows if my interference would have been of much use?"

"Captain Denalguez," said Faithorne, "we have here in London a large firm of pickle manufacturers, called Crosse & Blackwell. Both of these gentlemen have made enormous fortunes. Can you conceive how they made them?"

"In the usual course of trade, I presume."

"No, sir; by attending carefully to their own business."

Denalguez flushed. "Your rebuke is just," said he; "however, to the point: my reason for getting Mrs. Warburton's letters was to give her the power of securing her future—peace of mind."

"Suppose," said Faithorne, "I accepted your—pardon me—somewhat Quixotic method of defending your friend, as sufficient excuse for obtaining my property—by force—that's putting it as temperately as possible, I think—what do you propose to do with her letters?"

"I propose asking you to find some safer means of delivery, than that from which I rescued them. I would offer to be myself the messenger, but I think it better Mrs. Warburton should remain in ignorance of my efforts in her behalf. Will you take them?"

"Certainly," said Faithorne. "Meanwhile, however, Mrs. Warburton will think I am keeping what I promised to return. Well, I confess I don't care particularly what Mrs. Warburton thinks. You may have expected, Captain Denalguez, that I should be ridiculous enough to challenge you. Oh, no! *Pas si bête* I do not risk my life in such a cause. You cannot help seeing that I have already the best of the situation."

"It is admitted already," returned Denalguez coldly, and then added to himself, "And it is for *this* that a woman throws away name, home and honor."

"You see," pursued Faithorne imperturbably, "the golden rule in life is to take things coolly. You are a good fellow, so am I, and I am glad to find that we understand each other perfectly. Why, it would be the height of nonsense to endanger our lives for a tiresome woman——"

"Then why hold a threat over her?"

"That, of course, is my business. And though I have no objection to your minding your friend Warburton's, I distinctly object to your interfering in mine. Your old-fashioned devotion, Captain Denalguez, makes me feel positively philanthropic, and I should like to do you a good turn."

"A good turn," echoed Denalguez, not a little astonished at what he considered to be the amazing impertinence of his visitor. However, he realized that he had brought the gay baronet to a tractable state of mind comparatively quick, and felt that he must be allowed some latitude.

"Yes," returned the man. "You are quite sure you are not a little in love with Mrs. Warburton, yourself."

"You tread dangerously near the boundary between right and insult."

"I am answered. The great advantage of this nineteenth century of ours, is that instead of killing each other first and then explaining afterward, we reverse the process, and it saves lots of trouble, and some life. Now, if we had lived in, say the fifteenth century, we should have fought and died, and the chronicles would have told our descendants how nobly we bled for nothing. Your explanation suits me—I have nothing left to explain, and—one moment, I have nearly finished—you say I am taking advantage of the advantage which I already possess. I will prove to the contrary. You do not take this trouble for Warburton alone—er—Marion Wurmsley is a charming girl."

"Sir Reginald Faithorne, that is enough," interrupted Denalguez. "You presume. So far as I have felt my own conduct justified yours, I have submitted to your insolence for friendship's sake, but there is a limit, even to my endurance, and be good enough to remember that, apart from the subject we have already discussed, I resume my independence."

"But I wished to tell you something interesting about Marion," said Faithorne.

"And I tell you, I do not desire to hear."

"A thousand pardons, it was really not mere impertinence that dictated my questions. Am I to understand that Miss Wurmsley is nothing to you?"

"Nothing," and turning on his heel, Denalguez walked to the window.

I have conveyed, or tried to convey at the outset of this story, that Sir Reginald Faithorne was in every respect a gentleman as far as birth and breeding were concerned. The delicious impudence with which he turned the tables upon Denalguez at this interview requires consequently a word of explanation. He had a feeling of intense appreciation for the perfect honesty displayed by Denalguez during the difficult interview just concluded. The evident struggle betwixt indomitable pride and the resolution to endure the consequences of his interference, inspired Faithorne with genuine admiration for this really good fellow whom he knew to be the victim of Thello's malice.

It will be remembered that he had overheard the treacherous fabrications of Ethel Marsden on the occasion of his visit to Wimbledon Lodge, when the malicious Thello took advantage of Marion's ignorance, innocence and youth, to undermime with a few artfully contrived phrases the girl's confidence in her Spanish lover.

When Maurice Denalguez closed the colloquy with the laconic, heart-broken negative above recorded, Sir Reginald Faithorne arose to go.

"In ending this interview," said he, "I must say to you, Captain Denalguez, that I wish we had met under other circumstances, and I give you my assurance that Mrs. Warburton shall have no annoyance from me, unless she herself provokes it. One word more. Does Mrs. Marsden know that you have the letters?"

"No," replied Denalguez, "she does not know I have the letters."

"You asked why I threaten. I give you my word that if Mrs. Warburton's very innocent follies ever become known, it will be entirely through her own avowal of them." He bowed to Denalguez, who returned his salutation, and turned towards the door, which at that moment was opened by a servant, announcing Mrs. Warburton. Finding herself face to face with Faithorne, she started violently and turned color, but recovered her presence of mind immediately. Denalguez came forward, saying,

"This is indeed a surprise, the more pleasant for being entirely unoocked for."

"I fear I come at an awkward moment," said Edith. "You are busy."

"On the contrary," returned Denalguez, "let me present to you Sir Reginald Faithorne."

"Oh," said Faithorne, "Mrs. Warburton and I are old friends."

She bowed to Faithorne, and then continued: "Philip was obliged to go away this morning, so he asked me to call and tell you about tonight. He says you must come to father's and he will not be denied."

"I cannot go to your father's," returned Denalguez shortly.

"But you must," pleaded Edith. "My husband will think that I am a poor advocate if I do not succeed in winning you over."

"Captain Denalguez cannot resist such a pleader, I am sure," put in Faithorne. "Your husband, Mrs. Warburton, is indeed a lucky man. It is the sight of such happiness that makes one inclined to give up bachelorhood. I have been thinking for some time of settling down," continued he, with meaning, "and you have decided me."

"I don't see what you have been waiting for," said Edith shortly.

"Well," continued Faithorne, "you cannot be blind to the fashion that it has become for young married women to have a 'slave.'"

"Is he a slave?" put in Denalguez, who had resumed his seat at the writing-table.

"Yes," pursued Faithorne, "and a dangerous one, but manageable under ordinary treatment. He only kicks over the traces when he is pulled up too short. It is this custom recognized, tolerated and unchallenged, that has kept me from marriage. Egad! It makes a man careful, but I decided yesterday, and I do not regret my first steps in the right road."

"Do I know the lady?" said Edith. "When may I offer my congratulations?"

"Soon,—very soon," said Faithorne, nodding sagely, "and now good-bye."

A servant entered at the moment, bearing a card which he gave to Denalguez.

"In the library?" said the latter. "Pardon me one moment, Mrs. Warburton. An important message from my chief. Will you excuse me?" and replying to Edith's bow, he left the room and the two together.

## CHAPTER XI.

The moment Denalguez' back was turned, Edith Warburton's manner underwent an entire change. Turning abruptly, she said to Faithorne who was standing near the door, "Why did you not send my letters, as you promised?"

"I did send them," replied Faithorne, tapping the pocket where the bundle of letters lay.

"I have not received them."

"Really?"

"How can you be so cruel?"

"I promised to send your letters, I sent them—there ends my share of the matter."

"But Ethel says that she has not got them," continued Edith, almost feverishly. "If she says so, it must be true—you did *not* send them!"

"I will not say that that is a falsehood," said Faithorne gravely, "but I must say that you are asserting what is not true in the rudest way possible."

Edith did not seem to notice his words, but began pacing restlessly to and fro between the window and the fireplace. "I cannot rest till I get those letters," she said. "Why *was* I so foolish as to write them?"

"It *was* imprudent," assented Faithorne, coolly.

"Never mind," broke out Edith. "I will endure this no longer. I will tell my father, and you must tell him too, that I have only been reckless and blind, but not sinful. You will do this?"

"I think not," said Faithorne laconically.

She turned upon him, flinging out her arms in a gesture of despair. "Do you mean to say," said she, "that you *refuse* to speak the truth?"

"My dear," said Sir Reginald Faithorne, imperturbably, "you are too impetuous. You chose yesterday to take care of yourself, and released me without much ceremony from any further allegiance. Pardon me if I remark that I have been your tame cat as long as I intend to fill that domestic office. If you think you can play with fire and remain unscorched, you are mistaken. There may be salamanders, but assuredly you are not one."

"Why did you pursue me, and, with the rest, persuade me that I was doing no harm? I never meant wrong."

"No harm," echoed Faithorne, with a dry laugh. "Charming, all you women are! You expect to take up the major portion of a man's time, and even exact an account of his actions, reserving to yourselves the right to kick him out with a good deal less notice than you give your servant."

Edith Warburton had dropped into a chair. "I have deserved my punishment," said she, "but I ask so little of you—only tell my father——"

"Why tell your father what would only pain him, and of which he is in ignorance? I have never paid you any more attention than your sister; indeed during my intimacy it has been my constant care to appear more interested in Marion than you. We have been no little helped by Thello. Besides, look at it from another point of view: you wish to conceal your little escapade, and start by insisting on proclaiming it to the world. Could anything be more idiotic?"

"Oh," broke forth Edith, hysterically, "can you not understand? It is not enough to know that your fault is hidden. I want to cry aloud that though I have been weak and wilful, I have not been so, past retreat. As soon as I awakened and realized my error, I broke from the meshes of my folly, that might have become sin. I awakened—do you hear—it was I——"

The calmness of Faithorne was in singular contrast to the agitation of the other participant of this interview, and he now cut in calmly with the remark, "And you still think because you have not paid your fare, that you had not reached very near the end of your destination! Well, well, you travelled free, you ought to be comforted. Be calm, I have only been teaching you a little lesson. Here are your letters."

As he spoke, he took them from his pocket and held them out to her. She snatched them eagerly from his hand; Faithorne watched her with a quiet smile. A servant entered the room bearing a card which he gave to Edith. It was one of Ethel Marsden's and upon it was written in pencil: "*Ask me in. I want particularly to see you and Captain Denalguez.*" As she read it, Denalguez himself entered the room by the opposite door, and going to the table took up two or three papers that lay upon it preparatory to going out again.

"I have only to consign these papers to my visitor," said he to Edith, "and I shall be with you again. Sir Reginald," added he to that gentleman, who had risen to his feet, "may I ask you to wait a few moments."

"I am entirely at your service," said Faithorne, dropping into his seat once more.

"You know," continued Denalguez to Edith as he made once more for the door, "it is only duty of the most pressing kind that could make me leave you in this way."

"Captain Denalguez," answered she, "do you mind my asking a lady in for a moment? She has just sent a card, saying that she wants to speak to me. She is an old friend."

"Can you ask?" interrupted Denalguez. "You are at home. Do you wish to see her privately? Please give any orders you choose. I hope you will do me the honor of presenting me to your friend. Pardon me for a moment—I shall be with you again," and he went out of the room.

"Ask the lady to come in," said she to the servant, who still waited. And she added to herself, "How did she know that I was here, I wonder." Then walking to the fireplace she threw the letters into the fire that was blazing there.

The next moment Ethel entered the room. On seeing the two together, she merely nodded to Faithorne, saying as she passed him, "Hello! made it up?" And Faithorne nodded briefly as he walked over to sit in the arm-chair by the table, and taking up a paper began to read. The two women greeted one another.

"My dear," said Ethel, "what luck. I was looking everywhere for you, when, passing here, I saw your carriage at the door. I stopped and asked your man whose house it was, and when I heard, nothing could have induced me to go. I made up my mind that I would see your husband's friend. Where is he? I will tell you some day why I am so interested in him."

"And you really have never met him?" said Edith.

"Never, of course," answered Thello. "If I had, why should I be so anxious to see him?"

"Well," said Edith, "I will present you in form. Were you much bored by the emissary from Russia after I left you yesterday?"

Ethel gave a little silvery laugh. "Oh, my dear child," she said, "it was a most ridiculous thing. You know we were talking when the servant announced him, and I never looked at the card. However, you remember I said not at home, and then I said that

496

I would see him. Imagine my surprise when I came back to the drawing-room after leaving you, I found that he was a particularly charming friend of mine." Thello did not observe that at this point in the discourse, Denalguez had quietly reëntered the room and was standing, waiting until she should have finished her speech, to be presented.

"A man whom I have known for years," she went on, "and I wouldn't have missed seeing him for anything. He was an ancient sweetheart of mine, and it made me feel quite old, looking at him and thinking of the years that we have been friends. You must know him—I must present him to you. I am sure that you will delight in him, for he has been all over the world. Talk of adventures——" she stopped suddenly as she raised her eyes and caught those of Denalguez fixed upon her face. She uttered a little involuntary gasp, and Edith, following the direction of her eyes, said quietly,

"Mrs. Marsden, Captain Maurice Denalguez."

Denalguez bowed gravely, and advanced with a twinkle in his eye, as he said, "My pleasure in welcoming a friend of Mrs. Warburton is doubled by that friend being you, Mrs. Marsden. I am indeed fortunate on my return to receive as my first guests, the wife of my dearest and best friend, and the most fascinating woman in London, who is so well known to so many of my intimate friends."

Whilst he said this, Thello had recovered her presence of mind, and her purple eyes were now dancing with a mixture of excitement, amusement, and fury.

"It is charming of you," said she, "to forget that I invaded your sanctum, but I have wanted to meet you for a long time. However, I never thought that our meeting would be under such dramatic circumstances. It seems unfortunate, does it not? that Mr. Warburton doesn't like me, for Edith and I are such old friends."

"Oh, my dear," said Edith, "it is no use speaking of Philip to Captain Denalguez; each to the other is a paragon of all that is right."

"Of course, of course," said Ethel, "but it is such nonsense—the idea of poor little *me* being dangerous. Do you think, Captain Denalguez," she added, turning to him with her head on one side like a mischievous parrot, "do you think that I could do anyone any harm?"

"What a question!" said Denalguez.

"That is no answer," continued Thello, "well——?"

"Well," said Denalguez, as if he were revolving a deep problem, "I know that if you were to smile upon me too bewitchingly you would indeed be dangerous," and he drew out of the pocket of his coat the handkerchief he had captured from Thello the day before and showed it to her, concealed in his hand as he spoke.

Thello, whose greatest redeeming quality was perhaps her unconquerable sense of humor, burst out laughing to the no small mystification of Edith, and her laugh was answered by Faithorne, who rose at this moment with a copy of a society weekly in his hand.

"And what is amusing *you*?" said Thello, looking at him a trifle viciously.

"Today's *Tattler*," answered he. "It is delicious. Have you read it?"

"Not this week's," replied Ethel. "How goes it?"

"Why," said Faithorne, "the Bad Fairy has had a terrible set-down."

"Oh," said Denalguez, "a story for children, I suppose—a fairy tale?"

"Oh, dear no," said Faithorne, "but an anonymous story which all London is discussing at this moment. It is called 'Arcadia *versus* Hades,' and it is a modern story for grown up children, served up week by week in the form of a myth. The scene is Arcadia—in it we have Phyllis weary of Corydon—not, however, that she is pining after any particular Strephon."

"If she indeed resembles her earthly prototype," interrupted Denalguez, who had caught the spirit of the fable, "she probably complains that the lambs are too spotlessly white, the crooks too gold, the ribbons too blue, and Corydon too faithful."

Thello answered promptly, "And she would be right. One cannot live entirely on caramels. I should die without my olives." The last sentence was accompanied with a flash from the wondrous eyes.

"There is the Bad Fairy who tries to lead Phyllis away," explained Faithorne, looking steadily at Thello. Then turning his eyes on Denalguez, "A good fairy, who tries to save her——"

"And," broke in Thello, "a mischievous fairy, who complicates matters."

"Why," asked Denalguez, "did Phyllis wish to leave Arcadia?"

"She did not wish to leave it," put in Edith at this point abstractedly, "at least not till she was taught to believe that it was stupid and dull."

"Phyllis was quick at her lessons as all good little girls should be," put in Ethel, maliciously.

Faithorne was about to continue his reading in answer to Denalguez' questions, when, catching Edith's eye, he handed her the paper, and said:

"You read it to us, Mrs. Warburton."

She took the paper mechanically and read: "She allowed herself to be taken away blindfolded, but in spite of the excitement of the journey, she could not quite shake off her misgivings. When she had travelled a long way, she began to miss the loving care Corydon had lavished upon her, and which had been so much a part of her life that it had become unheeded. She found in the new land so many jostling hither and thither that she became afraid, and a restlessness to be at home, at peace, overtook her. At length she tore the bandage from her eyes, and saw not far before her a ledge of rocks that divided the two lands. She hesitated a moment, then turning her back upon the new, tried to find her way back to the old land, unaided and alone."

"Poor Phyllis," and she laid the paper down, and it dropped to the floor as she leaned back in her chair, and Faithorne stooped to pick it up.

"Well," said Thello, "Phyllis is so weak I have no patience with her. I should have gone over if it had been headlong."

"And that," said Denalguez, who was somewhat mystified, "seems to be the end of the story; Phyllis is saved."

"No," said Faithorne, a fragment of a smile twitching up one corner of his mouth. "The Bad Fairy is not so easily beaten, as this last sentence will show," and he made believe to go on reading where Edith had left off: "Phyllis turned sadly from the land she had dreamed was so beautiful, wondering if Corydon would forgive her, and if he were slumbering as she had left him. Meanwhile the Good and the Bad Fairy were hurrying on far in advance of poor Phyllis. The Good Fairy hoped to get back to Arcadia and keep Corydon asleep until Phyllis came home, but the Bad Fairy travelled faster, and on the road found a power- ful Talisman which was to awaken Corydon. Which will reach Arcadia first?" And he closed the paper as he laid it down upon the table.

A light was beginning to dawn upon Maurice Denalguez. "I shall watch with much interest," said he, "the fortunes of Arcadia."

"So shall I," said Faithorne.

"Well, good-bye, Captain Denalguez," said Ethel, "I must go now, but I am so glad to have met you—at last. I am always at home at five—come when you can—and soon. Are you ready, Edith?"

"Yes," said Edith; then adding to Denalguez, "You have no message for Philip?"

"Yes," answered Denalguez, who had been thinking deeply. "Will you give him a letter for me? I won't keep you a moment."

"Why, of course," replied Edith, and she seated herself in an arm-chair by the window. Thello was sitting at the fireplace, and Faithorne came and leaned over the back of her chair. He pointed to Denalguez as he said, softly:

"How did he get the letters?"

"Didn't he tell you?"

"No, but I bet you were sold somehow."

"Do you think so?" said Thello, opening her purple eyes wide, and turning up her face so that there was about four inches between her own and Faithorne's; "where are the letters now?" she continued.

"Safe—burned," answered he, "admit that you are beaten."

"No one is infallible," returned Ethel, with a light laugh; "by the by, Faithorne, do you mean to do as you said yesterday afternoon—marry?"

"Most assuredly," replied that gentleman. "I proposed formally this morning, and I am to receive my answer tonight."

"Cunning of you, wasn't it," returned Thello, "to keep the girl going whilst you were making love to Edith." Then after a little pause, she looked up at him again and said, "You are a sweet thing."

"Yes, I am nice," returned Faithorne in the same tone. "You see," he continued, "a man must take care of his character, and if Edith had thrown me over and I had had nothing in reserve, I might have done something desperate."

"Gracious," said Thello, "what do you call marriage?"

"When a man has lived as I have," returned Faithorne, "he knows where to find a wife *and her friends.*" As he spoke, Thello's eye fell upon the little note which Faithorne had enclosed with the letters, which Denalguez had left upon the table at her side. Denalguez himself was writing at a *sécretaire,* his back turned towards them.

"I wish," said Ethel, "that you would find my purse for me; I put it down somewhere a moment ago."

He came around her chair and leaned over the table to get the purse from the other side where it lay. As he did so, she snatched up the little scrap of paper, and thrust it into her muff. "Phyllis, my dear," said she, turning to the unconscious Edith, "look out for yourself!"

Denalguez was reading over the note he had written, which concluded with the words—"so you see, my dear Philip, there must be reasons stronger than you can guess for my refusal to be present tonight. I cannot possibly——" he was interrupted by the entrance of a servant, announcing Mr. Wurmsley.

"Captain Denalguez," said the new-comer with hurried pomposity, as he advanced into the room, distributing greetings all around as he came, and not seeming to notice the incongruity of the party assembled. "I come an unbidden guest, but——"

"You are no less welcome I am sure," interposed Denalguez, with some show of agitation, wondering what horrible mischance could have brought Edith's father there at that moment.

"I came," interposed Edith in turn, "to make sure of Captain Denalguez for you tonight, papa."

"If I had known that," said Mr. Wurmsley, "I need not have intruded. The fact is, I have determined there must be no mistake about tonight. You see, Captain Denalguez, Philip Warburton would find no pleasure if you were not of our party. The reception is for nine o'clock. The family only—and of course you are one of us—will be at dinner, we can then have a chat before the guests arrive. To tell you the truth, I have a particular reason for desiring the presence of my relatives and intimates, apart from the pleasure of their company. I need not make a secret of what is to be announced tonight. I have been asked for my daughter Marion's hand, and I was to give my answer tonight. I give it—my consent,—now." He took Faithorne's hand in his as he spoke, and amid the astonishment of the others, the silence was almost audible.

"It seems strange, my dear Reginald," continued he, with much unction, "that we should meet like this. It was an impulse that brought me here, and it would be nonsense to keep you in suspense when my answer is 'yes.'"

Even the imperturbable Faithorne was embarrassed for a moment, as he answered, "I am much honored, I am sure. May I ask the privilege of being the first to speak to Marion?"

"Most assuredly, most assuredly," said Mr. Wurmsley. "I do not believe in saying to a girl, 'You are to marry Mr. So and So.' A lover should plead his own cause."

By this time Thello had recovered herself, and advancing to Faithorne, she said with her adorable grin, "Let me be the first, Sir Reginald, to say how glad I am to know of your good fortune, though I am not altogether surprised. I should be dull indeed if your devotion had escaped me." And then dropping her voice, she said as she resumed her former manner, "You are a sweet thing."

"Yes," returned Faithorne as before, "I *am* nice."

Maurice Denalguez had been watching Edith anxiously whilst the above colloquy had taken place. She had seemed on the point of speaking once or twice, but words seemed to fail her. Now Sir Reginald Faithorne came to her side, and looking her in the eyes, with an expression that for her seemed full of threat, though to the others his manner seemed naught but most courteous, he said, "You will congratulate me, will you not? We have always been such good *friends* that I cannot doubt your welcome."

"My God," exclaimed Denalguez to himself, as she still remained silent, "will she not speak?" A few moments later, after what was getting to be an embarrassing pause, Edith took her departure with her father, and Sir Reginald Faithorne, offering his arm to Mrs. Marsden, led her to her carriage.

## CHAPTER XII.

The evening of the same day was destined to be a momentous one in the lives of all the actors in this drama. At the house of Mr. Botolph Wurmsley, a family party had assembled, which was to be followed by a reception later on, and though the thing had been comparatively unforeseen, Mr. Wurmsley promised himself the satisfaction of making the announcement of his daughter's engagement to Sir Reginald Faithorne, under circumstances highly gratifying to his self-esteem.

The dreary dinner was drawing to a close, and Marion, who had excused herself, was sitting in the drawing-room alone. She had thought that Denalguez would be of the party, and shrinking from meeting him had dined alone. She was mistaken, however, for Denalguez had clung to his resolution not to attend, hoping to be able to see Philip Warburton and to ascertain if possible the exact state of that gentleman's mind, and the extent to which he was informed in regard to the events which were happening around him, principally with himself as their objective point.

Marion sat in the drawing-room alone, reflecting deeply; and the world seemed a very strange place to her just then. She knew Maurice Denalguez had come back, for Edith had mentioned having seen him. Her father had been dropping ominous hints all day, and she gathered that she was at that moment the object of some scheme in her father's mind, of whose nature she was unable to form any conjecture, though her experience of her father's schemes for the welfare of his daughters caused her a certain vague alarm.

"What can be the surprise," said she to herself, "that father said I was to have tonight, with his odd remarks about being a 'strange little girl,' and 'keeping her father in the dark.' He said it was something very important. There is nothing I think important now. There might have been long ago," and the child sighed deeply as she looked out of the window at the people passing and repassing in the cool of the summer night, in the park just over the way. "And yet," continued she to herself, "it does not seem to be so very long ago, either," and taking a little letter case from her pocket, she drew therefrom an oft-folded and unfolded letter, which she smoothed out tenderly and read to herself as she had done, probably, many hundreds of times before.

"My dear Mr. Wurmsley," it read, "I do not know whether you are prepared for this communication from me, but I will be brief. I want you to give me your daughter Marion for my wife. No promise has been given or asked between us yet, but I do not fear, if you will give your consent, of gaining hers.

"Maurice Denalguez."


She read the signature over again, as she pressed her lips to it, and then refolded the paper and restored it to its place.

"How happy I was when this came," said she. "And with what pride I said to Edith on her birthday, 'A letter came from St. Petersburg today for father. I know it is asking after me,' and not ten minutes afterwards I knew that my hopes were killed. How cruel it was of him, and how kind Mrs. Marsden was to that poor little girl." As she thus reflected, the object of her reflections entered the room.

"Aren't you surprised to see me at this unusual hour?" said Thello as she greeted the girl. "The fact is, I have had nothing in the world to do between my quiet dinner, which takes me no time at all, and your party later on; so I thought I would come and play a game of piquet with your father, as I had not been able to dine here."

"I was just thinking of you," returned Marion, "and of a subject—*you* know—which I have always avoided. It is not a pleasant one to me as you may imagine. Do you ever sit dreaming over the fire and reading pictures there?"

"Sometimes," returned Thello, beginning to feel a trifle uncomfortable.

"I do often," pursued Marion, in the same tone. "I can never look for long into the fire without thinking of some one, and it seems to me it is the same thing as I sit here and look out of the window into the park. I see him all the time." She paused for a moment, and then went on in the same unheeding tone. "Wasn't it curious that you should have told me about that girl being wronged by him when you did not even know that I knew him, much less"—and her voice sank to a whisper—"how I loved him? You did not guess how your words nearly broke my heart, did you?"

"Come, come," said Ethel Marsden, becoming more and more uneasy; "you must not have such sad thoughts tonight of all nights."

"Think how lucky it was," pursued Marion, not noticing the interruption, "that you happened to tell me just then. In a few days it would have been too late. Could you believe it? he had proposed to my father for me that very morning. I never could have supposed a man could be so wicked."

"It is very dreadful," said Thello, taking refuge in a pained expression of face which she simulated to perfection.

"I am going to ask your advice, Mrs. Marsden," went on the girl. "I think I ought to tell Philip how deceived he is in Maurice Denalguez. You know Philip doesn't know that he proposed for me. No one knows—when father told me—what was in the letter—I only answered, 'I refuse, and I hope you will not persuade me.' Don't you think it would be right to tell Philip?"

The perturbed condition of Thello's mind was, fortunately for her, not apparent in her face, as she answered, "Well, my dear, you know it would be a little awkward for *you*. Of course *I* might; but then your brother-in-law and I are not on very cordial terms. There is no use disguising the fact. Since the fuss on Edith's birthday it has been extremely unpleasant. We never meet, but I know he is still unjust to me. When they come in after dinner, we can easily avoid each other."

"Perhaps you will not believe it," said Marion, "but I was very near disliking you once. I am so fond of Philip that I suppose I was prejudiced; but when you told me about that girl, I knew you must be tender-hearted and good to try and cheer her when you had so much else to do. I am only glad—yes, very glad—that I was warned in time," and turning, she walked over towards the fireplace to hide the tears that she could not suppress any longer.

"Goodness me!" said Thello, looking after her, with some anxiety, "this young woman will spoil all my plans if I am not careful. Do you know," continued she, aloud, as if suddenly starting a new train of thought, "I do not care to see Philip Warburton before the other people come. Is dinner over, do you think?"

"Scarcely," said Marion. "Philip rushed in from the city just in time. His servant brought his things, and he is going to dress directly after dinner, so you are not likely to meet. I will go and see how long they are likely to be. Do you know that Edith is quite ill? I made her lie down, and now she is asleep. I hope the rest will do her good. I told Philip he was not to have her wakened. But everything seems to have gone wrong tonight, there seems to be something dreadful in the air. It is as if there was a gloom over us."

"Edith ill!" echoed Ethel Marsden, "well, it is getting late. Don't you think you had better go to her? Don't mind me, run away; but, by the by, about what you asked me—I don't think you had better speak to Philip just at present. Men are queer creatures and look at things in a different way from women. Leave it alone for a little while."

"Well," answered Marion, "I was sure that you knew best, and would tell me the right thing to do. I think I will go to Edith if you are sure you do not mind?"

"Not a bit," replied she, and the girl left the Machiavelian Thello alone.

Left by herself, Thello dropped into the seat which Marion had vacated and began to think over the events of the day. As the recollection came back to her, her little malicious smile parted her teeth again, and she remarked to herself,

"How I enjoyed this morning, as soon as I recovered from the shock of finding the Count Guerravillia, who adored me yesterday, was my mortal enemy, Maurice Denalguez—today. First trick to you, Captain Denalguez. Will the next be mine, I wonder? You worked hard enough to keep Edith's fault from her husband, but your work was crude. I wonder if anyone would take so much trouble for me?" She rose with a little gesture of indignation, and began pacing the room with her characteristic and hesitating little glide. "Why should such a woman, with neither heart nor brain, be tenderly cared for, as though she were something finer than the rest of creation?—and Philip Warburton, with his virtuous pride, did not think me good enough to associate with his wife! We shall see how it will be in the end. I can awaken Corydon and spoil Phyllis' return, though the Good Fairy thinks my talisman is lost—sleep on, dream on, my Arcadians, in your fancied security—you shall wake at my bidding. Oh! my puppets, I hold you in the hollow of my hand, and though the hand is small, the grasp is firm." She sank into the chair again, the strain somewhat removed by motion, and pursued her chain of thought. "I have so much satisfaction within my reach, that I do not know where to strike first. What will be the result of awakening my Arcadians? It will dispose of Warburton and dear, delicate Edith, but it will also effectually stop Marion's marriage with Faithorne, leaving her free. Explanations might then take place between her and Denalguez—might, yes, but *must not!* —*shall* not! That will be my task. I am sorry that I must hurt that child, Marion, but it is war, and I will not be beaten."

As she came to this conclusion, the object of her cogitations came running in.

"Oh, Mrs. Marsden," said she, "what shall I do? Captain Denalguez has just called and asked to see me, and I do not know what answer to make. I want to be determined, for I know he is unworthy and has behaved most basely. But he is so handsome, and so clever, and it is so long since I have seen him that I fear I shall break down. If he should question me, he might find out I had been to see that girl, and I should be so ashamed. Of course I know there was no harm in going or you would not have taken me."

"No harm," echoed Ethel, "no, my dear, but very indiscreet, as I told you when you insisted on going—and I am afraid your father will be very angry with me when he knows——"

"But he will not know——"

"You cannot prevent his knowing—if Captain Denalguez learns of your visit——"

"Captain Denalguez shall not learn it from me, I promise you. You give me strength, Mrs. Marsden. I might have shown some weakness if I alone had to suffer rebuke for the impulse that led me thither, but the thought that you might be blamed for what was an act of charity and kindness, will keep my lips sealed. No entreaties shall gain from me the knowledge I possess. You do not doubt me, surely?"

"My dear child," said Ethel, "no one could possibly doubt you. See, your hair is all tumbled. Come and make yourself tidy before seeing Captain Denalguez. It would not do for him to see you looking so excited. Ask for him to be sent here." As she spoke she had rung a little hand-bell and a servant came in.

"Ask Captain Denalguez to come in here," said Marion, and the servant left the room.

"Now run away and put your hair straight," said Thello, and Marion preceded her through the *portières*.

"How lucky I am," said Thello to herself, as she followed her. "This unexpected move would have ruined my whole plan. But now I am on safe ground again."

She followed Marion out of the room as Maurice Denalguez was shown into it by another door.

Denalguez's state of mind was decidedly mixed. "I wonder," said he to himself as he looked around the room and ascertained that it was empty, "if I am wrong in seeking an explanation from Marion. My pride at first said 'no;' but through all the misery of this morning there came to me a hope that she had not refused me for another. Whatever be the reason, no other love taught her to forget mine. She does not know yet, I suppose, that tonight her hand will be sought by Faithorne. The man was honest after all in asking me if I had any claim on her. I wonder if I am doing the right thing by him in coming here now?" He walked up and down the room twice before answering himself. As he came to a full stop, in front of the looking-glass, he said, "Yes, for if she means to accept him tonight, my visit cannot possibly affect her decision."

He stopped as in the glass he saw Marion enter the room behind him. She was obviously nervous and ill at ease, and he permitted a moment to pass before he let her know that he had seen her. Then he turned slowly, and bowed with ceremony. She returned the salutation, and sank into a chair.

"I have till now," began Denalguez, approaching the girl, "accepted your strange disposal of me, but I will not let today pass without making an effort to understand it. What is it that has become between us, Marion?"

She remained silent, and he made a little gesture of despair.

"Are you happy?" he continued.

"Yes."

The reply was almost inaudible, but Denalguez's anxious ear caught it, and man of the world as he was, he could not restrain a momentary heart-throb as he read in her tone the denial of her words.

"Why did you treat me so cruelly?" he said at last.

"Ask your own heart."

"I find no answer there, or I should not seek it from your lips. Tell me, what have I done?"

"It is a matter I do not choose to discuss," said Marion, firmly, rising and moving away from him. He followed her a step, and then he said,

"But, child that you are, you cannot—you must not dispose of our lives in that passionless way. Remember," and his voice became very grave, "if I leave you now, you send me to a bitter, hopeless existence." He paused, and as she gave him no sign, he took another step forward, and exclaimed almost roughly,

"A man at my age cannot begin a fresh life with the dawn of each day. Even *you* have not done that, or I should not be here." Then controlling himself again, he went on. "Can it be that I, by my own pride, have robbed myself of your love? I should have sought you before to ask your reasons, but it was the knowledge that I had done nothing that could offend you that made me acquiesce in what was to me inexplicable. I have always been honest with you, I told you what my past had been when we first met. You were but a child to me then, yet how full of womanly sympathy. As we grew more to each other, I told you that my life was no fit mate for yours, that I, whose love was beaten and bruised, had no right to ask a resting place in your fresh young heart. You set aside my fears, you gave me hope."

He became silent, and seemed waiting for her reply. He waited in vain for a few moments, then he continued in a harder voice. "What could have been your reason for deceiving me so? It is neither just nor natural. Once more, will you tell me your reason for rejecting me?"

"And once more I reply," returned Marion at last, an accent of despair in her voice, "that there is no need that the reason should be discussed. The kindest thing you can do is to let me forget. Do not force me to say what I think of your pretended ignorance——"

Denalguez interrupted her with a movement of his hand. "I have done—and I beg that you also will spare me any more on this subject. I thought that I had sounded the depths of misery in my life, but I had yet to encounter the cruelty, the wanton cruelty, of a child. And believe me, Mademoiselle, you will forgive me for my intrusion before I shall forgive myself."

He moved towards the door, and lifted the curtains. His back was towards her, or he would have seen her lips frame the word, "Maurice," before she turned and disappeared through the curtains. When Denalguez looked around, she was gone, and he, too, went out by the opposite door. As he did so, Mr. Wurmsley came bustling into the room by the door through which Marion had made her escape, and then an excessively funny thing happened.

The *portières* over the other door at the end of the room, parted, and Thello Marsden smiling, *insouciante*, as ever, stepped into the room. To the reader, who is beginning to know Thello almost as well as the writer, it is not necessary to say that she had been an interested observer of the whole of the scene which was just completed. The two confronted one another.

"Surely," said Mr. Wurmsley, as he greeted her, "that was Captain Denalguez' voice. Where is he? Marion, too, where is she? Marion!" he called, moving towards the door.

Thello interposed. "Are you calling Marion?" she said ingenuously, "I have just sent her to find something for me. She will be back in a moment."

"Good," returned the old gentleman. "My dear Mrs. Marsden, you are so kind and unceremonious to come in so early. Why, you are like one of my own children."

"That is very nice of you to say," returned Thello; "but why don't you kiss your eldest daughter?"

"My youngest, I protest," returned old Wurmsley delightedly, as he stooped down and kissed the cheek that Thello turned up to him as she stood on tiptoe for the purpose.

"I told you," continued she, "that though I could not dine with you, I would come in for the reception, and I am quite half an hour too soon for that, but I thought we could have a game of piquet. You beat me so shamefully the last time we played."

"It is charming of you," returned the old gentleman, "to think of an old man. I wish you had dined with us. My son-in-law was very late, he has only just gone to dress, now. Do you know, I cannot imagine why Edith is so strange and nervous. We insisted on her lying down. It was nonsense, her trying to go through dinner, and she consented. Do you know, I want to thank you for your help. Frankly, if you had not been clever enough to have seen Sir Reginald Faithorne's attention to Marion, and had not told me that you were sure she cared for him, I should have been puzzled what answer to give him this morning. Much as I desire that my daughter in marrying should attain rank and position I should never think of sacrificing her happiness to my pride. Thanks to you, however, my dear Mrs. Marsden," and he took her hand with much paterfamiliarity, "I was prepared. Girls are extraordinary creatures! Dear me, dear me! I never should have guessed from Marion's manner that she cared for Faithorne. Ah, well, well! a man who is left with a daughter to marry off, is a pretty helpless specimen of humanity."

Old Wurmsley's gentle babble was interrupted by the entrance of a servant, with a packet which he carried upon a salver.

"Some letters," said he, "that Mr. Warburton's servant has just brought, thinking they may be important."

"Place them on the table in the library," said the master of the house, "and bring coffee. And now, my dear Mrs. Marsden, if you will pardon me, I have some business papers to get ready before Faithorne comes."

He went to the door, and left the room as Thello answered, "Why, of course. Here is Edith—are you better?" she added, addressing the latter who had just entered the room, and sank into an arm-chair.

"I wish I had died this afternoon," said Edith. "Upon my honor, I do. How am I to stop this scandal?"

"Which scandal?" asked Ethel innocently.

"How can you ask?" returned Edith. "This abominable marriage. It cannot be—it shall not be! but what can I do?"

Ethel looked at her for a moment with her pretty head on one side, and then she replied, in her clear, incisive tones.

"Wait for about an hour until there are plenty of people here, and then confess. It would be just like you to choose such a moment for your repentance; it would place so many people in an awkward position. It is always good to have as large a crowd as possible to witness one's domestic smash."

"But there is no time to lose," replied Edith, not noticing Ethel Marsden's sneer. "Oh, to think," she continued, rising, "that Marion should be made the victim of the revenge *he* has chosen."

"There is no reason she should be regarded as a victim," replied Ethel, delicately licking the tip of her finger, and applying it in little dabs to her fan, to repair some imaginary tear. "Her position will be far better than yours. Faithorne is rich, young, popular, clever, and it is quite possible that he is very fond of her——"

"Oh, for pity's sake, stop! It drives me mad to hear you talk of this marriage as possible."

"You are too sensitive, my dear. When Faithorne told me last night that he was going to propose for Marion, it struck me as the best way possible to end all suspicion about you."

Edith sprang to her feet. "And you think that I will buy my peace at such a cost? Good heavens, Thello!"

"I know, of course, that it must wound your vanity to find Faithorne in love with your sister, but the fact remains, that a man should prefer openly to adore a beautiful and innocent young girl to secret interviews, at imminent risks, with a married woman, is a peculiar taste, of course—but it exists, nevertheless."

"You say that he is in love with her—and she——? is she not to be considered?"

"Certainly," replied Thello, in the same tone as before. "But are you quite sure she will dislike this marriage so much? Have you any reason to suppose that it will be in any way repugnant to her?"

Edith had dropped into her chair again.

"There has been little confidence between us lately," said she drearily. "God help me, I cannot tell what is best."

"That, my dear," observed Thello, "is a self-evident proposition, or you would see that this marriage is a special providence for you, and you had better think seriously before you break it off."

"What you suggest is infamous."

"To put it plainly, my dear Edith, because Faithorne has been—well, let us say 'attentive,' in his manner to you, you have construed his feeling into something deeper. Believe me, he has been no more devoted to you than he has been and is, to me, for periods of about two months in every year; but I know how to estimate his nonsense, and you do not. You choose to take for earnestness his 'man of the world gallantry,' which means positively nothing. Of course I am assuming your flirtations to be as harmless as mine. Perhaps I am assuming too much."

Edith was sitting, looking at her from under her brows. She was silent for a moment, and then she said gravely, "Philip was right about you."

Thello threw back her head, and put both her pretty feet straight out in front of her upon a foot-stool, as she shut her fan with a snap and grinned softly.

"You make me feel my own unworthiness, sweet Edith," said she, "and I would not further contaminate you by a moment of my company if this were your house, but I think I shall have an amusing evening later on, and I do not mean to miss it. However," and she rose to her feet, "there is no need for me to bore you with a *tête à tête*, so fare thee well for the moment, my best friend and pupil," and Thello, humming some little snatch from some French opera or other, passed through the *portières* into the adjoining room.

"Who can I ask for counsel," thought Edith miserably, "and why did I ever ask it of her? She was right in one thing, however, it will never do to speak tonight. Marion may refuse Faithorne, after all. I will wait until tomorrow, I can decide that much at once." She was about to pass into the library when her father entered the room.

"Ah, there you are," said he, cheerfully, "let me look at you. Are you feeling better? Not much, eh?"

"Yes, yes," returned Edith, "I am much better. Father," continued she, "were you not very much surprised at Sir Reginald Faithorne's proposal?"

"Well," returned the old gentleman, "not altogether surprised. He has been here so much lately that when he asked me,

I wondered that I had not expected it. What other reason could bring him here so often?"

Edith was fidgeting nervously with a tassel, as she replied, "But is his reputation altogether what you would wish?"

"Oh," returned Mr. Wurmsley, easily, "I dare say he has been credited with a good deal more than he deserves, and will probably make a very good husband. If, as they say, he has been a bit wild, he will be the more ready to settle down."

"So you are satisfied?"

"My dear, I am more than satisfied. I have nothing, absolutely nothing left to wish for. You children have been very little trouble to me—have made splendid matches, and I am proud of you both. I should be hard to please if I were not satisfied."

He crossed over to the window, as Edith leaned back in her chair.

"I must wait," said she to herself.

A servant entered the room with coffee at this moment, and Marion coming in at the same time began to serve her father. She was so employed when Philip Warburton entered the room. Had his wife turned her head in his direction she would have seen at once that something was amiss. Philip Warburton was deadly pale, his lips were tightly clenched, and a strong furrow between his brows betrayed the fact that he was prey to some unwonted emotion.

It was mechanically that he took his coffee cup from Marion, and sat down near his father-in-law. Edith threw him a casual glance. He was sitting with his back towards her, and she said,

"You look worn out,—had a tiring day?"

"Yes," returned Warburton. "I have been much occupied all day, and I have just heard some bad news."

"Ah," said Wurmsley, "those letters that your servant brought?"

"Yes."

"Can you not forget your bad news for tonight?" said Edith.

"I am sorry I sent those letters to you, now," said Mr. Wurmsley, "for whatever it is, you can do nothing on the spot, and the knowledge of their contents will dispirit you. I hope that

Captain Denalguez will be here early, I did all I could to make him come tonight, I even called upon him personally, but he seemed uncertain."

"Oh," said Edith, "I shall be glad if he stays away, though I persuaded him to come for your sake. He might as well be here, however—you will be regretting him all the evening, so his absence won't benefit me much."

"You are mistaken," said Warburton with deadly emphasis. "My regrets will be for another friend. I am meditating how to help him."

"What is his position?" said Mr. Wurmsley.

Warburton rose.

"He is a husband," said he, "who has been deceived. I will state the case, and you—all of you—" and he looked from his wife to his father-in-law, "shall give me your opinion."

Edith was obviously uneasy.

"Perhaps you forget," said she, "that Marion is here?"

"I am sure," said Mr. Wurmsley, "Philip is not likely to say anything that she may not hear."

Philip Warburton went on.

"There will be a scandal, but justice must be done."

"I do not care for such stories," said Edith.

"You have suddenly become very sensitive," said her husband.

"I don't see why we should be bothered with other people's troubles."

"Listen," said Warburton, "and you will see. My friend married a woman with whom he was desperately in love. Gradually this husband was forced to the knowledge that his wife did not return his love. For a time he fought against his convictions until, try as he would, he could do so no longer. Of course a man does not see the light of his life die out without retaining some hope that it will live again. So with him—a faint, small hope would still creep in."

He paused a moment, and Mr. Wurmsley put in,

"Perhaps he was too suspicious in his disposition."

Edith was getting more and more anxious. She even seemed on the point of speaking to arrest her husband's words, but with a forbidding gesture he silenced her as he proceeded.

"He would not be discouraged. She was young, and he hoped that time with his patience and kindness, would bring a change. It did. She began by being irritable and faithful, she ended by being amiable and unfaithful."

Every one turned and looked at him as he spoke.

"She rewarded his devotion with treachery, and he only needed proof."

"Ah! there is the difficulty," put in Mr. Wurmsley.

"Which he suddenly and unexpectedly obtained," said Warburton.

"What has he done?" queried his father-in-law.

"Nothing yet. It is so grave a matter that one cannot be too careful. Now for your advice; the youngest first—Marion, in his place, what would you do?"

"I would forgive," said Marion, looking up from where she sat at her father's feet, "in the hope that repentance and gratitude might inspire what all else had failed to awaken."

"And you, sir?" said Warburton to Mr. Wurmsley, who was regarding the proceedings with a mild air of astonishment.

"Oh," broke in Marion, "it is Edith's turn to advise."

"I would not say a word in such a matter," said Edith, rising, "don't ask me."

"You say——" said Warburton to Mr. Wurmsley, as before.

"I—er—I——" began Mr. Wurmsley, "should just take her back to her parents—or friends. I should make them judge between us. I should say, 'See, the seed has blossomed, the fruit is ripe,—pluck it.'"

"Good!" exclaimed Warburton, "you have judged!"

Every one rose.

"What do you mean?" said Mr. Wurmsley.

"I say that you have judged, and I return her to you, for I am the man, and the woman is your daughter."

"Listen to me," said Edith. "Have you no mercy?"

"Do not let me look at you."

"You might have asked——"

"Asked!" echoed the man.

"It is not as you say!"

Warburton turned upon her. "And your lover," he exclaimed, "have you forgotten him since yesterday? Here are the proofs," continued he, turning to Mr. Wurmsley, and handing him a packet of letters. "Her letters to the man."

Mr. Wurmsley took them as if in a dream, and Philip Warburton, turning to all present, said: "Justice is done. Now to avenge myself. There is one man too many on the earth." He started for the door, and Mr. Wurmsley stopped him.

"Stay—stay—" said he. "I cannot believe it. You say these letters are your proofs. Who is the man? There must be some mistake." He feverishly undid the packet. "I cannot see," said he. "Read them."

Warburton let fall the letters, retaining in his hand a single slip, which he read as he crushed it in his hand and flung it to the earth:

"I return your letters, but I keep your peace of mind. Reginald Faithorne."

As he spoke the name, it was echoed by a servant, who threw back the *portières* and announced,

"Sir Reginald Faithorne."

Warburton walked up to him before Mr. Wurmsley could interpose, and as the unsuspecting baronet extended his hand as if to greet him, a sharp noise echoed through the room. Philip Warburton had slapped Sir Reginald smartly on both sides of the face.

Faithorne, thunderstruck for the moment, raised his arm as if to strike back, then catching sight of the women and remembering himself, he drew back a step, and indicating the ladies by a wave of the hand, bowed ceremoniously to every one in the room. Then he turned on his heel and left the house. The only member of the group left behind who seemed to realize the scene that had taken place, was Thello Marsden, who, standing in an artistic attitude half hidden by the *portières* leading into the library, had watched the entire sequence of occurrences, and grinned maliciously as the curtains fell over her retreating figure.

# CHAPTER XIII.

Midway between Calais and Ostend lies a little fishing village, half hidden in thickly grown woods. Once beyond the confines of the village itself, one loses one's self at once in a tangle of woodland greenery, where the earth is hidden by the thick growth of the underwood, as the skies are hidden by the interlacing of the branches overhead. Even that observant person known to the makers of guide-books and romances as the traveller, could easily mistake these woodlands for primeval forests, were it not for the continual intersection of alleys which seem to have been cut through the brushwood by countless generations of wayfarers. Several of these alleys led to—converged towards a clearing in the brushwood, covered with soft, green grass. The patch is of about half an acre in extent, and it is occupied on this warm August morning by four men.

They present a peculiar spectacle, taking into consideration the hour and the nature of the locality. All four were dressed precisely alike, that is to say, from head to foot in the most immaculate black, and their black frock coats and tall hats, standing out against the surrounding verdure, convey the impression of a conclave of legal crows.

The men are Philip Warburton, Maurice Denalguez, a young English friend of Warburton's, resident in Ostend, and the fourth, who is the senior of the party by at least a score of years, is recognizable at first glance by a certain grim calmness of manner, to be a doctor.

"Well," said Denalguez, as the four arrived upon the scene by one of the alleys through the brush, "we are here first at any rate. Pretty place, isn't it?"

"Yes," returned Philip Warburton, calmly.

"Are you quite decided what you are going to do about it?" queried Denalguez.

"Perfectly," replied Warburton. "My mind was made up long before I claimed and asked this favor of you."

"And what, then," said the young Englishman, "is to be the termination of this duel?"

Philip Warburton turned to him with a smile, as he said, "Possibly my death, but probably his."

"Ah, it is serious then?"

"Very serious. If I should fall," said Warburton, turning once more to Denalguez, "you will take me home to Edith. If he should fall, I will carry the news myself. If by any mischance both of us leave this place alive, remember, gentlemen, that today's meeting is entirely between ourselves—a matter that never occurred."

"Come, come," put in the doctor at this point, an old friend of Philip Warburton's who, much against his will and against his own convictions of what was right and what was wrong, had consented to cross the Channel with his friend and Denalguez to minister to Philip in case his ministrations should be needed. "Do not talk in this horrible way. Your honor has been compromised, my dear Philip, and though it is barbarous and old fashioned and ridiculous and unsatisfactory, you are quite right in seeking to have it avenged. But what the deuce!—you are not going to kill one another. Think of the scandal——"

"Yes," said Warburton, interrupting him sharply, "think of the scandal! I have thought of nothing else since it occurred."

The doctor shrugged his shoulders and turned on his heel.

"There they are," he said, pointing across the clearing as four similarly black figures arrived upon the scene.

The four new-comers, headed by Sir Reginald Faithorne, walked briskly across the glade one behind another, and Warburton and his three companions advanced to meet them in the same order. In the middle of the clearing they met, and stood in a row, facing one another, when with one mechanical movement every man removed his hat and saluted his *vis-a-vis* gravely. It was like some grim figure in a dance of death.

This formality over, the two principals turned their backs upon each other, and retired about twenty paces. Denalguez and Sir Reginald's principal second advanced towards one another and Denalguez spun a sovereign in the air for choice of position.

Sir Reginald's second won, and Denalguez rejoined Philip, who was buttoning up his coat, turning up his collar, and drawing his cuffs up out of sight under his sleeves.

Meanwhile the two other seconds had gone through the formality of examining and loading the pistols; and the two doctors, whilst they leisurely fumbled in their pockets for the keys of the two ominous looking cases they had brought with them, fraternized with the air of two men accidentally thrown together under distressing circumstances, which do not concern them personally.

The preliminaries being arranged, the two principals were placed back to back, and a pistol was given to each, which he held in the orthodox manner, with his elbow bent, the muzzle pointing to the sky. Even the trees seemed to hush their murmuring in deference to the drama of life and death that was proceeding beneath them.

The seconds retired, and Denalguez said in a low and distinct voice,

"Are you ready?"

The word "Yes" came simultaneously from both men. Warburton's short and incisive, Faithorne's languidly drawled.

"You will each walk ten paces as I count," proceeded Denalguez, "and at the tenth, you will turn and fire. One—two—three—four—five—six—seven—eight—nine—*ten*!"

Faithorne's second had won the toss for choice of position, and consequently Faithorne walked towards the sun and turning to fire, turned his back upon it; Philip walked in the opposite direction, and turning at the end of his ten paces, encountered the full glare of the morning brightness full in his eyes, and upon his pistol barrel. Nevertheless his aim was fairly true, and when the smoke of simultaneous reports cleared away, Faithorne was lying on the ground. Philip stood looking at him as if he could hardly realize exactly what had happened.

"Captain Denalguez," said Sir Reginald's second, approaching that gentleman, "you doubtless observed that my principal fired in the air."

"Yes, damn him!" returned Maurice Denalguez; and then, as the four seconds gravely saluted one another, Philip Warburton and his three companions left the field.

An hour later Sir Reginald Faithorne was carried into the inn at Roche-Mairie, and at the same moment, Philip Warburton and Maurice Denalguez, accompanied by the man of medicine, boarded the train for Calais.

"Why did you not kill him?" said Denalguez.

"It was the sun," answered Philip Warburton.

## CHAPTER XIV.

The summer and the autumn were spent when our story re-opens. Reopens in one of those little houses beloved by bachelors and young housekeepers, in Lower Eaton place, where Edith Warburton had hidden herself after that night that already seemed so long ago, that night when Philip had read in the drawing-room at her father's and had seemed to confirm Faithorne's message to her, "I return your letters, but I keep your peace of mind."

Edith sat in the boudoir which she had fitted up with such of her own belongings as she had brought from Wimbledon—sat in a listless attitude in a low arm-chair before the fire. To her own troubles she seemed by this time to have become thoroughly accustomed, and a new anxiety was filling her mind at the moment that we see her.

Her mind was occupied with her sister Marion, who had announced her definite intention of becoming a sister of mercy in an institution of ministering angels in the far east of the city, and no prayers or entreaties seemed able to turn her from her decision.

"Poor Marion," thought Edith. "She seems cheerful, but I cannot bear to think of her leaving the world in such a manner. It is little better than a convent that she goes into, and I dare not say a word. What argument of mine could influence her? She could so justly answer me with the example of my past. What use have I made of my life that I should presume to direct hers? What an example have I been to her! It seems years since I saw her, and yet it is only months. But I shall see her now, perhaps; that is to say, if she comes to say good-bye in answer to my entreaty. Oh, if I had only dreamed what my waywardness would have cost me, how different the world would have been to us all."

She sank into a reverie of forgetfulness, which was interrupted half an hour later by the entrance of Marion herself. The sight of the pale young face surrounded by the white and black draperies that all but concealed the golden hair, struck Edith with a sense of horrible contrast. The last time she had seen her sister, it had all been so different. Her resolution was not then made, and Edith had been taken to the south of France by her father, in the hope that change of air and of scene might have a beneficial effect upon her stunned senses. When she returned, Marion was already in the east, working with the sisterhood that she was now about to join.

Edith rose, and going to her, exclaimed,

"You have come in answer to my wish—in answer to my prayers! How good of you!"

"It was not good of me," replied the child-nun gravely and sweetly, "I wished to come and see you again, for we may not meet for so long, and besides, I want you to come to the Church today. I want you to be there when I am received into the sisterhood."

"You are to enter your new life today?"

"Yes. If you come quietly, no one would be any the wiser, and I shall be so much happier——"

"But, child," broke forth Edith impetuously, "don't talk so. It is dreadful. You must know that this new existence upon which you are about to enter seems like death—a living death, to those who love you."

"That is because they do not understand," returned Marion, gravely. "The life I leave is one sad memory, full of cruelty and disappointment; of shattered faith, and of foolish hopes which were but dreams. The life I begin today is one full of sweet re-alities, one made up of pure and steadfast ideals. Be sure, sweet sister of mine, that I shall be happy in my choice."

There was silence for a few moments between the sisters, and then Edith said,

"Tell me, Marion, if you do not mind going back for a few moments before you forget the past forever—why did you refuse to marry Maurice Denalguez?"

The young face hardened as the reply came slowly,

"Because I could not have been happy with him, nor he with me. Don't let us talk about my affairs that are over, for I must go very soon. Tell me, have you seen Philip?"

"No," replied Edith. "All that part of my life seems to be a blank. I know that he and Sir Reginald Faithorne fought, and that Sir Reginald was wounded, seriously, they say—that much I have gathered."

"Yes," said Marion, thoughtfully, "and they all say that he behaved wonderfully well after that night. He would not fire at Philip, and they say he might easily have killed him, had he chosen. He has been away ever since, has he not?"

"Don't speak of him," said Edith, rising. "It brings back my past that I would rather forget if I can. It reminds me, too, of the past further off than that, before I knew him when I was so happy. Don't remind me of it."

"But I want to remind you of it," insisted the child. "Do you think that I can be happy, knowing your trouble? I will never believe that you were wilfully wicked, and you may be quite sure that I never believed you did wrong."

Edith gave her a grateful hand pressure as she answered,

"And your child heart told you truer than the heads that called me guilty. I deserved to be thought the worst of—I was such a fool! I should like you to go to the altar with your mind and heart free from the burden I have brought to you. I will not try to exonerate myself from blame, but from sin. They told me— my friends I mean—I should be laughed at, if I didn't flirt as the rest. I was led away, step by step, through the fear of ridicule, till I told lies and deceived my husband to hide my folly. As each lie brought its multitude I was overwhelmed. But—there I stopped. To what end? Here am I alone, deserted by all but you. After that fearful night when Philip cast me off, I thought I could kill him for believing me guilty; but as time went on I knew I had given him every reason to believe the worst of me."

Marion put her arms round her sister as she asked,

"Why did not you defend yourself?"

"Because appearances were so terribly against me. I was utterly dazed at first to find he had those letters. I had destroyed all of them in the morning. Where those he had came from, I cannot imagine. It was all so sudden. Then when I came to myself, I thought he had judged me too hastily, and I felt bitter resentment. I was almost glad at the pain I knew he must suffer—forgetting his patience and my folly. Afterwards when I came to my senses, I feared him. Besides, what proof had I? A man never understands that a woman can commit any folly—may lie as I did, but will still hesitate to raise the fatal barrier. It is impossible to make a man believe this—oh, if regrets could expiate! I am so penitent!"

"Write and tell Philip so."

"I cannot. Do not ask me. Forget what I said except for the comfort it may give you. I am convinced if he had had any love or mercy in his heart, he would have spoken before this."

And Edith let her head drop on Marion's shoulder. It was pathetic to see this woman sheltered in the arms of this young girl. She whispered soothingly, as to a wayward child.

"Then let *me* tell him."

"No," said Edith, "you must promise me not to speak of me at all, till I am dead—promise. All I want is for you to know that you may still kiss me, for I still have the right to kiss you."

"Darling!" and the two sisters were locked in one another's arms.

When they had recovered themselves a little, Marion glanced at the clock, and Edith following her glance, said,

"Yes, yes,—I know. You must go now? Good-bye, and God bless you," and after a last kiss the two sisters parted.

Edith Warburton paced up and down the room a few times after her sister had gone. Finally she seated herself at the writing table, and tried to write. Hastily rising again, she went to the window.

"I cannot write," she said. "Why did she speak of Philip? I dare not write; but still, if I were quite sure that he would listen, I should like—but why should I think he cares for me any longer?"

She sank wearily into a chair, and her next conscious thought was one of the grim irony of circumstance, as a servant drew back the *portière* and announced, "Mrs. Marsden and Mrs. Beaufoy."

That Edith was surprised, is to use a miserably inadequate form of words, but she rose as if mechanically to meet and greet her visitors.

"Well, stranger," was Ethel Marsden's greeting, as she dropped into a chair by the fire opposite to Edith, and Clare Beaufoy took her seat between them.

"It is you who are the stranger," returned Edith, "for this is certainly a most unexpected pleasure. You could not expect to see me, since I have been away, and I have been very quiet since I returned. It is good of you to come and cheer up my loneliness."

"Oh," replied Ethel, airily, "I am not unforgiving, and besides it is interesting to note the effect upon an artless mind, of such a cataclysm as you have been through with that extraordinary husband of yours. I should have come before had I been able to."

"So should I," said Clare Beaufoy, "I have been intending to come day after day, but I have been so dreadfully busy. I have had five balls already this week which I had to go to."

"And I," echoed Ethel, "have had a house full of visitors, it seems to me, every day and all day."

"You receive—you go to the balls, all of them?" said Edith, looking from one to the other. "You are happy enough——"

"And you look more wretched than ever," said Clare.

"I have good cause," said Edith. "My sister has just left me, and I shall not see her again, perhaps for years. Poor little Marion! with her last good-bye she asked me to write to Philip."

"To your husband?" exclaimed Clare.

"What?" exclaimed Ethel.

"Just as I expected," remarked Mrs. Beaufoy, complacently, stretching out her dainty toes and burrowing in the rugs with her feet. "He sent her, of course. Don't you see that he is more in love with you than ever; that he is thoroughly penitent, and only looking for the slightest pretext on which to make peace?"

"Do you really think so?" said Edith Warburton eagerly. "I only pray that it may be so. I cannot go on living this ugly life all alone. What shall I do?"

"What a fool you are," said Ethel, "to worry yourself about the future! There is nothing but pleasure and freedom in store for you if you care to take it."

"Perhaps," said Edith reflectively, looking into the fire, "you would not see it any more than I do, were you situated as I am. Do you think you would like this? Look around you. How would you like this after the homes I had?"

"Well," said Clare, "it is your own fault that you are here. Why did you not stay at your father's after the row? There was nothing to prevent you."

"Do you think," said Edith, with a shudder, "that I would live in the same house with Marion after that night? Heaven knows I had done her injury enough. I would not live there, but if my father had only spared me his reproaches I might have seen more of Marion, and perhaps have prevented her sacrificing herself today." She paused for a moment, and then continued, staring into the fire, "I have never understood her refusal of Maurice Denalguez. There is some mystery in it, I am sure. Even just now, when I asked her why she refused him, she evaded the question. I may be morbid, but I cannot help accusing myself of being in some way the cause of this resolution of hers—of her seeking this death in life."

"Well," said Thello, smoothing her muff with one finger of her gloved hand, "I can relieve your mind of that burden. I have seen a good deal of your sister lately, and she has never been so happy as she has been since she decided on taking this step that makes you so miserable. I can assure you that much as Marion has thought of you, you have had nothing to do with her determination."

"Would that I could believe it."

"By the by," said Clare Beaufoy, "is there anything that I can do for you? I have been most anxious to see you to explain a thing which must have appeared strange. Of course I should like to have asked you to visit us, but I was afraid it might be a little awkward for you. My husband is so tiresome about that kind of thing. He is very indulgent, but he will not let me ask a woman who is separated from her husband to the house."

"And I," said Ethel, "am even worse off than Clare in that respect. Living alone as I do, it would compromise what shreds of reputation I have left if the heroine of the celebrated Faithorne-Warburton scandal were to be seen constantly at my poor little house. So you see, my dear, it has not been my fault that we have not met oftener."

"There is no need of any explanation," said Edith coldly, "I do not go out at all. Strange," continued she reflectively, "that you who taught me—goaded me—to defy my husband's wishes, should be so careful to comply with the wishes of your own, and to square your behavior with the lightest expression of the world's opinion. Surely it is scarcely practising what you preach."

"Goodness me," said Ethel. "Why, anyone would say that I had persuaded you to leave your home."

"Well, well," said Edith wearily, "we will not speak of the past, and if I seem changed and imbittered, it is only that I have neither the power nor the inclination to conceal the truth. I have had time to think in the last few months, and many things are clear to me now."

"Well," said Clare, getting up, "at any rate I do hope you quite understand why I have not been to see you before. I must run away now. By the by, Thello, don't forget that an old friend of yours is coming to tea with me this afternoon. Mind you are not late. Good-bye, Edith, be sure to let me know if I can do anything for you."

"Thank you, Mrs. Beaufoy," said Edith in the same tone, "I have all that is necessary."

And Clare, with a little shrug of her fur-clad shoulders, made a little mischievous *moue* at Thello, who grinned in reply, and left the room.

There was a short, awkward pause, and then Ethel remarked,

"By the by, I shall see your people tonight. Is there any message—any question—for them? Anything you want to know about them?"

"There is one question I should like to ask," said Edith, "have you ever heard how or where Philip got those letters? I had burned the letters myself just before you came into Captain Denalguez's rooms that day—the whole packet, which Sir Reginald had just given me."

"I have never heard it explained," said Thello audaciously, "but I have no doubt that the whole thing could be traced to Captain Denalguez himself. Did it never strike you as a peculiar coincidence that we found Sir Reginald with him that morning? I suspected mischief at once, and if you had said anything about those letters then, I might have helped you; but it is so long ago that it will be difficult to associate it with him now. There is one person, however, who might help you."

"Who?"

"Faithorne. I hear he returned some days ago."

"You forget what you are saying," said Edith, rising.

As she did so, her servant brought in a note which she read hastily.

"Marion wishes to see me at once. What can she have to say? Listen,—she says, 'Come back in the carriage. I will not keep you five minutes. It is my last request. Marion.' I must go, Ethel. Give me my hat and cape, Sarah."

"I have to be off, too," said Ethel. "I have to meet a friend at Clare's. I will come in again tomorrow and find out what has transpired, when we can decide better what is to be done in the future."

The two women left the house together, Edith in Mr. Wurmsley's carriage, which had come to meet her, and Thello in a hansom which deposited her at Clare Beaufoy's door in Ebury Street.

"My work is ended," said the little arch-conspirator to herself as she threw off her wraps and settled herself in one of Clare's lounges.

Clare had not returned, and probably had no intention of doing so, so Thello proceeded to make herself perfectly comfortable with her reflections and a cigarette.

"And by the by," continued, she, apostrophizing her boots, "it is not completed a moment too soon. I could not have prevented explanations much longer. I have kept away from Edith too long for safety, I think; but, however, she fortunately never had sense or pluck enough to send for Denalguez. He might have enlightened her a good deal about those letters, but I knew she would not think of him."

At this point her cogitations were cut short by the lifting of a *portière* which disclosed Sir Reginald Faithorne, looking at her with a sweet and cynical smile upon his handsome face.

Thello, without moving, greeted him with the first couplet of Costa's song,

> "Beau chevalier, qui partez pour la guerre,
> Qu' allez vous faire,—si loin d'ici—"

To which musical accompaniment he entered, and shaking her by the hand sat down opposite to her on the other side of the fireplace.

"Well, *beau chevalier*," said Thello, "what brings you here? The last place in the world you would be expected to choose for a *rendezvous*."

"I have come in search of information which I knew that either you or Clare would give me. I want to hear something of the history of the Wurmsley family since my departure. I suppose, however, I need only have come straight to you."

"*Quid pro quo*," responded Ethel, "I want to know some things too. Yours for mine?"

"It is a bargain. Ladies first, however; you always commanded me, continue to do so now."

"First, why didn't you shoot Warburton?"

"Good gracious, why should I? He had not injured me, there was not a reason in the world why he should die excepting your wish, and you forgot to lay that injunction upon me. Now look here, Thello, don't let us chaff any more, but tell me something: how was it that when Edith had burned her letters in the afternoon—I saw her burn them—Warburton produced apparently a duplicate set in the evening?"

"You *saw* her burn them?"

"Yes."

"Did she count them?"

"No, she merely glanced over them, and threw the whole bundle into the fire."

"That is exactly what I expected. Women are so careless with their correspondence! You know I am somewhat of a collector of autograph manuscripts—I selected two of the most interesting as worthy of my collection."

"Do you realize, Thello Marsden," said Faithorne, "that you place yourself in my hands absolutely when you tell me your secrets like this?"

Thello laughed.

"Oh, I am not afraid," said she merrily. "I know you are as bad as I am"

"You flatter me," said Faithorne, bowing gravely. "I really cannot take so much credit to myself. I feel that it is not due——"

"Your usual modesty, my dear Rex. Oh, you're a sweet thing!"

"Yes," assented Faithorne, "I *am* nice."

"I'm delighted to see you back," pursued Thello. "You are the only person that I can speak out to, and with all this on my mind, I have been so bottled up that I ache to tell the truth to somebody. It is a positive luxury."

"Why don't you indulge yourself oftener? It is not at all painful when you become accustomed to it."

"You are simply horrid!"

"Yes, but to continue. You have been strangely inconsistent, Thello. Your fixed plan on the day of the Warburton row was to secure my marriage with Marion. The same evening you overthrew that plan yourself. You upset the marriage and diverted your attention from Denalguez to Warburton; now if

I may be permitted to ask a wholly irrelevant and ridiculous question—why?"

"Because I am a woman, and unfortunately cursed with a temper. Still there was more method in my madness than appears at first sight. As you very justly say, I determined that your marriage with Marion would suit me perfectly——"

"Thank you, Thello. It is nice to earn the approval of a great mind——"

"Don't interrupt. Just before you came in that night Edith aggravated me all to pieces, and I lost my temper, so I fired my little shot—otherwise the two interesting specimens of Edith's handwriting. They would not have been so effective had I not found by accident—that is the truth—a small note in your charming fist, saying—but you remember the words,—it was extremely useful. You saw the effect of the explosion. The bomb had been fired the moment before you entered. I think you experienced some of the after shock yourself."

"Yes," replied Faithorne sardonically, "I made a note of the scene, I remember. I also remember that I was unprepared for that *dénouement*, but I cannot recall any letters of Edith's that could produce such a scene. There was not the slightest cause for Warburton's marital indignation—you know that as well as I do."

"That is the charm of the whole thing," said Thello, leaning back luxuriously. "Imagine Philip Warburton's feelings when he knows that Edith is guiltless of anything but an idiotic romance, which taken in comparison, with his present belief, he would be only too glad to pardon."

"Still," persisted Faithorne, "I don't see why he should be willing to accept such slender proof."

"Ah," said Thello, significantly, "you forget. Now you are able to judge dispassionately, take his side of the question. His wife had been sufficiently imprudent in her manner to cause him considerable uneasiness, if not absolute suspicion. He is a much more sentimental man than would be imagined; so between wounded love and the suspicion aroused by Edith's folly, his mind was in no state to judge. He could only feel, and imagine that he knew. Then again, it was not so much Edith's letters as your unconsidered words that did the work. You never dreamed how important your small note would prove, did you? That is the advantage of a fine, crisp style. You hardly expected to make such a success as a writer, did you?"

"Perhaps," said Faithorne, who struggled between an amused and an angry sensation, that made him hesitate between kissing and slapping his interlocutor, "you made the success for me, if success it was. You are certainly right on one point; I never intended those few words which I sent with Edith's letters for any purpose beyond frightening her a little. Two more questions, and I shall know all that is necessary. Was it not a little difficult to prevent Marion and Denalguez coming to an understanding?"

"Yes, dreadfully difficult, and I should never have succeeded with any other girl. Strangely enough, the strength of her love for him made it easier to keep them apart. In proportion to the height to which she had exalted him, was the depth to which he fell, when fall he did. That has been the only part of my work which has been distasteful to me, and I am very glad that it is ended today."

She rose, and walking to the fire kneeled down, spreading her hands to the blaze.

"How ended," said Faithorne.

"Marion becomes a bride today."

"What?" said Faithorne, rising and congratulating himself that his tormentor's back was turned to him. "Wedded today? And to whom?"

"To the Church," said Thello, looking in the fire.

"Great heavens!" Then changing his tone back to his former one of cynic half amusement he continued,

"I thought I might be of some use, but it seems to me you could have done very well without me."

"Before I answer your final question," said Thello, sinking back upon her heels and giving a twist to her body so as to half face him, "I want to know why you take any further interest in the Wurmsley family. The whole adventure has been rather disastrous for you; the only luck you have had in the matter was your wound not proving fatal."

"My interest," said Faithorne, rising and assuming the serious tone of a man who does not propose to allow his words to be ridiculed or his actions misconstrued, "is simply to discharge a debt of honor. When I returned to London the other day, I found that old Wurmsley had been financially crippled, temporarily, doubtless, but still sufficiently seriously. I supposed he would be burdened with the maintenance of Mrs. Warburton, whose scruples forbade her to stay in the house with Marion, and I felt it my duty to provide for Edith—silence! if you please, and let me finish—having been, without doubt, the cause of the separation. The difficulty was, to do this without her knowledge. Great caution was required, and that caution I employed. On making inquiry on my behalf, my agent found that provision was already made for her by——"

"Warburton, of course——"

"No, by Captain Denalguez. He cunningly contrived that her father, through whose hands the money passed, should believe that it *did* come from Warburton. Now I have told you the whole thing. Confidence for confidence. Tell me, why have you been so down on Denalguez? I am sure you don't mind telling me?"

Thello was silent for a few moments, during which she paced twice up and down the room.

"Well," she said at last, "I will tell you, though I must fall in your estimation, as it involves the rather humiliating confession that instead of being the very original person that you and everybody else take me to be, I had, like the rest of my sex, a weak spot; and what annoys me more than anything else is that it was the simplest of all weaknesses—love."

"Not possible!" ejaculated Faithorne.

"Oh," continued Thello in the same tone, "it was a long time ago. I knew a man who was remarkable for the most perfectly beautiful disposition I ever came across—he was very handsome into the bargain. He was the poem of my whole existence. There was only one bar to our happiness,—I was married."

534

Faithorne jumped as if he had been shot and looked at her incredulously.

"Don't laugh," continued the woman, "I told you before I began, that my confession would disclose a secret. I had in this case some strong scruples and principles. I do not know what we hoped, but our dream was pure and untainted by any suspicion of an alloy. It was impossible to know Prosper Denalguez and think of wrong. Though there seemed no end or aim to our dream, that was the hour of the supremest happiness I have ever known in my life. All went well till Captain Denalguez came back from abroad. He chose to think that I should ruin the boy—God only knows how much nearer the boy came to being my ruin! Maurice Denalguez set to work to poison his brother's mind. He succeeded, not in winning him from me, but in ending our dream—the boy shot himself."

She covered her face with her hands, and a strong shudder shook her. Faithorne, moved despite himself, rose, and laying his hand upon her head, smoothed back her hair, as he said:

"Poor Thello—poor little girl."

"Thanks," she said, as she took his hand and pressed it. Then she continued.

"Maurice Denalguez considers me the cause of his brother's death. I consider him his brother's murderer. Perhaps we share the responsibility. I expiated my part in the crime—tragedy—call it what you will—and he shall expiate his. That is our feud. And as he has robbed me of my love, so I have robbed him of his."

"So you, too, had a heart," said Faithorne with a half return of his old manner. "I thought you were born without such an incumbrance."

"It may have been so," said Thello, wearily. "It is probable that Prosper Denalguez, out of *his* great good heart, made mine. One thing, however, is certain," said she, tossing back her tawny head and recovering herself as she put another cigarette between her lips and proceeded to light it at the mantel-piece, "that I have none left, so respect me once more."

"Thanks for a very interesting story," said Faithorne, rising. "Though as you say, it is not original and rather destroys your individuality."

"Rather, but not quite. I am myself now."

"Well," said Faithorne, crossing the room and taking up his hat, "you are so fascinating that I forget time in your presence. I must be off, for I am very busy."

"Busy? What about?"

"Some private theatricals I am going to arrange. I shall make you take a part."

"What sort of a part?"

"Oh! a bad part."

"Very well," returned Thello. "Good-bye, come and tell me about it some other day," and Faithorne left the room.

She sank into the lounge as he left.

"Today," said she to herself, "ends my self-imposed task, and tomorrow I shall bid a definite good-bye to the Wurmsley family. Not a year ago Philip Warburton told me I was not good enough for his wife. I wonder what he thinks today?"

She gave a little laugh which ended in something suspiciously like a sob, as she concluded,

"And my year of planning and scheming brings me only weariness. Ah, well. Like all realizations, it is disappointing— disappointing."

# CHAPTER XV.

The following afternoon, true to her promise, whilst Edith sat in her rooms in South Eaton Place, Ethel Marsden broke in upon her.

Well," said she, cheerily, as she entered, "what was it all about yesterday?"

"You may well ask," replied Edith, "there is much to tell; at last I know the cause of that child's retirement from the world. She has been driven to it; driven to it by a man's deception, and that man is Captain Denalguez."

Thello, anxious to know more before she committed herself, half turned her back as she deposited her cape upon a vacant chair, and Edith continued.

"You who have seen my sister so often must have known of her struggle between her love for him, and what she believes to be right. Can you tell me, Ethel, if she has ever sought, or if he has ever offered any explanation? She only told me of her reasons for refusing him, but how the knowledge came to her she would not say."

"I believe," replied Ethel, "that Marion was so convinced of Captain Denalguez's guilt that she refused to see him or in any way discuss the subject. He has not been a lucky friend of your family. If you remember, your troubles dated from his arrival."

"That is true," said Edith thoughtfully, "but why should he hate me? I had done nothing to rouse such a feeling."

"Oh, to do him justice," returned Ethel, "I think it was from a false idea of taking care of Warburton more than from any consideration of you, good, bad or indifferent. And then again, perhaps he thought that you had told Marion not to marry him."

"And so sought revenge?—it may be so—it may be so."

"By the by," said Ethel, "I have an idea that might be useful to you. Before I tell it I must ask a question. Do you care to say by whom your income is supplied?"

"Why," said Edith, wonderingly, "I thought you knew—by my father, of course."

"I am sorry to distress you," said Ethel, "but your father can scarcely keep himself. This is one of Marion's reasons for her decision. She saw but one alternative to being a burden upon him, and marriage——"

"But this is impossible! I have had more money than I needed. My father could not have been so foolish,—he certainly would not have been delicate to such an extent as to rob himself, apart from the fact that he has all along sided with Philip, and has shown but little sympathy for me."

"Your father allowed Warburton to provide your income—that is, he believed the money came from him, but Warburton was not so generous. Your luxuries have been supplied by Captain Denalguez."

"What?"

"By Captain Denalguez."

"Can you prove this?"

"Certainly, ask Faithorne. I saw him recently, and he said that for some mysterious reason or other, he was going to call upon you. I dare say that Denalguez felt that you were in some way dependent upon him."

"Oh," exclaimed Edith, indignantly, as she arose, "that I should have been snared into accepting anything from him. It seems as though my heart would break, and I am so helpless! Why can't I work—work—work?"

"So you can," said Ethel, "go on the stage. With your name and the associations connected with it, you would make a *furore.*"

"Don't be absurd—I can't act."

"Of course not. You would not make any money if you could."

"But I am so awkward,"

"The very reason why you would succeed. People nowadays go to the theatre to be amused; you could do that. Why, the girl who would play your maid would know more about acting than you are ever likely to know."

"Then why should they engage me?"

"Why, because you are a curiosity."

"But I might learn with study," said Edith as the idea took possession of her. "And I would work so hard. I might make my own fortune, or at least my own living. But my father—and my husband—what would they say?"

"Oh, well, continue to take the wages of Captain Denalguez."

"Never! Tell me—how can I find out about going on the stage?"

"I have not the least idea now, but I will make inquiries for you if you like. You always dressed well—have you lots of clothes?"

"I suppose I should want a great deal of dress," said Edith thoughtfully.

Thello, seeing that Edith's head was turned the other way, grinned a little.

"It depends on the theatre, I imagine," she said laconically.

As Edith looked up as if for an explanation, the servant, opening the door, announced Captain Denalguez. As he entered the room and saw Ethel Marsden, he stopped short. The two women were not less astonished than he, and finally he broke the silence, saying,

"I embarrass you by my entrance. Have I had the misfortune to interrupt any fresh combination?"

"No," said Ethel, with an undisguised air of triumph. "Be reassured."

"I am *not* reassured," said Denalguez gravely. "Your very feebly disguised delight, the triumph in your face, shows me that I am no longer in your way."

By this time Edith had recovered her self-possession.

"Captain Denalguez," said she, "is it to exult over me that you are here?"

"Madame," replied Denalguez, "my feeling is an altogether different one, as different as my object in being here. It is on your husband's behalf that I have come."

"You come from my husband?"

"As I should only detain you about five minutes, I am sorry my visit is inopportune. I will try to find you alone some day soon—or perhaps you——"

"Pray don't let me drive you away," said Ethel Marsden; "I am particularly anxious to see you myself, and with Edith's permission, will run away now, and come back after a while. You will not refuse me a few moments, Captain Denalguez, I am sure?"

"Certainly not," said Denalguez. "Only too charmed. I am still fond of studying human nature, and the material you provide is inexhaustible. I am still in search of knowledge."

He had moved to the door with her, and held it open. As she went out, she said:

"You shall obtain all you want in about ten minutes, I promise you. I shall be back soon, Edith."

Edith Warburton motioned her visitor to a seat, and seated herself, as she said:

"What does Mr. Warburton propose?"

"His proposal, if you call it so," said Denalguez in a matter-of-fact tone, "is simple."

A ray of hope illumined Edith's face as she broke in eagerly—

"He regrets having been so harsh—I mean so cruel——"

"Er—not precisely; but a woman, in fact your sister, spoke to him—pleaded for you. She feared your father would not long be able to protect you, and sought your husband's aid. He at once gave instructions to allow you——"

"That is enough! Captain Denalguez, it is not necessary for you to proceed. I intend to take no aid of the kind you suggest from Mr. Warburton. He possesses but one kind of gift that I would accept, and *that* he does not offer. Before you entered I made up my mind to refuse all further help from my father. In future I shall depend upon my own exertions."

"May I ask how?" said Denalguez.

"I intend to act," said Edith, with a show of bravery that she was far from feeling.

"Your intentions," returned Denalguez, "may be excellent, but the acting I doubt. Surely you are not serious."

"Perfectly."

"But, my dear lady, do you suppose the theatre to be a training school for women like you? Only two kinds of women *without* talent can succeed; one who is *in* society, and one who has forfeited her right to be there. By a series of misfortunes you are no longer in society, but I know that you have not forfeited your right to be there."

As he spoke the last gleam of hope died out in Edith's heart. When he was silent, controlling herself with a violent effort, she said to him in a strangely altered voice,

"I must thank you, Captain Denalguez, for showing me how disastrous the work I had hoped to obtain, would prove. You have at least succeeded in showing me that I should only have made myself ridiculous. I might possibly take heart of grace from the fact that you always mistrusted me. Perhaps if I had been brought up like other girls, it might have been different, but you know our mother died when we were quite children. Father did all he could for us, but what can a girl do without a mother's care? I grew up, I suppose, as selfish as they say I am. Every one flattered me and said I should make a great marriage, and when Philip Warburton came I was flattered by his proposal, by his wealth and by my promised position. Well, he gave me all he promised—more; but he was hard with me. I did not find in him the sympathy without which I cannot live. Even you, a stranger, almost, have pursued me as though I had done you some great injury——"

Denalguez silenced her with a gesture.

"Stop," said he, "you do me an injustice. *I* pursue you? Believe me, I did more to save you than I would ever have done for myself. I suffered insult, humiliation, even my own self-contempt."

Edith was about to speak when he motioned to her to keep silent once more.

"I would suffer so again," continued he, "to save Philip all that he has borne, and I would give much to know whose hand it was that struck the blow. My own plan was merely to show you how dangerous was the path you had chosen, and I believe you would have been saved, which was the only object of my hopes. Fate, however, ordained that it should be otherwise."

He ceased speaking, and Edith on whom his words had evidently made a profound impression, said gently,

"Thank you. I fancy that if I had had a true friend, such as you have been to Philip, and, in these latter days, to me, my life might have been different."

Then with a change of manner, she continued,

"I have something to say to you that I cannot tell you now, I am too upset. It is not, however, about myself. As far as I am concerned, tell Mr. Warburton that I refuse his money."

She steadied herself as she spoke, grasping the back of a chair, and said as she moved to the door,

"I have a packet that has been entrusted to me for you. If you will wait a moment I will get it. You will wait, will you not?"

"With pleasure," and Denalguez was left alone.

Not for long, however, for almost as she left the room, Ethel Marsden entered it.

"You see I have come back to keep you company," said she. "Am I not thoughtful? You don't seem very enthusiastic over it. If you remember, Captain Denalguez, the last *tête à tête* that we had you were warmer in your enthusiasm—more *empressé* in your attentions, though I did not then know the way to your heart as well as I do now."

"You know the way to my heart!" echoed Denalguez. "Never!"

"Do you feel inclined to bet about it?"

"No."

"You are wise, Monsieur, you would lose."

Maurice Denalguez did not attempt to conceal the disdain which he felt at the moment for the woman who sat before him, but nevertheless experienced the uncomfortable sensation that he was fighting against hidden weapons, and there seemed no means of making her show her hand.

"You know," pursued Thello, "I have only to say one word."

"Indeed," said Denalguez, "it must be a very terrible one."

"No," replied Thello, looking him straight in the eyes, "not very terrible—to you at any rate. It is simply the name of a pure, charming, innocent young girl—Marion."

In spite of himself, Maurice Denalguez started, and he half turned, so as to hide his face from her as she continued,

"You see I *do* know the way. You loved her very much, and it is your dream to wed her. Though she jilted you, your heart has remained with her. It is strange that such a weak little child should so enchain 'the Galahad,' Captain Maurice Denalguez—I might almost say 'the Don Quixote.' Well, well, you love her in spite of yourself, and she has contemptuously refused you. Do you know why?"

"I do not wish to discuss the matter," said Denalguez, "but she could have had but one reason,—that she did not love me."

"You are wrong," said Thello shortly. "Her love is as deep as yours."

"Mrs. Marsden," said Denalguez, turning to her once more, "don't let us fence in this matter. What have you to say? There is some ingenious torture or other hidden beneath your information. You would not have told me of her love if you did not think you could sting me with the assurance. Speak."

"When you seek knowledge, you must do as all scholars should—walk before you run. Patience, my dear friend—patience! I have something to say as you justly suppose, but I am going to take my time. There were but two people in the world who knew Marion's reason for refusing you—one was Faithorne, and you would not listen to him. The other is myself—will you listen to me?"

"Have at least the mercy to speak!"

"Marion loved you, and all the time that you were away she thought of nothing but your return. She had but one dream—to be your wife. That would have made *you* too happy—it would not have suited *me*. I had to make matters right. I thought of the worst things that I could say—and I said them."

As she said this, Edith appeared at the door, but the two were so engrossed with their conversation that they did not notice her entrance.

"And do you mean to say," said Denalguez, "that she could believe your—your lies?"

"Oh," said Ethel, in the tone of one giving a simple explanation, "it required, of course, a certain amount of ingenuity. I found a young girl, innocent, ignorant, stupid. A girl who had suffered a common fate, but who did not know the name of her betrayer. I agreed to take care of her on condition that she said whatever I told her to say. Marion, whose pity I enlisted for her, went to help and comfort her. The girl told her that the man who deceived and abandoned her had gone to Russia—was in the Embassy, and that his name was—Denalguez."

"Great God! No one but a child could have believed such a story. You chose your victim well!"

"You have had some evidence of Marion's obstinacy. Witness, for instance, her refusal to give you any satisfaction."

"I should like to kill you," said Denalguez calmly, looking her in the eyes.

"You sought for knowledge—take it. It was I who separated Edith from Philip Warburton. It was I who kept and sent him two of her letters, knowing that she was guiltless of all wrong. It was I who kept you and Marion apart, and today, Maurice Denalguez," and she rose and came close to him, "you have expiated your share in Prosper's death. I vowed you should, and I have kept my oath."

A groan behind them seemed almost a welcome diversion, as they both turned and saw Edith.

"And it was I," said she, as the two kept silence, "that brought this woman into communication with my sister. Oh," continued she, addressing Denalguez, "don't say that there is no hope. Can we not go to her?"

Denalguez drew himself up as he replied,

"You are right. This is your work. This woman," said he, pointing to Ethel, who stood like an avenging demon, her hand upon the mantel-piece, "has ruined your sister's life as well as yours. You were warned against her. Did she lose one iota of her pleasure or position when she bade you defy those who loved and respected you? God forgive you for your share of today's work. As for you," continued he, fiercely, turning to Ethel Marsden, "don't imagine that your sex will protect you. Between us from this moment, it is war—without mercy—war to the knife. I warn you!"

"That is understood," said Ethel calmly. "You and I have played the game of vengeance for a long while. Sometimes the luck is in your favor, sometimes in mine. You should be too good a gambler to mind losing. You have held some good cards, but it is my turn now. You have lost me some cards, some diamonds, in the game, but I have taken your best card—a Heart. At last we are quits."

"I know now," said Edith, interrupting her, "how I have been a tool of this woman. Try to forgive me, for my agony is almost more than I can bear. Think what I must suffer, knowing myself to be the cause of such misery."

With the obvious truth of the words thus wrung from her, Maurice Denalguez softened in spite of himself.

"You must not plead to me, poor child," said he. "I must have been mad when I spoke to you just now. It is I who am the true cause of this—woman's—work. If she had but visited her cruelty on me alone; if she had but spared the rest of you."

As he finished speaking, and took Edith's hand in his, Sir Reginald Faithorne was announced.

Taking in the situation at a glance, he approached Edith and said as he bowed gravely to her,

"I see my entrance would be an intrusion if I had not a sure passport. Look up, at least, Mrs. Warburton, and tell me that I may try to earn my pardon for my share in this deplorable business?"

Edith remained silent, whilst Ethel, who had been quietly buttoning her gloves, looked up at him with a glance of keen anxiety. It was Denalguez who broke the silence.

"Sir Reginald Faithorne," said he, "once by my pride I prevented your telling me what, had I listened, would have obviated all the distress that followed that meeting. This is no time for lengthy explanations. I ask you as man to man, for God's sake, end this suspense."

"Marion will return to her life in your world," said Faithorne, quietly.

"It cannot be," ejaculated Ethel Marsden.

Faithorne silenced her with a wave of his hand.

"She was led to take the step she decided on," continued he, "by a treachery, which, unfortunately, cannot be properly punished, but the failure of the plot at the moment of success, will be a considerable blow, I think, to Mrs. Marsden."

Edith looked up at him eagerly.

"You would not say this only to comfort me," she said. "Are you sure of what you say?"

"Perfectly,—upon my honor. You may expect to see her here at any moment."

"Oh," said Edith, "I have prayed so for help, and it has come—has come from *you*, of all men in the world. Thank God!" and she turned and went to the window.

"Since when," said Ethel, with a little preparatory cough, "has Sir Reginald Faithorne become the defender of the good, the true and the beautiful?"

"Since you took the liberty of making me an unwilling accomplice in your infernal schemes," replied the baronet. "You were too clever yesterday, Mrs. Marsden. The open avowal of your malice would have sickened me, had I not at once determined to avert it if human power could achieve so much. I sought the help of those whose help was all-powerful, and we succeeded in a very short time in crumbling your edifice of lies."

"Curse my tongue," said Ethel venomously, all the worst passions of her nature coming into her face as she spoke. "Your morality is delightful, Sir Reginald. I never saw any signs of it before, and I did not know you were gifted with such a troublesome thing."

"A man, however bad he is," returned he gravely, "has always enough of that troublesome thing to enable him to appreciate a good woman."

Ethel laughed.

"Curious that I never saw any of it until now," she said.

"Well, you see *you* hardly inspired it. I told you yesterday you were to play a part in my private theatricals, and I have kept my word. Your part is not a pleasant one, is it?"

"Well, if it comes to that, yours is not much better, though, by the by, when you come to think of it, it is a comic part, is it not? You were always very sensitive to ridicule. It seems to me that the Wurmsley family have made you a greater fool—have made you more utterly ridiculous than you will be able to bear very easily. Do you know I quite feel sorry for you."

"I do not deserve your pity, Mrs. Marsden, I am indebted to you for so much, and I have paid my debt by marring your plot so completely. You have done just the reverse from me. You made mine. I could never have finished my story without your aid. By the by, you did not know that *I* was the author of that romance that interested you so much—'Arcadia, versus Hades,' though you complimented me yesterday on my fine, crisp style. I felt unworthy as I told you then, for you provided most of the material."

A little spasm of malice crossed Thello's face, as she remarked,

"I cannot bear the purity of this atmosphere. It is positively stifling. You people are too good for me."

"I am dreadfully afraid," returned Faithorne, "that we share your opinion. Er—can I take you to your carriage?" and he opened the door.

"Take care," said Thello, as she passed through followed by him, "that I never get the chance to avenge my failure."

When they were gone, Edith turned from the window and came to where Denalguez stood, as she had left him.

"Can you forgive me," said he, "for speaking so unkindly to you just now?"

"Yes," replied Edith, "your heart is good and true, I know. You would have saved me if you could. It is no fault of yours that you failed. I wonder," said she, looking up at him, a dazed expression in her eyes, "if there are many people like me, who come to grief for no sin save being a fool? Why could not I see last spring what I see now? Oh, for the months that can never return!"

She covered her face with her hands for a moment, and then laying one hand upon his arm, she continued softly,

"Happiness will soon be yours. You can spare a few minutes to my misery. Since I have been here alone, how I have prayed for a word to show that I was remembered. My heart choked me when you said you came from him—I thought my prayers were answered—but no. He offered me only an allowance. I want the love of which I once thought so lightly, and that now I would give my soul to regain, and he offers me instead—money. I decline the offer!" continued she, drawing herself to her full height. "When I am dead, which I trust will be soon, tell—my husband—that—since he last spoke to me in love I have learned more good than evil."

At this juncture the door opened softly, and Philip Warburton appeared. Edith, engrossed as she was, did not catch the sound that he made in entering, and at a gesture from Denalguez he remained out of sight behind them.

"It was then that he told me I should learn who really loved me. Tell him I have learned. Tell him I have learned to know him, and have—learned to love him in return."

"You have told me yourself," cried Warburton, coming forward. "Marion, thank heaven! could not keep her promise to you. She told me of her visit to you yesterday, and that my love might conquer my pride. Ah, love," said he, coming close to her and taking her in his arms, "why did you not send for me before?"

A voice—Marion's—was heard in the passage, asking for her sister, who, disengaging herself from her husband's embrace, ran to meet her.

"You will forgive me," said the little girl, "will you not," as she threw her arms around her neck, "for telling Philip everything that I promised not to tell him?"

"Forgive you, sweetheart?" said Edith, "it is I who ask your pardon. And you," she continued, turning to Denalguez, "can you ever forgive me?"

"My reward," returned he, "is in seeing you reënter Arcadia, confident that you will never more weary of its sweet security. But if you owe me aught, in payment give me a place in your graceful land where dwells my love."

THE END.

# A PARTIAL LIST OF SNUGGLY BOOKS

MARCEL SCHWOB *The Assassins and Other Stories*
MARCEL SCHWOB *Double Heart*
CHRISTIAN HEINRICH SPIESS *The Dwarf of Westerbourg*
BRIAN STABLEFORD (editor)
    *Decadence and Symbolism: A Showcase Anthology*
BRIAN STABLEFORD (editor) *The Snuggly Satyricon*
BRIAN STABLEFORD (editor) *The Snuggly Satanicon*
BRIAN STABLEFORD (editor) *Snuggly Tales of Hashish and Opium*
BRIAN STABLEFORD *The Insubstantial Pageant*
BRIAN STABLEFORD *Spirits of the Vasty Deep*
BRIAN STABLEFORD *The Truths of Darkness*
COUNT ERIC STENBOCK *Love, Sleep & Dreams*
COUNT ERIC STENBOCK *Myrtle, Rue & Cypress*
COUNT ERIC STENBOCK *The Shadow of Death*
COUNT ERIC STENBOCK *Studies of Death*
MONTAGUE SUMMERS *The Bride of Christ and Other Fictions*
MONTAGUE SUMMERS *Six Ghost Stories*
GILBERT-AUGUSTIN THIERRY *The Blonde Tress and The Mask*
GILBERT-AUGUSTIN THIERRY *Reincarnation and Redemption*
DOUGLAS THOMPSON *The Fallen West*
TOADHOUSE *Gone Fishing with Samy Rosenstock*
TOADHOUSE *Living and Dying in a Mind Field*
TOADHOUSE *What Makes the Wave Break?*
LÉO TRÉZENIK *Decadent Prose Pieces*
RUGGERO VASARI *Raun*
JANE DE LA VAUDÈRE *The Demi-Sexes and The Androgynes*
JANE DE LA VAUDÈRE *The Double Star and Other Occult Fantasies*
JANE DE LA VAUDÈRE *The Mystery of Kama and Brahma's Courtesans*
JANE DE LA VAUDÈRE *The Priestesses of Mylitta*
JANE DE LA VAUDÈRE *Three Flowers and The King of Siam's Amazon*
AUGUSTE VILLIERS DE L'ISLE-ADAM *Isis*
RENÉE VIVIEN AND HÉLÈNE DE ZUYLEN DE NYEVELT
    *Faustina and Other Stories*
RENÉE VIVIEN *Lilith's Legacy*
RENÉE VIVIEN *A Woman Appeared to Me*
TERESA WILMS MONTT *In the Stillness of Marble*
TERESA WILMS MONTT *Sentimental Doubts*
KAREL VAN DE WOESTIJNE *The Dying Peasant*

www.ingramcontent.com/pod-product-compliance
Lightning Source LLC
Chambersburg PA
CBHW020225110726
47898CB00004B/1158